PRAISE FOR N S DOLK

"*Silent Hall* is very nearly a perfect nove. had been anywhere near as inventive and challenging to the norm."

James A Moore, *author of* Seven Forges *and* The Last Sacrifice

"Love this story."

H D Lynn, *author of* The Corner Store Witch

"This is a very special debut novel. The quality of writing takes this tale way beyond a simple fantasy adventure."

Strange Alliances

"An excellent debut from a new author. What a lush world of magics and peoples, gods, and dragons. What's more, the author set it all in a patriarchal world, yet delivers some rather feminist notions in a very organic way. Likewise, there are nuggets about racism and even domestic violence, but done so subtly and woven in so smoothly that they don't stand out as such. They just blend in to make a much rounder story that has a lot more to say than the typical medieval-patriarchy fantasy. A delightful surprise, and cleverly done."

Women of Badassery

"If you are a reader of fantasy, I highly recommend *Silent Hall*, the first in Dolkart's new series. Read it because you like a comfort read. Read it because you like to read about close friends succeeding together. Read it because you appreciate the value of ethical interaction that is so lost in most of the fantasy literature coming out today. Read it for its cleverness, read it for its endearing Talmud like study of a fantastical theology... Read it because it's raining outside. Whatever. Read it!"

Dirty Little Bookworm

"I believe any fan of epic fantasy, or anyone who just like a well written, focused character driven story, will enjoy this book."

The Bookworm Speaks

N S DOLKART

Among the Fallen

GODSERFS BOOK II

ANGRY
ROBOT

ANGRY ROBOT
An imprint of Watkins Media Ltd

20 Fletcher Gate,
Nottingham,
NG1 2FZ
UK

angryrobotbooks.com
twitter.com/angryrobotbooks
Chariots of Laarna

An Angry Robot paperback original 2017
1

A catalogue record for this book is available from the British Library.

ISBN 978 0 85766 569 0
EBook ISBN 978 0 85766 571 3

Set in Meridien by Epub Services.
Printed and bound in the UK by 4edge Limited.

*In memory of Gretchen Therrien, Tom DePeter
and Bob Mitchell.*

PROLOGUE

"Your dress is torn." Mother scrunched her lips together. "You've been climbing again."

"No, I–"

"Don't lie to me," Mother snapped. "You know what happens to girls who lie."

Dessa bowed her head while Mother inspected her hands. "I'm sorry."

Mother sighed and took up her needle. "Just be careful, all right? And don't ruin the wedding. We don't want the Highservants to think they've made a mistake."

"I saw a dragon today," Dessa said. "It was flying so high in the sky..." She lifted her arms to indicate how high.

"Stand still," Mother said, "and don't tell stories." When she was done sewing the tear in the dress, she sat back and smiled. "You'll make a lovely bride."

"I'm not even a woman yet," Dessa grumbled.

"Nor should you be," Mother answered. "We've waited too long with you as it is! Any longer and the villagers might start noticing you! What if one of *them* wanted you? What could we say?"

"It's not fair," Dessa complained. "They get to marry whoever they want, and wait as long as they want."

Mother shook her head. "Life isn't fair," she said. "Go ask your Grandma if she wants some soup."

Grandma was out weeding in the garden, tugging indiscriminately at weed and herb alike and gathering them all in her left hand. Dessa ran up to her and gave her a kiss.

"Sweet child," Grandma said, her face wrinkling with pleasure. "Where is your husband?"

"I don't have one yet," Dessa said.

"You must tell him to be careful," Grandma warned, dropping her pile of plants and taking Dessa by the shoulders. "I saw his doom today."

"I don't have a husband, Grandma," Dessa said soothingly.

Grandma's eyes flashed, and she did not let go. "They will be the end of him," she insisted. "The black dragon and the she-wolf. I saw them, Iona! They will be the end of him!"

"Grandma, I'm Dessa. Iona is my mother. Come inside and have some soup."

Dessa took her grandmother by the elbow and led her indoors. The old woman calmed down the moment she saw Mother. "Oh, Iona, there you are. We were looking everywhere for you."

"What were you telling Dessa?" Mother asked, guiding Grandma into a chair and bringing her a bowl of soup.

"She was telling me not to marry," Dessa said.

Mother shot her a warning glance. "Nonsense, Dessa. Don't tell lies. Mother, I think you'd better stay here indoors with me."

Grandma nodded. "Of course, dear, I would never leave you alone. I have to take care of you, don't I, now that your husband is gone?"

"Belkos isn't gone, Mother. He's just having the nag re-shod today, that's all. He'll be back by suppertime."

Grandma lifted the bowl of soup to her lips and slurped at it tentatively. "Enjoy him while you can, dear."

Mother sighed. "I think you'd better stay inside for the rest of the day. You look tired."

Grandma seemed surprised. "Do I?"

Mother lowered her voice. "I'm worried something will happen."

"You worry too much."

"I have to now," Mother said, exasperated. "You don't anymore. And Dessa's hopeless. You don't know what I have to put up with, Mother. Do you know she was climbing trees?"

Grandma's placid demeanor vanished. "Where? Did anyone see her?"

"No, Grandma," Dessa insisted. "And I did it the hard way. I promise!"

"Let's see your hands."

Dessa hesitated, but Grandma snatched up one of her wrists and turned her palms up. Then she slapped her. "Your skin is torn, you little liar!"

Mother rushed forward, crying, "Mother, stop! Torn skin is good, remember? It means she was telling the truth."

Grandma let go and Dessa scurried away from her, sobbing. "The truth?" Grandma asked confusedly.

"The truth, Mother. Dessa's a good girl. You shouldn't hit her."

"I didn't hit anyone," Grandma said.

"The red priest take you," Dessa muttered.

"What did you just say?"

Why did Grandma's hearing have to be so sharp?

"Nothing."

Grandma's eyes flashed again and she advanced on Dessa. "I'm sorry, I'm sorry," Dessa cried, cowering against the wall.

"Stop, stop!" Mother said, holding Grandma back. "I'll take care of it, Mother, I promise I will."

At last, Grandma relented and went back to her soup. Mother was shaking.

"Wait until your father comes home," she warned Dessa. "Honestly, can't either of you control yourselves? How will we survive if neither of you can keep out of trouble? I'm going to have to keep your grandmother indoors after this, Dessa, but what am I supposed to do with you? You should know better."

Dessa bowed her head, ashamed. She had been afraid – she hadn't been thinking.

"I'm sorry, Mother," she said, and turned her claws back into hands.

1
CRITON

The room was already spinning when he opened his eyes. Criton groaned, trying to focus on a single spot to slow the world down. It had been like this for the last two weeks, ever since the red priest of Ardis had robbed him of flight and watched him plummet to earth. Every time he woke, it felt like a struggle to come back from the dead. His vision blurred, his head felt heavy, and the spinning – well, maybe it was slowing down a little.

He sat up slowly, still trying to focus on that spot in the thatching. When he dared to look down, he found Bandu sitting across from him, nursing Goodweather.

"It still hurts," she said, concerned for him.

"It doesn't exactly hurt," Criton tried to explain, "and it's definitely better than it was, but..."

"But still bad."

"Yes, it's still bad."

Bandu sighed. "Rest is good for me too. You can take her soon?"

Criton began to nod, but stopped. Nodding brought the dizziness back. "Give me a few minutes," he said, "but I'll take her."

He sat there, getting his bearings, until Bandu rose and handed Goodweather over to him. "I sleep now," she said.

Goodweather had fallen asleep while nursing, thank God Most High, and she did not wake up when Bandu transferred her to Criton. Criton held her at his shoulder, rubbing her back absentmindedly with his scaly palm. He needed water, and he needed to relieve himself, but in what order? He stumbled out of the hut, carrying his daughter in his arms. He found Narky already at the well, pulling up a bucket of water.

"How are you feeling today?" Narky asked. "Good enough to travel?"

"What's the hurry?" Criton said, trying not to groan. "We have what we need here, and for once nobody's trying to kill us. Except my head."

Narky frowned and lifted the bucket onto the stones. "We should be moving already. I feel it here." He tapped at his chest.

Criton looked around, trying to open his eyes all the way. The abandoned village had suited their needs perfectly these last two weeks – did they really have to leave so soon? They had stayed here once to give Narky time to heal, back before the villagers had left for the dubious protection of a wizard's fortress. The villagers hadn't bothered taking the straw mattresses when they left, and some of the thatched roofs would easily last another ten years. It was a perfect place to rest – why should Narky, of all people, spoil that?

"My head's not all better," Criton said obstinately. "Could you hold Goodweather a minute? I need a drink."

Narky looked like he might refuse, but Criton didn't give him an opportunity. He placed his daughter in Narky's unwilling arms and took a long gulp of water straight from the bucket. Goodweather stirred a little, and Narky's eyes widened in panic.

"Don't worry," Criton said. "I'll be right back." And over Narky's whispered protests, he went to find a place to piss.

When his head had cleared, he found that he was still rocking from side to side as if Goodweather remained in his arms. That was what it was like now – taking care of his daughter had become a reflex. A sweet, happy reflex.

He couldn't stop thinking about her. Goodweather was

growing so beautifully, and not just in size. She had begun to smile too, the briefest of smiles that filled him with joy one moment and disappeared the next. He had no knowledge of babies besides what few stories Ma had told him about himself as an infant, and he had not known to expect these tiny fleeting expressions. He wondered which would grow faster – her little body or her little smiles.

"Take her, take her," Narky insisted when Criton returned. "She won't hold her head up; I don't want to break her neck accidentally."

Criton took Goodweather back, holding her head against his shoulder and bouncing gently from side to side. "I'd have thought you knew about these things better than I did," he said. "You watched animals give birth and everything, didn't you?"

"And helped them, sometimes," Narky confirmed. "Lambs aren't so damned helpless, though. She's more than a month old already – a sheep would be running around by now!"

Criton shrugged, and Goodweather stirred. A little wave of heat met his shoulder and died away again, returning every few seconds in a steady rhythm. Hiccups.

"Where would we go?" Criton asked after a while.

Narky scratched at his chest. "Wherever your God takes us. It's generous of Him to let us rest for a while, but do you honestly think he could be done with us already? He's bound to show us the way soon enough."

"Do you count yourself among the servants of God Most High, then? I thought your theory was that Ravennis still lived."

"He does," Narky said. "He must. Until that last Oracle turns up dead, I won't believe He's really gone. So of course I'm His servant first, but what's that got to do with anything? People worship more than one God all the time."

Criton shook his head. "Not with God Most High. His worshippers follow Him alone."

"According to who?" Narky asked pointedly. "What's-his-name who wrote that scroll Psander gave you? He also told you Dragon Touched were monsters who should be wiped off the face of the earth. And you almost killed me when I said he could have been right about *something*."

Goodweather stirred. "I didn't almost kill you," Criton muttered.

"You're not the one to judge that."

Luckily, Hunter spared Criton the need to answer by arriving just then, carrying a saddle over one forearm and a sack in his other hand. "Take this," he said to Narky, handing over the sack. "It's all the food I could find that's still good."

"Why did you bring back a saddle?" Narky asked. "We haven't got any horses."

"Phaedra asked me to bring her any leather I could find," Hunter said. "There wasn't much left but this."

Criton sighed. "She's going to try leather now? That'll be a good deal heavier than the tree bark."

"But it won't fall apart," Hunter pointed out.

Phaedra had become obsessed with writing down what they had learned in their travels, but her attempts at creating makeshift books had met with abject failure.

Narky peeked inside the sack and grimaced. "This won't last us more than a day or two."

"Most of what wasn't burned has been picked clean by now," Hunter said. "And the battlefield is already overrun with vines. Between the scavengers and the Yarek, we're lucky I found this much."

Narky looked knowingly at Criton. "We should leave tomorrow, whether we have your God's guidance or not."

"Phaedra won't be happy about it," Hunter commented, "but I can tell her we're leaving soon. Where are we going?"

Goodweather began to cry.

"That depends on Criton and his God."

Criton went to bed that night hoping for a vision from his God, but it was not God Most High who spoke to him as he slept. Instead, the prophet Salemis appeared to him. The great dragon was flying so high above the clouds that his shadow seemed to span half the world. The air was thin and cold, but

Salemis seemed to have no trouble staying aloft. When he saw Criton, still somehow lying in bed so far below, he almost smiled.

"Are you feeling better?" he asked.

"I'll be fine," Criton said, still asleep beside Bandu. "Are you visiting the heavens?"

"I will be returning soon," the dragon answered. "Are you well enough to travel?"

"I think so."

"Then gather your friends and go north. I will meet you in my old home, by the mountains of Ardis."

2

PHAEDRA

Hunter's dagger was not the best tool for this kind of work, but Phaedra considered herself an expert in perseverance. She carefully slid the blade back and forth, back and forth, working at the space between the saddle's seat and its frame. Slowly, painstakingly, the top layer of leather began to part from its base, and with each stroke, Phaedra moved the dagger more easily. When she finally dropped her tool and held up the single, pliable piece of leather in her hands, she found that it was still too thick to easily roll up like a proper scroll. But makeshift parchment was better than none; with a steel nail or a sharp rock, it would mark easily enough.

They ate what Hunter had brought with him from the ruined camp. Phaedra spent the meal lost in thought, composing her first words. When she had finished eating, she took a flint shard off the ground, settled the leather in her lap, and scratched into it:

I am Phaedra Merchantsdaughter, of the once-great island of
Tarphae. Here is what befell my people, both those who perished
and those few who remain beside me.
*   I must begin my account with the circumstances under which*
we left Tarphae behind. In the year before the plague, I had
developed a youthful obsession with Atel the Messenger God,

*and I was eager to visit the Atellan abbey known as Crossroads
on a pilgrimage. On the eve of Karassa's summer festival, I
booked passage for myself and my nursemaid Kelina on a
fishing boat headed for Atuna. Four others joined us there:
Hunter of House Tavener, Criton of the Dragon Touched, Bandu
of the woods, and Narky.*

*Unbeknownst to the rest of us, or indeed to the fisherman
who had promised us passage, Bandu brought with her the wolf
Four-foot, concealed under a blanket. Shortly after we left the
harbor at Karsanye, this wolf escaped from its hiding place. In
the chaos that ensued, my poor Kelina fell out of the boat and
was drowned. Bandu was eventually able to calm Four-foot,
but not before the fisherman gave him a long cut with his knife
– a cut that would eventually become infected and mean the
animal's doom.*

On and on Phaedra wrote, her lettering growing smaller and
smaller as she grew more practiced with the flint. When she
next looked up from her work, the sun had nearly set. She let
out a sigh of contentment and got up to stretch her uneven
legs. *I've barely even begun,* she thought happily.

She slept well that night, better than she had slept in ages.
In her dreams she was dancing with the carefree joy that she
had lost the day her nursemaid Kelina had drowned. Her feet
glided along effortlessly and the music went on and on, though
the musicians were nowhere to be seen among the crowd that
surrounded her, watching her glorious performance. They had
never seen anything like it before, she knew. They would go
home and tell all the world what they had seen.

In the morning, Phaedra did her best to roll up her makeshift
scroll, and joined her friends as they prepared to leave. She
had woken late, and seemed to have missed the morning's
argument.

"Where are we going?" she asked Narky.

"Ardis," Narky told her, looking somewhat ill.

"The Dragon Knight's Tomb, really," Hunter explained. "It

came to Criton in a dream. It's awfully close to Ardis, either way. I think we should ignore it, but I've been overruled."

"We can't go around ignoring the Gods," Narky said. "Certainly not now, and certainly not this one."

Phaedra nodded, noting how different both Narky and Hunter sounded from the young men she had met last yea ckat40 r. They seemed to have taken up each other's sides of the argument.

"You don't believe in Criton's vision?" Phaedra asked Hunter.

"I do believe him," he said. "But going near Ardis means death, either for us or for a lot of Ardismen. I don't want to be a part of it."

"We may not need your sword, with Salemis there," Criton said hopefully.

"My sword broke," Hunter reminded him. "I don't plan on taking another."

The others all stared. They stared, but Phaedra was proud. The last time she had spoken to Hunter about his calling, he had been full of despair. His place as the islanders' protector was a constant burden on him, and yet when Phaedra had said that one day he might be able to lay down his sword, he had responded, "But I don't know how to *do* anything else!"

Now that despair was gone. He had made the decision to build himself a new life, and whatever it might turn out to be, he already looked happier for it.

"The army the red priest raised is gone," Criton pointed out. "There'll be no scouts to watch for us when we near Ardis, and nobody who sees will dare confront us. They'll have heard stories by now."

"That's true," Phaedra said, weighing in. "As long as we don't go through Ardis itself, we may well be safe. Especially if Salemis meets us there."

"We can go," Hunter said. "Just don't expect any more killing out of me."

There had been a time when Phaedra loved to travel. Now her ruined ankle turned her pleasure sour; made her legs uneven, her hips disjointed, her back stiff and achy. She wished they still had a horse, and felt selfish just thinking it. They all still had their lives, didn't they?

They spent weeks slogging northwards in the dry heat, sleeping in the open with only clothes for pillows: the straw mattresses were too hard to carry, and all the tents that had gone up around Silent Hall had been burned when the dragon Salemis came to the islanders' rescue. They did not bother asking for shelter at the houses they passed along the way, for these were the families whose menfolk had died in the fire. It was a miserable journey in more ways than one.

They chose to give wide berth to the city of Anardis, a move that was as necessary as it was disappointing. Phaedra desperately wanted to know whether the Great Temple of Elkinar still stood, and how its high priestess had fared in the months since they had last seen her, but Anardis too had citizens who would blame the islanders for their misfortunes. In fact, the entire region of Hagardis had cause to hate them. Phaedra dearly wished Criton were leading them somewhere else.

They were deep in the territory that had belonged to the God Magor – but was it still His? Phaedra wondered whether the loss of the red priest's army had been enough to break Magor's power in the region. If so, who would benefit? Magor's worshippers respected power, and His defeat had been the work of God Most High, yet it seemed highly unlikely that the people of Hagardis would turn to the dragons' God. There was too much bad blood.

There was no doubt the islanders were getting noticed as they traveled north, but it seemed no one dared confront them. They foraged as they went – stealing, really – but nobody who saw them did anything but stare. It made Phaedra feel like they were somehow not a part of the world they traveled through.

When they reached the southern outskirts of Ardis, the people's reactions to them grew stranger still. Men and women gasped, and children pointed. "O see, the prophet speaks truth!" one woman cried.

It was not the reaction they had expected.

They grew bolder. At the next tributary village, they stopped and asked for food. Far from the aggression they had dreaded, the people there treated them as exalted guests, fed them a feast of lamb and dates and sweet wine, and offered them lodging in the house of an elder.

"The prophet spoke of your arrival," the elder explained. "Whether you're angels or men, you're welcome here."

"Thank you," Phaedra said, leaving the half-asked question unanswered. "When did you see this prophet?"

"Ten days ago. She appeared out of a cloud of dust, black of hair and white of skin, and said that you would be coming from the south to herald the beginning of a new age. A one-eyed man, she said, with skin black as night and four companions as dark as himself, speaking words of truth. Have you any words for us?"

The islanders looked at each other. Whoever this prophet was, it was not Salemis.

"The dragon Salemis has been freed," Criton said, "and God Most High has defeated Magor in battle. As the Oracle of Laarna said, the Gods Themselves will be judged in the coming days."

The elder and all the other villagers nodded meekly and asked no more questions. Phaedra wondered who this mysterious prophet might be, and why she had singled out Narky, but she did not have to wonder long. When the islanders left the village the next morning, their walk took them past a Temple of Magor, closed and abandoned. Some vandal had chalked an enormous sigil on the wall beside the door, an artless pictograph of a bird in flight.

A symbol of Ravennis.

3

NARKY

"It's the Oracle."

Only two of the three priestesses that had made up the famed Oracle of Ravennis had been executed when Laarna fell to the Ardisian army. The Graceful Servant, the one in the middle, had survived somehow. Now she had resurfaced, and was being hailed as a prophet. Narky had been right: Ravennis still lived. But in what form?

The battlefield outside Laarna had been riddled with the bodies of crows. They had believed Ravennis dead, or whatever passed for dead among the Gods. Was it possible He had recovered already? His servant was certainly wasting no time converting the men of Hagardis to her religion. How quickly Magor's triumph had been erased!

The next town they came to treated them just as well as the first. After the Oracle's visit, their very arrival seemed to prove her God's power to them, and even the most devout of Magor's worshippers began to doubt their own God's might. After all, wasn't Magor supposed to have defeated Ravennis for good? If Ravennis remained and Magor's high priest did not, who could argue that the God of the Wild was as strong as ever?

When Narky asked, nobody knew exactly where the Graceful Servant had gone. North, many thought, but to where? At the next town, however, the people pointed Narky west, to Ardis.

"The prophet said that the one-eyed man would follow her to Ardis while his companions traveled on," an elderly woman told him. "She said her God had marked you as His."

Narky nodded. "She's right," he said.

It was Phaedra who objected the most. "I don't understand," she said that night. "I'm as curious as you are about Ravennis, but don't you think we should stick together? We know now, from both Salemis and the fairies, that God Most High really is supreme among the Gods. He's been our protector more than Ravennis has – Salemis is the servant who really saved us, and he said to meet him at the Dragon Knight's Tomb. Bestillos might be gone, but Ardis is still the city of our enemies. Why don't you stay with us, at least for now?"

Her argument was weak, and she knew it. He could see the pleading in her eyes. The five of them had been together for over a year now, the lone Tarphaeans in a sea of pale angry faces, and parting had begun to feel unnatural – that, and inherently dangerous. He understood, and he felt the same way, but his God had spoken.

"Criton's God might be the biggest and the strongest," he said, "but Ravennis owns me. His mark is on my chest, Phaedra. If He says I ought to go into Ardis alone, that's what I'm going to do."

"We may never see you again."

The truth of her words struck him hard. She was afraid of losing him for good.

"The Dragon Knight's Tomb isn't far from Ardis," he said, but it was a feeble answer. He looked at his friends, friends he had never thought he would have, and his heart ached. When he had first met them all, he could hardly wait for them to part ways. But parting had been impossible – first Ravennis had held them together, and then Psander, and now the others felt like a part of him. Yes, they had separated before, but always with a plan to regroup afterwards, and Narky had never been truly alone since he'd first stepped into that fishing boat in Karsanye, hoping to escape justice. This time was different. This time his

God wanted him alone.

What awaited him in that city? He couldn't pretend he wasn't terrified of being away from the others, of being at the mercy of his enemies, *in Ardis*. Could Ravennis even protect him there? He hadn't protected the Youthful Servant or the Venerable one.

But he had no choice. He dared not defy his God. Ravennis had spared him from His wrath once, but that had been for an honest mistake. Or a dishonest one, really, but a mistake nonetheless. In any case, Narky doubted his God would forgive open defiance.

He said his goodbyes the next morning and set off at a brisk pace, afraid that if he didn't hurry it would give his fears the chance to paralyze him. He tried not to wonder what the God of Fate had in store for him. He wondered instead what it meant to be the God of Fate when another God, the dragons' God, reigned supreme in the heavens. The fairies had convinced Narky well enough that God Most High really did live up to His name, so what was Ravennis' role? Did He not command fate, but instead guard it somehow; watch over it; decide what to reveal and what to keep hidden? To what purpose had Ravennis angered Magor, if He knew that His Oracle's words would lead to the destruction of His city of Laarna? Had it been some kind of trick?

He should have discussed it with Phaedra when he had the chance. Even when she didn't have answers, discussions with her were always clarifying. He hoped she didn't waste too much time writing the islanders' story – her talents were wasted on recording the past. He wondered what she would make of herself. He hoped he didn't die before he saw her again.

But back to Ravennis. After seeming to lose to the God of the Wild, He had instead outflanked Magor and was now stealing His followers. Narky had always thought himself unworthy of his God's favor, but these new developments presented another possibility: perhaps Ravennis had chosen him *because* he wasn't righteous; because he was the sort of man who shot his enemies in the back. Did his refusal to fight fair make him a more suitable tool for the God of Fate?

He hoped it was not too blasphemous a thought, but whatever this maneuver against Magor had entailed, it was devious. Surely the Keeper of Fates had an unfair advantage over the other Gods, even if it was only greater knowledge and not actual control. After this trick, what would be his God's next move?

Whatever it was, he was now a part of it.

Ardis rose in front of him, walled and imposing. Was he even going to be able to get in? If the guards at the gate were less reverent than the villagers in the outskirts, his journey was about to come to a sudden and disappointing – if not at all unexpected – end.

Two guards stood rigidly outside the gates of Ardis, their short spears and shields at the ready. Narky wished his friends were still beside him. It wouldn't have made him any safer, but it would have made him *feel* safer.

It was hard to breathe. If he didn't do this now, his panic would take hold of him. With a silent prayer to Ravennis, he walked up to the nearest guard and forced himself to speak.

"Um," he said. "I assume you know who I am. Can I enter, then?"

The guards stared at him silently. They probably couldn't believe that he had delivered himself like this. A few seconds dragged by, and Narky couldn't bring himself to meet their eyes. What was taking them so long? Were they dumb? Were they trying to decide what to do with him? Maybe they just liked to see him squirm.

Or maybe they hadn't heard of him. "My name is Narky," he said. "I'm one of the Tarphaean islanders who fought against Ardis at Silent Hall – that is, at the wizard's fortress. I'm sure you heard what happened there, or maybe even saw…"

Even at the gates of Ardis, the towering Yarek was just visible on the horizon. Narky waved his arm in that direction and kept right on talking, letting his nervousness spill across his tongue.

"The prophet of Ravennis left a message for me to follow her here," he said.

The guards still did not move, and when he looked up, he saw the fear in their eyes now. Terror, even. Something was very wrong here – were these men even alive? They seemed incapable of motion, besides the frightened little movements of their eyes.

"They're paralyzed," said a voice from up ahead, and a plump middle-aged woman strode toward him. Her hair was as black as his, though there were many gray strands mixed in, and her skin was as white as any mountain clanswoman.

"Not to worry," she said, "it's only temporary. Many of the Ardismen have not yet converted, but Ravennis guides and we follow. In the case of these men, He guided me to poison the wine they drank with their noonday meal."

Narky stared much as the guards were doing. "You're the Graceful Servant," he said dumbly.

The woman smiled. "Welcome to Ardis."

4

BANDU

Things got quiet after Narky left. The pack had lost a member, and everyone was too sad to speak. It was not like when Four-foot had died. Then the others had closed around Bandu out of sympathy, but they had hardly known her and had seen Four-foot only as people had always seen him: a wolf, a wild animal, a monster with teeth. Losing Narky was more shocking to them, even though he wasn't dead.

Not yet, anyway. Maybe his God would protect him, maybe not. Bandu had a low opinion of Gods. Even Criton's God Most High did not impress her as He did the others. So, He had created the world. So, He was more powerful than all the other Gods. So what? Was He kinder than They were? The fate of the dragons spoke otherwise. So what if He had defeated the Yarek, built the mesh that separated the heavens from the earth, made a world that could sustain her existence for a time? It had to all be *for* something, and if it was not for kindness then it was no good. Bandu did not worship things just because they were big.

She wondered if Criton really understood how she felt about his God; how she hated the way it consumed his thoughts. But then, it was wrong to blame the God for that: Criton was the sort of man who could only really care about one thing at a time. That wasn't his God's fault.

It was Criton's fault. He hardly knew a thing about this God of his, but now it was all that mattered because the God *belonged* to him, to the part of his family that he wanted to call his own. That was what really bothered her.

She knew he loved her, of course, and that he loved Goodweather too. Just not enough. If he lost them he would tear his hair and mourn, but he would heal one day and do his best to replace them, just the way he had replaced his father with a dragon half the size of a mountain.

Maybe that was forgivable. After all, she had tried to replace Four-foot too. But she had failed, she realized now. Criton was no replacement for Four-foot. The wolf had wanted only to live and to be with her; Criton was more complicated.

She still missed Four-foot terribly. The wizard Psander had offered to help Bandu tear her way into the underworld to retrieve him, but she had not done anything about it for months, and now she was gone. She had moved her fortress into the world of the elves and left the islanders to their troubles. Bandu almost hoped the Kindly Folk would eat her.

They traveled northward in subdued silence, all but Goodweather. Goodweather still cried, still scratched when nursing, still breathed sparks when she hiccupped. Bandu tried binding her hands so that she wouldn't scratch so hard at least, but the girl had a way of wriggling out of the bindings and finding flesh to press her razor-sharp claws against. Bandu had wanted the pregnancy, and wanted Goodweather still, but she had to admit that she hadn't really considered those tiny claws when she and Criton had mated.

At last they came to the foot of the mountain in which Salemis had once lived, in a cave now called the Dragon Knight's Tomb. The climb was not hard – at least, it was far easier than it had been when Bandu was still pregnant. Yet as they came nearer the cave, they began to hear voices up ahead.

"Who could that be?" Hunter asked, automatically reaching for a sword that wasn't there. He frowned at his empty hand for a moment and put it behind his back. "It sounds like a whole crowd."

"This is where Salemis said to meet him," Criton said stubbornly. "There's nothing for us to fear up there."

Nobody responded. They were all quiet, feeling the emptiness where Narky's voice should have been. Bandu did not know what he would have said – she had found some time ago that she could ignore him half the time without missing anything important. Still, his absence felt wrong.

They trudged the rest of the way up to the mouth of the cave, listening to the sounds that drifted down to them. Whatever the argument was about, it ceased when they reached the entrance to the Dragon Knight's Tomb, as those inside turned to look at them and fell into silence.

There were some thirty people in the cave, and they were all Dragon Touched. They were disguised as Criton so often disguised himself, but Bandu could see through such things. Their pale continental skin melted into golden scales beneath her gaze, and their frightened eyes turned an almost radiant yellow. Even outnumbering the islanders more than seven to one, they could not conceal their terror. How long had they hidden in the shadows of Ardis? Did they expect the islanders to turn them in?

Criton stepped forward, and Bandu was suddenly afraid. Her mate was not the last of his kind after all. Would he abandon her for this new family?

He cleared his throat and let his hands turn back into claws. "My name is Criton, the son of Galanea. We are here to meet Salemis."

A murmur went through the crowd. "It's true, then?" one of the women said. "My daughter thought she'd seen a dragon a few weeks ago."

"The Ardismen who fought in the south have been saying for weeks that they were attacked by a dragon," said one of the younger men. "I told you all then, but you wouldn't believe me!"

"The Dragons' Prisoner is free, then?" a gray-haired elder asked.

"He is," Phaedra said. "We freed him from his prison beneath the world of the elves, and he rescued us from the armies of Magor and Mayar. He told Criton he would meet us here."

It was hard for Bandu to tell whether the Dragon Touched were more excited or more afraid to hear that the dragon would be coming to meet them in this place.

Goodweather made some very upset noises, but those had less to do with Salemis than they did with her wet bottom. Bandu gave her to Criton. She wanted him to remember that he had a *real* family to worry about.

He knelt on the cave's floor and began to unbind the baby's clothes, but was unable to keep his mind on the task at hand. "If you didn't know Salemis was coming," he asked, looking up, "why are you all here?"

"I called the meeting," the elder said. "Even with Bestillos gone, turmoil is dangerous for our people. Who knows who may rise to take his place?"

"You come here to worship too, don't you?" Phaedra asked her suddenly. "We found a goblet here once…"

The elder nodded. "It is a site holy to God Most High."

Criton looked up again, though he was still not finished changing Goodweather's swaddling clothes. "You still worship God Most High," he breathed. "I – we – we are servants of God Most High too, but we know nothing of his worship. My mother did not teach me of our people's God."

Hunter made a noise of sudden understanding. "You're Dragon Touched," he said to the crowd.

"Yes," the elder said, and for a moment she too dropped the disguise. But only for a moment. "Bestillos' purge was not complete. Some of us managed to hide ourselves. As long as we kept out of the red priest's sight, no one else could see our true forms. We have been hiding for a generation now – I have been the midwife to every child born in our community. We teach our children to hide their heritage before we let them leave our homes, and we marry them to each other while they are still young so that no outsider can know of us.

It has kept us alive so far."

"How many are there?" Criton asked.

"Each family has sent one person to this meeting," the midwife answered. "There were only thirty-eight who survived the purge, but we are nearly two hundred now."

Criton stood up. "Salemis is free, and God Most High has arisen. We should not need to hide any longer."

There was a murmur of approval from the younger generation of Dragon Touched, but the elder answered coldly, "That is not a decision to be made hastily. If Salemis is indeed alive and free and coming to meet us here, we can decide that together after he arrives. You have risked our lives once already, Criton, son of Galanea. After years of quiet, your appearance drove the red priest half insane searching for the remnants of the Dragon Touched. How many times have the Ardismen nearly discovered us? Now here you are, telling us to openly announce our presence!"

"I'm sorry my being here brought danger upon you," Criton said, "but I'm not sorry for what I've done. I'm not sorry I came here, and I'm not sorry that Salemis is free, and with God Most High protecting us, I'd be glad never to disguise myself again."

Half the Dragon Touched seemed ready to cheer, but they did not, out of respect for their elder. "I wish I could agree with you," the woman said, "but I was here during the purge. If the Dragons' Prisoner himself comes here and tells us to follow your advice, then I will trust that it is the will of God Most High. Until then, you are only a dangerous young man."

"We can wait," said Hunter, putting a hand on Criton's shoulder. "We only came here to meet Salemis."

"Are you *all* worshippers of God Most High?" asked the same young man who had spoken before. "Even the... even the rest of you?"

Bandu shook her head, but Phaedra answered for them. "We know little of God Most High," she said, "but Criton is our countryman, and the Goddess of our homeland has abandoned our people. We hope to find favor in your God's eyes."

The crowd nodded along, and even the elder looked pleased. Phaedra always knew how to talk to people.

They waited there together, talking, for more than an hour, and still the dragon did not come. Criton and Phaedra passed the time asking questions and getting acquainted with the Dragon Touched, learning their ways, and telling them about themselves. Bandu knew she should join them – it was important to Criton, and he was bound to want to stay with these people for a long time – but for now she stayed back, holding Goodweather and trying not to panic. There were too many people here, too many eyes looking at her. It was agonizing.

Hunter seemed to feel similarly, but he at least could listen to the others without getting tired of it. Bandu couldn't bring herself to listen to Phaedra telling their story – her story – to these people, or to join Criton in caring about how the Dragon Touched worshipped their God. She just wanted to go somewhere quiet and hide.

"May I see the baby?" one of the women asked, and Bandu clutched Goodweather closer to her. "What's his name?"

"She is Goodweather," Bandu said, and the woman apologized for guessing wrong, as if Bandu cared.

After another hour, the crowd began to grow smaller as people went home to their families, afraid of what might happen if their neighbors noticed them gone for too long. Hour after hour went by, until only the elderly midwife remained with them, standing in the mouth of the cave and looking for Salemis in the darkening sky. Apparently her name was Hessina, and she was the matriarch of a family called the Highservants.

"The Highservants are the priestly line of the Dragon Touched," Hessina told them. "My father was High Priest before the purge, before the worshippers of Magor tortured him to death and tore the temple down. I thought I would never see it rebuilt, but if Salemis comes to fight for our cause, how can we lose? We may not have believed every rumor that came our way, but there's no denying that very few soldiers came back from the battle in the south. If Salemis was there, I can see why. What happened exactly?"

Phaedra repeated the story of the battle at Silent Hall, with even more detail than before, and also gave Hessina the leather she had been scratching on all these weeks. "I wrote it all down here," she said. "Please, keep it."

Bandu sighed. If these dead animal skins with the words on them were so wonderful, why did Phaedra have to repeat herself too?

Goodweather had fallen asleep in Bandu's arms, so she laid the baby down on their empty sack of food and stretched her weary muscles. She ought to make Criton do more of the carrying.

By this time they had waited so long that the sun had set. Hessina stood and stretched. "Salemis will not come tonight. We can return tomorrow morning."

It was an invitation, and Criton looked tempted, but Bandu shook her head. After all this, Goodweather was finally sleeping, and Bandu had no intention of waking her. "We stay tonight," she said.

Hessina nodded and made to leave them. "May I escort you?" Hunter asked. "It's almost dark; the climb will be treacherous."

"I know my way."

They settled down in the cave and tried to sleep. It was no good, and not because the ground was so hard. Criton kept her awake with excited chatter about how wonderful it was not to be the only Dragon Touched, and how much he looked forward to learning even more about their ways.

"You were not only the one before," Bandu pointed out, gesturing to Goodweather between them.

"You know what I meant," Criton said. "I don't just have a child now; I have a people."

"You have people before too," she answered. "Us."

Criton growled in frustration and said, "Bandu, stop. You know what I'm saying. Stop misunderstanding me on purpose."

Bandu did not answer. It was useless. Maybe tomorrow he

would realize that he was the one who was doing his best not to understand, ignoring her because he didn't want to admit that she was right. He didn't want to talk about the way the search for his 'real' family kept him from making one – kept him from giving Bandu and their daughter the attention they deserved.

She slept fitfully, as she so often did now – Goodweather kept waking up wet and hungry, and though the baby soon fell asleep again, it always took Bandu longer than it ought to. The last time Goodweather woke her was around dawn, and Bandu looked around the cave trying to decide whether to rise or to try to squeeze in another hour or two of sleep before her companions awoke. She thought she could hear wing beats in the distance, but she couldn't quite decide if they were real or if it was her imagination.

Then the ground shook, and she heard the dragon's claws scraping against the stones outside. Not her imagination, then. Salemis was here.

5

SALEMIS

It hurt to leave his mate; it always had, and it always would. There was no feeling that could compare with the touch of Eramia's divine presence in the world above, without a mesh of sky to come between them. What a reward God Most High had prepared for him, to open the heavens at his arrival! To leave now was pain itself.

But he had to leave, at least for a short time. His Dragon Children were waiting for him. If he did not return, who knew what they might think in his absence? What they might do? They needed his leadership, even if only for a moment, to set them on the path that his God intended for them.

So he left his God and his love and returned to the world that had hatched him, the world that now belonged to humanity. He arrived just as dawn was breaking, landing outside his former home for what must surely be the last time. That was all right – he would not miss it here. Now that he had seen his love's home in the heavens, this mountain struck him as unspeakably dismal.

But it was nice to breathe proper air again, to feel the satisfying way it filled his lungs as he called his descendants to him. His voice rang off the mountains that had once been his enemy Caladoris, echoing in the valley between until he was sure all of Hagardis must have heard him. But his words were intended for his descendants alone, and only they would know what they were hearing.

The islanders who had rescued him, children of Tarphae, stumbled out of the cave that had once been his home, and was now a tomb.

"You're here!" the dragon child Criton exclaimed.

"I am here," Salemis agreed.

"Have you come to lead us?"

He had known they would ask this. Of course they would, poor things.

"No," he said. "I have not come to lead you."

The boy looked crestfallen. "Do not worry," Salemis told him. "God Most High is with you. This world is not for me anymore, but that does not mean the heavens have abandoned you. Lead your people well, and our God will watch over you."

Criton had been nodding sadly until he heard this last piece of encouragement. "*What?*" he cried. "*I* can't lead the Dragon Touched – I only just found out they exist!"

"I understand," Salemis answered. "You have nonetheless been chosen."

"But I *can't!*"

Salemis dismissed his objection with a hiss. "It is decided," he said. "God Most High has chosen you to lead His people. Will you defy His wishes?"

Criton's eyes widened, and he shook his head. "But why me?" he asked.

"I am a prophet," Salemis told him, "but I am not God Most High. Only He knows why He has chosen you."

"But why would He keep something like that from us?" Phaedra asked. "Shouldn't Criton know what's expected of him?"

Salemis looked down at them with sympathy. "Our God created the elves' world Himself," he said. "More than that – He watched the elves explore the world He had made for them; He taught them to sing and to pray and to write poetry; He guided their growth and gave them their castles as gifts. But still they wanted to live in the heavens, to join the Lower Gods or to replace Them, and when He told them they could not, they threatened to rebel. He and the Lower Gods had to create a new world to protect those creations that were salvageable. The first dragons were among these.

"God Most High no longer guides His creations as closely as He once did. Even when He intervenes on your behalf, He will not speak to you of it. It was partly His attentions that drove the elves to madness."

The islanders looked sullenly at each other, but he knew they understood. They had seen the madness of the elves first hand, and would not deny that the younger world was better without the risk of succumbing to it.

Salemis gazed down upon the valley, where groups of his descendants were now streaming toward the mountain, a few of them already beginning to climb it.

"It is almost time," he said. "Soon I will give the Dragon Children my message, and then I shall return to the heavens, possibly forever."

"Please," Phaedra said, "tell us about the heavens before you go."

Salemis had to turn his head away lest he laugh too hard and incinerate them all. "The heavens are indescribable. I would not know where to start."

"Then just tell me, was the sage Katinaras right about the Gods? Are They genderless? Do They have no families? Are They all equally ageless?"

"These are too many questions to answer at once," Salemis told her. "The Gods are genderless if They choose to be so; They have no bodies that we would recognize, and do not reproduce the same way that we animals do. They sometimes take on masculine or feminine aspects, but that is entirely by choice, and is not immutable. They are not ruled by physicality, which makes Them very flexible. Those that tie Themselves to your world can be greatly affected by the actions that Their followers take. Even God Most High has changed since I last flew these skies."

The islanders gasped. "How?" Criton asked.

"He has grown more forgiving."

The Dragon Children had gathered sufficiently by then, so Salemis turned to face them, raising his voice so that all could hear. "I am Salemis," he said. "I am the one you have known as the Dragons' Prisoner, the prophet of God Most High. I have returned to you for a time so that you will know the words of the God Above All. Listen to these words, for the age of petty gods is coming to an end.

"God Most High has told me that the Dragon Touched will rise to become a great people, but I will not be leading you. My place is in the heavens now. Our God knows that you have followed His ways even in hiding, and has told me to elevate His servant Hessina as His High Priestess. Heed her in all matters of ritual and worship, as it will please your God.

"As for your leadership in matters of war and peace, God Most High has sent His servant Criton, the son of Galanea and a son of Tarphae, to lead your army and show you your path. Respect him, and you respect your God.

"My time here is at an end. Trust in God Most High and follow His path, and you cannot fail."

With that, Salemis leapt from the mountain, gliding for a time on the warm summer air before beating his wings and rising up toward the heavens. If he missed anything, he thought it would be the good, fragrant air of this world. Perhaps if his God allowed him to, he would return sometimes, just to feel it in his lungs. But then, he didn't want to weaken the mesh by visiting too frequently.

Besides, his love awaited him. Why should he ever leave again?

6

NARKY

The Graceful Servant led him through streets and alleys, twisting and turning through Ardis until she finally unlocked the door to a small house and let him in. It was dark inside, dark enough that Narky stood helplessly for a minute while he waited for his eye to adjust. It was a long wait.

"Most of the Ardismen do not know what I look like," the Graceful Servant said.

"You do sort of blend in," Narky said. Besides her distinctly Laarnese coloration, her features were not particularly memorable. In the dark, Narky found that he was already forgetting them.

"I have been spreading my teachings carefully," she said. "Those who would learn more come here, where none can see each other. If one or more is captured, they will not be able to identify each other."

"Fair enough," Narky said, "but won't they be able to lead people here?"

"Could you?"

"No, but I don't live here. If I'd lived in Ardis all my life–"

"–then you would find your memories escaping you even as I led you here." The Oracle's voice was almost smug. "There is nothing to fear. We will not be found until we are ready, and besides, we will be ready very soon."

That sounded pretty ominous. "Ready for what?"

"Ready for the open. Ready to convert thousands to the worship of Ravennis, Keeper of Fates and God of the Underworld."

"God of the Underworld?" Narky repeated. "I thought there was no God of the Underworld."

Laughter in the darkness. "You were right, but things have changed. There were too many Gods in the heavens, and nobody to watch the dead. The Keeper of Fates decided to seize that role, for all fates must end in death. You helped Him, you know, by burying my sisters at the foot of His temple. That is why He brought you to Laarna: not to prevent the city's destruction, but to witness it."

Narky felt sick. A city full of people. A city that Ravennis had essentially sacrificed to Himself. Narky hoped its citizens were being rewarded in the afterlife. It was the least their God could do.

"What was your part in this maneuver?" he asked.

"Just like yours, mine was to stay alive; to keep a thread of His power tied to this world while He established His kingdom in the world below. But that is nearly done. Soon He will require us to join Him, to sacrifice ourselves in His name and cement His place not only in the underworld, but in this world as well."

Perhaps Narky was going to throw up after all. His stomach seemed to be plunging down further into his abdomen – it was only a matter of time before it came back up.

"That's what we're preparing for?"

"That is what we are preparing the world for," the Graceful Servant replied, sounding almost giddy. "Our fearless deaths will inspire the people to entrust their souls to Ravennis. All the people of the world will pay Him tribute, in life as in death."

"But how about God Most High?" Narky asked desperately. "I've spoken to fairies, and to the dragon Salemis, and they both say that God Most High is supreme among the Gods. Ravennis owns me and I am His servant in all things, – "*whether I like it or not*" – but is this plan realistic? How could Ravennis or His new followers stand up to God Most High?"

The Graceful Servant laughed again, a high carefree sound that was more terrifying for its levity than any more malevolent laugh could have been. "How many generations has it been since God Most High was active in the world? How many more before He withdraws His attentions again? There will come a time when the world has forgotten God Most High, but they shall never forget Ravennis, king of the world below. One day, when you and I are both long dead, the world may come to believe that Ravennis *is* God Most High."

Narky thought of Criton, his anger and his determination. "Not among the Dragon Touched," he said. "They're not completely gone – my friend is one, and he has a child already. They'll never abandon their God."

"The *Dragon Touched*," the Oracle scoffed. "How many of *them* will there be? Not enough to convince the world that we're wrong. God Most High may reign supreme in the heavens, boy, but Ravennis will have the earth."

Why did Narky find this all so horrifying? Ravennis *was* his God, after all. Why shouldn't his God cheat and manipulate His way into power, especially when power and survival were synonymous as far as the Gods were concerned? And yet... the implications bothered him. For all that he had come to terms with his own tendency to take advantage whenever possible, he wasn't that way on purpose. He had been trying his hardest to leave that part of him behind. Was it really possible that the God who had rescued him from himself now wanted him to embrace that side of his personality?

This woman was a zealot, there was no doubt about that. Even the thought of sacrificing herself to her God's ambitions seemed to fill her with nothing less than delight. Had the destruction of Laarna driven her mad, perhaps? He didn't want to believe that she was right about *everything*.

For one thing, he didn't want to die. Certainly not soon. He hoped that Ravennis would settle for just one holy martyr and leave Narky out of it. The fact was that at this point he had little choice but to do whatever Ravennis wanted of him, even if that meant dying painfully in the near future. It seemed so wrong that his God's survival should make him feel worse off, but there it was. It had been bad enough when all Narky had to fear from disobedience was becoming crow food; that had been before Ravennis took charge of the underworld. Now Narky could be absolutely certain that sooner or later, his God would get him. If Ravennis did find cause to punish him for disobedience, Narky might spend eternity being torn apart by holy birds every day, or every hour. He was trapped.

The door opened and a man's silhouette became briefly visible before whoever it was stepped inside and the door shut again, plunging them back into darkness.

"Teacher?" the man called. His voice cracked a bit. "Are you here?"

"I am here," the Oracle said.

"The priests of Magor are asking for you. They want... a confrontation."

The Graceful Servant chuckled. "Let them wait. First with apprehension, then with anger. Then with desperation, and then with resignation. By the time I appear before them, they will have given up hope."

"But Teacher, they will call you a coward!"

"Death does not come when you call it," she replied calmly. "But it comes."

"Yes, Teacher."

The door opened again, and the man stepped out. When they were alone once more, the Graceful Servant opened a door on the other side of the room and ushered Narky through it into a dimly lit bedroom. There was a cot here, and a window that had been bricked shut and now served mostly as a shelf for candles. The bricks were not mortared, and were spaced far enough apart that some small amount of light slipped in through the cracks.

"You can stay here for a time," the Graceful Servant said. "We will bring you what food you need, and there is a chamber pot beneath the bed. The man who killed Bestillos must not be known to the masses, not yet. Rumors of your presence will spread as it is; the gate guards saw you, after all, even if they could not move. When you go with me to the meeting with Magor's priests, they will quake at the sight of you."

"So I'm a monster for frightening crowds now," Narky said, sitting heavily on the bed, "and until you're ready to use me, you're going to keep me locked up."

The woman looked at him curiously. "Do you prefer it that way? To be an imprisoned monster, to take no responsibility for the role Ravennis has given you? Our God has chosen you above all others, has placed His mark upon your chest! Will you take no pride in His favor? When you slew the champion of Magor, the man who brought fire and slaughter past the gates of Laarna, did you not glory in the task Ravennis set before you?"

Narky stared at her in the dim light. "You amaze me!" the Oracle cried. "Have you not done these deeds by choice?"

"I chose not to let my friends die," Narky snapped. "I don't know about you, but Ravennis hasn't ever told me what He's up to. He showed me mercy, and gave me a second chance. He saved me. But He's never explained Himself. I've just been doing what seemed right to me, trying to stay alive and follow whatever signs Ravennis sends me, and be… better. Better than I am."

He lapsed into silence, surprised and ashamed at how quickly his defiance had turned to confession. When the Graceful Servant spoke, her tone was softer.

"You may not deserve your redemption," she said, "but Ravennis is more merciful than the Gods above. Nobody in this world is good enough to join Them in the heavens, but Ravennis became Lord Among the Fallen so that we could share His mercy in the world below. Only through His love can we find kindness in the afterlife."

Narky's eyes widened as he began to understand. "That's what Ravennis told you?"

The Oracle nodded.

"And what happens to those who don't find favor in His eyes? What's the afterlife like for them?"

This time she only shrugged, a smile creeping across her lips.

"Gods above," Narky breathed. "Gods above and Ravennis below. It's not for His sake that you're trying to convince people to worship Him, is it? It's for their own sakes."

Another nod. The Graceful Servant's eyes shone with the power of her belief, and as he looked into them with his own single eye, he began to feel that same strength growing within him.

"We have to succeed," he said. "Life in this world is short, but the afterlife doesn't end! People have to know that only Ravennis can reward them in a way that lasts. My friends who worship God Most High are making a mistake – they're only thinking about this life and not the next! I have to tell them. We have to make them understand that the favor of other Gods is meaningless! We have to spread the word!"

"Yes, we do," said the Graceful Servant, and her eyes twinkled in the dim light. "Welcome to the brotherhood of Ravennis. We are truly glad to have you."

7

CRITON

When Salemis had disappeared among the clouds, Criton and his companions began their climb down toward his people. It took some effort – a part of him wanted to crawl away and hide. What would be worse: for his kin to reject his leadership, or accept it? He didn't feel at all prepared to lead the Dragon Touched, but he still wanted their respect. What would he do if they laughed at him, or gently listened to his words without giving them any weight? If Salemis said he was ready for this, he thought the Dragon Touched ought to accept that. But would they? After all, he couldn't quite accept it himself.

They were in sight now, all climbing toward him. His chest tightened in panic, and his breathing became heavy. How could Salemis have done this to him? How could his God? He had been so hopeful that Salemis would tell him what to do when he got here. Now he'd been abandoned.

Bandu was at his elbow. "I am here. They don't hurt you."

Criton looked down at her. "You'll protect me?" he asked, smiling weakly.

Bandu nodded, still looking down the mountain at the approaching crowd. Her face remained serious. "I always protect you."

They faced the descendants of Salemis together, while

Hunter and Phaedra stayed a short distance behind. The Dragon Touched arrived not long afterwards.

"Are you Criton?" the first asked, a big solid man in his thirties, with long brown hair that reminded Criton of his Ma.

Criton nodded.

The man regarded him seriously. "My uncle was named Criton, and he had a daughter named Galanea, who fled her home as a girl before the purge. Can it be that you are my cousin?"

Criton nodded, stunned. "This is my family," he said, by way of hasty introduction. "My wife Bandu, our daughter, our friends Hunter and Phaedra and – and that's all of us."

"Who are you?" Bandu asked defiantly, pulling the top of her dress down so she could nurse Goodweather. Criton could hear Phaedra wincing at Bandu's immodesty, and hoped she wasn't shocking them too badly. He desperately wanted to make a good impression.

"I am Belkos," the man said. "My daughter is engaged to Hessina's grandson."

"Really?" Phaedra asked. "How old is she?" Hessina had said the Dragon Touched married their children to each other early, but Belkos still seemed a bit too young to have a daughter of marrying age.

"Eleven," Belkos answered. "Letting them wait longer is too dangerous. If even one of us intermarried…"

He broke off, eyes widening as he realized what he had said. Obviously Criton's mother had intermarried. She had been pale like Belkos, her hair brown and wavy. Criton… was different.

His feelings about his mother's choice were more complicated now than he had even realized, and far too complicated to talk about in front of this crowd. Only Bandu would understand. She had a way of cutting through all the subtleties of a thing and plucking out its beating core.

But Bandu! Criton had intermarried as well; maybe *that* was why Belkos had broken off so awkwardly. Did the Dragon Touched already disapprove of his marriage?

"I understand," Criton said, hoping to reduce the tension. "Your community might have been discovered."

"Anyway," a tall woman said, "there will be no more hiding now."

"Right," Criton agreed. "Salemis says God Most High is with us. As long as He's with us, we have nothing to fear."

They continued the descent together and were soon surrounded by Criton's kin. Criton had to admit that it felt strange to suddenly be one among many, to have a whole community where his scales and claws and fire breath were the norm. And yet... he still didn't fit in. The Dragon Touched clearly saw him as a foreigner: exotic and unreliable. His darker skin put a greater distance between him and them than his scales and claws had ever put between him and Bandu.

Being named as their leader only made things worse. They would never have chosen him of their own volition. Even as a decree handed down straight from God Most High, it was pretty presumptuous. How could he possibly lead these people? He hadn't suffered with them; hadn't had to hide like them; had never lived among them. It took imagination and focus for him to relate to their struggles, and they surely understood him even less.

Why had God Most High chosen him? Was it some kind of misguided reward for freeing Salemis? In Ma's stories, the hero was often rewarded with the throne of a far-off kingdom. Sometimes he achieved this by marrying a princess; sometimes he turned out to be the long-lost heir to the throne. Would she have been proud to see Criton living one of these stories? Maybe. But it didn't feel like a reward now that he had it.

Hessina was at the center of those who had not climbed up to meet them, but people made room for Criton and his friends to get by. "So," Hessina said when she saw them. "Here is the boy who is meant to lead us. Come, Criton. Let us confer about the fate of your people."

There was an edge to her voice, though Criton could tell that she was doing her best to be civil. Naturally. She had led her people thus far, and was now being relegated to high priestess when before she had been everything. Criton sighed.

"We haven't got much time," he said. "I don't know if the Ardismen heard or understood Salemis, but plenty of them will have seen him, and seen us. How long do you think it'll take them to raise a new army?"

"I'm no strategist, but surely a week or two at least," Belkos said, "and longer if they want a big one. But they're dangerous to us even in total disarray. We have, what, sixty, seventy men and boys old enough to fight? A mob tonight could come close to wiping us out."

"Do we have weapons?" Criton asked. "Can we defend ourselves?"

Hessina shook her head. "We lost all these things in the purge. Our neighbors have spears and armor, those who came back from the south alive and those who never left. In this season they tend their fields in the day, and at dusk they set their fires and spear-dance until the light dies. It is a rite of Magor."

"Then we should take their weapons now, before they can prepare themselves."

"It cannot be done," Hessina said. "If you would attack now, they would raise an alarm. We would lose half our number before we were armed. The Ardisian women fight as fiercely as the men, and can wield a spear as well. Attack one house and the spears of the whole village will be set against you."

Phaedra made a noise. The islanders knew better. "I didn't say we should attack," Criton said. "I said we should take their weapons. You know your neighbors well enough, don't you? You know the way they look, the way they speak. What's to stop you?"

His new kin looked at him in confusion. He would have to show them. So he made his hair grow longer and straighter. He lightened it and his skin, reworked his face, shortened and broadened his body as well as he could without tearing his clothes, and, with a touch of Psander's illusion, made those clothes look more like those he saw around him. When he was done, he could easily have been Belkos' twin.

He clapped his cousin on the shoulder and surveyed the awed faces that surrounded him. "Don't tell me you've never done this?" he said. "You've been hiding your dragon blood for ages now, making yourselves look more like your neighbors, and you've never tried *being* your neighbors?"

"We've been *hiding*," Hessina snapped, "not practicing transformations or playing dangerous tricks on our oppressors."

Still, Criton could see that she was impressed – she and the rest of the community.

"Cousin!" Belkos cried. "That's ingenious. We can simply walk into our neighbors' houses and take their weapons and armor while their families look on!"

"But what will we say to them?" a younger man asked. "What excuse can we give for taking up their arms?"

"We will say," Criton answered, "that the Dragon Touched have returned."

8
PHAEDRA

"This isn't our fight," Hunter said. They were standing on the outskirts of the crowd while Criton discussed strategy with his cousin and the other Dragon Touched. "The Dragon Touched don't even want us here, Phaedra. And I love Criton like a brother, but I won't kill for him again. Not for him, not for anyone. The lives of the men I've killed are already too heavy for me to bear."

Phaedra nodded absently. There would be war, and soon. For all that she did not want to leave Criton and Bandu, she did not belong in a war either. They had already left Narky to his fate in Ardis – did Bandu and Criton matter more than he did, that she should abandon one and not the others?

The trouble was that Bandu needed her. As hard as it was to be human among the Dragon Touched, it would be so much worse to be the *only* human among the Dragon Touched. Bandu was suspect for being black, suspect for being human, suspect for being Criton's wife. *Criton* was more suspect for being married to her. It would be a very difficult time for her, and Phaedra felt wretched for wanting to leave.

And yet... she had things she wanted to do, things to learn that she could never learn from the Dragon Touched. The elves and dragons, Psander had said, grew their magic like a muscle of the body that could be exercised or neglected, but would grow

49

naturally without any effort. Wizardry was not like that – it was a form of knowledge. With enough discipline and instruction anyone could learn it, and Phaedra meant to.

In the heyday of academic wizardry, Phaedra could have found any number of wizards to teach her the basics; now the only living wizard was trapped in another world. Phaedra's hope was that there were still other sources from which to learn: lesser magicians, or books that Psander had failed to gather in her library. With their natural magic, the Dragon Touched would be of no use in that regard.

"You want to leave Hagardis?" Phaedra asked.

"Yes," Hunter said. "This is no place for me now. It's no place for anyone who refuses to fight."

"Where do you plan on going?"

Hunter looked embarrassed. "I didn't have any particular place in mind. I thought maybe I'd take a ship to one of the outer islands where I can actually blend in, and try to learn a trade. But I don't know where exactly, or even what trade I ought to take up." He hesitated. "Would you go with me?"

"To take up a trade and start an ordinary life?" Phaedra asked. "No. We've escaped the lives we were supposed to have, Hunter. We have the chance to insist on something meaningful. I mean to try piecing together what remains of academic wizardry. I think God Most High might allow it, since He let us rescue Psander from the other Gods."

Hunter looked skeptical. "You want to be another Psander?"

Phaedra shook her head. "Psander did what she did to *preserve* knowledge. It's too late for that here. Most of the writings that weren't destroyed are in her library. I'm not going to reach her level of knowledge or power even if I work at it my whole life. But the Gods created a world full of magic, and I want to know how it works. I want to know *why* it works."

"So where will you go when you leave here?"

Phaedra thought about that. "I don't know. But I think I would have to start in Atuna, because of all the trade that goes through it. You can buy ink and parchment there, instead of having to make it yourself or to scratch your thoughts on heavy leather. After that, I guess I'll have to seek magic wherever I can find it."

Hunter studied her face with a look of profound gravity. "That sounds dangerous, Phaedra."

She smiled at him. "And what's so new about that?"

"There were five of us before. Now there will only be two."

"You're coming with me, then?"

"Do I have a choice?"

"Of course you do."

Hunter didn't answer, and they fell into silence. After a time, Phaedra said, "We're not traveling as a group anymore. Criton and Bandu are staying here; Narky's gone already. You don't have to stay with me. You can find an island to live on, stop wandering, stop protecting us all and think about yourself for once. You hate traveling. You hate fighting and killing. I don't want you to give up on finding a new life for yourself."

Hunter sighed. "I don't hate fighting. I love it, really. It feels natural to me. It's living with what I've done afterwards that I hate."

Phaedra felt for him, but what could she say? She could not guarantee that if he came with her, he would not have to kill again. Nor could she guarantee that she would survive without him. It was all a gamble. And it was her gamble, in pursuit of her goals. How could she intentionally put herself in danger and then ask Hunter to keep her safe?

"Go to your island," she said.

Hunter did seem tempted, but then he shook his head. "I'm not sure I can," he said. "I... I don't know if I'm ready to be alone. I only have four friends in the world, and..." He stopped there, defeated.

Despite herself, Phaedra was happy. She might have been lost without a friend to steady her, and he was right – he may easily have been lost without her too.

"You can join me," she said. "I'd love for you to join me. But I don't want you to kill for me, and if that means that I die, I forgive you in advance. I don't need you torturing yourself. I'd rather travel alone than make you hate yourself for what you're doing."

"Thank you," Hunter said, "but you know I'm not going to let you die."

"Well then," Phaedra said, "I'm not going to let you kill."

He smiled wryly, but said no more.

They said goodbye to Bandu and Criton, though they had to wrest the latter away from his new-found kin in order to do it. Criton seemed disappointed, and Bandu outright mournful, but neither seemed terribly surprised. It was possible they had realized this would happen before Phaedra had.

So they embraced their friends and parted, keeping their goodbyes short. "I hope you find what you're looking for," Criton said, because of course, he himself had done just that.

Bandu hugged Phaedra with tears in her eyes. "Learn slower," she whispered, cryptically.

The journey to Atuna lasted three weeks at Phaedra's slow pace – three weeks of tension intermixed with boredom. She and Hunter already knew what each other were thinking much of the time, and neither had the stomach for smaller conversation. Besides, Hunter had always been the brooding type, and not much of a conversationalist at the best of times. As for Phaedra, she was suddenly, awkwardly afraid of talking too much. She was too aware of the difference between a woman traveling with friends and one traveling with a man, and she didn't want to explore the meanings of her choices more than she had to. She had enough to think about, trying to compile everything she knew about magic.

According to Psander, the magic of dragons was completely innate, a part of their nature just like it was part of the Gods' nature. This was not particularly useful to Phaedra, as far as she could tell. The elves were another matter. Their magic certainly *seemed* innate, but if that were the whole story, how would Bandu have learned to replicate it?

Then of course there was Psander. Phaedra tried listing

the feats of magic that Psander had performed within sight, and found that they were maddeningly few. The wizard had dismissed her illusory mask in the blink of an eye, far too quickly for Phaedra to observe any action on her part. She had created a light in her palm, much as Criton now could, but that seemed to have taken her little more than some amount of concentration. All the great magical works had been performed either long ago or behind closed doors: the construction of Silent Hall; the wards that protected it against the watchful eyes of the Gods; the fashioning of the magic-siphoning charms – all these Psander had done outside Phaedra's view. The wizard had claimed she would be generous with her knowledge, but perhaps old habits died hard.

Phaedra wished she still had something to write on. It would have been helpful to record her thoughts someplace where she could review them. Maybe when she and Hunter arrived in Atuna, she'd have an opportunity to buy writing supplies.

Though, come to think of it, how would she pay for them? She and Hunter had no money left, and nothing to barter: Hunter's expensive weapons and armor were gone, and most of Phaedra's belongings had been lost in the mountains. They would have to earn their living once they got there, but how? She could theoretically have done as she'd planned to a year ago and earned her living as a weaver, except that she didn't even have the means to buy a loom anymore.

By the time they finally arrived, both of them had sunk deep into melancholy. Phaedra still desperately wanted to write her thoughts down, so she asked after parchmenters and scribes, hoping to make some arrangement. Thus, to her surprise and delight, she learned of a scribe who was in need of an assistant. He worked near the great Atunaean customs house, writing detailed notes for the traders and financiers, recording debts and exchanges, and at times becoming an arbiter between men with competing claims. It was perhaps the least interesting thing one could do with a pen and ink, but the scribe paid well for Phaedra's assistance, and it gave Phaedra plenty of access to ink, parchment, and the cheap reed paper that was an Atunaean specialty.

The scribe paid Phaedra twice a week, and the commissions were high enough that she was able to expand her definitions of what counted as a necessity. There was only so long the man could tolerate his assistant looking so disheveled. Phaedra had explained her appearance by saying that she was in mourning for her lost nation, but in truth the anniversary had passed already. The days were growing short. Now she washed and trimmed her hair, and teased it up so that it rose from her head in a frizzy ball of curls. It had been a popular style on Tarphae, easier to keep up than the thousand-braid style that her nursemaid Kelina had so faithfully maintained. How Phaedra missed her.

She bought new clothes too, to replace those she had worn out with rough travel. She was tempted to commission something truly beautiful that might flatter her curves the way her old dresses once had, but she resisted. There would be no dances for her, not now, and she meant to begin traveling again as soon as she had somewhere to go. She had to be sensible.

The scribe had a small room for her to sleep in, but Phaedra was neither able nor willing to extend its use to Hunter. As such, Hunter had had to find his own work at the docks, loading and unloading the shipments that came in nearly every day from the islands and other coastal cities. She saw little of him until the evening after her fifth payment, when he appeared outside her door and told her there was a witch on Mur's Island.

"Come with me," he said. "I'll show you."

Phaedra snatched up a candle and followed him through the darkening streets, wondering where they were going. It was a warm night, probably one of the few pleasant ones left before the rainy season started in earnest, and she did not yet miss the shawl she had left behind, draped over the corner of her bed.

"All sailors carry charms," Hunter said as they walked, "but you have to see this one. The man says his auntie gave it to him. He said she makes them herself."

He brought her to a sailors' inn, a sprawling, stinking building crowded inside and out with men of all sizes and colors. It was only when they arrived outside the door that Hunter suddenly froze, stricken with horror and embarrassment. Phaedra had come along with him unthinkingly, excited at the thought of what he might show her, and now he of all people had put her in danger.

This was not a place for women – only whores came anywhere near there, and that only because they had to. If Phaedra came in with him, people would assume that Hunter had paid for her. If she lingered outside, it would be even worse.

"So he's in there?" Phaedra asked, trying not to seem frightened or angry, trying not to scream *why have you brought me here?* because she knew well enough why. He hadn't been thinking, plain and simple. An innocent mistake, until someone got hurt. At the very best, she would never find another job in Atuna. She worked with a customs scribe – someone here was bound to recognize her.

Hunter nodded wretchedly. "I–" he began, but he sputtered to a stop. There was no excuse, and an apology would do no good.

Phaedra came to a decision. "I'm your sister," she said. "We're going to go in there, we're going to find whatever it is you came to show me, and tomorrow we're going to take the first ship away from here. If we can find one to take us to Mur's Island, all the better. If not, we're still leaving. All right? Don't forget, I'm your sister."

He swallowed. "All right."

Phaedra caught his hand in hers and they approached the door together. It was propped open by an earthenware jug that stank of liquor, spit and vomit: a distillation of everything Phaedra expected to find inside. She kept her eyes on Hunter's back as he pulled her in with him, imagining the stares as she went limping along behind him. It smelled ghastly in there, and men whistled and jeered at Phaedra as she passed. Someone's hand gave her left buttock a sudden squeeze, and she yelped and turned, but could not locate her aggressor. She looked to Hunter and found him still focused on navigating the room. He hadn't even noticed.

They weaved through the crowd, passed into a narrow hall where they had to physically push by the patrons, and entered a small room with a large bed. The bed already had two men sleeping in it, with room for two or three more. On the side opposite the sleepers sat an islander, conversing with a continental man with an enormous red beard. The two turned when they saw Phaedra, and fell to silence.

"This is my sister," Hunter said awkwardly. "Could you show her your bird charm?"

The islander smiled at Phaedra. She doubted he believed Hunter's story. "Happily," he said.

He reached into his tunic and withdrew a string of shells. On the end was a delicate octagonal pendant made of twine and what might have been cormorant bones – Phaedra remembered the cormorant as sacred to one of the Gods of Mur's Island, though she could not recall the God's name. Tig, maybe? A small piece of driftwood was strung from one side of the pendant to the other, with a tiny beak bone loosely screwed to it. The beak was so small it must have been from a chick, and the screw was made of whittled shark tooth. There was no metalworking tradition on Mur's Island.

"Look at this," Hunter said, as the man placed the pendant on his palm. Slowly, the beak turned to point east.

"It always points home," the islander said, his accent thick and familiar. Phaedra's father had had business partners in Mur's Island, and their Atunaean had always been strongly accented and heavy with the effort of foreign speech. They had talked business with her father in their own language, which he had never taught her. Like Tarphae as a whole, Phaedra's father had always looked west.

"Always? No matter where you go?"

"No matter where. It always points home."

She stared at the little pendant, wondering what it had been that had transformed it from a few pieces of bone and twine into this wondrous thing. She was suddenly glad that Hunter had brought her here. Forget her reputation in Atuna – this was real magic! If charms like this were still possible, then so were her dreams.

Hunter thanked the man and they left again, pushing their way toward the door and freedom. Phaedra breathed deeply as they reached the cooler air outside, glad to have escaped without more unpleasantness. Hunter walked her back to her home before returning to the inn to sleep, promising to ask everyone he met if they knew of any ships leaving for Mur's Island. Phaedra went to bed with a smile on her face. Tomorrow they would abandon this noisy, dirty city, and sail away to meet a witch. The thought delighted her.

9

Hunter

He did manage to find a merchant ship the following day that would eventually be stopping at Mur's Island, though that destination was not the first on its trade route. Phaedra, unlike Hunter, had managed to save enough money from her work to book their passage. She also had new clothes, and some extra coin left over. It was enough to make Hunter rethink what sort of trade he ought to pursue. While he had neither Phaedra's passion for reading and writing nor her aptitude, his education had still involved practicing these arts until he was competent. It would certainly beat working at the docks.

The ship carried olive oil and guardian wood and steel, which the captain meant to exchange for salt and spices and tukka gum, for medicinal tonics and mineral cures, for pearls and nacre. The smell of the lumber made Hunter miss home again; in its day, Tarphae had been known for its high-quality guardian trees and its tukka gum, which was both edible and a major ingredient in ink. Mur's Island was known for its pearls.

Sailing had a poor effect on Phaedra. It clearly brought back memories of her drowned nursemaid Kelina, and she spent the first few hours below deck where she would not have to face the ocean that had taken the old woman. Hunter would have joined her, but the rocking motion bothered him less in the open air than it did in the musky darkness below.

So he stood up on deck, watching as the ship crashed through the waves and listening as the sailors called to each other in pidgin Atunaean and sang songs to keep their rhythm steady as they hauled on ropes or bailed out the hold. Every man had his task. At any given time, each knew where he belonged.

Hunter didn't. He admired Phaedra for the way she was always adapting to her circumstances, making new plans and choosing new goals, and never, ever, giving up. He admired her, and he envied her. For better or for worse, his friends had all found their callings. God Most High had plans for them, or else like Phaedra they had plans for themselves. Only Hunter had no plans, and now that he had done his part in fulfilling the Dragon Knight's prophecy, he suspected that no God particularly cared what happened to him.

The following afternoon, as Hunter was trying unsuccessfully to nap and Phaedra was teasing at her hair with a steel comb, a crewman stuck his head through the hatch and called them above deck. They stumbled up the steep ladder-like stairs, wondering if the ship had reached its destination already. When they reached the top, they found that it hadn't.

Even before their eyes adjusted to the sunlight, they could hear crewmen praying. Hunter blinked and stared. Though the sky above the ship was blue, a ring of angry clouds had gathered, some hundred yards out to sea in every direction. The waves underneath these clouds reared up like menacing giants, the waters under the ship remained calm. The ship sailed on, and the unnatural weather moved right along with it.

"What does it mean?" the captain asked, more to himself than to anyone else.

Hunter and Phaedra looked at each other. "God Most High has blessed our journey," Phaedra said. "This is a sign of His power, and His favor."

The cook had abandoned the galley to watch the unnatural weather, and he now turned to Phaedra. "Who is this God Most High?"

Phaedra told him what she knew: that God Most High had

slain the Yarek in days of old and built the elves' world out of its carcass, that He had created the mesh between the worlds, and that the dragons had worshipped Him and their descendants still did. Lastly, she told the captain of how she and her friends had brought Salemis back into this world and gained his God's favor.

"I think Hunter and I are responsible for those clouds surrounding your ship," she admitted. "Both Mayar and Karassa have declared Themselves our enemies. But it looks like even here, God Most High protects us from Them. Apparently, Their strength even in Their own domain is impotent compared with His."

The captain gulped. "Change course," he called to the helmsman. "We're going to Mur's Island first, and may God Most High find favor with us."

The crew obeyed without a word of complaint. They were terrified, and who could blame them? Not one but two Sea Gods were trying to tear their ship apart and cast them into the depths of the ocean – what would happen if God Most High stopped protecting them? If they insulted Him by treating Hunter and Phaedra poorly? It didn't even stop there – what if He lost interest in the ship once Phaedra and Hunter disembarked? Would Mayar and Karassa lose interest too?

Phaedra spent the rest of their voyage telling the crew everything she knew about the dragons' God. The sailors listened eagerly and never interrupted, which Hunter supposed must be a welcome change for her. By the time they reached Mur's Island, half the crew had made vows to worship God Most High alone.

Hunter found his new God's activity confusing. Salemis had once claimed that the Gods never slept, least of all God Most High; and yet, if He had not been asleep before, why was He only now asserting His presence in the world? Why had He not protected them from the earthquake when they returned to Tarphae, or from the rough seas on the way back to the continent? Or had He been protecting them then too, but more subtly? If so, why was He being so unsubtle now? What had changed?

It must have had something to do with Salemis' return to the world. Although Hunter couldn't understand why this might be so, it stood to reason. The event that had cast Psander's fortress into the world of the fairies, in exchange for rescuing Salemis and giving the Yarek a foothold here... it must have somehow prompted God Most High to take a more active role. That was a relief, certainly, but Hunter still wished he knew why.

Three abnormally sunny, breezy days later, they reached Mur's Island. Hunter hadn't known quite what to expect of it: on Tarphae, Mur's Island had been known as a backwater. From a distance, it looked beautiful. Ivory beaches stretched all along the shoreline, and the waters were a perfect clear blue. Some cormorants sunned themselves on a rock. Past the dunes, a fishing village was nestled into the edge of a wood. A number of skiffs bobbed cheerfully across the water, their owners waving as the merchant ship approached. It took Hunter a few minutes to realize what was missing: a dock.

The helmsman steered the ship around the island until they came to a small town – or a somewhat larger village, really – with something resembling a pier. Even so, the waters were too shallow for the ship to approach. Instead, they filled a small boat with jugs of oil and lowered it into the water. Hunter and Phaedra climbed down after the captain and two of his crewmen, and they rowed their way to the shallow dock.

They stepped onto the sand, thanking the captain, and walked toward the village while the sailors were still unloading their cargo. Or perhaps walking was the wrong word. After their time at sea, the ground beneath Hunter's feet was too solid, almost brutal, and he fell to his knees in the sand when it refused to move under him. Phaedra managed to keep upright, albeit barely. She tried to stop and steady herself for a moment, then changed her mind and limped along the beach much faster than Hunter could follow. She seemed to have decided that her forward motion could not be controlled and had to be fully embraced instead.

Hunter stayed there on his hands and knees, feeling the sand between his fingers. When he rose, Phaedra was well ahead of him, approaching a young man of about their age. The man smiled, a reaction Hunter hadn't seen since they'd left Tarphae a year ago. It was good to be among islanders again.

"I am looking for an auntie who makes charms," Phaedra said. "Out of cormorant bones?"

"Auntie Gava," the teen said. "She lives by Perrinye. I take you?"

It was a request for coin, and Phaedra obliged. They followed him across the beach, past the village – perhaps it was the capital? – and into the woods. The boy's name was Tamur, and he was a pearl diver. His Atunaean was weak but passable, and he told them a bit about his work as they walked – how long he had taught himself to hold his breath underwater, and which sand was best for seeding. This last was difficult to understand, both because of Tamur's accent and because Hunter hadn't even realized there *were* different kinds of sand.

He found his mind wandering. What would it be like to live here, on an island so far away from the major cities and ports that made up civilization? If Hunter decided to stay, how long could he bear it?

They forded a shallow stream and turned vaguely leftward, bound to meet the shore sooner or later. Phaedra was doing remarkably well despite her limp; she even seemed to be enjoying their walk. The ground was getting rockier, though, and they were traveling uphill. When they passed the tree line, they found that the hill turned into craggy cliffs up ahead, sloping down to the sea on the left. At the bottom was another fishing village, which must have been Perrinye. Perched on the rocks above was a small hut, built out of what honestly looked like driftwood.

"She lives up there," Tamur said, "but you better take her a gift. Nobody doesn't go without something for her."

Hunter and Phaedra looked at each other. "Like what?"

"Like food."

"Could you buy us some and bring it here?" Phaedra asked. "I can't walk much farther."

She paid him again and he scurried eagerly down the hill toward Perrinye. Then Phaedra sat down on a rock to wait. "Thanks for coming with me," she said to Hunter. "I don't know what this is going to be like, but I'm glad you're here."

"Of course," Hunter answered, and after that there didn't seem to be anything left to say.

Tamur returned some time later with a bucket of assorted mollusks, covered over with seaweed. Hunter took the bucket while Phaedra thanked the boy and gave him a tip, and they turned back to the driftwood hut.

Hunter's knuckles barely made a sound on the spongy wood of the door, but the old woman who lived there must have had sharp ears. The door opened soon afterwards, and they stood face to face with Auntie Gava.

She was a tall woman, slightly hunched though she was, and her dress was covered in beads, bones, and other small objects that clacked together as it swayed. Her long gray hair was bound only loosely in the back by what might have been dried woven seaweed. She was bulky too, with a formidable heft that told of strength despite her years. Hunter was not sure what exactly he had expected, but this Auntie was far more imposing than anything he had imagined.

She spoke to them first in some of the languages of the eastern archipelago, and switched to Atunaean only when it became clear that they didn't understand a word. She clearly hated that – she spat out the Atunaean words like they were each a bad bite of fruit or a seed half-eaten by insects. At least she spoke it, though.

"I don't know you," she said bluntly. "What do you want with me?"

Hunter looked to Phaedra, who said meekly, "I was hoping you could show me magic."

Auntie Gava began to shut the door again, but Phaedra put

her hand in the way. "Please," she said.

"I've got no use for you," the woman said. "Move your hand or I break it."

"Go ahead," Phaedra answered, finding her voice. "If I can't study magic, I may as well lose my hand too."

That stopped her. Hunter could see Auntie Gava reassessing them through her cold dark eyes. She looked extremely skeptical. She was going to ask what was in it for her, Hunter was sure, and he doubted that a bucket of oysters would be enough. But then she surprised him and said, "Come in then."

She stepped back and they entered her hut, which was small enough to seem crowded with just the three of them inside. There was no furniture whatsoever – the nearest thing to a bed was the single blanket rolled up in a corner. The floor was littered with junk: bones and mollusk shells, pebbles and sticks and seaweed. Gava took the bucket from Hunter and sat down on the floor, clearing a space for herself with a thoughtless sweep of her arm. Hunter and Phaedra sat gingerly across from her, or beside her – it was practically the same thing in here.

Auntie Gava took up a flint knife and began shucking oysters, popping them open with an expert twist and sucking out the contents. She did not offer any to them.

"You want to learn magic," she said after a time. "Where are you from? You look all right, but you only speak Atunaean?" She said the last word as if it disgusted her.

"We were from Tarphae," Phaedra said. "And we've been on the continent for the last year, ever since the plague that killed our people."

Gava slurped another oyster. "That would do it. Atunaean is all you know, I'll bet. Not even a word of Estric or Lago, and definitely no Tigra. You're rich too. Fancy words. Tarphaeans always wished they didn't live on an island. The richer they are, the more they talk like it."

It was an undeniable truth, put forward in the ugliest way possible. For all that they worshipped Karassa and looked like the other islanders, the people of Tarphae had always looked to the continent for their culture and learning. Tarphae was the westernmost island in the archipelago, and aspired to the kind of power that the great cities of the continent were known for.

"Our wealth is gone," Phaedra answered. "What we have now are our skills and our wits."

"And you want to learn magic."

"And we want to learn magic. Or, I do."

"And you?" Gava asked Hunter. "You're along for her, yes?"

"Yes," Hunter admitted, though he didn't like her implication.

"And what makes you think you can learn from me?" she said to Phaedra, and again her implication bothered Hunter. She was questioning Phaedra's aptitude as a student, not her own skill as a teacher. Blunt. Rude.

Phaedra took a breath and recited a speech that she must have prepared beforehand. It was far too formal for their surroundings, but at least she didn't falter once she'd committed to reciting it. She said, "I have seen a continental wizard conjure fire in her hand, and summon books from her shelves with no more than a gesture. But she's gone elsewhere, to the world of the fairies. I have seen more amazing things than could fit in a thousand stories. I want to learn, and I am willing to learn from you or from anyone. Only time will tell if I shall succeed."

Auntie Gava put her knife down and met Phaedra's eyes. "You talk too fancy," she said. "You say the right things, mind, but too fancy. My magic isn't fancy, not like your words. I doubt it'll suit you. But we'll see. You want to try to learn from me, I'll show you what I do here."

10
PHAEDRA

The first thing Auntie Gava did was to finish her oysters, maintaining her unhurried manner. When she was down to the last one, she reached into a fold in her dress and pulled out a thin coin.

"See here," she said.

She slid her knife in beside the hinge and began to pry the oyster open, stopping as soon as there was a gap between the two halves of the shell. Then she slipped the coin inside and pressed the oyster back together with her fingers. It was imperfect, but good enough to keep the coin from falling out again.

She said a word in her language three times. Then she marched out of the hut and climbed partway down the rocks. Phaedra and Hunter followed dutifully. "Now we bury it," Gava explained. "Here, boy, move this rock for me."

Hunter did as she said, and when he had cleared a space, the old woman dropped her oyster in and told him to cover it up again. It wasn't even a proper burial – they hadn't dug into the ground – but when the oyster was no longer visible, Gava began to climb back up to her house.

"What now?" Phaedra asked when they got there.

"Nothing," Auntie Gava said. "That's it."

"What did that word you said mean?"

"Prosperity."

"Is it supposed to bring prosperity to you, or to the whole island?"

Gava shrugged. "Doesn't really make a difference. When things go well, people share."

"Is there some way you can tell when it's working?"

This time, Gava laughed. "Sure. People do well, they come and bring me things."

"And if they don't do well?"

"Then you try again. You just need more oysters and more coins, that's all. If they've got 'em, I've got time to bury 'em."

"Then how do you know when it's magic and not luck?"

Gava looked at her sternly. "This is luck magic, girl. If it works, it works; if it doesn't, it doesn't. The luck and the magic are the same thing."

"Oh."

"I don't know what notions you've got," Gava said, "but you can't separate magic from the world and say, 'this part's magic, this part's normal.' Magic is part of the whole thing. It *is* normal. The Gods are all magic, and They made this place."

Phaedra nodded, but she knew her disappointment was showing. It was all well and good for Auntie Gava to say that magic was normal, but she hadn't seen what Phaedra had seen.

"The Gods put this place together on purpose," Auntie Gava went on. "Some places They made it pretty, some places They made it ugly. They make it how They like it. If you want to do magic, you take a look at what They made, you try to get some of the pieces so they fit together better than before, and that's it. You've got magic. It's not fancy."

It took all Phaedra's self-control not to argue with the old woman. Whatever one might say about magic, it was definitely fancy. Psander's library, Criton's fire, even Bandu's connection with plants and animals – they were all miraculous, all aesthetic. How could anyone be so prosaic about magic?

But then, maybe she wasn't being fair. Auntie Gava and Psander did seem to share a general attitude toward life. They might have more in common than met the eye.

"Can you show me how you make the sailors' charms? The ones that point back here?"

"What, I'm your private teacher now? Just because I let you watch doesn't mean I'll go out of my way just to show you things. You gave me some oysters, not a fortune in gold. I only make charms for people who need them."

"I'm sorry," Phaedra said. "That's fair. I'll just watch whatever you're doing."

She spent the rest of the day watching and listening without interruption as Gava went about her work. She watched the old woman coax her fire back to life, listened carefully to the songs Gava sang as she prepared her meals – it could all be important. Auntie Gava might not pulse with power the way Bandu, Criton, and Psander all did, but she had been doing this for years, and she sang her songs and performed her rituals with all the confidence that Psander had shown in her own domain.

Her attempt to reconstruct magic theory wasn't off to such a bad start, Phaedra decided. Gava's perspective was useful, especially since Phaedra could compare it to what little the wizard Psander had told her. Psander had spoken of magic as a series of rules that existed above and alongside the "ordinary" rules of reality. She had never revealed what these rules might be, but one did begin to taste their flavor, the longer one watched her. Phaedra thought back to the time a few months ago, when the islanders had tried to open a route to the fairies' world. The Goddess Eramia had given Hunter a flower to help them find their way through to Salemis, and Narky had suggested that Criton bleed on it: "It seems like the kind of weird thing Psander might have you do."

It had worked, too. Once Bandu had added her fairy magic, the gate to Salemis' prison in the elves' world had opened. There had been a kind of poetry to their method, and it had worked.

Phaedra's new theory was that this poetry was essential to

magic, that magic itself might *be* a kind of poetry. She doubted that Psander would have put it that way, and Gava would probably have objected too, but it was a theory that resonated for her. So much of the magic she had seen in the last year was, for lack of a better term, *appropriate*. Even Gava's prosperity magic, unrigorous though it was, had that same underlying appropriateness to it. Whatever the details, Phaedra thought that this must be the basis of Psander's "magic theory."

Right or wrong, at least Phaedra had a solid hypothesis now, and a framework with which to test it. If magic was truly a kind of universal poetics, then somehow or other, she ought to be able to manipulate the world through thoughtful composition. For now, she'd observe Auntie Gava in the hopes of witnessing a piece of demonstrably effective magic – something she could practice on. After that, she would have to proceed through trial and error.

Auntie Gava's lack of rigor was excruciating, though. She treated every mundane task as if it were magical and every magical task as if it were mundane. The worst part was that she did it that way on purpose – as she had said, she didn't believe there *was* a dividing line between the two.

In the late afternoon, when Phaedra was already starting to wonder about where they were going to sleep that night, a man with Atunaean coloration came running up from the village to tell the old witch that his wife had gone into labor. Gava made him stay while she cut off a lock of her own tangled hairs and braided a charm for the baby out of it. Phaedra watched, fascinated, as the old woman washed the charm with a few drops of blood taken from her thumb, and presented the man with a necklace just big enough to fit over a baby's head.

"Never let the babe take this off," she warned, "and if it comes apart before six years have passed, you come back to me. My old blood will protect your child from the demons."

The man took the charm gratefully and paid her in gold. Atunaeans were the ruling class here, and Phaedra suspected that this was a massive overpayment compared to what a native islander would have given her, but Auntie Gava did not even thank him. She just took the money and watched him run off, leaving Phaedra to ask what all that had been about.

"Your parents never told you about demons?" Gava asked disgustedly. "It's a wonder you people survive at all."

Phaedra *did* know about demons, at least from the perspective of continental religion, but none of what she knew explained what Auntie Gava had just done with her hair and blood.

"Please," she said, "tell me about them."

"Demons like to steal babes and children and take them off to their demon halls. My old blood keeps our young ones from being found."

"Have demons stolen children here before?"

"Not in generations, girl, but they used to, before we aunties started warding them away."

"What do they look like?"

Auntie Gava sucked on her bloodied thumb and rolled her eyes. "How do I know? I keep them away; I don't invite them in."

Phaedra nodded. She thought she knew exactly what demons looked like. She thought they looked like fairies.

The word "fairy" was a misnomer – the denizens of the first world changed their complexions depending on the lighting. In the dark, their skin was not only pale but luminescent; in daylight, it turned blacker than night. Phaedra and her friends had only barely escaped them a few months ago, rescuing eight human children in the process. The fairies had meant to eat them.

Phaedra was amazed that she had never made the connection between elves and demons until now. Demons were a well-known part of religious lore, a part that Phaedra had always vaguely considered metaphorical. They were supposed to be the cursed children of evil Gods, living to torment humanity through temptation and guile, guiding lovers to ruin or sailors to their deaths. But Auntie Gava said they stole children, and that changed everything. The more she thought about it, the more Phaedra realized how obvious the connection should have been to her. Of *course* elves and demons were one and the same. The people of Mur's Island were right to fear them, and they were lucky to have aunties like Gava to protect them.

There being no place for them to sleep in Gava's shack, at sunset they clambered down the rocks and wandered into the village below, more or less begging to be lodged. A generous widow took them in, and they blessed her in the name of God Most High. Hunter, as usual, had no trouble sleeping, but Phaedra was too excited about her theory to sleep well. If she was right, then magic was an art. She would learn it like a new dance, step by careful step, until she was confident enough to improvise. What glorious days she had ahead of her!

They awoke late, luxuriating in the island's relaxed atmosphere. It was nice to be away from the continent, away from the stares, and from the instant recognition that the five black-skinned youths must be those cursed wanderers from Tarphae. Here on Mur's Island, she and Hunter blended in, at least until they spoke their flawless Atunaean. In any case, the freedom from recognition was priceless.

They ate with their hostess, a breakfast of dried fish and seaweed, and went down to the beach for a stroll. Phaedra had it in her head that they might find some gift for Auntie Gava, but in the end she and Hunter spent more time talking than they did searching for gifts. They had barely spoken for days, but now Phaedra could see that Hunter was worried about something, though he seemed willing to let her chatter on endlessly about her theory of poetic magic. After a time, she gave up on letting him bring his worries up himself and asked him outright what the matter was.

He grimaced. "I don't want to distract you."

He was too stoic for his own good; always had been. "Hunter, the last time you tried to keep everything inside, you forgot to feed yourself and nearly fainted. What's the problem?"

She had embarrassed him. She was a bit sorry about it, but it did get results.

"I don't know how we're going to get off this island," he admitted. "Not that we shouldn't stay as long as you need to, it's just... I don't have anything to do here. They don't need any of the skills I have. And we're going to want to leave eventually, right? How long until another ship comes by? How are we going to pay for our passage on it?"

Phaedra had no answers for him. She was making progress here; was it selfish for her to hope *not* to leave any time soon? After all, Hunter had known from the start that this was what she wanted. That was why he hadn't wanted to admit to his concerns.

They walked on, the silence between them growing. They were both being selfish, both feeling bad about it, and why? It wasn't as if some sea captain had actually offered to sail them elsewhere.

"I keep thinking about Bestillos," Hunter said out of nowhere. "He'd have killed me if Narky hadn't shot him in the back. I keep thinking through our fight, over and over again. He was faster and stronger, but his technique wasn't perfect – I should have been able to beat him."

Phaedra studied him curiously. Bestillos had not been the sort of man to surrender. Had Hunter defeated him in combat, it would have been another death for him to carry.

He seemed to read her mind. "I know," he said. "It's still true, what I said before. I don't ever want to kill a man again. But I still think about it sometimes, just for myself, like I used to when I was learning to spar with my brother. I used to think about fighting all the time, and it felt good."

"I can imagine," Phaedra told him. "I've seen you fight, Hunter. It was terrible, but it was also like a dance in some ways. Beautiful."

He looked at her with such relief and joy that she wanted to weep. "Exactly. You *understand*. When I tell myself that that part of my life is over, it's like saying I'll never dance again."

Oh Gods above, there were actually tears in her eyes. She could hear Hunter gasping at his own thoughtlessness, then floundering wordlessly as he searched for a way to apologize. But of course, there was nothing he could say.

It took an effort to compose herself, with Hunter standing there awkwardly, remorsefully, watching her. When she could trust her voice not to crack, she said, "I don't think you should stop. You haven't been crippled. Can't you still enjoy it, as long as you don't fight to kill? Maybe you could find someone to spar with."

Hunter nodded hopefully. "My father had a swordsmaster who trained me and my brother. Maybe I can do that – find a nobleman with sons, who needs someone to..." he broke off, looking past her.

A group of five men was running toward them. Three of them were continental. Could it be? Why were those sailors still here – hadn't that merchant ship left almost as soon as Phaedra and Hunter had come ashore?

The sailors reached them, and, to Phaedra's shock, seized them by the arms. "You're coming with us," one of them barked. "You brought this curse upon us – now it's your job to lift it!"

11

DELIKA

Delika knew there was something wrong with Galdon the moment he set foot inside the door. Her adoptive father *looked* all right, and he walked with the same heavy gait as always, but while she couldn't explain precisely what it was, she knew there was *something* wrong.

Or maybe it was her imagination. Rakon didn't seem to have noticed anything – he just kept on picking burrs out of his pile of wool, keeping his head down like he always did. He was better at that than Delika was: she was always sticking her nose out, and getting a beating for it.

She missed her parents. She would probably never see them again, and it was her own fault because she didn't know where they lived. The black islanders had asked, and she hadn't been able to answer. So they had brought the children they could back to their different homes and left Delika, Rakon, and Caldra here.

They had tried to bring Rakon back to Laarna first, but it was gone. His parents were probably dead, which was even worse than for Delika in some ways, but in other ways it was better. Delika knew that her parents were alive somewhere out there, missing her, but the world was too big for her to find them.

It was the same for Caldra, but Delika didn't like her, so she didn't care.

She had thought it would be better here than it was. When the islanders had brought Adla and Temena home to Galdon's brother-in-law, Galdon and his wife had said they would happily raise the last three children as their own, since they couldn't make any themselves. So Delika had thought, foolishly, that it would at least be nice here.

And it had been, for about a week. But then the red priest had come, and whatever he'd said to them, he'd scared them so much that now they spanked the children whenever they talked about the past – especially when they talked about the islanders. Well, Rakon and Caldra were good at pretending that the islanders had never existed, but Delika wasn't. The big one called Criton had saved her from drowning, and she didn't think it was right for her to try to forget him. But whenever she talked about him, well, out came the switch.

Galdon was looking for something by the doorway, and getting frustrated that he couldn't find it, but instead of telling them what it was and demanding that they help him look for it, he was trying to do it subtly, as if he didn't want to keep them from their work.

"What are you looking for?" Delika asked, knowing that it would likely get her in trouble. She couldn't help it.

He looked startled at first, trapped even, but then he frowned. "Did you move my spear?"

She shook her head. Why did he want it? "It's still there," she said, pointing.

He went and got it. "You're a good girl," he said.

"I know you're not him," she answered.

Galdon froze. "What?" he asked.

Rakon's head snapped up so he could glare at her, but Delika ignored him. She'd said it already – if she was going to get in trouble for it, it was too late anyway. "You're not him," she said. "You're someone else. Why do you want his spear?"

At that moment, Galdon's wife Sina came in with Caldra and their baskets of vegetables. "Oh, Galdon," she said in surprise, "I didn't realize you were home! Did something happen?"

She was between him and the door, and Delika could see the terror flash across his face. "The Dragon Touched are back," he said, walking toward her. "We need to drive them off before it's too late."

The Dragon Touched! That meant Criton! Wait, was *this* Criton? Delika squinted at him as if she could force him to turn back into himself, but it was no good. Not-Galdon met Sina at the door, gave her a quick kiss, and fled.

Delika wanted to scream at him to take her with him, but it was too late. He was gone. Sina looked frightened, but she only put her basket on the table and stood with her hands on her hips, staring at Delika. "You've let Rakon do all your work for you, haven't you?"

"That wasn't Galdon," Delika said, trying to deflect. "That was someone else, and he took Galdon's spear! Maybe it was–"

She stopped herself, but it was too late. Sina knew that she had been about to say "Criton." Now Delika was in *so much trouble*.

"What makes you say that?" Sina asked, poison in her voice.

Delika didn't even answer. She backed away around the table, slowly at first, afraid of Sina's hand and of the switch that it might soon hold. Sina marched toward her, already reaching out to catch her adopted daughter. Delika kept backing away from her, then suddenly changed direction and sped underneath the table and out toward the door as fast as her legs would carry her. She had to dodge stupid Caldra on the way, but she ended up being glad for the other girl's presence, because Sina actually *did* crash into her while giving chase, and had to stop for a moment to pick the girl up and apologize. By that time, Delika was gone.

She tried to find the man who had pretended to be Galdon, but she couldn't spot him anywhere. Had he already transformed into someone else? He wasn't Criton – she didn't want to believe that Criton would visit her new home just to steal a spear and run away. But he was *like* Criton. She was sure of that.

She had to find a place to hide before Sina could catch up to her. She had already turned a corner so that she wouldn't be seen from the door, but that wouldn't be enough. Where could she hide? If she tried running into a neighbor's house, they'd recognize her and bring her back.

Ahead, she saw the Temple of Magor. She hated the place, since it was the fault of Magor's priests that her new parents had started hitting her, but it *did* have lots of little corners to hide in. That, and Sina would never expect her to go there. Delika ran for it.

When she slipped inside, panting and out of breath, the priest was busy pouring sacrificial blood from the altar's four blood-collectors into the big metal vat in the corner. His back was to her, so she had time to hide under one of the benches without him noticing. Then she crawled forward a few rows so that she wouldn't be visible from the door, doing her best to calm down and stop panting.

The priest went about his business, totally oblivious to Delika's presence. She watched him over the top of the bench in front of her as he cleaned the altar, swept the floor around it, and rearranged various items she couldn't see from her vantage point. She tried to breathe more quietly. There was a commotion outside, and she was afraid that Sina and the real Galdon might be looking for her, but then there were some cries and thuds and she realized that it was a fight. Even the half-deaf priest heard it, because he grabbed his spear and turned toward the door.

Before he could leave, another man came rushing in. "What's going on out there?" the priest asked him.

Delika turned to see if she could spot the other man, but he was still too far away. She could only see his feet, which were big and dirty and wearing sandals, just like any man's feet might have been.

"The Dragon Touched are back," the man said. He sounded young, and familiar. Which of her neighbors was it?

"What?" the priest cried. "Impossible!"

"Come and see for yourself," the man answered, coming closer. Now she could see his hair peeking out above the benches. She might have seen more if she moved a little, but she didn't want either of them to notice her.

The priest strode forward, but as he reached the other man he gave a sudden cry. "See?" the second man said. "I told you."

The priest's knees hit the ground in front of where his feet had been, and the second man's feet took a step or two back, transforming before her eyes into scaly claws. There was a grunt as he yanked something out of the priest, and then the old man was lying prone on the ground, staring straight at her. He wasn't dead yet, and his expression turned to surprise and then to worry as he saw her there, hiding under her bench. But he didn't say anything, and soon the butt end of a spear came down on his head and quieted him for good.

The second man laughed and ran to the altar, breathing flames at it and at the statue of Magor behind it. She got the briefest look at his face as he ran by, and she knew it instantly. It was her teenage neighbor Pilos, who lived with his wife and parents only a couple of houses down from Sina and Galdon. If he was like Criton, how many of her other neighbors were like him too?

Delika tried not to move, tried not to breathe. She didn't want Pilos to notice her. Criton was good, Criton had saved her, but that didn't mean that *all* these people were good. This one had just murdered a priest.

She wanted to run away, but she was afraid that he would catch her and kill her just like he'd done to the man on the floor. So she stayed while he lit the altar on fire, lit the statue on fire, lit the temple on fire. She stayed until he ran laughing from the building, and it grew hot and smoky around her. And by then, it was too late.

The smoke was everywhere by the time she crawled out from under her bench, and the flames too. There were casks of oil by the door, and their tops were aflame – they'd probably burst soon. Delika crawled away from them toward the burning altar, not knowing which way to go. A piece of roof fell down behind her, smashing the bench she had just crawled out from under. When she raised her head even just a little, the smoke choked her. She coughed, and sank lower to the floor.

Where could she go? There were killers outside, and flames inside, and soon she would burn just like that statue of boar-headed Magor. The benches were on fire already. Her skin and lungs felt like they were burning too.

At last, she remembered the vat in the corner. She sucked in a big breath from the good air near the ground, and ran as fast as she could for it. When she reached the vat she fell down again, winded. She felt weak, and her back was so hot – oh mother, it was burning! Her dress was on fire!

Delika coughed, sucked once more for air, and climbed into the vat.

12

BANDU

The men did not stay long. Off they went to get their weapons, with Criton in the lead, leaving Bandu and the baby with the Dragon Touched women. That was no good. The women all avoided her gaze like they were afraid of her. One might have thought she was the one with claws.

Hessina muttered something under her breath, apparently praying. Bandu did not catch the whole prayer, but she kept hearing the word "arise," over and over again. When she thought about it, it made sense that the Dragon Touched should pray like that: others may have believed their God to be dead, but the Dragon Touched only thought He was far away and inattentive. Salemis had even said something like that once. What had it been? That for his God, people's lives passed in the blink of an eye?

It certainly didn't feel like the blink of an eye, waiting like this for her mate to return. Goodweather had woken up and was crying for the breast again. Bandu felt Hessina's eyes on her as she fed her daughter. She met the old woman's gaze and asked, "You have young once?"

The old lady looked surprised, but then her expression softened. "Six. It was a joyous time, before the purge."

"Does your mate help then?"

"Not much. He had duties serving my father, the High Priest."

That explained a few things. "Your father is High Priest for your God? This is how you are important."

Hessina's eyebrows shot up. "Yes. I don't mean to be insulting, but where did Criton find you?"

She didn't mean to be insulting? If she hadn't begun that way, Bandu wouldn't have known that she *ought* to be insulted. Now she was annoyed.

"Criton is lucky he 'finds' me," she said. "You and your God are lucky too. You think Criton wakes up Salemis? I wake him up. You think Criton grows Goodweather's seed so the dragon can come back to this world? I grow the seed. I do these things while you are still hiding. You should be happy and say thank you."

"I apologize," Hessina mumbled. "I did not mean–"

"You think Criton should not love me," Bandu pressed on, not letting the old woman recover. "You think he should love only his kind. You are wrong."

Hessina tried to shrug this off. "When you've lived to be my age and seen some of the things I've seen, you may begin to see things differently. I am grateful for what you have done to help us, and am sorry if I suggested otherwise. But people should stay with their own kind. I make no apologies for thinking so."

"Everyone say your kind is dead," Bandu pointed out.

"Perhaps now that Criton has learned otherwise, he will take a second wife."

Second wife? Bandu felt that like a kick to the stomach. Phaedra hadn't said anything about second wives. She had said that marriage was when people promised not to have others. Or, hadn't she? Maybe Phaedra hadn't said exactly that, but it was what Bandu had understood. How much had Phaedra neglected to tell her?

If marrying was only a promise for her and not for him, then it was no good. Besides which, whatever marriage was *supposed* to be, Criton *had* promised not to have others. If he broke that promise, he could not have her. Not unless she could have others, anyway. But then, that didn't work, because she didn't want anybody else.

She had thought that she and Criton were the same: two wild things without any family except each other. But Criton wanted more. He had always wanted more. And now there were others of his kind who wanted to take him away from her.

Her fury stretched itself in all directions. Below the earth, something answered. Roots connected to roots – the Yarek was listening. It owed her a favor. Did she want it to eat this woman?

It took some strength to resist. Bandu would have liked to see Hessina dragged away beneath the ground to become food for plants, but she knew better. This woman did not deserve that, not for this crime, and besides, Bandu might need that favor someday.

She looked south into the distance, where even now the Yarek was visible. It was taller than the mountains of the Calardian range, so tall and wide that it might have been a pillar holding up the heavens. It amazed Bandu – the great tree seemed so much larger than Castle Goodweather, its parent in the fairies' world. Parent *and* child, maybe – it was hard to tell with these ancient beings. God Most High had torn the Yarek into two pieces in ancient times. Those two halves, Castles Illweather and Goodweather, were the cornerstones of the fairies' world, while their roots made up that world's foundation. The tree before Bandu's eyes had come from Goodweather's seed, but she could see that the new Yarek was stronger, more whole. Less kind.

Maybe the new Yarek's size should not have come as a surprise. This younger world was not built of gnarled old roots; it was made of soil, soil that was rich and yielding and had never known the Yarek. Of course the great tree would take advantage.

Hessina, following her gaze, went back to praying to her God. "You who struck down the Yarek of old, who conquered Your enemies before the first dawn, defeat Your detractors now so that they will not scoff at Your name. Arise, our God, and Your enemies tremble; lift Your hand, and they scatter like chaff in the wind."

Bandu switched baby Goodweather from one breast to the other and smiled a bit to herself. She wondered what Hessina would think if she knew the story behind her daughter's name.

There was a fire growing in the village nearby. Even from here, she could see people running. Whether or not Criton's plan had worked, it had clearly led to some sort of fight.

Bandu considered staying and watching, but she was tired of Hessina's company. Criton might need her help, for all that he wanted her to stay behind to protect Goodweather. Bandu thought she could protect both.

Figures were running out of the smoke, but none of them were Criton. The fire was spreading, too, jumping from house to house. Was Criton trapped in one of those awful wooden houses, with a roof of burning thatch above his head?

She broke into a run. The wind whistled in her ears, warning her to stay away. It was fighting against her now, trying to keep her back. "Stop," she said through gritted teeth. "Stop blowing. You make the fire worse. *Stop.*"

The wind calmed at her words, and she ran on. At least the clouds of smoke were rising straight up to the sky now. Without the wind blowing it in all directions, she could see that the source of the smoke was somewhere in the middle of the village. That was bad. Even with a calm wind, the fire would spread unless it could be put out. Bandu clutched Goodweather to her chest and kept on running, past frightened livestock and fleeing villagers, past barns and sheds and houses, until she turned a corner and almost ran headlong into Criton's cousin.

There was a ragged line of Dragon Touched men facing the blaze, with weapons in their hands and rags over their mouths to keep out the smoke. Belkos had clearly only just recovered from a coughing fit – he was still in the process of standing up straight after having been doubled over, and his breath came in gasps.

"They're still there!" he wheezed. "Who the hell set fire to Magor's temple?"

Nobody answered, and Belkos began to stumble forward. There was a shout of, "Where are you going?" and Criton came running to his cousin's side, carrying a shield and spear. He hadn't noticed Bandu yet.

"My family!" Belkos cried. "My Iona! Our house is on that side of town!"

Bandu stepped forward. "Take us there."

Criton saw her, and his expression turned to horror. "Bandu! What are you – you brought Goodweather *here?*"

"So take her!" Bandu yelled at him. "She's yours too. You have your fighting things now – go watch Goodweather while *I* help your cousin and his family."

Criton did not take the child; his hands were full. Instead he made a frustrated sound and said, "Never mind. We can go together."

They followed Belkos as he made an arc around the burning buildings, hurrying toward his house. "They might still be all right," he said. "I'll *kill* whoever set that fire! The rout's no good if our village burns down because of it, and the townspeople are fleeing us instead of helping! At least the wind has calmed down now. Thank God for that!"

Yes, Bandu thought, *thank your God for calming the wind. What do* you *know?*

Goodweather had woken up during the run, and was wriggling with discomfort. She did not like this heat. Bandu raised her to her shoulder, where her grip was better. "Be quiet," she pleaded, and for once her daughter obeyed.

They hurried on, townspeople scattering as they passed, until they came to Belkos' house. A Dragon Touched woman, her scales hiding under a layer of magic, was trying to load her family's possessions onto a wheelbarrow, shouting orders at her daughter while her mother looked on. She saw Belkos and cried out, tears in her eyes.

"Thank God you're here!" she said, then recoiled as she took in his spear and realized he was undisguised. "What's happening, Belkos?"

Bandu did not listen to his answer, because the woman's mother was staring at her. "She-wolf," the old woman spat. "Black Dragon. They have come."

Bandu locked eyes with her. The old woman did not flinch as others did, but stared right back, unblinking and unashamed. In fact, it was Bandu who became disquieted and had to turn away. There was something less than sanity in the old woman's eyes, and Bandu got the impression that whatever was missing had been replaced with magic.

"Come," Bandu said to Criton. "Kill the fire with me."

"You don't kill a fire," Criton muttered, but he came with her.

The lack of any breeze may have helped to slow the flames' progress, but the blaze had nonetheless expanded – there was only one house now between it and Belkos' home.

"So what's the plan?" Criton asked. "I've *made* fires before, but I've never fought them."

Bandu patted Goodweather on the back and thought about it. "Without wind, the fire doesn't jump far. If this house doesn't burn, it is good."

Criton looked at her incredulously. "Yes, but how can we keep it from burning?"

Bandu was about to answer, but just then Goodweather made a sudden attempt to fall out of her mother's arms, flopping backwards with a motion that no spine should have allowed. Bandu did not let her fall, but the baby began to scream anyway, a cry of pure infantile anguish.

"Take her," Bandu snapped. "I can't think."

Criton obeyed, dropping his new shield and spear to take the baby from Bandu's arms. Bandu touched the walls of the house, trying to quiet her mind. Between the heat and Goodweather's near-constant nursing, she was beginning to feel light-headed. She wished she could abandon the fire for a moment and go find a well – there must be one around here somewhere, and she badly needed a drink of water. Her mouth was as dry as the wall she was leaning against.

A strange thought came to her, the beginnings of a plan. This house was made of trees – dead trees, yes, but if they could only be made to remember…

She pressed both her palms against the wall and closed her eyes. She felt her dry mouth, licked her lips, and tried to make the walls feel her thirst. *You must be thirstier than I am,* she told the wall. *Long ago you have roots that reach down to where wells are born, and you drink and drink and grow and grow. Do you remember? Your roots then are not so short like now.*

Remember how you are alive then? You should let your roots grow again, so you can drink. The water is waiting for you!

The boards in this wall did not have roots anymore, but when she told them otherwise, she found them open to persuasion. She commanded them to let their roots grow deep again, and she could feel the wood groaning as it tried to obey. One of the boards beneath her hands splintered with the effort, and dug into Bandu's right hand.

Yes, she told the wall encouragingly, *like that. But don't dig into me to find your water, dig into the ground! There is water there, so much more water than in me. Take it! Let your roots grow down to it!*

They were trying, she could feel it in her hand. The splinter was actually sucking at her as the rest of the boards tried to grow roots. It was small enough that she decided she should let it, if that meant that it would remind the others how it was done. And when at last the roots burst out of the boards and into the ground, she felt their triumph echoed in her pain.

Down and down the roots grew, searching for the water that had been promised them. At last they found it, and Bandu leapt back from the wall with a yelp. How greedily they had begun to drink, both from the ground and from her!

Criton ran to her side, asking if she was all right. Bandu nodded. "I'll take her," she said, reaching for Goodweather with her left hand. "Pluck that out from me!"

Criton did as she said, passing their daughter over and then inspecting her right palm closely. "That's kind of a thick splinter," he said, pinching the end between clawed fingers.

"This is going to hurt."

He was right about that much. It definitely hurt. When he had pulled the splinter out, he muttered an oath and held it up for her to see. The wood had divided into three tiny squiggly roots partway into her hand. Bandu licked her wound and handed Goodweather back to Criton. The baby was miserable in this heat.

Criton threw the root away and looked up, finally noticing what she'd done to the house. "How did you do that?" he marveled.

She looked back and smiled. Water was running down the outside wall as the boards drank and drank from the underground well, lifting more water out of the ground than they could possibly absorb.

"Take Goodweather back to Belkos," she said. "Tell him they are safe."

She touched her good hand to the wet wall and reminded it to share with the roof. Then she picked up Criton's spear and shield and followed him back to his cousin's house.

Belkos and his wife were still loading the wheelbarrow, keeping one eye on the fire's progress, when Bandu and Criton arrived. Their daughter stood motionless, a long dress draped over her arms, staring at the rising smoke.

"Don't worry," Criton said, "the fire won't come here. Bandu's seen to that."

Belkos' wife looked incredulous. "What? How?"

"The She-wolf makes houses weep," the old woman said darkly.

13

Dessa

Grandma didn't like that witch Bandu; that was part of what made Dessa love her. She didn't trust Grandma. Mother always said that she should be grateful because Grandma and Grandpa had protected Mother when she was Dessa's age, and without that, there would have been no Dessa. But at least Grandpa had been nice. Grandma was mean.

Mother said it wasn't her fault. She hadn't always been this way. Mother was probably right – Dessa could almost remember a time when she had loved Grandma more than anyone. But now she never knew what to expect, whether Grandma would smile at her or hit her, and when she did hit, she never said sorry. Dessa always had to say sorry. It wasn't fair.

So when she saw Grandma looking at Bandu with such hatred in her eyes, Dessa decided that Bandu must be wonderful. And she was – look what she had done with that house! Even the nasty name Grandma gave her sounded impressive. The She-wolf. It was like something out of a story.

Bandu was short and skinny compared to the other women Dessa knew, but that didn't make her any less impressive. She looked like no one Dessa had ever seen before – her skin so dark it was almost black, her clothes dirty, her hair a tangled mass. She didn't look like someone who could be punished for climbing trees. She looked like someone Dessa wanted to be.

Mother made Dessa help with the packing, since Grandma wouldn't leave off staring at Bandu and her husband. That was so unfair, Dessa wanted to scream. Grandma wasn't even talking; she was just standing out there glaring while Father talked. If Dessa had been allowed to stay outside, she could actually meet Bandu!

Dessa wasn't even sure why they were still packing, if their house was safe from the fire. She must have missed something Father had said while she was watching a building cry. Were they going somewhere? What was going on?

She hurried to finish, but by that time Bandu and her husband were gone. "Where's Chalkstone?" Father asked when he came indoors.

"She ran off during the fire," Mother told him. "She was too wild for me to control, and when I turned my back on her for a minute, she was gone."

"I thought I'd tied her up well," Father said. "Partha? Did you see her go?"

"What's that?" Grandma asked. "I don't know who you're talking about."

"The horse," Mother answered.

Grandma just stared at her blankly, for so long that Dessa was almost sure she couldn't remember the question. Then she said, "I didn't know you had a horse, dear Iona."

Mother made a frustrated sound and turned away.

Dessa hoped she'd have the chance to meet Bandu properly soon, and she couldn't wait to talk to Vella about her. Vella was six years older than Dessa, and she was the person Dessa admired most in the world. She was generous and kind, and even though she was married, she still found the time to talk with Dessa about whatever might be troubling her. These days, it was her impending marriage that bothered Dessa most, and the fact that she would have to leave her home and her family so soon.

Vella helped with that too: Dessa was betrothed to her little brother, Malkon. The fact that the two of them would soon be sisters-in-law was the one nice thing about the whole situation. Even so, Dessa was afraid. Vella and Malkon's parents lived a whole town away. Dessa would be seeing much less of Vella after the wedding, even though they'd be sisters-in-law. She'd be completely alone in a town full of strangers.

Vella tried to make it better for her. She told Dessa stories about her family, reassured her that her grandma Hessina wasn't as scary as she seemed, and did her best to make the move to another town seem normal. After all, if Vella could live through it, so could Dessa.

Now Dessa wondered if she might not have to live through it at all. Everybody she knew seemed to be packing, preparing for some big trip somewhere. From what she heard, it sounded like all the Dragon Touched everywhere would be going together. So she wouldn't be separated from her parents, at least for now. Might her wedding also be postponed, or even better, cancelled?

Dessa's father said that everyone would be gathering that night in front of the weeping house. Where would they be going after that? He didn't know. "Wherever Criton leads us," he said. "God Most High has placed our people in his hands."

It was a strange thing to say, and the way he said it was even stranger. He sounded almost giddy about it.

Mother was *not* giddy. She was worried. Dessa didn't know who to trust about how to feel – Father always said that Mother worried too much, but he was acting too weird right now for her to trust him. Should she be afraid of what was coming?

She and Mother spent the next few hours making bread and wrapping it up for the journey while Father went to find Chalkstone and Grandma watched them bake, muttering angrily to herself. Wherever they were going, Dessa wished they could leave Grandma behind.

They all gathered that evening just as Father had said, bringing their things and their animals with them. Every Dragon Touched person Dessa knew and some she didn't stood before the weeping house while Vella's grandma purified Criton the old way, sprinkling him with bull's blood and counting aloud so that everyone could hear she was doing it right. Dessa had never seen this ritual before, having grown up long after the Dragon Touched went into hiding. She'd only heard of such things, and now watched in fascination. Neither Criton nor Hessina were wearing a disguise – their scales shone in the firelight for all the world to see. Did this mean Dessa's people would be leaving the shadows for good?

And did that mean she wouldn't have to marry yet?

Bandu was standing not too far away, and Mother waved her over. "Would you like me to hold the baby?" she asked.

Bandu nodded and handed her infant over, stretching her back. "Thank you," she said.

Dessa felt paralyzed. Here Bandu was, standing right next to her, and she didn't know what to say. "I want to be your friend" was too blunt, and "Thank you for saving our house" would sound stupid, especially since it sounded like they would be leaving it soon. Besides which, Bandu would just answer "You're welcome," and then they'd be right where they started.

In the end she settled on, "I can hold the baby too if you like." That prompted an appraising glance and a small nod, which was enough to delight Dessa no end. Mother never did hand the baby over, but Dessa was glad to have been considered worthy anyway.

In the meantime, she was starting to gather more about what was going on. Her people were coming out of hiding for good, and would have to find allies to help them retake their homeland. Criton was going to take them northward first, to find allies on the northern plains. They would leave tomorrow.

Dessa was almost certain that that meant she would not have to marry Malkon any time soon. As happy as she was at the thought, there was also a sadness that caught her off guard, because if she didn't marry Malkon, she wouldn't be Vella's sister-in-law after all. She had already started thinking of her as a sister, and had loved the way Vella kept reassuring her that her family would love Dessa. They could still be friends even if the marriage never happened, but it wouldn't be the same.

On the other hand, she was already related to Bandu, sort of. Father said that Criton was his cousin, and that meant that Bandu was family too. Wouldn't Vella be jealous! She was sure Vella would be just as fascinated by Bandu as she was.

She spotted Vella in the crowd, standing beside her husband Pilos. Did she dare to go join them? Pilos had always sort of frightened her: he was so aloof and disdainful. He was the same way with Vella, and possessive too – that was part of what frightened Dessa about getting married. What if Malkon would be the same way with her? Vella said he wouldn't be, that he was a nice boy, but Dessa wasn't convinced that such a thing existed.

Dessa was halfway there before she realized that Pilos' parents were right behind him. She *hated* Pilos' parents. They always acted as if Dessa's engagement was an attack on them – it had been quite a coup for them to marry their son to Hessina Highservant's eldest grandchild, and they jealously guarded the place that gave them in the community. They were always polite to Vella, since her inclusion in their family gave them status, but they also did their best to keep Dessa from her.

Now they would hate Dessa even more, because the Dragon Touched suddenly had two leaders instead of one, and Dessa was related to both. Or, at least, she would be if the wedding still happened – maybe she ought to marry Malkon after all, just to beat them at their stupid game. It was a tempting thought.

In any case, they'd all seen her walking toward them, so it was too late to turn back. She had wanted to tell Vella about everything that had happened to her today, and everything she'd seen, but instead she walked up and said, "Vella, do you want to come meet my new cousins? Criton's related to us, you know, and his wife said I could hold their baby! You should come meet her!"

Vella gave her in-laws the sort of look that said, "This girl's not really my friend, but what can you do? She looks up to me." Then turned back to Dessa and said in an indulgent tone, "Sure, Dessa. I'd be happy to."

She kept up the act until they had put half the crowd between them and her in-laws, and then she said, "Criton's related to you?"

Dessa nodded. "Wait till you meet his wife, the witch. She's *so amazing.*"

But by the time they got to where Bandu was standing, the crowd was quieting down to hear what Criton himself had to say about their future. Dessa tried to give a hurried introduction, but her mother shushed her and Bandu just nodded absently and turned to look at Criton while he spoke.

"Today we armed ourselves," he said, "right under our enemies' noses. But if we want to take Ardis, we'll need more than weapons. We'll need an army. So tomorrow, we'll start off northwards. I've heard that the people of the northern plains used to be enemies to the Ardismen, so I'm hoping they'll willingly rise up to help us take Ardis back.

"They might not, though, so I want us all to be prepared. If we're going to build an army big enough to beat the Ardismen, we can't let every other village turn us away. We need a reputation as frightening as the red priest's was, so that people will be *afraid* not to join our cause. That means we'll have to make an example of anyone who refuses to help us. Do you all understand?"

There was a murmur of assent from the crowd, but Dessa wasn't sure she understood. Was Criton saying they'd have to kill everyone who didn't join their army? That *couldn't* be what he meant, could it?

"I hope this war will be short," Criton said, "but there's no way of knowing. We'll just have to trust Salemis that God Most High is with us and will protect us from our enemies."

The adults around Dessa nodded solemnly. That seemed to be the end of Criton's speech, because he thanked everyone and took two steps toward the crowd before suddenly freezing. He was looking at something behind Dessa and to her left, and as she turned to see what it was, she heard frightened cries and gasps of, "Is it an omen?"

A little girl was walking toward Criton, and she was covered head to toe in blood. She had been on the outskirts of the crowd at first, and with all eyes on Criton, few had seen her as she approached. Now there was horror and confusion. Was she real? Or a ghost? A vision of things to come?

The girl couldn't have been older than six, seven at the most. There was no expression on her face as she approached, dripping, dripping. She was leaving a trail of blood behind her – did that mean she was real? Either way, Dessa shuddered at the sight of her.

She looked back at Criton, who had the same look of horror on his face that most of the others did. But as the girl got closer, his expression suddenly changed.

"Delika?"

At the name, the girl broke into a run. Criton bent toward her, and she hurled herself into his arms, sobbing. Nobody in the crowd knew what to make of that. Neither did Dessa, but unlike the others, she was too curious to gossip and wait. Bandu was already walking to join Criton and the girl, and Dessa followed.

"I didn't even realize," Criton was saying. "I should have known, but I never thought – how did this happen?"

Dessa couldn't quite hear the response, muffled as it was by the girl pressing her whole face into him, but she thought Delika said something about the fire in the temple.

"Where are the others?" Criton asked suddenly, kneeling and pulling her away so he could look at her. "Rakon and Caldra, and Adla and Temena?"

The little girl shook her head. "I don't know. I ran away."

Criton sighed. "They'll be gone then, either way. I hope they're all right."

Suddenly, she rushed in and hugged him around the neck again. "Please let me stay with you!"

"Of course," Criton said. "Bandu? Is that all right?"

Bandu nodded, and said nothing. Behind Dessa, a voice spoke.

"You two know this child?"

It was Vella's grandma, Hessina Highservant, and she was just as formidable up close as Dessa had feared she would be. Even from afar, she had seemed terribly judgmental and severe, and proximity only reinforced that impression. The rest of the crowd might react with horror or fascination or wonder or trepidation at the blood-soaked girl who had thrown herself on Criton, but Hessina didn't. Hessina only *disapproved*.

"This is Delika," Criton said. "We rescued her from the elves, and from Mayar..."

"She stays with us," said Bandu. "You don't care."

The "you don't care" was a command, not a statement. Dessa loved the way Bandu talked.

"Well," Hessina said, "as long as you take responsibility for her. But for God's sake clean her up."

Criton looked relieved that Hessina wasn't giving him any more trouble. He turned back to little Delika with a smile.

Dessa was relieved too. More than anything, she was glad that Delika was a real girl and not some terrible omen of things to come. Because if she *had* been an omen – well, Criton's whole neck and chest were covered with blood.

14

NARKY

For three hellish weeks, Narky stayed hidden in the room the Graceful Servant had prepared for him. It was not the accommodations that bothered him – the bed was fine, and the meals they brought him were good. The problem was the crushing boredom. He wished someone had taught him to read, so that he could at least try to amuse himself with the books that were in his room. Not that he thought they'd be especially interesting if he *could* read them, but anything would be better than sitting alone on his bed and waiting for news.

The Graceful Servant or one of her followers always gave him updates on the situation outside whenever they visited to bring him food or take out his chamber pot, whether there had been any real developments or not. He got to know a few of the other followers who came to visit him: Ptera, the young widow who had turned to Ravennis in her grief; Taedron, the big, nervous man who always called the Graceful Servant 'Teacher;' wispy Magara, whose voice was so gentle and soft that it put Narky on edge. They were all clearly intimidated by him, whether because of his history or his general appearance, it was hard to say. Narky found that he preferred the Graceful Servant's company.

On Narky's third day in the room, Ptera passed along rumors of a dragon north of the city, supposedly trying to raise an army of its own with which to conquer Ardis. From this Narky gathered that Salemis must have visited his former home and met the other islanders there – the talk of an army was clearly ridiculous. The next day, the story was that some of the Dragon Touched had survived the purge, and were sure to try to take back their city. Someone had spotted Criton, then.

The Graceful Servant was pleased with all this nonsense. She said, "The people no longer trust Magor to protect them. They see an enemy in every shadow, a dragon in every cloud. Can they cling to their God for long? Just a little longer, and we will show them how weak Magor truly is. When Ravennis reveals His might, the people will flock to Him as their true protector in this world and the next."

"Let's hope so," Narky said. It was hard to feel hopeful after three days lying low in a dark room.

On the fifth day, the news from outside was shocking. The Dragon Touched had raided several villages, stealing weapons from under their servants' noses, and even sacked the town closest to the Dragon Knight's Tomb. Reports on their numbers ranged from hundreds to thousands – it was no longer possible to believe that all this fuss was about Criton alone. There must have been a community of Dragon Touched hidden out there after all, a community that Salemis had rallied during his visit. Criton must be overjoyed.

How had Bestillos missed them all? The red priest had had no difficulty seeing through Criton's disguise, and Bandu had insisted that he could track them by the smell of Criton's magic. A clan of hundreds, of thousands, all lurking near Ardis undetected seemed impossible to reconcile with his knowledge of the red priest's power.

But villages did not sack themselves. A community of Criton's kin must exist, and they were beginning to assert their power, just as the followers of Ravennis meant to. It appeared as if Magor really was doomed. The vultures were circling. Or the ravens, rather.

The days passed slowly, as Narky spent his waking hours

waiting for news that didn't come. The Ardisian Council of Generals sent scouts to assess the strength of the Dragon Touched army, but apparently these had yet to return. The generals were raising a massive army of their own, while in the shadows, the Graceful Servant and her followers spread their gospel throughout the city. The time was nearly at hand – they had to prepare the populace for the great confrontation between them and the priests of Magor.

Then at last the day came. The Graceful Servant came to get him, bringing with her a hooded black robe.

"You want me to put this on?" he asked. If the idea was that he could travel through the city unnoticed that way, it wasn't going to work: his dark hands and face would still be visible to anyone who looked. What was the robe for, then?

"The priests of Ravennis wore these garments," she replied. "Do you object?"

Narky sighed and took it from her, and she left the room to wait for him to change. The garment was long, at least, and would hopefully keep him warm in the chillier weather. But Ravennis forgive him, he didn't want to be a priest! Was that what the Graceful Servant wanted from him? If she thought he could do it well, she was very much mistaken.

When they stepped out of the house, Narky was nearly blinded by the light outside. The sky was overcast, but that only meant it was uniformly white and unbearable. Though the alley struck him as deserted at first, soon he and the Graceful Servant were joined by a small crowd of other Ravennis worshippers, and together they set off. People gasped and stared as they marched through the streets as a unit, squeezing through countless alleyways before bursting out into the temple square. It was uncomfortable how right the Graceful Servant had been: though the prophetess of Ravennis stood no more than three feet away from him, all eyes were on Narky. His presence had made the desired impression.

The Ravennis worshippers fanned out, and the Graceful Servant stepped toward the Great Temple of Magor. The temple was a gigantic, hulking edifice of painted stone, with murals of hunting scenes visible past the outer support pillars. There were stylized spearheads seeming to burst out of the roof above each pillar, and the tip of each spearhead was painted a very convincing red. A large permanent altar stood in front of the temple, with gold-coated boar's tusks at its four corners. The sight of it reminded Narky of the Boar of Hagardis, and he suddenly wished he had a spear to hold onto. At least then he'd have something to do with his hands, besides letting them hang impotently at his sides.

"Priests of Magor, I challenge you!" the Graceful Servant cried, and her voice boomed throughout the square and echoed off the temple's walls. It was magic; it had to be. Like Bestillos, the Graceful Servant was not just her God's High Priestess, but His chosen, His representative on earth.

At first, no priest came to answer her challenge. A crowd of citizens, however, was beginning to gather outside the temple, watching to see what would happen. For a good five minutes the Graceful Servant and her pupils stood watching the crowd grow, waiting for the priests of Magor to show their faces. The Graceful Servant even repeated her challenge, mocking the priests with her tone. Why hadn't they come out yet? It made them look weak.

Finally, five priests emerged from the temple, all carrying spears and dressed in red robes. "Who are you to challenge us?" asked their leader, a thin man in his forties. His voice was deep and gravelly, and it did not boom like the Graceful Servant's, but cut through the air as if all distance was illusion.

"I am the Graceful Servant of Lord Ravennis, Keeper of Fates and Lord Among the Fallen. God of the Underworld."

The priest let out a bark that never quite became a laugh. "The God of Laarna, you mean. Laarna, which was destroyed, and its Oracle slain. I am glad to finally meet you face to face, woman. I was beginning to think you no more substantial than your dead God. And yet, here you are. Where did you hide to avoid the fate of your sisters, eh, Graceful Servant? In a stable, with a pile of horse dung to disguise you?"

"Your High Priest Bestillos was no more observant than you are," the Graceful Servant answered. "Perhaps that is why he was so easily killed. Magor's chosen, killed by a boy with a crossbow, a servant of Ravennis. Here he stands today, the slayer of your champion, defying Magor's power in His own city. You mock me to cover for your God's weakness, a weakness that only grows more obvious by the day."

There were whispers and gasps from the crowd as she introduced Narky, but the Graceful Servant barely paused before she moved on. "You have mentioned my priestly sisters," she said. "I was there when our God spoke to us and commanded the Venerable and Youthful Servants of Ravennis to stay behind and die, so that He might conquer the underworld through them. That was their task, and they performed it unquestioningly. If Ravennis had chosen to let them live, they could have evaded Bestillos as easily as I did."

The priest of Magor opened his mouth, but the Graceful Servant went on in her booming voice: "Perhaps Magor lost His eyes when the Boar of Hagardis was slain. Or before, since He tried and failed to eliminate the Dragon Touched. He has certainly lost His strength now, when the Dragon Touched no longer cower in fear but go rampaging across the countryside. I have come here to demonstrate, before all the people of Ardis, that Ravennis is a greater God than

Magor ever was, and that it is His protection the people should be seeking."

At last, the Graceful Servant stopped to let Magor's priest speak. "Those are bold words," he said. "Especially coming from a so-called 'Oracle' of a God whose people were slaughtered and enslaved. I am glad you have come here to us, so that we can teach you a lesson and demonstrate to all your deluded followers that Magor still reigns in Ardis."

At this the other priests raised their spears to the heavens, as if the very existence of their weapons proved their God's power. It was a ridiculous, theatrical gesture, but Narky had to admit that the crowd responded to it.

The Graceful Servant clearly didn't care. "Magor's power is broken," she laughed. "Ravennis, who rules the land of the dead, will soon rule over Magor as well. If you do not believe me, then believe the words of Narky of Tarphae, who slew both the Boar of Hagardis and your God's High Priest."

The square went silent in anticipation of Narky's speech. It was extremely intimidating. Narky had never spoken in front of a crowd before, and he keenly felt the hundreds of gazes that were directed at him. He froze for a moment, a moment that seemed to last for hours. But nobody spoke in his place, and at long last he took a deep breath and addressed the crowd.

"Everything she says is true," he said, speaking at the top of his voice and wishing that he could project it the way the Graceful Servant did. "I killed the boar, and I killed Bestillos. The Oracle of Laarna told us the truth those months ago – the Gods are being judged, and Magor has been judged most harshly. Even His victory at Laarna was an illusion: Ravennis outmaneuvered Him. The people of Laarna sacrificed themselves to make Ravennis the God of the Underworld, and now He can reward them in the world below while Magor's power here in our world crumbles.

"Magor is dying, people. The dragon Salemis burned His army. The boar is dead, and Bestillos is dead, and even the Dragon Touched seem to be coming back to life. I'm only a farmer's son from Tarphae, but Ravennis has marked me and guided my hand, and raised me above the highest of Magor's servants. If I were you, I'd abandon your old God – He can't protect you in this life, and only Ravennis can save you in the next. Join us before it's too late."

There were murmurs among the crowd when he finished, some of them angry. But nobody had thrown anything at him, so Narky considered his speech a success. Even the angrier Ardismen were afraid of being wrong and having to face Ravennis when they died.

The priests of Magor hissed. Their spokesman said, "Nonsense.

Ravennis is a dead God, slain by Magor's hand. Two of the three Oracle priestesses were killed in Laarna, and the last has come to us here, pretending that her God still has power? We will accept your challenge, woman, and when we are done, you will be slaughtered like a lamb and bound to the doorway of the temple like your sisters were in Laarna."

With that, the five priests raised their voices as one and cried, "O Great Magor, show these people Your power!"

Nothing happened. That was a relief – Narky had been afraid that he might get struck by lightning or something. He looked to the Graceful Servant. She wasn't mocking the priests just yet. How long would she wait?

The ground suddenly shifted under Narky's feet, and he stumbled back as a hole opened where he had been standing. Rats poured out. Narky hurriedly backed away from them, but they all ran at the Graceful Servant. The woman didn't budge. Before the swarming rodents could reach her, a flock of ravens appeared as if out of nowhere and dove straight at the rats, snatching them off the ground in a cacophony of caws and squeals. People gasped and the ravens flew away over the Temple of Magor and disappeared into the city. In a battle of miracles, Ravennis had won the first skirmish.

Now the Graceful Servant raised her hands in the gesture of her God's priestesses, her thumbs and middle fingers pointed toward each other. "O Ravennis," she prayed, "send a message of Your power to these people."

There was a screech from above and Narky looked up, along with everyone else, to see the frightening visage of a crow-angel hurtling down toward the temple. Like the others Narky had seen, it looked like a pale man with enormous black wings, bald and naked and sharp-toothed. The priests stumbled back as it landed on Magor's altar, talons and pointed teeth bared.

The angel screeched at the priests again, then turned from them to address the crowd.

"Here is the Lord of Fate's message," it cawed, but its words were cut off as Bestillos' successor stabbed it through the back with his spear. The angel made a horrible noise and curled in on itself, shrinking and curling until it was just an ordinary crow skewered on a spear.

"Whatever that monster meant to say," the priest said, "I think we're better off without it."

Narky half expected him to be killed on the spot, but Magor must still have had at least enough power to protect him. Perhaps Narky should have expected that, but he hadn't, and the ramifications of it still amazed him: Ravennis had provided a miracle, and the priest had effectively countered it with a pointed stick.

The Graceful Servant glared at the grinning priest. Then she raised her voice and cried, "Ravennis, if You really are the Lord of Fates and the King of the Underworld, if You are truly undefeated among the Gods, show this man – show these men their deaths. Reveal to them the manner of their demise and let them see what awaits them in the world below!"

There was a hush among the crowd, as a look of real fear came onto the priests' faces. Then the high priest began to laugh. "How weak your God is, to be making threats He can't act upon! I'm to kill myself with a sword three days from now, am I? Well, then. If that comes to pass, let every man of Ardis turn from Magor and worship the Crow God of Laarna. Otherwise, Servant, I will see you bound to the pillar behind me and whipped to death."

The Graceful Servant smiled back, oozing patronizing indulgence, but for someone standing as close as Narky was, it was hard to miss the look of hatred in her eyes. "Liar," she hissed under her breath.

His heart sank. The Graceful Servant had made a terrible mistake, one that Ravennis could not save her from. Perhaps the God of Fate had granted her request, but that couldn't stop the priests from lying about it. Who really knew what that man had seen? There was no point in the Graceful Servant objecting to his words – an argument over what vision the priest had received was one overbalanced in his favor. He had cleverly chosen a 'vision' of his death that he had maximum ability to control, and now there was very little the Graceful Servant or even Ravennis Himself could do about it.

"We shall see what the coming days bring us," the Graceful Servant said, with great poise. "Until then, make peace with your God, but turn to mine before it is too late, for it is Ravennis who will watch over you when you pass on. Farewell, doomed servants of Magor."

They left the square, followed by a large portion of the crowd and the stares of all. Narky was trying not to panic, going over their encounter with Magor's priests again and again. Phaedra had always insisted that men had free will, no matter how the Gods tried to manipulate them. He was starting to see her point, and to see why people were such valuable tools in the Gods' wars. Here was an argument over which God was more powerful, an argument in which the Gods themselves had had a say, and yet it seemed like it would be won not on godly might but on human tactics. There was something darkly amusing about that. It would have been more amusing if he'd been on the winning side.

As they neared the house, the citizens who had followed them began to peel off, looking vaguely confused. The magic of the place was keeping them from finding it. Impressive. The Graceful Servant had told him about it before, without him really believing her. Now that he saw its effect on the citizenry, he had to admit that it was pretty amazing.

By the time they arrived, there were only five of them: Narky, the Graceful Servant, Taedron, Ptera, and Magara. A pair of lamps flared as they entered, bathing the room in warm light. They closed the door fast behind them.

"That went well," Narky said. "What the hell do we do now?"

"The high priest lied," the Graceful Servant said, explaining to the others what had already been obvious to Narky. "He was never supposed to kill himself, and certainly not this week. Ravennis should never have let him speak like that."

She sat down and sank her head in her hands. "I am to

blame for this reversal: I told Ravennis what I wanted instead of offering myself as a vessel for His power, and the priest of Magor took advantage of my poor choice. If I had trusted in Ravennis to provide a miracle of His choosing, this would not have happened."

"Sure," Narky said, "but what's our plan now? That priest out-thought us, and now it's going to look like Ravennis has no power here. I don't suppose we can force him to kill himself?"

The Graceful Servant shook her head. "It is time for you to leave us, Narky. Tonight, before our enemies can move to stop you. Your part here is done for now, and if both of us are martyred at once, the church of Ravennis will have no leadership. I am ordaining you as a priest, to be high priest after my death. Go to Anardis, and convert that city to the worship of our God."

Anardis. The City of Elkinar. A city that had blamed the "cursed islanders" for its bad luck; a city that Narky and his friends had been forced to flee before its people could deliver them into the hands of their enemies. Surely, Narky was the worst-suited messenger for bringing the Lord of Fate's message to Anardis.

Not that he had any intention of switching tasks with the Graceful Servant.

"Why Anardis?" he asked instead. "Why not some other city? Why not Atuna?"

The Graceful Servant looked astounded, as if Narky's question was too foolish to be believed. She asked, "What greater symbol is there of Magor's power than that tributary city, the city that the red priest brought to its knees last year? To lose Anardis is to lose all semblance of worldly power, to be truly isolated and confined to one city. Ardis does not have the strength to put down a second rebellion: though Bestillos burned half the city, the walls of Anardis still stand. Without Magor's chosen as its high priest, Ardis no longer has the power of intimidation on its side. You will be safe there."

"And you? Will you really stay behind here and let the priests of Magor flay you?"

The Graceful Servant nodded, her eyes glowing. "Of course. What have I to fear? The priests of Magor can only hurt my body for a short time. My God will reward me forever."

Her faith and her confidence were astounding. Narky had to wonder whether he would ever show the kind of serenity she did in the face of certain death. Somehow, he highly doubted it.

"How can I even get out of this city?" he asked. "I can't exactly slip out unrecognized."

"One of the night watchmen is a man of the faith," the Graceful Servant replied. "He will let you out without raising an alarm."

"And how will I know which one is him?"

"I will go with you," Ptera said. "He was one of my husband's friends – I know him well. I converted him and his family."

"Take Ptera with you to Anardis," the Graceful Servant said. "Those who stay with me may well perish. Ptera's a clever girl, and her faith is strong. The Keeper of Fates needs her in this world for now."

Narky scratched above his bad eye uncomfortably. "That's... I mean, a man and a woman, traveling together without being married... it's not like I can tell people we're related."

The Graceful Servant smiled patronizingly at him. "I never suggested such an arrangement. Take Ptera as your wife. She has already told me she's willing."

Narky looked back and forth between them, unable to register his shock. When had they had this conversation? Why hadn't he been involved?

He had thought himself oversensitive to flirtation – after all, he had once thought himself in love just because a girl had been nice to him. Back then, he had built up each conversation in his mind and imbued every word and glance with far more meaning and emotion than they deserved. Narky had confronted that girl's lover, and eventually murdered him, all because he had taken her unexpected friendliness far too seriously.

But there had been no flirtation here, not that he had

detected. So when, exactly, had Ptera told the Graceful Servant that she was willing to marry him? Narky would like to have known how that topic had even come up between the two of them. And, nerves aside, he wished he knew how he felt about the whole thing. It was too shocking for him to process.

"I..." he said.

"You will do as I say," the Graceful Servant answered, cutting him off. "You will marry Ptera, and together you will go to Anardis to spread Ravennis' teachings. Our God will guide you once you are there; you will know when the time is right to return. Ardis will be His before the year is out."

"And you..."

"I will be with Ravennis. Don't worry, you will see. My martyrdom will change everything in this city – it will open a path for you. By the time you return, Ardis will be begging to hear your holy words."

Narky nodded, though the voice in his head remained stubbornly skeptical. How could the loss of their God's prophet change anything for the better? Why should Ardis clamor for Narky's teachings after they had tortured and humiliated the Graceful Servant, even up to her death?

And what the hell *were* his teachings, anyway?

15

HUNTER

Hunter had no chance to struggle – the sailors were holding his arms too tight. If he had known what they were planning... but then, he still didn't understand what was going on.

"What curse?" he asked them. "What are you talking about?"

"Your God won't let us leave this damned backwater island!" one of them answered. "Every time we weigh anchor, a tempest keeps blowing us to shore. We almost got shipwrecked this last time, so the captain says, 'Find those two kids from Tarphae and bring them back. Their God doesn't want us leaving this place without them.'"

Hunter looked over at Phaedra. Well, that answered that question: God Most High wasn't going to make them wait for another ship or even pay for their passage. It was a shame for Phaedra that the crew had found them so quickly, but then, it would have been too cruel to force these men to stay here a fortnight while the two of them shucked oysters and watched an old woman cook her meals and wash her clothes and take naps. For all that Phaedra might be developing very interesting theories about how magic worked, he was glad it hadn't taken the sailors too long to find them. He was even a bit relieved.

Now if only they'd stop squeezing his arms like that.

"Please let go," Phaedra begged. "You're hurting me."

The sailors who were holding her obeyed, and even Hunter's

captors eased up a little. "We're coming with you," Hunter told them. "You don't have to drag us."

They went along meekly, Hunter supporting Phaedra on the uneven ground. If only her ankle hadn't been shattered on Mount Galadron, when they were unknowingly risking their lives to explore a giant ant hole. If only he or the others had known how to set it before it healed wrong. If only he hadn't said that thing about never dancing again.

They eventually reached the dock and were rowed back to the ship. The captain looked relieved to see them, but his relief soon turned to anger as he was finally able to vent his frustration and fear.

"We should have left you in Atuna, you wretches! You may as well be pirates, the way you've hijacked my ship!"

"I'm sorry," Hunter said. "We didn't know."

"You didn't know," the captain repeated, disgusted. "Well, we're never letting you on shore again. Not on this voyage. Not until you can assure me that your God will leave us alone! If we can't have fair weather without you on board, we're just going to have to make you stay. I don't care if I have to chain you to the mast; you're not leaving my ship."

Phaedra said something, to which the captain barked, "What's that? If you have something to say, girl, speak up!"

"I said I wouldn't recommend that."

The captain's face went red. "Are you threatening me?"

"No," Phaedra said. "I'm saying that we don't control our God – He controls us. We had no idea God Most High would keep you here, and we have no idea where He wants us to go next, but I'm pretty certain that wherever we're meant to go, He's going to guide us there. If you try to control our movements instead of taking us wherever our God wants us to be, He's going to find another way. I don't mean to threaten you, but I can't believe that God Most High would take enough of an interest to force you to wait here for us without getting offended if you imprison us. I don't even know why He's taken such an interest in our voyage, but He clearly has. If you would treat your own Gods with caution and respect, you should treat ours with double."

The captain struck her across the face with the back of his hand, and she fell to the deck. Immediately, the hands of the crewmembers seized Hunter's arms to restrain him. It shouldn't have been necessary: Hunter knew full well how precarious his position was. He had wanted to help Phaedra up, not retaliate. But the crew pulled him back, and Phaedra was forced to climb to her feet by herself.

The captain had the look of a man who knew he had crossed a line. He was clearly terrified of what God Most High might do to him, and at the same time giddy with the freedom of transgression. With that blow, his logic had changed dangerously: God Most High might well punish him, but if He meant to do so, there was little the captain could do about it. That meant his fear couldn't control him any longer.

Phaedra, on the other hand, was all control. Though tears were streaming down her cheeks as she struggled back to her feet, her voice was level and strong. "I don't know if my God will punish you for that," she said, "but I will pray that He doesn't. I've seen what happens when Gods punish men."

"Your God won't sink this ship with you on it," the captain answered. "As soon as the other search parties return, we'll be back to our regular trade route. It should be an easier voyage than usual, what with your God keeping the bad weather at bay."

The man's bluster was enough to enrage anyone, but Phaedra remained calm. If anything she grew calmer, and her look was one of pity, not anger.

"I'm sorry we've brought trouble to you and your crew," she said. "I don't want to see anything bad happen because of the way you've treated us. Please believe me that it's not too late to repent. We have a friend who lives today because of the power of his atonement."

The captain looked tempted, hopeful, relieved. Then his expression hardened. "It's thoughtful of you to say so," he said.

"I'll make a sacrifice at our next port."

He turned away. "Put them below."

And just like that, they were confined below deck for the rest of the voyage. Days went by as the ship went from port to port, trading goods for coin and other goods. The crew brought them food and took their waste, treating them with embarrassed deference. At the first major port, half of them left the ship. The others told Hunter and Phaedra that they meant to do the same soon – they respected the islanders and their God, and didn't want to wait to see what would happen to the ship and its captain. But for Hunter and Phaedra, this only made the voyage worse. Each crewman who left was replaced with one who didn't know the prisoners' story, and didn't have any cause to fear God Most High. As the captain grew bolder, his crew only grew more obedient, and by the start of the third week, he and the cook were the only original crewmembers who remained.

And why shouldn't the captain be bold? The stormy season should have begun by now, and yet, to judge by the gentle rocking of the ship, the weather remained fine. If the captain's gambit was working just as he'd hoped, maybe the islanders' powerful God didn't mean to punish him after all.

Hunter wondered whether God Most High had indeed forgotten about them, or whether this latest reversal was all part of the plan. He wasn't sure which possibility worried him more. Now that the crew was made up of men who echoed their captain's blasphemy, he found himself simultaneously hating them and fearing for their lives. After the miracles God Most High had already performed on his and Phaedra's behalf, He seemed bound to intervene again soon enough.

Hunter hoped He would be merciful.

It was miserable being confined below decks, even though there were no cells in which to hold him and Phaedra. They stayed in the same old sleeping bunks as before, in a compartment they shared with six crew members. But the crewmembers got to leave, and he and Phaedra didn't, and that made all the difference. Without access to the fresh air above, Hunter developed a constant, low-level nausea that would sometimes quite unexpectedly grow out of control. One moment he would be talking with Phaedra, or perhaps trying to rest, and the next moment he would have to stop whatever he was doing and focus all his energies on keeping his stomach down.

Then one morning it finally happened. Hunter awoke before dawn to the sounds of a fight abovedeck. It was all the stomping that woke him, but soon there was a piercing scream and then Phaedra was awake too, fumbling about in the near-dark with short, fearful breaths. Hunter's brain was still processing the situation – they had dropped anchor two days ago at Belinphae, an island on the western end of the archipelago, not far from Tarphae, and they hadn't moved since. Much of the crew would still be ashore at this hour – he and Phaedra were alone in their compartment. Now there were voices above, barking orders. The anchor was being lifted – they were setting sail.

An unfamiliar head appeared at the hatch. "Anyone down there, you just stay. The fight's all over, and my friends and I are up here waiting to stick anyone who feels like starting another. We'll be away from here by breakfast time, and then we'll let you up."

"All right," Hunter called back. "We'll stay. We don't want trouble."

The man snickered. "Oh, you've got trouble already."

16
CRITON

They washed Delika with buckets from the well, but had no dry clothes to change her into, so they wrapped her in a blanket from Belkos' house while her own clothes dried. The more he gathered about what had happened to her, the more horrified he became. How proud he'd been that he'd found a caring family to adopt those children!

She'd hidden herself in the Temple of Magor, poor thing, and had climbed into a vat of sacrificial pigs' blood when it burned. Apparently, Magor's priests used the blood in some of their rituals, watering it down just enough so that it wouldn't congeal. It still took some scrubbing to get it off Delika's skin, though.

Iona helped them, while Dessa held Goodweather. Criton secretly wished Iona and Belkos would offer to adopt the girl, but he knew they wouldn't. Delika was his problem now, and Bandu's – the fact that they had only become parents a few months ago was irrelevant. Besides which, the girl had sought him out personally, and the last time he'd tried to get her adopted had turned out disastrously. He and Bandu might be only ten or eleven years older, but they would still have to be parents to her.

It might not be *so* bad, though, he thought, as he changed the clothes of a wailing Goodweather. At least Delika could talk.

The next morning, the Dragon Touched began their journey northward. Traveling in a caravan with them reminded Criton of a time nearly a year ago, when the islanders had left another village with all of its inhabitants and made for the shelter of Silent Hall. His people moved just as slowly as those villagers had, traveling as they were with children and livestock, and setting up tents each evening. It was even more or less the same time of year, perhaps a month away from the start of the rainy season.

Of course, that didn't make the two journeys identical. Psander's villagers had been looking for a protector, and they had found one. For the Dragon Touched there would be no shelter, no safe haven at the end of the road.

On the other hand, now he was here with family, venturing into the northern plains with a clan of his own kin. That made him happy in a way he had never felt before.

Bandu was less happy, though he could tell that she appreciated how good it felt to him. And it helped that Iona and Dessa kept offering to hold Goodweather, or to change her clothes, or to help Bandu bind the baby to her back with wide strips of cloth. He had less time to devote to his infant daughter, now that he had to lead his people and watch over Delika too. The girl clung to him like he was still the only thing saving her from drowning. Even when he met with Hessina or with his cousin to talk about strategy or ask about their religion, Delika wouldn't leave his side without a good deal of cajoling.

That caused its own troubles for him and Bandu. He could tell that his wife resented his inattention to Goodweather, and his supposed favoring of Delika. But what could he do? Goodweather didn't really care who changed her swaddling clothes, and it was barely even his choice anyway. He had duties to his people, and duties to the girl who had braved fire and blood to find him, so at least for now, Goodweather would have to come third. There was nothing he could do about that, and he wished Bandu wouldn't give him so much trouble for it.

Besides, he was doing his best with Goodweather. He held the child plenty, and changed her clothes often enough. He gave her as much attention as he could afford.

But he spent most of his time getting to know the members of his new community, and learning their ways. He had once read a screed against the Dragon Touched that had been written by a friar of Atel, claiming all manner of evils for Criton's people, and he had always wished that he knew which parts were true and which weren't. Now he had the opportunity to find out, and even with his troubles multiplying and Delika clinging to his side, he did not squander it. He asked Hessina all about the worship of God Most High, and she was happy to oblige.

The friar's screed had apparently been right about at least one thing: the respect and worship of other Gods was anathema to God Most High. His worshippers weren't permitted to use other Gods' ritual objects, and they didn't eat other Gods' sacred animals. Magor's pigs, Ravennis' crows, Karassa's jellyfish – they were all forbidden. Criton gasped when he heard this, because he and his friends had all eaten from the Boar of Hagardis, but Hessina assured him that her purifying ritual had wiped his transgressions away.

Even so, he worried. What if he ate other sacred animals without realizing it? He didn't know which animals were sacred to which Gods – what else should he be avoiding? Luckily, Hessina was well versed in these things. Sharks and whales were sacred to Mayar; moths to Elkinar; falcons to Atun; mules to Atel; hares to Eramia; cats both great and small were sacred to Pelthas. There were other animals that she knew were forbidden without knowing which Gods they belonged to: ants and termites, cockroaches, scarabs, snakes, lizards, jackals – the list seemed endless.

"Eat what the rest of us eat," she said at last. "You'll be fine."

Criton wondered what it meant for God Most High to be so firmly in opposition to all the other Gods, but Hessina disagreed with his characterization. It wasn't a matter of opposition, she said. The "Lower Gods" weren't rivals to God Most High,

They were more akin to disobedient servants, who would all eventually be punished.

"Are there some He won't punish?" Criton asked. "Are some of Them allies?"

"God Most High does not need allies," Hessina answered. "But He is merciful, and will tolerate those who obey Him."

Criton nodded, but it seemed as if she could no sooner answer a question than he thought of another. "Does God Most High have special holy days? When do you give sacrifices?"

Hessina sighed at that. "In the old days, we used to make offerings during the draconic festivals. After the purge we started making our sacrifices on Magor and Elkinar's holy days, whispering the prayers of dedication so that our neighbors wouldn't suspect us of worshipping any God but their own. But the draconic calendar is not the same as the common one. In the end we lost track of where we were on it, and when that happened, we lost our own holidays."

That was so unspeakably sad that Criton forgot what other question he had meant to ask.

The northern plains through which they traveled were a flat expanse of mostly grasses and farmland, their farmers and herders paying taxes to Ardis without any conceivable benefit to themselves. Criton meant to put an end to that, but in a way he too had chosen for his people to prey on these poorest and weakest of their neighbors, building their army and their reputation on the backs of the desperate. Especially now, at harvest time, his decision to raise an army from these plainsfolk was too cruel. If he took all their able-bodied men just as they were most needed for the harvest, in a few months there would be starvation.

But what could he do about it now? His people had to survive, so they needed an army. He had chosen his path.

It only took them a day to reach their first village, a hamlet of no more than twenty houses whose people immediately surrendered upon hearing the conditions Criton offered them. Criton took a man from each house and some livestock besides, and the Dragon Touched continued on their way. The livestock were mostly sheep and pigs, the latter of which would of course be useless to the Dragon Touched, but perhaps it was a good thing that their allies would have a food supply dedicated to them alone. Hessina wanted to demand that the pigs remain behind, but Criton overruled her. It was bad enough that he was raising his army here. He wanted the northerners to think of the Dragon Touched as allies, not tyrants.

The men from this village did not have weapons of war, but they took sticks, hoes, whips, or whatever else they could use in a fight without harming their families' ability to harvest their crops. Criton doubted these tools would be much use against an Ardisian army, and he hoped it would be a very long time before they all found out. But that day was bound to come sometime. The Ardismen would catch up to the Dragon Touched eventually, and besides, the Dragon Touched would meet resistance among the plainsfolk too, sooner or later.

In fact, the very next village they came to met them with scythes and spears, held by a ragged line of men who yelled at them to keep away. Criton steeled himself and led his kin in the assault.

It was too easy: the Dragon Touched slaughtered their resisters, seized their families and their property, and moved on. Criton put his cousin in charge of dividing the spoils, with instructions to give special privilege to the northerners who had joined them. It was the best way he could think of to encourage more plainsmen to ally with the Dragon Touched.

Even so, Belkos insisted on giving Criton and Bandu a flock of sheep, as well as the widow who had owned them.

"My Ma didn't raise me to own slaves," Criton told him.

"It doesn't matter," Belkos answered. "You're our leader. It's expected."

"They expect me to own a person and call it normal."

"By the old laws," Belkos said, "slaves were kept only until they had repaid their debts. Would you be happier with that? What debt do these people owe, do you think?"

"How about a year of service?" Criton asked. "Or until we take Ardis, whichever is sooner. For all of them. We're only punishing them for not helping us against Ardis, after all."

"Good," Belkos said. "Then let these people serve us until then."

Criton accepted that, even though it still bothered him. At heart, he knew that these townspeople had done nothing wrong, that it was terrible to punish them at all. But this was war. He was a leader now, a leader of his people, and if the Dragon Touched didn't develop the sort of reputation that would cause villages to surrender and bolster their camp with fighting-age men, they would all perish. The Ardismen would crush them.

Besides, with all his new obligations, he didn't have time to herd all those sheep himself.

So he made an arrangement with their new slave Biva, one modeled on the relationship between Psander and her villagers. Though he and Bandu theoretically owned both the sheep and the woman who herded them, in practice they let Biva keep both her autonomy and her sheep in return for a share of the milk, wool, and meat. They did not speak of her husband, whom his men had killed, and Criton did his best to pretend that she was just a neighbor who owed him money. She ate and slept separately from his family, and their only contact with her was transactional. In a year's time, they would part ways and never speak to each other again.

Criton took to war easily. He did not have the trained, fluid motions that Hunter had displayed time and again, but he was good at the simple, brutal work of beating down an opponent's defenses and sticking him with something sharp. He liked to intimidate his enemies with an early burst of fire, then slip his spear past their guard and finish them off. It was a dumb trick, and unfair to boot, but if he had learned anything from Narky and Bestillos it was that winning didn't have to be fair. And as long as nobody who fought him survived, there was nothing wrong with using the same technique over and over again. It would be new and surprising every time.

Village after village, town after town was given the choice: cooperation or death. And it worked: the ranks of the Dragon Touched were swelling, and over time, fewer and fewer people resisted them. Their growing numbers slowed them down, of course, what with the livestock they were herding and the difficulties of coordinating such a large group, but that was a good problem to have. The important thing was that they really were raising an army, ragged though it was. Their reputation preceded them now, and there were whole villages that welcomed the Dragon Touched with open arms and gladly joined their cause, hoping to free themselves from their southern oppressors. Slowly but surely, Ardis was losing control over its tributaries.

As the weeks went by, Criton began to develop his own reputation among the plainsfolk. They called him the Black Dragon, just like Belkos' mother-in-law had, and his enemies cowered at the sight of him. For the most part, he didn't mind: the name made him sound powerful, even awe-inspiring. Who could stand up to the Black Dragon in battle? It was a catchy name, too. Soon a number of his kinsmen were using it, and even Hessina occasionally asked him semi-sarcastically, "What does the Black Dragon think?"

On the other hand, being the Black Dragon also made him less of a person. If his enemies were frightened by the idea of him, all the better, but he should have been more than an idea to his own kin. It was alienating, and he didn't deserve to be alienated from the family he had wanted his whole life. He could feel that added distance turning him into a harder person. He didn't think his mother would have liked that.

It helped in the evenings to retreat to his own tent with Bandu and Delika and the baby. They all loved him in one way or another, and not because he symbolized anything to them. It was frustrating to have Delika there sometimes, since her presence made it harder for him and Bandu to be intimate, but he appreciated her presence anyway. She was a talkative girl, which could be nice when Bandu was in one of her quiet moods, and despite all she'd been through she smiled and laughed much more easily than the two of them did. If Bandu's presence was full of love and of wisdom, Delika's was full of joy.

And there was need for joy. This war of conquest did not sit well with Bandu. It struck her as savage and pointless – what did the Dragon Touched need all these sheep and slaves for, anyway? Criton tried to explain how it was really about gathering force, a necessary step toward defeating Ardis, but she didn't seem to care for that goal either.

"Why your people need Ardis?" she asked. "Why not go far away where they don't try to kill you?"

"They want us dead everywhere," Criton reminded her. "Ardis is where we belong."

"So you kill other people and take their things? Why? Ardis is *that* way!"

"I know, but they're too strong for us right now. We're building an army, Bandu, just like Bestillos did when he moved against Psander."

Bandu gawked at him. "Like Bestillos? Let me remember you something."

"Remind."

She waved a hand dismissively. "Let me remember you something: Bestillos is a wicked man. Very, very wicked. You hate him. So why you want to do things his way?"

"Because that's how it works! The world hates us just for existing. Just for being. We need an army, and this is the only way to build one right now."

Bandu rolled her eyes. "Does Bestillos' army help him?"

"That's not fair," Criton answered. "We had Salemis then, and the element of surprise. But Salemis said he wouldn't be coming back. We *have* to build an army."

"If your God is so strong, he can send Salemis back. Or he can do something Himself instead. You want to make army the red priest's way, the wicked way. Why your God helps you if you are wicked like Bestillos?"

"I'm not wicked like–" Criton began, but it was no good. Whether she was being purposefully obstinate or not, he knew very well that she couldn't see the distinction between borrowing an enemy's tactics and borrowing their wickedness. And when it came right down to it, *was* there such a distinction? It was hard for the Dragon Touched to remain morally superior when they were emulating their enemies.

Her words nagged at him all that day and the next. His strategy was a good one – wasn't it? The Dragon Touched and their allies were over a thousand strong now, with some four hundred warriors among them. The plainsmen who had joined of their own volition now owned slaves and livestock, and fought with as much zeal as any of the Dragon Touched warriors. It was the right way to fight a war, he had come to believe. The only way. They would still be far outnumbered if they faced Ardis now, but with a few more weeks to grow...

The next day, word came from the south. The first towns to ally with the Dragon Touched had been sacked. Ardis was coming for them.

The news threw the camp into disarray. The men who had allied with the Dragon Touched now spoke of leaving to protect their homes. A council of their elders, one from every town and village, came together and demanded that the Dragon Touched do something to protect their families from the Ardismen. There was no question what that 'something' might be. Criton hadn't thought his people ready for a confrontation, but it seemed they had little choice: they had to face Ardis now, before any of their allies could desert.

Hessina said he was being too hasty. Ardis was goading them into an open fight long before the Dragon Touched could be ready for one. Criton agreed with her logic completely, but it didn't change his calculus. This was as clear a sign as they were going to get. The time had come to prove their faith in God Most High. The Ardisian army was rumored to be two thousand strong – in battle, they would outnumber the Dragon Touched five to one. But if this was what God Most High wanted, so be it.

They turned back southward. All talk turned to battle tactics, and Criton rediscovered his kin's weakness in harnessing their magic. He had thought his own magical skill limited, after seeing all that Psander could do, but the truth was that he had taught himself a lot. He could summon a light. He could change his appearance, clothes and all. He could fly. The Dragon Touched universally knew how to hide their draconic heritage, and breathing fire came naturally enough, but that seemed to be all. Was it the three decades of repression, or an actual lack of talent that kept them from using their magic as he did?

He hadn't flown since the battle at Silent Hall, when the high priest of Magor had ended his flight with a single word of command. It had taken him over a month to fully recover from his fall, and he was not eager to take to the air again, but flying would have made for an amazing advantage over the Ardismen now that Bestillos was gone. Ah, well. He could still do it himself, if he found the courage to, but it seemed that there was no hope of his commanding a flying army.

Hessina insisted that his greater magical ability was a gift from God Most High. Perhaps she was right, but he would have rather his God granted these abilities to *all* the Dragon Touched, so that their enemies' greater numbers wouldn't be so devastating an advantage. It was bad enough that nowadays only an eighth of his force even *was* Dragon Touched.

Their tactical options were limited. Outnumbered as they were, there was no sense in keeping some part of their force in reserve. He would have liked to throw up his hands and say that God Most High would take care of everything, but his allies had no reason to trust in God Most High as of yet, and he needed their support. If he couldn't find a way to embolden them while demoralizing his enemies, it would be a rout. Or, worse still, the majority of his army that wasn't Dragon Touched might panic and turn on his people. No, he couldn't leave the tactics to his God.

It was Bandu who gave him the idea, by pointing out that the food supplies were soon going to run low if they didn't start eating pigs. There had been a feast after every victory, and after every northern village joined their cause. It was a way of keeping their allies happy; of convincing them they were on the right side of this war. But Hessina had not allowed these feasts to include pork, so the supply of sheep had dwindled while the number of pigs grew. Criton wondered if this was a metaphor for the foolishness of recruiting an army the way they had, and that was when the idea came to him. A metaphor. Yes.

Pigs were Magor's animal, and the Dragon Touched had access to an enormous number of them. The plainsfolk kept stores of rendered grease that they used to cook their meals. And the Dragon Touched could breathe fire.

Criton sent scouts ahead as the Dragon Touched and their allies marched south. It would take some time to coordinate the display he had in mind, and he didn't want to be surprised by the Ardisian force before he was ready for it. He hoped the plainsfolk wouldn't give him any trouble about the use of their pigs.

They did, of course. Criton called their leaders together that night, once they had made camp. The elders listened to him as he explained that he meant to light their pigs on fire and drive them toward the enemy, and they scoffed at him.

"How are you going to make sure they don't run back at us?" an elder named Paedros asked. "Once you light a pig on fire, there's no telling which way it'll run. If you think they'll all charge toward the enemy, you're a fool."

"I'm no fool," Criton insisted, feeling ever more foolish as he said it. But these were desperate times, and he was prepared to try any tactic, no matter how unorthodox. Their survival depended upon it. "They ought to at least run away from the direction of the fire, right?"

The elders looked at each other. "Probably," one said.

"But not necessarily," Paedros added.

"I think they will," Criton said, "and keep in mind that we don't need them to charge the enemy in unison. The point isn't to use the pigs as part of our army, it's to send a message to the

Magor-worshipping Ardismen. They'll watch their God's sacred animals burning and squealing and running away from us, and they'll understand that we mean to do the same to them."

"And if half the pigs turn on us instead?" another elder asked. "What message will that send?"

"You've managed to herd them up to now. Make sure that doesn't happen."

"They haven't all been on fire up to now!"

Criton sighed. "If you like, I can ask Bandu to help you. My wife has a way with animals."

That quieted them down. Even among the Dragon Touched, Bandu had a reputation as an unpredictable foreign witch. The plainsfolk feared her even more, knowing that this was how their fire-breathing allies spoke of her powers.

"Again," Criton said, "the goal is to shock the Ardismen into forgetting that they outnumber us. If we don't face them like we're afraid we might lose, they'll start to wonder whether we know more than they do. Let a few pigs run the wrong way – as long as they're mostly running at the Ardismen, we'll have gotten the point across. By the time our armies meet, *they'll* be ready to run."

There was silence at first. Criton was not sure whether he'd convinced them – they kept looking wordlessly at each other, as if they were elves and could hear each other's thoughts.

"That may be true," Paedros conceded at last. "We can try it, if you'll compensate us for our lost animals."

Criton promised that they'd be well compensated in spoils once they defeated the Ardismen, offering them a greater share than they had taken from their conquests so far. It was a fair offer, since they were bound to win such spoils if they defeated the Ardisian army. Once he'd left, he let out a great sigh of relief. He had thought it foolish of God Most High to put him in charge of this army, but maybe he was better at the tasks of leadership than he had realized. That was somewhat reassuring.

In any case, he felt confident in his battle plan. The Dragon Touched and their allies would not fight like a force outclassed, would not stake out a position on some hill and wait for their foes to try to overwhelm them. They would set Magor's pigs aflame and then charge their enemies, giving no time for tactics and no room for maneuver. They would fight like people who knew that with God Most High at their backs, defeat was impossible. And when they did that, Ardis would believe them.

He couldn't wait.

17

GENERAL MAGERION

As far as Magerion was concerned, the council spent far too much time discussing the Dragon Touched threat, and not nearly enough talking about the threat from within. The generals argued over how long it was taking to raise their army – which was quite a long time, delayed as they were by the harvest. They argued about the ideal field of battle too, as if they would have a choice, and lastly about who should command the force that faced down the Dragonspawn. Some of the talk was worthwhile, but to Magerion's mind, a lot of it was meaningless.

The Dragon Touched had moved north, gathering their strength for the inevitable battle with Ardis, so it was probably true that the sooner Ardis marched out to meet them, the better. Still. Most of the council's disagreements were about ego, not strategy.

Had he still been alive, Bestillos would have resolved these questions easily. He would have dominated the discussion, and doubtless led the army himself. Now that he was gone, everyone wanted the chance to supplant him as the champion of Ardis.

Magerion was the exception. He had never minded the priest's dominance, nor his greater visibility. Bestillos deserved it, after all, for having led the Great Uprising that put them all in power in the first place. Championing Ardis was a job for someone theatrical, and Magerion was not one for theatricality. He thought the others were overly concerned with the dramatic reappearance of the Dragon Touched, when the death cult of Ravennis threatened to tear Ardis apart far sooner, from the inside.

The cult had grown so rapidly that the other members of the Council of Generals had yet to register its importance. Or perhaps they believed on principle that the Ravennis worshippers shouldn't be taken seriously, after the way Magor had trounced Ravennis at Laarna. Whatever the reason, they were being foolish. Magerion had been listening to the death cult's followers, and he had seen yesterday's confrontation with the priests of Magor. These people were dangerous. Their theology would appeal to the masses now that Bestillos was gone – it already *was* appealing to them. The army of Ardis had been routed by a *dragon*, for Magor's sake. If the dragons' God was still alive after centuries of abuse, and still so vital that He had summoned up a dragon and a whole clan of Dragon Touched out of nowhere... well, who was to say that Ravennis was really gone?

And if the cult of Ravennis won over the people of Ardis, what would happen to its current rulers?

Magerion had been a young revolutionary during the Great Uprising, when Bestillos had led the people in toppling their king and his Dragon Touched lackeys. The dirty secret of those days was that thousands of Ardismen had been true believers in God Most High right up until the forces of Magor had won – the Magor-worshippers had been in the minority. Perhaps the others had forgotten, but Magerion still remembered how the people had turned on their God and His representatives. Men who had prayed next to their Dragon Touched neighbors in wholehearted devotion had quickly, so quickly joined in the slaughter once the tide had turned against the Dragonspawn. Why shouldn't something similar happen again, if the followers of this death cult were to prevail?

Yet none of the other generals saw the danger. They were still arguing over who ought to lead the forces that took on the Dragon Touched – it looked like General Xytos might well win that argument, but Choerus and young Scrofa still weren't letting it go. Magerion decided at long last to interrupt them.

"Why don't you all go?" he suggested. "All three of you. There is glory enough for everyone, presuming you win. What I ask is this: leave me a hundred picked men with which to defend the city. We have deadly enemies right here in Ardis that we ignore at our peril."

"Enemies?" Xytos asked. "This isn't about those Ravennis-worshippers again, is it?"

Magerion nodded, and the other men sighed and rolled their eyes.

"A hundred men," he insisted. "Then you won't have to listen to me repeating myself. Besides which, if Magor is with you, you won't need another hundred. And if He's not, another hundred men won't do you any good."

"And if we are evenly matched?" Scrofa said. "What then? What if Magor and the dragons' God both watch silently, or if They both intervene equally?"

"Then when you have fought the Dragon Touched into the night, and both sides pull back to regroup, you will be glad not to come home to a city overrun with Laarnan death cultists."

Xytos smiled. "At first I was concerned about our convening a meeting without replacing Bestillos first, but I see the priests of Magor are well represented."

"Bestillos was a true general," General Stellys said, frowning. "He wasn't on our council to represent the priesthood."

"True," Xytos agreed, "but he represented them anyway. And now Magerion appears to have taken up the cause. Have your hundred men, Magerion. We'll make do without you."

They moved onto other topics, , and the next day Magerion went to meet with Bestillos' successor as high priest. He found High Priest Melikon surprisingly optimistic about the prospect of exterminating the Ravennis death cult, especially considering what they both agreed they were up against.

"The people are losing faith, it is true," Melikon admitted, "and there is some truth too in the death cult's philosophy. Ravennis was clearly not defeated as we had thought – the miracle of the crows proves that much. But with the failure of our death-prophecies to materialize, and with your men rounding up Crow God worshippers for public executions, this revolution will be over before it begins. Then Ravennis will truly be dead, and the faith of Magor's followers will be restored."

The men Magerion picked for his anti-Ravennis cleansing were all either personal loyalists or members of his clan: his sons Mageris and Atlon, his nephews, close friends and distant cousins, all people who owed him their positions in society. Their mission would involve slaughtering their neighbors – he could not afford doubters.

They started with that leftover Oracle, the so-called Graceful Servant. Magerion had expected her followers to keep her hidden until he could torture her location out of them, but he had thought wrong. The Graceful Servant delivered herself to them the very next day, striding up to the Great Temple of Magor as if she believed herself untouchable. She cooperated fully as they tied her to one of the temple's pillars, and though her mouth was full of prayers to her God, she did not pray for Ravennis to save her. Rather, she locked eyes with General Magerion and prayed for Ravennis to bring His truth to the world, and to grant His followers peace and joy in the world below. It was unsettling. Though an enormous crowd had gathered to view her execution, Magerion felt that she was saying something directly to him. It wasn't a plea, either – if anything, she seemed triumphant.

He had her flayed. After that, he had her lieutenants found and flayed as well – all those who were known to have associated with the Graceful Servant were put to death in as public and painful a way as possible. The priests of Magor delighted in this, but Magerion grew more and more uneasy as time went by.

The Oracle's followers all did their best to follow her example, praying to their God to reward them in the underworld rather than to save them, and their unnatural bravery was having an impact. Many found the cultists' attitudes inspirational. It was Laarna all over again: no matter how many of His worshippers they killed, Ravennis only seemed to grow stronger.

The trouble was that Ravennis' worshippers weren't universally reviled by the city's leaders. The priests of Elkinar declared neutrality in the conflict, having received no directive from their high priestess in Anardis to take one side or the other. Without the Elkinaran priests' help in chasing Ravennis from the city, the Crow God's worshippers found enough of a safe haven to persist.

To make matters worse, the biggest prize had already escaped him. Narky the Black, the one-eyed slayer of Bestillos, had vanished as if he had never existed. Rumor had it that he had escaped the city even before the Graceful Servant's death, fleeing under the cover of night. High Priest Melikon might laugh that Ravennis' champion had fled in terror, but as far as Magerion was concerned, the point was that he was *alive*. He didn't have to be brave to be dangerous. From what Magerion had heard, Bestillos had been shot in the back.

He began questioning Ravennis worshippers about Narky before killing them, but it seemed that anyone who knew anything was long dead. The general had to own up to his poor planning on that front.

Not all the Ravennis worshippers were suicidal, of course. A good many of them practiced their religion secretly, when none of Magerion's men were around. He would take that. The fact that his men were driving the death cult into the shadows and not the other way around was in itself something to be thankful for. The question was, how long could this situation last?

The army of Ardis had marched off two weeks ago with all the fanfare that that entailed, parading out of the city with three generals at its head. As Magerion saw it, there were only two possibilities now: either Generals Xytos, Choerus, and

Scrofa would crush the Dragonspawn and return triumphant, in which case the Ravennis worshippers would likely remain underground for another generation… or else they would lose. If they lost, he was sure the citizens of his city would abandon Magor and embrace the Raven God of Laarna, and if that happened, Magerion's head was bound to be discovered atop a spear before long.

The Graceful Servant began haunting his dreams. Night after night, he dreamt that he rose from his bed and went to stand below her corpse at the Temple of Magor. Even skinless, even tied to a pillar of her enemy's temple, there was an awful majesty to her.

"You cannot resist us forever," she would taunt him. "Ravennis knows your destiny. Ravennis *is* your destiny."

When he tried to reply, his voice came out a caw and he discovered that he had been transformed into a raven.

He slept less.

He ordered ten of his men to try to track down Narky the Black, wherever he had disappeared to, though at this point he was not sure what to do with the man once he had him. The Graceful Servant had endured public humiliation, torture, and death, and still had the power to keep Magerion awake at night. He was no longer sure this monstrous cult *could* be beheaded.

He was beginning to understand that no matter what he did, it would not be enough on its own. For any of this to be worthwhile, Magor would eventually have to demonstrate His supremacy. So long as the situation with the Dragon Touched lay unresolved, all of Magerion's efforts against the cult of Ravennis could only postpone a revolution, not prevent it.

So he joined the priests when they prayed for victory against the Dragon Touched, repeating their words so many times that he could have led the prayers himself. He prayed when he awoke in the morning, and went to bed with still more prayers on his lips. He prayed as if the power of his worship alone could give Magor the strength to keep fighting against His enemies. And maybe it would – who knew how these things really worked?

Let Magor give His generals, Xytos, Scrofa, and Choerus, the strength and cunning to win their war against the Dragon Touched, and win it soon. Magerion could try to keep the death cult at bay until their return, but victory was not his to aspire to.

And he couldn't hold out forever.

18

CRITON

"You are wicked! Your thoughts are wicked!"

Bandu hated his plan. She hated it with a passion so strong he could barely comprehend it.

"Why you do this to pigs? Why you kill them and not to eat, and not to give to your God, and not to do anything, just to kill? It is wicked, wicked, wicked!"

Goodweather was wailing too, while Delika cowered in a corner of the tent. Criton took the baby from his shouting wife and rocked her from side to side, for all the good it did. He was sure the whole Dragon Touched camp could hear them.

"Your God is wicked like you?" Bandu demanded. Criton winced to think of who might be listening. Who might hear her say such things. Probably everybody.

"Answer me! He is wicked like you?"

"God Most High isn't wicked and you know it," Criton hissed. "This is blasphemy, Bandu – how well do you think I can protect you?"

"If your God isn't wicked," Bandu retorted, "then He hates what you do to pigs. He punishes you for being so wicked to them. You take fat from dead ones and use it to kill more, to *murder* them."

"It's not murder," Criton said. "You had it right the first time."

"No, murder is wickeder than kill. I know your words."

Criton sighed. "They're just pigs, Bandu. Murder is for people."

"If your God likes this," Bandu spat back, "He is wicked. If your God is good, He hates this."

Criton was glad he was holding Goodweather, or he might have struck her. His anger was starting to take over again, in that dangerous way that had only ever led to pain for them both, but which he somehow remained powerless to stop. He had struck Bandu once, and she had shunned him for more than a month afterward – he couldn't let that happen again. Yet how dare she claim that God Most High could not support him and be good at the same time?

"This," he said, his voice rising, "will demoralize our enemies and bring us victory. We're planning to slaughter our enemies on the battlefield, Bandu. God Most High won't mind if we slaughter some pigs too, on the way."

Bandu glared at him, but she spoke no more blasphemies. She only took Goodweather from him and left him to calm down without them. Eventually, he did.

The Dragon Touched met the army of Ardis two weeks later, in a field flatter than an altar top. There were very few hills in this country anyway, though the Calardian range still stood imposingly in the distance. A light rain fell on the armies as they faced each other across the field, the Dragon Touched wary and the Ardismen gleeful.

The entire multitude of the Dragon Touched and their allies stood together in a mass, Criton having declined to keep the women and children separate. Even so, his people were easily outnumbered by the army across the field. The Ardismen banged their spears against their shields as they marched forward, still too far away to begin their charge. The Dragon Touched slathered lard on pigs.

When they were no more than a hundred yards away, the Ardismen sent forth their champion. He strode forward, spear held high, his shield emblazoned with a gold-leaf depiction of the boar of Magor standing before a city gate. Criton wondered if that was a family crest or a symbol belonging to the Ardisian Council of Generals. Either way, it was impressive.

"I am Scrofa," the man cried, "general of the Ardisian council and slayer of dragons! Send me your champion, Dragonspawn, to be a sacrifice upon this sacred battlefield. Magor stands with me!"

For a moment, Criton was sorely tempted to take the bait and enter into single combat with this man. Did he think Criton would be intimidated by this dragon slayer nonsense? Whatever position General Scrofa held, he clearly wasn't old enough to have been active during the purge of the Dragon Touched. Criton would have loved to drive a spear through him personally.

But no. The Ardismen were known for their warriors, and this was one of their generals. All of Criton's war experience amounted to one dumb trick that he used over and over again. A fight against Ardis' champion would be no more equal than the size of their respective armies.

General Scrofa turned back to his troops as if to say, *see what cowards these Dragon Touched are?* "Send me a champion," he cried again.

Criton lit a pig.

It didn't even run in Scrofa's direction so much as diagonally away from Criton, squealing pitiably as it first approached the Ardismen, then turned away from them again. Finally it collapsed.

On Criton's signal, the plainsfolk stepped back and the Dragon Touched breathed fire on the rest of the pigs, keeping up a steady flame to dissuade the animals from turning back toward them. It was mostly effective, as the vast majority of the pigs surged toward the enemy and not at the rest of the Dragon Touched army. It wasn't perfect, though: Criton was nearly run down himself, and had to leap into the air to keep from being trampled. He stayed there, hovering, and called the attack.

The Dragon Touched charged.

The Ardismen charged too, but their ranks were already

broken. Though many of the pigs were collapsing before they ever reached the enemy, they had done their job admirably: the most disciplined force in the world was fighting on the same level as the Dragon Touched and plainsmen. Warriors from both sides dodged around flaming sows, slipping in the mud and the wet grass, and most of the Ardismen were too afraid of offending their God to put the pigs down and get them out of the way. Their ranks broke around Magor's dying animals, and when the two armies met, the disorganization turned to chaos.

Above it all, Criton searched the crowd for Scrofa. He found the Ardisian general a little nearer than he had expected, already showing his deadly efficacy with spear and shield. Two men lay dying at the general's feet as he ducked and thrust at a third, never slowing his onslaught. Criton was glad he hadn't chosen to face General Scrofa one-on-one: the man was fast, fearless, and a cunning fighter.

But he wasn't looking up.

Criton dropped toward him feet first, readying his spear. The spear was seven feet long and sturdy, but not terribly useful at this angle, what with the general's helmet and armored shoulders as the only real targets. That was all right, though. Criton meant to surprise him with a hard landing and a burst of flame before skewering him through the chest.

The first half of the plan worked marvelously. Scrofa didn't even notice his approach until the last moment, when the man he had been fighting saw Criton coming and backed off. He looked up just in time for Criton to land on his shoulders, sending him sprawling. He dropped his weapon and his shield in the process, but he was fast – God, he was fast! He wriggled back away from Criton's first spear thrust and sprang to his feet, unarmed but back in a fighting stance. He had a short sword in his belt, but didn't draw it yet.

Criton didn't give him the chance. He advanced, jabbing at the general with his spear. Amazingly, Scrofa managed to evade him even while moving closer, catching the spear by the haft and nearly yanking it from Criton's grasp. Criton panicked and shot back into the air, but Scrofa held tight, forcing him to remain suspended directly above, unable to escape. The general pulled at the spear with a frightful determination, trying to drag Criton nearer the ground.

Criton was straining too hard to effectively breathe fire, but though his muscles were being taxed to their limit, his magical strength suddenly grew to accommodate his needs. Instead of pulling Criton down to earth, Scrofa found himself pulled off the ground, and together they began to rise.

If this turn of events surprised the general, he didn't let on. Hand over hand he climbed up the wet spear toward Criton, even as the wind and rain blew at his face and the two of them rose farther and farther into the air. They were actually speeding up – where was this extra power coming from? Was this what an intervention from God Most High felt like? Scrofa should have let go when it was still safe to; now, even if he killed Criton, he might well be injured by the subsequent fall.

But Criton had no intention of dying. He meant to live, and he meant to live victorious. Just as Scrofa got to the top of the spear and reached for his arm, he caught his breath enough to blow fire in the general's face. There was nowhere to dodge to, so Scrofa simply grunted through the pain and tucked his chin down to avoid the flames, his hand falling back to the spear's haft.

This would likely be Criton's only chance. Once the general caught his arm, he didn't doubt that Scrofa would be able to snatch that sword from his belt and deal a death blow. He didn't mean to wait for that to happen.

"Goodbye," Criton said, and let go of the spear.

They had not risen high enough for the fall to kill Scrofa outright, but that hardly mattered. The whole battlefield had seen them rise, and the whole battlefield saw Scrofa fall. He cried out as he hit the ground, probably breaking a leg or two in the process, and the Ardismen, whose front lines had backed up to give him enough room to land, were in no position to prevent an opportunistic plainsman from leaping forward and driving a spear through his chest. The army of the Dragon Touched hollered out its triumph and surged forward, and the Ardismen broke and ran. Just like that, the battle became a rout.

The Dragon Touched and plainsmen chased their enemies across the fields, slaying every Ardisman they could catch. Criton flew above them, leading them onward, until the pursuers began to thin out for lack of endurance. Then he called off the pursuit and came back down to earth.

He landed to cheers. Belkos lifted him up and his men carried him back to the camp on their shoulders, reveling in the victory despite their well-earned exhaustion. Criton laughed, giddy with his army's triumph. Who could deny God Most High now? And who could deny that He had chosen the right man to lead His people in battle?

Bandu's warnings had all been nonsense – the dragons' God had clearly blessed their army, whatever she said. She might still scowl at him for a few more days, but what did that matter? He had images of the Dragon Touched marching their army through the gates of Ardis and taking back their city. If they could win this battle, no army could stop them.

Hessina's son Kilion disagreed. "I have made a count of the bodies," he told Criton later that evening, during the victory feast. The rain had thankfully ceased, though its chill remained. "We lost thirty-eight men, seven of them our own kin, and killed an even hundred and eighty. At that rate, we'll run out of men before they do."

Criton frowned. He was an odd one, Kilion, a man who exuded quiet diligence even as Hessina, his mother, was all force of will. Criton had thought at first that he was simply too terrified of his mother to speak up, but it seemed that his voice barely rose above a whisper even when she was absent. It was as if Hessina had kept all the force of personality to herself and left none for him. What kind of a man spent the first moments after a great victory counting bodies?

"We routed our enemies and killed their general," Criton

pointed out. "You're saying we have to do *better?*"

"If we mean to outlast Ardis, yes."

Belkos, who had overheard, came to Criton's defense. "We humiliated the Ardismen today. How many more times do you think they can be humiliated before they refuse to meet us in battle? And what other fool would take up arms against us now?"

Kilion shrugged. "The army of Ardis is still five times our size."

"You are wrong," Bandu interjected from her seat beside Criton. "We are here too."

"We're only counting combatants," Criton said. "Only people who can fight. I know *you* could fight if you wanted to, but the other women? The children? And what would people say if we had to rely on women as a part of our army?"

"They say our army is bigger."

Criton smiled, though he knew he shouldn't. "I don't think that's what they'd say."

"So what do we do now?" Belkos asked. "Do we chase them down, even though they still outnumber us?"

"Of course," Criton said. "We can't give them time to regroup. If we can catch them tomorrow, they'll have to fight with less than their full army. God willing, after another defeat, half of them will desert."

Belkos frowned. "We can't catch them at our children's pace. Are we leaving them and our wives behind?"

Criton didn't answer. He sat silently, saying nothing, knowing that every moment made him look more foolish. It was absurd that he hadn't even considered how much faster the Ardismen would be, having left their wives and children safe at home. Now, he realized, he was faced with a terrible choice: if the Dragon Touched held to their current strategy and moved together as a unit, the Ardismen would have time to recover from their surprise defeat. If they separated the warriors from the rest of the camp and advanced more quickly, there was the chance that they might drive the Ardismen all the way back to their city walls – but there was also the chance that they would be outmaneuvered, and see their families massacred. How likely was that worst of possibilities? How unlikely would it have to be to make the risk worth it?

Delika was looking at him fearfully, already anticipating his abandonment. Bandu just looked frustrated. It would be a lot of work for her to watch both children at once.

"No," Criton said at last. "No, let them stay with us. If that gives the Ardismen time to recover from their losses, we'll just have to live with that. I'm not going to risk our families' lives on the assumption that the Ardismen will fight us honorably. Their army is so much bigger than ours, what's to stop them from sending a quarter of their force to attack anyone we leave behind?"

Relief passed across Belkos' face, and then shame. Despite himself, he had clearly been hoping Criton would say something like that. They were giving up on the biggest opportunity they had to finish off the Ardismen once and for all, and they both knew it, but their families were more important than a swift victory.

Besides, who cared if the Ardismen regrouped? Bandu had been wrong – God Most High had favored Criton's tactics, and would favor His people forever. They couldn't lose.

19

NARKY

Getting out of Ardis was as easy as Ptera had said it would be. Her connection nodded when he saw them and turned the other way as they slipped past the walls. Then it was a long trudge down the open road, with only the moon's light to guide them.

Narky didn't say anything – he was far too self-conscious. Ptera expected him to marry her, and he wasn't sure how he felt about it. He had never imagined himself with a continental girl, and certainly not with a woman so many years his senior. How many years, actually? Eight? Ten? He wanted to ask her, bluntly, just as he did with all awkward questions, but he couldn't bring himself to risk the trouble it would cause. She'd likely find it insulting, after all, and what if it turned out he wanted this? He didn't want to ruin their marriage before it had even begun.

He wished he still had Phaedra to talk to. She would have been able to clarify his position, to show him where his duty lay. Why did he have to be cut off from his friends, the only Tarphaean who had to figure things out for himself?

He'd finally, finally gotten used to being part of a group rather than outside one, and it had felt so good. The others didn't all like him – certainly not all the time – but they had still been friends to him, every one of them. They had supported him, and fought for him, and taught him how to live. They had valued his opinions and tolerated his poor manners, and whatever he said, he had secretly loved being with them all. Now he'd been given this ridiculous responsibility of leading the church of Ravennis, and he wouldn't even have his friends' support to get him through it.

Ptera wanted him to rely on her instead. The Graceful Servant had *commanded* him to rely on Ptera. But could he?

This marriage was so far from what he'd imagined for himself. He had known all along that he had no chance with Phaedra, and he had never meant to return to the archipelago, but still, a continental wife? He had thought it more likely that he'd stay lonely and unloved forever.

So shouldn't he be jumping at this opportunity? Sure, it was sudden, but so had been his exposure to Bandu's dimly lit nakedness, and that hadn't stopped him from wanting to see more.

It was the motivation that bothered him. What reason did Ptera have to want to marry him? Was it a matter of ambition? Attraction? Sacrifice to the cause? And had it been Ptera's idea, really, or the Graceful Servant's? He didn't like *that* idea at all.

"Why?" he said aloud.

Ptera turned to him. "Why what?"

"Why did the Graceful Servant say I should marry you? She said she'd talked to you about it already – why?"

She blinked at him, her features so bright in the light of the full moon that it reminded him of the fairies. It was outrageous of him to connect the two, but he couldn't help it. He felt as though he was Ptera's prey, just as the islanders had been prey to the elves. What a ridiculous exaggeration on his part.

But was it, though?

Yes, yes it was.

"What did the Graceful Servant say to you about me?" He was trying to be gentler, but it wasn't coming out that way. "Was this her idea, Ptera, or was it yours?"

Another long pause. "Hers," Ptera admitted at last. "She said that you would be vulnerable to other people's influence so long as you were unmarried, and that this way, your head would be clear to make better decisions. She thought you should marry within the faith as soon as possible."

Oh.

"So you're just doing your duty, then? That's disgusting."

She shook her head, smiled tentatively. "Sometimes Ravennis gives us the opportunity to choose which duties we prefer."

That made Narky laugh. "I see. So I'm better than being tortured to death. Can't argue with that."

"You're too hard on yourself."

Ptera's face was serious, and Narky suddenly realized what it was that made that face distinctive: her left eye was ever so slightly higher than her right. It was striking, now that he noticed it. He couldn't decide whether it bothered him or not.

"You're a handsome boy," she continued, "and no one's done more than you in the service of Ravennis. Why shouldn't I choose you if I get the chance?"

He had no answer for her. It was the most flattering thing anyone had ever said to him, and he didn't know what to do with it. Was that really how she saw him? A handsome boy, despite his lack of muscles or height or chest hair, despite his prominent scar and missing eye? His instinct was to be skeptical, to wonder what she was concealing from him, but nothing made sense. If she didn't really find him desirable, why had she connived to marry him? Even if it had been the Graceful Servant's idea in the first place, it sure didn't sound like she'd resisted.

Still, he hated not having a say in the matter. They had ambushed him, the two of them, and they expected him to simply fall in line and bind himself to Ptera for the rest of his life. No amount of flattery could cover over that fundamental truth. He was traveling to Anardis with a woman whose help had likely saved his life already and whose support he would certainly need in the days ahead – he could hardly afford *not* to marry her and keep up his end of the bargain. But it was a bargain she had made without him.

It was best to have out with it. "I don't like what you're doing to me," he said. "You haven't really given me a choice, the two of you. I'm not such a bastard that I'd send you away, and you're taking advantage of it."

Ptera winced. "I'm sorry you feel that way."

"I do."

They walked on in silence. Oh Ravennis, what was he going to do about this? He was wide awake, but his legs were growing tired. Where would they sleep tonight? *How* would they sleep tonight?

Ptera seemed to have read his mind. "We don't have to sleep together if you don't want to. I think you'd like me if you gave me a chance, but I don't want you to think you have no choice. We can sleep separately, and I'll still be your ally in all things. Ravennis is more important than me or you."

He nodded unhappily. That was the other thing. She was supposed to help him spread the word of Ravennis – how was he supposed to tell her that he didn't know what that was?

The biggest trouble with spreading the word of Ravennis was that Narky wasn't sure how he should relate to God Most High. Ravennis was Narky's God, Ravennis owned him, but Criton's God was the true power in the world, the builder of the mesh, the slayer of the Yarek and so on, and it was His prophet who had rescued the islanders from Bestillos and his army. Was Narky supposed to pretend that God Most High had had no role in his salvation?

And that was only the beginning. Whatever relationship Narky had with Criton's God, the real question was what relationship *Ravennis* had with God Most High. The Graceful Servant had viewed God Most High with something bordering on contempt, as if He was some doting old fool who would eventually tire of the world and wander off somewhere. That didn't strike Narky as right, but where did the truth lie? Was Ravennis an ally to God Most High? A rival? A high-level servant? Or was He perhaps a sort of divine parasite, feeding off God Most High's plans to further His own agenda? Narky worshipped Him and belonged to Him, but he was allowed to wonder. It was his *duty* to wonder, if he was to be Ravennis' high priest.

He wished his God would give him a sign, perhaps appear to him in a dream and explain what was expected of him. If Eramia could appear to Hunter in a river, why shouldn't Ravennis appear to Narky in a dream? Would the Keeper of Fates really leave him to his own devices on this most important of missions?

He hadn't been left *just* to his own devices though, and so his thoughts wandered back to Ptera. What was he to make of her? She certainly knew how to say the right thing. She was trying her best to win his heart, despite their bad start. He had to admire her effort, at least.

Did he find her attractive? It seemed almost like a silly question – he had never *not* found a woman near his age attractive, at least attractive enough to distract him a little. She was no Eramia – the girl, not the Goddess – and no Phaedra either, but those were awfully high standards. Yes, her hips were narrow, and her hair was limp and brown, but her face was fascinating to look at now that he had discovered its secret. It pulled him in. And she had something that neither Eramia nor Phaedra had ever had: she wanted him.

They stopped at a house that had Ravennis' mark painted on its door. After a little while, the bleary-eyed owner answered their knocks and gave a little yelp when he saw them. Narky barely had time to explain who they were before the man said, "My wife and I will sleep in the barn. Please, take our house and may Ravennis bless us all."

Ptera thanked them, and a few minutes later they were alone inside, staring in the darkness at the single bed.

"Shall I take the floor?" Ptera asked innocently, and Narky shook his head. Hunter would have offered to take the floor himself, and he would have thought to do it before Ptera said a word. Narky, unfortunately, was not Hunter.

"I think there's room enough for both of us," he said. "We can lie head-to-toe."

"All right," Ptera said, but they both just stood there.

The dry season was coming to an end, but it was a warm night for the time of year. In weather like this, Bandu would have stripped her clothes off without a thought. No! He shouldn't have thought about that. Now he didn't feel like sleeping anymore.

Ptera was staring at him. "I heard that Ravennis gave you a sort of mark," she said at last. "May I – may I see it?"

"I don't think you'll be able to in this dim light," Narky said, but Ptera just stood there waiting until he gingerly took his shirt off. She stepped closer and ran a hand along his chest, feeling the ridges where Ravennis' mark had cut into his skin.

"I didn't realize it was so ornate!" she said.

"He nearly killed me," Narky told her. "When I repented for what I'd done, He let me live and gave me this."

Ptera nodded. She didn't ask him what he'd done. She also didn't take her hand off his chest until he gently pushed it away. She was testing him, he thought.

"Thank you," she said, and went to lie down in the bed.

Narky lay himself down by her feet and did not sleep. He kept thinking of her hand touching his skin, and of the fact that she wanted him, she wanted *him*, and she was right here beside him. He had resented Bandu once, for keeping him up at night without even realizing it, but how could he resent Ptera when she had made it clear that he could have her if he would only ask? If he could not sleep for thinking about her, he had only himself to blame.

He sat up in bed.

"You win," he said. "I want you."

20

PHAEDRA

Pirates. Kidnappers. Where was their ship headed now? She
and Hunter sat on their bunks, unable to do anything but
worry. Perhaps they were in their new God's hands, but who
was to say whether He had really planned this? It didn't feel
particularly like they were in His hands – it felt like they were
in the hands of men.

Piracy had always been a danger in the archipelago, but
there had been a treaty struck when Phaedra was young,
making every island responsible for patrolling its shores and
harbors for pirated ships and goods in an effort to eradicate
the problem. Its effectiveness had made her father rich, since
investing in merchantmen had swiftly become a much less risky
proposition. But the problem had never gone away completely,
and now it had become *their* problem.

Did they want a ransom? There would be no one to ransom
her and Hunter. Was it the ship and its cargo they were after?
If so, the two of them were completely expendable. And if this
was God Most High's punishment for the captain, Phaedra
failed to see how it could improve the lives of His servants.
Before, they had been trapped. Now they were likely doomed.

Their new voyage lasted a few hours before their captors
called them above deck. Up the ladder they went, limbs stiff
and aching, blinking in the morning sun. There were men

around them, and a good number of them too, but Phaedra could not focus on them, because she saw now where their ship was headed.

It was headed for Tarphae.

Someone had repaired one of the docks in Karsanye's harbor, and to this they were headed at full speed. Phaedra's heart pounded thunderously in her chest and she had to force herself to breathe. The cursed island. Home. Apparently it was now a pirate haven.

The ship's captain was still alive, but he was tied to the mast. A half dozen other sailors knelt beside him, staring terrified at the pirates who had taken their ship. The cook wasn't among them, though he had been on the ship last night. Had he been killed and thrown overboard? That wasn't necessarily surprising, but it was undeniably horrifying.

The pirates were predominantly young islanders around Phaedra's age, but their leader was far older. His beard was flecked with hints of gray, while his eyes sported the beginnings of crows'-feet. He smiled as his crew forced Phaedra and Hunter to kneel beside the others.

"Hello there," he said. "My name is Mura. You haven't heard of me; nobody has, except my friends and a sizable number of dead men. Now, let me tell you what is going to happen. There are nine of you now. Three will not survive the afternoon. The rest may live a good deal longer if you obey my every command and make no attempt to free yourselves. Do you understand?"

They all nodded dumbly. Mura's men tied their hands behind their backs, and soon they were being helped onto the new dock. Phaedra winced as her foot touched the planks, terrified that Karassa would notice her presence and take offense. But nothing happened. Was God Most High shielding them from the Goddess' vision?

How long had these pirates been using Tarphae as their refuge? The island had been deserted when Phaedra and the others had come back for their king, and that was only a few months ago. Karassa had tried to swallow them with an earthquake, and now even Her great capital of Karsanye was mostly rubble.

But out of this rubble, the pirates had built an altar. It was made of uneven stones, probably from the remnants of the nearest building, and it stood just past the end of the docks, waiting for them. *Three of you will not survive the afternoon.*

Which of them would Mura choose for his sacrifice? Surely, God Most High would not have protected her and Hunter all this time just to allow them to be sacrificed to Karassa. Even so, Phaedra knew better than to complacently assume His continued protection. It was too easy to accidentally offend a God, and if they ever lost that protection, their first and only warning might well be their deaths.

Hopefully He was still protecting them, and Mura would choose others instead. The captain would be a tempting target, Phaedra was sure. He was also responsible for the crew's defiance toward God Most High, so if Mura *didn't* choose him, it would mean that the dragons' God had had no part in this latest turn of events. That was too frightening to contemplate, so as horrible as it was to hope for anyone's death, Phaedra dearly hoped the captain would be chosen.

But after him, it was anyone's guess who would most appeal to Mura's bloodlust. The tallest ones? The brawniest? The weakest? It all depended, she supposed, on what he meant to do with those who survived.

In the end Mura did choose the captain, and two continental sailors besides. The three sailors who were islanders heaved a collective sigh of relief, while the last remaining continental shifted his gaze from person to person, looking hunted. Mura smiled at this and turned back to the captain, unsheathing a long knife from his belt.

Phaedra closed her eyes while the horrible deed was done, squeezing them together so hard that tears formed in the corners and blurred her vision even after she opened them again. She wished her hands had been unbound so that she could cover her ears as well. What she heard made her want

to bury her head in a pillow and never take it out again. The
screaming, the pleading, the gurgling... she felt sick.

A sudden burst of heat made her open her eyes. All three
dead men on the altar were wreathed in flames.

"The Goddess has accepted our sacrifice!" Mura cried.
"Praised be Karassa, who protects us and grants us the use of
Her islands."

"Praised be Karassa," his men echoed. This wasn't their first
time, Phaedra thought. That only made it more horrifying.

"God of Dragons protect us," she muttered under her breath.

The heat of the altar was intense, despite the lack of any
visible fuel. The flames ate greedily at the bodies, turning them
to ash before her eyes. Karassa was taking to these pirates'
sacrifice far better than anything Phaedra had ever seen on the
holy days of her childhood. How easy it had been for Her to
discard the Tarphaeans and start anew!

Phaedra felt a true hatred for Karassa growing within her.
To think that they had spent months worrying that some other
God had overpowered Her to slay Her people! Phaedra hoped
the Oracle that had warned of a Judgment of the Gods had
been right – Karassa deserved to be judged, and judged harshly.
May God Most High cast Her out of the heavens!

When the bodies were little more than charred husks, Mura
collected some of the ashes in a bag that had been hanging
around his neck, tucked into his shirt. That struck Phaedra
as odd. Did the ashes have a ritual purpose? The Tarphaean
priests of Karassa had never collected the ashes of a sacrifice to
Phaedra's knowledge, and Phaedra's knowledge was extensive.
These ashes were different, of course, and not just because they
were made from the corpses of men: they were a direct sign of
the Goddess' favor. They were the kind of thing Psander might
have used to bolster her home's defenses.

Was Mura a wizard? Phaedra had been wondering what
God Most High meant to do with her and Hunter, but now
it suddenly seemed clear. In one blow He had punished the
captain and crew for imprisoning her and Hunter, and brought

her to a place where she could learn more of magic! If she could survive the place, anyway.

The pirates dragged the prisoners to their feet and led them roughly onward, through the rubble of Karsanye. Her captors had no sympathy for Phaedra's handicap, shoving her nastily when she fell behind, and slapping Hunter when he asked to help her.

"What good is she to us?" one of them asked Mura. "You should have sacrificed her, too."

Mura ignored the man. He strode ahead, leading the way through the ruined city, and then past its borders and out into the countryside. After another hour's walk, Phaedra spotted their destination: a farmhouse and mill on the edge of the Sennaroot river, active with people and animals. These pirates were also farmers, then?

Not exactly, it turned out. The farm and mill ran on slave labor, its seven workers overseen by four more of Mura's followers sporting weapons and whips. This was where the pirates came for supplies and safe harbor in between raids. It was also where Phaedra and the others would be staying.

When they got closer, Phaedra spotted the six graves outside the farmhouse. The pirates had been courteous, then, when they arrived here, and had buried the former inhabitants. They must have thought it necessary for securing Karassa's favor. Phaedra wondered if they were right, or if the Goddess had watched them with amusement as they reverently buried the very same people that She had so carelessly slaughtered.

Mura caught her gaze, and seemed to read her mind. "Do you worship Karassa?" he asked.

The four remaining sailors all nodded vigorously. Phaedra felt Hunter's eyes on her, waiting to take his cue. He was like that, Hunter. Never comfortable being the first to speak.

"No," Phaedra said, assessing the situation and deciding that Mura was unlikely to be deceived. "But I respect Her power."

That seemed to be the right thing to say. Mura laughed a big, genuine laugh and said, "Who wouldn't, after what She did here?"

He knew, then. How?

"Oh yes," he said. "It was Karassa who drowned the people of Tarphae; She told me Herself. She came to me in a dream and invited me to claim Her island, if I would devote all my worship to Her. She has provided for us ever since, and in return we have given Her sacrifices and kept Her holy days, as will you."

Phaedra nodded along with the others, and said nothing more. If Mura ever found out that she and Hunter were Tarphaean, that would be the end of them. He'd be delighted, *honored* to sacrifice them to the Goddess of their childhood.

One of the overseers, who introduced himself as Bennan, surveyed the new captives about their skills. Luckily, Hunter had the sense to lie and say that he had grown up as a merchant's son. It was at least a plausible background for such an obviously well-bred person, and it didn't encourage anyone to pick fights with him the way that the truth might have. If he had told them of his nobility, it would only have made them want to further demean and humiliate him. If he'd told them of his combat training, they'd surely have taken it as a challenge.

Phaedra was able to be more truthful. She told them of her grandfather, the master weaver, and of her mother who had taught her the craft. Her father really had been a merchant and financier, so she claimed that her mother had been his second wife, and that Hunter was her half-brother. Bennan nodded and told her she would be mending clothes. Hunter, like the other men, would have to work in the fields.

The separation was nerve-wracking. Setting foot in the farmhouse, Phaedra felt the same pervasive danger she had felt in the Atunaean sailors' hostel. She was inside – trapped! How could she protect herself in a place like this, surrounded by these young men with their hungry stares, without even Hunter's protection?

One of Bennan's companions led her to a room with a pile of clothes and a sewing kit, and told her to get to work. "My name is Terrin," he said, standing at the door. "I'm the cook here. If you want to eat, you'll be good to me."

Phaedra nodded, and he left. She stared at the door, momentarily paralyzed by fear and dread. She didn't have any plan, and she badly needed one. She knew she could find the strength to tolerate any ordeal – the ants of Hession's cavern had proved as much – but not without a plan. Without some way forward, all she could do was despair.

She picked up needle and thread, and began patching a tunic. It was simple work, work that didn't require any real skill and left an unpleasant amount of room for thought. It didn't take a weaver to sew on a few patches here and there – all it took was basic competence.

If only she had the same level of competence when it came to magic. She didn't need Psander's ability to ward a castle against the Gods, she just wanted to protect herself and Hunter. God Most High may have had plans for them, but He wasn't likely to do much more than keep them alive – would He even notice if they were harmed more subtly? Gods were not well known for Their subtlety.

What if there were some way to alert Him? If God Most High could be coaxed into taking a more personal interest in them, she wouldn't even need her own magic. Normally, this kind of coaxing was accomplished through sacrifice and prayer, but there was nothing here for her to sacrifice. Would He listen to prayer alone?

"O God Most High," she mumbled, so as not to be heard by anyone nearby, "God of Dragons, Builder of the Mesh, Constructor of Heavens: help me. Protect me among my enemies – among *Your* enemies. Turn their evil intentions from me and Hunter. Save us from their gazes."

Her hands began to tremble, and she put down the needle. Could God Most High hear her, or was His attention elsewhere? Was there something she could do to amplify her message?

She thought of Auntie Gava, burying her oysters under the rocks; of Psander, who had called magic theory a framework for reusing the Gods' magic for one's own purposes; of Narky, who had justified his suggestions by saying that they seemed like "the kind of weird thing Psander would do." She thought of Mura, whose magic seemed to rely on Karassa's favor. She had all the tools she needed, she was sure of it. She just needed to figure out how they went together.

"The Gods are all magic," Gava had said, "and They made this place. You take a look at what They made, you try to get some of the pieces so they fit together better than before, and that's it. You've got magic."

You've got magic.

What she really had was her prayers, a needle, and a pile of clothes that needed mending. It would have to do.

Phaedra took up her needle again, and began sewing her prayers into her seams. Nobody who had even the most basic domestic skills would have let the pile get this big, and that meant that nobody would be checking her work before they wore it. She made an extended prayer out of multiple garments, picking up the thread wherever she had left off on the previous one. She whispered the prayer as she sewed it, giving it the power of her voice as well.

God Most High, protect me from the men who wear these clothes. Turn their thoughts away from me and my friend, Hunter of House Tavener, and shelter us from their gazes. Let them feed us and forget us, never knowing that they have forgotten. Make them memory boxes like Bandu's, and put all thought of harming us inside, locked tight with a thousand locks and a thousand missing keys. God of Dragons, Slayer of the Yarek, who made the seas calm for Your servants, nothing is impossible for You. Say the word, and it will be so.

It took hours to complete the prayer, and when she was done only a third or so of the garments had been mended. Her fingertips were bleeding from having been poked with the needle, and her eyes throbbed from staring so intently at such short distances. But she was on the right track, she was sure of it. Whether or not her prayers would be answered, she did not doubt that God Most High would hear them.

A noise made her look up. Terrin stood in the doorway, grinning at her. He pulled off his tunic.

Phaedra threw him a mended one. He caught it, surprised, and looked down at the garment. Phaedra held her breath. Terrin seemed confused for a moment, like he wasn't sure what the mended tunic was for. Then he put it on.

"You've made progress," he said, looking around and noticing the shrunken pile of torn clothes. "Keep it up."

And just like that, he left.

Magic, Phaedra thought. *It works!*

21

BANDU

At first, Criton's war went well for him. After a few days the Ardisian army regrouped and tried to fight them again in the open field, but they were too afraid of Criton and his God. Their ranks broke before the Dragon Touched even reached them, and they lost more men in the stampede than in the fighting.

But the victories didn't last. When they regrouped a second time, the Ardismen stopped trying to confront the Dragon Touched and split their army, sending one half to burn the plainspeople's villages while the other stayed behind to keep Criton's army from catching up. They killed any stragglers who fell behind the camp, so the Dragon Touched couldn't hurry to save the northern villages without leaving their slowest and weakest to die. Criton refused to let that happen, so they moved at a crawl instead.

In the meantime, a sickness spread through the Dragon Touched camp, slowing them down further and making everyone miserable. Criton had the worst of it, coughing and wheezing and blowing sparks everywhere. The sparks were all he produced, though – his fire was gone. He wasn't the only one, either. Most of the Dragon Touched had lost their fire. They were lucky the Ardismen hadn't found that out yet.

Bandu feared for Goodweather's life when she saw all the breathing troubles Criton and his kind were having, but luckily she and the children were spared the sickness. "Your God is angry about the pigs," she told Criton. "You are sorry you don't listen to me."

"But we won the battle!" he objected, right before another coughing fit left him gasping for breath. "God Most High favored us!" he croaked.

"He doesn't now," Bandu pointed out. "You should say sorry, like Narky does. If Ardismen know your God is angry, they kill us all soon."

"Our God isn't angry," Criton insisted. "It's just a cold with a bad cough."

"You burn pigs," Bandu said. "Where your fire is now?"

Criton sighed, which turned into more coughing. "Maybe you're right. I'll make a sacrifice and ask for forgiveness."

"Good," Bandu said. "Ask me too. You don't listen to me when I tell you before."

He made an aggravated sound, but then he said, "You're right. I'm sorry. I promise I'll listen to your advice from now on."

Bandu decided that that would do.

She was glad he was listening to her now, at least. She was also glad about the sickness, as long as Goodweather had been spared. If Criton's God was punishing him for what he'd done, then maybe He wasn't so bad after all.

Criton made his sacrifice the following day, giving his God three of Biva's ewes. Hessina gave another, as did several elders among the plainsmen. It bothered Bandu that they should repent of needlessly killing animals by killing more animals, but it must have been what God Most High wanted, because Criton and his people all recovered from their illness within a day or two.

What did Gods do with all those animals people gave Them? Did the fires that burned the animals' bodies act like a frog's tongue, catching an animal's essence and sucking it into the heavens for Them to eat? Bandu might be able to forgive the Gods for all that death if They were only eating.

Anyway, she was still angry at Criton, whether God Most High forgave him or not. It wasn't just about the pigs. Criton was more concerned with killing Ardismen than he was with making her happy, and he spent more time with Delika than with his own daughter. Some of that wasn't his fault: Delika clung to him whenever she could, and Goodweather preferred Bandu because Criton couldn't nurse her. But it was also more than that. Criton actually avoided the baby. Bandu thought he was afraid of Goodweather, not because of the girl herself but because of his own instincts. He didn't trust himself with her.

Sometimes Bandu didn't trust him either. When Goodweather's clothes were wet and she awoke with a long, continuous wail, Criton would jerk up angrily and change her with hatred in his eyes. He always calmed down a little while after the baby did, and then came the shame and fear. What if he had hurt her this time? He hadn't, yet, but he had been close. He was always close.

Bandu, on the other hand, was growing to love their daughter more and more. Goodweather smiled now, sweet thing, real smiles that expressed such joy it pained her. The girl was happier to see her mother's face than Bandu had ever been about anything, as far back as she could remember.

But Criton hardly noticed his daughter when she wasn't screaming, because he was too busy parenting Delika. He was more comfortable with the older girl, and why shouldn't he be? He didn't have to guess what she wanted, because she could tell him. She also didn't wet herself, didn't wake him up at night, and didn't respond to inattention by screaming. But for all that Bandu understood this preference for the older girl, she still hated it. A man shouldn't love someone else's little girl more than his own.

At least Bandu did have help with the baby, even if it wasn't usually from Criton. His cousin's wife Iona was full of helpful advice for how best to calm Goodweather or bind her safely to Bandu's chest while traveling, and her daughter Dessa was always asking if she could hold her baby cousin. Dessa also came now and then with her friend Vella, whose younger brother was supposed to have married Dessa later this year. Vella was about Bandu's age, and was herself married to some man Bandu never saw, a soldier in Criton's army. She wasn't as helpful as Iona or as friendly as Dessa – she mostly seemed afraid of Bandu. But she came, and she was usually willing to carry Goodweather, and Bandu would take all the help she could get.

Certainly if the rest of the pack had been more welcoming, Bandu would not always dream of taking Goodweather away and leaving Criton with his not-daughter and his war. She wouldn't wish that she still had Four-foot instead of him. But the pack was *not* welcoming. Almost everyone looked at her with suspicion, and even Belkos' family wasn't always nice – Iona's mother was worse than anyone else in the pack. She hated Bandu, and never bothered to hide it.

"I know why you're here," she would hiss. "My daughter will not be widowed."

That was a new word, but nobody would explain it to her. Iona would only apologize for her mother and tell Bandu to ignore her, which was her one piece of advice that was not at all helpful.

Criton didn't want to tell her either. She asked him, after Delika and Goodweather had both fallen asleep, and all he said was, "It's not important."

"Yes, it is."

"No, it's not," he insisted. "Whoever told you you'd be widowed is a liar and a fool. You shouldn't listen to people like that."

"She doesn't say that."

Criton snorted. "Of course she doesn't *say* that she's a liar, Bandu."

"No, not she is a liar. Not that I am."

Even in the dark, she could tell he was frowning. "You're not making any sense. You're not going to be widowed, Bandu! Don't worry about it."

She wanted to hit him, but she didn't. "She doesn't say that! She doesn't say I am widowed."

"Then what are you worried about? I'm going to be fine, Bandu. We're all going to be fine."

"You don't answer me."

"Don't be angry."

"I *am* angry."

He sighed. "To be widowed is to lose your husband."

"Lose where?"

"Nowhere. It's to have him die, Bandu. If I die, you'll be a widow."

Bandu groaned. "Stupid," she said. "Stupid words. All your words for me are stupid. First Phaedra says I am virgin, then we mate and I'm a wife, and if you die I am widow? Why do all your words for me care so much about you?"

"I don't know," Criton said. "I'm not sure why it annoys you so much. Anyhow, you wanted to know what it means to be a widow, and I told you. But you don't need to worry about it."

"You don't tell me when to worry."

She turned away from him. Criton only thought about himself sometimes. Too many times. Maybe she should have mated with someone like Hunter, who only thought about other people. But then, Hunter hadn't interested her.

Anyway, now she had her answer. But why did Iona's mother think that Bandu and Criton were going to kill Belkos? As far as Bandu could tell, Criton's cousin was his closest friend now. They talked about their war all the time together, and there was more to it than that. For Belkos, Criton was a leader to be proud of: his cousin was head of the pack. For Criton, Belkos was his closest connection to the family he had always wanted: his *cousin* was a part of the pack.

Belkos was also the cause of Bandu's connection to Iona and Dessa, her only real friends among the Dragon Touched. No matter how she looked at it, she couldn't find a reason for the old woman to think that she and Criton meant to kill him. It made no sense.

But she couldn't just ignore it the way Iona and Criton wanted her to. Iona's mother may have lost much of her sense, but that didn't make her harmless, and it might not even make her wrong. Her magic was so strong Bandu could smell it. Maybe the old woman saw something in them that was really there, something they didn't even know about. Bandu couldn't ignore that possibility. It worried her.

Criton was under a lot of strain these days. His plan to catch up with the northern army of Ardis wasn't working, but nobody could agree on what they wanted him to do instead. The plainsmen wanted him to hurry to protect their villages, even if it meant losing a few stragglers to the Ardismen's southern army. Belkos wanted him to deal with the southern army first and then move straight on to Ardis while the northern force was still distracted. And of course, Bandu wanted help with Goodweather, and Delika wanted Criton to take her along no matter where he went.

The short days and rainy weather weren't helping anyone's mood either. Everyone in the camp was miserable; many took it out on Criton.

"What am I supposed to do?" he asked her one evening as they were making camp. He was holding Goodweather while Delika played with rocks and Bandu tightened the canvas on their tent. Criton was no good with tents.

"This isn't sustainable," he went on. "We can't do anything with that army on our tails. We're going to have to attack them, try to drive them off. Then we can deal with the other half."

"Yes," Bandu agreed. "You can't help other people if we go so slow."

"The trouble," Criton said, "is that there are still more of them than there are of us, and they'll be ready for us if we try to attack them. Their scouts will tell them when we get close. Hessina thinks they'll avoid our full army if they can – their old general Xytos is known for his patience. He'll wait for the plainsmen to desert us if he can, and only face us in an open battle if he has to. So we should try to catch him, I guess, but if we do fight a battle and lose, we're all doomed.

"Maybe if we could surprise them somehow, we could drive them off for good. But even if we attacked at night, they'd be ready for us – their scouts are everywhere. We're lucky their General Xytos is so cautious, or they'd have ambushed *us* by now."

Bandu nodded thoughtfully. "Night is good, I think."

"We don't have any scouts at all," Criton confessed. "I figured we couldn't afford to lose any. I've just been flying straight upwards in the evenings to see where they've lit their fires, and that's how we know where they are."

"That is good enough!" Bandu said. "If you know where they are, that is good. You can fight them."

"They'll know we're coming though!" He was repeating himself, and his voice was becoming a whine. She loved him, but this was very annoying.

"Maybe they know you are coming," she said, "but they don't see good at night. You can go with only Dragon Touched, and send plains people after."

Criton looked at her as if that was the dumbest thing he had ever heard. "We can't lead a raid with *just* the Dragon Touched, there aren't even sixty of us who can fight anymore! It's not a number that can attack a force of twelve hundred!"

"It is," Bandu insisted. "Their eyes are no good at night. We do just like when Narky kills Bestillos: you are Hunter, and plains people are Narky. You say that Ardis people know you are coming, and everyone is ready? Good! So everyone goes together first, and Ardis people see you and they are ready. But then, after, you go a different way with Dragon Touched only. You breathe fire and make noise and they all go that way. Then plains people go from other side and surprise them, and they run away."

Criton considered that. "So you want to use the Dragon Touched as a decoy?" he said. "That... well, it *could* work. And it's better than waiting for our allies to abandon us. I'll bring it up with the others."

"Good," Bandu said. "I talk to Iona about watching Delika and Goodweather then."

Criton had begun to nod, but suddenly stopped when he realized what she meant. "Hold on, what? You're not coming with me, are you?"

"No," Bandu explained. "I go with the plains people. They need someone to show them the way and help them be quiet, and you're no good for that. You need to go with your kind so the Ardismen think you have everyone. So I go. I can talk to Iona now."

She saw his face turn sour. "I do this," she said. "You don't stop me."

"I don't want to stay with Iona!" Delika said suddenly.

So she had been listening to the two of them after all. Of course she had. Bandu took Goodweather back from Criton and left him to argue with Delika while she went to ask Iona about watching the children.

She wondered if Criton would give her any more trouble about joining the plains people when they made their attack. He was probably worried that they wouldn't let her go with them, but she didn't think that would be such a problem. She knew she wasn't a member of their pack, but she also knew they were afraid of her. They called her "witch," which Iona had said was a bad name for a woman who used magic. That meant they were afraid, she thought. Anyway, Bandu *did* use magic, and she was used to being called wicked. She suspected that the plains people would be too afraid to say no to her, and that was enough. She didn't need them to like her – just so long as they did what she said, they could call her whatever they liked.

They weren't really one mass, of course. There were many clans from many villages, and she and Criton would have to convince each and every one of them to let her lead them in the raid. When she had sorted out her arrangement with Iona, she made Criton take her with him to talk to those elders. It was long and frustrating and took two full days – the plainsmen preferred to be led by one of their own, and they preferred to be led by a man – but in the end, they agreed just as she had thought they would.

What convinced them was the story of the weeping house, which many of them had heard from the other Dragon Touched and which Criton told them again anyway, just in case. For all their objections, the story was powerful. It was one thing to be led by a foreign woman, but no one could say they didn't want to be led by a miracle worker.

And so, two nights later, Bandu led an army through wet grasses toward the enemy camp. The whole of the army had gone together to a spot maybe half a mile from where the Ardismen had set up tents, so that the scouts would tell their leaders that all the Dragon Touched were coming. Then the Dragon Touched themselves split off, and it fell to her to lead the plainsmen the rest of the way.

First, she asked the wind for its help in keeping their steps silent. A breeze picked up and began whistling in their ears, blocking out the sound of their shuffling feet. Good. As long as they could still hear the battle when it started, this breeze was their friend.

They approached as quietly as a three hundred man army could. There was only a sliver of moon, and they stole forward in the darkness, straining their eyes to catch the first light from the Ardisian camp. When they had come as far as Bandu dared, and the lights of the camp were readily visible, she gave the order to stop. She whispered it through the wind, which made many of the plainsmen stare shocked in her direction. But they did all stop, and they did it without anyone having to yell out a command or make a hard-to-see hand signal in the dim light. They would be glad they'd let her lead them.

The camp looked asleep from here, to Bandu's surprise. Criton had thought they would be ready for an attack, but apparently he had been wrong. This might be easier than they had expected.

The Dragon Touched made their attack a few minutes later,

and Bandu quickly saw her mistake. The Touched came in unexpectedly from the west, but the Ardismen were far more ready than they looked. A guard sounded the alarm long before the Dragon Touched reached him, and masses of soldiers streamed from their tents fully armed and ready for battle. It wouldn't take long at all for Criton's group to be overwhelmed.

Bandu whispered her command and the plainsmen broke into a run, making no sound except for the pounding of their feet and the laboring of their breaths. The closer they got, the more Bandu wished she had given the order sooner: the Dragon Touched were so, so outnumbered. For all their blazing breath-fires, it wouldn't be long before the Ardismen killed them all.

But the tactic worked. The Ardismen didn't call a second alarm until Bandu and the plainsmen were practically on top of them, and by then it was too late. They weren't ready for the real army to appear out of the night, running them through from behind. Bandu wasn't in the front by the time they arrived – the others ran too fast – but she was still there in time to join the battle. She drove her way through the crowd and toward the clump of Dragon Touched, swinging the farming tool she had been given to fight with – a hoe, did they call it? Whatever it was called, she used it to smash people in the head.

The Ardismen broke quickly, even quicker than she had expected. They made their retreat in total confusion, trampling each other in their hurry to escape. The Dragon Touched and plainsmen cut them down as they fled into the night, slaughtering them by the hundreds. Another battle, another rout.

We can win this war, Bandu thought. *Nobody can stop us.*

22

NARKY

They had glorious sex that night, and then again the next morning. Now that he had given himself permission, he couldn't get enough. Ptera had been married before and knew exactly what she liked, which was wonderful since it meant he didn't have to guess. The morning was also a better time for it, because he liked seeing everything. He sorely missed his left eye – he'd have grown ten more if he could have.

When they finally stumbled out of the house that morning, they asked the older couple whose bed they had borrowed to witness their wedding. It was a slapdash affair – Narky might have been high priest of Ravennis, but he had no knowledge of the old Laarnan wedding rites, so he had to invent new ones himself. To his secret shame, he modeled them after Bandu and Criton's ridiculous wedding, with an exchange of vows and a few words connecting the whole thing to their God. He told Ptera and their witnesses that the Lord of Fate had decreed that they should be married long before any of them had even been born, a claim that he was not sure he even believed. It was plausible enough, sure, but did Ravennis really care that much about His servants' affairs?

They set out again. Now that Ptera was officially his wife and he was no longer preoccupied with the question of whether or not to marry her, Narky found that he was desperate to know more about her history. He barely knew *anything* about her! How long had she been married before? What had her first husband been like? Why hadn't she had any children, if she had all this experience with lovemaking?

He was going to ask her about all of it – he just hadn't figured out how to yet. He was still trying not to be too blunt, at least not until she knew him better. Besides which, if he had the chance to improve himself a little bit, and before she could really get to know him – well, he was going to take it.

To think that the Graceful Servant had thought that marrying Ptera would make him *less* distracted! Now his thoughts were consumed with the tactics of tact and the dangers of upsetting his bride. What if, over the next few days or weeks, she discovered that she didn't actually like him? That would mean a miserable life for the both of them, and it also wasn't terribly unlikely. What did she really know about him? Nothing. No more than he knew of her, anyway.

But she seemed happy enough so far, and Ravennis below, she was beautiful with her clothes off. Whatever anger he had felt toward her and the Graceful Servant for arranging this marriage, it was gone for now. If it could last, this was the life for him.

He tried again to imagine what Phaedra might say if he told her which questions he meant to ask Ptera. The question about the children was definitely the wrong one to start with, he was sure she would have said that much. How about her first husband? No. Questions on that subject might bring up painful memories, besides which, what if her first husband had been better than Narky in every way? It wouldn't have taken much.

He had probably been tall. Tall and muscular and manly, and better in bed. He'd probably swept Ptera off her feet, and now she was trying to make do with a mere shadow. She called Narky a boy; her first husband had been a man. Maybe he'd died doing something suicidally brave, like wrestling a lion away from a small child. Or maybe he'd died by drinking too much and falling in a river. That would be better.

Narky wished she would volunteer something about the man. He didn't want to have to ask, to open the old wound all by himself. Why couldn't she make this easy for him?

What if he made his questions as generic as possible? He didn't think Phaedra would have objected if he asked a really basic question in a soft tone of voice. How about, 'Can you tell me about your first husband?' That was a nice, simple request, not judgmental or prying in any way. He rehearsed it in his head.

He was about to ask it when Ptera said, "You don't regret it, do you?"

"Huh?"

She sighed. He shouldn't have made her have to explain herself – that was already a mistake.

"Marrying me," she said. "You're right, I didn't even talk to you about it before we sprung it on you. And I'm much older than you, and I've been married before... is it all right?"

The question brought back all his resentment, so plainly laying out the reasons that it had been justified. He almost said "No," and left it at that. Instead, he took his time before answering. Yes, she had done the wrong thing, but hadn't he been thinking just a few minutes ago about how happy he was with the result? If he drove her away, that would be his own doing, not hers. If he wanted more mornings like this one, he had to find a way to salvage the situation.

"I don't know yet," he said. "I wasn't angry today until you asked me."

"This morning was good, right?"

He nodded. "Yeah, it was good this morning. So far, it's not so bad."

She sighed again, and seemed to accept that. He didn't want her to look so unhappy, but then, he also didn't want her to think that he was no longer mad at all – or that it was all right to cut him out of decisions she made for the two of them.

"It's got nothing to do with your age," he told her. "I've got no complaints with your looks or anything like that."

She smiled wryly at him. "Thanks, Narky, that's quite a compliment."

He felt his face get hot. "Sorry, I... This is how I talk."

"I'd noticed."

"You had?"

She laughed at that, and Narky couldn't think of anything else to say. She had already noticed how blunt he was – did that mean he should give up on trying to be tactful with her? That would certainly make things easier. Still, he was surprised at how much disappointment was mixed in with his relief. Perhaps he ought to keep trying anyway.

On the other hand, if she was already aware of his manner of speaking, that sort of gave him permission to ask his awkward questions, didn't it? He hoped so. As a test, he asked, "What was your first husband like? I know I'm young, but I don't want to live in his shadow."

She raised an eyebrow at him. "You're not in his shadow, Narky. He barely cast one."

"Yeah? I bet he was taller than me, and stronger and everything."

"Well, yes."

"So?"

She sighed. "It was no good, Narky. How can I explain it?"

"Try. Did he hit you or something?"

She shook her head. "He wasn't a brute, he just wasn't right. At all. He married me after Magor's fertility festival because he said he liked how I looked under him, and I was young enough that I thought it was a compliment. We had a few decent months, but it went sour fast. We just didn't get along that well, and he was annoyed at how long it was taking me to conceive. He was actively looking for a second wife when he died.

"He wasn't cruel," she added hastily. "He'd have kept supporting me either way. But I wasn't exactly looking forward to the rest of my life."

Narky swallowed. "So... when you say it took you a long time to conceive..."

"I didn't conceive at all," she said tersely.

"And you were married for...?"

"Three years."

"How did he die?"

"A man killed him," she said disgustedly, "in a fight over a woman. His brothers avenged him, and killed both his killer *and* the girl. Then the girl's father stabbed one of *them*, and the priests of Magor had to step in and threaten to eradicate all three of our families before the feud resolved itself. The whole thing was stupid from top to bottom."

"Oh."

He felt foolish now that he knew the story. "I thought you'd turned to Ravennis out of grief," he said.

"Over *him*? No."

"Then..."

"Even before he died," Ptera said, "I was starting to question my allegiance to Magor. The God of Strength seemed to want me to be powerless, now and forever. And then suddenly my husband was dead and the Graceful Servant appeared at my door, offering me a place in the church of Ravennis and the eternal protection of a God who cared about me."

She smiled with the recollection. "She gave me this name, Ptera, and it suits me better than my old one did. Did you know that I was the first Ardiswoman she converted? She said that our God had special plans for me, and that I would help her build a church that would last for the ages. And now here I am."

"Yeah," Narky said. "Here you are."

They fell into silence again. He was going to have to get better at talking to her. They kept starting and stopping, leaving more unsaid than he could really process.

"Anyway," he said, "I'm glad you don't have any children I didn't know about."

"I may not have any with you either, Narky."

He shrugged. "We can worry about that later, or never. I'm not ready to be a father yet anyway. I've seen a bit of what it's like."

Her expression was priceless, a mixture of shock, confusion, tentative relief. "Really? You don't care?"

"What do I want with a baby?" he asked her. "I can barely handle myself right now."

She clearly couldn't tell if he was joking or not. He wasn't. It was a relief to know that they wouldn't be following Criton and Bandu's path any time soon. Gods, how he had hated spending time with that yowler of theirs.

It might be different with one of his own, of course. Gods knew, Criton and Bandu didn't seem to have noticed how hideous their child was. Parenthood seemed to cause a sort of blindness in that respect. Even they had noticed how loud it was, though.

In any case, maybe by the time it came up for him and Ptera – if it ever did – he'd feel differently about it. For now, he wouldn't have minded a guarantee that she *wouldn't* conceive for a little while.

"So," he said, "what is Magor's fertility holiday like?"

He shouldn't have asked. Ptera was clearly trying to find a way to avoid the question, or at least avoid telling him all the details.

"It's much kinder to men like my first husband," she said, helpfully leaving off the obvious follow-up, *kinder to them than to men like you.* "The Graceful Servant called it barbaric, and she wasn't really wrong. It could be good, though, and it definitely taught me a lot about lovemaking. I'm sure that makes you uncomfortable."

It did, but he wasn't about to admit it. If they had had an orgiastic holiday on Tarphae, he was sure he'd have grown up even more miserable than he had been already.

"You're really good at what you learned," he said diplomatically.

"Thank you."

There was nothing to say to that, so they stopped talking yet again. These frequent silences were killing him.

"We should get off the road," he said after some time, just so he could hear *something* beside crickets. "We don't want to meet anyone who will tell Magor's priests where we are."

They did as he suggested. They stopped only at doors marked with the symbol of Ravennis, which grew more common as they traveled farther south. The cult of Ravennis seemed to have grown fastest in the lands between Ardis and its southern neighbor, Anardis. Magor had been widely worshipped in Anardis before His defeat at Silent Hall, and yet the people there lived far enough from their northern neighbor not to feel immediately threatened by Magor's priesthood. Some doors they found marked with both Elkinar's moth and the crow of Ravennis. It seemed that, at the very least, Ravennis was rapidly displacing Magor as the secondary God of this area.

What would Narky's reception in Anardis be like? Did they still blame the Tarphaean islanders for the destruction of their city at the red priest's hands? Would Narky be seen as a representative of his God, or as a symbol of their weakness and subjugation?

He had stalled long enough: he ought to tell Ptera about the last time he'd been to Anardis. The islanders had come there last year after Phaedra broke her ankle, hoping that the priests of Elkinar would be able to heal her. Which they had, sort of. When they had arrived, Phaedra had been completely unable to walk. The high priestess Mother Dinendra had rebroken the bone and set it properly, and now she could walk with a limp.

The islanders, Narky explained, had had a reputation back then for bringing bad luck wherever they went, but Mother Dinendra had shielded them from those who wished to see them gone. They had spent weeks in the inn across from Elkinar's temple, visiting every day to help in the rooftop garden or, in Phaedra's case, to read. But then the army of Ardis had come through the gates, preempting any plans the Anardisians' king may have had for breaking free of their dominion. The islanders had fled without saying goodbye, leaving the city burning behind them. He didn't know if Mother Dinendra had survived, or if so, how she felt about the islanders and their "bad luck" now.

But the two of them were about to find out.

The first thing Narky noticed as they approached the city was the wall. The city wall had never come down, it seemed. Criton had thought once that Bestillos might be chasing him, trying to slay the last of the Dragon Touched, rather than taking the time to fully subjugate Anardis. Did the wall's presence mean he was right? Had the red priest really tried to chase them so soon after taking the city?

He and Ptera approached with caution. The gate was wide open, and Narky could already see the devastation that had been wrought by the fire the Ardismen had set. Many of the old houses were still there, burnt-out husks that would serve as a reminder of that day's events for years to come. Others were new, or had blackened sides where the fire had passed by without destroying them.

He took a deep breath and walked up to the guards who stood by the open gate. "I am Narky of Tarphae, High Priest of Ravennis. I'm here to speak to Mother Dinendra, or whoever is high priest of Elkinar in these times."

The men's hostility was unconcealed, but they didn't turn him and Ptera away. "Mother Dinendra still lives," one said, "not that you wanderers of Tarphae would have cared should the Ardismen have slaughtered her as they did so many others. Ravennis is respected here, but you are not. Enter, but know that you are not welcome."

He supposed that was as pleasant an interaction as he could have hoped for. They entered the city and went straight to Elkinar's temple, trying to ignore the many stares they received along the way.

The temple's sides had been blackened by the fire, and none of the hanging greenery that he remembered was visible on its roof. Had the priests' rooftop garden perished in the fire?

One of the younger priests, Father Taemon, met them at the door. "I am here to speak with Mother Dinendra," Narky told him.

The priest said nothing and was about to turn away when Narky added, "You're the one whose wife was having a baby when Ardis came. How is your family?"

Taemon looked surprised. "They're well. I thank you for asking." He bowed slightly. "I'll tell Mother Dinendra you're here."

They stood outside the triangular building, waiting. What could Narky say to the High Priestess of Elkinar to make up for the misfortune they had brought to Anardis? He had to keep reminding himself that Dinendra hadn't believed any of that stuff about the islanders being cursed. She had thought her nephew, the king of Anardis, was to blame, because of the way his actions had goaded their northern neighbor into attacking them. Did she still feel that way? He hoped so.

Mother Dinendra arrived a moment later, opening the door and looking beyond and all around Narky before accepting that he and Ptera were the only ones there. The elderly high priestess was a welcome sight in this place. "You've lost your friends," she said. "And gained a new one. What's this about your being High Priest of Ravennis now?"

"The Graceful Servant named him high priest," Ptera answered. "And Narky has gained more than a friend: I'm his wife."

Dinendra smiled indulgently. "Welcome, Narky's wife, and welcome to you too, Narky. But what did you do with the other islanders?"

"They're among the Dragon Touched in the north," he answered. "At least, I assume they are. I left them before they got there."

"And now you have returned to Anardis. Well, come in."

They entered the dimly lit hall of worship, where pillar-chimneys stood waiting for worshippers' prayer notes, each pillar containing an oil lamp. There were three women inside praying, one of them noticeably pregnant. They stared at Narky, their gazes unfriendly at best.

"We can speak in the library," Mother Dinendra offered,

"and you can tell me what brings you back here."

She led the way, slowly and carefully, to the chamber beyond, which was perhaps even dustier and more disorganized than Narky had remembered. Scrolls and codices were stuffed onto their shelves in a jumble, joined by earthenware jars, empty bowls, half-spent candles, and various other kinds of debris. In a corner sat a familiar sack of plaster and a pile of rags. It was here that Mother Dinendra had bound Phaedra's ankle, allowing her to walk again, though with a limp. At the time, they hadn't realized how permanent that limp would be: Phaedra had hoped that Psander might heal her ankle with magic someday. Those hopes had been dashed upon their return to Silent Hall.

"What happened to your garden?" Narky asked the priestess.

"The temple walls are made of stone," Mother Dinendra said, "but the garden was flammable. We were able to bring some of the clay pots down to the library, but we had to cast the heavier ones off the roof to keep the fire from spreading to us. So the garden remains, but the hanging plants that you'd have seen from the street outside are no longer. We will replace them eventually, I'm sure. There would be no better symbol of Elkinar's resilience than the display of new plants to replace the old. Elkinar's cycle continues, as it always has."

Narky nodded. "I've noticed that my God has taken up residence in Anardis as well. Have the worshippers of Magor all converted on their own?"

"Almost. If Bestillos' humbling of our city made Magor less popular here, his death dealt a mortal blow to the cult of Magor in Anardis. The temple was defaced within days, and its priests fled. Ardis might have punished us for that, but we sent our tribute early to placate them. Without Bestillos, and with our city walls still standing, the Council of Generals chose to accept our payment with grace."

Ptera made a subtle noise that caught Narky's attention and made him put off what he was about to say. "Does Magor's defaced temple still stand?" she asked.

"It does."

He saw the meaning in her eyes. "We can claim it for Ravennis," Narky said. "Good thinking."

She smiled. "Thank you."

"You'll be staying in Anardis, then?" Mother Dinendra asked.

"Yes, at least until Ardis is ready to welcome us back."

The old woman eyed him skeptically. "And when will that happen?"

"When Criton slaughters their army."

23

HUNTER

The first couple of days were the hardest. Phaedra disappeared into the house and didn't come out again, while the field slaves and their overseers worked and ate and slept outside. He worried about her constantly – what were they doing to her in there? But there was nothing he could do besides pray for God Most High to protect her, and hope that his prayers would be enough.

The overseers were cruel, violent men, and quick to use the whip. It stung more, knowing that this land may well have belonged to his father: House Tavener owned much farmland on the outskirts of Karsanye. His father had taken him and Kataras out to the fields when they were children, but Hunter hadn't shown enough of an interest to be brought back. Neither had Kataras, really, but as the eldest son, Lord Tavener had forced him to learn about managing their lands anyway.

Hunter wondered whether the slaves his father owned had been treated like this. He hoped not, and he honestly doubted it. Under the Tarphaean system of slavery, slaves could bring suit against their masters for unreasonable treatment and win back their freedom. Hunter hadn't always retained what his father had taught him of Tarphaean law, but this much he remembered: the contracts by which men sold their families into slavery were taken seriously. Any breach of contract could be prosecuted.

He didn't remember what qualified as mistreatment under the old Tarphaean law, but he was pretty sure his captors would have been in breach of contract. They allowed no rest during daylight, and beat their workers on a whim. When one of the continental sailors collapsed, they threw him in the river and watched as he nearly drowned trying to get out again. By the end of the day, every prisoner was aching and weary, and the continental men had sunburns.

On that first day, they built a barn for the captives to sleep in alongside the six sheep and one cow that the pirates had somehow found and brought back here to supply them with labor and, hopefully, milk. Hunter was surprised, frankly, that any domesticated animals had survived the last year without turning wild or being eaten by predators. Farming had always seemed like such hard, tedious work to him that he had imagined a whole year's neglect would surely ruin everything. And yet, even if only a hundredth of Tarphae's crops and animals could be recovered, that would be more than enough to feed such a small group of people.

He was glad of the barn, in any case. The rainy season might have held off for him and Phaedra while they were on the ocean, but the unnaturally fair weather didn't last for long. No sooner had they erected the barn than the downpours began. But if he had thought that would spare him from laboring outside, he was wrong: the overseers gladly sent their slaves out in the deluge to catch river fish.

By the second and third day, though, Hunter began to notice a mysterious change in the pirates' attitude toward him. In short, they stopped paying attention to him. He still did as they directed, not wanting to test the limits of their leniency, but the difference was noticeable. The whip never touched his body again, and he was able to be occasionally inefficient without fear of violence. The other captives looked on him with envy and loathing, but they also began praying to God Most High. They might not know *how* Hunter was being protected, but they had some very concrete suspicions about *why*.

Mura returned a few days later, collecting men to help repair the new ship. The hull had apparently sprung a mysterious leak – he suspected foul play, but could find no motive for sabotaging what was, as far as anyone knew, the only way off the island. Almost as soon as he had arrived, Mura sniffed the air and announced that something was wrong.

"Somebody's been casting spells here," he told Bennan. "There's magic so strong I can smell it."

"Really?" Bennan said. "I haven't noticed anything unusual."

Mura gave him a long stare, frowning. "Gather everyone," he said at last. "The slaves too. We're going to get to the bottom of this."

While Bennan was gathering the others, Mura commanded Hunter to build a fire. The ground was muddy, but he seemed to want a bonfire outside, so Hunter chose the driest spot he could find and made a few trips to the woodpile in the barn. Mura did not light the fire with magic this time – perhaps that required Karassa's intervention – so Hunter had to do it by hand. By the time he had set the tinder alight, everyone had gathered around.

Everyone but Phaedra.

Hunter felt that familiar fear gnawing at him, the same fear he had felt when Phaedra had fallen into the ants' nest in Hession's cavern. What had happened to her? He prayed that she had somehow escaped, but he didn't really believe that was possible – not with her limp, and not without a word to Hunter first. Had they hurt her? Had they killed her and forgotten even to taunt him about it?

No. No, he couldn't believe that. Why would God Most High protect him from these men, while allowing her to die? That just could not be. It was all wrong.

Mura noticed Phaedra's absence as well. "Where is she?" he demanded.

"Where is who?" asked Bennan, playing dumb. There was only one 'she' on the island, besides Karassa.

"The girl. This one's half-sister."

Bennan looked sheepish. "Oh, her. I'm sorry, Mura. I forgot all about her. She must still be up in that attic."

"Get her."

Hunter allowed himself to breathe a little. They had simply forgotten her. It was hard to believe, but it was true. Somehow, Bennan and the others had managed to *forget* that there was a woman living among them. Hunter was no wizard, but he was starting to understand what Mura meant by "magic so strong I can smell it."

Had Phaedra had some sort of breakthrough, and laid an enchantment on their captors? He couldn't imagine who else would have done such a thing, and it would explain the overseers' lenient treatment of him. So what had changed? What had Phaedra discovered?

Mura paced in front of the fire while everyone waited for Bennan and Phaedra to return. They arrived a short time later, Bennan mumbling an apology. Mura gave the two of them a contemptuous glare and commanded the whole crowd to look into the fire.

"Karassa," he intoned, "let the nature of this enchantment reveal itself to me." He added three foreign words, pulling the pouch from under his tunic and sprinkling some of its ashes in the fire.

The flames leapt skyward for a moment, drawing Hunter's eyes upward. A vulture was circling overhead. An omen? If so, then for whom?

His heart was pounding. What if Phaedra really was behind this enchantment and Mura found out? God Most High may have protected the two of them from Karassa and Mayar, but hadn't Phaedra always said that humans had free will? That was the whole point of the mesh, wasn't it – to protect people from too much interference by the Gods? Could anything really stop Mura from killing them if he set his mind to it?

"Look into the fire!" Mura spat.

Hunter glanced about, startled and frightened, but luckily Mura was not just talking to him: several other people were as distracted as he was. One or two of them were overseers, which was also lucky. If none had been, Mura would likely have punished all the captives without even waiting for his fire ritual to bear fruit.

Hunter turned his eyes back to the fire, wondering what he was supposed to be seeing. He hoped that whatever Mura had planned, it wouldn't work. But now that he was really looking, he saw that the embers were glowing green as if they'd been burning copper. Mura threw in another handful of ashes, and the flames turned a startling purple. At the third handful the fire flashed such an intense white that Hunter shut his eyes involuntarily, an after-image of the fire still glowing beneath his eyelids.

"An enchantment of the mind," Mura said, probably to himself and yet loud enough to be heard. "No surprises there – far too inattentive to be natural. Well, I can fix that."

He turned away from the fire and began circling behind the crowd, sprinkling holy ashes on each of their heads. He was mumbling the whole time, and when he got close enough for Hunter to hear him, it became clear that these words were in no language Hunter had even heard before. Were they real words in *any* language?

Hunter began to feel something, a tugging at his mind. He thought the ashes must be acting as a wick, trying to tease the enchantment out through their heads. The sensation went away fairly quickly, but then Hunter was pretty sure he hadn't been a target of the original enchantment. Perhaps this was having more of an effect on the others.

It sure didn't seem like it, though. Mura was growing increasingly frustrated. "Karassa," he pleaded, "aid Your servant. Break the shackles that have imprisoned these men's minds and give them the freedom to think as before. I cannot do this alone!"

He threw another handful of ashes in the fire, but this time, nothing happened at all. He tore the pouch from his neck and flung the whole thing in, but the flames only burned on, unchanging. Mura stood there with a look of disbelief, watching his pouch of sacrificial ashes, his sacrifice of sacrifices, blacken and disintegrate to no effect.

"Listen, the lot of you," he shouted. "I'm going to get to the bottom of this, and when I do, whoever cast this spell on my men will suffer like no one has ever suffered before. I will offer him to Karassa piece by bloody piece, all while he lives and watches. If magic will not break the enchantment, death will."

With that he stalked away indoors, leaving his men and their captives looking wonderingly at each other. "Mage Mura is angry at us," the cook said dumbly.

"As well he should be," Bennan answered. "We let ourselves get enchanted, and now he has to fix it. You just pray he figures it out before he starts cutting *us* into pieces. I've never seen his magic fail before."

"Best to keep away from the house," said an overseer called Tarphon. "I don't want to get in his way."

The others agreed, so they all spent the next few hours outside, fishing and tending to the livestock. "We need to leave tonight," Phaedra whispered when she and Hunter were briefly next to each other. "It's not safe to stay, and I think an escape might be possible."

"On what ship?"

Phaedra shook her head almost imperceptibly. Nobody had noticed them talking yet, and there was no reason to change that. "Even if we have to live in the forest, it's better than staying here with Mura."

"You think we can make it far enough away with your limp?"

They separated for a minute, seeing Bennan glance in their direction. When the danger of their conversation being witnessed had passed, Phaedra said, "I think we'd better find out."

They had to wait until late that night to make their attempt. Shortly after their conversation, Mura returned from the house and took a lock of hair from every person on the estate, presumably so that he could use them to identify whoever had cast the spell on his men. However he meant to use the hair, he was apparently waiting for morning to do it, because they heard nothing more about it that night. That was a great relief: the two of them had no intention of waiting to find out whether his second ritual would identify Phaedra as the culprit.

They made their attempt shortly after midnight. Hunter slipped out of the barn while its watchman was relieving himself against a tree, and set off to get Phaedra from the farmhouse. It was midmonth, and the moon was bright overhead. He slunk over to the house, keeping low so that he would be harder to spot. Nobody stopped him. The cook, Terrin, was on watch at the house tonight, but he seemed to be half asleep in his chair by the door. What had Phaedra done to these men?

Whatever it was, Hunter had no complaints. He had been on the cusp of thinking this might be *too* easy, but that was nonsense. Being caught would mean their deaths, whereas escaping would save their lives – there was no such thing as "too easy."

Something touched his shoulder and he spun around, his heart pounding. It was Phaedra. "I was starting to worry you wouldn't make it," she whispered. "Let's get out of here."

They picked their way around the house until they were sure they could not be seen from either the house or the barn, then picked up their pace. The moon was bright enough that they were able to find their way with little trouble, breaking from the road once the farmlands and tukka orchards gave way to true forest. Hunter kept looking back in case they were being pursued, though of course they weren't – if nobody had noticed them leave, they weren't likely to be missed till morning.

But for all that they had a tremendous head start, he worried about Phaedra's slow pace. She had grown used to traveling with a limp, but that mostly meant that she stopped to rest and stretch her muscles far more often than he'd have liked. He took the time during one of these breaks to find her a good walking stick, but though she seemed to appreciate it, it didn't much improve their speed. They walked on.

The hardest part came when the initial excitement and anxiety of their escape finally wore off, and they were left sleepily plodding along, trying to keep their eyes open and focused and to get just one more mile farther away, and then another, just past these trees and after that, those ones. The night winds were chilly at this time of year, and all Hunter wanted to do was to curl up in some reasonably dry place and fall asleep.

At long last, when Phaedra had decided that they should go no farther that night, they curled up back to back on the most level patch of ground they could find and passed swiftly into unconsciousness.

When they awoke, a familiar face was staring down at them.

24

PHAEDRA

Phaedra blinked, trying to place that face. It was a skinny continental face with close-set eyes and long brown hair, and it belonged to a girl who must have been at least a year or two younger than Phaedra. Where did she know her from?

"I know you," Hunter said to the girl. "You're from that village that Psander took in! How did you get here?"

"She sent me through," the girl said. "She wanted me to get some things to help her fight off the elves."

"Like what?" Phaedra asked.

The girl looked uncertain, as if she thought Psander might not have wanted her to say. "Like what?" Phaedra repeated.

"Like relics from your lives. You islanders. She said you'd been to the elves' world before and survived, and if I brought her some of your things she could use them against the elves."

For a moment, Phaedra just gawked at her. Psander meant to use relics from the Tarphaeans' lives – from her life – to fight the fairies? How was Phaedra supposed to feel about that? Except, obviously, she wasn't supposed to feel anything about it. She wasn't meant to know.

She vaguely remembered having fed this girl, back when Psander's villagers had all been sick and weak from the wizard's overreliance on their latent magic. Psander had made them pendants that siphoned off unused magical potential and used it to buttress her wards, and upon the islanders' last visit they had found the villagers too weak to stand.

"Have you all recovered from the pendant-sickness, then?"

The girl nodded. "Mostly. Psander had us take the charms off after we got to the world of elves, so she could look them over and make some changes. They don't make us as weak anymore, and we also don't wear them all the time – we go one week on, two weeks off, in cycles. It's not so bad now, and if it keeps the elves away, that's worth more than anything we could give."

"How have you held them off?" Hunter asked. "They even knew you were coming!"

"They didn't know where, though," the girl said. "We had a few days before they found us, for Psander to turn her wards around."

"Turn her wards around? What does that mean?"

"I don't know. It's what she said."

They went silent for a time, until Hunter pointed out that they had to keep moving if they were to stay ahead of Mura's men. The village girl was confused. "Psander said the island would be empty when I came."

Phaedra explained the situation, and that ended the questions. They fled deeper into the forest. The girl followed them, occasionally consulting with a map she had brought with her. It was a strange sort of map that seemed to be marked differently every time Phaedra glimpsed it. It was made out of a patchwork of five or six pieces of cloth sewed together. Just over half of it was covered with signs and squiggles that shifted as they walked, but the other almost-half seemed to be permanently blank.

"Those are your pieces," the girl explained when she saw Phaedra looking. "They're all supposed to go empty like that when I'm close enough to something of yours. These two parts must be from the two of you."

"I see." The material this map was made from looked familiar somehow… Ah, that was it. They were patches of bed sheet. Psander must have made this map out of the linens the islanders had slept under when they came to Silent Hall. It was poetic magic, just as Phaedra had suspected: Psander was looking for relics from the islanders' homes, so she had used the material she had that was closest to being their home at Silent Hall. Phaedra would never have thought to have done that, but it made fine sense now that she recognized it.

"What's your name?" she asked the girl.

"Atella."

"Did Psander choose you for your name?"

The girl looked confused, though she shouldn't have. Atel was the God of travelers and messengers, and it was too fitting for a girl named after Him to be sent back to this unfamiliar place to seek and find relics of its native children. There might have been some magical benefit to sending a girl with a name like that. But then, perhaps you had to be a student of magic to recognize such things.

"How are you going to get back to Silent Hall when you're done here?" Hunter asked.

"I'm supposed to find my way back to where I came through, and if I'm in time it'll open for me. I've only got eleven days to find everything and get back, or Psander said I could be lost for years."

Elevens again. Phaedra wished she could make them all add up. Everything that had to do with the world of the elves seemed to come in elevens, but there was no rhyme or reason to it as far as she could tell. Perhaps Psander could explain it all, if she had mastered the theory of elevens so quickly.

"We'll go back with you," Phaedra said. "It'll save you time finding things to represent me and Hunter."

That, and it would get them away from Mura.

"Thanks," Atella said. "I hope we can get back in time."

Phaedra smiled reassuringly at her. "We will."

It was an incredible, overwhelming relief to think that Psander might once again save her and Hunter from their enemies and pursuers. Phaedra had thought that she and Hunter were trapped on the island for good this time, but now there was the possibility of leaving this world behind and seeing Psander again! In eleven days, she might sit in Psander's library and learn how the wizard worked her magic without the support of a patron God.

So far, the magic Phaedra had done was more similar to Mura's terrible rituals than anything else: just as Mura seemed to rely on Karassa's blessing for his power, so Phaedra had relied on God Most High. Their magic was at best an amplification of their prayers, a way to get more attention from their respective Gods than they might have warranted otherwise. Yet this was obviously *not* the way Psander worked – she didn't have to rely on some God's favor to disguise herself, or to summon a flame, or to make her fortress invisible. Phaedra wanted to know how she did it.

On the other hand, what if it was this non-reliance on Them that had turned the Gods against the academic wizards, after a centuries-long tradition of tolerance? Perhaps magic was *supposed* to rely on the blessings of Gods, and it was the decoupling of magic from worship that had both empowered and doomed Psander's colleagues.

They followed Atella's shifting map until another of its patches went blank, in a part of the forest that looked like any other. There were guardian trees here, and a healthy undergrowth of plants that Phaedra could not identify – she had never been that interested in plants. She scanned the trees and forest floor for any reason for them to have stopped. What could be here, among the guardian trees, that could be called a relic of the islanders? It must be something of Bandu's, but what? What significance did this place have? Was it the place where she had met Four-foot? The place her father had left her when he first brought her to the forest to live or die without him? Was it the place where the fairies had first abducted her, some eleven years ago?

Atella didn't seem to know any more than Phaedra did. She turned round and round, looking lost. "What's here?" she asked despairingly.

"I don't know," Phaedra said.

Hunter beat about in the underbrush, looking for anything that might be hidden among the vines and bushes, but it was no good. There was nothing there to be found.

"What do we do?" Atella asked.

"Take some of everything," Phaedra suggested. "Some dirt, some bark, some leaves and twigs. If we leave without what you're looking for, Bandu's part of the map will start working again, won't it?"

The girl looked relieved. "I think so. Oh, thank you!"

She pulled her satchel around and began harvesting little pieces of their surroundings. "We'd better get moving soon," Hunter pointed out. "Mura can't be that far behind us."

"Do you think we could try to find a road again?" Phaedra asked. "If they're tracking us, they won't still be on the roads anymore."

"It's worth trying," Hunter said. "Besides which, I'm not Criton – I can't catch us a dinner with claws and fire. We can try throwing rocks at birds, but I think we'll have better luck foraging around the old towns."

He was right. The three of them proved completely incapable of hunting for themselves, and the little streams they found along their way were not deep enough for fish, though their water was sweet. They walked in the direction they thought most likely to lead to a road without taking them back toward Mura's outpost, but they found none that day, and broke for the night still surrounded by trees. Atella luckily had brought dried meat, hard bread, and cheese with her on her journey, but it was meant to last her a week and a half, and they had to share it in tiny portions to make it last. They settled down to sleep still desperately hungry, shivering in the cool winter night and listening to the howling wolves.

The wolves made Phaedra think of Bandu and her wolf Four-foot, who had died of an infection so short a time after saving the islanders from Magor-worshipping highwaymen. Phaedra had always found the wolf terrifying, but she knew how Bandu loved him, and she loved Bandu. She missed the other girl, her generous soul, her insight, and even her infuriating lack of understanding about the norms of civilization. Bandu would surely have felt at home here, and Phaedra would have felt at home with Bandu.

It was too hard, having all split up like this. Phaedra had lost her first family, found a new one, and now lost that one too. Would she ever see Bandu or Criton or Narky again? She wished she knew what they were all up to, or at least that she could have gotten some assurance that they were all still alive. Who knew what had transpired in her absence?

She thought the wolves might be getting closer – their howls seemed to be becoming louder and louder. She prayed to God Most High to protect her, Atella, and Hunter while they slept. But her prayer felt hollow, so she got up and scratched it into the ground all around them with a sharp rock, reading it through three times, both for the power of the repetition and to make sure she was satisfied with her wording. That would have to do, she decided. She was a novice at magic, but Criton's God had shown them such favor so far that hopefully He would forgive her amateurish work.

They awoke the next morning and moved on, coming at last to a path that led them to a village. The village square was full of bones, where villagers had died during the divine plague and then been preyed upon by birds and wild animals. Some skeletons were mostly intact, others scattered by the rougher scavengers who had fed upon their flesh. The blackened bones of a ram still lay upon the altar in the center of the square, grinning at them.

They went into the houses, looking for the stores of grain that had never seen another sowing season. It was an eerie feeling, walking into other people's houses unannounced, knowing that the owners were inevitably among the bones outside. They found what they needed, though, and spent most of the day grinding flour and baking hard bread for their journey. She thought that would still give them enough time to collect everything Atella needed – from what Phaedra knew of Narky's past, his village couldn't have been more than a day or two away. With Psander's map to guide them, they ought to reach it with still five or six days left before their eleven-day window closed. That ought to give them just enough time to get back to Karsanye for something of Criton's before returning to the forest and, hopefully, Silent Hall. The only trouble was that Mura and his people still existed, and, unless he gave up and turned back, might catch the three of them at any point along the way.

They left the village that evening and soldiered on despite their lack of rest, stumbling down the road weary and half asleep. They were glad they did: after dark, they spotted a light no more than a day's journey behind them. Mura might not have reached the village tonight, but he surely would tomorrow morning.

How many men could he possibly have with him? Presumably he had left his captives behind with overseers to guard them, and taken a small group to track down the escapees. He would kill them when he found them, that much was certain. Hunter wouldn't give up without a fight, so he would die first, but Phaedra would be sacrificed and her ashes harvested for more spells. She had no idea what they'd do with Atella. Probably the same.

They didn't sleep at all that night. When Atella tried to sit down and rest, Phaedra snatched the map from her and kept limping on, forcing her to rise and follow. Mura and his men would be much faster than them – the only way to outpace them was to never ever stop.

By midday the next day, Phaedra was seeing things she was pretty sure weren't there. The fairies on their horses, pursuing them through the woods – that was a memory, right? But she kept thinking she saw or heard them, riding toward her and the others with their sky-nets and elvish sickles ready for slaughter.

By early evening, when they arrived at the village that Atella's map indicated as Narky's, Phaedra could have sworn the skeletons in the yard were moving. She shied away from them as she passed through, afraid that they might snatch at her. The map led them just out of the village before Narky's corner went blank.

"I don't understand," Atella said, tears streaming down her face. "There's nothing here but a clump of trees."

Phaedra's vision was blurring too, and her eyes kept closing. She slapped herself in the face. "There has to be something. Narky isn't like Bandu – places aren't important to him. Whatever's here, it's concrete."

Hunter nodded. "I'll look in the trees, you look on the ground. Atella, check that stream over there."

"Where?"

Hunter blinked a few times. "Sorry. Just help Phaedra look on the ground, then."

This would have been much easier had they slept before their search. Phaedra kept finding things that struck her as full of significance, only to realize a moment later that they were simply rocks or sticks or blades of grass with interesting coloration. She crawled about on the ground, examining every pebble and trying not to be fooled by her own imagination. Even when she found what she was looking for, she almost ignored it on the assumption that it wasn't really there.

But it *was* there. No matter how many times she blinked or felt it with her fingers, she had found the front half of a crossbow bolt. Someone had snapped the thing somewhere near the middle and flung it away – the other half must be around here somewhere. Phaedra knew what it was, and she knew why it was important: it had been pulled from someone's body after Narky had put it there.

"I have something!" Phaedra cried. "Come here. We need to find the other half."

"It's an arrow?" Atella asked, looking confused.

"A crossbow bolt," Phaedra corrected her. "Find the other half."

She did, lifting it out of the grasses a few minutes later. "So this is it? This is what we're here for?"

"This is what we're here for."

Phaedra didn't tell her any more than that. Hunter seemed to have figured out the bolt's significance on his own, but it was not the sort of thing one said aloud. They knew that Narky had murdered someone, probably not long before they had met him. They had learned it not from his mouth but from a prophecy, one that had referred to Narky as *he who was murderer*. Narky had been the one to point out the other verses' resemblance to the five islanders, but though Hunter had claimed to believe that he himself was the murderer for the things he had done in self-defense, Phaedra thought he must have realized the truth by now. Narky had fled his home after killing someone; that was why he had been so desperate to get on the boat that took them to the continent. Here then was the crossbow bolt that had turned Narky into a murderer, and saved his life.

"So," Hunter said, rubbing his eyes. "So. What... how are we supposed to get to Karsanye now? Our enemies are between us and where we need to be, we haven't slept – there's no way I can fight them off. What do we do?"

Phaedra sighed and looked around. A dark cloud was coming across the island from the east, promising rain and maybe lightning too.

"We go back the way we came," she said. "And we pray."

25

NARKY

It took them almost two months to convert the former Temple of Magor into an acceptable temple of Ravennis. At first they worked alone, but as word spread of their presence, new followers of Ravennis began volunteering their support. Narky and Ptera set them to work destroying all the statues and figurines that had been so prominent in Magor's temple and painting over the devotional murals with pitch. It didn't look beautiful by any means, but it would do.

During their breaks, Narky preached. Phaedra had once read him a scroll by a priest of Ravennis, and he did his best to recall what he had learned from it. He was lucky that the people of Anardis knew even less about Ravennis than he did, because they never complained about his spotty knowledge, and when he didn't know the answer to one of their questions, he could always invent one. He wasn't much of a public speaker, but he was quick on his feet, so he would give only the barest of speeches and then spend the rest of the time answering questions.

The personal quarters of Magor's temple had had room for four priests to live there at one time, but Narky and Ptera kept it to themselves for now, luxuriating in its space and making prodigious use of the beds. They pushed two of these together to give themselves more room to sleep once their lovemaking was done, and slept more comfortably than Narky had in his life.

They made love constantly. The excitement of being newly married was mutual and overwhelming, and Ptera's reactions convinced him that he was getting better at it. He had never felt so confident, so alive.

He was starting to really like Ptera. She was a schemer like him, even if she wouldn't admit it, and they shared a similar sense of humor. It was a wonder he hadn't discovered this back in Ardis, or perhaps it was no wonder at all. He had barely spoken to her at the time, except when she was delivering news. Their similarities hadn't come up.

Twice a week, Narky would go to visit the Great Temple of Elkinar and speak with Mother Dinendra. For all that she had forsworn politics, she was a very practical, political sort of leader, and Narky was convinced that her support was the key to converting Ardis. Elkinar had a real and widely-accepted presence there, and as Magor's power waned, Dinendra's influence in Ardis was not to be overlooked. What her priests taught, the people would accept.

The trouble was Dinendra's second-in-command and likely successor, Father Sephas. Sephas was a true theologian – Phaedra had loved him – and he would not accept the notion of an alliance between their two priesthoods without an airtight theological reason for thinking that Elkinar and Ravennis were really allies. Dinendra liked Narky and enjoyed their meetings, but she agreed with Sephas on this matter, so unless Narky could somehow convince him on a theological level, her support would remain tacit.

He thought he could manage it, if he just framed it the right way. Elkinar and Eramia were supposed to be siblings, and the islanders had guessed that Eramia and Ravennis must have been working together to fulfill the Dragon Knight's prophecy and bring about a Judgment of the Gods. It was the Oracle of Ravennis that had told Hunter's father to send him to the continent, Ravennis who had kept an eye on Narky and marked him with His power. Eramia, in the meantime, had goaded the island's patron Goddess just as Narky and Hunter, Phaedra, Bandu and Criton were about to leave. As a result, the five of them had escaped the island at the last possible moment, sealing their fates as wanderers of the continent. Without this, the dragon Salemis might never have been rescued, and Magor's army never destroyed.

Narky even wondered sometimes whether Eramia had had a direct hand in turning him into the prophesied murderer. The girl he had loved back in his village had been called Eramia too, and it was her lover Narky had killed. How much of a coincidence could that possibly have been?

The trouble was that Elkinar did not seem to have had a part in any of this, for all that His sister was so deeply involved. But then, perhaps that shouldn't have surprised anyone. Phaedra had once told Narky and the other islanders about a theory that all the familial relations between Gods were invented by people, just as the Gods' genders supposedly were. According to this theory, the Gods were all equally related or unrelated, but had been grouped together thematically into 'families' because people understood the world better that way. If this was true, there was no real reason to expect Elkinar to be on Eramia's side.

It was interesting that Elkinar and Ravennis were not said to be brothers, considering that Narky would have thought Their domains must overlap quite a lot: the God of the Life Cycle and the Lord of the Underworld should have had a lot in common. But then, Narky was no theologian – he was just some poor sap who'd been named high priest by an Oracle who should, of all people, have known better.

At least he had Ptera to talk to about it, if he ever had the courage to tell her how little he knew. He thought that if he could only speak freely, as he had with his friends, he might talk his way through to something really meaningful. But he didn't dare reveal the depth of his ignorance – not yet, anyway. For all that she might enjoy him physically, he knew that it was his supposed connection to Ravennis that had attracted her to him in the first place.

So he stayed silent, and learned nothing, and felt once again like a coward. And all the while people came to him with their gifts and their labor, and looked up to him as if he knew something. What would they do if they ever realized how little he deserved his position?

Of course, he also felt ridiculous for failing to appreciate their respect, now that he finally had some. He'd left home less than a year and a half ago, and look how far he'd come! In Tarphae he'd been miserable, alone, disrespected, and full of self-doubt. Now here he was: High Priest of Ravennis, happily married, sought out by followers for his wisdom… and still full of self-doubt.

Was this something immutable about his personality? He should have been confident, considering how well things were going. The new Temple of Ravennis was looking less and less like a painted-over Temple of Magor, and worshippers were beginning to come by not to help convert the building, but to make sacrifices. They made sacrifices when a loved one died, begging the Lord Among the Fallen to watch over their departed family members in kindness, and they made sacrifices when things went well for them, thanking Ravennis as the Keeper of Fates. Narky did his best for them. They weren't exactly wrong to come to him: no living person knew more about what Ravennis had been up to than Narky did. The trouble was that only he seemed to realize what a tragedy that was.

For there had been news from Ardis: the Graceful Servant had been publicly executed, as had every other follower of Ravennis that could be found. General Magerion had been given free rein at home while his companions on the council were at war, and he had made his focus the persecution of the Ravennis worshippers. The remarkable thing was that the cult had survived, even in Ardis. He knew this because a trickle of Ardismen kept making the pilgrimage to Anardis and Narky, to give sacrifices and receive guidance on how to proceed. It had happened just as the Graceful Servant had predicted: she had been martyred to their God, and it had only made Him stronger.

Narky wished he had a good answer for the Ardismen who came to him. His instinct was to tell them to stay away from Ardis, to save themselves and, if possible, their families, and make new lives in this safer city. Ardis was fighting a two-front war against him and Criton's army, and things were bound to get worse before they got better.

But he couldn't say that. It didn't matter that the cult of Ravennis was growing in Anardis, and that the people here were safe for now: Ardis was the prize his God wanted. The Graceful Servant had ordered him to come back someday soon, to wrest Magor's city from its doomed God and make His punishment complete. The Ravennis-worshippers left in Ardis were there to pave the way – they could not flee.

So Narky told them to go back, and to keep converting their friends and neighbors in secret. Yes, many of them would be captured and killed, but Ravennis would watch over them in the underworld, and He would favor all those who had died in His name. He told them to show no fear, no matter what happened. Life was short; Ravennis was eternal.

His followers loved that. He wished he did too.

It was wrong of the Graceful Servant, wrong of Ravennis to make Narky His High Priest. Narky was a coward and a coward's son, a man who would never give his life voluntarily for *any* cause. Ravennis was forever, yes, but life was *now*. How could such a man be asked to send people to their deaths, to encourage them to *love* their deaths? It was too cruel, to them and to Narky too.

But this was what his God demanded of him, and he could not shirk his duty. He'd had Ravennis angry at him before, and didn't ever want to put himself in that position again.

If only the priests of Elkinar had been able to grant their support and not just their neutrality, Narky might have felt that he could send his followers back to Ardis as the vanguard of an army instead of as martyrs. He must try to convince them. It might be hard, but the options didn't get any easier from there. It was certainly better than the Graceful Servant's path.

This time when he and Ptera visited the Temple of Elkinar, Narky did not shy away from theological debate. They were all sitting crowded around the library table, sipping a strong wine that had been donated to the temple, when Narky asked, "Have you wondered why there haven't been any real fights between the followers of Ravennis and the followers of Elkinar? A new God has come to power here in Anardis, but Elkinar doesn't seem to mind."

"Well," said Mother Dinendra, "I don't mind taking a little bit of credit now and then. I've practically encouraged Magor's followers to turn to Ravennis as a secondary God, once it became clear that they would not turn over their whole being to Elkinar. Magor always satisfied people's needs for a God of power and domination, and Elkinar was never one to fill that role. Our priests are healers and midwives, and our God a sustainer of balance. Let Magor's place be filled by your God – as long as there is life-sustaining balance, Elkinar can never be threatened. That was my theory, anyway."

"Are you saying you think your God has stepped aside to let Ravennis in, just because Elkinar hasn't historically been the only God of Anardis? Why shouldn't He try to take more?"

"Because 'taking more' is not Elkinar's way!" Father Sephas scolded. "He is not some crafty nobleman, always maneuvering for more power. All of life is His domain."

Narky snorted. "In one breath you say that He has no interest in power, and then you turn around and say He's in charge of all of life. If claiming all of life as your domain isn't maneuvering for power, what is?"

Mother Dinendra's countenance hardened. "Have you come today to insult Elkinar in His own temple?"

That stopped Narky short. Why was he so bad at this? He was trying to build a theological argument for a pre-existing alliance between Ravennis and Elkinar, one that he thought was really good, and his base rudeness was getting in his way.

Even Ptera was staring at him, aghast. She hadn't understood what he was trying to do either – he'd done a truly terrible job of explaining himself.

His mistake was that in his attempt to point out how welcoming Elkinar had been to them, he hadn't expected Sephas to push back against the very notion of godly ambition. That had thrown him off, and he'd fallen back on his usual argumentative style. Idiot. If he was going to make this work, he had to control himself.

"I'm sorry," he said. "I haven't come to insult Elkinar, but to exalt Him for the warm welcome He's shown to me and my God. I only meant to say that Elkinar didn't *have* to be so welcoming, He *could* have tried to fill Magor's role by Himself and become the only God of Anardis. Instead, He and His servants have welcomed us into His city and even into His house, this temple. I meant to express my gratitude."

"You are young," Mother Dinendra said indulgently. "Tact is not one of the strengths youth has over age."

Narky nodded, relieved. "Thank you. You're absolutely right."

Father Sephas waved a hand. "Go on, then. Let's start from the point you were trying to make."

Narky looked to Ptera for strength and tried to regain his composure. "Well," he said, "in any case, Elkinar *could* have made a play for sole patron of Anardis, but He didn't. You might say that's because ambition isn't in His nature, but I think He's been uniquely welcoming to Ravennis. I can't imagine that He'd have supported, say, Atun, if the Sun God had tried to capitalize on Magor's weakness here."

"Perhaps not," Dinendra conceded.

"I think it's not a matter of Elkinar lacking for ambition. I think He *wants* Ravennis here."

"You think They are allies," Father Sephas concluded. "Yes, Narky, we've heard this from you before. You even make a very good case for it–"

"That's not what I'm saying," Narky said, to his own surprise.

"I'm saying They're the same God."

The room went silent. Narky closed his eye and waited. Would Ravennis slay him for saying what he'd just said? Would Elkinar? What had possessed him to say such a thing? He was practically *begging* the Gods to smite him.

Nothing happened. Narky opened his eye. They were all staring at him. Of course they were.

"What?" Ptera asked.

"I think," Narky said, and stopped. His hands were shaking. "I think that may have been a prophecy."

"What do you mean?" asked Father Taemon.

No God had smitten him yet. How could he make sense of this?

"I don't think those were my words," he said. "I mean, I said them, but they just came to me as I was saying them, and, well, and They haven't killed me yet. Is it – is it possible that Ravennis and Elkinar are one and the same?"

"We've had no reason to think so," said Father Sephas. "Up until now."

"But it's possible."

"Anything is possible, if the Gods say it."

"No," Narky said, "I mean, yes, but I think it's plausible too. When I was with the other islanders, two Gods were clearly guiding us: Ravennis and Eramia. We had no idea why those two should be allies, but Eramia and Elkinar are brother and sister, right? If Ravennis *is* Elkinar, the alliance makes perfect sense.

"When my friends and I came here, to Anardis, it was the priests of Elkinar who took us in and sheltered us before Bestillos invaded. And it was Elkinar's sister Eramia who gave us what we needed to find the Dragons' Prisoner and rescue him, and to destroy the armies of Magor and Mayar. I think this really is a prophecy. I think Elkinar is the sole God of Anardis; we've just been worshipping His two halves.

"Their domains are perfectly complementary. Keeper of Fates; God of Birth, Life, Death, and Rebirth; God of the Life

Cycle; God of the Underworld. They're the same God."

"If what you say is true," Sephas asked, "how could Magor not have known it? Why should He and Elkinar live in peace even as Magor sent Bestillos to destroy Laarna?"

"I–" Narky began, but he had no answer, nothing beyond the fact that he had said the two Gods were one, and neither had killed him for it. "I don't know," he finished.

"Thank you, Narky," Mother Dinendra said, indicating the end of his visit. "You have given us a lot to discuss – it will take much more than an evening, I think, to tease out the various implications of what you have said tonight. It may be too early to assume that neither God has taken offense, but if in a week's time you still have not been punished, we may have to accept that both Elkinar and Ravennis endorse your statement. Hopefully by then we will have arrived at a good theological explanation."

They bowed to their hosts and left, still trying to process what had been said.

"She's being too cautious," Ptera said during their walk home. "Ravennis spoke through you. Anyone could see that."

"Not everyone, I guess. And she's right that I don't have all the answers. I don't think it'll hurt for them to spend a week figuring out what all this means."

Ptera's mouth twisted. "And making sure that Elkinar remains the dominant half here in Anardis."

"You think so?" That gave him a lot to think about. Ptera didn't stumble into her words the way he did – she always thought before she spoke. If she thought that power-hunger played a role in Mother Dinendra's thinking, she wasn't just saying so reflexively.

Ptera gave him a look that expressed just how naïve his question sounded. "She has a priesthood to protect."

"You're probably right," he said, when they got indoors. "And she'd be wise to make sure of it, really. Who knows if what I said tonight was even true?"

Ptera stopped dead, one hand already reaching for the door

of their bedroom. "Are you telling me you were lying?"

He shook his head. "Of course not. Ravennis put those words in my mouth – I'm sure of that much. But what if *He* was lying? For all I know, the two of Them have been separate Gods all along and now He's trying to swallow Elkinar while He's got the chance. The Gods can shield us from each other – if this is a surprise attack, Elkinar won't be able to smite me unless He wins the struggle with Ravennis first."

"Narky!" she cried. "Do you even know what you're saying?"

He smiled. "You're only just getting to know me, Ptera. This is how I talk."

"But you're accusing your own God of treachery! You're His high priest, Narky, you can't go saying–"

"Do you think I know how this all works?" Narky snapped. "I'm seventeen, Ptera, for the Gods' sake! I'm not a theologian, and I was nobody's holy man until the Graceful Servant told me I was going to be high priest. I'm just trying to figure out the truth for myself, and to follow Ravennis' path wherever He leads me. If He's been Elkinar all along, great! If He's trying to usurp and co-opt Him, that's fine by me too. Ravennis is my God no matter what. But until He gives me clear guidance, I have to make guesses and talk these ideas through so I can figure out what I'm going to do about it. If He has a problem with that, He can send me a clear message for once and tell me what to do!"

Ptera was staring at him silently, her expression inscrutable. He wished he knew what she was thinking.

"I don't know what's going on right now," he admitted, "and if you want to know what I *think*, it's that we'll never really know. If Ravennis swallows Elkinar, there'll be no way to know for sure that They weren't the same God all along. I think Mother Dinendra is right to be wary of my prophecy. Our Gods might be united, but They also might be fighting in a life-or-death struggle as we speak, in which case Elkinar can't afford for His own high priestess to give up on Him. She can't trust me; she's doing the right thing for her God."

He could tell that Ptera didn't agree with him about something, but about what? Why wasn't she saying anything?

"I don't know," he sputtered on, unable to stop talking. "Maybe it's over already. Maybe They weren't the same God before, but They are now. The thing is, if it *is* a fight, and the fight isn't over, this could get really ugly. Even if Ravennis can shield me from other divine powers, an independent Elkinar might be able to tell Mother Dinendra the truth – assuming for now that the truth is different from what I said it was."

At this, Ptera finally spoke. "Stop doubting yourself, and stop doubting our God. Ravennis doesn't lie, Narky."

He shrugged. "Ravennis made the world think He was dead, then wormed His way into Magor's territory and started undermining Him from within. He made me shoot a man in the back, or at least rewarded me for doing it myself. You can say that Ravennis doesn't lie, but what do we know? No straightforward, honorable God would have chosen me for His high priest."

To Narky's surprise, Ptera caught his face between her hands and kissed him hard. With her hands still firmly on his cheeks, she said, "I love you, Narky, but you don't understand yourself at all. I'm sure you have all sorts of flaws, but dishonesty isn't one of them! Whatever His reasons, Ravennis didn't choose you because you're a good liar. What man in your position would admit to his wife that he doesn't know what's going on? What high priest would speculate that his God chose him for nefarious reasons? You can't even hold your thoughts inside you for long, let alone mask them in deception. The truth shines through you."

"Thanks," Narky said. "Are you going to let go of me now?"

"No," she answered, and kissed him again. There was no more talk of Gods that night.

In the morning, however, the work began. Ptera was right, after all: it wouldn't do for Narky to doubt his own God. Even if the prophecy wasn't strictly true yet, Ravennis would want him to act as though it was.

So Narky called a festival in honor of the prophecy he had been given, and sent Ptera to spread the word throughout the city. The priests of Elkinar were caught flat-footed – they had apparently not settled on a response yet, nor had their God given them any visions to contradict Narky's prophetic words. As such, Narky was able to spread his message of the Gods' unity for two full days without any story competing with his. That was perfect: without disagreement from the priests of Elkinar, people assumed that Narky's version of events must be true. When they asked him what would become of the two separate priesthoods, Narky demurred magnanimously, saying that the One God had yet to guide him on such political questions. The priesthoods need not merge overnight.

As for the people's everyday practice, Narky told his followers to dedicate all future prayers and sacrifices to "Ravennis, who is Elkinar". He defied the priests across the way to find a reason for complaint – after all, wasn't he doubling the number of prayers and sacrifices directed at their God? Of course, it was quite possible that Ravennis and Elkinar had always been one. That was what Ptera thought. But if there *was* a struggle in the heavens, he meant to win it for Ravennis.

The next time he and Ptera visited, Father Sephas was furious. "What is this you've been spreading while our backs were turned? We were to coordinate our teachings!"

"I'm sorry," Narky said, "I thought you were just waiting to see if Elkinar struck me down. He still has time to, you know. I'm sure if He smites me tomorrow, the people will reject my teachings without any argument."

Ptera was right – he was terrible at concealing his thoughts. That had come out far more biting than he'd wanted it to, and exactly as biting as he'd meant it.

"Be careful," Father Taemon said. "The Gods can work through men as well, and this is still Elkinar's city."

Narky's stomach clenched. Oh Ravennis below, why hadn't he thought of that? If Narky was beaten to death here in the Great Temple of Elkinar, who would deny that his teachings had proven false? Could he make a break for it if he needed to?

Mother Dinendra smiled innocently at him. "I'm sure Narky didn't mean to offend us. He is young, and has yet to learn tactful speech. He was not raised to be High Priest of Ravennis, but had the position thrust upon him."

"Yes," Narky said, sizing up the room. "I apologize."

Without Mother Dinendra, who was old and frail, there were still five priests of Elkinar and only Narky and Ptera to face them. What's more, the door behind him was closed – he doubted he could get it open and slip out before they were upon him, and of course, there was Ptera to consider too. And even if they did escape, where would they flee to? The very act of running would be seen as a defeat for Ravennis, a proof that Narky's teachings had all been lies. There was no way around it: he was at the priests of Elkinar's mercy.

"We have a theological quandary here," Mother Dinendra said. "I have discussed it with Father Sephas and we see two distinct possibilities: either Narky's words the other night were truth, and Elkinar and Ravennis are one, or else Ravennis is attempting to usurp Elkinar's place in the heavens even as He festers in the world below. If I had to guess, Narky, I would say that you were operating under the latter assumption."

Narky gulped. "I considered the possibility."

"And yet," Mother Dinendra said, "you are as ignorant of the truth as we are. Without Elkinar's word on the matter, we can't know whether the right course of action is for us to join our priesthoods together or, if you'll pardon me Narky, to kill the two of you immediately."

"Ravennis doesn't lie," Ptera said, but her voice shook with fear.

"Well," said Mother Dinendra, "therein lies the quandary. If our Gods are truly one, then to kill the two of you would be unspeakable blasphemy. Elkinar may well do to us what Karassa did to Tarphae. I would rather not risk it, which is why I had *suggested* that we take a week to sort out the truth. By spreading word of the prophecy, however, Narky has forced our hand."

"If you guess wrong," Narky warned, "it'll mean the death of your people."

"If I guess wrong on the other side, it'll mean the death of my God."

Narky fell silent. His talking wasn't helping. He hadn't thought that Mother Dinendra was especially attached to her God – she had told him once that she had only joined Elkinar's priesthood as a way to keep herself and her children out of politics. Only now did he realize how little contradiction there was between that fact and the possibility that she might take her role as high priestess of Elkinar seriously.

"What are you going to do?" Ptera asked.

"Barring an answer from the heavens," Dinendra said, "I'm going to have to devise a test. Luckily, just such a test has presented itself."

"It has?"

The old priestess smiled. "Oh, yes. I received word today that General Magerion of Ardis is on his way here with a hundred men. Apparently, he wishes to take Narky back to Ardis with him. Ravennis has proven quite well that He can take advantage of His followers' deaths, but if He is truly one with Elkinar, He will also be able to sustain their lives. So I propose that you go with Magerion peacefully, and see what happens.

"I do not enjoy being rushed, Narky, so let me be clear and precise this time: today is the seventh day of the eighth month. If in a year or more you come back to Anardis and give a sacrifice on Elkinar's altar, then it will be proof that our Gods are one."

26

BANDU

The Ardismen never recovered from Bandu's ambush. Though their general had escaped, their army did not reform, and after two days in pursuit, Criton turned the people northward again. By now, a steady trickle of refugees was joining them, bringing news of the second army's movements. Criton did not think it would take long to catch them.

He was wrong. The second army managed to slip by them and hurry homeward, and Criton was left trying to chase them down with no real hope of catching up. Belkos said they should march straight down to Ardis and besiege the city. Bandu begged Criton not to try.

"They are so many more than us," she said, "and they have walls. You can't win there, but you already win here! They are too afraid to fight you. The plain people are happy without Ardis. We can make a new home for the Dragon Touched here!"

But Criton would not listen. He was angry because the second army had gotten away from him, and it was no good talking to Criton when he was angry. He stopped listening. Even Delika avoided him for a day or two, and Bandu wouldn't let him handle Goodweather until she was sure he'd be able to control himself. That made him even angrier, which made her trust him less, and on and on it went.

She relied even more on Dessa and Vella to help her, since

Iona's time was often spent now taking care of her mother. Partha was getting worse, it seemed. Her balance was bad, and she couldn't walk so fast, so she rode on a friend's mule when the camp was moving, and made demands of Iona whenever they stopped to rest. It was enough to make Bandu glad that she had no mother of her own.

Dessa split her time between visiting Bandu and helping take care of her grandmother, but Vella was available almost every evening. She still seemed scared of Bandu, but at least she was useful. She doted on Goodweather, really, and she also had much more patience for Delika than Bandu did. Bandu was too unkind to her.

Vella and her husband were not close the way Bandu and Criton were, for all their fighting. They were not friends, and from what Bandu could tell, they spent very little time together. That was the problem with choosing mates the way the Dragon Touched had – parents chose mates for their children not to make them happy, but to keep them safe. This might have worked to keep their neighbors from finding them, but it was too easy to make mistakes and pair children who didn't like each other.

It would not always be this way, at least. Dessa had been supposed to marry Vella's younger brother, but that had been put off when the Dragon Touched went to war. There was no time for weddings and no need to hide now, so Dessa might even get to wait until she was Bandu's age and could choose for herself. Dessa was very happy about that.

But then, Bandu sometimes wondered if even that was old enough – sometimes she thought she might have chosen Criton too soon. She loved him, and the two of them knew each other better than they knew anybody, but he was not a good mate – he was easily distracted, he let his worries spill onto Bandu and their daughter, and of course, he had never been good at controlling his anger. His father had broken that in him.

He *wanted* to be better, of course – that was why she hadn't left him yet. He always tried, or almost always, and if he failed…

well, it was still his fault, and she didn't forgive him for it. But at least it was understandable.

It scared her how little she wanted him sometimes. She had once needed him so desperately that any separation had been painful, but now... well, she had changed. Baby Goodweather needed her more than Criton did, and she took up so much of her mother's time and energy that Bandu had less interest in trying to fix Criton. Now if he said or did something bad, or ignored her when he should have been paying attention, Bandu just rolled her eyes and went to someone else for help.

Sometimes she dreamt she had Four-foot back, and could live just with him and Goodweather in the shadow of the Yarek. The wolf and the tree would protect her from harm better than any army could, and they would never make her feel like the pack was more important than she was. That was how life should be. Why couldn't Criton have given her a life like that?

She knew why, of course: because he would have been miserable all alone with her. As much as he loved her, being alone with a mate and a child was not his dream. He too had grown up in isolation, but his isolation had been very different from hers, and he had hated it in a way that she knew she would never completely understand. He had always wanted to be part of a big pack that loved and accepted him – he needed the Dragon Touched even more than they needed him. Bandu couldn't ask him to abandon the people he had been looking for all his life.

But then, when had Criton ever asked Bandu if she wanted to be part of a Dragon Touched army? If the pressures of being part of this pack were too much for him, serve him right! Maybe if things got bad enough, he'd be willing to try it her way for once.

She had never felt so powerless as she did now, among these people, with a baby to take care of. It was one thing to choose a mate and then rely on him for support, and it was another thing entirely to have to rely on help from his cousin's family so that she wouldn't be overwhelmed. It was one thing to travel with a pack that didn't always understand her, and it was another to be surrounded by people who called her a foreign witch.

When she needed reassurance, Bandu looked to the Yarek. It was always visible, at least from here, stretching from the ground to the sky like a living pillar holding up the world. It was her connection to who she was, and it was ready to help her if she called.

But though she drew strength from its presence, she never reached into the earth again to speak to it. She was afraid of what it might offer her. It may have come from Goodweather's seed, but it wasn't like a child. The Yarek was dangerous, much more dangerous than people realized. It wasn't just a tree, and it didn't really hold up the world. It split it.

But it was tempting to look toward it anyway whenever she felt misunderstood. Unlike the Dragon Touched, the Yarek was grateful for what she'd done on its behalf. Unlike the Dragon Touched, it did not fear her. And unlike any person she had ever met, it did not fear the Gods.

Bandu didn't fear the Gods either, not the way other people did. All her kind worshipped the Gods out of fear, because that was what They wanted. There was good reason to be afraid, of course – Bandu had seen the Gods do great and terrible things – but that only made her angrier about Their meddling. It made her want to stand like the Yarek and cry, *You cannot destroy me. You can cut me down and tear me to pieces, but I will always grow back.*

She did not say these things to Criton.

She wondered if Hessina knew; if that was why the high priestess was so unwelcoming to her. Could she sense that Bandu did not respect her God? Was that why they all shunned her, why they seemed so afraid of her? Maybe it wasn't her foreignness that bothered them. Maybe it was her fearlessness.

One evening, when they had all made their camp again and Criton was out with Delika, learning prayers or rituals or something from Hessina, Bandu decided to make Vella tell her what made her so scary. The other girl was playing with baby

Goodweather while Bandu arranged the bedding for the night, and Bandu turned on her and asked, "Why you're so afraid of me?"

Vella's eyes widened in horror. She looked trapped.

"You are always afraid of me," Bandu said. "I don't do anything to you, but you are afraid anyway. Why?"

"You're a bit intimidating," Vella answered quietly. Her face was starting to turn red.

"Then why you come here, if you are so afraid?"

"I like coming here."

Bandu didn't believe her. "You don't look like that. You don't look happy – always you're scared of me just like everybody else. Why do you come here?"

"Do you want to see less of me?" Vella asked meekly.

Bandu made a frustrated sound. "No, I want you to answer."

"Because you're so beautiful," the girl nearly whispered.

"What?"

"I said, because–"

"I hear you; I don't understand. What do you mean, I am beautiful? Why that makes you afraid?"

Vella stood shakily and handed Goodweather back to her. "Do you want to hold her again? I have to go."

And like that, she fled.

Bandu stood holding Goodweather for a long time. What had just happened between them? Did Vella want to be Bandu's mate? She hadn't said so, but that was what it seemed like. But Bandu already had a mate, besides which, she hardly knew Vella – the girl had always been too afraid to talk to her. It almost made her laugh, though, to think that she had thought Vella could explain why everyone was afraid of her. She had assumed that Vella had the same reasons as everyone else, but that obviously wasn't true – she was fairly sure the other Dragon Touched weren't afraid of her because she was beautiful.

It was a nice thing to hear, that someone besides Criton thought she was beautiful. The thought made her smile. She liked Vella much more now that she knew why the other girl had been shy with her. Bandu thought they might talk a lot more after this, since Vella had apparently said the thing she'd been so afraid to say before. She looked forward to it. It had been so lonely thinking that everyone hated her.

But she did not see much of Vella for the next few days. Maybe the girl was too embarrassed to see her.

In the meantime, the Dragon Touched camp moved closer to Ardis by the day. As time went on, Criton was beginning to admit that his plan for attacking made no sense. He had won his battles against the Ardismen by making them run away, but as he said now, no army would run when its city was at its back.

Not everyone agreed. Sitting in the tent where they held their meetings, Criton's cousin said that the Dragon Touched ought to march straight to the gates of Ardis and demand that they open, just as the gates of Anardis had opened to the red priest.

"And what if they don't open their gates?" Criton asked. "If they shoot arrows at us, and throw rocks, and never open the gates? What'll we do then? We've won our battles so far, with the help of God Most High, but we've won them by making our enemies flee us. For those in Ardis, there is nowhere to flee. I'd love to think that they'd surrender to us, but we can't afford to assume they will."

"What do you mean to do, then?" Belkos said. "Give up on Ardis? Settle in these lands and worry about them attacking for the rest of our lives and our children's lives? Let them laugh at our God, and say that He was unable to overcome a stone wall? We can't do that."

"You can," Bandu pointed out, burping Goodweather.

Belkos pointed at her angrily. "Why is she here? She's not one of us; she doesn't represent any clan of Dragon Touched or plainsmen. Who does she speak for?"

"I value her judgment."

His cousin snorted. "I don't."

"It was her idea that won us the fight against Xytos' army!"

Criton cried. "How can you say she doesn't belong here?"

"We didn't win on your wife's tactics," Belkos said. "We won because God Most High willed it. She doesn't even worship Him! Consult with her in the bedding of your tent if you feel the need, but she doesn't belong in this council. Think for yourself and speak for yourself, cousin – God Most High named *you* our leader, not this girl wife of yours."

Criton looked into Belkos' eyes for a long time, while Hessina, her son, and the elders of the plainsfolk all stared at Bandu. Their gazes made her angry. Why shouldn't she be here? She was no less a leader than Hessina's timid son, and she had done as much as anyone to help these people win their stupid war. What's more, she had had to beg Iona to watch Delika for her – or really for Criton, but he was always ready to foist the girl on Bandu for these sorts of occasions – so that she could come to this meeting and be heard.

She secretly hoped Criton would lose control and yell at his cousin, maybe even threaten him. She knew from experience how frightening it could be when Criton lost his temper, and Belkos had insulted both of them, on purpose. He deserved to be scared.

Instead, Criton just sighed. "You'd better go, Bandu."

"No." He had promised to listen to her, after the pigs. He had promised!

Criton's eyes flashed. "Go, Bandu."

Bandu stood up, barely able to contain her shock and her fury. "You are sorry later," she said.

"The longer it takes you to leave, the sorrier I'll be."

27
CRITON

Hessina was the first to speak after Bandu left. "You need a new wife, Criton. A Dragon Touched wife. Bandu presumes too much."

Criton resisted telling her to mind her own business and tried to turn the conversation back to Ardis, but the others would not let him. "Your high priestess is right," said Endra, an elder from one of the larger clans of plainsmen. "My first wife was like yours: she thought she could control me. Take another wife, and she'll realize she has nothing you couldn't find elsewhere."

Another elder, Kana, added, "She'll hate your other wife for it, though. Two is not enough. Two wives will become enemies, and their rivalry will consume all your happiness. Take at least a third, and maybe a fourth. They'll learn to live together and be kind to you when they realize that a fight between two of them will only benefit a third. Take several more wives, Criton. The Dragon Touched have married all their older girls away already – take a few from among our daughters while you wait for your own to mature."

Criton shook his head. Their advice was all self-serving, besides which, it was horrible. Criton had promised. These men just wanted to weaken Bandu's influence, and to raise their own. They wanted to bind their families to the leader of the Dragon Touched, to strengthen their positions and claim a larger say over the decisions of the group.

But then, what was wrong with that? A handful of plainsmen had already made marriage pacts with the Dragon Touched for after the war, and a good number had pledged themselves to God Most High and begun abiding by Hessina's rules for them. Perhaps the time had come to cement these alliances, to call the plainsmen Dragon Touched as well and stop treating them as if they were lesser allies for their lack of claws. Even if it meant sacrificing his promise to Bandu not to take another wife, might it not be worth it? He was the political leader of his people. Could he afford to be so selfish?

He could see the disapproval in Hessina's expression – she didn't want him to marry outside his kin. But she was letting her prejudices get the better of her: the political benefits of accepting the plainsmen's offers were unmistakable. Right now, this alliance was held together only by the common enemy of Ardis, and by the fear that otherwise the Dragon Touched would maraud across the plains themselves. If Criton cemented his alliances with a few marriages, he could then call the northern plainsmen a *part* of the Dragon Touched. Then his people would not even be so many fewer than the Ardismen.

Besides, what if the elders were right? What if the addition of wives could actually improve his relationship with Bandu? There had been tension between them, always. The other women could help with Delika and Goodweather, and make the times when Bandu was angry with him more bearable. And if that made him more patient, might it not be worth it for her too?

"I'll think about it," he promised the clan leaders. "Now can we please get back to the question of Ardis?"

"So long as God Most High takes our side," Belkos said, "we can't lose. Everyone knows how Bestillos took Anardis without the loss of a single soldier. It was the fear of him that opened the city's gates, not the strength of his army. What has given us our victories over the Ardismen time and again? Their fear of us."

"Their fear of God Most High," Hessina corrected him. "It is the God Above All who granted us these victories, and set His terror upon the soldiers of Ardis. Do not take our God for granted, as our ancestors the dragons did."

"We shouldn't doubt Him either," Belkos countered. "You think you know better than He does whether we're worthy of taking Ardis? Let our God judge our readiness. If He favors us, we can't lose."

"But if He doesn't favor our attack," Criton pointed out, "we're unlikely to get a second chance. If we assume that God Most High wants us to conquer the city and we're wrong, the Ardismen might easily take advantage and annihilate us entirely. Our God hasn't actually told us we ought to take Ardis, and we've been wrong about His wishes before. All Salemis said was that if we followed God Most High, we would be safe. But for that, we need to know where He's leading us."

"Where to, then?" Belkos said. "If not Ardis, then where?"

"To the Dragon Knight's Tomb," said Hessina. "We will pray for guidance in the holiest place we know, and camp at the base of the mountain. It is near enough to Ardis to show them our lack of fear, and defensible in battle should they choose to risk another confrontation. We can stay there until God Most High lends us His guidance."

Kana turned to Criton. "What say you?"

"I say she's right," Criton answered, standing up. "Now I need to go and speak with my wife."

"Will you follow our advice?" asked Endra. "Will you marry a daughter of the plains?"

"Or several?" Kana put in.

Criton sighed. "You can put together a list, if you like. Women whose marriage to me would satisfy everyone here. I don't promise I'll take any of them."

He went back to his own tent, where he found Goodweather asleep and Bandu pretending. She hadn't bothered to go get Delika back – the girl must have been asleep in Belkos' tent by now.

"Bandu," he said, putting a clawed hand on her shoulder.

"Don't talk to me," she snapped.

"I'm sorry," he said. "But that meeting was necessary, and you weren't helping."

"Don't talk," Bandu repeated. "I don't care."

"Don't stop talking to me over this," Criton said. "That's not going to help either of us."

Bandu said nothing.

"Bandu, you can't keep doing this to me."

Silence.

"They want me to take more wives," Criton said, "and I have half a mind to listen to them."

He'd expected that to make her turn around and look at him at least, but she only stiffened and kept her face turned away from him.

"It makes sense," he said. "If I do it, it'll signal to the rest of the Dragon Touched that the plainsmen aren't just allies, they're brothers. Our people will intermarry and we won't be a big conglomeration of allied clans with the Dragon Touched at the top. We'll be one people. Bandu, are you listening? It makes sense, and the only thing stopping me from doing it is you. If you don't want me to take other wives, you have to say so. You have to talk to me."

Bandu did not turn. Why did she have to be so stubborn? They both knew that she hated the idea – if she had changed her mind, she'd have said so. Had she resigned herself to his doing whatever seemed right to him? Her body language didn't strike him as resigned.

Well then, it was her job to dissuade him! He wasn't going to spend the night arguing with himself.

"Fine," he said, "we'll talk about it in the morning, when you're ready to act like a civilized person."

He hated going to bed angry, but there was nothing for it. He lay down beside her, facing the opposite way, and went to sleep.

When he awoke, Bandu was gone.

28

Hunter

They stumbled back the way they had come, toward Karsanye and toward their enemies. Phaedra led them in a prayer to God Most High which she seemed to have composed herself. Hunter and Atella repeated the words after her as they shuffled down the road, trying not to collapse in their exhaustion. After a couple of times through, Phaedra realized that they could set her prayer to a tune that had once been popular at Tarphaean dances, so they sang it instead. Hunter was not very tuneful, and Atella was altogether unfamiliar with Tarphaean music, but Phaedra was very musical herself and her voice was clear and precise, so they soon caught on nonetheless.

Hunter kept his eyes down, watching his feet move, because whenever he looked up at the way ahead, his eyes blurred and he became dizzy. Even with his head down, he kept seeing things moving at the corners of his eyes, things that clearly weren't there. Stars shooting past. Giant insects. The disembodied heads of men he had killed.

He focused on the road.

If they were bound to be caught anyway, he wondered, why couldn't they just go to sleep? They'd had a sunny day or two now, and the dusty road looked like a perfectly good place for it. He imagined lying down with his head on that rock over there, and he nearly cried for wanting to. But no: if they slept, they could not pray, and they needed the prayers more.

Besides, the rock was shuddering. Gods, he needed to sleep.

If people had free will, as Phaedra was always insisting, then what good would all their prayers do them? God Most High could not force Mura to let them go, nor could He make them merciful. Could He? Maybe he could. Phaedra was very knowledgeable about these things, but she wasn't infallible.

Hunter chose to believe that the God of Dragons could do anything. It was easier to pray that way, and easier to stay awake too. To stay awake, and pray.

He thought he might be losing his mind.

Phaedra led them through repetition after repetition of her prayer-song, and Hunter began to grow impatient for Mura's men to meet them here already. What was taking them so long? They ought to get on with it, so he could see if God Most High would really answer their prayers. Did he dare to look up and try to spot them?

He chanced it, lifting his eyes from the road and willing them to focus, focus on *something*. He blinked. He stopped walking. He slapped himself in the face.

"Phaedra," he said.

Karsanye was standing before him, not half a mile away. He knew those ruined buildings. He slapped himself again, blinked again, again, again, again. His foolish eyes wouldn't stop seeing the city.

"Phaedra," he repeated, and the girl stopped and looked up.

"Karsanye?" she said. "How is that possible?"

Hunter fainted.

It was night-time when he awoke, still lying in the road. Phaedra was asleep beside him, with Atella softly snoring on her other side. They had apparently decided to sleep instead of rousing him, a decision for which he was extremely grateful. In fact, he thought he might sleep some more if he could – he had a bit of a headache still. He'd had the headache since sometime yesterday, he thought, but it had been so low on his list of problems that he'd barely noticed it before. Now he looked at the road ahead, saw that Karsanye was still there, and went back to sleep.

He woke to rain falling on his head. He groaned and sat up, wiping the mud off his cheeks and looking around. It looked to be dawn, though he couldn't be sure. The clouds were dark.

"How long have we slept?" Phaedra asked in a panicked voice. "We should go!"

"We should," Hunter agreed, rising to his feet and shielding his eyes as he gazed toward their ruined city. "How did we get here?"

"God Most High brought us here. He shortened our path somehow."

"I know, but how? Or why?"

Phaedra frowned. "I wish I knew. He's sent miracle after miracle, and I can't believe that it's because He wants me to learn magic. We must have something big we're supposed to do, He just hasn't revealed what it is yet. Let's find some shelter. Maybe Psander will know."

Psander. Would they truly be seeing her again, just a few short months after her departure from this world? He had hoped never to see the world of fairies again, and with that hope had come the assumption that he would never see Psander either. Wrong and wrong.

They took shelter under a tree until the rain lessened from a downpour to a steady patter. If God Most High was protecting them here, would He be able to do so in the world of the elves? Bandu had said – and everyone who knew anything about it had agreed – that instead of a mesh between the heavens and the fairy world, God Most High had built a wall. The Gods no longer had influence in the world of the fairies. If Hunter and Phaedra found themselves endangered there, there would be no miracles to rescue them.

At least it sounded like Psander was still alive, for now. That had hardly been guaranteed when they had helped her transport Silent Hall to the other world.

"Well," Atella said, "whatever reason your God has saved us, I'm very grateful to Him. I'd make a sacrifice, if I had an animal."

"Pray to Him," Phaedra suggested. "It's not much, but it'll have to do."

The girl nodded. "What do I say?"

So Phaedra led them in a thanksgiving prayer and they resumed walking toward the city. Atella tried to follow her map, but she needn't have: Hunter and Phaedra both knew where they were going. The only remaining patch on Atella's map belonged to Criton.

Up until he had joined them on the last boat out of Tarphae, Criton had lived with his mother in the prison of his father's house. Criton's father had hidden him from the world by claiming that his wife was deathly ill, and that only he could tend to her. Knowing Criton's side of the story, it hadn't taken them long to guess who his father had been. And that meant they knew where he lived.

It had been a two-storey house, but the earthquake had reduced it to two walls and a pile of rubble. Phaedra steered them to the door that still stood in one of the two walls – Criton's mother Galanea was bound to be somewhere in that pile of rubble, undevoured by scavengers who could not shift stone. There would be more of her than bones, and they had no desire to find out how much more.

But the door was locked, a sad irony that did not escape Hunter. So they went around after all, picking their way over the wet stones and hoping to find something that would represent Criton's essence, besides the corpse of his mother. There were plenty of objects in the rubble, so they collected as many as they could – the leg of a chair, the remains of what might have been a tapestry, feathers from some pillow that must still be trapped beneath the stone. But once they were a few feet from the house, the last corner of Atella's map always came back to life. They hadn't yet found what they were looking for.

"I sure hope…" Phaedra said, and didn't finish. Hunter knew

what she was thinking, even if Atella didn't.

"It'll be some object," Hunter insisted, in an attempt to reassure the both of them. "It has to be."

Atella raised a hand to stop them. "Do you hear that?"

Someone was whistling.

They scrambled to get behind one of the walls, praying that no one would find them. "Mura's ship is still at the docks," Phaedra whispered. "There must be some sailors around here."

They waited until they couldn't hear anything but their beating hearts, and then waited some more. When they felt the danger had passed, they left Atella as a lookout while they continued their search. That cut their manpower by a third, but at least Atella was still able to make runs back and forth away from the building to test each item they found. But every time she left them, the map came back to life.

The clouds passed, and the sun came out. Eventually Phaedra gave up her part in the search and sat down on the ragged edge of one of the walls, resting her uneven and aching legs. Hunter was left to pick through the rubble on his own.

"Try over there," Phaedra would say now and then, and Hunter didn't know if she had any special reason for indicating the spots she did, but he obeyed anyway.

He had just painstakingly freed a mangled pair of hearthside tongs when Atella called out to him.

"This is it!" she said. "You found it!"

Hunter dropped the tongs with an annoyed grunt – how many heavy stones had he had to lift to get the useless things out? – and stumbled his way over the wreckage to see what Atella was talking about. He couldn't even remember what the last item he'd given her had been.

Phaedra got there first. "Really?" she said.

It was a broken wooden bucket, with a metal handle bent and dangling from one side. A little rainwater had managed to collect at the bottom.

"The map stayed blank," Atella insisted. "See for yourself."

They walked twice as far from the house as usual, just to

make sure. "If there's a story behind this," Phaedra said, "I don't know it."

"Well," said Hunter, "let's get out of here."

They left Karsanye for the forest, making sure to avoid the route that led to Bennan's farm.

"I wonder what the map would have chosen for us," Hunter said, "if we hadn't been here ourselves."

Phaedra pondered that silently, chewing on one of their soggy breads. It was late afternoon by now, and Hunter had lost track of how many days they had left before their window closed. For one thing, he didn't know how long they had slept on the road. It could have been sixteen hours or forty. Considering their state in the days before, he didn't want to assume that it was the lower number.

"Do you think we'll be able to find the place where I met you?" Atella asked. "Because I'm completely lost."

Hunter looked to Phaedra, who shook her head. "I've been hoping that God Most High will lead us there. The mill has to be somewhere northeast of here, but I don't know how far west we'd gone before we met you. I wish Bandu were with us – she'd know."

Yes, Hunter thought ruefully, she would. Even on the continent, Bandu never failed to find whatever was needed at the time, be it food, water, or a safe path through the mountains. She probably knew the forests of Tarphae better than the wolves did.

Hunter had known that he would miss the others, but he hadn't realized how much. There were holes in his life where they belonged, just as there were holes for his parents and brother, and a hole for the man he had thought he would become. He had imagined once, vaguely, that the king's army would become a second, realer family the next time Tarphae went to war. That war had never come, but his need for its comradeship remained. He had grown to appreciate being one of five, but now even those five were dispersed. Phaedra alone was not enough.

"This way," Hunter said. "We should go north first and see what we reach."

He was no tracker, but he had studied a map of Tarphae some years ago, back when the thought of being invaded had been exciting rather than horrifying. When he thought back to those times, studying the maps, he realized that he could still visualize all the little blue squiggles that represented rivers and streams. If they went north early enough, they were bound to meet the Sennaroot river that ran past Mura's mill. From there, he might be able to retrace their steps.

They followed his instincts and his lead, and within an hour or two they found a little stream that ran northwest. They drank there, pondering their next move. Hunter was sure that this stream was too narrow to be the Sennaroot, especially after the morning's rains. It must be a tributary, in which case it should meet the river at some point. He thought if they came to the place where the rivers met, he'd know how to proceed from there.

So they crossed the stream and followed it westward as the clouds and rain returned, turning the whole world gray. The stream did meet a larger river not long thereafter, much to Hunter's relief. If memory served – and if this was indeed the Sennaroot – there would be a ford not too far upriver. They changed directions again.

As they walked, Phaedra asked Atella what interactions the people of Silent Hall had had with the elves.

"They're horrible," Atella said with a shudder. "Their queen came to talk to Psander, and promised to leave us alone for ten years if we'd give her four 'breeding pairs.' Psander said they want to eat us. She said no to the queen, but every week or two she comes back with her guards and asks again. We didn't want to go outside after the first time she came, but we had to cut down the trees and try to farm or we'd have had nothing to eat. Psander made a ward that tells us when the elves are close, so we run back in when they're coming."

"They have a queen?" Hunter asked. "We met a prince, but I

didn't know they had a queen."

"I don't know anything about a prince. The queen is so frightening I can't even say, and her guards are just as bad. They have no tongues, and they clack at you."

"Did Psander let them in?" Phaedra asked, horrified.

"No, I saw them from the walls. Everyone told me not to climb up there and look, but I thought I wasn't afraid."

Hunter shook his head. "The elves are worth fearing."

"I know that well enough now. You don't have to tell me."

They spent that night in the forest, which was somehow infinitely less comfortable than the road had been the night before. Hunter suspected that this had very little to do with the wet ground and much more to do with their better-rested state before they went to sleep this time. Whatever the reason, Hunter awoke cold, wet, and sore. His neck was stiff, his right arm numb from having been used as a pillow, and when he tried to rise, he found that one of his feet was still asleep. It tingled for nearly a minute after he got up, and hurt whenever he stepped on it.

The others followed his lead for the rest of the day, and for the entire afternoon he felt that they were maddeningly close to the spot they were looking for. He had brought them as far as his memory for maps could take him, but that still wasn't enough to take them the rest of the way. At best, he had narrowed down their location to somewhere within two or three square miles of where they wanted to be. He missed Bandu even more.

Phaedra went back to praying, and Hunter began to wonder whether she might wear Criton's God out with all these requests for successively smaller things. God Most High had shortened their path to Karsanye and thus allowed them to evade their pursuers – could He be bothered to help with this last insignificant task, which any competent woodsman would have been able to figure out on his own?

On the other hand, why shouldn't He? If God Most High had taken them this far, how strange would it be for Him to abandon them right before they could reach their goal?

Hunter didn't ask Atella any more about Psander's dealings with the fairies, but that did not stop him from thinking about them. He had felt guilty knowing that the islanders' salvation from the armies of Magor and Mayar had come at the cost of exposing Psander and the villagers to a world full of child-eating demons – Auntie Gava's term for the elves had been a good one. But he had had the comfort, at least, of not being forced to think about it terribly often while he and Phaedra were busy following her quest for magic. Now he had to face the reality of what they had done to Psander and her villagers, and it was horrifying.

He wished he could believe that Psander knew what she was doing; that she could stand up to the elves and win; that she could protect herself and those she had come with. From what he'd heard so far, it seemed highly unlikely. The very fact that Psander was relying on Hunter and his friends as magical ingredients for her wards was damning. After all, it wasn't as if the islanders had actually *defeated* the elves – their greatest success had been in running away. If Psander was building her wards on the strength of such questionable victories, she must be desperate. An arrow from Narky's life; a bucket from Criton's; a handful of dirt to represent Bandu – these were not the stuff of powerful magic. For the Gods' sake, Psander would be getting Hunter and Phaedra in the flesh, and it *still* wasn't worth much of anything.

"When did Psander tell you she was a woman?" Phaedra asked suddenly.

"The day after we arrived," Atella said. "That was a shock to everyone. It sounds stupid, but we all felt safer when we thought she was a man."

"Well," Phaedra said, and then cut herself short. She had been shaking her head, but now she stopped. "Yes," she said. "That *is* stupid."

There was silence for a time, a silence Hunter did not understand. He had the sense of a second conversation occurring outside of his hearing, a conversation in which somehow Phaedra's insulting words were not rude but complimentary, encouraging. Such was Phaedra's expression, anyway.

They kept walking, turning whenever Hunter thought they had gone too far in one direction. At this point they were not so much on their way somewhere as they were attempting to find a place that looked familiar.

They still hadn't found such a place by nightfall, when the cooler air brought forth a stagnant mist that rose up from the ground and made any further navigation impossible. So they huddled together, trying and failing to find a comfortable position to sleep in. Just as Hunter finally began to drift off, his back against a tree, the wind picked up and roused him halfway with its cool touch on his cheek. He opened his eyes and yawned.

The wind was doing something very strange up ahead, swirling the mist round and round in an ever-growing spiral. Hunter scrambled to his feet. He knew what an entrance to the elves' world looked like.

"Get up!" he cried to the other two. "We're here – we found it after all."

The girls got up hurriedly, Atella grabbing her satchel as she rose to her feet. Together, the three of them walked into the swirling mists. Psander awaited.

29

GENERAL MAGERION

The word of Xytos' defeat shook Ardis to its foundations. How could a city famous for its warriors be losing to an enemy that had appeared so completely out of nowhere? First a dragon and now the Dragon Touched were proving that the greatest warriors in the world could not stand against them, that all talk of their extinction had been very premature. It was shocking. How short a time ago had Magor's city been paramount in the world, its people respected and its army feared? One moment, High Priest Bestillos had been like a demigod, conquering every city that resisted or denied Ardisian might. Now he was gone, and it seemed as if Magor had gone with him.

What good was a leader like Magerion against a reality like that? What chance did his city have, with the Dragon Touched defeating their armies and the worshippers of Ravennis trying to devour them from within? Perhaps it was time to prioritize his enemies differently. He had worked for nearly two months to prevent Ravennis from expanding on His foothold in the city, but he did not fear Ravennis the way he feared God Most High. He had spent his youth in an Ardis ruled by the latter, and he did not mean to go back.

Magerion had succeeded so far in keeping Ravennis and His death cult at bay – that much, at least, he had accomplished. But even if the worshippers of Ravennis did not respond to

Xytos' defeat with jubilation – after all, it was their brothers too who were dying in these battles – the Dragon Touched were nonetheless strengthening their hand. How long until revolution swept Ardis? How long until the Great Temple of Magor fell?

Magerion had no intention of dying in a second purge. His family, his clan, had risen to a place of prominence in the city on the strength of his leadership, and he would not let them down. It was time to switch sides.

The cult of Ravennis could not afford to turn down the support of a man like Magerion. He could bring them an aura of legitimacy and the allegiance of a powerful clan – he would be indispensable. So what if he had spent weeks now slaughtering their worshippers in the most public and gruesome ways he could devise? Their God was a sneaky one – He would see Magerion's sudden change of heart as a major coup, regardless of its motives. The only question was how to engineer this change of heart in such a way as to deliver the city to him in one clean stroke.

The priests of Magor had to be gotten rid of, that much was a certainty. But would Elkinar then rise from His slumber and make a play for God of Ardis? It was possible. What Magerion needed to avoid was a power vacuum, a moment when the fate of Ardis was unclear. He needed to make sure that none of the other generals survived the new order to take sides in a conflict between Elkinar and Ravennis.

He wanted to get them together somehow, to gather Magor's priests and the Council of Generals in the same place, where a surprise attack by his loyalists could wipe them all out at once. But how best to arrange such a thing?

It was his scouts who brought him the solution. Narky the Black had escaped to Anardis and was now spreading the message of his cult to the people of that city, where once again Elkinar's priests seemed to have taken a stance of neutrality. Perhaps they had learned from Magerion's example that killing the Ravennis worshippers did not always have the desired effect. Or maybe their God was secretly dead, and no one had told them.

In any case, Narky was the key. The capture of the young high priest of Ravennis could draw both the generals and the priests of Magor to a meeting, and the black priest could bless Magerion once he'd disposed of them. It would be perfect.

But first he needed to capture Narky, and that might not be so simple. With Bestillos gone, the people of Anardis could not be counted upon to capitulate to an Ardisian general who had no army to back up his demands. A hundred men would not do for that purpose – but perhaps the priests of Elkinar could help him. They might be officially neutral, but they stood to gain a lot from Magor's collapse, unless the cult of Ravennis could co-opt the Wilderness God's following. They had every incentive to get rid of Black Narky.

But how to get a message to them without tipping him off? If Narky discovered that Magerion and the priests of Elkinar were in communication with each other, he was liable to run off and disappear again. Conversely, if Magerion revealed that he was seeking Narky's aid and not his elimination, word was bound to get back to Ardis long before he was ready for it. It was far too risky a thing to be so open about. This had to be very delicately done.

In the end he settled on his niece, who was a great devotee of Elkinar and very friendly with His Ardisian priests. She would travel to Anardis as a pilgrim and deliver the high priestess of Elkinar a message: Magerion would be coming to town in another week with a hundred men, so that he could take the pesky Narky away from their city and bring him to justice. He would be much obliged if the priests of Elkinar would send the boy out to him when he arrived.

In the meantime, he informed General Stellys of his plan to capture the high priest of Ravennis. "Why do you bother?" Stellys asked. "You executed their first leader, and dozens after her, and what good has that done you? What good has it even done Magor? The cult hasn't died – if anything, it's grown stronger. Why not just leave them alone?"

"And pretend that that would make them go away?" Magerion retorted. "Black Narky is more than just their latest leader, Stellys; he's the man who killed Bestillos. He's their proof that their God survived Magor's victory at Laarna and came out the stronger for it. A public execution of Narky would do more than humiliate the cult of Ravennis – it would unravel them."

"So you say. I say they'll just find another leader. These people lost their army, their city, and their famous Oracle. They saw their God's sacred birds fall dead from the sky, and they still insist their God is greater than the one that killed Him. *Nothing* can convince people like that, Magerion. No matter what you do to them, they'll find a way to call it a victory."

Magerion twisted his mouth to conceal the smile that was trying to creep onto it. "We'll see."

When he left the city, his hundred men with him, he had still told no one of his true intentions. He informed his men on their third night outside Ardis. They were shocked at first, but eventually they fell in line. Who cared if they had been slaughtering cultists yesterday, so long as Ravennis accepted their conversions and rejoiced at their support? Human life was cheap to the Gods, and to Magerion's loyalists, it didn't honestly matter which God ruled the city so long as He ruled through Magerion. For with the other generals gone, Magerion would be the sole ruler – the new king of Ardis. His clansmen would be royalty, his loyalists favored in all things. Who among them could object to that?

When Magerion was king and Ravennis ascendant, Ardis would again be strong enough to turn its attention outward, to the defeat of the Dragon Touched. Ravennis could unify the city as a weakened Magor had failed to, and then Ardis could face its enemies with the backing of a rising God rather than a declining one. With Magerion's leadership, his city could make this transition without wasting its manpower or resources on a prolonged civil war. His Ardis would be stronger than the one that had purged itself of the Dragon Touched so many years ago.

When they arrived at Anardis, Black Narky was waiting for them. He was standing outside the gate with his wife and a crowd of followers, and as Magerion's army approached, he parted with the crowd and came forward to meet them.

Magerion did a quick reassessment of the situation. He had more or less expected the priests of Elkinar to deliver the man to him in chains, yet here he was, walking toward the men of Ardis of his own volition. Had his God already told him of Magerion's plans? The general had thought that he was using Ravennis and His cult to his own ends, but perhaps he had it backwards. Perhaps he was a tool of the Gods after all.

But no, Ravennis had not told Narky what to expect. When the two met face to face, the young man struck him as barely holding in his terror. "You came here for me," he said. "Well, here I am."

"Yes," Magerion agreed. "Here you are."

Black Narky was much younger than Magerion had expected, and shorter than he had remembered. But then, he had only seen him the once, from a distance. In person, the High Priest of Ravennis was an average-sized teenager, neither particularly impressive physically nor wise beyond his years in any obvious way. Magerion had to remind himself that it was this boy who had killed Bestillos and this boy too who had slain the Boar of Hagardis. There was clearly more to him than met the eye.

Speaking of eyes, from what Magerion had heard, nobody knew how Narky had lost his left one. The rumor he'd heard most often was that Narky had given it to his God in exchange for wisdom. Up close, Magerion could see what nonsense that was. He could tell a scar from a blade when he saw one: that eye had been slashed by some enemy, not sacrificed to a God. It had been burned too – it looked a mess. But it was not so recent a scar that Narky could have lost it in the fight against Bestillos. It had been healing for a few months longer than that, Magerion thought.

Narky was clearly uncomfortable with the way Magerion was looking at him, sizing him up. Magerion let it stay that way for a little while, savoring the feeling of power that came from intimidating a high priest. He and Narky would be partners, but he now knew that they would not be equal partners. That was a pleasant surprise.

"Well?" Narky said at last. "Are we going to Ardis, or...?"

"We are," Magerion assured him. "And I thank you for coming out of Anardis on your own, and not wasting my time. Is this your wife?"

The girl nodded. "Yes, general. My name is Ptera."

"You moved quickly," Magerion noted. "Did you smuggle him out of Ardis as a wedding gift?"

Ptera's lips tightened, but Narky said, "More or less."

Some of Magerion's men grinned at this, and his son Atlon actually laughed. Mageris, the younger of Magerion's sons, did not. He had admired the late high priest of Magor greatly, and had once been given the honor of tracking the Tarphaean islanders alongside his idol. Mageris would obey his father, but Magerion knew it would be a long time before he would forgive him for betraying Bestillos' legacy. Among his men, his own son was the least happy about his new alliance.

Well, Mageris would have to get over it. Bestillos was dead, and the Tarphaeans were clearly favored by the Gods. Of the forces threatening Ardis, both were led by islanders – the cult of Ravennis by Narky, and the Dragon Touched by his erstwhile companion, whom the people called the Black Dragon. Perhaps Narky would have some insight on how to defeat his former friend.

Magerion waited until evening to tell Narky of his intentions. Let the boy think he was a prisoner. Let him think he would be martyred as the Oracle had been. The memory of this moment might keep him from overstepping himself later.

When the camp was set and a fire burning, Magerion called Narky over in front of his men and told him he was needed. "I have a task for you, before we arrive in Ardis."

Narky gulped visibly. "Yeah?"

"Yes. My men and I haven't known your God except through slaughtering His followers, but that will not do now. We will soon be bringing you before the priests of Magor and the full Council of Generals, and we must be better prepared for the task ahead of us. You can help us with that."

"I can?"

"You can. I have had a vision, a vision that I need you to help me fulfill. These hundred men are my closest kin and most faithful friends. All are loyal to me and will do as I tell them. I want you to teach us about Ravennis, and convert us to the worship of your God."

The boy's jaw dropped. For the first time in what felt like ages, Magerion laughed.

30

VELLA

Vella spent much of that night crying. It was the terror, the terror and the relief. She had opened up her heart in a way that she had never done before – opened up her heart, and endangered her life.

What would her husband do to her if he learned of her desires? He would probably kill her. Even with Vella's lineage, nobody would stop him.

She hoped Bandu knew not to tell a soul. She was unpredictable – it was part of what made her so enchanting. It always felt as if she could see through Vella, as if she could look into her and *see*. But of course, she hadn't known. She hadn't known, or she wouldn't have asked.

Would she? Vella never knew what was going on in Bandu's head. Maybe she had known, but wanted Vella to admit it out loud.

Oh, Vella didn't know. All she knew was that she had finally told someone, and she had told the only person who mattered. Her sobs were sobs of happiness. Happiness. And fear.

She was saved, for now, by her husband's indifference. Pilos didn't even ask why she was crying, he just lay down and snapped at her to shut up and go to sleep. She tried and failed, but he didn't press the issue, just grunted his annoyance and took his own advice. An hour later, Vella was still crying.

What did Bandu think of her? She desperately wanted to know, and to ask Bandu if she felt the same way, but she was too afraid. What if Bandu rejected her? What if she didn't even understand? One could never be sure from the way she talked. Sometimes it seemed like she was simply letting people's words wash over her unexamined, while at other times she seemed to understand a good deal more than had even been said.

Vella was too afraid to go back and talk to her. She felt like a coward and a fool, and she tried telling herself that she was just going to go walk beside Bandu while they traveled southward, maybe offer to hold Goodweather for a bit – but her courage always failed her.

It would have been all right had her life been otherwise bearable, but it wasn't. She and Pilos had consummated their marriage last year, but hadn't made love since – had never really made love. There was no love between them, and never had been. She resented his treatment, and he seemed to resent her very existence. If he had fallen in love with someone else – and perhaps he had – then she would hardly have felt betrayed, since he had never loved her to begin with. But not everyone felt that way, and Pilos in particular did not do well with humiliation. She hoped, for her own sake, that he never found out.

So she didn't go to see Bandu, didn't play with Goodweather or change her, didn't walk beside them as they moved south toward Ardis. And she lived a week of utter misery.

Then one night she awoke with Bandu kneeling beside her. Vella had slept in her clothes, it being a chilly night, and she stumbled out of the tent after Bandu as hurriedly and quietly as she could. Pilos turned over, but did not wake.

"What are you doing?" she whispered, suddenly realizing that Bandu had Goodweather strapped to her back, atop a traveling pack. Oh God. "Are you leaving? Are you here to say goodbye?"

"No," Bandu whispered back. "I don't say goodbye. I want you to go too."

Vella gasped. Her heart was beating so fast it was starting to feel irregular. It was actually hurting her chest. "You want me to come with you? Where? Who else is going?"

"Only Goodweather."

"But where are you going? Bandu, we can't just–"

Bandu caught Vella's head with both hands and kissed her, longer than it took to make her point. "Just come."

Vella followed Bandu out of the camp, her head in a blur. There was a watch, but the guards didn't seem to notice them as they left the tents behind. The moon was high – it couldn't have been much past midnight. They walked and walked until Vella lost her sense of direction entirely, but Bandu seemed to know where she was going. They came to a stream, which Bandu began to ford before abruptly changing direction and following the current northward – it had to be northward, because Vella thought it must be the same stream that their camp had crossed yesterday evening. Why were they going north? She splashed after Bandu, but they soon turned again – was it eastward?

"Bandu, where are we going?"

"Away."

"Away to where?"

Bandu didn't answer, and on they went. How long had they been walking? The moon was a good deal lower than it had been when they started out.

Vella repeated her question. "Away to where?"

"Away from Criton. He doesn't follow us here. He can't smell magic like I can, and this is the wrong way for him."

"But why? Why are you leaving him? Why take me with you?"

Bandu stared into her eyes in the moonlight. "I need your help. And I like you."

The second part sounded like an afterthought, but Vella pushed that down. It was too late to turn back. She was lost now, the camp was nowhere in sight, and she had no story to tell her people if and when she did find them again. She was at Bandu's mercy, a thought that thrilled and terrified her in equal measure.

She had to believe that Bandu didn't just want her help with the baby. "You like me," she repeated.

Bandu nodded. "I can mate with you," she said. "I don't want Criton now."

The more Vella allowed herself to think, the more complicated this was getting. It wasn't just the baby, it was Criton too! Did Bandu really love her, or did she just want to punish Criton? Now the thrill was wearing off, and Vella was just terrified. What had she gotten herself into? Why had she followed Bandu?

Bandu kissed her again, but Vella pulled away. "You don't love me," she said, and her heart sank as she said it. She knew it was true.

Bandu shook her head. "I don't know you yet," she admitted. "You are so quiet."

"Then why did you bring me here?" Vella almost shouted at her. "Why are you doing this to me?"

"Maybe I don't know you now," Bandu answered, "but I like you. You like me. You want to be my mate, and I don't want Criton now, so this is good."

"No," Vella groaned, "no, this isn't good. You're angry at Criton, but you can always go back if you change your mind, because he loves you. My husband hates me, Bandu. If I go back now, he'll kill me."

"Criton wants other wives," Bandu said quietly. Goodweather stirred with a soft moan.

Vella bowed her head. "I'm sorry," she said. "But you didn't have to take me with you."

Bandu pulled a strap over her shoulder and began to take Goodweather off her back. "I don't have to," she agreed. "I *want* to. If your husband hates you, why you want to stay? You don't. You are not happy there. That's why you come with me."

She sat down with Goodweather and began to nurse her. Vella sat across from them, grateful to the earth for its stability. Dawn was breaking, and her world was falling apart. And what would replace it? Nothing real, it seemed. Nothing true.

"This isn't going to last," she said. "You're just going to go back to him when you're done with me."

Bandu shook her head. "Never. Criton is not a good mate."

"It doesn't matter. You'll go back."

Bandu made a frustrated sound. "Why nobody listens to me? I don't go back, Vella. You want me to say again? I don't go back!"

She laid Goodweather's wrappings on the ground and gently lowered the baby onto them. Goodweather had gone back to sleep.

"You don't even know me," Vella said. "You brought me out here to be your lover, and you don't even know me."

"So tell me about you," Bandu said. She motioned the ground next to her.

Against her better judgment, Vella joined her. She felt suddenly afraid.

"Tell me about you," Bandu repeated, but what could Vella say? Where could she start? The whole of her life seemed insignificant now, and when she tried to think of something to tell Bandu, she couldn't think of anything worth mentioning. She had been with her parents, and then she had been with Pilos. Her childhood had been pleasant, and she loved her parents, but she also resented them for having chosen Pilos, and besides, she didn't want to talk about her parents or her husband, she wanted to talk about herself! But what was there to say?

Bandu kissed her again, so tenderly it made Vella weak. "Don't be afraid," she said, but Vella had no choice in the matter.

The sun rose and they lay down together, exhausted from their walk but nowhere near sleep. Vella tried to let go of her fears and live in the beautiful moment, the moment that she had not even dared to imagine. They kissed and kissed, and then Bandu's hand found her and Vella gasped, but didn't stop her. Bandu looked into her eyes the whole time, unashamed of what they were doing and confident, always confident in her power over Vella.

It was too much, too strong. Vella's head snapped back and she shouted, the fire escaping from her lungs and out into the world. Each cry sent another burst of flames up toward the trees, but Bandu didn't stop until one of those cries awoke Goodweather. Then she rose and changed the baby's clothes, lifted Goodweather with one arm, and went back to the stream to do the washing. Vella lay on the ground waiting for them to return, drifting in and out of sleep, feeling more relaxed than she could ever remember. Then Bandu came back with Goodweather strapped to her chest and the washed clothes hanging from a stick, and told her they had to go.

Vella sat up slowly, languidly, savoring her last moments of delicious relaxation. "When are *you* going to sleep?" she asked.

"Later."

They walked on, Vella following meekly, not knowing what destination Bandu had in mind. What sort of town would be welcoming to the three of them? Did such a place exist?

Bandu seemed confident that she knew where she was going, so Vella chose to trust her. Besides, the farther they walked, the greater the distance between them and Criton.

After most of a day, they reached a town whose men had pledged themselves to the Dragon Touched. Vella told them that she and Bandu had been sent there to rest, since the army's pace was too much for them, and she was relieved when their hosts accepted this explanation without too much suspicion. All the men of fighting age were gone, so there was more than enough room for Vella and Bandu. They thanked their hosts for their generosity and lay down in comfort, if not in privacy.

Bandu fell asleep before Vella did, Goodweather cradled in her arms. Vella watched them sleep, her heart aching. Could this last? She wanted to believe that Bandu would never go back to him. She wanted to believe that the two of them could make a life together, that they could care for each other and for Bandu's child without the angry world tearing them apart. Oh, how she wanted to believe!

31

NARKY

Narky could hardly believe his good fortune. Magerion was not here to kill him, to torture him to death, even to humiliate him! Ravennis was executing yet another of His maneuvers, and it was glorious.

Most of Magerion's men were very amenable to being taught about Ravennis. They learned His ways the same way they might have learned to use a new weapon – with a sort of professional, utilitarian engagement. They asked about the underworld – everyone always did – but they were more focused on the here-and-now. How would their everyday practices have to change in order to accommodate Ravennis instead of Magor? What animals did Ravennis favor in sacrifice?

Narky told them that they could continue sacrificing the same animals as before, so long as they left the eyes for Ravennis. He had grown more comfortable with inventing new practices during his time in Anardis. Nobody would be judging him, he had learned, for the ways in which his teachings might differ from the old Laarnan practices. He was the high priest of Ravennis, and it was assumed that Ravennis spoke through him. If the men of Laarna had worshipped their God differently, perhaps they were the ones who had been wrong. They were all gone now, after all.

Magerion was just as engaged as his men were, listening

attentively and asking the occasional question himself. This mass conversion may have been a power-play on his part, but he was still taking it seriously. He had apparently decided that Magor's defeat was inevitable, and he meant to be on the winning side. While Magerion the man frightened him, Narky was quite sympathetic to this line of thinking.

Narky was relieved that his martyrdom no longer seemed to be a major part of Ravennis' plans, but he was still nervous about the days to come. The plan was for him to remain a prisoner right up until the moment when Magerion and his men turned on their former leaders. What if their coup failed? What if it succeeded, but Narky was killed in the struggle? Would Ptera take up the mantle of high priestess?

It wasn't such a bad thought. Ptera might not have the reputation that Narky had, but she knew as much about Ravennis as anyone, and in some ways her faith was much stronger than Narky's. She certainly never questioned that Ravennis was a good and moral God, whereas Narky had his doubts on that front. She would make a fine high priestess, if it came to that.

He hoped it wouldn't. Ravennis might protect him in the land of the dead, but Narky preferred to take his sweet time getting there.

As they neared Ardis, word got out that Narky had been captured, and people began meeting them on the road to cheer Magerion or jeer at Narky, or else just to stare. Narky hated those last ones the most – he wished he knew what they were thinking. Were they worshippers of Ravennis, watching despairingly as their high priest returned to Ardis in captivity? Were they Magor worshippers, come to watch their God's triumph but suddenly struck with suspicion? Or maybe they were all witless fools, gathering to gawk at the soldiers and captives just for the spectacle of the thing. Either way, he hated their presence.

When they arrived in Ardis a few days later, an enormous crowd was waiting for them. Magerion had sent messengers ahead to tell of Narky's capture, and people of all ages lined the streets to watch the procession go by. Narky and Ptera had been put in chains for the occasion, and walked with at least three spears pointed at each of them. This was all for show according to Magerion, but Narky was still keenly aware of his vulnerability. The general's son, Mageris, was one of those with a spear, and it was terrifying to realize that he had the power to kill Narky quite suddenly should he choose to. By the look of him, he was strongly considering it.

Narky had recognized Mageris by his voice as one of the men who had been waiting for the islanders when they got back from their first conversation with Salemis. His father might be a shrewd and ambitious man, a worshipper of whichever God was likeliest to increase his power, but Mageris was a Bestillos loyalist. Narky didn't trust him.

They reached the Great Temple of Magor, where the priests and the other members of the Council of Generals were waiting for them. The crowd cheered them on as Narky and Ptera were marched inside. The bulk of Magerion's men stayed outside to control the crowd while the general, his sons, and the others who shared the duty of guarding the prisoners entered the temple.

The Great Temple of Magor was a magnificent building, its walls covered in murals and painted friezes depicting victories for the God and His city over various enemies. Here, a band of soldiers led a jackal-headed Goddess in chains toward the throne of the Boar God. There, a young High Priest Bestillos rammed his spear through the chest of a mounted Dragon Touched warrior. Narky even spotted a corner where someone had recently added a scene of Laarna's destruction, with Bestillos standing before the twin pillars at the entrance to the Temple of Ravennis, a flayed Oracle lashed to each. Above this scene, the boar of Magor trampled on a desperate-looking crow, its wings spread as if in an attempt to escape.

If everything went the way it was supposed to, Narky would have the privilege of watching these works of art destroyed.

He would have that boar repainted as a corpse, with its eyes pecked out and the raven perched triumphantly on its back. He would tear down Magor's statue at the temple's center, behind the altar, and... and first he had to survive the afternoon.

The soldiers forced Narky and Ptera to their knees as a group of men came forward to meet them. These were the same five priests of Magor that Narky remembered from the Graceful Servant's confrontation, and three other men who must have been members of the city's Council of Generals. These were dressed formally, their armor polished and their swords hanging from their belts in ornate decorative scabbards. A boy stood behind them, near the altar, holding the priests' barbed spears.

"Welcome back, General Magerion," said Magor's high priest, "and congratulations on your capture of Narky the Black. His sacrifice will be holiest to Magor, and send a message to his brother the Black Dragon that there is no escaping Ardisian might."

"Perhaps," said one of the generals, turning a critical eye on the two who stood beside him. "But if we wanted to send that message to the Dragon Touched, defeating them in battle would have worked better."

"Quiet, Stellys," said the older of the two. "You have not fought the Dragon Touched yourself, nor have you worked to suppress the cult of Ravennis as Magerion has done."

"You let the Black Dragon rout you, Xytos. I'd call that worse than doing nothing. And Choerus didn't even engage with our enemy before fleeing homeward."

"Which is why Ardis still stands," the one called Choerus retorted. "With Xytos' army routed and the Dragon Touched between me and our home, our enemies could have easily stormed the city and burned you alive if I hadn't outmaneuvered them and made it here first. Only fools criticize without thinking."

High Priest Melikon ended their quarrel with a clap of his hands. "Save your arguments for later," he scolded. "Ardis faces enemies both within and without. Today marks our victory against the former – defeat of the latter is bound to follow. The day is Magerion's."

"Thank you," Magerion said. "I believe this day is getting better and better."

Melikon nodded. "Today marks the end of the death cult of Ravennis. With them no longer weakening our people from within, Magor will once again bless His city with victory. The strength of Ardis will be restored."

"No," Magerion said, "not restored. Renewed. Ardis can never be what it once was. It must become something new and stronger."

Every muscle in Narky's body tensed. It was coming. Soon.

"I don't follow you."

"Then let me show you," Magerion answered, and with a sudden leap forward he thrust his spear straight through Melikon's stomach. The other generals cried out and drew their swords, but Magerion's retainers skewered all three of them before they could do much more than that. The remaining priests of Magor scrambled to retrieve their spears from the boy by the altar, but Atlon hurled his spear into one of their backs while Magerion drew his own short sword and whistled for his men outside to join them. The priests of Magor and their young assistant were quickly surrounded and dispatched.

Narky looked over to find that Ptera had squeezed her eyes tightly shut. Narky would have loved to do the same, but his sense of self-preservation wouldn't let him. What if one of Magerion's men turned on him? What if he had to dodge a stray spear thrust or worse, an intentional one? So he watched the horror that unfolded before him and sighed in relief when all of Magerion's former colleagues were dead.

When it was over, Atlon helped Narky to his feet and untied his hands while another of Magerion's men did the same for Ptera. Magerion turned toward them. "Are you ready?"

Narky shook his head. High Priest Melikon was staring at him, clutching at the spear that had gone through his belly and was poking out the other side. He was trying to say something.

Narky approached him warily – he wouldn't have put it past the man to have hidden a knife in his palm on the off chance Narky got close enough for a kill.

"It's happened," Melikon gasped, barely audible over the sounds of the agitated crowd outside the temple.

"It has," Narky agreed.

"Just like she showed me," Melikon continued, his voice getting weaker with each word. "Only she never showed me who. I only saw the spear, and felt... betrayed... surprised..."

"You should have expected it, then," Narky said. "The Graceful Servant showed you the death Ravennis meant for you, and you didn't even guard against it? You're an idiot. I'd have spent the rest of my life suspecting *everyone*."

Melikon blinked and looked up into his eyes. "I thought if I killed her... a prophecy is only..."

Narky nodded. "A prophecy is just a God's boast, sure. But you didn't kill Ravennis, you killed His servant. That's not the same thing. Not even close."

Melikon closed his eyes and said no more, waiting for death to take him. Narky turned away.

They stepped out into the sunlight, where the crowd stared at them all in shock. They had heard the screams, but the soldiers outside the temple had held them at bay until it was all over. Now they just stood, waiting for someone to explain away the sudden horror.

Magerion raised a bloodstained hand. "Magor has fallen," he announced, "defeated by Ravennis, Keeper of Fates and God of the Underworld. The senior priests of Magor are all dead, beside our failed leaders Xytos, Choerus, and Stellys. A new age is upon us: the age of Ravennis. All will worship Him or be put to the sword."

There were gasps, and muttered exclamations, but nobody was brave enough to object aloud. Magerion turned to his men. "Round up the families of the slain generals and tell them that they can pledge their loyalty to me and be named nobles, or refuse and be slaughtered. Narky, as high priest, I leave the conversion of the city in your hands. Wherever a worshipper of Magor refuses to give up the old religion, don't hesitate to have him slain. Tell me or my men, or do it yourself – I don't care, so long as the city unites under Ravennis and under me."

Narky nodded, and the old general looked at the crowd and smiled.

"So begins my reign," he said, aloud but clearly to himself. "Ardis has a king once more."

32

DESSA

Dessa couldn't believe Bandu and Vella had left her behind. Why, why would they have gone off together and not taken her too? They hadn't even told her that they were going – they'd just disappeared one night without warning, leaving Dessa to cope all by herself. How could they?

She'd thought Bandu was so wonderful. She'd ignored Grandma's warnings, and why shouldn't she? Grandma had said Bandu and Criton would take Dessa's father away, not her best friend!

Nobody knew where they'd gone – not Criton, not Vella's parents, not Pilos or his awful parents. Dessa kept trying to think back to what had happened over the last few weeks, what warning signs she might have missed, but there was nothing. Vella hadn't even visited Bandu in days and days! Could they have planned this so far in advance?

No, she was sure they hadn't. Vella knew that Dessa could keep a secret – if she and Bandu had been planning to leave together, she'd have said something. It was comforting to think so, anyway. Maybe it had been a sudden emergency, and they'd had to hurry off without any time to tell Dessa about it. That would have been almost excusable. Almost.

So what could she do now? Who was left for her to care about, now that the two people she admired most were both gone? That little girl Delika didn't even care. Mother suggested that Dessa talk to Malkon about it, since he was sure to be missing his sister too, but that was such a grown-up way of looking at things. Having 'things in common' didn't help anything, it was just an excuse to try to shove the two of them together. Dessa had just lost her two favorite girls – she didn't want to talk to some boy about it.

Instead, she avoided talking to anyone. Mother found that distressing, but she didn't push Dessa too hard because she also had Grandma to worry about. Grandma was getting worse and worse – she sometimes thought that rocks were mushrooms and tried to eat them, or else she would try to leave their tent without being properly dressed. Now when Mother said Grandma "wasn't herself," Dessa believed her.

She was still herself *sometimes*, though. Sometimes she would look at Dessa with such clarity and speak with such sense and purpose that it was hard to believe her mind was really going, that she wasn't just pretending the rest of the time.

"I know I'm going mad," she said once, when Mother and Father were busy and Dessa was alone with her. "I can feel it slipping away, Dessa. It's horrible, just horrible. I'm sorry I can't be like I was. Once…"

She broke off, sobbing. "I'm sorry."

Dessa gingerly patted her on the back. That only made Grandma cry harder, but Dessa didn't know what else to do, so she kept going. "You'll be all right, Grandma," she said.

"No, I won't," Grandma insisted, wiping her eyes. "Don't lie to me, child. This never gets better, it only gets worse. I'll lose more and more until there's nothing left."

Dessa didn't know what to say to that. She had never considered what it would be like to go mad, and she hadn't realized that you could *know* you were going mad, hate that it was happening to you, and be unable to stop it. She suddenly felt bad for having hated Grandma before. Mother was right: it wasn't her fault.

"We'll take care of you, though," she said. "We won't let you eat rocks or anything."

"What?" said Grandma, looking up. "What rocks?"

"You try to eat rocks sometimes."

"I do not."

Dessa should have known better than to take the conversation in this direction. "Oh," she said. "You're right. I'm sorry, Grandma, that was a mistake."

Grandma smiled. "It's all right, child. We all make mistakes."

We sure do, Dessa thought.

She told Mother about their conversation, and Mother nodded sadly. "It's very hard for her," she said. "It's hard for all of us. I hope you'll be kind to her, Dessa, and don't take what she says sometimes to heart."

"I'll try," Dessa told her. "But Mother?"

"Yes?"

"Why does she hate Bandu and Criton so much?"

"I don't know, maybe they remind her of someone."

Dessa didn't think that was very likely. There weren't any other Dragon Touched who were dark like Criton, and she didn't believe there could be anyone in the world who was quite like Bandu. But then, there was no telling what was going on in Grandma's mind. She called Dessa 'Iona' sometimes, and at other times she thought that Mother was *her* mother. For all Dessa knew, maybe the Tarphaeans *did* remind her of someone – someone who was nothing like them.

But it was Grandma who had called Criton the Black Dragon, so she had to have recognized that his skin was darker than any of the other Dragon Touched. And the fact that she kept saying Criton would kill Father didn't have anything to do with her confused memories. That scared Dessa. What if Grandma was right? It was hard to believe – Father was so warm and solid, and he and Criton seemed to be the best of friends. But grown-ups could change quickly. There was a whole level to them, underneath the surface, that Dessa couldn't understand. So she worried.

She would have liked to pretend that Grandma was just

confused again, that she was mixing Father up with Grandpa, who really was dead. But then, she couldn't have been mixing up their deaths, because Grandpa had died peacefully in his sleep.

Still, Grandma *was* going mad. Maybe she had just dreamt something, and thought it was real. That seemed likely enough. Just so long as it was a nightmare and not a prophecy, it would be all right. And it *had* to be just a nightmare. Why would God Most High give a prophecy to a madwoman?

33

PARTHA

That feeling of slipping, slipping. For Partha, losing her mind wasn't a sudden snapping, it was a grueling ongoing process: an assault on her *Partha-ness* that raged on and on as she faltered and retreated, falling back from each position as it became impossible to hold. Her husband had been a soldier, a captain, so she thought of it in his terms. Her husband, her husband – oh God, what was his name? Belkos? Belkos! No, that wasn't right, that was someone else's husband. Shit!

At first she had thought it was simply her memories slipping away, but it was far worse than that. They were failing to form in the first place now, dying stillborn before she could catch hold of them and drag them into the light. This whole thing was like sleeping on a hill. Every day you woke up lower down than you remembered.

And it was infuriating, losing her mind. People thought she would do something crazy just because she couldn't catch it, whatever it was. Her mother watched her day and night, told her what to eat and what not to – she was a nuisance, really. Partha could take care of herself, she was a full grown woman, except... had she just called Iona her mother? That was a mistake, a terrible mistake. She hoped she hadn't made it out loud. She didn't want Iona to catch on to the fact that something was wrong with her – there was no telling what would happen to her then.

Her eyesight was going too, along with her mind. Or not exactly her eyesight, since her eyes could still see, but her mindsight. The things she saw with her eyes made less sense to her now. She would say, "Careful, Iona! Don't step in the hole!" and Iona would turn to her and say, "It's not a hole, Grandma, it's my black wool coat. I took it off while we were putting the tent up." But Partha couldn't trust her, of course, because Iona was always lying. Here she was, lying again, because she had called Partha "Grandma" when Partha knew damn well that Iona was her daughter, the insolent girl.

But while her ability to see and understand faltered, she was receiving visions in its stead. That should have been a holy thing, except she thought she might be stealing them. Or maybe not stealing, that wasn't right – it was more as if she was standing on the wrong path, on *their* path, and intercepting them by mistake. Was that holy, or unholy?

She saw that devil, that Black Dragon, giving her little girl a mealy-mouthed apology for killing her Belkos. It was a fake apology, she knew. He didn't even mean it, the liar! And that witch, the She-wolf, she had scurried off into hiding somewhere, but she was the one responsible for it all. Partha could feel her presence *inside* the Black Dragon, influencing him, sustaining him.

That was the only true thing she knew, at least until it slipped away too. She was afraid it might if she didn't keep thinking about it. Sometimes the vision was blurry, the words indistinct, and all she could remember was that those two had betrayed her. They had killed her father, Belkos.

No! Damn her, that wasn't right either! But it was close, close enough. The point was that they had done it to her, either long ago, or later on. It was the betrayal that mattered. She had to sustain her fury, because someday it might be all that sustained *her*.

But more often than Partha was angry, she was frightened. There were times when the fear of losing herself pushed all other thoughts to the side and she wept out of sheer terror, unable to hold onto the parts of her that mattered – unable to even explain which parts they were. She clung to the notion of the Black Dragon's betrayal like a reed on the edge of a cliff, not because it was strong or even important, but because it was all she could reach. The fear of falling governed everything.

Sometimes she prayed for her God to take her before she could lose any more. She didn't know how old she was – seven, maybe? – but she knew she was old enough to die. They probably wouldn't even weep over her grave, just say, "Too bad about that girl Partha," and move on. They were all liars and false friends anyway.

This one here, this one who was pretending to be Partha's daughter – Partha knew better than to trust her. She might pretend that she was a dutiful daughter, just looking after her poor aging mother, but it was all a game. She was after something – was it her money? She had hidden Partha's real daughter away somewhere, and was trying to ingratiate herself.

"I know what you're really after," Partha told her. "You can't fool me."

Not-Iona sighed. "And what am I after, Mother?"

Partha didn't know for sure – it *might* have been the money, but it might also have been something else, so instead of answering, she repeated herself. "You know what you did. You can't fool me. You're not really her, you're one of *them.*"

"One of who?"

"You know who."

It was morning, time for them to help her onto that horse of theirs; the horse they had stolen from the *real* Iona. Partha considered resisting, but then she decided it might be best to go along, to pretend that everything was fine. She didn't want to tip her hand too early.

She was tired of riding that damned horse day in and day out. Her arse was sore. They were trying to tire her out so that she'd give up and they could steal her money. She had gathered it up off the ground, but they had somehow changed it so that it all looked and felt like little rocks and pebbles. They wanted her to give up and abandon it so they could make off with it and turn it back into money afterwards. She was onto their tricks.

Now the little one was angry at her for some reason, giving her nasty looks as if Partha had done something to her. "Stop looking at me like that, you horrible little girl," Partha said to her. "What did I ever do to you?"

"You chased Bandu away," the girl said sullenly. "You were mean to her. Maybe that's why she left. I bet you're happy."

"Dessa!" her mother scolded. "How could you say such things to your grandmother? Apologize. Now."

"I'm sorry," Dessa mumbled, obviously not meaning it.

Was the She-wolf gone, then? Partha hadn't known. She hadn't known, and she actually *didn't* feel happy about it. She was sure it was a trick – the witch would stay away until Partha couldn't recognize her anymore, and then she would strike when Partha was defenseless against her. She knew that Partha's memory was failing, and she was taking advantage of it. Partha tried to resist, but she was already having trouble visualizing the girl. It was fiendish and underhanded, and it played on her weaknesses. If she forgot the She-wolf, forgot to hate her, what would remain?

Not much, she feared.

34

CRITON

It took him far too long to realize that Bandu had really left him, and by that time he had little hope of tracking her down. He spent over an hour wandering through the camp, insisting that she must simply be elsewhere – lingering with Iona while picking Delika up, or visiting Biva and her flock of sheep, or perhaps washing Goodweather's clothes somewhere nearby. But nobody could remember seeing her, and though he felt her presence when he came to the stream's edge, he could not tell in which direction she had gone.

What began as bewilderment quickly turned to panic. She was gone! She had left him! Would she ever come back?

The others could not understand his desperation. None of the Dragon Touched had liked Bandu except for Belkos' wife and daughter, and Kilion's daughter Vella. Speaking of which, Vella had disappeared too. It was Kilion, rather than his son-in-law, who discovered her absence and brought it to Criton's attention. Kilion looked absolutely sick about it; he was the only person who seemed to care almost as much as Criton did.

Where had they gone? Had they left together, or was there some other explanation for their simultaneous disappearance? Had one gone in chase of the other?

He questioned Belkos' daughter Dessa, who was friends with Vella, but she didn't know anything. Neither did little Delika, and worse, she seemed viciously glad to have Criton to herself. But he shouldn't get mad at Delika for that – she was so young, too young to understand or care that his heart was breaking. His panic meant nothing to her.

Criton wished Bandu hadn't taken a friend with her. He was increasingly sure that that was what she had done, and it worried him. If she had been alone with Goodweather, she might grow tired and lonely without Criton and come back to him. But like Phaedra, a woman friend would probably encourage her to stay away longer.

And he deserved it; that was the worst part. He had made a promise to Bandu that he would never take another wife, and then talked openly about breaking that promise for the sake of a political message – and, he had to admit, because he had secretly hoped that Bandu wouldn't mind the idea of his taking multiple wives. After all, he had thought to himself, the notion of exclusive marriage hadn't come naturally to her: it had taken Phaedra to explain the concept.

That secret hope had been quickly dashed, but he had still thought that she would argue, that she would force him to choose her above all others. He hadn't expected her to forfeit.

What was the matter with him? He didn't even *want* other wives, not really. It may be a good idea politically speaking, but there were other ways to encourage camaraderie between the Dragon Touched and the plainsfolk. And though the idea had intrigued him, he hadn't taken it all that seriously – and clearly not as seriously as Bandu had. Now he was miserable. He only really wanted Bandu, couldn't she see that? When would she return to him?

There was nothing he could do now to bring her back. He wanted to send out a search party, but he knew that if Bandu didn't want to be found, no search party would find her. Besides, Hessina and the elders wouldn't approve of his sending such a party. They didn't want her back. It was all he could do not to scream at them.

Bandu's absence only made them press harder for him to

take new wives, but he put them off. The very thought made him sick now. It was the threat of his betrayal that had chased her away – if he followed through, he feared that she would never come back.

At least she knew how to find him. The Dragon Touched were hard to miss, and she knew where he was headed. That was all he had now, the hope that she would seek him out in a month or two and let him apologize to her for what he'd done. Until then, all he could do was to pretend everything was fine, to raise triumphant Delika as if she was his only daughter and to lead his people as if half his soul hadn't disappeared overnight.

He led his people back to the Dragon Knight's Tomb, just as Hessina had suggested, encountering little resistance on the way. The people fled before him, leaving their houses and farms for the protection of Ardis' walls. The army of Ardis seemed content for now to hide behind those walls as well, and the Dragon Touched reached Dragon Knight's Tomb without incident. There Hessina asked – or, rather, demanded – that Criton accompany her into the tomb alone. He had less energy for disagreement without Bandu at his side, so he left Delika with his cousin again despite all her protests and ascended the mountain at the old woman's side.

At first, Hessina didn't even talk to him. She knelt by the Dragon Knight's sarcophagus, praying silently to herself. Criton tried to do the same, closing his eyes and trying to find the words for a prayer. But the only prayer he could think of was *please send Bandu back to me.*

At last Hessina shifted, causing Criton to open his eyes. "You wanted to speak to me?" he asked warily. The last thing he needed right now was a lecture, but he was sure he was about to get one.

"I am sorry for what has happened between you and Bandu," she said, grimacing as she sat on the hard floor of the cave. "I understand your pain. But you do not have the luxury of grief. You must marry again, and soon. Speak to Kana and the other elders, and marry the women they suggest to you."

"I thought you were against intermarriage."

She sighed. "Hession was my ancestor," she said, indicating the tomb. "I'm sure you didn't know that. Though not Dragon Touched himself, he was married to a Dragon Touched woman, and my lineage traces back to them. Our people have never been pure in that sense – there have always been intermarriages. Despite my reservations, I have come to the conclusion that such intermarriages are necessary for the survival of our people.

"That means I owe you and Bandu an apology. Though she was not well suited to living among us, you were not wrong to marry a girl from your own island."

"You didn't make her feel very welcome," Criton said bitterly.

"I know."

"She left me because I was considering listening to you. I promised her when we married that I'd never want another woman, and you made me question that promise. You practically chased her off yourself!"

She eyed him sternly. "My suggestion was not wrong, Criton. It still isn't. I think that with time, you'll come to understand the wisdom and the necessity of marrying again. You are no longer simply a man, but a symbol. You owe it to your people to marry the women the plainsmen suggest to you, to give us the strength of the plainsmen's numbers and turn them to our ways. I believe it is for this purpose that God Most High chose you to lead us – I am too old to make political marriages."

"Or maybe He chose me because I make better decisions than you do."

He had meant to insult her, to make her hurt for the way she was scratching at his wounds, but to his shame and fury, she only regarded him with that disapproving gaze that made him feel like a child, one who could be indulged now and punished later.

"Your tactical decisions have helped our cause more than they've harmed it," she said. "But this one choice is more important than any of those you've made so far. If you do not marry the women the elders suggest to you, our people will suffer."

"We'll see."

She spoke on, unfazed. "I do understand your grief, Criton, whatever you may think. A first marriage is special. My husband had no other wives, but from watching others, I can tell you that more wives are unlikely to make you happier. They may dislike each other, or dislike you, and you may well curse us, your elders, for suggesting this course of action. But these marriages are a political necessity. You must realize that."

She sighed. "You should know that while I did not especially like Bandu, I did not bear her any ill will. She was an impediment to you politically, but I know her abandonment has hurt you, and I am sorry for that."

He hoped she could see the hatred in his eyes. "You knew she'd leave me."

"Of course not. But we should look to the future. Our victory is close."

"Really? You think we can take Ardis?"

"God Most High will not abandon us. Now that I am here, I am sure of it. Soon Ardis will fall, and we can make its citizens pay for what they did to us. Which brings us to the second thing I wanted to say. As with your marriages, I want to be sure that you understand what we must do, and why."

That sounded ominous. "Has the plan changed? When we take Ardis, we'll reward our allies and settle in to live as we used to."

"No," the old woman said, her face grim. "It will not be the way it used to. We used to live in relative peace, protecting the king and protected by him as well. Now there can be no peace, not so long as the worshippers of Magor live within those walls. They slaughtered us, Criton. You were never here to weep with us at our losses, but there is no punishment too severe for those who killed our people."

Criton recoiled from her. "What are you saying? You want us to slaughter the whole city? We're not monsters. The goal is to live in Ardis righteously, not to destroy it ourselves!"

Hessina shook her head. "We cannot live with the Ardismen after what they did to us. I had five sons, Criton. Five. Eight grandchildren. Kilion was my youngest, the only one I was able to save. All the others were killed – my sons, my daughter, and all their children and babies. We *cannot coexist* with the Ardismen. As long as we live, they will be our enemies. As long as *they* live, they will be a danger to us. They will dream of murdering us in our beds."

Criton said nothing. The story of Hessina's family – even the short version – was devastating. He had once witnessed the red priest executing an entire family. He had watched children die then, and the horror had been unfathomable. But now, as a father, these things affected him so much more deeply. The reality of Hessina losing her children and grandchildren was so overwhelming it robbed him of his power of speech. He nearly burst into tears thinking of those children, and of his own daughter now absent. Goodweather had been a frustrating chore right up until the moment that she became a hole in his heart.

It was that pain that brought him back. He shook his head, choking on his grief and on hers. Hessina was justified in her hate, but she was also wrong. She could not ask him to inflict her experiences on other parents, other grandparents. Whatever she said, he would not accept that as the only way.

Hessina was studying him. "You've given me a lot to think about," he told her. "I'll ask God Most High for guidance, but you should know that I disagree with you. I'm not going to become the kind of killer Bestillos was. Not willingly, anyway. If I can find a new arrangement with the Ardismen, a peaceful one, I'll take that peace over the kind of victory you're hoping for."

"This is the victory we have *all* been hoping for," Hessina said vehemently. "Our people will not settle for less."

Criton frowned. "Then I'll have to convince them. Maybe *this* is why God Most High chose me to lead the Dragon

Touched – because I'm willing to make peace with our enemies when others won't."

The old woman's eyes flashed. "Nobody who grew up before the purge will accept your position on this, Criton. You are young and idealistic, and foolish. Don't imagine for a moment that your stance will be popular."

"Thank you for your guidance," Criton said acidly. Then he closed his eyes and pretended to pray so as to cut off any more communication.

Bandu would be happy with his position when she found out. She had never believed this war was necessary, and would never have endorsed the slaughter of an entire city. If by some miracle he succeeded and the Dragon Touched made peace with their enemies, she was bound to hear about it and come back to him.

Wasn't she?

35

PHAEDRA

They came through the mists right into the courtyard of Silent Hall, where they were greeted with cheers by Atella's people. Psander was there too, looking both pleased and astonished at Phaedra and Hunter's presence. "Oh, well done, Atella," she said, and to Phaedra added, "I did not expect you two to be on Tarphae – what were you doing there?"

"We'd been taken there," Phaedra answered. "Karassa has turned our home into a haven for pirates. Without God Most High's protection, we'd have been sacrificed to Her as soon as we touched shore."

"And yet here you are."

"Here we are."

Psander took Atella's bag and thanked her. "You surpassed my expectations, and even my hopes."

Phaedra found herself a bit overwhelmed. This was so much more a homecoming than she had expected, certainly more a homecoming than their return to Tarphae had been. Even the villagers, once suspicious of the Tarphaeans for their association with the Gallant Ones, now looked on her and Hunter with admiration and hope. The whole group of them had gathered to witness Atella's return through the mists, and they looked just as happy with Phaedra and Hunter's surprise appearance as Psander did.

It was early morning here, unlike on Tarphae, which confused Phaedra somewhat. The hours of the two worlds had been more or less aligned before, from what she could remember. Had she been wrong about that, or had the release of Salemis somehow thrown this alignment off?

A young boy spoke up. "Are you here to save us?"

It was a heartbreaking question, and one that Phaedra did not know how to answer. If the situation was as dire as Phaedra feared it was, nothing could save these people.

Hunter stared at her. He'd been waiting for her to answer, she realized, and her hesitation had already caused a ripple of fear to spread through the crowd. He turned to the boy. "Yes," he said. "We're here to save you."

The tension remained among the adults, but the boy smiled. "Good. We need you."

You *need us most of all*, Phaedra thought. The boy was right around the age that elves preferred for their food.

It was good to see the villagers looking so lively. The last time Phaedra had seen them, they'd all been too weak to stand. So far, the move into the fairies' world seemed to have done them more good than harm. The trouble was that they couldn't expect it to last.

How reckless of Hunter, to say that they were here to save these people! They were neither of them some devastating weapon that could hold the elves at bay. Psander's interest in them as such was a mark of her desperation. And yet, looking at Hunter's face, Phaedra was surprised to see confidence there. It might make no sense, but he clearly believed himself. He thought he could save them.

Perhaps this was what Hunter needed, what he'd been looking for all along. He had wanted to lead the army of Tarphae once, and when that dream had died, he had fought to protect the remaining islanders from whatever dangers they encountered. Now Psander's villagers needed rescuing from the elves, who meant to capture them and breed them and eat their children. What better fight could Hunter join?

They broke their fast all together in the courtyard, joined even by Psander. She had apparently been much less aloof from the villagers since revealing her true nature to them, and a sort of camaraderie had developed in the months since then. Hunter asked the villagers about their interactions with the elves so far, and Phaedra was relieved to hear that nobody had yet been taken. As Atella had told them, Psander had set up wards that alerted the villagers whenever elves were near, and they would flee for the protection of Silent Hall any time the alarm sounded. What protection the walls offered them was unclear, but Psander's reworking of her God-evading wards had apparently been effective so far. Phaedra hoped she would explain how she'd done it.

When they had finished with their meal, Psander asked Phaedra and Hunter if they would like to speak privately with her. To Phaedra's shock, Hunter declined. He was polite about it, but firm: he preferred to stay with the villagers. Phaedra was left to talk to Psander alone.

As they walked to the wizard's library together, Psander asked her to explain how she and Hunter had come to be once more on Tarphae. So Phaedra told her of the events of the last few months, and of her ambition to recreate academic wizardry for herself.

"I am glad you came here," Psander said, "and it is a great relief to know that God Most High sent you. My old mentor was right, then: the dragons' God is alive and well, and growing more active in the world. If that is so, and He sent you to me with His blessing, then there is hope after all. I had grown desperate."

"I know," Phaedra told her. "I figured if you had sent Atella to find ingredients that would represent us islanders, the situation must be dire. All we ever did to the fairies was escape from them."

Psander eyed her skeptically. "You give yourselves too little credit. My understanding was that Bandu had bested the elves in one of their games, Criton had defeated one of their living castles in a battle of wits, and Hunter had slain more than one elf in hand-to-hand combat. I'm sure if all this is true, your support and Narky's were not immaterial."

"Thank you," Phaedra said. She felt herself blushing. Psander clearly respected her; respected all five of them. Phaedra knew that Narky would have scorned her for feeling so flattered, but she couldn't help it. Psander did not express respect for people often, and she respected *them*.

"But I will admit," Psander added, "your overall assessment was correct. I reached for these shadows of you because I am running out of tools. Any day now, the fairies may recognize our weakness and slaughter us all."

"How have you kept them away so far?" Phaedra asked. "Atella said you turned your wards around, but your wards were for keeping the Gods from seeing you. I don't understand how those could be useful against the elves, even reworked. My conception of magic is as a sort of universal poetics, where ingredients are all representational. Am I missing something?"

The wizard shook her head. "You are not. My wards *are* useless against the fairies. But they don't know that, and their lack of knowledge is what has kept us safe so far. Atella is repeating what I told her, which is more or less the truth. I have reversed my wards entirely: where once they were keeping my hall invisible to the Gods, they now project a *feeling* of the Gods' might. That is all. When the elves come to my walls, they feel that projection and, so far, they have chosen caution. I have not told the villagers this truth because their minds are so easy for the elves to read – they have not learned to guard them as I have."

"But you're telling me?"

"I am telling you. And that means that I cannot let you leave my hall until you have learned to protect your mind."

Phaedra gaped at her. "You'll teach me?"

Psander smiled at her shock. "You have proven yourself fully capable of learning, and I am in need of an assistant. I will be glad to teach you everything I know."

36

HUNTER

Hunter stayed with the villagers when Phaedra went to talk to Psander. He asked them about their food stores, their foraging habits, their ability to avoid starvation, and found that they had adapted themselves quite quickly to their surroundings. Psander had deemed it too dangerous to go out hunting, and they had responded by becoming quite good trappers. They set their traps well within Psander's wards of alarm, where the elves could not ambush them, and they caught enough meat to supplement their remaining stores of grain while they waited for more to grow. They had cleared most of the tents out of Silent Hall's courtyard so as to leave room for a small field of wheat and oats, and the displaced families had moved into Psander's tower. They had also cleared away space for a modest vegetable patch just outside Psander's walls.

The trouble with trapping was that nearly every animal in this world seemed to be omnivorous, if not altogether carnivorous. If the villagers were too late in checking their traps, they were liable to find their prey already feasted upon by a great blue cat, or an unfamiliar pig-thing, or a flock of pigeons.

When he asked them to show him what defenses they had in case the elves did eventually attack, they pointed to the walls.

"That's all?"

"That's all."

"Then you need weapons."

They had axes, at least, for chopping wood, but they were not balanced the way a weapon ought to be, and Hunter knew how fast the elves could be with their war sickles. So he set off with Atella's father and two younger men to gather boughs for halfspears and quarterstaffs. He had learned stick fighting as a boy, before Father had given him his sword, and he thought he could teach it passably. Besides, he knew nothing of forging swords.

They would want weapons with some reach on the elves anyway – the elves were fast, brutal fighters, and the villagers would need every little advantage they could find. When the boughs were gathered and cut, Hunter set himself to teaching anyone who had time to learn. He started with the simplest drills, repeating them over and over until his students dropped their staves out of exhaustion. Then he had them gather more, smaller branches so that the children could practice with them too.

It would take months for the villagers to be even passable with their weapons, divided as their time was between training, trapping, and farming. He knew that. He also knew that in an actual fight, the elves would have every advantage. So when they broke for the evening meal, he set about devising a way to turn the elves' advantages against them.

Phaedra tried to talk to him while they were eating, but he had to apologize multiple times for inattention. His mind was fully engaged with the problem of fighting the elves, and he could not be distracted. He gathered only that Psander had offered to train Phaedra in magic, and that she was very excited about it – of course she was. He congratulated her and went straight to bed.

He awoke before dawn and went outside to repeat the drills he had taught the villagers, adding some other ones and refamiliarizing himself with the weapon. At his peak, Hunter's swordsmaster had always said, a warrior would become one with his weapon. He would stop thinking and engage fully with each moment, seeing and responding to the slightest motions of his opponent with a perfectly blank mind. Now Hunter tried to build a further step on top of that: he tried to train himself to think while he acted, but in ways that contradicted his motions. If he could teach himself to cut high even as he *thought* about attacking low, then he could turn the fairies' mind-reading against them.

It was surprisingly difficult. With his swordsmaster, he had reached the point in his training when one no sooner thought of an attack than one had done it. He frequently found himself accidentally letting his actions match his thoughts, or vice versa. The village children, watching from the walls, must have wondered why he kept making frustrated sounds after each perfectly executed cut.

But he needed this to work. If he could master his new contradictory-thought fighting style, then one day his students would too. The elves would find them far more capable of defending themselves than they expected.

His life became a never-ending cycle of military preparations, both internal and external. He began introducing his theories into his training of the villagers, hoping to skip straight over the empty-minded fighting that had taken him years to learn. Most of the villagers were frustratingly slow to learn even the basics of stick fighting, but he thought that could have been expected. His swordsmaster had always called him an exceptional talent – he could not expect others to catch up to him so quickly.

"Cut low!" he would bark at his students while they were practicing a high parry. The trainees looked at him with annoyance and confusion, but he had already explained his reasoning, and could only tell them to keep not-quite-ignoring his instructions.

"Memorize my words," he would say, "visualize what I am asking you to do. But do the opposite."

The villagers hadn't realized that fairies could read minds – it had shocked and horrified them when Hunter had explained the truth. Their reactions to that information convinced him to wait before explaining how nearly impossible elves were to kill. He had seen elves survive beheadings, which made him wonder if they were altogether immortal. He didn't *think* so, but he couldn't know for sure.

He hoped it wouldn't matter. Mortal or not, elves were still made of flesh and bones – bones that could be broken. If an elf was crippled and incapable of fighting, that was sufficient. A live elf might even be useful to Psander, if they could capture one.

Psander watched with apparent amusement while he tried to train the villagers. She clearly didn't believe they would ever be able to resist the elves in arms. He meant to prove her wrong. What did Psander know of armed combat, anyway? Many of the villagers were coming along quite well, by Hunter's standards: Atella's father took naturally to the training, as did a pair of brothers who were grandsons of old Garan, and there was one nine year-old girl, Tritika, who imitated Hunter with such adroitness that he was sure she would be quite formidable given five or six years. He hoped they would live that long.

Of course, there was no knowing how well everyone was doing on the mental side of the training, visualizing movements other than those they were making. Gods knew, Hunter was having enough difficulty himself. At best, he could manage a mental-physical split about half the time, and that was never mind the fact that he had no proof the technique would work at all. He was relying on the assumption that these mental acrobatics would confuse the elves more than a closed mind would have – if he was wrong, then all was for naught. The elves had probably spent hundreds of years mastering the use of their long-handled sickles. Weapons training alone would never overcome them.

There were other benefits to his interactions with the villagers, though. Hunter and his friends had first met them a year and a half ago, when they had generously helped nurse Narky back to health, and sheltered and fed the islanders while they waited for the boy's recovery. They were good, kind people, and yet they had grown suspicious of the Tarphaeans after they had joined with a group of bandits on Psander's orders. Later, the wizard had used ingredients the islanders had brought her to make charms that sickened the villagers while bolstering Silent Hall's defenses. And then, to cap off their betrayal, Hunter and his friends had helped transport them all to the horrifying world of the fairies.

During all this time, the islanders had taken advantage of these people just as Psander had, and barely given them more thought. Now Hunter was finally getting to know them, making friends, sharing meals, and working with them in the courtyard and the vegetable garden when he wasn't too busy teaching them to fight. He inspected traps with his new friends, chopped wood with them, lived his life with them.

He even considered moving to live with them instead of in his room in Psander's tower, but that would have taken him farther from Phaedra. True, she spent most of her time now holed up with Psander learning the mysteries of the universe, but she still stopped by sometimes to talk, and to give him an update on her progress. He didn't want to lose that.

He thought he loved Phaedra. No, that was a lie – he *knew* he loved her. Seeing her so happy only reinforced how important she was to him, how much he liked to see her so excited about her life. She was radiant, her troubles forgotten as she limped hurriedly toward the library, day after day. He wanted her to look that excited about him.

He had never expected for them to come back to the elves' world, let alone for them to be happy there, but strange as it was, they really were both happy. Phaedra wasn't the only one benefitting from their time here – training the villagers to fight the elves filled Hunter with such purpose that he sometimes forgot that he had not always meant to be a combat trainer. Here was the aspect of his life that had gone missing when Tarphae was drowned. Here was the nation he would fight for, the army he would lead in battle. His answer to that little boy, Emmer, felt true: he was here to save them.

Even the older villagers believed that now, and the admiration and respect they showed him made him feel stronger, wiser, more attractive. He wondered if Phaedra could tell.

He was out one day checking on traps with Atella and her father when the alarm sounded. Or perhaps 'sounded' was the wrong word – it was more like a very loud *feeling*, telling him that one or more elves had passed within the range of Psander's wards. Hunter and his companions immediately broke into a run, cursing. They had been right on the edge of the wards' range for that particular trap – if they were unlucky, they might not make it back to Silent Hall before the enemy did.

They were lucky this time. They made it to the fortress just as the door was closing, and after some small amount of shouting, Psander opened the door to let them in. "You were cutting it awfully fine," she scolded them.

"We ran back as quick as we could," Atella's father said, panting.

"You were almost too late," Psander answered. "They're just testing the boundaries now, but they still would have loved to catch you outside these walls."

"They're testing the boundaries?" Phaedra asked, horrified. She had come hurrying along behind Psander to open the gate to Hunter and the other two. "Can we afford for them to do that?"

"Not at all," the wizard answered grimly. "These tests are building up to an attack. But I don't see that there's much we can do about it. Today's scout will try to sniff out the nature of our defenses, as will each future one, and they will report back to their queen. If I could capture them before they returned home, I would."

That stopped Hunter in his tracks. "I can," he said.

Psander looked at him appraisingly. "Are you sure?"

"Is there just one of them?"

She nodded. "So my wards tell me. If they have found a way to make my wards lie to me..."

"Hunter," Phaedra said, but when he looked at her, she said

no more. She was smarter than he was – she knew full well that letting him try to capture the scout was worth the risk to Hunter's life. If he couldn't defeat an elf in single combat, he was of no use to the people of Silent Hall. And anyway, if *he* couldn't defeat an elf, they were probably all doomed.

But her eyes expressed more than resignation, and more than pain at his risking of himself. They expressed trust. Belief. Love.

Atella brought him a staff, and Psander opened the door for him. Hunter took a deep breath and stepped back outside.

He walked as far as the edge of the trees before he stopped. He had seen elves disguise themselves as thorny bushes once, and had no intention of being caught off guard. "Come out and fight me," he called into the woods. "You want to test our defenses? Test me."

A gentle breeze blew out of the forest, but no one answered his call. Hunter stood waiting. Had the elf scout failed to hear him? Was he being ignored on purpose? Or was this long wait only a ploy to make him nervous?

"Maybe you've heard of me," Hunter shouted. "I am Hunter, who beheaded Raider Two of the Illweather elves, who rescued human children from that castle and left this world in triumph. If you're too afraid to face me, I don't blame you."

A buck trotted into sight, standing among the trees and staring at him. Hunter eyed it skeptically. He hadn't seen any deer here before, and he expected this animal to turn into his elf scout any moment. "What are you waiting for?" he asked it.

The creature bared its teeth at him – sharp, pointed teeth that never belonged to any deer. Then it lowered its antlers and galloped.

Hunter didn't have long to realize that this creature was not going to transform into the expected human shape before it was practically upon him. He tried to imagine smashing its head in while he crouched and swung at its legs instead. His blow connected with a sharp crack and the animal ploughed into the ground beside him. He rose quickly and went for the head this time, jabbing his staff into the base of its skull. The creature began to crumple forward, but it was already transforming as it tucked in its head, did a front somersault, and rose as a man.

In the daylight the elf's hair and skin were blacker than night. His hair flowed past his shoulders, and he wore clothes that looked like they were made of silver. In his hands he held one of the cruel elvish sickles that Hunter had grown all too familiar with. He looked, dismayingly, no worse for the wear despite Hunter's blows. Then he grinned, baring those same pointed teeth, and leapt to the attack.

For a time, Hunter forgot all about his new strategy and let his mind go blank, acting and reacting on instinct alone. He blocked and thrust, dodged and swung, never planning his next move until he was already doing it. He was glad then for every obsessive moment he had put into his training over the last few years: even against the ancient warriors of this godforsaken world, he could hold his own. The staff might not be his weapon of choice, but he still fought like a natural.

The trouble was, so did the elf. Hunter's opponent dodged or parried each attack Hunter sent his way, grinning all the while. No droplet of sweat shined off his unnatural skin as the elf leapt and spun, pressing the attack. Soon, Hunter began to realize his disadvantage in this fight – he might be just as fast, but his weapon was inferior. It cracked as he was blocking one of his opponent's swings, and then broke in two.

Hunter retreated, still blocking his opponent's blows with what now amounted to two jagged clubs. He considered throwing one of the clubs at the elf warrior, and saw the elf react to the possibility with a slight adjustment of his weight. The technique could really work, then! Hunter feinted with his mind again, and swung both clubs together at one of the elf's hands.

It was a ludicrously small target, but he hit it nonetheless. His opponent cried out in pain as Hunter broke his fingers and then, with another hard swing, knocked the sickle out of his hands altogether. Hunter dropped the club in his left and swung again, this time for the head. His swing should have ended the fight, but the elf raised his good hand and caught the club in an iron grip, twisting until the splinters forced Hunter to let go. So he changed tack and leapt after the sickle.

He got the sickle off the ground just as the elf landed his first blow on Hunter's skull. There was a cracking sound – from the wood, thank goodness – and his vision went fuzzy for a moment, but Hunter was not one to let this throw him. He jabbed upward and retreated, getting his bearings. The elf advanced again. As he did so, Hunter swung for his legs with his mind, and with his body, aimed instead for a killing blow.

The blade was sharp, and his aim was true. The elf, caught off guard, missed his parry, and the sickle cut through muscle and bone until his head tumbled from his shoulders.

The elf's head screamed as his body collapsed, then glared at the man who stood above it. "How?" the head screamed.

Hunter pulled a splinter out of his hand and picked the elf up by the hair. "You're too confident that your mindreading is an advantage. You shouldn't trust everything you see."

The elf gnashed his teeth at him even as blood dripped out of his remaining sliver of neck. "You will pay for this. Your ploy can only work once, and then–"

"It'll work as many times as it needs to," Hunter interrupted. "I'm taking you to Psander, elf. You'll be lucky if you can still *think* by the time she's done with you."

He walked back to the fortress walls, where a crowd was watching from the battlements – not just the villagers, but Psander and Phaedra too. He held up the head and sickle, and his audience erupted in cheers and applause.

It was the moment of glory that he had spent years imagining, and it came with all the pride, all the emotional power he had dreamt it would. This was how he would have felt if Karassa had never turned on his people, if Hunter could have gone on to live as the king's champion just as he had meant to. It felt incredible.

But hadn't he left all this behind? He had thought his days

of killing were over – was it different now, just because he was killing elves instead of people? The fact that the elf could talk even after being beheaded did nothing to lessen the savagery of Hunter's victory. He was still waving a head around, indulging in the primal glory of having slain an enemy with his hands. And what if the Kindly Folk only lasted an hour without their heads? What if their seeming immortality was itself an illusion? Would he feel remorse then? He didn't think the elves' deranged foreignness should give him an excuse to feel good about killing.

"My young will grow up fatherless," the elf said, and Hunter looked down at him in shock. He had never considered the possibility that elves might have children. Did they? Could it be true? Or was the elf simply trying to make him feel worse, reading his thoughts and striking where he found a weakness?

"Of course we have children," the elf admonished him. "We are older, wiser, and more worthy than you, but we are still your cousins. We were made by the same cursed Gods who made you."

"Then why aren't there more of you? If you have children, and you live even after your heads have been cut off, why isn't this world completely full of you?"

The elf didn't answer. Was it a sign that Hunter had caught him lying about having children? Or did it mean that elves *could* die, and this one was too afraid to reveal the fact of their mortality? Hunter reached the gate of Silent Hall, which now stood open to him. Luckily, he would not have to guess these answers on his own. That was what Psander was for.

"You put too much faith in your Psander's abilities," the elf scoffed. "She cannot protect you for long."

Hunter swung the head into a wall, just hard enough for the elf to get the point. "Keep underestimating us," he suggested. "That's how you end up like this."

37
Bandu

Bandu had no intention of staying in town for long, whatever Vella might think. It was a good place to stop for now, but she did not like living with so many people around to look at her, to stare, to wonder, to judge. She would be happier, she thought, in a forest or maybe the mountains, where she could live away from all these people. It had been one thing to travel with her pack, with just the four other islanders, but the last few months had been too much for her. She did not like living with these crowds, with what her kind called "civilization." If it hadn't been for Criton, she would have fled all these crowds long ago.

She had let his needs outweigh hers for too long, and though she'd done it out of love, it had been the wrong choice. Criton probably thought she had left because of his promise to her, because he had told her he would never want others and then he'd changed his mind. That was a part of it, but their problems had been building since long before, in some ways since the first time they had kissed. He had never cared more about her than he did about his dragons, his heritage, his imaginary family. She had worried it might be that way, but because he was also brave and strong and did his best to protect her, she had overruled her good sense and stayed with him. Until now.

Now she knew how much of a mistake it had been, and she vowed to trust her instincts better. So if her instincts told her it was time to go back to the forest, that was what she meant to do.

Maybe she could take Vella and Goodweather back to the Yarek, to live in its shadow and under its protection. Nobody was likely to bother them there, and she was confident of her ability to find food. But that was a long way to go, and she was not sure Vella would want to be quite *that* far away from her home. She didn't want to do the same thing to Vella that Criton had done to her, valuing her own desires so high above her mate's.

The trouble was that Vella was so out of her depth that it was hard for Bandu to be sure what the girl even wanted for herself. She wanted Bandu, of course, but what else? Bandu was not sure Vella even knew.

They were probably the same age, really, but Vella was still so much younger than her. She still compared everything to her life with her parents, which sounded as if it had been nicer than anything Bandu could relate to. What was it like to have parents who loved you like that, who fed and clothed you and even tried to make you happy? Bandu could only guess. It had made Vella younger and sweeter than Bandu or Criton, and more fragile. Bandu smiled when she thought of it. In some ways, Vella reminded her of Hunter.

She hoped Goodweather would grow to be as sweet and playful as Vella was. Perhaps if they loved and cared for Goodweather as Vella's parents had done for her, she would have that same sweetness to her that Bandu so appreciated in her new mate.

It was amazing to even have these thoughts. Before, she had worried about what influence Criton and his people might have on their daughter; now she felt free to dream of how she and Vella would raise the girl on their own. What would she be like, their Goodweather? Would she have her father's bravery? His obsessiveness? Would the wind whisper to her as it did to Bandu?

Bandu liked to watch Vella play with the baby. She would

cover Goodweather's eyes with her claw and then pull it away, and the two of them would laugh and laugh. Play came so naturally to her, in a way that Bandu could recognize and admire but never understand. She tried to play the same game with Goodweather a few times, but the baby just looked confusedly at her and Bandu never really knew what was supposed to be so funny to begin with.

Vella was a good mate too, gentle and loving without any of Criton's impatience. She looked at Bandu almost worshipfully when they were alone together, and Bandu liked the way they mated. It was different, and very nice. She took a special delight in making Vella breathe her fire – Vella had learned as a child to suppress that fire, and it only came out when she lost all ability to think. The downside was that this meant they could only mate when they were out 'taking a walk' together with a sleeping baby, because they didn't want to accidentally burn down the house they'd been allowed to sleep in.

She was glad when the townspeople started looking at them suspiciously, because it gave her an excuse to drag Vella away from there. Vella was too used to the comforts of beds and pillows, and did not like to travel. But she was no fool, and didn't argue when Bandu said it was time to go.

So they left, taking some provisions with them, and continued on their journey. To Vella's delight, they found a place to stay before nightfall that had a roof and a bed. It was a woodcutter's house, sitting on the edge of a small wood. Vella was worried at first that the owner would come home and find them there, but Bandu pointed out the thin layer of dust on the table and the empty hooks above the doorway. The owner had been among those who marched against Psander behind High Priest Bestillos. He would not be coming back.

It was a good place to stay, dry and safe from animals but not too close to other people. There was even an overgrown vegetable garden outside, which Vella knew more about tending to than Bandu did, and it did not take Bandu long to find the well that the unknown woodcutter had dug out in the woods. He had abandoned his food store along with the house, so between that and Bandu's foraging, they ate quite well. The food store was all dried grains and lentils and chickpeas, and Bandu was glad for Vella's experience cooking these things. She even knew how to grow them, she said, if they stayed here long enough.

Bandu was not sure what she thought of that. She knew Vella wanted to stay, but she did not like the idea of staying quite this close to Criton and his people. If and when his war ended, he would eventually hear that they had passed through that town, and this house was less than a day's walk from there. But for now, she supposed it would do. Vella was so happy.

At least, she seemed happy. Sometimes Bandu would catch her looking pained and miserable, and every time she asked what was wrong, Vella would say, "You're not going to go back to him, are you?"

And Bandu would say no, and Vella would nod a few times and try to smile, saying something like, "Forget about it." And then a few days later it would happen again.

That was one bad thing about Vella: when something bothered her, she would keep talking about it over and over again, even when there was nothing left to say. It was fair for her to be afraid that Bandu might change her mind and go back to Criton – Bandu was afraid of the same thing, sometimes – but what good did it do for her to keep coming back to it? Bandu was growing to love her more and more as time went by, but having to keep reassuring her about this was frustrating.

"I don't go back," she would say. "Criton is never a good mate."

"But do you love him?"

"Yes, but he is a bad mate, so I don't go back."

That answer always upset her, but what did she want, for Bandu to lie? Of *course* she loved Criton – he was a part of her pack, and always would be. He had comforted her after Four-foot died, had protected her from their enemies more times than she could count, and for all his problems, he had made beautiful little Goodweather with her. If only for that, she would never stop loving him. That didn't mean she wanted him as a mate again.

But that was more than Vella could understand, not knowing their history together. Bandu had neither the words nor the patience to explain how she felt, and she worried that trying would only hurt Vella more. She might feel bad for not being part of Bandu's pack.

Bandu wondered sometimes whether the rest of her pack would like Vella, if they ever got to meet her. She thought Phaedra and Hunter would. Vella was kind and gentle, and Bandu thought they would have a lot in common. In any case, they were unlikely to object to her even if they didn't like her at all. They were both dishonest in that way, with the funny sort of dishonesty that most parents apparently taught their young, where you didn't say what you thought if it wasn't friendly enough.

Narky was much more honest in that way. He also didn't seem to like anyone, at least at first. You had to force Narky to like you – it didn't happen on its own. He still didn't like Bandu, as far as she could tell – though there was no doubt that he respected her, and from Narky, respect was almost as good.

Would he respect Vella, if he ever got to meet her? Bandu wasn't sure. She didn't think he would appreciate her gentleness the way Bandu did. A lot of things were different when you had a baby to think about, and wanting to be with someone gentle was one of those things. It had been easier to stay with Criton before she had had Goodweather's safety to worry about.

She felt bad now, because Criton loved Goodweather too, and Bandu had taken her away. If it had been the other way around – if Criton had been the one running off in the night, taking Goodweather with him – Bandu wouldn't have slept until she had her daughter back. Criton probably felt the same way, and it was wicked of her to have done that to him. But then, it had been wicked of Criton to take such bad care of them. She was sure she had done the right thing. She just wished she could have done it without hurting him.

This was one of those things she couldn't talk to Vella about, because Vella didn't like knowing that Bandu cared so much about Criton. She wouldn't understand Bandu's complicated thoughts, not with Bandu's halting speech, and that meant there were some conversations that shouldn't even be started.

That caused its own problems, though. Criton might have been bad for her, but Bandu had always been able to tell him how she felt. It was lonely keeping her thoughts to herself, and she didn't think it was right for a mate to make her feel lonely.

So that night she told Vella everything, as best she could. It was just as hard as she had expected, but at least Vella didn't interrupt. When she was done, the other girl looked her in the eye and said, "I don't know why you're doing this to me."

"Doing what?"

"Torturing me. You took me away from my family and my people, and now you're telling me you feel bad because of *Criton?* That's not right."

"That *is* right!" Bandu insisted. Vella had clearly understood her words perfectly, so why did she think otherwise?

"I mean that it's not fair," Vella snapped, noting her confusion. "It's not fair to me. You don't feel guilty for wrecking my life, so why should I care how guilty you feel about leaving your husband? It was all your idea!"

"You think I break your life? So why you come with me?"

"Because I love you. That doesn't give you an excuse to be selfish."

Vella was right, but if Bandu couldn't tell her how she felt, even about Criton, then that meant she couldn't tell anyone. The thought made her feel lonelier already.

"You don't want me to tell you what I feel."

Vella sighed. "No, no, I didn't mean it like that. Of course I want you to tell me how you feel, it's just... you hurt me this time. I wish you cared as much about me as you do about Criton."

"I do," Bandu said, but she knew Vella didn't believe her.

Bandu hated fighting. She *hated* it. It had felt like all she and Criton did sometimes was fight with each other – was this what it would be like with Vella too? Would they stop speaking for weeks sometimes, and only start again when Bandu weakened? Maybe Bandu should not have a mate, if it would always be like this. Maybe she should have left Criton by herself.

"*You* are not fair," she said. "You don't want me to care about Criton, but he *makes Goodweather with me*. If he is important to me too, that is not bad. I don't want him anymore, I want you. I can still *think* about him."

She thought Vella was going to say something, but she just sat there, eyes shining. "You're right," she said at last. "I'm sorry. I get jealous sometimes."

And just like that, their fight was over. Bandu leaned over and kissed her, and they lay back down. Nestled between Vella and her sleeping baby, Bandu marveled at how much better she felt now. This was not like with Criton after all. This was nothing like with Criton. Somehow, instead of causing hours and days of pain, this argument had brought them closer together.

"You don't need to be jealous," she told Vella. "You are good for me, better than Criton. And I love you."

38

Narky

The next few days were bloody and decisive, as Magerion moved with blinding speed to consolidate power and eradicate his enemies before anyone could organize an opposition. Narky was given a squad of six men as guards and servants, and he led them in defacing the Great Temple of Magor and rounding up workers to recreate it and rededicate it to the glory of Ravennis. The artist who had painted the temple's murals converted as soon as he was called for, and hurriedly volunteered to rework or paint over every image in the building. The statues of boar-headed Magor were attacked with hammers until they were little more than rubble-covered pedestals. Within a week, Magor's one great city belonged entirely to Ravennis.

It was everything a dishonorable God could want.

Narky became high priest to the whole city, and the people flocked to him with fear in their eyes. They wanted him to tell them that Ravennis would be magnanimous in His conquest and kind to His former enemies. Narky was happy to oblige. So long as people gave themselves freely to Ravennis before their deaths, he told them, He would watch over them kindly and lovingly in their final rest. But those who opposed Him would be subjected to eternal torment, at least until their Ravennis-worshipping descendants prayed to Him for leniency on their behalf. Narky felt he had to add this last bit, because otherwise all those who had died before Ravennis came to Ardis would be doomed through no fault of their own. He had no idea if it was true.

He was growing more comfortable inventing doctrine though, as he spent more time in the role of high priest. Given his God's clear ability to put words in his mouth if need be, every sentence that Narky uttered on his own now carried the Keeper of Fates' implicit approval. The lack of further divine intervention suggested that Narky was guessing right about the true teachings of his God – or else that Ravennis didn't particularly care. Either way, he no longer worried that his teachings would conflict with his God's position.

What did worry him was that Ardis was now undergoing its *second* mass conversion in thirty years. What if Magerion somehow lost control, and Narky got swept away in the backlash? The old artist who was repainting the temple told him a bit of the city's history, and it turned out that the Great Temple of Magor – now of Ravennis – had been built on the same site where God Most High's great temple had once stood. The architect for the new building had been murdered once it was finished so that he could never design any building greater than Magor's temple. That sounded horrifying to Narky, but the artist said it with a certain pride. That was easy enough for him – his painting services didn't come with an end date.

The temple wasn't the only building that had been transformed during the "Great Uprising." The armory across the square had once been the Ardisian Hall of Records, where the Dragon Touched and the royal family had kept all the documents of state, from histories and rare, precious texts of academic wizardry, to tax records and bills of sale. When Bestillos and his followers had come to power, pillaging the Hall of Records had been their second act after tearing down the temple of God Most High. They had burned every document in the building, torn out half the shelves, and turned it into an armory. Narky could only imagine how much that would have horrified Phaedra.

Though his position seemed secure enough for now, he'd

have felt better about it if he'd had better relations with the priests of Elkinar. He was too afraid to even meet with them, after the way Mother Dinendra had humbled him. They were staying neutral for now, and if he made it through the year, they would have to accept the merger of the Gods and become his underlings. But a year was a long time. In the meantime, he ought to make sure they didn't hate him.

Here Ptera was indispensable. She acted as his liaison to the Elkinaran priesthood, representing his gospel without insulting their faith or intelligence, which was likely more than Narky could have done. Narky envied her tact, and wished sometimes that he could secretly go with her just to see how she did it. He hoped he'd learn from her over the years.

A second bloody week came and went, and Magerion sent Narky a messenger saying that he would be needed for the coronation. Probably owing to Narky's youth, Magerion was handling all the details himself, and the messenger intimated that Narky would need to do little more than show up on time to crown and bless the new king. That sounded easy enough, so Narky asked no further questions and sent the messenger back with his acceptance.

After all, the coronation was probably the least of their worries. Magerion's takeover came at a particularly perilous time: the Dragon Touched were on the move. The latest reports were that Criton's army was already marching for Ardis, bent on destroying the city. With any other people, the notion of such a small army threatening Ardis would have been laughable. With the Dragon Touched, it was credible. Criton's people had yet to lose a battle, despite their modest numbers, and though the bulk of their army was northern plainsfolk, it did not take many flying soldiers to imperil a city's defenses.

Narky worried about his inevitable confrontation with Criton. Such a confrontation would come, he knew – he would have to somehow convince his friend to leave the city alone, despite the very real claim the Dragon Touched had over it. It wouldn't be easy – he and Criton hadn't always gotten along so well. He still had memories of Criton's clawed fingers closing around his throat from when the two had argued over a scroll, and in the case of Ardis, all of Criton's strengths and weaknesses as a person were aligned: his insane bravery, his short temper, and that childlike confidence that he was the hero in his own story. They all pointed toward a confrontation.

Narky hoped he would be able to appeal to Criton's overall decency and generosity. If Ptera had taught him anything, it was that flattery really did work. Maybe he could appeal to Criton's sense of himself as a hero, by telling him that only he could bring peace to the region. Narky hoped that would work, especially since it might well be true.

He supposed he ought to be thankful that Criton was in charge at all. It was hardly a given that the one foreigner among the Dragon Touched would be the one to lead them, but just as the islanders' reputation had once led to doors being slammed in their faces, now their reputations were opening new doors. People didn't even call them by their names anymore: they were the Black Dragon and the Black Priest. In theory, this latter title could have been a reference to Narky's robes – Bestillos had been known as the red priest, after all – but everyone knew that was nonsense. Narky would have been the Black Priest even if he'd been wearing mauve.

Magerion wore him like a talisman. Narky was doubly strange, the foreign priest of a foreign God, and he got the impression that he was expected to bring some kind of foreign magic to the service of Ardis. He was their answer to Criton.

But Narky knew better. He had no magic, and his powers of persuasion were limited at best. He was friends with Criton, sort of, and that was all.

What's more, Magerion seemed to be under the false impression that Ravennis could protect the city against God Most High. Narky, who had spoken to elves, to a wizard, and to the dragon Salemis all face to face – well, he knew better. God Most High had not gotten His title by accident.

If they were all lucky, Ravennis might be a high-level servant to the dragons' God. He was allied to the Goddess Eramia, after all, and she was married to Salemis. If they were unlucky then that alliance might have been merely temporary, but either way, Narky did not think his God could ever stand up to Criton's in battle. He would be crushed like a bug.

He could see how, from Magerion's perspective, it might seem as if Criton and his God had prevailed in war only because Magor had been terminally weakened, caught between two stronger Gods. Magerion thought that by aligning with the other of the two, he would be on even ground against the marauding Dragon Touched. He was so, so wrong.

Was Ravennis powerful? Definitely. He had lost Laarna and its Oracles, and still lived – if you counted being Lord of the Underworld as "living". But God Most High had power on a different order of magnitude. He had abandoned the *dragons*, on purpose, without fear of being consumed by His rivals. The dragons, who had themselves killed Gods in battle! If there was a comparison to be made between the two, it was not to Ravennis' benefit.

The trouble was that Narky was terrified of explaining this to Magerion. If he thought he had chosen the wrong side, the new king of Ardis might well execute Narky and start all over again. He might ally with the Dragon Touched and welcome them into Ardis, just as another king had done generations ago, and lift them up as his prized advisors and lieutenants. It would cause much whiplash for his other subjects, but they were all afraid of him now, and they would not stop him. Then Narky would have failed his God completely, and he would reach the underworld as the most hated of creatures. He would probably be tortured and tormented until the day Ravennis was destroyed by some other rival, and then the new God of the Underworld might well torture him too.

Narky had no intention of failing his God. One way or another, he would have to dissuade Magerion from battling the Dragon Touched, without revealing the true supremacy of God Most High.

But first, the coronation. Magerion held it in front of the armory, an unsubtle message if ever there was one. Though it was drizzling, citizens flooded the square to watch Narky place the old crown of Ardesian kingship on Magerion's head. The crown was an interesting story in itself: it had been sitting atop the statue of Magor in the temple, and Narky had assumed that it was gold leaf over stone until someone told him that it was in fact the real crown. Magerion's men had removed it before the statue was destroyed, and the old artist had explained that it had been placed there after the tyrant king's death, as a symbol of the end of the kingship and the beginning of Magor's reign. Of course, it had taken many months to carve the statue, so the red priest had held onto the crown until then. That didn't surprise Narky in the least. Council of Generals or not, it seemed that Bestillos had been in charge all along.

Now Narky placed the crown on Magerion's head, and blessed him in the name of Ravennis below. Magerion rose to deafening cheers, whether genuine or forced it was not clear to Narky. To some degree, it didn't matter. Magerion didn't seem to care about his city's love, only its obedience.

The city would be safe under his rulership, the new king told the crowd. The weakness of Ardis had been vanquished with the last of the red priests, and the city would soon know glory again. The crowd loved that, and they roared their approval. Narky had to hand it to Magerion: the man knew how his city wanted to be ruled.

The tyrant king of Ardis had once had a great palace within the richer quarters of the city, but this had long been torn down and disassembled for its stone. Magerion instead invited Narky and Ptera back to his house, a mansion two stories tall with beautiful decorative weapons and shields adorning the walls. There they dined on choicest veal and discussed their next moves in the war.

Criton's army had come all the way to the Dragon Knight's Tomb, and Magerion wanted to strike at him there despite the unfavorable terrain. He was afraid that given time, the Dragon

Touched would summon the great dragon that had once lived there, and which had incinerated so many Ardismen. The Dragon Touched had won all of their battles so far, despite their army's unimpressive size. With a dragon, they would be unstoppable.

They were unstoppable anyway, but Narky didn't say that. Instead, he suggested that Magerion offer a truce. What if it was too late, and Salemis was already on his way? Better to make peace now, when the terms would be more favorable and the Dragon Touched might be convinced to settle for the territory they had already conquered.

"Peace?" Magerion scoffed. "There can be no peace with the Dragonspawn. They will not have forgotten that Ardis was once theirs. They will not have forgotten what we did to them."

"No," Narky admitted, "but they can't hope to rule the city through armed occupation. Even if we surrendered, a few targeted murders a year would chase them out again."

Magerion shook his head. "You are naïve. They have found allies in the north, allies who would be happy conquering our territory and tilling our fields. They could burn our houses, slaughter every last man, woman, and child, and start from the beginning. Ardis isn't the buildings, boy, it's the land."

That was sobering. If such widespread slaughter was an option, how could the Dragon Touched ever be persuaded to give up? Criton might hesitate to sentence another Tarphaean to death, but that didn't mean he would turn his people away from their only goal just because a friend's life was at stake. Besides which, Narky had always been a mediocre sort of friend.

Yet surrender was impossible with Magerion as king. "Let me pray for guidance," Narky said. "The God that outmaneuvered Magor will have an answer for us."

Magerion shook his head. "Pray while our soldiers march. With the Keeper of Fates' blessing, they will destroy our enemies before any dragon comes to their rescue."

"No," Narky begged, "please. Ravennis hasn't given us His blessing yet. At least wait until He sends us an omen."

"He sent us an omen," Magerion said. "He made me king."

39

PHAEDRA

The apprenticeship was everything Phaedra had imagined it to be. Having discovered the essence of magic theory for herself, Phaedra was able to skip directly to the practice of individual techniques and the elucidation of the theory behind each. Psander was not a patient teacher, but neither was Phaedra a patient student, and their progress was rapid. If magic was poetry, Phaedra was finally being taught composition.

That was certainly how she thought of it, though Psander took a different view. She talked of magical "resonance" as if it was a natural force, when to Phaedra even that choice of words suggested poetry. The more a composition resonated with the natural ugliness or beauty of its context, the more powerful it became. The trick – and the thing that set academic wizardry apart from any less rigorous form – was controlling one's composition with such precision as to yield the desired effect and no more.

This had been the major work of the academics: testing and retesting individual techniques in specific contexts until the effects of their magic could be reliably predicted. Many of the scrolls Psander gave Phaedra to read dripped with the tedium of their authors' work, and yet there were few things more exciting than to read about a discovery in a book and to be able to prove its worth within minutes.

Under Psander's tutelage, Phaedra quickly learned how to replicate the ghostly light that had once impressed her so; she constructed her own flawed illusions and practiced her wizard sight; she even learned how to call books down from the impossibly tall library shelves. This last task turned out to be deceptively easy: all the effort had gone into threading the ghostly tethers that connected each book to its spot on the shelf and to the library floor. Pulling on those tethers was as simple as widening one's weak magical field and calling out the right name.

Phaedra's training was not all rote, of course: the principles of magic theory allowed for plenty of improvisation. This improvisation was most effective in areas where the wizard had a deep knowledge of the related symbology, and for Phaedra, that field was travel magic. She had spent a year of her life deeply obsessed with Atel the Messenger God, and she knew the imagery of His domain better than she knew anything. Whenever she read about a travel-related spell, her mind would fill with dozens of modifications that could make the spell more effective under varying circumstances.

The hardest training, and the most necessary, was in the realm of mental defense. There were two components to such a defense: detection, and willpower. Pushing a known intruder out of one's mind was actually fairly easy, Phaedra discovered – one fought that fight on one's home turf, after all. It was detecting the intrusion in the first place that caused all the difficulty. It was like training oneself to recognize a dream before anything implausible happened. It did not come naturally or easily, no matter how often Psander attacked. She had the humiliating habit of slipping past Phaedra's defenses undetected while Phaedra was studying a book, and then reading aloud from its pages using Phaedra's own eyes. Psander might be across the room and facing the other way, but all of a sudden she would speak the very words Phaedra was reading, and Phaedra would know that she had failed her test yet again.

The elves, Psander insisted, were stronger in their mental

attacks and at least as stealthy, but Phaedra had reason to believe that she was exaggerating their subtlety. For one thing, it was much easier to catch an intruding Psander when Phaedra knew she was being tested. The elves could be expected to make an attempt on Phaedra's thoughts any time they were present, so she would already be on the lookout whenever she was near one.

"True," Psander said suddenly. "But that's no excuse to leave yourself unprotected in the meantime."

Phaedra groaned and pushed her out again.

She was glad, though, to be learning from Psander. Phaedra's spellcasting on Tarphae had had the desired effects, but it had relied entirely on God Most High's willing intervention. This state of things, it turned out, was to be avoided.

"You used the most inherently dangerous form of magic there is," Psander said when Phaedra told her of her exploits. "Gaining the attention of a God is extremely perilous, Phaedra. You're lucky God Most High didn't smite you on the spot."

Phaedra looked at her incredulously. "Might He have?"

"Of course. The Gods are made of such powerful magic that They are liable to burn any creature that gets too close to Them. They *are* made of magic, you know, as far as we can tell. Corporeal bodies may or may not be sustainable on Their side of the mesh. In any case, we must keep our distance whenever possible, even those of us who don't already have a target on our backs. The attention of a God can be disastrous at any time, *especially* if you are attempting to perform a feat of magic. The fact that you may be practicing devotional magic is no defense. One false move, one mislaid cue, and They will destroy you."

That was alarming, if true, but it didn't seem to match up with Phaedra's experience. "I don't know," she said. "God Most High kept the sea at bay on our behalf even before I learned to enhance my prayers with magic. He went to the trouble of keeping the merchantman from leaving Mur's Island until we were aboard. Do you really think He'd have turned on me a few weeks later over a poorly executed spell?"

"Yes," Psander said. "And it wouldn't have been the first time, either. God Most High in particular is said to have once struck down His own high priest over a misworded sacrifice. You are intensely lucky that you didn't get burned."

While Phaedra spent her days learning from Psander, she was happy to see that Hunter was putting his time to good use too, training the villagers how to fight with staves and spears. She doubted the training would do the villagers much good, but no one could deny its positive effect on Hunter. Gone was the brooding, melancholy man she knew – Hunter had a project now, and he was as focused on it as Phaedra was on her own. She thought this must have been what he was like when he had first learned to use his sword – intense, tenacious, obsessive – except that he was also making friends among Psander's villagers, set as he was on training them. In her few breaks from studying, she would watch him from one of the tower windows as he drilled his students or practiced by himself, or even helped out in the garden. She could tell he was growing into his own, and she was glad.

Psander used much of Phaedra's reading time setting up new wards in an attempt to dissuade the elves from attacking. It was a miracle that they had waited this long, but Phaedra supposed they could afford to be patient. From what Psander told her, it sounded as if Silent Hall had arrived in this world much nearer to Castle Goodweather than to Illweather, and the Goodweather elves might well have been concealing Psander's arrival from their enemies. Either that, or the two elven camps were still negotiating what to do with Psander and her people once the fortress was breached. Phaedra hoped not.

Phaedra told Psander about Auntie Gava, and how the old woman had warded the "demons" away with her own blood. Psander was impressed.

"That is a very clever ward," she said. "Now that I've seen something of the elves, I have to admit that we academics spent far too much time trying to learn *about* them and far too little time trying to protect ourselves and the world *from* them. We never liked to give hedge witches credit, but if Mur's Island hasn't seen an elven raid in so many generations, their 'aunties' have done far more for them than the academics did for our own people."

"Can we use Gava's ward to keep them away now?"

"No, not here. It is far too late to keep them from detecting us, and for once they don't seem to be looking for children. My impression is that the queen of the elves means to set up a breeding program."

Phaedra tried not to think about that.

For now, the greatest danger came from the possibility that the elves might soon realize how illusory Psander's defenses were. If a fairy scout discovered the extent of the deception, they were all doomed.

So when a scout did breach the outer wards and Hunter volunteered to capture it, Phaedra didn't have the luxury to object. Instead she waited on the battlements with Psander and the entire village, hoping. Hunter was just visible, standing right before the tree line with his staff.

"He'll do it," Atella said, a little further down the row. "He'll win."

They were able to see the whole fight from their vantage point. They gasped when Hunter's weapon snapped, and broke into cheers when he disarmed his opponent. But when Hunter cut off the elf's head, Psander snorted disgustedly.

"I'd have preferred it if he'd captured one alive," she said.

"He did," Phaedra told her. "We're not even sure elves *can* be killed."

Sure enough, it soon became obvious that Hunter and the elf's head were carrying on a conversation. "Amazing!" Psander exclaimed, sounding more genuinely surprised than Phaedra had ever heard her. "I wonder."

Psander was not a talkative woman, but she couldn't help speculating, while Hunter brought the head back to the fortress, about how and why elves might survive their beheadings.

"Do you suppose their souls remain in their heads because

this world has no underworld?" she asked. "If that were the case, one would expect us also to survive beheadings here. That seems unlikely, but we have yet to fully disprove the possibility. Alternatively, could it be that the elves' souls are sturdy enough that they don't even need a functioning body to cling to? What does it mean that the body has stopped moving, while the head still speaks?"

Phaedra asked, "Will you be able to learn the answers from this one? Is there some way to make sure the head won't lie to you?"

"Maybe," Psander said. "If so, it will take some experimentation. There are known potions for truth telling, but I possess the ingredients for none of them, and what's more, I am uncertain of whether such a potion would have any efficacy without a stomach to digest it. I will have to learn my answers through interrogation and experimentation."

They greeted Hunter at the base of the tower, where the elf's head met them with rageful obscenities, sharp teeth gnashing. Psander shoved a rag in its mouth. "You will be less useful to me if I have to cut your tongue out," she told the elf, "but I will do it if I must. I'm sure the tongue of an elf would make for a fine ingredient if it turns out I have one lying around."

The elf looked hatefully at her, but he stopped trying to speak. "Should we bring the body in too?" Hunter asked.

"Absolutely. I have a long table in my study – Phaedra, show him the way. I'll bring the gentleman's head myself."

With the help of a few village men, they retrieved the elf's body before some scavenging beast could devour it and brought it up the stairs to Psander's study. The wizard's study was a large room near the top of the tower, past the heavy door that had once stymied the Tarphaean islanders in their attempt to interrupt one of Psander's experiments. Psander had cleared the raised stone slab that stood in the middle of the room, so they laid the body down there beneath its head. They wanted to stay to watch Psander work and perhaps to ask about the various bottles, vials, and tools that lined the walls, but as soon as the body was positioned on the table, Psander said, "Everybody out."

Phaedra was about to reluctantly file out with the others when Psander said, "Not you, Phaedra. You can stay. I'm too accustomed to working alone – I forgot about you."

"Oh," Phaedra said, sighing with relief. "Thank you."

"You're welcome. Now hand me that bottle over there. Yes, the grain liquor. And that dish, too. Let's see if we can't set some ground rules for our friend."

Phaedra did as she was told, and Psander was soon pouring a clear liquid into the dish. The elf's eyes followed her movements, showing only contempt.

"I hope to learn a lot from you over the coming days," Psander told the elf, "but I want to be very clear about what I expect from our conversation, and that is first and foremost civility. You may lie to me all you please without consequence – I expect plenty of lies. But if you open your mouth to curse me or my people, if you say a word of denigration or abuse, here is what I will do. I will lift you up by the hair, and I will place you in this dish. Do you want to know what that feels like?"

She did not wait for a response – the elf's mouth was still stuffed with that rag, after all. His eyes betrayed no fear, no doubt, no curiosity as she followed through on her threat, placing the head chin-deep in the alcohol.

It must have been agony, because Phaedra suddenly felt his presence in her head as he lost control and let out a long psychic wail. She covered her ears instinctively, though it had no effect – the scream went ringing on and on in her skull until she finally gathered her wits and banished him from her mind.

She dropped her hands again and looked back to the table. The elf was making a muffled sound through the rag in his mouth, and tears were dripping from his eyes as he squeezed them shut against the pain. Psander had turned from the elf and was looking on Phaedra with disappointment. After all their training with mental defense, she still hadn't been prepared. She would do better in future, she promised herself. Now

Phaedra knew what an elf's presence felt like, she would notice it even when it was subtler.

With a grimace, Psander lifted the elf's head once more and placed it back on the table. She waited calmly while the elf slowly recovered, then pulled the rag out of his mouth and said, "Do I make myself clear?"

"Ohhhhhhhh," the elf moaned, still weeping. "Clear, yes."

"Good. I'm going to start with some very simple questions. What is your name?"

"Olimande."

"And your orders here were?"

The elf stared up at her defiantly.

"I'll answer that one, then," Psander said. "Your orders were to test my defenses, to learn how they worked and how they can be avoided or dispelled. Have you satisfied yourself on that account?"

Olimande's head wobbled on its remaining portion of neck, and Phaedra was fairly sure he was trying to shake it. "Hunter got to you first," she said. "And after that, you weren't paying attention."

"The raids will not end," the elf said. "We will find a weakness, and then our queen will destroy you. She will eat your heart herself, wizard."

"That is always a danger," Psander admitted magnanimously, "but I am beginning to doubt it, frankly. After all, I am about to learn a good deal more about her than she knows about me."

"I will tell you nothing."

"You've already told me that your queen means to eat my heart. So now I must ask, why? Is there something special about my heart, of all organs, that is more precious to her? I have eaten heart, though not a human heart, obviously, and it was neither tender nor especially enjoyable. If she hopes to eat my heart, therefore, I imagine that it must be for symbolic reasons and thereby magical ones as well."

"You understand nothing," Olimande sneered.

"Nonsense," Psander replied. "You have every incentive to

turn me away from the truth. When you call me a fool, that is when I can be most confident of your lies."

The elf had nothing to say to that. Psander really was on the right track, then. If the fairy queen wanted to eat Psander's heart, that meant there was a special power in the act.

"Perhaps I ought to try eating *your* heart," the wizard mused. "Would it give me an advantage of some kind?"

"There is no advantage you can gain over us," Olimande said. "Sooner or later, we will devour you."

Psander raised an eyebrow. "Why this fixation on eating us? I recognize the symbolic power of doing so, but you have yet to connect it to a specific purpose, which suggests that it is not part of a given spell but a ritual of some inherent value to you. Is eating a human's heart a method for permanently absorbing their magic, or perhaps their soul? If it's a matter of absorbing people's souls, then your own souls must not be kept in the heart at all, but in the head somewhere. Otherwise, it would be your body that was moving without your head, rather than the other way around. Could your own souls be stored in your brains, rather than your hearts?"

The elf closed his eyes. "I have said already, I will tell you nothing. You will learn no more from speaking with me."

"Mmm," Psander said. "Then I shall have to begin experimenting. Phaedra, there is a saw on the far wall, second shelf. Hand it to me, will you?"

40

CRITON

Criton had sent scouts to watch the city of Ardis, so they were ready when the assault came. They had moved their livestock to the other side of the mountain, supervised by a few hand-picked youths, and had themselves hiked up to secure their dominance of the high ground. They waited for the Ardismen to come creeping up the mountain in the hope of surprising their quarry, whom they believed were still asleep. Then Criton's men came down on their assailants with a roar, routing them before the two sides could even come to blows.

More Ardismen fell to them that night than at any other battle. They had to wait until morning to properly assess the devastation, but when they did, the results were astounding. Only six of Criton's men had lost their lives. On the Ardismen's side, it was nearly four hundred.

"Enough hesitating," Belkos said to him when the count had been made. "It's time to march on Ardis. If they know what's good for them, they'll surrender."

"Let's bury our dead," Criton said. "We can discuss our next move after that."

If that was the best he had, he must be getting truly desperate. His people were growing suspicious. He had told himself for long enough that he was being prudent, cautious, when in fact he was simply reluctant to commit to the destruction of Ardis. And why shouldn't he be reluctant? He knew what the rest of the Dragon Touched didn't: that Narky was in there.

They had left Narky on the road to Ardis, where his God had separated him from his friends and sent him into the city of their enemies. There had always been the question before of whether he had survived – the Dragon Touched had kept no prisoners, and Criton knew nothing of what had been happening inside the city. But he hadn't failed to notice that many of the dead Ardismen from this last raid wore raven charms.

How cruel would it be if Narky had survived his inevitable struggle with the worshippers of Magor, only to be caught in the slaughter of a Dragon Touched victory? It was one thing to kill Ardismen – they had shown the Dragon Touched no mercy a generation ago, and Hessina and Belkos insisted that they deserved no mercy in return. But it was another thing to condemn his friend.

Criton had so few friends now. Narky had left; Phaedra and Hunter had left; even Bandu had left, and taken Criton's daughter and another man's wife with her. Belkos was his friend, of course, as well as his cousin, but somehow it was not the same. Delika didn't count either – she saw him as a sort of father, not a friend. Only the other islanders knew him for who he was. Only they knew *Criton*, and only Criton had friends – no one could be friends with the Black Dragon.

But there was no way he could say all this to Hessina or Kilion or Belkos or anyone. So what if Narky was in Ardis? Why should Criton's people care? He wasn't the only person in the city who didn't deserve to die. To condemn a city was to condemn its peaceful dissidents too, and its innocent children. Criton still had memories of Bestillos spearing the little princes of Anardis. The Dragon Touched would do the same in Ardis, when they breached its walls – to pretend otherwise was naïve. Hessina had told him as much. That was what victory looked like.

Had Criton become a hard enough man that he could

welcome such horror? Why should Narky's presence have been the only obstacle left, the only signpost to remind him of the nature of the path he was on?

It was too late now anyway. After this victory, the Dragon Touched and their allies expected to take Ardis. They had fought this war for that purpose alone, and Criton did not think he could dissuade them. So when the Dragon Touched had buried their dead, Criton told his people that it was time to march on the city. At this point he thought they might have done so even if he'd told them to march the other way, but at least this way his cousin smiled at him instead of frowning.

Narky met them on the road late that afternoon, flanked by a few guards under a banner of peace. He was dressed in black robes, and looked very official. Official, and nervous.

Criton was relieved to see him. He wondered if he could keep him as a "prisoner" so as to save him from the pillage of Ardis. It was worth considering. In the meantime, he had the meeting tent erected and called for the council of elders to gather there and hear what Narky had to say.

When everyone was in attendance, Narky began his speech. "I'm here on behalf of Magerion, King of Ardis, who wants to broker a peace between our peoples."

Hessina interrupted him. "Ardis has no king. Magerion is only one general among many."

"Oh," Narky said. "So I guess I'm the one who's been away for months, pillaging the countryside? Because if I were, I wouldn't have any idea what was going on in Ardis."

Criton winced. With Narky's diplomatic skills, they'd be lucky if Hessina didn't insist upon a public execution before they even reached the city.

"The other generals are all dead," Narky went on, "and so are the priests of Magor. Under Magerion, the entire city has converted to my church. Ardis worships Ravennis now."

"Are we supposed to care?" Belkos snarled. "Ardis is still Ardis. Its people are still our enemies. No new God can change that."

"Let me respectfully disagree," Narky said, sounding in no way respectful. "It's Magor who stood up against your God when Bestillos and the generals came to power, and Magor who tried to exterminate your people. Magor was your enemy, but Ravennis has only helped you. Criton can back me up on this – we left Tarphae together. Ravennis helped us get off the island, and Ravennis kept us together afterwards. Our Gods are allies. Magor tried to destroy you, and Magor tried to destroy Ravennis. Or were you too busy hiding to hear about what happened to Laarna?"

If Hessina or Belkos had been in any way open to Narky's arguments, he lost them with that last gibe. Criton was glad the elders of the plains were there to keep the two of them from tearing Narky apart.

"We know what happened at Laarna," Kana said. "We had heard your God was dead."

"My God *is* dead," Narky said, "just not in the way other Gods have died. He rules the underworld, while your God rules the heavens. There's no conflict between the two, unless you insist on starting one."

Belkos waved him off. "We haven't fought and bled all this time to make peace on the eve of our victory. Ravennis may not be Magor, but He's still taken the side of the Ardismen."

"Isn't that the whole point of war, though?" Criton nearly begged. "To make peace on our terms?"

"The point of *this* war," Belkos answered, "is to take Ardis."

Hessina turned back to Narky. "You say our Gods are allies? You are a fool. God Most High needs no allies. If you and your God stand in the way of ours, you will both be crushed."

"Maybe," Narky said. "Or maybe God Most High will abandon you if you condemn His friend, just as He turned on the dragons for condemning Salemis. A God as powerful as yours doesn't rely on His people to survive. He can always start again."

Those words struck a blow. The council fell silent, pondering Narky and his threat. Then Belkos said, "Kill this man. He may be your friend, Criton, but he's here to spread poison and doubt. He and his God are liars and cowards – they know that their armies are useless, so they're trying to defeat us from within. Kill him and take Ardis – God Most High will bless us."

"The alliance could be real," Criton said. "Magor and Ravennis have been enemies all along."

"That doesn't make his God and ours friends," Endra pointed out.

"Kill this man," Belkos said again. "Put his ugly head on a spear and drive it into the heart of Ardis."

"Listen to me," Narky said, beginning to sound desperate. "I'm the man who killed Bestillos while Criton was lying helpless on the ground. Ravennis gave me strength, and guided my aim. I'm one of His fingers. Ravennis did as much to rescue Salemis from his prison as God Most High did – without Him, the Dragon Touched would still be in hiding and the plainsmen would still be paying Ardis tribute. You can call Ravennis your ally, you can call Him your God's servant, you can call Him God Most High's son, I honestly don't care. Whatever you want to call Him, He's been on your side."

"That's a very convenient position for you to take," said Hessina, "now that we are at your gates. Where was this alliance two nights ago, when your army tried to surprise us as we slept?"

Narky bowed his head. "I tried to stop that. Magerion thought that Magor's weakness was responsible for your victories, not God Most High's strength, so he figured by aligning himself with a stronger Ravennis, he could beat you. I told him he was wrong, and that Ravennis wouldn't bless the attack, but... it didn't work. I'll take responsibility for not convincing him. I'm here because he's learned his lesson, and is willing to make peace with you."

"Willing!" Belkos laughed. "You hear that? The new king of Ardis is *willing* to make peace with us. Magerion, who was the red priest's lieutenant during the purge, who slaughtered our parents and brothers – he's willing to make peace with us, now that we're about to give him and his people what they deserve."

He spat on Narky's face. "Here's your peace."

Narky wiped his face with his robe, and Criton could see the rage building within his friend. "Criton," Narky asked, "who is this idiot? Can you send him away?"

"Belkos is my cousin," Criton said. "My mother was his aunt."

"Wow. I guess your side got the decency *and* the brains."

Criton folded his arms. "If you want us to make peace with Ardis, you're doing yourself more harm than good. Apologize to my cousin, or this meeting is over."

Narky looked back at him with something like distaste. He'd expected more indulgence from Criton, as if they were back with the others all together, where everyone would forgive him for being blunt. He was reassessing now, and it clearly pained him.

"I apologize," he said, keeping his good eye locked on Criton. "Please forgive me, all of you. I wouldn't want the Dragon Touched to react to my personal rudeness by murdering thousands. So many people are relying on the Dragon Touched to be merciful, the way your God is supposed to be."

"Our God is merciful," Hessina cut in, "but only to the repentant. A city that abandons the worship of a cruel God only to turn to an underhanded one has shown no signs of repentance. Frankly, Ardis does not deserve our mercy."

"Your king sent an army first," Kana agreed, "and when that failed, he sent us his city's rudest messenger to *argue* for peace when he should have been pleading for it. Your lack of respect is staggering."

Criton loudly cleared his throat, hoping to cut off any further escalation. "We'll talk it over and give you our terms," he said.

Once Narky had been led away, the others turned on Criton. "Our terms?" Belkos asked, his voice shaking. "Our terms are that they die! We're not going to let Ardis and its leaders mock us just because you're friends with their high priest!"

"Narky made good points!" Criton objected. "He's not the most polite person I know, but he's one of the smartest, and he's no liar. He believes what he says."

Hessina snorted. "What he says is nonsense."

"How do you know? How do you know Ravennis isn't a servant of God Most High, just as we are? Has our God told you otherwise?"

Hessina shook her head, but she didn't look any less skeptical.

"You don't know, then," Criton said. "I was there when Narky killed Bestillos, and I was there when he killed the giant Boar of Hagardis. I think his argument about Ravennis being a servant of God Most High is a good one. What if he's right? What if God Most High has judged Ravennis worthy of serving Him in this world and the underworld? Our God reigns supreme in the heavens – He doesn't need Ardis. What harm will come to us from offering peace terms?"

"You're young," Belkos said, "and you're foreign. It's easy for you to say that Magor was responsible for the purge, but we remember those days. It wasn't Magor who killed our families, it was the Ardismen. After what they did to us, they think that running to another God will protect them now that we're here to take our city back? Our God is merciful, but Ardis doesn't deserve His mercy. It definitely doesn't deserve ours."

"The purge happened almost thirty years ago," Criton countered. "When you take the city, will you spare those too young to have participated in it? No, you'll kill everyone you can get your hands on, and thirty years from now, the remnants of the Ardismen will try to take *their* city back and punish the people who killed *their* parents."

"Let them try," Belkos sneered. "You think the children of Ardis deserve our mercy because only their parents and grandparents sought to wipe us out? What do you think these children will try to do when they're of age?"

Hessina nodded. "A guardian tree doesn't produce carob seeds, Criton. A poisoned tree bears poisoned fruit."

"That's an argument for perpetual war."

"No," Belkos said, "it's an argument for winning *this* war once and for all. If God Most High is on our side, our enemies will never rise again."

Criton turned to the plainsmen. "Do you agree with this? The Ardismen have been your enemies and your overlords for generations. Do you think we should ignore their pleas for mercy?"

Endra spoke first. "I think with favorable enough terms, a peace might be granted. If Ardis were to pay *us* tribute, and if their walls were to come down as those of Anardis once did, I think that might be suitable. With tributes of gold, bronze, and stone, a city of the Dragon Touched could rise in the north."

"It is a possibility," Kana agreed.

Criton turned back to Hessina. "Our God has named you our leader in matters of religion. What religious tribute would you require the Ardismen to make, if we were going to make peace with them?"

He could tell that Hessina didn't like the question, but she found it unable to dismiss as the others turned to her expectantly. He had asked it well, he knew, reminding her that she was a religious leader and not a political one, and that their God had entrusted him with the authority to make peace as well as war.

At last she said, "Abandoning Magor is not enough, if they have simply adopted another false God in His stead. The people of Ardis would have to accept God Most High as the Lord Above All, and the master of their new patron God. If your friend Narky is serious about saving Ardis, he can stand before his people as the high priest of Ravennis and proclaim that his God is subservient to ours, a heavenly lieutenant tasked with the mission of bringing God Most High's order to the world below. If the people embrace this teaching and repent of their actions in the purge, Ardis will be worthy of God Most High's mercy."

Endra raised his eyebrows. "That's a lot to ask."

"It's perfect," Criton said. "Narky has the authority to make God Most High's supremacy official dogma for the worshippers of Ravennis. If he wants to save Ardis, he'll do it. He suggested the idea himself; let him own it."

They spent the next hour discussing the specifics of the proposed tribute Ardis would have to pay, and then sent for Narky. He grimaced when he heard their conditions, but promised to deliver their message to Magerion and return with his answer. Then he left with his guards, and it fell to Criton to calm his cousin.

Hessina might have given Criton her blessing to negotiate terms despite her skepticism, but Belkos was inconsolable. "You're selling our victory away for smoke and vapor," he said. "This decision will doom us. Our grandchildren will be slaves."

"That's ridiculous," Criton said. He didn't understand his cousin's anger – why should Belkos be so attached to this war when even Hessina was willing to see where Criton's negotiations would lead?

"Magerion may not accept the terms," Kilion pointed out. He had been nearly silent throughout the meeting, but apparently he too was bothered by Belkos' irrationality.

"That won't forgive what you've tried to do here," Belkos said. "You would give Ardis away for nothing."

"How can you say that?" Criton asked. "If Magerion accepts our terms for peace, it'll mean the end of Ardisian rule over the north, a yearly tribute in gold and stone, and the elevation of God Most High even among the worshippers of Ravennis! How could you dismiss all that?"

Belkos looked at him with contempt. "All those things would be ours if we conquered Ardis as we always meant to. There's nothing they can give us that we couldn't take ourselves, but with the surrender of Ardis to Magerion and his people, you leave open the possibility that some day they'll stop paying the tribute, that their religious doctrines could change or their new God be abandoned, and that they will seek to destroy us again. You are selling us for nothing."

"We're selling them their own lives for peace," Criton said. "It seems like a fair enough trade to me."

But Belkos only stormed out of the tent.

"Give him time," Hessina counseled. "He too will be glad when this war is over."

Criton nodded absently. He wondered.

41

PHAEDRA

Phaedra did not stay to watch Psander take a saw to the elf's head. It was the most she could do just to ask Psander how her interrogations were going the next day, when the wizard poked her head into the library.

"Most profitably," Psander answered. "The elven anatomy appears to be built much the same as ours, and yet now that the head has been removed, it is operating on magical rather than anatomical principles. I believe – though I do not yet know – that the head gathers all the magic into itself upon severance and uses it as a backup system until, presumably, it is either reattached or destroyed. From what I've gathered so far, the magic is stored in the heart prior to severance, which is why the elves believe that devouring a heart will increase one's power. Presumably, now that the magic has transferred from heart to brain, the elven way would be to devour the latter."

"Oh," Phaedra said, trying to keep her disgust from showing. "Do you plan on… doing that?"

"I'll admit I've considered it," Psander said, "but I think there is more to be learned before I take such final measures. Olimande can still talk, you know, even with the top of his skull removed. And with greater access to his brain, I think I may be able to disinhibit him and improve the quality of his answers. I shall have to be very careful, but I think it can be done."

Psander finally seemed to take note of Phaedra's discomfort as she said this, and twisted her mouth thoughtfully. "Perhaps while I am conducting my experiments, you should take the opportunity to conduct some research of your own. Independent research used to be a staple of magical schooling, back when such a thing existed. I believe we will both be glad to see you put to good use here in the library rather than getting in my way upstairs."

Phaedra nodded. "That sounds perfect."

"What have you been reading this morning?"

"Nothing in particular," Phaedra lied. In actuality, she had been scanning the first few lines of scroll after scroll and codex after codex, searching for any sign of healing magic. Psander had once told her that healing magic was a lost art, that there was no way to fix her ankle, and yet Phaedra knew that *some* texts still existed from the days of academic healing magic – after all, she had brought Psander just such a scroll from Anardis. *Developments in Magical Surgery* it had been called, and she doubted it was the only one of its kind.

So far, her search had been unsuccessful. Besides *Developments*, which covered magical techniques for wound cleaning and ultra-localized cautery, the only other scroll of healing magic that Phaedra had found so far described a rather horrifying surgery for the male anatomy. She was very glad that she had put that one away before Psander came in.

"I meant to ask you," she said, pointing to a side table piled high with scrolls. "What are all those doing there? Were you researching the underworld?"

"I wasn't," Psander answered, "though I had meant to at one time. In return for her help with the Boar of Hagardis, I had promised Bandu that I would tell her how to retrieve her wolf from the world below. It's a ridiculous notion, of course – you don't risk your soul for an animal that was barely going to last the decade anyway. But for a brief while, I thought I might have time to research the question."

"But you won't now," Phaedra said with disappointment,

noting the finality in Psander's voice. The wizard might have opened her tower to the villagers, might have finally revealed herself to them, but that didn't mean she had changed. Promises meant nothing to her, except as tools for getting what she wanted.

"No," Psander agreed, "I won't. There has always been a more pressing concern, and I imagine there always will be."

Phaedra looked over at the pile of books. "Then I will."

"You will do no such thing. I've given you all the tools you need to be truly useful – I won't have you squander your skills on such frivolity when there is much more urgent work to be done. It won't be long before I'll be sending you back, after all."

"What?" Phaedra cried. "You need me to go back? Why are you only telling me this now?"

She could have answered her own question. Psander never volunteered information until it was convenient for her to do so, and she never acted out of the goodness of her heart. Bandu called her a wicked woman, Narky called her a blackmailer and a manipulator, and neither of them were wrong. It was the thing Phaedra disliked most about her mentor, even as it was nearly inseparable from the quality she admired most: Psander's unapologetic use of power.

After a meaningless, defensive answer to Phaedra's second question, Psander went back to answering the first. "When we first arrived here," she said, "the ground shook, and so did the sky. Was there no such effect in the other world?"

"The sky shaking?"

Psander nodded. "It only happened here, then. Had it happened on your side, you would have known. A skyquake is not a subtle effect. If you stay here for long enough, you're bound to witness one – which, I assure you, you don't want to do."

"I trust you," Phaedra said. It was hard to imagine quite what a skyquake would be like, but that only made the concept more frightening.

Psander went on: "I assumed at first that the skyquake was

a temporary aftereffect of our arrival. But there was another soon afterward, and another three months after that. The first came during an assault by the Goodweather elves, and I'm sure it was that more than anything that convinced them my wards were too strong to be overpowered through sheer numbers. The coincidence is responsible for our survival.

"Even so, the phenomenon itself is extremely ominous. I have had some time since then to determine what causes these skyquakes, and I believe that this world is being dragged closer to yours, to a dangerous extent. Our arrival here and the introduction of the Yarek on the other side have bound the worlds closer together, and they are moving closer still. As far as I can tell, if the connection isn't loosened then the two will eventually crash, most likely killing everyone on both."

Phaedra couldn't help but gasp – it was too terrible to believe. Would God Most High really have allowed the islanders to plant the Yarek's seed in their soil even if it meant the eventual destruction of both worlds?

"Then why haven't we seen any skyquakes on our side?" she asked. Surely, Psander had made some mistake.

Or maybe she hadn't. It was true that God Most High had been kind to Phaedra and her friends so far, but that didn't mean she could know His motives. Maybe the islanders had been *meant* to bring about the worlds' end?

"I had assumed," Psander told her, "that there had been skyquakes on your side as well. I cannot pretend that I understand the situation fully, but my first guess is that this world's much smaller size makes it more vulnerable to such disturbances. Presumably as the two worlds move closer together, your side too will begin to see these effects."

"But you think we can fix this?" Phaedra asked, sounding desperate even to her own ears. "You think we can stop the collision from happening?"

Psander shrugged. "Maybe. In any case, it seems wise to try."

"So what will I be doing?"

"Sealing gateways," Psander said. "I have come to believe

that the gateways between the worlds are not only areas of thinner mesh but in fact points of connection, tethers that keep the worlds from drifting apart. The new one between my hall and Tarphae seems to have thrown off the balance, but presumably sealing some of the other gates will have an effect similar to cutting loose a mooring line – the distance between the worlds should grow with each severance until eventually the system becomes stable again.

"This newest connection will be the strongest, of course, built as it is on the Yarek's power. It may take the severing of many gates to make up for the one new one. But to cut the connection at my hall would be to cede all power over interworld travel to the elves, and I am unwilling to do that – besides which, a severance may be a good deal more difficult to accomplish here than elsewhere. In any case, my preference is to sever the connections at the other gateways instead, releasing some of the tension while leaving me in possession of the only active gate.

"The flaw in this plan, of course, is that I'm still afraid to leave my house. I may be safer here than in my previous location, but I cannot afford to meet any elves without the protection of my walls and wards. Your presence solves this problem. If you could go back and seal the gateways from the other side, it would put both of us at lower risk without lessening our effectiveness. That is my hope, anyway."

Her words were heartening. As long as they had a plan, Phaedra felt she could move mountains. "How do I seal a gate?" she asked.

"That's the bad news," Psander said, gesturing to the walls of books that surrounded them. "Your guess is as good as mine. Nobody's ever attempted to close a fairy gateway before – I'm proud enough for having learned how to open one. It is up to you to answer your own question if you can, and in the meantime I will study Olimande to determine if and how an elf can die."

"Wait!" Phaedra cried, realizing that her mentor was about

to leave. "Can you at least point me to the right shelf?"

Psander thought for a moment, but then she shook her head. "The answer itself is in none of my books – as I said, to my knowledge nobody has done anything like this before. The hope is that you will find something tangentially useful in this library, and use it to develop a spell of your own. I cannot tell you where this inspiration lies – if I could, I'd have done it myself. If it were me, I might start with accounts of the War of the Heavens, since that was the last time the mesh underwent significant changes. But that is only a thought."

With that she exited, leaving Phaedra to a roomful of books. Phaedra stared up at the shelves that rose so impossibly high and felt nothing but despair. Even if the answer *was* here somewhere, what were the chances she would find it?

She laughed sadly to herself, a puny "huhuh" that dissipated into the many folds and crevices of the stacks that surrounded her. Who would have thought that she could ever feel so intimidated by a pile of books?

She started where Psander had recommended, with accounts of the War of the Heavens. But her mind kept wandering, and whenever she thought a scroll was about to tell her something useful, it would veer off into some other topic entirely. How had the mesh been torn at the war's onset, and how had it been repaired at its end? The dragons had torn it, the latest scroll attested. The Gods had repaired it. And without another word on the subject, the author would turn to a discussion of casualties or of human reactions or of the Gods-damned weather.

It was horrendously frustrating, and all the while that little side table kept calling out to her. Psander had promised Bandu that she would research the underworld, and then she hadn't. But Phaedra was Bandu's friend – didn't she owe it to her to read those books? Psander might have abandoned Bandu and her hopes and dreams, but how could Phaedra? She might even have the opportunity to visit Bandu and Criton someday soon, after she returned to her world. And it would have been one thing if her reading so far had turned up some hint of progress, but it hadn't. More and more, the fact that Phaedra had to save their world felt like an excuse.

Besides, even Psander didn't know where to look for their answers. What if the clue to the sealing of gates was hidden somewhere in those books about the underworld?

Phaedra went to bed that night dreaming about that pile of books, the only part of the library that Psander had deemed "frivolous." When she awoke the next morning, she promised herself that she would devote this day, just this one day, to reading through them. If there wasn't anything useful there, she'd have only lost a day.

To her slight shame, she found the books in Bandu's pile endlessly fascinating. Her mind didn't wander once as she read account after contradictory account of journeys to the underworld, or of what steps people took to avoid getting there in the first place. The first scroll she read was the story of a man who had gone down in search of his dead wife, only to return empty-handed. In the second scroll, the same man came back victorious. The contradictions were maddening, and yet each reversal only made her want to read more.

Over the course of the day, a picture of the world below began to emerge. It was a depressing picture, to be sure. The general consensus was that the dead spent the eternity of the afterlife sleeping, dreamless and inert. Most of the clerical sources Phaedra read were preoccupied with the question of how to avoid this miserable place. The followers of the Sun God cremated their dead, hoping that Atun would take their souls up into Himself instead of letting them sink into the earth; Mayar's followers had a similar reason for their burials-at-sea. There was a southern vulture God whose worshippers performed sky-burials. There were others who didn't seek to avoid the underworld, though: Atel's priests buried their dead much as the Tarphaeans had, and called death the Final Journey.

The second most common theme after avoidance was in the many stories about journeys to the underworld and back.

And yet, while these stories were common, there was only one man whose success was entirely verifiable: Maira, the wizard-king of Parakas, had retrieved his wife from the underworld some hundred and thirty years ago, a success that had been much celebrated at the time. When she came across the fact, Phaedra's heart leapt. Here finally was the information Bandu had sought! Even if she never used it to bring back Four-foot, she would know that Phaedra had kept Psander's promise for her.

So yes, dinnertime had come and gone and Phaedra was starving and weary, but surely this merited a second day of study.

That second day began with another fascinating reversal: though the contemporary accounts of Maira's feat all agreed that he had succeeded, there was no agreement on how. The wizard-king had told his story to scores of people, and each version was notably different from the others. The monsters and demons Maira had bested on his journey seemed to change with the telling, as did the manner of his victories. Phaedra tried to determine which version of the story he had told first, but even that wasn't exactly clear. Unfortunately, the rescued wife didn't seem to have contributed to any of the accounts. She had apparently gone silent within days of her return and refused to speak to anyone besides her elderly mother, who had taken their conversations with her to the grave.

The most awful scroll Phaedra read that day was a list of wizards and heroes who, inspired by Maira's success, had attempted similar journeys over the last century-and-a-half and never come back. Most of them had been trying to bring back children, those they had lost to disease or accidents or, in one case, a grisly murder. It broke Phaedra's heart to read summary after summary of the tragedies that had prompted grown men – and they were almost exclusively men – to willfully hurl themselves into the abyss in the hopes of seeing their beloved sons and daughters once more. When she was finished reading the scroll, Phaedra found that she had no strength to keep researching the matter. She skimmed a few more scrolls to see if she could find the method by which Maira had journeyed to the underworld, but gave up before she found it. After reading that horrifying list, the idea of helping Bandu reach the underworld was no longer appealing to her.

So she turned back to the question of the gateways, unsure, as always, of how to proceed. How many gates were there? How many would she have to seal to make up for the new one? And were they like simple threads connecting the worlds, or could each gateway on the fairy side connect to multiple human-side gates? If they formed a sort of web, then would closing a gate on just one side even work?

She had spent too long with books – she couldn't think straight anymore. Psander was still shut in her lab, conducting Gods-knew-what horrible experiments on Olimande's head, so Phaedra went to talk to Hunter instead. He was resting in his room after dinner, staring at the ceiling. "Am I disturbing you?" she asked.

"No," Hunter said, sitting up hurriedly. "I was just thinking about you, actually."

"Really?"

Hunter nodded and stood, looking self-conscious. "I was going to ask if you'd... like to marry me."

Phaedra gawked at him. She opened her mouth, and closed it again. She was dimly aware that she must look like an idiot, but she couldn't so quickly adjust from the conversation she had expected to have, to... to this.

"We're finally here," Hunter continued nervously, "and you're learning magic just like you meant to, and as bad as it is in this world, I think we could make a life together if we wanted to. *Do* you want to?"

Phaedra was still staring, but she forced herself to speak. "This is so sudden," she said.

"I'm sorry," he said. "I didn't mean for it to be sudden. I thought you might already know how I feel, but I guess I'm not that good at expressing..."

"It's all right," she said, awkwardly.

"So... do you want to...?"

"No," Phaedra said, and responded to his wince with one of her own. "I can't, Hunter. Not right now, anyway. There's no telling if we'd conceive as quickly as Bandu and Criton did, but I can't afford the risk. None of us can afford it, really."

"We can't?"

"We can't."

She told him then what Psander had told her about the skyquakes, and of the mission she would soon be leaving on. Additional complications were decidedly unwelcome.

"Oh," Hunter said, and his disappointment was painful to behold. "No, I guess that makes sense."

They stood there in silence, the pain between them growing. Hunter opened his mouth to say something, but Phaedra interjected, "I don't know," and he closed his mouth again. She had imagined him about to ask whether she might marry him sometime in the future, assuming Psander's plan succeeded. Now, regardless of whether this had indeed been his intended question, they both knew it was the question she had answered.

"I see," Hunter said.

"I'm sorry," she said, and left him alone in his room.

She felt terrible. She loved Hunter like family, and she had always been attracted to him. He was such a sweet, gentle man, and he *was* good looking. In another life, under different circumstances, she thought she might have married him without a moment's hesitation.

But the more she thought about it, the more Phaedra realized she had made the right choice. It wasn't just the current circumstances: she didn't think she'd *ever* be ready to leave her studies behind and devote herself to raising children. As terrible as it felt to admit it, she would rather live Psander's life than Bandu's.

She had always assumed that she would have children one day. But that assumption was now a relic of her old life on Tarphae, of the days when her options had been limited by her parents' imagination. Had things gone as they'd been supposed to, had Tarphae never been cursed, Phaedra would have returned home after last year's pilgrimage, married whomever her parents had chosen for her, and had however many children the Gods chose to give her. But that wasn't her life anymore. What's more, she didn't *want* it to be her life.

Now her life was magic. It was full of questions she had never thought to ask as a girl, and answers to the ones she had. Let others marry and have children – there was no lack of children in the world, but there was a distinct lack of wizards. There would be no time for babies during her mission, and there would be no time for them afterward either. How could she ever go from a quest to save all of humanity to a normal life of marriage and pregnancies and childrearing?

And if she did, how could she do it without growing to hate the man who had asked it of her?

She lay awake that night, too overwhelmed to sleep. She ought to talk to Hunter again. She ought to explain that her inability to settle down with him was not only for now, but forever. But he would be asleep by now, and she could not go and wake him. It would give him false hope for a moment, and in the most vulgar possible way. She couldn't do it.

But she couldn't sleep either.

Instead she rose, conjured a ghostly candle in her hand, and stumbled to the library again. This time she didn't make any attempt at rational strategy, but pulled scrolls and codices off the shelf at random and read each one only until she tired of it.

It was in a book about trees that she finally found what she was looking for. It wasn't even a magical text, but an agricultural one – in one section, the author discussed trees' ability to heal and grow, telling the story of a woodcutter who had come across an iron nail fully embedded in the bole of an oak, invisible until the tree had been cut down.

The mesh, Salemis had once said, repaired itself. Why, then, was it thinner in some places than in others? At the gateways it was thin enough that at certain times the elves could tear at its fabric and use it for their nets – at least until the healing mesh drew those nets back into itself. There must be something in those places keeping it thinner, continually wearing it down. There were nails hidden somewhere in the wood.

Phaedra put her book down. The mesh was nothing like a tree, and so this book could teach her nothing about it – all it had done was to trigger the right thought.

When she made her report to Psander after breakfast, the wizard frowned. "I'm not sure I follow you," Psander said. "We already knew that the mesh was thinner at the gateways than in other places. How has this changed anything?"

"It's changed everything!" Phaedra cried. How could Psander not see it? "What I'm saying is that if the mesh naturally heals, any section that's thinner than the others must be a place where there's a hidden irritant continually wearing away at it. If we could find that irritant and remove it, the mesh would close the wound on its own!"

"But what would such an irritant look like?"

"It's probably something different at each gate. For the new one, it could be Silent Hall or the whole island of Tarphae, or even the Yarek itself. I can't remove any of those, but I think I can break some of the other ones if I know what I'm looking for. You said once that the wizards' tower at Gateway was built around an old elven gateway that already existed – what did *that* gateway look like? How did they know it belonged to the elves?"

"There was a pattern there," Psander answered, leaning against a lectern. "A sort of echo of the fairies' world, as I recall people saying. It manifested sometimes in dreams and sometimes in physical phenomena. I was once instructed to count the leaves that had fallen in the clearing, and found there to be a hundred and twenty-one of them – eleven times eleven. It wasn't any single structure, like a circle of stones or anything of that nature."

"I'll bet there was still something more specific causing it all," Phaedra said. "I might be able to find it if I went back there."

Psander's mouth twisted, but then she nodded. "We might not do any better than that as far as theory goes, not without experimentation. I'll show you how I open the gate in the courtyard, and we can plan for you to leave tomorrow."

"One more thing, please." Phaedra raised the scroll she had taken from the side table, the list of failed attempts to breach the underworld. "This list only has two women on it, and thirty-two men. I thought you said there had been many female academic wizards before you, but if there were, then why didn't they–"

"I said no such thing," Psander answered, cutting her off. "I said only that there had been female wizards before me, which indeed there had been. But it was not a large number, even in the best of times. The community of academics was never welcoming to us – it was a fight for every book and every apprenticeship. When I told you there had been others, I did not mean to imply that I was unexceptional."

"Oh," said Phaedra. "I see. And now there's just you and me."

"Yes," Psander said with a slight smile. "If we survive the coming crisis, I'm sure much will be written about that fact. If others do not write it, we shall have to write it ourselves."

She looked cheerful enough that Phaedra risked asking her about Olimande – and regretted it immediately.

"I may yet eat his brain," the wizard answered. "He seems to have run out of useful things to tell me."

Phaedra shuddered. "Do you think that would actually help?"

"It might," Psander said. "Power is power, and if the elves mean to gain it by feeding on us, we may as well return the favor."

"Has he taught you anything about how to fight the elves off?"

"Yes. It seems that if an elf is not decapitated but pierced through the heart, the magic will bleed out into the world, killing him and returning that magic to the plant-beast this world is made of. The elves have a tradition of decapitating their enemies in battle in order to humiliate them, but only slay each other under very rare circumstances. Battle is a kind of sport to them most of the time."

"But not against us."

"No," Psander said, "of course not against us. They see us as lesser beings, and they envy us for the attention the Gods have shown our world, short-sighted as that makes them. They think we deserve death more than they do."

"Auntie Gava called them demons," Phaedra said. "I think she's right."

"Knowing what we do now? Undoubtedly. If you are successful in closing all the other gates, it will save countless lives not only from our colliding worlds but from the elves as well."

"There's a lot I still don't understand," Phaedra confessed. "I've been assuming so far that the gateways are like tunnels, but do you think they might open in more than one place in our world?"

"Not as far as I know," Psander said, "though I have hardly had the time to verify that. The gate to Tarphae is the only one I have been able to open so far. I frankly would have expected to be more closely connected to the Yarek and my home's previous location, but I suppose one can also see why the new thread connecting us to our world might attach itself to Tarphae instead. Much of the power that brought me here came from Tarphae one way or another: there were the five of you, of course, who performed the final magic, and it was Karassa's unwilling contribution – as harvested through the tears of your king – that pushed us over the threshold into this world.

"I know what you're thinking," she went on, and Phaedra made a frantic sweep of her mind before realizing that it was just a figure of speech. "When I send you back to our world, I will have to send you right back to Tarphae, where you will have to evade the pirates and find your way safely off the island. I wish there was another way."

"There is," Phaedra said, "but it's going to take a lot more power since I won't be using the stronger gate here. I'll need Olimande too, I think. Illweather and Goodweather obey the elves."

Psander lifted an eyebrow. "If you plan to journey to one of their castles, I cannot condone that. I cannot afford for you to get yourself killed."

"I'm not going to the castles," Phaedra said. "I'm going underground. There's a gate down there, among the roots of the world, that leads straight to the Dragon Knight's Tomb."

42

BANDU

Bandu had never been so happy. In all the ways that her relationship with Criton had been bad, the one with Vella was good. Bandu was beginning to realize how lucky she was that Vella loved her.

Goodweather was thriving too. She was learning to crawl on her own, dragging herself along with her arms since she had not yet mastered the use of her legs. She sometimes tried to stand too, pulling herself up to her feet while holding onto Bandu or Vella or a table leg, but such efforts usually ended with a fall and a wail. Then Bandu would scoop her up, or Vella would, and within a minute she would be back to smiling and babbling.

She was babbling a lot now. At this rate, Vella said teasingly, she'd be talking better than Bandu soon. Bandu didn't like that joke, but she knew Vella hadn't said it to make her angry, so she decided that it was all right.

The babble didn't mean anything yet – Goodweather was only experimenting with the sounds she could make. Her cries, on the other hand, were distinct and meaningful. Bandu could tell hunger cries from sleepy cries, lonely cries from hurt cries. Vella couldn't quite, but she would look to Bandu for her cues and it would generally turn out all right.

They were not always happy, of course. Vella still missed her family, for all that her feelings about them were complicated. She talked of them sometimes, telling Bandu stories of the way they had raised her, and especially of how tender her father had been. Bandu hadn't had much of an opinion of Kilion, who had never given her more than the occasional sympathetic glance, but apparently he was a kind and thoughtful man. He was with his children, anyway.

Bandu avoided talking about her childhood, or about Criton. Instead she told Vella about the others, Phaedra and Narky and Hunter. Vella said they sounded like Bandu's real family, which was right. Bandu might have no parents, but she *did* have a family.

Vella was horrified to learn that Bandu did not know how to read. "How could Phaedra not have taught you?" she asked, and when Bandu told her that she didn't want to learn, Vella would not take that for an answer.

"All the Dragon Touched teach their children to read," she insisted. "We were advisors to the king once. Everyone has to learn."

"I don't," Bandu said. "Dead people shouldn't talk."

Vella clearly found that statement confusing, so Bandu had to explain how Psander had had animal skins full of the words of dead people. Bandu did not think it was right for dead people's words to remain after they were gone.

Vella didn't care. "I'll teach you," she said. "I'm sorry, but not being able to read – it's like being a child, for us. You have to at least try."

So Bandu tried. She hated it. A week of lessons yielded no progress whatsoever. She couldn't tell the symbols apart – they were just meaningless shapes that didn't look anything like what they were supposed to: a camel, a fish, an ox, an eye, and so on. Each made a sound related to its shape, but it was hard to remember what those sounds were when it took such creativity to recognize the pictures.

"Why I do this for you?" she complained. "I never use this."

Vella looked at her sternly. "Of course you'll never use it if you don't learn it. That doesn't mean it isn't useful."

Bandu tried kissing her, but Vella pulled away. "You can't get out of learning to read that easily."

Sometimes Bandu missed Criton.

"How it helps later?" she demanded, not bothering to hide her skepticism. "I never read from dead animal skin, history and lies and bad things. Phaedra reads those, and she can tell me things if I need them. You can do that too – you don't need me to read also."

"And what if I have to go somewhere, and I want to leave you a note to tell you where I've gone? You can't always rely on other people, Bandu. If you don't learn how to read, someday you'll wish you did."

Bandu doubted she was right about that, but there was no dissuading her, so she did her best. Her best wasn't very good, but as long as she was trying, Vella showered her with praise and affection. That made the struggle easier, at least.

She did sometimes resent Vella for forcing her to tire her eyes and her mind; for torturing her with the symbols even when she wanted to relax; for taking even the moments when Bandu was nursing her daughter to test her knowledge. Vella scratched the letters into the wall beside their bed, formed them out of rocks in the garden, used them to count the days. The letters didn't only make sounds, they also represented numbers, and Vella drilled Bandu in those too. She began dreaming at night that the symbols were chasing her through the forest, shouting their names at her. The whole thing was exhausting.

They fought about it sometimes. Bandu didn't like being forced to do anything, and the fact that Vella did it in order to help her was no consolation. Bandu couldn't imagine ever needing to know how to read, and it felt sometimes as if Vella was trying to punish her for not having had parents who taught her such things. She didn't mean it as a punishment, of course, and that was important... but it wasn't everything.

Still, despite the pressure from Vella and the inevitable arguments that resulted, Bandu couldn't help but notice how much happier she was here than she had ever been with Criton. Vella never stopped engaging with Bandu's feelings, never refused to explain herself, and never, never turned violent. They would come out of each fight happier with each other than they'd been before, and that was more precious than anything. When Goodweather grew older, Bandu would teach her to look for that in a mate.

And over time, Bandu had to admit that Vella's lessons were working. When she forced herself to, she could sound out most of the words Vella scratched into the ground for practice, and she nearly cried when she discovered one day that one of the phrases Vella had carved beside their bed the week before was "I love you, Bandu." Vella did not stop teaching her after that, and the lessons didn't get any easier, but Bandu stopped resenting her for it. If it hadn't been for Vella's persistence, Bandu would never have discovered the joy that old words could bring.

Then one morning, Bandu awoke to Vella shaking her. "What's wrong?" she asked.

"I had a nightmare," Vella said. "Could you tell me if you think it means something?"

Bandu nodded, feeling suddenly afraid. She had had a prophetic nightmare once. She had misunderstood it at the time, and it had cost Four-foot his life.

"It started like one of my regular bad dreams," Vella confessed. "You told me you were leaving me and going to find Criton. I have dreams like that sometimes. But this time, you left me holding Goodweather, and she looked up and asked me if you were ever coming back. And I wanted desperately to say 'Yes,' but somehow I couldn't. And she said, 'We never should have left.'

"Then my grandmother was sitting alone in a room, crying. I wasn't holding Goodweather anymore, and I went to try to reassure my grandma, and put a hand on her back, and she turned to me and said, 'I feel sick.' Then she started heaving, and she opened her mouth and black feathers came pouring out. There was blood in the feathers too, it was really frightening and disgusting. I could still see it happening even after I turned away from her, because you don't see things with your eyes in dreams. I think there was more, but I can't remember it now. What does it mean, Bandu?"

Bandu shook her head. "Hessina is all the Dragon Touched. Black feathers are Ravennis, or maybe Narky. Narky is from Tarphae like me, he goes to Ardis before we meet your kind. Maybe Narky is Ardis? Your people try to eat Narky, and that is bad for them. I don't know why Hessina is crying before the feathers."

"And the first part?" Vella asked. "Where you left me with Goodweather and went back to Criton?"

"That never happens," Bandu said firmly. "I don't want him, I want you."

Vella looked dissatisfied, as well she might. In her dream, Goodweather had said that they shouldn't have ever left. They shouldn't have left, and now the Dragon Touched were about to do something foolish. Was it too late to stop them?

"Bandu. Tell me what you're thinking."

Bandu didn't want to say it. Vella was happy here. *She* was happy here. She would have been glad for Vella and Goodweather to be the only Dragon Touched, the only people she saw for the rest of her life. But she did not want Goodweather to grow up as Criton had, believing herself and one parent to be the only two Dragon Touched in the world.

"I think if we don't go back, they try to take Ardis and it is very bad for them. I think if they lose their war, then we are never safe. You are not safe, Goodweather is not safe. Maybe I am looking for Criton in your dream because I want to say don't try to take Ardis. Sometimes Criton listens to me."

Vella looked horrified. "Don't go," she said. "I can't live out here without you, hoping and praying that you'll come back. Don't do that to me."

"I don't go without you," Bandu answered. "Your dream is wrong. You come with me."

"I can't, Bandu! You don't understand! My people don't take

kindly to adultery – there's no telling what they'll do to us if we go back together!"

"What is adultery?"

"It's what we've been doing, Bandu. Making love together when we're married to other people. My husband could kill us in front of everyone and no one would stop him!"

"I stop him," Bandu reassured her. "They don't know what we are doing together, because they are not here with us. We tell them we leave together because you love Goodweather, and they don't know anything else. Criton is angry, but he doesn't hate us, and if Pilos hates you and wants to kill you, I stop him. Don't be afraid."

There were tears in Vella's eyes. "I *am* afraid, Bandu. Let's stay here. *Please.*"

Bandu looked at her new mate, so beautiful and so frightened, and relented. "You don't want to go," she said, "even if all your people die?"

"We don't know that that's what it means," Vella insisted. "All I know is that if I go back, they'll kill me. They'll kill us both, Bandu. Don't go."

Bandu kissed her and stroked her hair, loving the way it flowed so smoothly down from her head, straight and silky. "If you stay," she said, "I stay. Criton can save your people by himself."

43

PHAEDRA

Now that Phaedra had learned the basics of magical composition, learning how to open a gate turned out to be fairly simple. In many ways it was like tugging on one of the invisible threads that summoned the books in Psander's library down from the shelves. The difficulty was in finding the weak spot and gathering the strength to pull on it. That would be harder at one of the older gates than it was in Psander's courtyard, so Phaedra would need a source of external power. But Psander assured her that that would be no obstacle – she planned to cremate Olimande's body, and between that and the elf's head there would be plenty of fuel for the spell.

To be truthful, Phaedra was extremely uncomfortable with that fuel source. Psander might have no qualms with killing a captured elf for the sake of a spell, but Phaedra did. As odious as the elves were, they were sentient beings – they were essentially *people*. The thought of harvesting a prisoner's life for magic horrified her.

It was worth doing anyway: her mission was to save two worlds, after all. It also helped a little that the elves were mortal enemies, and there was no doubt that Olimande would have done the same to Phaedra had their situations been reversed. But while that might be enough to convince Phaedra that the deed had to be done, she couldn't bring herself to view it with the same utilitarian coldness that seemed to be Psander's default emotional state.

She wished she could consult with Hunter, who had struggled with his own moral questions and seemed to have found some happy equilibrium in training the villagers to defend themselves. But if she spoke to him about that, she would have to have that other conversation with him too, the one where she dashed his last remaining hopes of marrying her. She had put it off for too long already, and now that she was leaving, could put it off no further.

Well, it had to be done. She could start with the easier part, at least, so that was what she did, telling him of her qualms with using the elf's body and life as ingredients.

"Am I being unreasonable?" she asked. "Should I just learn to live with this?"

Hunter answered, "It sounds like you'll have to live with it, if you're going to do it at all. But that doesn't mean you can't hate it, and never use someone's life that way again unless you're forced to. Don't become like Psander. Don't stop hating it, or start taking it casually. Feeling every death is a good thing, I think."

"It really is horrible," Phaedra said. "I know it's necessary for me to get back to our world and save it from colliding with this one, but that doesn't make the killing any better. It just makes it all more miserable somehow."

Hunter nodded. "Now you know how I've felt."

"But you don't feel that way anymore?"

He frowned. "I didn't say that. Psander is using the elf about as cruelly as I imagined, and I feel complicit in that. It's training the others that makes me feel better. Teaching them how to defend themselves is a worthy goal – I can throw myself into it without feeling guilty. We all deserve to live just as much as the elves do."

He said it with a passion she had rarely heard from him. "You're not coming with me," she said. Hunter only quietly shook his head. Phaedra had known it all along in the back of her mind, had even conceived of her mission as a lone one, but only now that it had been said could she really acknowledge it. There was no reason for him to come with her anymore – he had found the life he wanted, and she had already refused to join it.

He saw the look on her face. "It's not because of that," he said. "I promise. I still love you – I wish you could stay. But even if your work is more important than mine, these people still have to be defended. They need me."

Phaedra sighed. "You're right, you're right. Oh Hunter, I'm going to miss you."

He smiled sadly. "I hope so. Will you come back to me, when this is all over?"

"I..."

It was too painful, what she had to say. He clearly meant to wait for her, however many years it took. And she did love him, she realized. She loved him deeply – just not as deeply as she loved the life she had found. She would not sacrifice it to him, even if she might someday be tempted to. He had to know.

"Hunter," she said, trying again, "I love you. I do. But I can't marry you, not now and not later. We couldn't consummate it – I don't want any children, ever. I don't want anything that would keep me from studying wizardry, or theology, or anything I set my mind to. I shouldn't have to hate you for doing that to me, and if we had any children, I would. You deserve better."

Hunter looked devastated, but he was as stoic about it as ever. He had never been one to rage or argue, and that did not change now. All he did was to nod dejectedly and nearly whisper, "I understand. Please come back anyway, if you can. I'll miss you."

She gave him a hug and went to pack.

The next morning, as Phaedra was filling a satchel with dry food, Psander came to her with the urn of ashes from Olimande's body, his head resting on top. She had replaced the top of his skull, but Phaedra knew that if she pulled on his hair it would come off like a lid, and the thought nearly caused her to vomit. She took the urn gingerly and tried to think of something else.

Olimande's head was asleep, or at least pretending to be. Phaedra closed her own eyes and checked to make sure he wasn't reading her mind. He wasn't. The elf must really have been asleep, then. Maybe Psander's interrogations had tired him out.

"Before you go," Psander said, and hurried back upstairs to fetch something. She returned a short while later with the bag of objects they had helped Atella to collect.

"You were right about these," she said. "They will be more useful to you than they are to me. They will not be needed for my wards, in any case. With the information I have extracted from Olimande, and with Hunter's continued assistance in defending the fortress, I believe we will be safe for the time being."

Phaedra took the bag from her. If she was to give Bandu her report on the underworld, she would have to find her somehow. The dirt inside would help with that. The broken arrow and bucket would be useful too, if she ever had to find Narky or Criton. The latter was unlikely to be a problem, since Criton and Bandu were bound to be in the same place, but she supposed one could never be sure.

Every soul in Silent Hall came to see her off. Phaedra bid farewell to them all, saving Hunter for last since she had all but parted with him already. What more was there to say? There was so much pain in his eyes.

She pulled him close and gave him a kiss. "I'm sorry," she said.

"Good luck," he replied.

She left him there and struck out into the forest with Olimande's urn in her left hand and a knife in her right. Every ten steps she stopped to carve a sigil onto a tree trunk. It was a simple sigil of her own design, a lit candle to symbolize her line in the Dragon Knight's prophecy: *let she who is dark bring light to the people.* Ten steps were to avoid the elves, who counted in elevens, while she worked her magic to draw the attention of the plant life. This world was built on the roots of the original Yarek, and it was the plants that would have to come to her aid if she was to find the gateway she was looking for.

When she reached the eleventh tree, she carved two sigils instead of one so that the total number would skip to twelve. She wasn't sure how effective an evasion it was – Olimande woke up while she was carving the twelfth sigil.

"What are you doing?" he asked. Phaedra could feel him trying to probe her mind, but she was ready this time, and he found himself locked out.

"Tell me what Psander has done to you," she deflected.

"She has sawed me open and broken that of me which lies and deceives. She has made me more obedient. And she has hurt me, more than anything I could imagine. She has made me welcome death."

"I'm sorry," Phaedra said. "That's horrible."

"But you benefit nonetheless," Olimande said. "You may be sorry for me, but you still enjoy the rewards of my subjugation. I have been hurt and humiliated and damaged beyond repair, and it only makes me a more useful tool for you."

Phaedra winced. "That's true. Does it help to know that I'm trying to save both our worlds from colliding?"

"It does not," he answered. "I would just as soon see all the worlds destroyed, mine and yours and the Gods' world too. There is no merit in any of them."

Phaedra finished carving her sigil and walked on, counting steps. "You can feel that way, just so long as you help me save them anyway."

"I have no choice in the matter."

At the eighteenth sigil, Phaedra began to notice the trees and undergrowth subtly reaching for her – whether out of attraction or malice, she didn't know. Either way, she was starting to get the attention she wanted, and she stepped up her pace. The effect grew stronger, and by the thirty-fifth sigil, the roots and branches of the forest were actively – if, thankfully, slowly –

trying to wrap themselves around her. At the thirty-sixth sigil, the ground shook and split, and a gigantic elder root rose out of it toward her.

"Tell it to stop!" she cried, and Olimande obeyed. The root paused, already halfway around Phaedra's body. "We need to get down to the heart of the world," she told it, though she was not sure it understood. "Ask for me, Olimande."

When he did, the root snapped back into action, wrapping itself around her with a strength that threatened to shatter her ribs. "Safely!" Phaedra shouted, but though the root did not squeeze any harder, neither did it loosen its hold. It lifted her into the air, and with a sudden, gut-wrenching force, plunged back into the ground. It was all Phaedra could do to keep from dropping Olimande and his urn – she let go of her knife and slapped her hand down on his head to keep it from being lost. The top of his skull shifted beneath her fingers. Still she held on, and the Yarek's limb dragged her down into the heart of the world.

The world of the elves was built upon the carcass of the plant-beast that had once threatened the Gods. Its heart was a mass of tangled roots, where the opposing goals and personalities of the elves' living castles came together and intermingled in a sad mimicry of their former unity. It was musty and dark, and Phaedra felt very much entombed. When the plunging and plummeting ceased and the root let her go, she struggled to keep her balance on the uneven roots. "Thank you," she said, to Olimande and the Yarek both.

"Muh ouh," Olimande replied.

Phaedra summoned a light, and groaned. The top of Olimande's skull had slid partway into his brain, which had scratches and scorch marks on it already from Psander's various manipulations. "Can you speak?" she asked.

"Ubbib," Olimande said, and Phaedra cursed. There was such pain in his eyes, so much that it crowded out even the hatred.

"I'm so sorry," she said.

She placed him down on a root and went about her work,

sprinkling the elf's ashes here and there in the sequence she and Psander had developed to wring the most power out of the poor elf's body. One pinch here, one there, two here, three there, five here, then eight, and then back down to five and so on. It was a sequence with power of its own, mimicking the shapes of ferns and plants of all kind, and when she was done counting down, she had thrown pinches of the elf's ashes in eleven different directions. The air was growing hazy, and Phaedra concentrated her newly acquired wizard's sight until she could see the threads of mesh glowing before her. She caught one and pulled, calling on the magic of the fallen elf as the hole widened and a mist rose from within it, glowing with the daylight that lay beyond.

She was about to step through when a root sprang into her path. The Yarek wanted its tribute.

"I thought you would take it yourself," Phaedra whined, but the Yarek only responded by putting a second root in her way. So Phaedra turned back to Olimande's poor miserable head. "The Yarek wants me to feed you to it," she told him. "I'm so sorry."

"Muh bub," Olimande replied, and his presence at the edge of her mind was pure in its hatred.

She lifted the head and presented it to the Yarek formally. "Take this elf, his power and his soul, back into you," she said, "and let me pass into the world the Gods built for my kind."

The roots that had impeded her took the head gently from her hands. Then they curled around it and crushed it. Phaedra winced and shut her eyes. When she opened them, her way was clear.

She limped through the mists and stepped into the light beyond.

44

NARKY

"Tribute!" Magerion snarled. "Ardis does not pay tribute."

"You're right," Narky said. "Getting killed is much more dignified."

The king's retainers made angry noises and looked to Magerion for an order, but after a meaningful pause, Magerion waved them off. "Don't take our enemies' side, Narky," the king warned. "High priest or no, I can have you executed as a traitor."

"At which point," Narky said, "you'd be an enemy to Magor, Ravennis, *and* God Most High, and you'd be damned no matter who won the divine struggle."

Magerion's eyes flashed, but he didn't make any more threats. "You counsel me to choose safety over dignity," he said. "That strikes me as going very much against the spirit of Ravennis' teachings. Are you not ashamed? You may wish to resign and let someone more capable take your place."

Narky didn't think much of these rhetorical traps. He answered: "Our church used to have a more capable leader, a truly great one who prized victory and glory over life. You killed her, and now you're stuck with me. Don't try to wriggle out of it. Ravennis knows you well. He gave you a priest who understands you and shares your motivations. I think you ought to make the most of that."

The king narrowed his eyes, but Narky could tell that he was pleased with his answer. He was getting to know Magerion better, and the king was, at least, *slightly* less intimidating now that Narky knew how to gauge his reactions. Less intimidating, but no less terrifying. He could still order Narky's death any time it suited him.

"You think your God is incapable of defending us," he said.

"I think Ravennis cares more for the reality of winning than for its appearance. Laarna's martyrs are now celebrating their God's victory while Magor's worshippers suffer endless humiliation in the underworld. Look past the obvious victories and losses – half of them aren't real. As long as the city stands, Ardis hasn't lost. If Ravennis wants us to keep fighting this war, He'll give us an omen. Otherwise, take what peace you can get from the Dragon Touched. It didn't turn out well for you the last time you ignored my advice."

Magerion sat in quiet contemplation for a time. "You may be right," he said at last. "Tribute is not death, and we may not have the strength to win this war. Since Bestillos died at your hands, Ardis has suffered defeat after defeat – it is no wonder that we are too weak to stand against the Dragon Touched. A few years' respite would give us a chance to recover. How long do you suppose we'll have to pay this tribute before we are strong enough to resist them?"

Narky shrugged. "As long as it takes for them to displease their God. It'll happen eventually, and when it does we should strike with all the force we have before they have the chance to get in His good graces again. The dragons fought a war without God Most High at their backs, and that's why there's only one left."

"And what of that one? Will it come back?"

"I don't know – from what I hear, he came down to talk to the Dragon Touched and then left again. It would be useful to know what he said."

"Tribute it is, then," Magerion said. "We will put off this war until we have greater strength and more information. It should not be hard to find spies who will pose as deserters and followers of the dragons' God, and we will be prepared should the Dragon Touched falter in their worship. Tell me, then, of your friend's terms."

Narky told him everything, including the requirement that he go before the people and announce God Most High's supremacy. The king frowned. "And you think Ravennis would permit His high priest to call Him a servant? You told me Ravennis and God Most High were allies."

"I don't think the difference matters as much as you think it does," Narky said. "I'll tell you what the Graceful Servant told me: it's been centuries since the last time God Most High was active. He's active again now, but who knows how long that'll last? The Graceful Servant said that there'll come a time when the world has forgotten God Most High, when people might even believe that Ravennis *is* God Most High. I don't think He'll mind if I call Him a servant to God Most High this year, or this decade, or this century. His scope is long."

Magerion looked disgusted. "You would live as a slave your whole life, content because your descendants might one day conquer."

"I'm already a slave to Ravennis," Narky said. "This hardly changes anything."

Magerion nodded. "That may be true. But I am no slave, and my children and grandchildren will not live as slaves. Even so, we will accept this tribute as a temporary solution to our problems. If the Dragon Touched cease their hostilities and leave to settle in the north, we will accept their terms for now. Let us hope that they displease their God soon."

Narky breathed a sigh of relief. "You'll let me tell Criton that we'll take his deal?"

"Yes," Magerion said. "But we must watch for those omens you spoke of. If the Dragon Touched displease their God, we strike. And if you learn that Ravennis means for us to fight this war now after all, do not dare conceal it from me. Ardis has taken Ravennis as its God – if I learned that you have deceived me about your God's wishes just to aid your countrymen among the Dragon Touched, your life will be forfeit, as will your wife's and any children or even friends that you may possess. Your countrymen are enemies to this city, Narky, and though that may yet save Ardis during this time of the Dragon Touched conquest, I will not pretend that I trust you for it."

"I understand," Narky said. "You've got nothing to worry about. If Ravennis wants a war, I won't hesitate to say so. He owns me."

He went back to his new temple, where Ptera was just finishing a communal service. When he told her that Magerion had accepted Criton's peace terms, she nearly shouted for joy. "Thank Ravennis, Narky, you did it! After that night raid, I was sure Ardis would fall."

Two of Ptera's cousins had died in the raid on the Dragon Knight's Tomb, and though Narky hadn't really known either of them, their deaths had been devastating to her. She came from a large family, it seemed, and she was close even with her cousins in a way that Narky couldn't quite fathom. He hadn't even been that close with his father.

The family was proud of Ptera for marrying him, but Narky got the sense that they didn't really see him beyond his role as high priest. Maybe that was for the best – not everybody who knew him liked him.

Sometimes he thought that only Ptera and Magerion realized how young he was. It was as if everyone assumed he was Ptera's age or something. Or maybe it was just that they respected him, and nobody at home ever had. Whatever the reason, all that respect felt wrong to him.

Ptera frowned when he told her about the teachings he would have to adopt to be in keeping with the terms of the peace, but unlike Magerion, she had no problem understanding Narky's reasons for agreeing to those terms.

"You're right," she said, "it doesn't matter if you have to tell people that Ravennis is subservient to God Most High. The dragons' God has no image and only the monstrous Dragon

Touched as His representatives – even those who believe Ravennis to be His servant will choose to worship the servant and not the master."

"That may be true," Narky said. "In any case, I doubt Ravennis will be the servant forever, no matter what the Dragon Touched want me to say. It may sound ridiculous, but I think the Graceful Servant might have been too cautious when she talked about the future. It looks like we're going to last the year, and that means Elkinar's priests will have to admit I was right: whether They started that way or not, Ravennis and Elkinar are the same God now. It's possible that Ravennis will even absorb God Most High one day, especially if we can spread His worship beyond Hagardis to the rest of the world. You never know."

Ptera smiled. "You're so ambitious, Narky. I love that in you. Ravennis chose well."

"He's the God of Fate," Narky said, smiling back. "He knows what He's doing. Besides, does it count as ambition if I don't expect to be here to see it happen? It's not like I'll still be high priest then – I'll be long dead."

"That's a comforting thought," Ptera said. "So when do you leave?"

"Tomorrow," Narky said. "We'll tell Criton that Magerion accepts his terms, and then it'll just be a matter of figuring out what order things happen in. Magerion wants to wait until after the Dragon Touched have withdrawn before he sends the first tribute payment. The Dragon Touched will probably demand that we send the payment first. But at that point, the details don't really matter so much. It'll be over."

"You've done well," Ptera said. "Get some rest."

"Don't I get some sort of reward?" Narky whined. "Besides rest?"

Ptera laughed. "Oh definitely, either before you leave or after you come back. I haven't decided which yet, but at this point the details don't matter that much."

She was only teasing – their sex that night was never in

doubt. It was wonderful to think that as long as Ardis stood and no further disasters interrupted them, he'd have a full lifetime of this. That happy thought sustained him until he reached the Dragon Knight's Tomb, at which point he was forced to stop thinking about his wife and concentrate on the task at hand.

Magerion had sent his son Mageris to watch over Narky during the proceedings, which was an annoying reminder that the king didn't trust him. But besides that, all seemed to go well at first. Narky had consciously left his spear behind for this journey, calculating that the gesture of trust would put the Dragon Touched more at ease. It seemed to work. They welcomed him and Mageris at the base of the mountain, and four guards climbed alongside them to the cave where the Dragon Knight had been buried. Narky wondered if the Dragon Touched had ever looked inside the great stone sarcophagus – if they had, they'd have seen that the knight's journal was missing, and that the hand that had rested on it was all out of order where the islanders had scattered its bones in their hurry to read the knight's writings. Not that they would know who had committed this act of desecration, unless Criton told them.

Criton and his council were waiting for them, and Criton was already arguing with that idiot cousin of his. "My mind is made up," he was saying as Narky and Mageris entered. "God Most High chose me to lead our people, and as long as I have that authority, this is the path we'll follow. Hello, Narky."

"Don't let me interrupt," Narky said. "I'm sure my news can wait."

Criton regarded him coolly. "Speak, Narky. For God's sake."

"Magerion has accepted your terms," Narky said, "as have I. He stands ready to begin sending his tribute once you've moved back north and chosen a site for your new city."

Criton looked to the members of his council. "That won't do," the old lady said. "He thinks he can trick us into leaving with no more than a promise."

"You've asked for stone, among other things," Narky pointed out. "I don't know what good that would do you here if you mean to build a city elsewhere."

"And you?" the woman asked. There was some commotion outside, so she spoke loudly to be heard over the noise. It made her voice sound even harsher as she said, "Have you already told your followers of your God's servitude?"

"Not yet," Narky admitted. "But if you'll give me your assurance that the Dragon Touched will make peace with us, I'll make that announcement as soon as I get back. I've only had just enough time to act as a messenger between you and my king. He accepts your terms. Will you hold by them?"

"Yes," Criton said. He turned to one of the guards. "Pilos, you'll go back with Narky to verify that everything happens as he's said, and to collect the gold part of the tribute. The stone can be sent later, as you say, once we've chosen a site for our new city. Does anyone object to this arrangement?"

He said it while looking at his cousin. Before anyone could answer, a voice said, "Excuse me, everyone," and they turned to see another Dragon Touched man step in with Phaedra at his side.

"Phaedra!" Criton called joyously. "You're back! Where's Huh-guhhhh…"

Narky saw the expressions on the faces in front of him change to horror, and he spun back around to see Criton standing with his cousin's claws lodged in his throat, gurgling as the blood dripped down his neck. Phaedra screamed.

"There will be no demon's bargain," Belkos said, his face contorted with hate. "Ardis will fall!"

With that he yanked his hand back, leaving Criton to collapse, throat torn open.

Narky's instincts were all wrong. He ran toward Criton, as if there was something he could do to save him, while Mageris took advantage of the confusion to stab one of their guards and flee. Narky had definitely made the wrong choice – he couldn't save his friend, and the other Dragon Touched were faster than him anyway. Some pounced on Belkos and subdued him while others crowded around Criton, staring down at what their kinsman had done.

He was dying. There was nothing they could do. Soon one of the remaining guards was on top of Narky, pushing him to the ground and tying his hands behind his back.

"Did you catch Mageris?" Narky asked, his head in a blur.

"Your companion?" the guard said. "Not yet."

"Then you'd better," Narky told him. "Holding me hostage won't do you any good. If you want a chance at peace, you have to keep Magerion from finding out what's happened."

The guard shouted something, and his fellows gave chase. But even if they did catch him, Narky thought, it didn't much matter. Their one chance to avoid catastrophe already lay dying on the cavern floor.

45

Partha

Belkos went to his death defiantly, spitting and ridiculing those who had condemned him. "I saved you from lives of slavery!" he yelled at the crowd, a disbelieving smile on his face. "I did what no one else was willing to do, and you're executing me for it! Have you all turned upside-down? When the Ardismen come to enslave your children, will you throw flowers at them? Will you give them a welcoming feast? What's the matter with you all?"

"Our God gave us a leader," the old priestess answered him, "and you murdered him. Do not pretend that you have done some holy thing."

She sounded so familiar, that priestess. Did Partha know her from somewhere?

Someone threw a rock at Belkos, and then suddenly everyone was doing it. Iona wailed and held her daughter back as the people stoned her husband and left him buried there under the rocks that had killed him. Partha watched too, horrified and yet relieved, suddenly emptied of the anxiety that had been pressing on her since that first awful vision. If Belkos was dead, that meant it was almost over. Almost over.

She couldn't spot the Black Dragon among the crowd, but she knew this was his fault. He had connived and tricked them all into doing it, and now any minute he would appear and give Iona his mealy-mouthed apology. Partha was so sure of it that even when the stoning was long over and she was alone with her grieving daughter and granddaughter, she couldn't remember if it had already happened or not.

"Grandma was right," the young girl sobbed into Iona's chest. "It's Criton's fault they killed him."

Iona just shook her head and wept.

"It's the She-wolf too," Partha told them, but her daughter turned on her. Wait, no. Not her daughter – Iona was her daughter. What was the word she was looking for? It wasn't "niece," she didn't think.

In any case, the girl pulled away from Iona and glared at her. "Bandu's not even here! She hasn't been here in weeks, remember? She took Vella and she disappeared."

"Vella?" Partha asked. "Who's Vella?"

That made the young one so angry that she screamed and ran from the tent. Oh – Dessa! That was her name! Dessa was furious for some reason.

"Don't worry about her, Mother," Iona said, her voice as dead as her husband. "She'll come back."

"If you say so, dear."

Iona was always trustworthy, and this Iona was clearly the real one. Thank goodness she had returned! If only her husband hadn't been killed by that horrible man and his horrible black wife. Iona deserved happiness, poor thing.

She was staring straight ahead, her eyes fixed on the tent pole. "I can't believe he did it," she said. "I can't believe they took him from us."

"They always wanted to take him," Partha told her. "That Black Dragon–"

"The Black Dragon is dead," Iona snapped. "Belkos murdered him, Mother, that's why they stoned him. None of this is Criton's fault."

Her words baffled Partha – why would Iona lie about this, of all things? Belkos couldn't have killed the Black Dragon, because the Black Dragon was supposed to apologize for all this! Or had he done it already, somehow? She was confused, far too confused. Just like that, all the anxiety came rushing back. Something was very wrong here, and she couldn't see where she'd made the mistake. Were her visions lies too? Why would her God do that to her?

Tears sprung to Partha's eyes. "I don't know what's happening to me," she confessed, and the shame of it swept over her like a flood. "Help me, Iona. I don't understand it. What's happening to me?"

Iona's eyes finally met hers, and they were full of knowledge and pain. "The same as with everyone," she said, and nearly choked. "The whole world is going mad."

"But I don't want this! I hate this!"

"I know," Iona said, and she put both arms around Partha and held her close. "Me too."

46

PHAEDRA

It was like a bad dream: she had returned from the world of the elves just in time to watch her friend die. Criton was gone by the time they'd even bandaged his neck, slipping away into the world beyond. Moments ago she had thought that Olimande's demise was the worst thing she would experience in her life, and it wasn't even the worst thing she was experiencing *today*.

They buried Criton outside the cave, in a grave as deep as the rocky ground would allow. His kin and a huge crowd of human plainsmen all gathered to mourn the man they called the Black Dragon, piling stones atop his grave until the mound was nearly as tall as Criton had been. Little Delika was there, much to Phaedra's surprise, and she threw herself weeping on the stones until one of the Dragon Touched men gently pulled her away. But still Bandu did not come.

Over the next few hours, the situation became clearer. Bandu was gone, having left Criton for reasons nobody knew or was willing to tell her. Goodweather was with her, as was the wife of another Dragon Touched man. Belkos, the cousin who had murdered Criton, was sentenced by his kinsman and stoned to death, after which a much smaller funeral was held. The murderer's family cried and could not be comforted – they had lost two beloved family members in one day, and there was nobody close to them who hadn't taken a hand in the second death.

Narky, now a prisoner, explained the situation that Phaedra's arrival and Criton's assassination had disrupted. Criton had died at a crucial moment, just as he was about to end the war the Dragon Touched had waged against Ardis. Magerion, the new king of Ardis, would take that murder as an omen from Ravennis, proving that their God wanted the war to go on until the Dragon Touched had been annihilated.

"Criton's bastard cousin thought the Dragon Touched should burn Ardis down and build themselves a new city on its ruins," Narky said. "If Magerion attacks them now, it'll give them an excuse to try. This is going to end really badly."

"Bandu needs to be told," Phaedra said. "I don't know what went on between her and Criton, but she's the only one who can bring him back."

"Bring him back?" Narky repeated. "That's possible?"

"It's possible," Phaedra answered. "It's also incredibly dangerous. We'd have to find an entrance to the underworld, which I don't know how to do; then the journey down is its own trial, and beyond that, no one knows. There'll almost certainly be a price for bringing him back, but I haven't the faintest idea what it might be. As far as I know only one person has ever brought someone back from the underworld, and his story of how he did it changed depending on who asked. The nature of the place may even have changed since then, for all I know."

"It has," Narky said. "Ravennis has taken the underworld as His domain, where His worshippers are rewarded and His enemies punished. That's the good news. If my God wants this peace as much as I thought He did, He'll be very supportive of a quest to bring Criton back."

"You don't think this really is an omen then?"

"If it's an omen, it'll be from God Most High and not Ravennis. I could see the point of sacrificing Laarna, and then the Graceful Servant, but Ardis? I can't see how that would benefit Ravennis at this point, and I think we can all agree that He's not planning on beating God Most High in battle."

Phaedra stopped him there. "The Graceful Servant is dead?"

Narky nodded. "I'm the high priest of Ravennis now. What did you *think* I was doing here?"

They had plenty of time to talk and catch up on each other's news: the Dragon Touched had no intention of letting Narky escape back to Ardis, but they clearly didn't know what to do with him otherwise. For now, they seemed to have settled uneasily on the notion that he was an important guest whom nobody had anything to say to, and who for some reason could not be allowed to leave. There had already been some talk of executing him instead, but that seemed to be on hold for now. Hopefully the side of mercy would prevail.

Phaedra learned from Narky about all that had happened in Ardis and Anardis, about the fall of Magor and the rise of Magerion and Ravennis, about Narky's marriage to Ptera and his acclimation to the role of high priest. In return, she told him of her travels with Hunter, and of all that had happened since they had last seen each other.

The Dragon Touched had no idea what to do with Phaedra, and did not seem particularly interested in detaining her, so it would be up to her to find Bandu when the time came. She conferred with Narky about how best to prepare Bandu for the underworld, should she choose to go. Narky kept wishing aloud that he could be more helpful – it seemed wrong that the high priest of Ravennis should have so little to contribute.

"Would you bless a token?" Phaedra asked. "For Bandu to take with her, as a symbol of your support?"

"I have this," Narky said, reaching for the silver chain around his neck, but Phaedra stopped him.

"Not symbolizing Ravennis," she said. "It's Ravennis we're trying to influence. I meant a token symbolizing you."

She opened the bag that Psander had given her, and took out the two thin pieces of wood that had once been a crossbow bolt. Narky gasped when he saw them.

"I can't bless that," he said. "Where did you get that?"

"It's what made you who you are," Phaedra countered.

"You wouldn't be here without it. You wouldn't even have worshipped Ravennis, and now you're His high priest."

Narky stared at the broken bolt for a long moment. Then he took it in his two hands and said, "Ravennis, as You know me, let this relic from my past stand for my presence as my friend journeys to meet You. Guide Bandu safely to You as if I were at her side, and return her safely to us, with Criton by her side. I ask this of You as Your servant, knowing that You are a God of Mercy as well as Fate, and that the Fates can bend if You so desire it. As I have asked, let it be so."

When he handed the pieces back to Phaedra she took them reverently. "That was beautiful, Narky," she said. "I had no idea you could compose such a prayer."

"Well," Narky said with a wry smile, "I've had practice."

Phaedra smiled back. She had always had a soft spot for Narky. He wasn't a fundamentally nice or decent person, but he wished he was, and so every gesture of kindness and generosity was a hard-earned victory, a triumph of intent over instinct. He had improved since she'd last seen him, and not just because he seemed more comfortable with himself. It was also good to see him more concerned about his wife in Ardis than about his own survival among the Dragon Touched. The craven boy she knew was outgrowing his past.

She had never asked him about the man he had killed with that crossbow bolt. As long as she didn't know the details, she could relate to Narky as he was in the present, without burying who he was now underneath that sordid history. All she knew was that it had been murder.

She parted with Narky late in the afternoon and set out to find Bandu. She did not take directions from the Dragon Touched, but set out northward so as not to be caught between opposing armies should Narky's assumptions turn out to be correct. She lay down to rest that night under a spell Psander had taught her to ward against rain, but the weather stayed thankfully dry, so she did not have to test it. In the morning, she set her tracing spell.

The major ingredient in the spell was the dirt that she and Hunter had collected with Atella in the area her map had indicated as somehow significant to Bandu. Phaedra wished she knew what that significance was, but the spell ought to function either way. She knelt, pulling dirt out of the bag by the handful. Thankfully, the soil quality was different here, and Bandu's rich black dirt stood out against the ground as Phaedra formed the intricate design that her academic forbears had developed. The design was meant to represent a world crisscrossed by roads, and its purpose was to draw on the Traveler God's power without alerting Him to the fact. The use of Bandu's dirt to draw the design itself was a forced modification, since the classic spell would have required Phaedra to destroy an item belonging to the individual she wanted to track. Phaedra knew of no way to destroy dirt, and she hoped this would do. When she had finished the design, she removed her right shoe and stepped barefoot in the center.

The spell worked beautifully. Almost as soon as Phaedra's toes had touched the ground, a second footprint, a left one, appeared on the ground in front of her. It was smaller than Phaedra's print, and it was dark like the Tarphaean soil. Phaedra slipped her shoe back on and began to follow Bandu's tracks.

The tracks went on and on, and it was hard not to worry about what awaited her at the end. What if Bandu refused to retrieve Criton? It worried Phaedra that they didn't know why Bandu had left him. She and Narky had acted as if Bandu's willingness to undertake the journey was a given, but was it? What if Criton had hurt her, or harmed their child? There were so many possibilities, so many potential reasons for Bandu to decide to let her husband stay dead.

And if she did refuse the journey that Phaedra suggested, did Phaedra dare to attempt it herself, given the risk that her failure and death might doom the entire world? If not, what right had she to ask Bandu to risk her own life?

There were other worries too – plenty of them. She worried that she hadn't studied enough to prepare Bandu – or herself for that matter – for the trials that awaited below. She had let that list of failures dissuade her from reading any more of Psander's materials on the subject – what if one of the scrolls she hadn't read held some essential piece of knowledge, without which any attempt to breach the underworld was doomed?

For one thing, Phaedra didn't even know how to find an entrance to the world below. The spell that Maira the wizard-king had used to reach his wife had clearly been much celebrated and publicized in wizarding circles in the years after his journey, but after so many had died using it, the wizarding council known as the Blasphemous Clairvoyants had restricted all access to it. The Clairvoyants had had their own seal, and Phaedra had dug through all of Psander's books that bore it, but none had included Maira's spell. She had *some* idea of how to develop a new spell, but that would carry its own risks.

After the second day of walking, Phaedra began rationing her food. It would have been easy to stop at one of the villages now allied with the Dragon Touched, but she did not know if her tracking spell could accommodate a detour. The footprints behind her always disappeared as soon as she had passed them, and she was afraid that straying from the path might cause the entire spell to dissipate.

Three days later, hungry and tired, she came to a woodcutter's cottage. Outside it, a Dragon Touched woman about her age was busily clearing space for a garden, with an infant on the ground beside her contentedly eating dirt. The infant was Goodweather – no doubt about it. She had dark skin and tight curly hair, and her face, though much developed since the last time Phaedra had seen her, was unmistakable.

"Hello," Phaedra said, and the woman jumped to her feet startled. "I'm looking for Bandu."

"Why?"

"I need to speak with her," Phaedra said. She felt she ought to save her news for when Bandu was present, and she wished the woman wouldn't eye her so suspiciously. "I'm a friend," she said.

"Yes, I see that," the woman said, wiping the dirt off her hands. Of course she'd know Phaedra was a friend: she was clearly an islander, and she had asked for Bandu by name – Bandu didn't have any enemies like that.

"Stay here," the woman added, "I'll bring out some food." She scooped Goodweather up and went inside, and Phaedra was left outside to wonder. When she came back with a bowl of vegetable soup in one hand and Goodweather in the other, Phaedra said, "I could have watched Goodweather out here, you know."

"Oh, no need," the young woman said, but she smiled tentatively and Phaedra could tell she was embarrassed about giving one of Bandu's friends such a cool reception.

Phaedra took the soup gratefully. "Is Bandu out foraging?" she asked.

A nod.

Goodweather, oblivious to the tension between the adults, gave Phaedra a big smile. "Is that a tooth?" Phaedra asked.

"It broke through the gums a week ago. I'm sorry – I'm Vella."

"Vella," Phaedra repeated. "I'm Phaedra. Did you come here with Bandu to be Goodweather's…?"

She had been about to say "nursemaid," but she broke off. She had seen Bandu feed the baby herself without any trouble, and Vella was too young and thin to have recently had a baby and lost it, as Kelina once had. Yet she was acting just as possessive of Goodweather as Kelina had been of Phaedra, almost like a second mother.

She ate her soup in silence.

As she was finishing with it, Vella looked up past her shoulder and said, "Your friend Phaedra is here," and Phaedra turned to see Bandu coming toward them, a pile of mushrooms in her skirt. She dropped these and ran to Phaedra, who rose to embrace her.

"I have bad news," Phaedra said. "Criton is dead."

Bandu let out a cry, looking horror-stricken. "He is dead?"

"His cousin Belkos killed him."

"No," Bandu said, "they are friends!"

"I know," Phaedra said. "But listen, it's worse than that. Criton was about to make peace with Ardis, to end their war. Belkos killed him before that could happen."

Bandu did not weep; she only shook her head and looked sick. "They want to eat Narky," she said nonsensically. "Vella, they kill him because they want to eat Narky, and Narky is Ardis."

"Narky is the high priest of Ravennis now," Phaedra corrected her. "The Dragon Touched have captured him. He's afraid the king of Ardis will take Criton's death as an omen and resume the war."

"Oh God," Vella said.

"If the king of Ardis sends his army against them again," Phaedra said, "the war won't end until one side or the other has been completely annihilated. Criton was the only one insisting that the Dragon Touched make peace with their enemies – the only one with enough authority, anyway."

Bandu and Vella looked meaningfully at each other. "This won't end well for my people," Vella said. "This won't end well for anyone. Bandu, we should have gone. We should have gone while there was something we could have done about it."

Bandu nodded, and she looked down at Goodweather with tears in her eyes. Goodweather had gone back to raking at the ground with her claws and bringing handfuls of turf to her mouth.

"There still is," Phaedra said. "That's why I'm here."

She told them about her studies with Psander, and of the research she had conducted on Bandu's behalf. The girl looked back at her and shook her head. "Criton is not my mate now," she said. "I don't want him. I want Vella."

Phaedra and Vella both winced. "Bandu," Vella said, "you didn't have to…"

"If Ardis is destroyed," Phaedra said, "Narky's wife will be killed, as likely will Narky, and thousands of others besides. If

Ardis triumphs, their army will come here too. You won't be safe."

Bandu nodded and wiped her eyes. "You want me to bring back Criton. He is not my mate and I don't want him, but you want me to bring him back."

"You don't have to go," Vella said. "Bandu, you don't have to go."

Bandu turned to her. "In your dream," she said, "your grandmother is sick. Even if your kind win, is still not good. This war is bad for them, is bad for Goodweather. In your dream I go to find Criton."

"And leave me with Goodweather!" Vella cried. "You never came back in my dream, Bandu!"

Bandu nodded, contemplating the situation in silence. "Tell me about the dream," Phaedra said.

When they had done so, Vella repeated, "You never came back."

"But she wasn't lost yet," Phaedra said. "You didn't say she felt lost, only that you couldn't tell Goodweather for sure one way or another."

"That's one way to look at it," Vella said curtly. "Or you could say that she won't come back, and I wasn't able to tell our daughter a lie."

Our daughter. Phaedra looked to Bandu, but Bandu said nothing.

"Bandu," Vella said, "Don't go."

"So many lives will be lost," Phaedra countered. "So many people will die."

Goodweather began coughing, and Vella lifted her and scooped the grass and dirt out of her hands and mouth. Bandu looked at them, and then back to Phaedra. She sighed.

"How do I go?" she asked.

Phaedra explained what she knew, while Vella wept and intermittently pleaded with Bandu not to leave her for this foolish mission. "We can leave this place and go into the mountains," she said, "or up into the far north where no

Ardisman will find us."

"Then your parents die?" Bandu asked her. "And your grandmother, and Dessa and Iona? If your kind make peace with Ardis, Goodweather has family and many places to go and nobody hates her. She can find mates who love her and not be like Criton's mother, always hiding. Vella, if I bring back Criton, I don't stay with him. He goes back to your people and has other women and I come back to you."

Vella passed Goodweather over to her and buried her head in her claws. Bandu took the baby and turned back to Phaedra. "There are animals you say that want to eat me when I go to find him. What else?"

"Well, for one thing," Phaedra said, "we'll have to find a way to get you down there at all. I have a suspicion that the Yarek could help if it chose to. Its branches breached the sky-mesh when it bore Silent Hall off into the fairies' world; it seems likely to me that its roots pierced the barrier into the underworld. If we could somehow convince the Yarek to help…"

"It helps me," Bandu said with confidence. "It already says so before."

Phaedra nodded and handed her the bag that contained Narky's bolt and Criton's bucket. "In that case," she said, "the rest is up to you."

47
BANDU

The Yarek was there when she reached for it. *Come to me where my trunk rises*, it said, *and I will let you into the depths where you wish to go.* When Bandu told Vella and Phaedra of that condition, Phaedra looked worried.

"That journey will take you weeks! Let's hope the war isn't over by the time you get back."

"*If* you get back," Vella corrected her. "Are you sure you want to do this, Bandu?"

"I am sure," Bandu told her. "Phaedra, you stay here with Vella until I am home. Help with Goodweather."

"I can't," Phaedra said. "I need to find and seal the fairy gates as quickly as I can. We may have decades or we may only have weeks, but I can't afford to–"

"Then I don't go," Bandu interrupted.

Phaedra sighed. "All right. But if you're not back in two months, I'll have to assume you're gone. And if Ardis wins and their army marches north, we're leaving and heading for Atuna."

Bandu left then, taking only the satchel that held Phaedra's relics and the food in her belly. In Dragon Touched lands she could rely on the northern plainsmen to feed her, and in the southern plains she could tell people that she was a friend of Narky's. Everyone had heard of Narky the Black Priest, and when people asked her where she was headed, she told them she was going to meet Narky's God and nobody questioned her.

The hardest part of the journey wasn't the travel or the wet weather, but the lack of Goodweather. Bandu's breasts grew hard and swollen after two days without nursing her daughter, and she had to painfully squeeze out some of her milk just to keep them from hurting all day long. She worried about how Goodweather was faring without her. At least she was old enough that she had started eating soft person-food.

It had been years since Bandu had been truly alone, at least for more than a few hours. It was freeing, but it was not pleasant. She missed Vella and Goodweather, she missed Criton, she missed Phaedra and Hunter and Narky. Most of all, she missed Four-foot. The wolf had been her companion since the time she was a little girl afraid in the woods, and it was wrong to travel without him or even the poor substitute of her own kind.

Would she see Four-foot in the world below? She hoped so, if only so that she could apologize. His death had been her fault, even if only indirectly. She wondered if Narky's God would let her bring Four-foot back with her too. It hurt that she had to prioritize Criton over him.

As the days went by and Bandu came ever closer, the trunk and branches of the great tree took up more and more of the horizon. It had grown markedly since the last time Bandu had been this close – how long before it stretched over the entire world? Its parent-self Goodweather had been her friend and ally, but she had no illusions that the Yarek's presence in this world was benign. The plant-beast was a weed that would worm its way into the foundations of this world and someday destroy it – at least, unless God Most High uprooted it again. It was strange how ambivalent she felt about the matter.

At last she neared the Yarek's base and stood among the burnt trees and burnt bodies where Salemis had routed two armies. The Yarek's trunk was wider now than Psander's fortress had ever been, towering before her like the affront to the Gods that its presence truly was. She felt its power, even here among the scorched and skeletal lesser trees, bursting like strong new shoots out of the ground all around her. The Yarek's magical presence was even vaster than its physical one.

When she reached its trunk, she found that the ground in contact with it had fallen away entirely, revealing a massive stairway of tangled roots that spiraled all the way around the trunk and sank deep into the earth.

Bandu took a deep breath and picked her way to the trunk across the uneven walkway that remained. She touched the live wood with her fingertips and said to it, *I am here. Will you help me?*

Of course I will, the Yarek responded. *Have I not told you that I mean to repay you for your efforts to bring me here, to your fertile new world?*

Then bring me to the land of the dead, she said, *and after that, bring me and whoever is with me back again.*

The great tree breathed its assent, a waft of sweet air falling upon her out of the branches above. *Descend,* the tree said. *You are safe with me.*

Down and down she climbed, round and around the tree until the sunlight disappeared and she lost track of the number of times she had circled the trunk. She lit no fire to disturb the mother of all plants, but kept her hand always on the bark, feeling her way down in the dark. After a time, she became aware of a sound beside her own, the creaking of massive roots growing further and further into the depths of the earth. And then another sound, a dissonant scratching as something large and multi-clawed scrabbled up the root stair toward her.

Show me what I can't see, Bandu asked of the Yarek, and she reached forward with her mind until it showed her what her eyes could not: an eight-legged badger the size of a bear, moving up the staircase toward her with horrifying speed. Bandu thought back to the guardians Phaedra had described for her, but none of them were anything like this beast. When it reached her it reared up on its hind-claws and said in the language of magical thought: *You are not permitted here. Go back or I will devour you.*

The creature had a steel collar around its neck. *Ravennis tames you,* Bandu said. *You don't stop me. I have His highest servant's blessing.*

A servant is still a servant, the badger said, licking its lips. *Speak my name and tame me too, or go back, else you will be eaten.*

Bandu stood her ground. *I give myself two names,* she said, *and they are both better than the name my father gives me. I don't need to know your old name – my name for you is stronger and truer: you are Eight-Claw the Coward, the First Who Runs. You do not stand in my way.*

The badger shrank away from her in fright. *That is not my real name.*

Go back where you come from, Bandu said, *or I call your real name Dust.*

Eight-Claw shuddered and obeyed, retreating until he had disappeared from her mind's vision. Soon he had disappeared from her imagination as well, shifting and fading in memory as if he had been only a dream. Maybe he *was* a dream, but on this endless stairway, such distinctions were essentially meaningless. Down here, a dream could kill just as easily as flesh could.

Now she heard voices from behind, calling to her from the world of the living. The first voice was Phaedra's. "Bandu!" it cried. "I forgot to tell you the most important part of what I learned! Come back – you're not ready for what's down there!"

Bandu ignored it. It was not plausible. Phaedra did not simply *forget* to give Bandu information. If anything, she sometimes forgot to stop.

"Come back!" Phaedra's voice called again. "It's new information really, I only just put it together from something Narky told me. Please, if you don't come back you won't know how to get past the final gate, and your soul will be trapped forever! At least wait for me to catch up!"

Bandu didn't even slow her pace. Did this new monster

think she was that weak, that doubtful of herself? It would learn otherwise.

Voice after voice called down after her, begging her to turn around, and Bandu ignored them all. When even Criton's voice cried that she had overshot her goal and that he was trapped on the level above her, she laughed scornfully at the second guardian's cowardly tactics and willed it to appear before her, which it promptly did.

It was a small creature, half Bandu's size and fragile like a doll made of reeds, which is what it might have been. Its figure solidified as she identified it, taking the form she had named: a wispy little reed-doll carrying a wicked inwardly-curved knife.

Why won't you turn? it squeaked. *I have slain more men than that badger ever did.*

Bandu laughed at its indignation. *Go away,* she said, but the reed-doll did not obey. Instead it lunged at her.

She stopped it with a kick that bent its upper half backward so far that it nearly folded in two. When it sprang upright again, she caught its knife and tried to wrench it away, but the weightless creature only rose along with the blade, clinging to it. *You cannot destroy me,* it hissed.

I don't care, Bandu told it. *Go away.* She wound her arm back and hurled the blade and the creature into the darkness. She never heard it fall.

She shook her head and kept walking, though at this point her descent was less physical than spiritual. Her callused feet no longer felt the roots beneath her so much as she *knew* that she was still descending. The physical world was receding behind her, a sign that she was nearing her goal.

Then, from her right, she heard a bark of greeting. It was Four-foot's voice, she recognised it in an instant. Going to meet him would take her away from the trunk, though – dare she lose contact with the Yarek? It was best to wait for Four-foot to come to her, if he could.

He could not – as the barks of greeting came closer, so did the sound of a chain being dragged. She felt the moment when he came to the end of his chain more than she heard it – it may as well have been *her* neck jerked backward by the unforgiving steel. Four-foot yelped, then growled, then whined. He could not reach her, and now she even saw him dimly, held by a chain that seemed to stretch back into eternity. There was a lock on his collar that kept it clasped around his neck. There was a key in it already, but without hands like hers, Four-foot could not turn it by himself.

Could she go to him? If it hadn't been for that key, if there had been nothing she could obviously do for her friend except comfort him, she would have done it without a second thought. But that key, it was wrong. It was a detail designed to tempt her, to trick her into thinking that she could free him without a fight. It was a lie.

But Four-foot was no lie, she was sure of that. She'd have known if he were a demon in disguise. She knew the wolf's voice, his *essence* too well to be fooled by some demon who had taken his form. He was really here, and he was really trapped, and he was really whining for her to come to him.

But if she stepped away from the Yarek now, her quest would be over. Maybe she would free Four-foot and maybe she wouldn't, but there was no doubt that the underworld would have won. It might swallow her as it had swallowed so many others. And even if it didn't, even if she survived, it would have managed to keep her away from Criton forever. The key proved it.

The trouble was that she did not *want* Criton, not like she wanted Four-foot. Rescuing him would not bring her the pure joy she would have felt with Four-foot alive once more. He was no longer her mate, no longer her companion; seeing Criton again could only complicate her feelings about him, and about Vella too. For Vella was right: Criton may have spoken of taking other women, but it was Bandu who had actually done so. If she rescued him from this dark place, she would have to face him again.

Four-foot barked again, to get her attention. She shut her

eyes tight, so tight that it squeezed tears from the corners. It made no difference – she could see him just as easily through closed eyes as through open ones. She wanted to go to him, wanted it desperately. How many months had she spent among the Dragon Touched, wishing she could have Four-foot beside her instead of Criton and his kin? This might be her only chance to make that happen.

But she couldn't go to him. She could not afford to save Four-foot and give up on Criton. The wolf could end no wars. He might have protected her against the dangers of Tarphae's woods, and even saved her friends from bandits once, but he could never protect Goodweather and Vella the way that peace would.

She opened her eyes again, for all that it didn't matter. *I come back for you,* she told Four-foot, but what if she was lying? She stumbled away down the stairway, weeping as Four-foot howled and whined behind her. His voice echoed in the darkness, on and on, no matter how far she went.

And then at last she came to the end, her path blocked by a wall of solid rock. There was a door in it, and in the door was a face. It could have been a man's face or a woman's, or then again, it might have been a dog's or a jackal's. The dream was growing less and less definite.

Whatever it was, it was looking at her through eyes of stone, waiting for her to say something. She could tell somehow that her first words would be very important, but she didn't know what they ought to be, so instead she waited, hoping that the door would speak first. It didn't.

Let me in, she said at last.

The jackal-person grinned at her. *I don't open for the living, unless they give me blood. Put your hand in my mouth and I will open for you.*

No.

Then I will not open. Turn back, girl-whose-pulse-beats-on. Go home.

Bandu stood, staring at the door while it stared back at her.

Then she reached into the satchel at her side and pulled out the two halves of Narky's bolt. *If you don't open for me,* she said, *open for your God. His priest blesses my journey.*

The door licked its lips with a great scraping sound. *That relic carries memories of a heart pierced and a life taken. Feed me the arrow and its memory, and I will let you pass.*

Bandu put both halves in the jackal's mouth, and gasped as the memory they held sprang to life in her mind. She got a sudden image of Narky releasing the catch on his crossbow, and of a big Tarphaean boy reeling and falling with the bolt lodged deep in his chest. She felt the wound as if the bolt had struck her chest too, and she collapsed to her knees, gasping for breath. Then the vision dissipated, leaving her to wonder about the circumstances that had led to Narky killing that boy.

Delicious, the door said, and swung backwards to let her through. Both halves of the bolt had vanished. Bandu took a deep breath, and stepped past the doorway into the underworld.

48

PTERA

Narky never came back. Instead, the king's son returned covered in the blood of other men, with the news that the Black Dragon had been slain by his own kinsman.

The first thing Ptera did was to suppress a scream. Being widowed had been nothing the first time, but to lose her second husband, her young Narky, was unthinkable. Had he been killed, or only captured? Would it make any difference? If Ardis won the war, the Dragon Touched would surely slay Narky out of spite. If the Dragon Touched won, they would slay him then too – him, and anyone else they caught.

The second thing Ptera did was to spread the word that Ravennis' temple was buying food. Magerion was probably mere hours away from ordering another assault on the Dragon Touched, and if that gambit turned out to be as disastrous as the last one, the city would soon come under siege.

Ptera did not go to talk to King Magerion. She knew that he would never listen to her, no matter her authority within the church – he had barely listened to Narky, and Narky was both a man and a prophet. It didn't matter what Ptera might say; Magerion would believe that the Black Dragon's death was an omen from Ravennis, proving that He favored war.

This, Ptera knew, was nonsense. If Ravennis had favored war, He would have told Narky so. At the very least, He would have brought Narky safely home to her, and allowed *him* to deliver the news of the Black Dragon's assassination. He would not, in His wisdom, have allowed Narky to be captured like this.

This was what Ptera thought: either the Dragon Touched assassin had been acting alone, without divine favor, or God Most High had decided to lure Magerion in so that He could condemn Ravennis and the people of Ardis to complete destruction. Under the first scenario, Magerion would be making a mistake. Under the second, he would be dooming his people.

Even so, Ptera had no intention of leaving the city. Ravennis could surely survive losing a second city if He had survived the loss of the first, and as long as Ravennis remained Lord Among the Fallen, Ptera must not fear death. Better to be a martyr in Ardis than to make her God think she did not trust Him.

So she had the church buy grain with the money that Magerion and his terrified fellow nobles had donated, and she gave sermons about the delights that awaited Ravennis' followers in the world below. People whispered about the grain, of course, but Ptera only smiled and carried on as if nothing was the matter. Either the king would order her to stop stockpiling food, or he wouldn't.

Within a week, the men of Ardis were marching off to war again, assured by their king that victory would be swift. Ptera hoped he was right – though if he was, what would happen to Narky? There had been no contact from the Dragon Touched regarding his release, but that was probably because they were in disarray after the slaying of their leader. Would their disarray be enough to give Magerion the victory he sought?

The people of Ardis were hopeful, but it took no special insight to sense their wariness. More than two thousand men had died since the day Bestillos marched south to punish a wizard, and the city was feeling their loss. When word came of a standoff on the mountainside, the relief in the city was palpable – yet how low had Ardis sunk, that simply failing to lose their army in its first week of combat should be considered a good sign?

The campaign dragged through another week, and another, as the army of Ardis proved unable to dislodge the Dragon Touched from their mountain. The swift victory that Magerion had promised was proving to be just as illusory as Ptera had expected: Ravennis did not truly support this war. Or if He did, He was opposed by an equally powerful force.

Then at last the word came. The Ardisian army had been routed again, and Magerion's son Atlon, who had been given its command, had died in battle.

The news destroyed the fragile equilibrium of the city, and the people came to Ptera in droves, hoping for words of comfort, at least, before their city went the way of Laarna. She gave them that comfort as best she could, and at every service, the crowd grew. Even Mageris, the king's second son, came to her to learn about his brother's fate in the world below – and, it went unsaid, about the fate they were all likely to face in the near future.

She spoke to him and to the others of the glories of Ravennis, and of the marvelous second lives that awaited them in His kingdom. But of course, that didn't change the fact that nobody *wanted* to die. Ptera certainly didn't, and it gave her great comfort to know that Narky hadn't either. If even the high priest of Ravennis didn't look forward to death, there was nothing wrong with her or with anyone for feeling the same way.

The Dragon Touched reached the city two days later, and Magerion ordered the gate closed. Those farmers who had not found their way within the walls were stranded outside, presumably begging for their lives. The Dragon Touched showed them little mercy.

The first assault on the city shook Ardis to its foundations. How many years had it been since these city walls had been tested? Over a hundred, probably; Ptera did not even know of a time when it had happened. Now they ran with blood and fire, and the sounds of war horns and clanging weaponry echoed into the night. Some of the city's women took up arms and joined their husbands and brothers on the wall, while the rest crowded into the Temple of Ravennis with their children. Ptera led them all in prayers until word came that the Dragon Touched had been repelled, at which point the women looked at each other in dubious relief, and she turned to prayers of thanksgiving.

The thanksgiving prayers were ones of Ptera's own invention. It was a sad fact that much of the Ravennian liturgy had been lost when the Graceful Servant was martyred. Though refugees from Laarna had no doubt settled in Atuna and elsewhere, Ptera and Narky had yet to meet any of them, and so they had been forced to develop prayers of their own. In some ways, though, it was not as great a loss as it seemed: the old prayers had been developed at a time when Ravennis was not yet God of the Dead, so the break from the past was perfectly excusable.

The Dragon Touched did not renew their assault the next day, so on Magerion's invitation Ptera spent the morning blessing the walls that had held them back. From her vantage point atop the gates, she was able to view the opposing army as it camped outside, nursing its wounds.

The army was small. If they had not humbled the men of Ardis so completely and repeatedly, Ptera would have thought the Dragon Touched too few to pose the city any threat. And yet, Ardis no longer had the kind of force to drive them away. The walls might hold or they might not, but no army of Ardismen would be leaving through these gates to break the siege. If Magerion could not buy the Dragon Touched off, the city would starve.

The king sent messengers suggesting an end to the war under new terms, but no peace could be brokered. The Dragon Touched were now led by their high priestess, Hessina, and she was less invested in the notion of peace than the young Black Dragon had been. The messengers told of how she had ridiculed their king for suggesting peace now, after he had so quickly withdrawn Narky's offer when he thought the Dragon

Touched were too weak to defend themselves. She would no longer trust Magerion's offers, she said – the war could only end with Ardis' destruction.

There was no word of Narky.

For the next few days, a double contingent of men patrolled the walls day and night. Yet for now, the Dragon Touched seemed content to starve them out. Two weeks passed without a second assault on the walls, even as the food supplies within them dwindled. After another two weeks, Ptera opened up the temple's food stores. But soon enough, her stockpile too was gone.

The king sent for Ptera now, for the first time since Narky's capture. Despite everything, the summons made her nervous. Ptera's family had been minor members of the king's clan, and they had always worshipped and feared their representative on the Council of Generals. Magerion was a powerful man, and a dangerous one.

She had thought, somehow, that he would never call for her, despite the prominence she had gained in Narky's absence. But, of course, she was the only representative Ravennis had in the city now. She would have to stand for the entire church. That meant she could not afford to be intimidated.

She saw now how much of an asset Narky's bluntness had been to their God. Her young husband was impudent and imprudent, but another man's power and stature could never prevent him from speaking. The Graceful Servant's power had been in her fearlessness; Narky's was in his bluntness. Where did Ptera's power lie?

She met the king on the walkway above the city gate, where he had been surveying the army that threatened to starve them all to death. He waved his retainers off as she approached, and the two of them made their own patrol of the city wall, alone.

"Our people have begun slaughtering their mules rather than feed them precious grain," the king said. "When the grain is gone too, it will be cats next, and dogs, and rats."

Ptera said nothing. She had prided herself once on her

strength of character and her quick wit, but now she was standing next to the man whose very name had made her parents quake. He hulked above her, his shoulders wide and his voice gravelly and deep. Though she was a strong woman herself, though she was here to represent her God and His church, she still could not speak.

"We are going to have to break this siege," the king said. "We have no choice. The Dragon Touched have defeated us every time we've met on the open field, but that is no excuse to hide behind our walls. I would rather our people died in battle than in starvation – I will not leave this world without bringing some of the Dragon Touched with me."

This time, Ptera found her voice. "They'll outnumber our army for the first time," she said.

Magerion shook his head. "Widows will have to take up their husbands' weapons for this final battle, and orphans their parents' tools of war. Everyone with legs to charge and hands to hold a spear must join us. That is why I called for you. What blessing can you give our people so that they will not fear the army they face?"

Ptera pulled her eyes away from his bulk and thought on this. Was there *anything* that could keep their people from fearing this calamitous final battle? What could Ptera possibly say to them that she hadn't said already?

Part of the trouble was that the people of Ardis were so new to the worship of Ravennis. They trusted Him, or at least, they trusted her, but Ravennis could not recover for them the feeling that they were *Ardismen*, the fiercest and most feared warriors in the known world. How could a God who had come upon them only in their weakness ever hope to remind them of their strength?

"Speak, girl."

The words hit her like a blow. Calling her "girl" was an attack on her, but it was more than that – it was an attack on Ravennis too. Blast her parents for teaching her to be intimidated by this man, and blast her own sudden shyness – she could not let him speak like that to a priestess. Afraid as she might be of Magerion, her faith demanded that he be chastised.

She could not be Ptera anymore, not right now. No. She was the Graceful Servant.

She stopped walking. "You can't call a priestess of Ravennis 'girl,' and expect our God to serve you. Do you think that Ravennis is so weak or so forgiving that He will ignore your disrespect, *old man?*"

Magerion was not accustomed to hearing such words from women. His first instinct was to raise his hand. But Ptera was ready, and she did not flinch. Instead she took a step closer to him.

"Ravennis does not fear you," she said, "and He does not serve you. Whether we drive the Dragon Touched away or whether we perish in hunger or in flames, your soul will soon pass into His halls, and you can expect to be judged according to your worth. Are you prepared for that?"

The king's hand was still up by his shoulder, but she was so close now that he could hardly have hit her with it if he'd tried. There was fear in his eyes.

"There is no time for you to switch sides," Ptera said, and the king himself flinched at her tone. She really was the Graceful Servant now, back in the flesh. "You have given Ardis to Ravennis," she said, "and He will not give it back."

"I... apologize," the king said at last, and when she would not step away, he did so himself. "But is your God – is our God content to let His second home on this earth fall, and His people starve, or will He help us? Will you do nothing to bless your city's cause?"

Ptera turned and walked on, forcing the king to follow. This game of imagining herself as the Graceful Servant really *worked*. An answer to his question presented itself quite suddenly, but she acted as if she had known of it all along and said confidently: "Our people need to know that it wasn't Magor that gave them strength. We should have a spear dance tonight."

"But spear dances were a sacred rite of His!"

"Magor is defeated," Ptera countered. "His people have turned to Ravennis. Why shouldn't Ravennis take His rituals too, if it suits Him?"

Magerion considered this. "A spear dance would hearten our people. Thank you, priestess. Consider it done."

That night, as the flames of a bonfire rose between the armory and the Temple of Ravennis, the men of Ardis displayed their prowess in sacred dance, spinning and leaping as if the Dragon Touched had never broken their confidence, never sent their brothers fleeing across the countryside. They danced and forgot the Dragon Touched – danced, and remembered Ardis.

The next day Ptera took up Narky's spear and joined Magerion at the gate, alongside every able-bodied man and woman in the city, and a few who were less than able-bodied. In size, their force would easily dwarf the Dragon Touched army, or any other army for that matter. It was enough to help them pretend that they would not break upon first contact with their enemies.

Magerion stood before them, dressed in scales of interlaced bronze and steel, polished to a magnificent shine. "The Dragon Touched think they can starve us to death," he said. "Today we show them what Ardis is, what the men and women of this great city can do to their puny little army. Today, this war ends."

Ptera cheered along with the rest, knowing that few of them truly expected to win, but willing to indulge in the fantasy. *Ravennis*, she prayed silently, *bring us to victory today. If You can do anything, bring these people home safely. Let us come to you another day.*

Perhaps Ravennis heard her. Perhaps He didn't.

The gates were opened.

49

Bandu

The first thing Bandu noticed when she stepped through the door was that the floor was made of stone, not roots. The Yarek's strength was enough to touch the underworld, but not enough to breach it. Beyond the door, she was on her own.

On this stone floor, bodies were piled. Hundreds of bodies, their skin a dark gray, were stacked one on top of the other all across the room, with only a narrow path leading between them. Now and then, one would mumble something or try to turn in its sleep, unsuccessfully. The bodies reminded Bandu of the ghosts she had seen on Tarphae a year ago, with no faces and no features. But they were solid. She accidentally brushed against one as she walked past, and there was no mistaking it.

There was an open archway in the wall ahead, and she passed from one chamber of bodies into another. There was no ceiling that she could see – the walls rose up into darkness. The second chamber was identical to the first, and when she came to a third, the only difference there was that the bodies here were not piled quite as high – they only came up to Bandu's waist and not her shoulder.

It was warmer than she had expected in the land of the dead – the kind of warmth that fogged the mind and made her eyes keep trying to close. But she forced herself to keep them open. She knew better than to fall asleep among the dead.

A screech from above made Bandu duck as a pale monster flew past her on raven wings, carrying another body in its arms. Bandu had seen these monsters before, with their bald heads and spiked teeth. Phaedra had called them angels, messengers from Ravennis. Two of these had attacked Bandu and her friends once. She knew how easily those talons could tear flesh, and that when these creatures died, they would turn back into crows.

But this one did not attack her. It only put its cargo down, almost lovingly, atop the other sleepers, and flew off into the darkness. Bandu stayed crouched for some time, until her body cried for her to stretch out, preferably on the ground, and her eyes began to shut themselves again. She rose, and pinched herself until a trickle of blood ran between her fingernails. The sting was enough to jolt her eyes open. For now.

She walked on, but before she could reach the next chamber two more angels swooped out of the darkness and stood before her on either side of the path. She was cautious in her approach, but the angels were faster than she expected. They caught her each under an arm and immediately lifted her into the air. Bandu wriggled in their grip, but it did no good. Higher and higher they rose until the chamber's walls came to an end and they flew over them through the darkness, sometimes veering left or right to avoid a collision with another body carrier. Bandu barely had the chance to catch her breath before they took a final turn over a high wall and lowered her to the floor. Then they screeched and flew away.

The new room was well-lit, with a rich carpet of woven feathers on the floor leading up to a majestic throne. On this throne sat the God Ravennis.

His body was like a man's, though easily three times too large, with the head of a crow. In His right palm He held an eye the size of a fist, a trophy she recognized. It was the eye of the Boar of Hagardis, which the Tarphaeans had given to Ravennis in the hopes that He might protect them from Magor. They had given other parts to other Gods, but apparently Narky's God cherished the gift nonetheless.

He nodded at her as she approached, and turned His head slightly to watch her. *I am glad you've come,* He said.

She knew His voice instantly. It was the voice that had whispered to her of Tarphae's drowning, the voice that had told her which water-leaf to hide in when she was a little girl trying to escape the fairies. It had always spoken to her through the wind, but she did not think Ravennis was the wind itself. He couldn't be. Could He?

Maybe He just wanted her to *think* He was the wind – He was tricky, Narky's God. Even now, He was lying to her with His presence.

Why are you showing me this body? Bandu asked. *It isn't real.*

Of course it is not real, Ravennis said. *We are not contained in bodies in Our world – that is why the Yarek's physicality was such a danger to Us. But the lower worlds are different. Yours requires physical manifestations. This lowest world is a place of dreams, and so I have fashioned this dream body to meet with you. I wanted to be prepared for your arrival.*

I am here for Criton, Bandu said, though He seemed to already know. *Give him to me.*

Ravennis laughed with a horrible cawing sound that grated at the soul as much as at her nerves. *You don't sound like you want him.*

I don't, Bandu answered. *But I need him back anyway.*

Ravennis turned His head all the way to the side to get a better look at her. *You don't want him? That will be a problem. Are you ready to pay the price for bringing him back with you?*

Yes, Bandu said, though she was very aware that she didn't know what that price would be. Phaedra had convinced her that this journey was necessary and that only she could make it, but she hadn't known what Ravennis would ask of Bandu, and so she had spent most of her time discussing the risks of the journey instead. What would Ravennis demand of her, now that Bandu was finally here?

I am glad you have come, Ravennis said. *You can help Me find him.*

His words confused Bandu. Did the God of the Underworld not know where Criton was? How was such a thing possible?

Ravennis answered her question without her speaking it. *I have been here less than a year,* He said, *turning the chaos that was here before Me into order. You will soon see how much work there remains.*

The God rose, towering above her. *Come,* He said.

His enormous strides took Him to the other side of the room within seconds, and Bandu found that she was with Him already, as if she had somehow been sucked into His wake. The wall parted as Ravennis approached it and they passed through onto a sort of balcony that jutted out into the chamber beyond.

It was not a room, this chamber, and it was not filled with air. The substance in which they stood was too thick, halfway between liquid and gas, and the bodies of sleepers were suspended in it as far as the eye could see, above and below for what must have been hundreds of miles. The bodies were surrounded in globes of faint light that changed colors and rippled outward in all directions, and where they met each other a light flashed or a sound boomed, or a sudden landscape appeared and vanished again. Raven-angels flew among them, moving them this way and that with some logic that Bandu could not discern.

What they are doing? she asked. She could not decide if the bodies were floating in a sky or in a sea, or if they were even floating at all. They all looked like they were lying down, regardless of whether they were upright or horizontal or upside-down. Sometimes they turned over.

They are dreaming, Ravennis answered. *The dead that you saw when you first came here are only the harmless ones, those who are safe to pile together as they sleep. My servants have been piling them up to make more room for these, the active dreamers.*

Bandu couldn't help but notice that some of the bodies were much smaller than the others. *There are children here,* she said. *There aren't in the piles.*

Yes, Ravennis said. *The dreams of children are too strong for the piles. Even in life, their dreams are more visceral. In death, they are dangerous. I have seen their nightmares come to life and devour the souls of other sleepers – those souls are now gone forever.*

As they watched, the ripples of three dreamers came together with a flash, and at their intersection a monster bubbled into existence. It rose from the mud, a patch of mud that hadn't even existed until it suddenly had. The monster had the head and body of a goat, but with three tails that looked like snakes, thrashing this way and that. It was brown and wet as clay, and it quickly turned on one of the dreamers above it and charged. Before it could get there, two raven-angels fell upon it and tore it to shreds. Then they took the dreamer's body and pushed it upward, away from the others.

The guardians of the underworld are some of the oldest dreams, Ravennis said. *They devoured their creators in days of old and broke free of their prison, but were too afraid to emerge into the light of the Gods. There are hundreds of them, patrolling the many entrances to this place. They see the dreamers as a treasure to be hoarded. I see them as children to be protected.*

A naked baby floated past them, giggling, its face a vision of pure joy. Its skin was the pale tone of the mountain clans, its cheeks rosy. One of the angels who had fought the goat-monster turned and flew toward it at a furious pace, its claws outstretched.

Your angels kill the good dreams too?

When they can, Ravennis said. *Sometimes a good dream turns bad, and that can be even worse than those that start that way.*

Bandu watched in horror as the angel approached the baby, screeching. They reached toward each other, baby and angel, and then the baby grabbed the angel's claws in its little fingers and pulled them off. The angel screeched again, trying to back away, but the baby floated forward excitedly and pulled its head off. The head and body shrank back into those of a crow, a transformation the infant watched in fascination. Then the baby lifted the crow's head to its mouth and gummed at its beak, cooing.

Do the dreamers know this is happening? Bandu asked.

They do not, Ravennis said. *They live immersed in their dreams, at least until one swallows them. Thankfully, that happens rarely. We are working to make it rarer still. With increased power in the world above, I will one day bring peace and justice to the world below.*

Justice?

Ravennis gazed down at her with His crow's eye. *There is no justice in death. Not yet. Whether the dead dream well or terribly is a matter of their own haunting, not their virtue. The anxious dream anxiously, the unrepentant proudly. I would have the virtuous dream well and grant nightmares only to the unworthy.*

Bandu wasn't fooled. *You want to punish Your enemies.*

Ravennis showed no outward sign of embarrassment. *Yes, so long as I am allowed to. If My Master wills otherwise, I know better than to disobey. The Gods above are only just learning the dangers of opposing God Most High.*

Bandu looked around. *Why there aren't any animals?* she asked. *These bodies are all of my kind.*

Your wolf is not trapped outside, Ravennis said, answering the question she hadn't asked. *The monster that appeared to you in his guise was preying on your desires. But he is not likely to be in this chamber either. The souls down here mostly segregate themselves, fortunately for all. Fewer are lost that way. There have been a few animal souls that appeared here, but We have moved them elsewhere. Human dreams are not kind to them.*

But let Me be clear, Ravennis continued. *I do not know where every animal dwells, just as I do not know where precisely Criton's soul has come to rest. There are whole realms in the underworld that My servants and I have yet to explore. The dragon souls, for instance, lie somewhere beyond this sea, and even I hesitate to seek them out.*

Bandu's estimation of Narky's God kept falling. For all that He was bigger and stronger than Bandu, bigger and stronger than Psander, or Salemis, or the queen of the elves, He was still so much smaller and weaker than she had expected. He didn't know where Criton was, He didn't know where Four-foot was – what *did* He know? He wasn't even one of the weaker ones –

that was the worst of it. She could see now why the Gods had been forced to cut Themselves off from the elves' world, why the dragons hadn't been afraid to fight Them, and why They had relied on Their own God Most High to defeat the Yarek. She was glad she had never worshipped these beings.

Bring me to Criton now, she said. *I don't like this place.*

We can search for him together, Ravennis answered. *As I have told you, I don't know where he is. Trust Me in this: I want peace in Ardis as much as you do.*

She looked up at Him skeptically. *Peace is good for the Dragon Touched too, and Criton's God is bigger and stronger than You. He doesn't tell you where to find him?*

He sent you.

Ravennis took her by the hand and pulled her off the balcony with Him. They navigated the sea of the dead together, inspecting the bodies they passed. None of them looked like Criton. They had no features any of them, and it was only by coming close enough to feel their dreams that Bandu was able to identify them as not-Criton.

There has to be a better way, Ravennis said. *Did you bring nothing that can help us?*

Bandu let go of the God's hand and reached into her satchel. The bucket was still there. When she pulled it out she found that it had mended itself. It was pulsing with power here in the sea of the dead, where dreams came to life. Its power drew the nearest sleeper toward her.

Is that him? Ravennis asked.

The body didn't feel especially like a not-Criton, but Bandu shook her head. *No. This is wrong.*

The God took her hand again and they flew off, or maybe swam. It soon became clear that the bucket's power was drawing all the sleepers toward it, and the monsters too. One terrifying white dog-thing came charging at them, roaring, "MOGAWOR!" – but the God of the Underworld only motioned it aside with the hand that held the boar's eye. The Mogawor creature retreated as if struck, and they moved on.

They seemed to drift forever through the sea of the dead, passing through varied dream-landscapes and waving away their more dangerous inhabitants until Bandu finally lifted the bucket and pointed. *That one.*

Among all those floating in the sea, one body in the distance was drifting slowly away from them. *How do you know?* Narky's God asked, sounding for a moment just like Narky himself.

Phaedra finds this in Criton's house, Bandu said. *Only bad things happen to him there. He doesn't want this bucket; he wants to get away from it.*

They sped toward the body. *You will have to catch him yourself,* Ravennis warned. *The souls of the dead are too delicate for Me to touch without destroying them. That is why I have these angels.*

Bandu and Ravennis were not the only ones who quickened their pace. By the time they reached Criton's soul, it was actively trying to escape them. Even in its sleep, it was kicking and thrashing and trying to swim away. Bandu released her hold on the bucket and caught one of the body's arms. It was cold and vaguely wet, and she nearly lost her grip as it tried to shake her off, but the arm was thinner than Criton's arms had been in life, and she was able to close her fingers around it. Then Ravennis was pulling them away, through drifting souls and nightmares, back onto the balcony and into His throne room. When they arrived, Criton's soul stopped struggling and stood somewhat limply at her side.

Ravennis let go of her hand and sat back down on His throne. *You have done well. But Criton's soul cannot survive leaving this place unless you pay for it.*

Bandu nodded to show she understood. *What do I pay?*

Criton's years among the living have run out. To bring him back, you must bind his soul to yours and let him feed off of you, taking a year of your life for each year he lives. Practically speaking, you will age at double the rate until he dies again, and if you die first, he will wither before his people's eyes and join you here before the day is through.

Bandu blinked, standing before Narky's God in shock. Criton did not deserve her years – he was not even her mate anymore!

He had never been right for her, had never made her feel safe –
why should she give half her life for him?

What would Vella say if she learned of this bargain? It was so
wrong. It was unfair. Why should peace between Ardis and the
Dragon Touched require this sacrifice of *her?*

Psander's words came back to her, from so long ago: "There
was once a great warrior mage, whose wife died while she was
still young. By magic, he tore his way into the underworld and
retrieved her, and she lived with him another fifty years."

Fifty years! Those could not have come entirely from the
wizard, could they?

Psander says there is a man who brings his wife back for fifty years,
she said. *Does he give those years from his life?*

No, Ravennis admitted. *That man had an infant son whom he'd
left behind when he took his journey. He traded the boy's years for
his wife's. She never forgave him. Will you give Criton Goodweather's
years instead of your own?*

Bandu recoiled. *Never.*

*Then I am afraid this is how it must be. I do not have the power to
grant him extra years Myself, much though I might like to. For as long
as Criton lives, he will feed off you. Will you bind yourself to him like
this?*

Bandu stood for a moment in uncertainty. How much did
she want this? Goodweather might live a long and happy
life even without the peace Narky and Criton wanted. The
Dragon Touched might win their war, for all that Vella's dream
suggested otherwise, and even if they didn't, Bandu and Vella
could flee into the mountains or further into the forest and
raise Goodweather without any fear of being tracked. Many
would die that way, but that was not Bandu's fault, for all that
her sacrifice might prevent it.

Or, she could accept the injustice of the underworld's price,
and save Criton's people. Vella would curse her decision, but
she would be secretly grateful for the results – she did not want
her people to die. And Goodweather would grow and flourish
in a world at peace, and might even meet her father again if

Bandu chose to let her. Was she willing to make this sacrifice for Goodweather's sake?

She was. Bandu sighed. *I do it,* she said. *Show me how.*

You know how to already.

Bandu nodded. She felt the flexibility of this place. She took Criton's hand and plunged it into her chest, through meat and bone, until it touched her heart. When she drew it out, her body closed itself up again and only the blood on Criton's fingertips remained.

"Come with me," she said aloud.

Ravennis opened a doorway through the wall for her. *Lead him up the stairway without letting go of his hand. He will grow more substantial as you go, but do not turn to see him until you are both standing in the sunlight. If God Most High wills it, it will be many years before I see you in My chambers again. By that time, I hope to be ready to receive you.*

50

CRITON

Criton groaned, trying to focus his eyes. His vision was blurry, and the light ahead was blinding. Where was he? Was that the entrance of the Dragon Knight's Tomb up ahead?

Bandu was holding his hand, pulling him along. That was nice. She was pulling him toward the light, though, and he would have liked to spend a little longer in the darkness, at least to let his eyes adjust. He tried to pull back, but her grip only tightened, and she dragged him harder up the stairway.

A stairway. That was odd. There weren't any stairs in the Dragon Knight's Tomb.

"Bandu," he said, "where are we?"

Bandu didn't speak, didn't even turn her head to look at him. She was still angry, then. He remembered the argument now: he had said he wanted to take another wife or two, and the results had been... predictable. So what was she doing back here? Had she forgiven him?

Slowly, slowly, his surroundings came into focus. They had almost reached the light by now, at the base of the tree. It must have been the Yarek, then, because it was far, far too massive to be anything else. These stairs were not stairs at all, but roots. He turned his head to try to see where he had come from, but there was nothing but darkness behind him.

"Bandu," he said, "what are we doing here? The last

thing I remember, I..."

It came back to him then. Narky, the Dragon Knight's Tomb, the sight of Phaedra and the feeling of Belkos' claws digging into his throat, breaking through skin and muscle, tearing into his windpipe. He had been dying not too long ago. Dying. And now he was here.

They reached the light, then the top of the stairway of roots, and finally the sweet dirt of the southern plains. It made no sense for him to be here; or rather, it made perfect sense, but it was impossible for him to believe it anyway. He *couldn't* have been.

"Bandu?" he asked. "Was I dead?"

Finally she turned to look at him. "Yes," she said, letting go of his hand. "I bring you back."

"Does that mean... that you forgive me?"

"No."

He had been trying to brace himself for a response like that, but it wasn't enough. He had allowed himself to hope.

"You are not my mate now," Bandu said. "You can take other women and do what you want. I don't care. I'm not yours and you're not mine. But now you go and make peace between Ardis and your kind."

She turned from him and walked back the way they had come, just until she could touch the Yarek's trunk. "Thank you," she said to the great tree.

He stood, watching her. "I still love you," he said.

She looked back at him coldly, so coldly. "That is sad for you."

They walked away from the Yarek in silence, together and yet not. "How long was I gone?" he asked her at last.

"A long time. I walk here to find you."

Over a month then. And in that time, how many had died? It was too much to hope that there had been no bloodshed in his absence – without his influence, his people might easily have decided to sack Ardis after all. But Bandu wouldn't have any useful news for him on that front. She hadn't stayed to find out what the Dragon Touched were up to, she had come after him.

He should have been so grateful for what she'd done. She'd *brought him back from the dead*, for God's sake. Yet her rejection still stung. It hurt more than anything he had ever known, more than having his throat pierced by his cousin's claws. It was hard to be as grateful as he should have been when she'd brought him back to such pain.

It was hot and dry that night, but Bandu didn't remove a single garment as they lay down on the ground across from each other. Criton kept apologizing for what he'd done, but she wouldn't listen. He begged her to forgive him, and she ignored him. She didn't care that he hadn't taken any other wives after she left him. She was unmoved by his tears. Finally, he made the mistake of asking what he could do to change her mind.

"Nothing," she said. "I love Vella. She is a better mate than you."

He sat up and gaped at her. "*What?* You took another man's wife as your, as your... as *your* wife?"

"Yes."

He lay back down with an angry thump. It was more than he could even process. Here he'd been, begging this woman to forgive him for *suggesting* that he might marry again, when she'd gone and taken another man's wife for herself! She didn't deserve his love; she didn't deserve his pain.

"How could you?" he said at last. "How could you be angry at me, and then go and do something like *that*?"

Now Bandu sat up. "I don't care what you think, Criton. I am not angry because you want other women. I don't *care* if you take others or don't take others. You are never good for me. Never. You can be angry about Vella if you want to be angry. I don't care. But if you try to hurt her, Criton, then I *kill* you."

"And Goodweather? What about her?"

"What about her?" Bandu repeated. "I take care of Goodweather before. I take care of her now. You have Delika now, and you can have other young with other women. If you make peace with Ardis and you tell your kind to be good to me and to Vella, then maybe you can help with Goodweather sometimes. I don't want her to be like you: she can know who her father is. She can love you. But I don't."

Criton had no response, no answer for her. He wondered what had become of poor Delika during his absence. Had Iona taken her in? Had anybody?

By the time he spoke again, Bandu had lain down and fallen asleep, her soft regular breaths unmistakable.

"I don't want Goodweather to be like me either," he said.

Criton did not count the days of their journey. Traveling with Bandu now, on the same route northward where they had once learned to make love together, was a painful affair. It was uncomfortable too: where once they had traveled this road with friends and a tent, now Criton had neither.

The villages that had once shut their doors against the cursed wanderers of Tarphae now opened those doors when Criton knocked, but he and Bandu always moved on as soon as they were fed. They couldn't trust the inhabitants not to try to kill him in his sleep. He was the Black Dragon now, after all, and what's more, they knew that he was *supposed* to be dead.

When Bandu had left him, it had broken his heart and shattered his confidence, but their relations now were so tense that it was a relief when Bandu finally left him again, striking out on her own sometime after they passed Anardis. It was so much easier to miss the Bandu who had loved him when the one who didn't was gone.

Criton only realized the next day that he hadn't asked her where she and Vella were living. He cursed himself then, because not knowing where she lived meant that he couldn't come to visit Goodweather either. Could he trust Bandu to bring their daughter to visit him instead? He had been a poor husband and an inattentive father, but he still loved the baby more than he could say.

He still loved them both, really. But Bandu would not have him, and her rejection freed him to make his political marriages. The notion no longer appealed to him, but it would have to do. Maybe he could find love again with one of the new wives the elders would choose for him.

He would have to be better to her than he'd been to Bandu.

Criton followed the road straight to Ardis, afraid that he would find a burning ruin there, or else a battlefield littered with the corpses of his kin. He breathed a sigh of relief when the city came into sight and he spotted the Dragon Touched camp outside it. He wasn't too late, then.

He arrived just before sunset, when the Dragon Touched were conducting their rituals to welcome the evening. If he had worried at all about what reception his people would give him, he needn't have. They greeted him with reverence, and brought him directly to Hessina's tent.

The high priestess regarded him with awe. "I prayed to our God for guidance," she said. "I did not expect this."

He soon learned of the losses his people had suffered in his absence, first at the Dragon Knight's Tomb and then during the disastrous assault on the walls of Ardis. Hundreds had died in that assault, not just plainsmen but true Dragon Touched as well. Criton winced at this description. His failure to marry any plainswomen had reinforced the feeling that the Dragon Touched were somehow above their allies, and that was a dangerous thing. He would have to speak to the elders, and marry the women they suggested as soon as possible.

He could not help but ask if Pilos, Vella's husband, was among the fallen. Was Bandu carrying on with another man's wife, or with a widow? It turned out that Vella was a widow – Pilos had died during the assault on Ardis. But upon learning so, Criton discovered that it didn't make him feel any better about Bandu and Vella. It might have made the whole thing worse.

He asked after Delika, and Hessina told him that her son Kilion had taken it upon himself to raise the girl in Criton's absence. Criton was surprised at first that it hadn't been Iona, but then on second thought, of course it hadn't. He resolved to visit Kilion's tent soon and reclaim her as his adopted child… but not yet. He had too many other problems to deal with.

The Dragon Touched did not have enough men to stage

another assault on the walls, so they had decided to fortify their position outside and starve the Ardismen out. Hessina had scorned an offer of peace from Magerion, but now she was having second thoughts. The Dragon Touched had never lost a battle in the open field, but their failure to storm the walls of Ardis raised the worrisome possibility that God Most High might have turned against them after Criton's death. Now even Hessina admitted that complete victory was unlikely, that she ought to have taken the bargain. And yet, Magerion was unlikely to renew his offer.

Criton's resurrection brought the hope of peace back to life. He had become a symbol of that peace in the weeks after his death, and whereas Hessina could no longer offer terms without signaling her army's weakness, Criton was uniquely suited to the task of rekindling the negotiations while still projecting strength. And yet, even this came with a price: where Criton had become a symbol of peace, Belkos' family had grown to represent war and hate, and had become increasingly ostracized within the community.

Criton put an end to that. He visited Iona with the elders in tow, and apologized for her husband's execution. It was ridiculous, on the face of it, to act as if he had killed Belkos and not the other way around, but the fact remained that Criton was alive now and Belkos was dead, and that it was Dessa and not Goodweather who would have to live without a father.

Iona accepted his apology with the grace of a martyr. Her mother and daughter did not – they took it as a vindication of their hatred for him. But there was nothing Criton could do except apologize again and move on.

He was horrified when Hessina asked him what he meant to do with Narky. He hadn't realized his friend was being held captive, and it seemed that even that much was a courtesy Hessina had extended to him as an islander and friend of Criton's, when the more popular option had been to give him a public execution before the walls of Ardis.

Narky shouted for joy when he saw Criton. "I knew it!" he cried. "I kept telling them that you'd be back, that Phaedra and Bandu would come through, but they wouldn't believe me."

"Bandu did bring me back," Criton said.

"So we can make the peace treaty happen now, right? You'll go with me and tell Magerion that you'll accept his tribute?"

Criton nodded. "And you'll tell your people that Ravennis is a servant of God Most High?"

"Gladly," Narky said. "Your coming back sort of proves that, doesn't it?"

Criton turned to Hessina. "You were right not to execute my friend. That decision is probably what saved you while I was away, and it'll make our peace possible now."

"Thank my son," Hessina said. "I was leaning toward execution, but he was very passionate about keeping your friend alive."

Criton's estimation of Kilion grew yet again. He had thought the man timid, but even in that he'd been wrong. Saving Narky, caring for Delika – these were not timid acts. His voice might be quiet, but it was a powerful voice for decency.

"Let's go," Narky said. "Let's go now and end this war."

"At dawn tomorrow," Criton said. "I need sleep."

He didn't get much. He was too anxious about the day ahead. He awoke well before dawn, and finding Narky in the same situation spent an hour in nervous chatter, going over what little they knew about Bandu's journey to rescue him. Narky was surprised that Bandu hadn't told Criton more, but Criton assured him that she hadn't, and when Narky asked him what had gone wrong between the two of them, he spilled his heart and told his friend about Vella.

After that, everything came out: his poor treatment of Bandu, her disappearance, and her final rejection of him, even after rescuing him from the underworld. Narky listened sympathetically, but he asked painful questions. Criton hated having to relive the way he had left Goodweather almost exclusively to Bandu's care, and how he had taken Bandu for granted – not only on the night she had left him, but really all along.

"I was a terrible husband," he admitted. "Just like I thought I'd be."

To his credit, Narky said nothing. Criton knew he agreed, but there had been a time when he would have had no qualms about agreeing much more vocally.

"It's no wonder Bandu hates me."

"She shouldn't," Narky said. "You're a good man. You saved us when we were trapped in Anardis, you saved us when we were trapped in Castle Illweather – you're braver and more loyal than anyone I know. It sounds like Bandu had good reasons to leave you, but that doesn't mean she has to hate you."

"That might be true," Criton admitted. "But it's still hard knowing that she left me because I deserved it. You can't imagine how much I regret it now."

Narky snorted. "I can't imagine how much you regret something? I killed a man, Criton. I shot him with my father's crossbow just a few days before you met me. After that, I stole this symbol of Ravennis from someone who was staying at our inn in Atuna. I hid it in my shoe, and I walked all the way to the Crossroads on it. Trust me, I know all about regret."

So Narky was the murderer from the prophecy. Criton wasn't exactly surprised that that was the case, but he was amazed that Narky felt he could admit it to him. "Who was he?" he asked. "Why did you kill him?"

Narky sighed. "I thought I was in love. He humiliated me for it, and... I was an idiot. When Ravennis spared me, I decided it was my chance to become a better person."

"I'm glad you took it."

"You helped," Narky said earnestly. "You and Phaedra and Hunter, and Bandu too. You all taught me how to be better, and I'm never going to forget that."

Criton smiled. It was good, so good, to talk to Narky again, not as leaders of men but as young men themselves; as people who didn't know. He couldn't think of a time when he'd enjoyed Narky's company more. They moved onto happier topics, and by the time they finished their conversation and left for the city, the sun had risen and was shining brightly in the east.

They took no guard, approaching the city together like brothers. As they walked, Criton rehearsed what he would say in his head, hoping that the guards at the Ardisian gates would listen to him rather than try to shoot him down. But the gates opened well before they arrived and an army came pouring forth, marching toward them ready for battle. It was an army like none Criton had ever seen before, more massive than even the one that had besieged Silent Hall. His first thoughts were panicked – with an army like that, would the Ardismen even care that he was offering them peace?

The closer they came, the more obvious it became that this was no ordinary army. At least two thirds of its soldiers were women, and half of them didn't even have weapons. They were marching on the Dragon Touched in a last act of desperation. But knowing what losses his people had taken, he couldn't have said who would win that final battle.

The army halted as Criton and Narky neared, and a man and a woman stepped forward to meet them. The man must have been Magerion. His armor was polished and majestic, and the crown on his head dispelled any doubts that might have remained about his identity. The woman, Criton soon learned, was Ptera. The looks that Narky and his wife exchanged filled Criton with sudden jealousy, so he willed himself to ignore them and concentrate on the Ardisian king.

"Black Dragon!" King Magerion called to him. "My son told me you were dead."

"I was," Criton answered. "But God Most High, who rules above all, commanded His servant Ravennis to release me so that we could bring an end to this war, which has wearied my people and prompted yours to march against them hopeless, desperate, and unarmed. So will you accept the terms I gave you before my death, and send all these people home in safety?"

All eyes fell on Magerion, the general and the king.

"Yes," he said. "I will."

51

NARKY

Narky made his proclamation that very evening, as the sun set behind the mountains. The square before the temple was so crowded that Narky thought a strong shove on one side might have knocked the whole multitude over, from the armory to the temple walls. With the king on his right side and Ptera on his left, Narky stood on the altar where once an angel had died and told his people that Ravennis, God of Laarna and of Ardis, Keeper of Fates and Lord Among the Fallen, was a servant.

"Ravennis Below interceded with His master above on our behalf," he told the crowd, "and through Him we were all saved. If not for the leadership of the Graceful Servant and the foresight of King Magerion, you worshippers of Magor would have been slaughtered like sheep, and your souls tormented for all eternity. Ardis still stands today because you turned to Ravennis, and He chose to favor you.

"The last time I was here with you, the man you call the Black Dragon had made an offer to our king and was willing to lead his people to peace. But when I went to accept his terms, his cousin killed him before my eyes.

"It was Ravennis who sent him back, Ravennis who took pity on our city and made this peace possible again. I'll say it again: only through Him was Ardis saved. Only through Him can we all be saved."

Narky surveyed the crowd, proud of the speech that he and Ptera had composed, and that he'd spent the last three hours memorizing. Nobody could say that Narky hadn't honored the terms of his agreement with Criton. He had been quite explicit about God Most High's supremacy – and yet, the Ardismen would not be turning from Ravennis to His master over this speech. Ardis still belonged to the God Below.

"And now," Narky said, "Priestess Ptera will lead us all in prayer."

He hopped nimbly off the altar while the men nearby – the king included – helped Ptera climb up it. While she led the crowd in prayer, Narky turned to the old man Criton had left behind to verify that he would be true to his word.

"You'll tell Criton that I kept my promise?"

"I will," the man said. He was an elder among the plainsmen, but Narky couldn't remember his name. Kenda, maybe?

"It's not the speech I'd have given," Kenda-or-whatever-his-name-was said, "but I'm not a priest of Ravennis. You kept your word. So long as your king delivers on his own promises, the peace between our peoples will hold for a generation."

Narky had hopes that it would. The first payment of gold was made the next day, and over the following weeks, shipments of stone were sent north to round out the first year's tribute. The Dragon Touched, in the meantime, withdrew from the gates of Ardis and moved northward as far as the Dragon Knight's Tomb. Per the agreement Criton had struck, the tomb would mark the southernmost point of his people's territory.

The treaty called for yearly tribute to be paid for only fifteen years, after which Ardis could consider its side of the bargain fulfilled. Narky had suggested the provision to Criton and Magerion, pointing out that it was the threat of a cessation of payments that had caused Ardis to make war on Anardis last year. If the treaty called for an end to the tribute payments within a reasonable span of time, there would be less temptation for either side to go to war again over the issue. The idea had appealed to Magerion for obvious reasons, and Criton too had accepted Narky's logic. Between that and his proclamation regarding their Gods, Narky felt personal responsibility for the treaty's success.

Perhaps the best part was how proud Ptera was of him for what he'd done. There was truth to her assertion that he had saved the city, for all that his part had been more minor than Bandu's or Criton's. And it was good, so good to finally settle into this life with her. Without war, capture, threat of execution, or fear of another religious betrayal by Magerion, he could finally exhale and begin enjoying his position as high priest. And in a year's time, Mother Dinendra would be forced to admit that Ravennis and Elkinar were one and the same, and the whole priesthood of Elkinar would be his to command.

To make things even better, Magerion seemed far less sure of his power over Narky than he had once been. Ptera had said something to him, something that had shaken him to his core. Though he clearly didn't like Narky or his wife any better than before, the king no longer viewed the priests of Ravennis as his tools to be used or discarded. What word would Phaedra have used? "Reverent," that was it. The king was reverent now.

There was another word at the back of Narky's mind, a word that would have applied to his situation now but that he was nonetheless afraid to use, afraid to even think about. Its power had haunted him all his life, but these last two years especially. To use it would have been an affront to his father's memory, and, he feared, an affront to the Gods as well.

But as the weeks went by, it was impossible not to feel it. For all his worries, there was no denying that feeling that he could finally breathe, breathe like a man who need never fear drowning. And one day, Ptera looked at him with those off-balance eyes of hers and asked how he felt, and it finally came out, bursting from its hiding place in his mind.

He felt safe.

52

DESSA

Dessa lay in her parents' tent, crying. She had such conflicting emotions, it was overwhelming. Anger at Father for sacrificing himself over something that everyone now agreed had been stupid. Guilt because she hadn't believed Grandma about Criton and Bandu. Guilt because she hadn't been able to stop their people from killing Father, and anger at Criton for being alive again when Father was dead. And above it all, sadness like she'd never known.

Bandu hadn't even come back to visit after rescuing Criton from the underworld. Dessa felt even more alone than before – Father was gone; Vella was gone; Bandu and Goodweather were gone.

If she had been more like Bandu, she could have gone to the underworld and brought Father back, just like Bandu had retrieved Criton. Maybe if she found Bandu, she could make her tell her how she'd done it. It wasn't fair that Criton should have a second chance just because his wife was a powerful witch and Dessa wasn't.

Mother didn't want Dessa to become a powerful witch. She wanted her to marry Malkon while she could, and join his family so that Father's taint wouldn't hang over her as it did his widow. Dessa wanted nothing to do with such plans. She didn't think she *could* live untainted anyway, not around people who knew about Father. Attaching herself to the Highservants would only make things worse.

Could she strike out on her own, and go find Bandu and Vella wherever they were hiding? Mother would have said she was too young, and would have forbidden it regardless, but hadn't Criton's mother left home at just such an age? Dessa didn't want to get married, and she didn't want to stay here and be hated. She had bigger plans for herself.

So she wrote her mother a note and left it where she'd find it, and then slipped away one afternoon while Mother was busy trying to calm Grandma. She took some food and some water and just sort of wandered off, trying to look like she was running an errand of some sort. At least for now, nobody seemed to notice her leave.

She knew that Bandu and Vella had disappeared while the camp was well north of here, but her sense of direction wasn't spectacular. All she knew was that she ought to head away from Ardis.

So she did, and spent her first night alone huddled in an empty barn, its animals already either eaten or carrying supplies for the Dragon Touched. She considered going back home that very night, but she knew that Bandu would have done no such thing. Bandu was always powerful, always confident. Dessa would be like her.

So she woke up the next morning and traveled onward, stopping whenever she needed to and foraging whenever she could. It was hard, but it was also good to be away from all the people who hated her over what her father had done.

She dreamt that Mother had found her and dragged her home to be stoned – she woke up shaking. But she got up, rubbed her eyes, and moved on. She always moved on.

Her legs got tired. Her stomach got empty. But still she traveled on and on, asking everyone she met whether they had seen two women like Bandu and Vella. Nobody had.

Even when she had been gone a week and a half and still turned up no sign of her friends, that little voice inside her would not let her give up. If she couldn't find Bandu, she could at least be independent like her. Maybe it didn't matter if she found her or not – so long as she made sure she was always eating enough and never falling asleep in dangerous places, she could still be *like* Bandu.

By God, she could be like her.

53

PHAEDRA

Phaedra stayed with Vella and Goodweather for over two months, waiting for Bandu to return. The wait was awful, but it could have been a good deal worse. Her relationship with Vella had grown more cordial, though Phaedra still sometimes caught her hostess looking at her with eyes that blamed her for the danger Bandu was in.

It was the words on the walls that softened their stances toward each other and turned them into tentative friends. Vella had been teaching Bandu to read, a feat that Phaedra had believed impossible until she saw the row of letters that Bandu herself had carved under Vella's set. Phaedra hadn't been able to hold in her respect and admiration for that – not that she would have wanted to. It was the first real smile Vella gave her, the one that lit up her face when Phaedra expressed such admiration and wonder at her work.

Phaedra couldn't have missed the *I love you, Bandu* that was carved above the bed, but she pretended to anyway, though she knew it didn't fool Vella. It was such an intimate message that she felt guilty for having read it at all, even though it was carved quite prominently on the wall. It showed the confidence with which Vella had written it – and the confidence with which she had assumed that the two of them would be entertaining no guests.

It was hard to escape the feeling that Phaedra was intruding on someone else's life. Particularly with Goodweather, who knew Vella but had no memory of Phaedra, it was clear that Phaedra didn't belong here – that her presence only made Bandu's absence worse.

Except, of course, on a practical level. Vella needed all her support just to keep Goodweather alive and healthy. The forced weaning that had taken place at Bandu's departure was a terrible transition, but they got through it together, taking turns consoling an inconsolable baby and trying to sneak another mouthful past her trembling lips. Phaedra had never realized an infant could give a person such a murderous look.

But she took to it in the end, and by the third week she was chomping happily on mashed chickpeas. All was apparently forgiven after that, and Phaedra even came to enjoy feeding her. The memory of an infant was short.

Phaedra's memory wasn't, though. Even in the midst of caring for Goodweather, she could not help but remember the mission Psander had sent her on, and worry about the length of this diversion. It was practically springtime already – just this week, Vella had planted the seeds for her garden! Could the world afford for Phaedra to spend another month waiting for Bandu, when she might have been sealing fairy gateways already?

And what if Bandu never came back? What if Phaedra had sent her to her death? Judging from the looks Vella gave her now and again, Phaedra wasn't the only one thinking about such questions. As much as Phaedra might blame herself if Bandu did not return, Vella would blame her more.

But Bandu did return in the end, looking so grim that Phaedra was afraid she might have failed after all. But no, she had succeeded. Criton was alive, and the region would know peace once more. It was the price of his return that had her looking that way, and when she explained it in her halting manner, Phaedra couldn't help but feel that Bandu blamed her for not having known. Phaedra had to beg her for details about her journey, which Bandu gave, incompletely. There were details that she claimed not to remember, and others that she gave only begrudgingly.

Phaedra recorded all she could, wary of forgetting anything that Bandu would supply. She was also wary of losing her work as she had lost her father's scrolls in Hession's cavern, so she found a sturdy branch in the woods to use for a walking stick and scratched Bandu's narrative in a spiral on its surface. Her story of the underworld and its sea of sleeping dead might well be the greatest revelation of the century, and Phaedra meant to carry it everywhere.

As soon as the staff was complete, she left Bandu and Vella to their life together. Bandu didn't want her to go at first. She had missed Phaedra as much as Phaedra missed her – couldn't she stay awhile longer?

But Phaedra could not. "I'll come back," she promised. "There are things I have to do first, but I promise I'll come back. All right?"

Bandu was reluctant to accept that. But Vella was not, and whatever Bandu's thoughts on privacy, Phaedra preferred to let them have their moments alone. So she gave Goodweather a final kiss goodbye and left them all to their reunion.

She walked first southward, the way that Bandu had come. There was a passage to the elves' world at the Dragon Knight's Tomb, which she ought to try and close, but that one might be best kept open until she had found a way to clear Mura and his pirates off Tarphae. Until then, the Dragon Knight's Tomb was her best and safest connection back to Psander.

So she made Gateway her destination instead. Her first exposure to the fairies had come by wandering through that passage, and it had been a terrible awakening to the dangers that lay beyond the mesh. It was fitting that she should try to close that gate first.

Phaedra had always been a social person. She made friends easily, had loved the dances and parties of pre-curse Tarphae, and would never embrace solitude as Psander had. But to her surprise, she found that she liked traveling alone. It was good to walk at her own pace, with no need to be self-conscious about her limp or her need to stop now and then to rest her legs, hips, and back. Perhaps she would learn one day how to fix that ankle of hers properly, and then she would walk and run and dance however she pleased. But until then, she still had magic. She still had learning. She still had power.

So she walked southward at her own pace, and when night came, she set a ward to protect herself from the rain and lay down on the ground to sleep. It was not such a bad life for her, the life of a wandering academic wizard.

It wasn't the life her parents had meant for her, of course. How they would have thrilled to hear that Hunter wanted to marry her! What would they have said, had they learned that she had turned him down? What would her friends on Tarphae have said? They would have thought her insane.

But marriage carried too great a risk of children, and she did not want children. If she hadn't been convinced of that already, Goodweather had confirmed it. The girl was delightful, but caring for her was incredibly taxing. Even without a pair of worlds to save, Phaedra doubted she would ever want such a responsibility for herself.

And she did have a pair of worlds to save. Gods help them all.

54

VELLA

Bandu was back, that was all that mattered. Yes, Vella wanted to pick at these wounds – she hated the sacrifice Bandu had made for Criton to live. The sacrifice they had both made, in a way. For peace, for safety, they had traded away years that might otherwise have been spent together. But there was no sense in bringing it up over and over, much though she kept wanting to. There was certainly no sense in bringing it up now.

Anyway, what was there to complain about when Bandu was back? Bandu was back! They would live together in peace and happiness for however many years they had left, and that was more than enough. It was more than Vella had any right to hope for.

So short a time ago, Vella had thought that she would never be happy. Now her heart was filled to overflowing. She had Bandu, and surely her people wouldn't dare to give them trouble when it was Bandu who had saved their nation. What more could Vella want?

Besides, it had been for Vella and her people that Bandu had made her sacrifice, and it would have been profoundly ungrateful to complain about it.

If only she could let these things go.

Bandu helped. Her grim mood vanished at their first kiss, and her high spirits seemed immune to thoughts of the future.

"You are so good," she kept saying. "So good all the time. I wish I have you sooner. Criton is never so good for me."

If Bandu could live in the present, by God, so could Vella.

Goodweather delighted at Bandu's presence, and spent the rest of the day squealing and waving her arms in excitement whenever her mother looked at her. It was a joy to behold.

"Now that she's weaned," Vella said, "we can make her a straw mattress on the floor and keep the bed to ourselves. She's sleeping better now."

Bandu nodded happily and said, "Tomorrow. I want everyone with me now."

So they didn't make love that night, but Vella didn't mind. Life was too good for her to mind much of anything. She lay in the bed, smiling to herself even as Goodweather wriggled and kicked in her sleep. What a beautiful world this was. She hoped it would never end.

ACKNOWLEDGMENTS

This was a much more tumultuous experience than the last time around. It was my first time writing a sequel, my first time writing on a deadline, and my first time submitting a draft I wasn't completely satisfied with. It took all manner of support to whip this novel into shape, and I'm profoundly grateful to those who gave me that support.

First and foremost, I need to thank my parents Claudette and Jonathan Beit-Aharon, and my in-laws, Vivian and Ken Dolkart, whose extensive babysitting gave me a lot more time to write without too severely increasing the burden on my wife. We both owe them a debt of gratitude, as does anyone who enjoyed this book. It might not have been written at all without their support, and certainly not on time!

I played my cards closer to the chest with this novel, but I also need to thank my family for their input into the book's contents. So thank you again to my parents and in-laws, to my sister Miriam and my brother Nathan and sister-in-law Becca, who were always willing to read multiple drafts, brainstorm improvements, and tell me honestly when they found a development disappointing. I can't stress enough how valuable it was to have readers like them in my corner.

I'd like to thank Paul Simpson for stepping into the role of my editor while Phil Jourdan was on sabbatical. His notes were detailed and excellent, and helped this book become what it is.

Lastly and most importantly, I want to thank my wife, Becky Jill Dolkart Beit-Aharon, whose support has been constant. She was the only person who read my first draft as I was writing it, gave me advice and encouragement every step of the way, and who would prompt me to talk my way through whatever problems I was having. When the deadlines grew short and the work stretched itself out before me, she gave me love and patience and even the occasional evening off from parenting. To say that I couldn't have done this without her feels like a ridiculous understatement – I couldn't have written the *first* book without her, let alone this one. And, true to form, she's reading this acknowledgments page as I write it, encouraging me to finish it with a perfect flourish and send it in already. So I will.

ABOUT THE AUTHOR

NS Dolkart is a graduate of Hampshire College in Amherst, MA. By day, he leads activities in a nonprofit nursing home; in the evenings he cooks with his wife and plays with their two children, and only late at night does he write his tales of magic and Godhood. He doesn't sleep much. *Among the Fallen* is Noah's second novel, the sequel to 2016's *Silent Hall*.

nsdolkart.com • twitter.com/n_s_dolkart

On the Edge of Darkness

A historian by training, Barbara Erskine is the author
of ten bestselling novels that demonstrate her interest
in both history and the supernatural, plus three collec-
tions of short stories. *Lady of Hay* was her first novel
and has now sold over two million copies worldwide.
She lives with her family in an ancient manor house
near Colchester, and a cottage near Hay-on-Wye.

For more information about Barbara Erskine, visit her
website, www.Barbara-Erskine.com.

BARBARA ERSKINE

On the Edge
of Darkness

HARPER

Harper
An imprint of HarperCollins*Publishers*
77–85 Fulham Palace Road,
Hammersmith, London W6 8JB

www.harpercollins.co.uk

This paperback edition 2009
1

First published in Great Britain by
HarperCollins*Publishers* 1998

A catalogue record for this book is
available from the British Library

ISBN: 978 0 00 728865 6

Set in Meridien and Photina by
Rowland Phototypesetting Ltd, Bury St Edmunds, Suffolk

Printed and bound in Great Britain by Clays Ltd, St Ives plc

Mixed Sources
Product group from well-managed
forests and other controlled sources
www.fsc.org Cert no. SW-COC-1806
© 1996 Forest Stewardship Council

FSC

FSC is a non-profit international organisation established
to promote the responsible management of the world's forests.
Products carrying the FSC label are independently certified
to assure consumers that they come from forests that are managed
to meet the social, economic and ecological needs
of present and future generations.

Find out more about HarperCollins and the environment at
www.harpercollins.co.uk/green

In a symbol lies concealment or revelation.

THOMAS CARLYLE

Glendower: I can call spirits from the vasty deep.
Hotspur: Why, so can I, or so can any man;
But will they come when you do call for them?

WILLIAM SHAKESPEARE, *Henry IV Part I*

Prologue

Time, the boy noticed idly, whirled in gigantic lazy spirals like a great vortex in the sky. Lying on his back on the short sweet Welsh grass he stared upwards into the intense blue, his eyes half closed, and let the song of the skylark carry him upwards. Beyond the clouds there was an intensity of experience which drew him on beyond the now, to where past and future were the same.

One day, when he was older, he was going to travel there, beyond time and space, and study the secrets which he knew instinctively in his bones were his hidden inheritance. Then he would fight evil with good and bring light into the dark.

'Meryn!'

His mother's voice, calling from the cottage down in the sheltered valley beyond the mountain where he lay, brought him to his feet. He smiled to himself. Later, after he had had his supper, when the long summer dark was descending over the hill, and the only sound was the occasional companionable bleat of a sheep in the distance or the quavering hoot of an owl drifting down the valley on silent wings, he would slip out of the cottage and run up here again to dream his dreams and prepare for the great battle which one day he knew he would fight out there, alone, on the edge of darkness . . .

PART ONE

Adam
1935–1944

1

'Why don't you take a knife and kill me, Thomas? It would be quicker and more honest!'

Susan Craig was shouting now, her voice harsh with despair. 'Dear God, you drive me to do this! You and your sanctimonious cruelty.' She was standing near the window, tears pouring down her face.

Adam, thin, skinny, and tall for his age, which was fourteen, was standing outside his father's study window, his arms wrapped tightly around his body, his mouth working with misery as he tried to stop himself shouting out loud in his mother's defence. The quarrel, growing steadily louder and louder, had been going on for what seemed like hours, and for what seemed like hours he had been standing there, listening. What had she done – what *could* she have done? – to make his father so angry? He didn't understand.

'Now you take the name of the Lord in vain as well! Is there no end to your wickedness, you stupid, senseless woman?' Thomas's voice too was almost incoherent.

'I'm not wicked, Thomas. I'm human! Is that so evil? Why can't you listen to me? You don't care! You never have, damn you!' His mother's voice was shrill, out of control, his father's a deep rumbling torrent of words designed to override and to annihilate.

The boy's eyes were blind with tears as he put his hands over his ears, trying to block out the sounds, but it was no use; they filled the echoing rooms of the huge old stone-built manse and spilled out of the windows and doors until they seemed to fill the garden and the surrounding village of Pittenross, the woods and even the sky.

Suddenly he couldn't bear it any more. Stumbling in his haste, unable to see where he was going for his tears, he turned and ran for the gate.

The manse stood at the end of a quiet village street, hidden behind the high wall which all but encompassed house and garden, save where, at the far end of the vegetable patch, the broad sweep of the River Tay rattled over shingle and rock. To the left of the house stood the old kirk amongst its attendant trees, its lawns and gravel paths deserted behind high ornate railings and an imposing gate. To the right the street, lined by grey stone-built houses, was silent and at this hour empty of people.

Adam ran along the street, cutting down through Fishers' Wynd, a small alley between high, blank walls, skirted some rough ground, half-heartedly gardened by the wife of one of his father's elders, hopped across the river by way of shining black rocks and stones and, climbing a wire fence, began to run up through the thick woods which clung to the lower slopes of the hill. He ran until he could run no longer, sure that if he stopped he would still be able to hear the sounds of his parents quarrelling.

The quarrels had been growing worse over the past few weeks. He had no brothers or sisters to share his burden, no other family in whom he could confide, no one in the village he felt he could talk to. His loyalty to his parents was absolute and somehow he knew that this was private, not something that anyone else should know about, ever. But he didn't know what to do, and he could not cope with what was happening. His beautiful, young happy mother, happy at least when he and she were alone together, whom he adored, had changed into a pale, short-tempered shadow of herself, whilst his father, always a large man, burly and of florid complexion, had grown larger and more florid. Sometimes Adam looked at his father's hands; huge, powerful hands, the hands of a labourer rather than the hands of a man of God, and he shuddered. He knew how hard they could wield the strap. His father believed in beating his son for the good of his soul at the slightest trans-gression. Adam did not mind so much for himself, he was used to it. Almost. But he was terrified, blindly, completely and over-whelmingly terrified that his father might beat his mother.

He never knew why they quarrelled. Sometimes at night, lying in his dark bedroom, he could hear the occasional word through the wall, but they made no sense. His mother adored the mountains and the river and the village and the life of a minister's wife, and she had dozens – hundreds, or so it seemed to her son – of friends, so why should she cry out that she was lonely? Why should she say that she was so unhappy?

Without thinking about where he was going, he had taken a

favourite path up through the trees, following a tumbling, rocky burn up the hillside, seeing flashes of white foaming water from rock pools and waterfalls as he climbed on between birch and rowan and holly, through larch and spruce, to where the woods thinned and the mountainside took over.

His pace had slowed now and he was badly out of breath, but still he ploughed on, following a sheep's track through the grass and prickly heather, skirting the rocky outcrops flung up millennia ago by volcanic and glacial fury. He was heading for the carved stone cross-slab, erected, so tradition had it, by the Picts, the people who had inhabited these hills even before the Scots came, to stand sentinel on the hill far above the village and the river. He always went there when he was miserable. It stood near a small wood of old Scots pine, part of the ancient Caledonian Forest which had girdled the mountains centuries before, and it was his own very special, private, place.

It had stood there on the flat top of the ridge, half circled by the old trees, for more than fourteen hundred years, rearing, at a slight angle to the vertical, over a view which on a clear day extended perhaps thirty miles to the south, to the north only two or three before the high mountains blocked the sky. On the face which turned towards the sun there was a huge cross, set within a wheel in the manner of the Celts, carved with intricate lacy patterns, the everlasting design which represented eternal life. On the back were stranger, heathenish carvings – a snake, a jagged broken stave, a mirror and a crescent moon – and of these symbols the village as a whole and his father in particular disapproved violently. Thomas Craig had told Adam that the symbol stones had been carved by worshippers of the devil, who had left them there on the high lonely hillside with their hidden message to all who came after them. Sometimes Adam used to think it was a miracle that the stone had not been torn down and broken and utterly destroyed – perhaps it was because it was too far from the village, too much effort to do it, or perhaps it was because secretly the people were afraid to touch it. He wasn't afraid. But he could sense its power – its special, wild magic.

Reaching the stone he flung himself down at its foot and, sure that no one could see him save the distant circling buzzard, he abandoned himself at last to his tears.

The girl had seen him coming, though. Often, before, she had noticed him, a boy about her own age, winding his way up through the heather and she had hidden, either behind the stone or amongst

5

the trees, or in the soft, drifting mists which so often descended on this place.

Three times lately she had heard him cry. It made her uncomfortable. She wanted to find out why he was so unhappy, to see him laugh and jump about as he had when he had brought the brown-and-white sheltie puppy with him. She had never approached him. She was not supposed to be here. Her brother would be furious if he knew she had strayed from his side, but she had grown bored with watching him carve the stone. The chisels, the small hammer, the punches, the tools of his trade laid out neatly on the heather with the rolled vellum template which he fastened to the stone to punch out the designs.

The dog had seen her and barked, its hackles raised along its back. She was puzzled by that. Dogs usually liked her. But she kept her distance. She didn't want the boy to see her.

His tears were exhausted at last. Sitting up he sniffed and, rubbing his face with the sleeve of his sweater, he began to look round. Far above him he could hear the lonely yelp of an eagle. He squinted up into the blue but the glare behind the clouds was too bright and he shook his head and closed his eyes. When he opened them he saw the girl for a fraction of a second, peering at him from the trees. Startled, he jumped to his feet.

'Hey! Hello?' His call was carried away on the wind. 'Where are you?'

There was no sign of her. He ran a few steps towards the trees. 'Come on. I've seen you! Show yourself!' He hoped she hadn't seen him crying. Blushing at the thought he peered amongst the soft, red, peeling trunks of the trees. But she had gone.

It was twilight when he retraced his steps reluctantly towards the manse. From the path amongst the thickly growing trees on the steep bank of the burn as it tumbled towards the river he could see in the distance the lamp already lit in his father's study window. Usually by now there would be a curl of blue smoke from the kitchen chimney but he couldn't see it yet against the darkening sky. Nervously he wondered if Mrs Barron had stayed on to cook supper as she often did, or was his mother, an apron tied over her dress, standing in the kitchen wielding the huge iron pans?

It was the back door he approached on tiptoe from the yard at the side of the manse. There was no one in the kitchen at all and no pans on the range. In fact the range was cold. With a sinking

6

heart he crept out into the back hall and listened, half afraid that the quarrel would still be in progress, but the house was silent now. Breathing a quick sigh of relief, he tiptoed through to the front and stood for one long, daring moment outside his father's study, then he turned and fled upstairs.

His parents' bedroom looked out over the wall towards the kirk. It was an austere room, the iron bed covered by a pale fawn counterpane, the heavy wooden furniture unrelieved by pictures or flowers. On his mother's dressing table, uncluttered by make-up or scent or powder sat, side by side, neatly aligned, a matching ivory-backed hair brush, a clothes brush and a comb. Nothing else. Thomas Craig would not permit his wife to paint her face.

Nervously Adam peered into the room, though he could sense already that it was empty. It was cold and north-facing, the room where he had been born. He hated it.

Normally he liked the kitchen best. With the warmth from the range and the smells of cooking and the cheerful light-hearted banter between his mother and Jeannie Barron it was the nicest and most cheerful place to be. When his father was out. When his father was at home his dour, disapproving presence filled the house, Adam's mother fell silent and even the birds in the garden seemed, to the boy, afraid to sing.

Standing in the doorway, he was about to turn away when he paused, frowning. Like a small animal, alert, suspicious, he sensed that something was wrong. He looked round the room more carefully this time, but in its bleak tidiness it gave no clue as to what might be amiss.

He had two bedrooms to himself. One, as sober and tidy as his parents', his official bedroom, was next to theirs on the landing. But he had another room, up in the attic, known to his mother and Mrs Barron, but not, he was almost sure, to his father, who never climbed up there. In it he had a bright rag rug, and several old chests for the treasures and specimens which formed his museum, his books and his maps. It was up here, alone, when he was supposed to be doing his school work in his official bedroom, that he led his intensely private life; it was here that he wrote up his notes and copied diagrams and studied musty textbooks which he had picked up in second-hand bookshops in Perth, all designed to lead towards his ambition to be a doctor, and it was here that he sketched the birds he watched out on the hills and here he had once tried to dissect, then to dry and stuff the dead body of a fox he had found in a snare. Jeannie Barron had soon put paid to that enterprise, but otherwise the two women had left him more or less to his own devices up there. Today however it did not provide the sanctuary he had come to expect. He felt restless and unhappy. Something was very wrong.

After only a few minutes' leafing half-heartedly through a book on spiders he threw it down on the table and went out onto the landing. He listened for a moment, then he ran down the narrow upper flight of stairs, then the broader flight below and went to peer once more into the kitchen. It was as cheerless and empty as before.

It was a long time before he plucked up enough courage to knock on the door of his father's study.

Thomas Craig was sitting at his desk, his hands folded before him on the blotter. He was a tall, rangy man, with a shock of dark hair threaded with silver, large, staring pale blue eyes and his skin, normally high-coloured, was today unusually pale.

'Father?' Adam's voice was timid.

There was no response.

'Father, where is Mother?'

His father looked up at last. There was a strange triangle of livid skin beneath each high cheekbone where his face had rested on the interlinked fingers of his hands. He propped himself wearily on his elbows on the desk, then cleared his throat as though for a moment he found it hard to speak. 'She's gone,' he said at last, his voice lifeless.

'Gone?' Adam repeated the word uncomprehendingly.

'Gone.' Thomas lowered his face back into his hands.

His son shifted uncomfortably from one foot to the other. An inexplicable pain had settled in the pit of his stomach. He didn't dare look at his father's face again, fixing his eyes instead on his own ragged plimsolls.

Thomas sighed heavily. He looked up again. 'Mrs Barron has seen fit to hand in her notice,' he said at last, 'so it would seem we are alone.'

Adam swallowed. His voice when he spoke was very small. 'Where has Mother gone?'

'I don't know. And I don't wish to.' Abruptly Thomas stood up. Pushing back his chair he walked over to the window and stood looking out into the garden. 'Your mother, Adam, has committed a grievous sin. In the eyes of God, and in my eyes, she is no longer part of this family. I do not wish her name to be mentioned in this house again. Go to your room and pray that her evil ways have not corrupted you. A night without supper will do you no harm at all.' He did not turn round.

Adam stared at him, barely taking in what he had said. 'But, Father, where has she gone?' Little panicky waves of anguish were beginning to flutter in his chest. He wanted his mother very badly indeed.

'Go to your room!' Thomas's voice, heavy with his own grief and anger and incomprehension, betrayed the depth of his emotion for only a moment.

Adam did not try to question him again. Turning, he ran into the hall, out through the kitchen and on into the garden. It was growing dark, but he did not hesitate. Loping round the side of the house he headed down the silent street towards the river once more. Slipping on the rocks in the dark he felt his feet sliding into the icy water but he did not hesitate, plunging into the woods and climbing as fast as he could up the hillside.

Once he stopped and turned. The manse was in darkness save for the single point of light, the lamp in his father's study. From where he stood he could see the kirk and the dark trees round it, and the whole village, where one by one the lights were coming on, the evening air hazed with the fragrant blue smoke from the chimneys. The village was friendly, busy, warm. He knew every single person who lived in those houses. He was at school with children from many of them, in the same class as five other boys all of whom he had grown up with.

He stood looking down for a few minutes, feeling the wind, cold now, on the back of his neck, and he shivered. There were goosepimples on his thin arms beneath his sweater. He felt sick. Where had his mother gone? What had happened to her? Why hadn't she told him where she was going? Why hadn't she taken him with her? Why hadn't she at least left him a note?

It was better to keep moving. Walking in the almost-darkness amongst the trees with the flash of white water on his right needed all his concentration. If he walked he couldn't think. He didn't want to think.

Turning, he scrambled on, feeling his wet plimsolls slide on the track, and he grabbed at the wiry branches of the larch which hung over him to stop himself falling as he headed for the stone.

It was completely dark when he reached the cross-slab at last. He doubled over, panting, aware that the moment he stopped moving the icy wind would strip away his bodyheat within seconds. He didn't care. The moment he stopped moving he could no longer fend off the misery which was flooding through him. His mother. His adored, lovely, bright, pretty mother was gone and, he shuddered at the memory of his father's words. What had she done? What could she have done? He wrapped his arms around himself, hunching his shoulders. He had never felt so alone, or so afraid.

She had never seen the boy come up here in the dark before. Behind the hills in the east a silver glow showed where soon the half moon would rise above the black rocks and flood the countryside with light. Then she would be able to see him more clearly. Quietly she waited.

Behind her, her brother Gartnait, five years her senior, was packing up his tools and stretching his arms above his head until his joints cracked. Between one moment and the next a black silhouetted moon-shadow ran across the ground at his feet. The light caught the gleam of an iron chisel and he stooped to pick it up.

Brid crept forward a little. The boy had a thin, attractive face with a child's nose still, but his shoulders and knees were beginning already to show the coltishness which would come before he developed the stature of a man. She stared at his clothes, colourless in the pale light, and she crept nearer. He never seemed to do much when he came up to the hill. Sometimes he sat for hours, his arms wrapped around his legs, his chin on his knees, just staring into space. A few times he had come up to Gartnait's stone and touched the carving with his finger, tracing the lines. Twice, in the hot months, he had stretched out on the hot ground and slept. On one of those occasions she had drawn closer, until she was standing over him and her slim shadow had touched his face. He had frowned and screwed up his nose and put his hand to his forehead, but he hadn't opened his eyes.

She could feel his misery. It was sucking at her energy, swirling round him in a cloak of black waves which lapped out into the darkness and touched her with its cold.

Perhaps her sympathy was so great it had become tangible; whatever the reason, he looked up suddenly, startled as though he had heard something, and he looked straight at her. She saw his eyes widen. Instinctively his hand brushed his cheek and he straightened his shoulders to hide his misery. His momentary fear at seeing a figure in the shadows gave way to relief when he realised it was the girl he had seen earlier and he made a brave attempt at a smile. 'Hello.'

She frowned. She did not recognise the word, though the smile was friendly. She stepped forward.

10

When she spoke to him it was in the language of her birth, the language of the ancient Picts.

His heartbeat had steadied a little. The exhaustion of the steep climb, for the second time that day, and then the girl appearing out of the darkness of the trees had made him gasp for breath. He stared at her, more puzzled than startled now. She had said something to him in words he didn't understand. Gaelic, he supposed, a language his father considered to be barbaric. He shrugged at her. 'I don't understand.'

Even in that dim light he could see the brightness of her eyes, the pert tilt of her nose and chin. She was wearing a rough dress which looked as though it were made of some sort of leather.

She shrugged back, mimicking him, and then she giggled.

He found himself laughing too and suddenly daring she moved closer and touched her finger to his cheek, removing imaginary tears. Her mime was clear. Why are you sad? Cheer up. Then her hands dropped to his and she gave a theatrical shiver. She was right. He was very cold.

He wasn't quite sure how he came to follow her. His misery, his cold, his hunger, all were persuasive. When she caught his hand and tugged at it, miming food in her mouth, he nodded eagerly and went with her.

He followed her towards the stone, his fingers brushing across the well-known shapes as he walked past it. There was a drift of mist across the path and he hesitated, but when she tugged again at his hand he went on, stopping only when he saw her brother. The tall young man, his tools now stowed in a leather bag slung over his shoulder, looked as startled as he was himself. He spoke quietly and urgently to the girl and she retorted with words quite obviously cheeky. It was then she introduced herself. She pointed to her chest. 'Brid,' she said firmly. She pronounced it Breed. 'Gartnait.' This was said thumping the young man's shoulder.

Adam grinned. He pointed to his own stomach. 'Adam,' he said. 'A-dam.' She repeated the word softly. Then she laughed again.

They walked for about twenty minutes around the shoulder of the ridge, following a faint deer track through the heather before Adam saw in the distance below them the flickering light of a fire. As they scrambled down towards it he smelled meat cooking. Venison, he reckoned, and the juices in his mouth ran. He hadn't eaten since lunchtime. He refused to think about the empty cold kitchen at home, concentrating instead on his new friends.

At the sight of their destination he frowned slightly. It was no more than a round ramshackle bothy, thatched with rushes, hidden in a fold of the hill beside a tumbling burn. The fire, he saw as they drew closer, was being tended by a woman, from her looks the mother of Brid and Gartnait, who, he had already guessed, were brother and sister. The woman, tall and slim, very erect when she straightened from poking the logs beneath her cooking pot, had hair as dark as her daughter's, and the same clear grey eyes. Throwing down her makeshift poker she made him welcome, a little shyly, and pointing to a fur rug spread on the ground near the fire indicated that he sit down. Her name, Brid told him, was Gemma. Gartnait, he saw, had gone to wash the stonedust from his hands in the stream. Brid too had disappeared inside the bothy. She returned seconds later with four plates and a loaf of bread which she broke into four pieces and laid on the plates near the fire.

The meal he was given was, he thought, the best he had eaten in his whole life. The bread was rough and full of flavour, spread with thick creamy butter. With it they ate – with their fingers – venison cut into wafer-thin portions by Gartnait's razor-sharp knife, mountain trout, cooked on slender twigs above the fire, and wedges of crumbling white cheese. Then there was more bread to mop up the rich gravy. To drink they had something which Adam, who had never touched alcohol in his life, suspected was some kind of heather ale. Mesmerised by the fire and the food and by his smiling though silent companions he drank heavily and within minutes, leaning back against a log, he was fast asleep.

He was awakened by Brid's hand on his knee. For a moment he couldn't think where he was, then he realised he was still outside. To his surprise he found he was lying warmly wrapped in a heavy woollen blanket. The fuzz of the wool was soaked with dew as he sat up and began to unwrap himself, but inside he was warm and dry.

'A-dam.' He loved the way she pronounced his name, carefully, liltingly, a little as though it were a French word. She pointed up at the sky. To his horror he could see the streaks of dawn above the hill. He had been out all night. His father would kill him if he found out. Frightened, he began to scramble to his feet.

Behind Brid her mother was bending over a brightly burning fire. Something was simmering in the pot suspended above it. He sniffed and Brid clapped her hands. She nodded and, taking a pottery bowl from her mother, spooned some sort of thin porridge into it. Taking it from her he sniffed, tasted, and burned his tongue.

As breakfasts went it was pretty tasteless, not nearly as nice as the meal the night before, but it filled his stomach and when at last Brid led him back the way they had come he was feeling comparatively cheerful.

The cross-slab was wrapped once more in mist as they passed close beside it and he walked onto the hillside and stood looking down at his own valley, still wrapped in darkness. Brid pointed, with a little smile, and Adam stepped away from her. 'Goodbye,' he said. 'And thanks.'

'Goodbye and thanks.' The girl repeated the words softly. With a wave she turned and vanished into the mist.

The manse looked bleak in the cold dawn light. There was still no smoke coming from the chimneys and the front door was locked. Biting his lip nervously Adam ran soundlessly round the side, praying under his breath that the kitchen door would be open. It wasn't. He stood there for a moment undecided, looking up at the blank windows at the back of the house. The awful misery was returning. Swallowing it down he turned and headed back into the street.

The manse might still be asleep but the village was stirring. The sweet smell of woodsmoke filled the air as he turned up Bridge Street and into Jeannie Barron's gate and knocked tentatively at the door. The sound was greeted by a frenzy of wild barking.

The door was opened seconds later by Jeannie's burly husband, Ken. A pretty sheltie was leaping round his heels, plainly delighted to see Adam, who stooped to give her a hug. The dog had been his once. But for some reason Adam had never understood his father had disapproved of his son having a pet and the puppy had been given to Jeannie. Ken stared down at Adam with a surprised frown and then turned and called over his shoulder, 'Jeannie, it's the minister's lad.'

Jeannie's kindly pink-cheeked face appeared behind him. She was wearing her overall just as she always did at the manse.

'Hello, Mrs Barron.' Adam looked at her and to his intense embarrassment his eyes flooded with tears.

'Adam.' She pushed past her husband and enveloped the boy in a huge plump hug. 'Oh, my poor wee boy.' He was almost as tall as she was but for the moment he was a small child again, seeking comfort and warmth and affection in her arms.

She ushered him into her kitchen, pushed her husband outside and sat Adam down at her table. A mug of milky tea and a thick wedge of bread and jam later she stood looking down at him. His pale face had regained its colour and the tears had dried but there was no disguising the misery in the boy's face. The dog was sitting pressed against his legs.

'Now, do you understand what's happened?' She sat down opposite him and reached for the large brown teapot.

He shrugged. 'Father said Mother has gone.' The tears were very near. 'He said she had sinned.'

'She's not sinned!' The strength of her voice helped him control the sob which was lurking in his throat. 'Your mother is a decent, beautiful, good woman. But she's been driven to the end of the road by that man.'

Adam frowned. Not recognising her metaphor he pictured a car, driven by a stranger.

Jeannie Barron scowled. Her fair hair leaped round her head in coiled springs as she wielded her pot and filled both their mugs again. 'How she put up with him so long, I'll never know. I only hope she'll find happiness where she's gone.'

'Where has she gone?' He looked at her desperately.

She shook her head. 'I don't know, Adam, and that's the truth.'

'But she'd tell you?' Adam was biting his lip.

She shook her head again. 'She told no one that I know.'

'But why did she leave me behind?' It was the bewildered cry of a small child. 'Why didn't she take me with her?'

Jeannie pursed her lips. 'I don't know.' She sighed unhappily. 'It's not because she doesn't love you. You must believe that. Perhaps she didn't know herself where she was going. Perhaps she'll send for you a wee bit later.'

'Do you think so?' His huge brown eyes were pleading.

Meeting them she couldn't lie to him and give him the reassurance he wanted. All she could say was, 'I hope so, Adam, I do hope so.' Susan Craig had been her friend but not her confidante. To confide too much in another was not in her nature. It was enough that she knew that Jeannie would be there for Adam.

It was as he was standing up to leave he remembered why they were here in her kitchen and not in the manse. 'Do you really not work for us any more?'

She shook her head. 'I'm sorry, Adam. Your father doesn't want me there.'

She would never tell anyone, never mind the boy, the vile, furious words the distraught man had flung at her when she had tried to defend and then excuse his wife's decision to leave. She put her hands on Adam's shoulders, her heart aching for the boy. With her

14

own family long gone and scattered round Scotland and one of them in Canada she had always thought of Adam privately as the child of her middle years. 'Listen, Adam. I want you to remember I'm here if you need me. You can come to me any time.' She held his gaze firmly. 'Any time, Adam.'

She had a shrewd idea what the boy was going back to and she didn't envy him. But he had courage, she had always admired him for that.

When he turned into the gate and approached the house this time the front door was open. He hesitated in the hall. The door to his father's study was shut and he glanced at the stairs, wondering if he could reach them in time on his silent rubber soles. He was almost there when he heard the door behind him open. Panic flooded into his throat. For a moment he thought, as he turned to face his father, that he was going to be sick.

Thomas Craig stood back, gesturing the boy into his study with a sharp jerk of his head. The man's face was grey and he was unshaven. As he closed the door behind his son, he reached up to the hook on the back of it and brought down the broad leather belt which hung there.

Adam whimpered, the ice of fear pouring over his shoulders and down his back, his skin already taut with terror at the beating that was coming. 'Father –'

'Where were you last night?'

'On the hill, Father. I'm sorry. I got lost in the mist.'

'You disobeyed me. I told you to go to your room. I had to look for you. I searched the village. And the riverbank, I didn't know what had happened to you!'

'I'm sorry, Father.' He was ashamed of himself for being so afraid but he couldn't help it. 'I was upset.' His words were very quiet.

'Upset?' His father echoed them. He pulled the leather strap through his hand and doubled it into his fist. 'You think that excuses disobedience?'

'No, Father.' Adam clutched his hands together to stop them shaking.

'And you accept that God would want you punished?'

No, he was screaming inside himself. *No. Mummy says God is the God of love. He forgives. He wouldn't want me beaten.*

'Well?' Thomas's voice came out as a hiss.

'Yes, Father,' Adam whispered.

His father stood for a moment in silence, looking at him, then he pulled an upright wooden chair out from the wall and placing it in front of his desk he pointed at it.

Adam was trembling. 'Please, Father –'

'Not another word.'

'Father –'

'God is waiting, Adam!' The minister's voice roared suddenly above his son's whispered plea.

Adam gave up. His legs shaking so much he could hardly move he went to the chair and bent over it, stuffing one fist miserably into his mouth.

Thomas Craig was a just man in his way, sincere in the austere, hard religion which he preached. He knew in some part of himself that the boy's misery at losing his mother must be as great, perhaps greater, than his own at losing his wife, but as he started to swing the leather strap down onto the child's defenceless back something inside him snapped. Again and again he swung the belt, seeing, not the narrow hips and scruffy shirt and shorts of a fourteen-year-old boy, but the figure of his beautiful, provocative, unruly wife. It was not until the boy slid into an ungainly heap at his feet that he stopped, appalled, staring down in disbelief.

'Adam?' He dropped the belt. He knelt beside the boy and stared in horror at the oozing welts which were appearing on the back of the boy's thighs, the long bloody stains soaking through his shorts.

'Adam?' He reached out his hand to his son's awkwardly angled head and drew back, afraid suddenly to touch him. 'What have I done?'

Swallowing hard, he backed away and moving blindly to his desk he sat down at it and picked up his Bible. Clutching it to his chest he sat without moving for a long time. On the blotter before him, torn into small pieces, lay the note Susan Craig had left for her son, a note Adam would never see.

In the hall outside, the long case clock ticked slowly on. It struck the half hour and then the hour and as the long sonorous notes echoed into silence Thomas stirred at last.

Lifting the unconscious boy he carried him upstairs and laid him tenderly on the bed and only then did he find the strength to walk into his own bedroom for the first time since Susan had left him. He stood looking round. Her brushes and comb lay on the table in the window. Otherwise there was no sign of her in the room. But there never had been. He had always discouraged ornaments and fripperies. He did not permit flowers in the house.

He hesitated for a moment then he walked over to the huge old

16

mahogany wardrobe. The righthand door concealed his own meagre selection of black suits; the lefthand door her clothes. More than his, but not many more: the two suits, one navy and one black, the two black hats which sat on the shelf above them and the three cotton dresses, washed and ironed again and again, with the high necks and the long sleeves and sober autumnal colours which he considered suitable for her summer wear. She had two pairs of black lace-up shoes. He pulled open the door, steeling himself to find the clothes gone, but they were there. All of them. He was not prepared to see them, not prepared for his own reaction. The wave of grief and love and loss which swept over him shook him to the core. Unable to stop himself he pulled one of the dresses from its wooden hanger and, hugging it in his arms, he buried his face in it and wept.

It was a long time before he stopped crying.

He looked down at the dress in his arms in disgust. It smelled of her. It smelled of woman, of sweat, of lust. He did not immediately recognise the lust as his own. Throwing the dress on the floor he pulled the rest of the clothes out of the cupboard into a heap, then he descended on the bed. He tore off one of the heavy linen sheets and bundled it around her clothes and shoes and even the two hats. He pulled open the drawers which contained her meagre collection of much-darned underwear and threw them in the pile, then he carried it all out of the room. The tangle of rusty wires and the iron frame which was all that was left of Susan Craig's beloved piano was still there in the garden behind the neat lines of vege-tables. Her clothes were thrown down there and Thomas poured paraffin all over them before setting them alight. He waited until the last thick lisle stocking had turned to ash, then he walked back into the house.

He did not climb the stairs to see how Adam was. Instead he walked into his study and stood looking down at the chair over which the boy had bent. He was full of self-loathing. The anger, the misery, the love which he mistook for lust which he had felt for his wife, were evil. They were sins. The most terrible sins. How could he tend his flock and rebuke them for their backsliding when he could not control his own? Walking blindly to the desk he picked up the strap which he had dropped there after he had given the boy the thrashing and he stood looking down at it as it lay across his hand. He knew what he must do.

He locked the door of the old kirk behind him and stepped down into the shadowy nave, looking round the grey stone building with

17

its neat lines of chairs and the bare table at the east end. A church had stood on this site for over a thousand years, or so it was believed, and sometimes in spite of himself, when he was alone in the building, as now, he could feel the special sacredness of the place. He was shocked to find this superstition in himself but could do nothing to rid himself of it. Enough light filtered in through the windows for him to see clearly as he walked halfway along the aisle and sat slowly down. In his right hand he carried the strap with which he had beaten his son.

He sat for a long time upright, rigid, his hands clenched, his eyes shut in prayer to the Lord. But he knew the Lord wanted more than this. He wanted punishment for Thomas's weakness. As the last rays of light died in the sky outside, throwing pale streaks through the windows onto the ancient stone of the walls and floor, he stood up. He walked to the front of the lines of chairs and slowly he began to remove his jacket and then his tie and his shirt. He folded them neatly, shivering as the cold air played over his pale shoulders. He hesitated for a minute, then he went on: shoes, socks, trousers, all meticulously stowed on the pile. He wondered for a minute if he should remove his long woollen underpants but the male body naked, like the female, was an abomination before the Lord.

Then he picked up the leather belt.

The pain of the first self-inflicted welt took his breath away. He hesitated, but only for a second. Again and again he raised his arm and felt the merciless strap curling round his ribs. He lost count after a while, glorying in the pain, feeling it cleansing him, feeling it wipe out all trace of his own vile sin.

Slowly the strokes grew weaker. He collapsed to his knees on the stone floor and the strap fell out of his hand. He heard the sound of a sob and realised it had come from his own throat. In despair he slid down until he was lying full length on the floor, his head buried in his arms.

When Adam woke he was curled face down on his own bed. He tried to move and cried out with pain, clutching at the sheet beneath his face.

'Mummy!'

He had forgotten. In the past when his father had beaten him she had crept upstairs later, secretly, and put iodine on his cuts and given him a sweetie to comfort him. But she wasn't here, and this time the pain was worse than it had ever been before. He tried to move and stopped, sobbing silently into the pillow.

The house was very quiet. He lay still for a long time as the blood congealed and dried and his clothes stuck to his back. After a while he dozed. Once he awoke with a start when a door banged somewhere downstairs. He held his breath, frightened his father would appear, then when he didn't he slowly relaxed again and once more sleep numbed his pain.

The need to urinate drove him at last from his bed. Moving stiffly, biting his lip to stop himself from crying out loud he made his way to the lavatory and, locking himself in, he unbuttoned his shorts. He was too stiff to twist round to look at his buttocks, but he could see the bruises on his legs, the blood on the cotton of his clothes. The sight frightened him. He didn't know what to do.

Creeping back into his bedroom he crawled back into the bed. When he woke again it was almost dark. Pulling himself up he crept to the top of the stairs and looked down. No lamps had been lit. Stiffly he tiptoed down. His father's study door was open. There was no one there and he stood for a moment, staring in.

He pulled an old raincoat from the line of hooks in the tiled vestibule and draped it round his shoulders, afraid he might meet someone, afraid that they would see what his father had done to him and afraid they would know that he had been bad.

He almost did not dare knock at Jeannie's door again, but he didn't know what else to do. As he stumbled up her front path his head was spinning. His feet felt as though they belonged to someone else a long way away. He raised his hand to the door knocker and grasped at the air, falling forward so his fingers clawed at the boards.

The dog heard him.

'That man should be locked up!' Ken Barron was pouring water from the pans on the range into the hip bath before the fire. 'He ought to be reported.'

Jeannie shook her head. Her lips were tight. 'No, Ken. Let be. I shall deal with this myself.' She had had to fight back the tears when she saw the state of the boy.

The bath had been the only way. He couldn't sit down in it, but she had him kneel in his clothes whilst she poured jugs of water over the thin shoulders and slowly worked first the shirt and then the shorts free of the dried blood.

When at last the wounds were clean and she had soothed them with Germolene she put one of her husband's clean shirts on the boy, cursing the roughness of the linen as she saw him wince, then she gave him some broth and put him in the press-bed in the corner of the room.

What she had to say to the minister would keep until morning. He was not going to get away with what he had done this time.

'Don't be a fool, Jeannie.' Ken was only half-hearted in his effort to dissuade his wife from visiting the manse the next morning. He had enormous respect for Jeannie's towering rages.

Her blue eyes were blazing. 'Just try and stop me!' Her hands were on her hips as she faced him and he moved back hastily and stood in the doorway, watching as his wife sailed off down the street, clutching Adam's hand.

The front door of the manse was open. She dragged Adam in with her and stood in the hall looking round. She could smell the unhappiness in the house, the lack of fresh air and flowers, and she shivered, thinking of the beautiful young English woman Thomas Craig had somehow won when he was training for the ministry and brought back to this house fifteen years ago. Susan had been full of the love of life, her hair bright, her clothes pretty and the high-ceilinged rooms of the two-hundred-year-old house had resounded for a while to the sound of her singing, to the piano she played so beautifully, to her laughter. But slowly, bit by bit, he had destroyed her. He forbade the singing, frowned at the laughter. One day when she had gone into Perth on the bus he had someone take the piano out into the garden and he had burned it as an abomination in the eyes of God, for was not all music frivolous and shocking if it was not played in the kirk? Susan had cried that evening in the kitchen like a child, and Jeannie, young herself then too, had put her hand on the bright hair, now tied back in a tight styleless bun, and tried in vain to comfort her.

Adam had been born ten months after Thomas Craig brought Susan to the manse. There had been no more children.

Her whole life was bound up with the little boy, but Thomas had views on his son's upbringing too; children should be seen and not heard; spare the rod and spoil the child.

Jeannie sighed. Adam was a bright child. He went to the local school and was now at the Academy in Perth. He made friends easily but, too afraid and ashamed to ask them home, became more and more engrossed in his books and his hobbies alone. The only love and happiness he had experienced in his home life had been sneaked behind the closed door of the kitchen, where his mother and the manse's warm-hearted housekeeper had in a conspiracy of silence tried to make the boy's life happy out of the sight of his father.

20

At the private life of the minister and his wife, Jeannie could only guess. She sniffed as she thought about it. A man who could order the shooting of a dog for covering a bitch in a country lane just because it was outside the kirk on the Sabbath, a man who ordered the village girls to wear their sleeves to their wrists even in the summer, was not a man at ease with sensual needs.

Thomas had seen them walking in through the courtyard from the window in the cold empty dining room. His clothes were immaculate, his shirt white and starched. There was no sign in his face of the pain he was feeling as he appeared in the doorway and confronted them. His eyes went from Jeannie's belligerent, tightly controlled expression to that of his son, white, exhausted and afraid. He did not allow himself to waver.

'Adam, you may go to your room. I wish to talk to Mrs Barron alone.'

He moved stiffly in front of her into his study and turned to face her at once, before she had a chance even to open her mouth. 'I would like you to take your old job back. There has to be someone to look after the boy.'

His words took her breath away. She had been ready for a fight. She clenched her fists. 'I nearly had the doctor to him last night,' she said defiantly.

She saw his jawline tighten, otherwise his face remained impassive. 'It will not happen again, Mrs Barron.'

There was a moment's silence between them, then she lifted her shoulders slightly. 'I see.' There was another pause. 'Is Mrs Craig not coming back, then?'

'No, Mrs Craig is not coming back.' His knuckles went white on the desk as he leaned forward to ease his pain. The scattered pieces of Susan Craig's note had disappeared.

Jeannie nodded in grim acknowledgement. 'Very well then, Minister. I shall resume my position here. For the boy's sake, you understand. But it must not happen again. Ever.'

Their eyes met and he inclined his head. 'Thank you,' he said humbly.

She stared at him in silence for a long moment, then she turned towards the door. 'I'd best go and light the range.'

2

For Adam the days that followed were different. His father spoke to him seldom, and when he did he was distant, as though they were polite strangers. The boy had his breakfast and midday meal in the kitchen with Mrs Barron. Supper was always cold. Sometimes he and his father would sit opposite one another in silence in the dining room; sometimes, when Thomas was out, Adam would put his supper in a bag, stow it in his knapsack and escape onto the hill.

The holidays were drawing to an end. In a few days school would start again. He was glad. Something had happened between him and his friends which he didn't understand. There was a new restraint between them – a slight embarrassment, almost an aloofness. He did not know that the news had sped round the district that Mrs Craig, the minister's wife, had run away to Edinburgh with – the selection was varied – a travelling salesman, a university lecturer (he had been staying at the Bridge Hotel for two weeks over the summer), or the French wine importer who had been visiting the Forest Road Hotel along the river and who had left two days before Mrs Craig had disappeared. Nothing was said, but when he caught sight of Euan and Wee Mikey whispering behind the shop and heard their sniggers, hastily cut off as he approached, he felt himself colour sharply and he turned away. They had betrayed him. His best friend Robbie would have understood, perhaps (Robbie being one of the few friends to whose house he was allowed to go) but Robbie had not been at home all summer and a year ago, after his mother had died, had gone away to boarding school. So, instead of seeing his friends for the last precious days of the holidays, Adam amused himself and concentrated hard on the thought of school.

He had always enjoyed school and he enjoyed his work. He hadn't told his father, yet, of his ambition to be a doctor, although he had no reason to believe the minister would object. In fact he would probably be pleased. Medicine was a respectable profession. Of one thing Adam was absolutely certain. He did not wish to go into the church. He hated the kirk. He hated the Sabbath. He hated the Bible and he hated the terrible guilt he felt about hating them all so much. Only one part of his duties as the minister's child had ever appealed to him and that was visiting the poor and sick of the parish with his mother. It was something she had done extremely well and in spite of her English background they liked her. She did not condescend or patronise. She was cheerful, helpful and not afraid to roll up her sleeves. The people respected her and Adam had swiftly absorbed the fact that half an hour in her company clearly did more for an ailing woman or an injured man than hours of preaching from his father. Sometimes they met Dr Grogan on their rounds and Adam would, when permitted, or simply not noticed in the corner of the room, watch. He had been only ten when his medical ambition first began to take shape.

A week after his world had changed so abruptly Adam, a packed lunch in his bag as well as his supper because Mrs Barron had gone on the bus to Perth to see her sister as she did every week, set off up the hillside towards the carved stone.

He had thought often about Brid and her brother and her mother and their kindness, but he had told no one about them. His natural openness, his enthusiasm, his love of life had all gone. The beating and the loss of his mother had changed him. Jeannie Barron could see it and her heart bled for the boy. She mothered him as much as she could, but he shrank a little from her when she hugged him. He tolerated her affection courteously but no more. It was as though he had closed down some part of himself and surrounded it in a protective shell. And the new Adam was secretive. He could have told his mother about his new friends. Without her there, he would tell no one.

It was a blustery day with an exhilarating autumnal bite in the wind. Besides his food and his field glasses, which were hanging round his neck on a strap, he had his specimen boxes with him – to collect interesting things for his museum – his bird book and a notebook and pencil, and he had stolen four slices of chocolate cake from the pantry. The three extra pieces were for Brid and her family. He knew Mrs Barron would see but he knew she wouldn't tell. His father didn't know the cake was there. Almost certainly he would have disapproved of it.

He reached the stone, panting, and swung his bag off his shoulders. He already had three birds to put in his notebook. Grouse, of course, skylark and siskin. He pulled the battered volume out, his thin brown fingers fumbling with the buckle on the outside pocket of the green canvas knapsack and, sucking the pencil lead for a moment to make it write better, he began to make his notes.

He had planned to eat lunch, to watch birds, and then in the afternoon to make his way down the far side of the hill to Brid's cottage.

The first part of the plan went well. He sat down on a slab of exposed rock, his back to the stone, facing the view down the heather-covered hill. It was growing brown in places now, the vibrant purple of the weeks before fading. He heard the lonely cry of an eagle, and putting down his wedge of pork pie he picked up his field glasses and squinted with them towards the distant cloud-hung peaks of the mountains behind the hill.

It wasn't until he had finished the last of his food, drunk half his ginger beer and folded the remains of the greaseproof paper neatly into his knapsack beside the carefully preserved slices of cake that he stood up and decided to go and look for Brid.

The sun was out now. It blazed down on the heather from a strangely cloudless sky. He sniffed. He had lived in this part of the world all his life and he could read the weather signs clearly. The wind had dropped. He would have an hour, maybe two, then he would see the mist beginning to collect in the folds of the hills and drift over the distant peaks, which would grow hazy and then disappear.

He stood for a moment, staring round, and then he lifted the glasses and began a systematic search beyond the stand of old Scots pine for the track which had led to the burn next to which Brid's cottage stood.

Spotting the track at last he set off, trotting confidently down the north-facing slope of the ridge, leaving the carved cross-slab behind him. He reached the trees and paused. The shadow he had thought was the track was just that, a shadow thrown by a slight change in the contour of the hill. He frowned, wishing he had taken more notice of where he was going when he had followed her before.

'Brid!' He cupped his hands around his mouth and called. The shout sounded almost indecent in the quiet of the afternoon. Somewhere nearby a grouse flew up squawking the traditional warning 'go-back'. He stood still. On the horizon the landmarks were disappearing one by one as the mist closed in.

'Brid!' He tried again, his voice echoing slightly across the valley. Disappointment hovered at the back of his mind. He hadn't realised how much he had been looking forward to seeing her and her brother again.

Pushing through the bracken, he headed away from the Scots pine downhill. The fold in the rock there looked familiar. If he remembered correctly he would find the burn there, running between steep banks. He was wading through the undergrowth now, feeling the tough stems of heather and bracken tearing at his legs, and he was out of breath when at last he burst through it onto the flat outcrop of rocks where, sure enough, the burn hurtled down over a series of steep falls to the pool beneath, the pool where Gartnait had caught the trout. He frowned. It was the right place, he was sure of it, but it couldn't be. There was no sign of the little rough cottage where they lived; where he had spent that fateful night. He scrambled down the slippery rocks: here. He was sure it had been here. He gazed round, confused. The grass was long and lush, watered by the spray from the falls. There was no sign of the fire.

It was obviously the wrong place. If he followed the burn down he would find the right one. He searched until it began to grow dark, becoming more and more annoyed with himself as his systematic crossing and recrossing of the ridge brought him back again to the same spot.

In the end he had to give up. He sat down and ate the pieces of cake himself, then admitting that there was nothing else he could do, he made his way back to the manse, tired and disappointed and depressed.

In the garden he hesitated. His father's study was lit; the shutters were fastened so he could not see in. Tiptoeing round to the kitchen door he cautiously turned the handle. To his relief the door opened and he crept inside.

He did not pause in the hallway. Running up the stairs as fast as he could on silent feet, he dived on up, past his official bedroom, unslept in now since the day his mother had left, and up again to the attic. There he had made himself a mattress with a line of old cushions and covered it with some bedclothes. Still fully dressed and wearing his shoes, he flung himself down on his improvised bed and pulling a blanket over his head he cried himself to sleep.

*   *   *

It was two hours later that he heard the footsteps below him on the landing. He had awoken with a start and he lay for a moment, wondering what had happened. He was still fully clothed. Then he remembered.

He tensed. There it was again. The sound of heavy footsteps. His father. Quietly he crawled out of the bed and, standing up, moved silently towards the door. His heart was pounding. The sounds grew louder and for a moment he thought his father was on his way up to the attic, then they drew away again and it began to dawn on Adam that his father was pacing the floor of the bedroom beneath him. He listened for a long time, then at last, careful not to make a sound himself, he climbed back under the blankets and humped his pillow over his head.

He did not sleep for long. At first light, he was awakened by the sound of a blackbird. He crawled out of bed and went to look out of the window. The churchyard beyond the hedge was grey. There were no streaks of sunlight yet above the eastern hills. He padded across the floor to the window on the opposite side of the attic. From where he stood he could almost see up the high hillside to where the cross-slab stood.

Making his mind up quickly he pulled a thick sweater over his sleep-crumpled clothes and let himself out of the room.

On the landing outside his parents' room he stopped, holding his breath. From behind the door he could hear the sound of husky broken sobs. He listened for a moment, appalled, then he turned and ran.

In the kitchen he grabbed the rest of the cake and a box of shortbread and another bottle of ginger beer from the cold floor of the pantry. Cramming them into his knapsack he paused for a moment to snatch Mrs Barron's shopping list pad and scribble, *Have gone birdwatching. Don't worry*. He propped it up against the teapot, then he unlocked the door and let himself out into the garden.

It was very cold. In seconds his shoes were soaked with dew and his feet were frozen. He rammed his hands into his pockets and sped towards the street and he was already across the river and at the bottom of the hill when the first rim of sunlight slid between the distant mountain peaks and bathed the Tay in brilliant cold light.

He did not have to search for Brid's house this time. She found him as he was sitting leaning against the stone, eating the last piece of cake for his breakfast.

'A-dam?' The voice behind him was soft but even so he leaped out of his skin.

'Brid!'

They stared at each other helplessly, both wanting to say more, both knowing there was no point. Until they found a way of communicating they were impotent. At last, on inspiration, Adam dived into his bag and cursing the fact that he had eaten the cake himself he brought out the shortbread. Breaking off a piece he handed it to her shyly. She took it and sniffed it cautiously, then she bit it.

'Shortbread.' Adam repeated the word clearly.

She looked at him, head slightly to one side, eyes bright, and she nodded enthusiastically. 'Shortbread,' she said after him.

'Good?' he asked. He mimed good.

She giggled. 'Good?' she said.

'Gartnait?' he asked. He had a piece for her brother.

She pointed to the cross-slab. 'Gartnait,' she said. It sounded like a confirmation. Jumping up, she tugged at Adam's hand.

He followed her, aware that with the sunrise had come the mist, wreathing through the trees and up the hillside. It had already reached the stone. He shivered, feeling it hit him like a physical blow as he walked after the girl. She glanced over her shoulder and he saw for a moment the look of doubt in her eyes, then it was gone, the mist was sucked up in the heat of the sun and Gartnait was there, sitting close to the cross. In his hand he had a hammer and in the other a punch.

'Oh, I say, you can't do that!' Adam was shocked.

Gartnait looked up and grinned.

'Tell him he can't. That cross is special. It's hundreds – thousands – of years old. He mustn't touch it! It's part of history,' Adam appealed to her, but she ignored him. She was holding out a piece of shortbread to her brother.

'Shortbread,' she repeated fluently.

Adam was staring at the back of the cross. Instead of the sequence of weathered patterns he was used to seeing – the incised circles, the Z-shaped broken spear, the serpent, the mirror, the crescent moon – the face of the stone looked new. It was untouched, with only a small part of one of the designs begun in one corner, the punch-marks fresh and sharp.

Adam ran his fingers over the raw clean edges and he heard Brid draw in her breath sharply. She shook her head and pulled his hand away. Don't touch. Her meaning was clear. She glanced over her shoulder as though she were afraid.

Adam was confused for a moment. The cross – the proper, old cross – must be there in the mist and Gartnait was copying it. He looked again at the young man's handiwork and he was impressed.

They sat together and ate the shortbread, then Gartnait picked up his chisel again. It was as he was working away at the intricate shape of the crescent moon, with Brid watching, giggling as Adam taught her the names of the plants and trees around them, that Gartnait suddenly paused in his chipping and listened. Brid fell silent at once. She looked round, frightened.

'What is it?' Adam glanced from one to the other.

She put her finger to her lips, her eyes on her brother's face.

Adam strained his ears. He could hear nothing but the faint whisper of the wind through the dry heather stems.

Abruptly Gartnait gave Brid an order which galvanised her into action. She leaped to her feet and grabbed Adam's wrist. 'Come. Quick.' They were words he had taught her already.

'Why? What's wrong?' He was bewildered.

'Come.' She was dragging him away from her brother towards the trees.

'Brid!' Gartnait called after her. He gabbled some quick instructions and she nodded, still clutching Adam's hand. The mist had drifted back across the hill and they dived into it as Adam saw two figures approaching in the distance. Clearly Brid did not intend him to meet them. In seconds he and Brid were concealed in the mist and their visitors were out of sight.

She led the way, confidently recognising landmarks he couldn't see and almost at once they were emerging near the spot where he had first seen her.

He looked round nervously. Surely Gartnait and the two strangers were only a few paces away behind the stone? He glanced back, seeing its shape looming out of the murk, touched now by the early morning sun. There was no sign of Gartnait or his unwelcome visitors.

'Who are they?' Adam mimed his question.

Brid shrugged. To explain was too complicated, clearly, and she was still afraid. She tugged his hand and, her finger to her lips, again headed down the hillside. Of Gartnait there was no sign.

The day was spoiled. She was clearly afraid and although she sat down near him when he beckoned her towards a sheltered rock from where they could survey the valley, which was still bathed in sunshine, in only a few minutes she had risen to her feet.

'Goodbye, A-dam.' She took his hand and gave it a little tug.

28

'Can I come again tomorrow?' He couldn't keep the anxiety out of his voice.

She smiled and shrugged. 'Tomorrow?'

How do you mime tomorrow? He shrugged too, defeated.

She shook her head and with a little wave of her hand turned and ran back up the hill on silent feet. He slumped back against the rock, disappointed.

She wasn't there tomorrow or the next day. Twice he went up the hill again and twice he searched all day for their cottage and for Gartnait's stone, but there was no sign of either. Both times he returned home feeling let down and puzzled.

'Where have you been all day?' His father was sitting opposite him in the cold dining room.

'Walking, Father.' The boy's hands tightened nervously on his knife and fork and he put them down on his plate.

'I saw Mistress Gillespie at the post office today. She said you hadn't been down to play with the boys.'

'No, Father.'

How could he explain the side-long looks, the sniggers?

He studied the pattern on his plate with furious concentration as if imprinting the delicate ivy-leaf design around the rim on his retinas.

'Are you looking forward to starting school again?' The minister was trying hard. His own eyes were red-rimmed and bloodshot, his hands shaking slightly. When his plate was only half empty he pushed the food aside and gave up. Adam couldn't keep his eyes off the remains of his father's supper. If he himself left anything he was normally the recipient of a lecture on waste and was told to sit there until he had eaten it. Seething with sudden resentment, he wished he dare say something, but he remained silent. The atmosphere in the room was tense. He hated it and, he realised it at last, he hated his father.

Miserably he shook his head as his father offered him a helping from the cold trifle left on the sideboard and he sat with bowed head whilst Thomas, clearly relieved that the meal was over, said a quick prayer of thanks and stood up. 'I have a sermon to write.' It was said almost apologetically.

Adam looked up. For a brief moment he felt an unexpected wave of compassion sweep over him as he met his father's eyes. The next he had looked away coldly. Their unhappiness was, after all, his father's fault.

*   *   *

'A-dam!' She had crept up beside him as he lay on the grass, his arm across his eyes to block off the glare from the sun.

He removed his arm and smiled without sitting up. 'Where have you been?'

'Hello, A-dam.' She knelt beside him and dropped a handful of grass-seed heads on his face. 'A-dam, shortbread?' She pointed to the knapsack which lay beside him.

He laughed. 'You're a greedy miss, that's what you are.' He unfastened it and brought out the tin of shortbread. He was pleased she had remembered the word. He glanced round. 'Gartnait?'

She shook her head.

As he peered round the cross-slab to see if her brother was there she wagged her finger. 'No, A-dam. No go there.'

'Why not? Where have you been? Why couldn't I find you?' He was growing increasingly frustrated at this inability to communicate with her properly.

She sat down beside him and began to pull the lid off the short-bread tin. She seemed uninterested in further conversation, leaning back on her elbows, sucking at the soft buttery biscuit, licking her lips. The sun came out from behind a cloud, throwing a bright beam across her face and she closed her eyes. He studied her for a moment. She had dark hair and strong regular features. When the bright, grey eyes, slightly slanted, were closed, as now, her face was tranquil yet still full of character, but when those eyes were open her whole expression came alive, vivacious and enquiring. Silver lights danced in her eyes and her firm, quirky mouth twitched with humour. She was peeping at him beneath her long dark lashes, conscious of his scrutiny, reacting with an instinctive coquetry that had not been there before. Abruptly she sat up.

'A-dam.' She was saying his name more fluently now, more softly, but with the same intonation which he found so beguiling.

He ceased his scrutiny abruptly, feeling himself blush. 'It's time we learned each other's language,' he said firmly. 'Then we can all talk together.'

She moved, with a graceful wiggle of her hips, onto her knees and pointed down the valley the way he had come. 'A-dam, big shortbread?' she said coaxingly.

He burst out laughing. 'All right. More shortbread. Next time I come.'

He hadn't planned to follow her. He just couldn't stop himself. He had spent the afternoon teaching her words, astonished by the phenomenal memory which retained faultlessly everything he told her. He taught her more trees and flowers and birds; he taught her the names of their clothes; he taught her arms and legs and heads and eyes and hair and all the items in his knapsack; he taught her walk and sit and run. He taught her the sky and the sun, the wind and the words for laugh and cry, and they had 'talked' and giggled and finished all the shortbread, and then at last she had glanced up at the sun. She frowned, obviously realising how late it was, and scrambled to her feet. 'Bye bye, A-dam.'

He was taken by surprise. 'But it's hours until dark. Do you have to go?'

It was no use. She shrugged and turning, with a little wave, she dodged behind the stone slab and out of his sight.

He leaped to his feet. 'Brid, wait. When shall I see you? When shall I come again?'

There was no answer. He ran a few steps after her and stopped in confusion. There was no sign of her. He retraced his steps to the spot where he had been standing and then turning, followed in her exact tracks. The afternoon seemed to have grown misty again. He stood, his hand on the stone, and peered ahead and suddenly there she was, running down the hillside in the thin sunshine. He set off after her, not shouting this time, deliberately following her at a distance and consciously noticing the way they were going.

She was following a clear track which he did not remember seeing before. He frowned, looking at the wood below him on his right. That was where the Scots pine should be. There were Scots pine, but too many – many many more than he remembered, unless they had already slipped unnoticed into a different valley. That was perfectly possible. One often did not see ridges and glens in the hills until one was upon them. He realised she was fast disappearing from sight and he plunged after her, aware of the strong smell of the heather and the baking earth and rock. Overhead a buzzard was calling, the wild yelping miaou growing fainter as it spiralled higher and higher until it was nothing but a speck in the blue.

The first he noticed of the village was the thin spiral of white smoke, almost invisible against the sky. He slowed down, trying to get his breath back, more cautious now. Brid was skipping unself-consciously about a hundred yards ahead of him as he ducked behind some low whin bushes. She stopped and seemed to be gathering some flowers, then she moved on, holding them in her hand, more decorous now. He saw her surreptitiously rub some dust from her skirt and run her fingers through her hair.

He hesitated for a moment, then he ducked out of his hiding place and ran a few paces further on, to throw himself full length behind a small outcrop of rock. From there he peered at her again. Two figures had appeared on the dusty track and he could now see the village more clearly. It consisted of little more than a cluster of small round houses situated around a larger, central one. He squinted to see the figures better and recognised the taller of the two as Gartnait. The young man stopped when he saw Brid and waited for her. From the way he stood, the flailing of his arms and Brid's sudden, obvious dejection, it was clear that Gartnait was angry.

Adam, who had been about to leap to his feet and admit to his presence, changed his mind abruptly. He lay where he was, his chin propped on his hands, watching. His vantage point allowed him to see the three figures – the third unknown to him – walk slowly back towards the village. Once there they stood and talked again animatedly for several minutes before at last ducking into a low doorway in one of the houses and disappearing from sight.

He stayed there for a long time, hoping someone would reappear. When it was clear they weren't going to, he began to crawl slowly forward, taking advantage of the clumps of long dried grasses as the only reasonable cover to hide him. Once he heard a dog bark. He dropped flat, pressing his nose into the dry earth, smelling its hot peppery sweetness. After a few moments the barking stopped, abruptly silenced by a curt command, in what language he could not tell.

He waited, holding his breath. There was no further sound and he raised his head again to find himself looking at a pair of soft leather sandals. Leaping to his feet in fright he found himself half suspended by the collar, face to face with a tall, white-haired man with fierce dark eyes, a fine aquiline face and a narrow mouth set in a tight-lipped scowl. The man barked a question at him and Adam wriggled desperately, half angry and half afraid.

'Let me go! I'm not doing any harm! Let me go! I'm a friend of Brid's.' He flailed out uselessly with his fists and the man put him down, transferring his iron grip to Adam's wrist. Turning he strode towards the village, pulling Adam with him. The boy wriggled harder, his initial alarm turning to real fear. The look in the man's eyes had been uncompromising and Adam knew that look well.

As they walked down the dirt track which served for a village street Adam saw faces at the doors. One by one the inhabitants appeared. Dark, shaggy-haired, dressed in strange bright-coloured woollen or leather breeches, the men were staring at him aggressively. Behind them he could see the women, most of them swathed in shawls, half hidden in the dark depths of the cottages, and suddenly he knew who they were. This must be a camp of tinkers – or real Romanies perhaps – from far away. He had seen tinkers, of course, in the village at home. Two or three times a year some of them would come, camping on the riverbank; they would mend the pots and pans of the housewives, and sharpen their knives, and then when the factor decided too many salmon had disappeared from the river they would move on overnight with their colourful vans and their ponies. He had heard that they had settlements somewhere over the hills where they went in the wintertime and this must be one of them. The realisation comforted him. Somewhere at the back of his mind had lurked a niggling fear about where Brid came from – a shiver, no more – something he couldn't put a name to. To find out that she was a gypsy was a reassurance. The tinkers were always friendly. They got on well with the village children at home and the folk all got on well with them. Except for the factor of course, and the ghillies.

He stared round, trying to see Brid and Gartnait, and finally spotted them at the back of the crowd. He felt a surge of relief. 'Brid!' he cried. 'Make him let me go!' He wriggled, tried to bite the hand holding him and received a cuff on the ear for his pains. The tall man had followed his gaze and was also staring at Brid. He pointed at her and shouted a command. The men and women around her fell back. Brid looked terrified. Slowly she moved forward through the silent, staring crowd and came to stand in front of them.

'Brid, tell him! Tell him I'm your friend,' Adam begged. The man's grip on his arm had not slackened. His head, Adam had noticed for the first time, was half shaven and there were dark tattoos on his forehead beneath the wild white rim of hair.

Brid shook her head. Covering her face with her hands she fell on her knees. Adam could see tears trickling from between her fingers. 'Brid?' He had stopped struggling, shocked by her abject terror.

It was Gartnait who stepped up behind her. He rested his hands gently on his sister's shoulders and spoke to the tall man, his voice calm and clear.

Adam glanced from one to the other. Both men, he noticed, were wearing silver bracelets on their arms. Gartnait had a sort of necklet around his throat and beneath his cloak the short sleeves of his tunic showed that he too had intricately coloured tattoos on his arms and an intricately wrought golden band above his elbow. It made him look exotic and foreign. Very glamorous. Adam found his eyes going from one man to the other. His father disapproved of jewellery. He thought it an abomination, as he thought so many things were which were clearly nice or fun or beautiful. His mother owned none save her wedding ring. He had never seen a man wear jewellery save for the tinkers in the village who sometimes wore earrings, and Lord Pittenross who owned the estate and wore a gold signet ring with a carved crest on the little finger of his left hand. Adam, in spite of his fear, was impressed.

The tall man's grip had slackened slightly as he stood listening to Gartnait and Adam snatched his arm away. He rubbed it defiantly, squaring his shoulders, feeling braver now. He gave Brid a quick grin but she was still kneeling with her hands over her eyes.

It was the turn of the tall man to speak now. He gestured at Adam, sweeping the boy with a withering look which took in his open-necked shirt, his shorts, his bare brown legs and his dusty sandals. It was then that the man pulled out a knife.

Adam gasped. Nearby, one of the watching women groaned. Gartnait went on talking calmly as though nothing had happened, but his fingers on his sister's thin shoulders had tightened until the knuckles went white.

Brid took her hands away from her eyes. Her face was very pale. 'Run, A-dam!' she cried suddenly. 'RUN!'

Adam ran.

He turned like an eel beneath the man's flailing hand and diving through the crowd fled as fast as he could back the way he had come. His sudden movement had taken them all by surprise and it was a moment before the tall man started in pursuit. But he gave up almost at once. No one else had moved.

Adam did not wait to see what happened. He pounded up the track, jumping over stones and heather, leaping from rock to rock across the burn and slithering down a gully which took him out of sight of the village. At the bottom he lay still, gasping for breath. His heart was hammering somewhere in his throat and his legs were trembling with exhaustion and shock.

When at last he raised his head and looked around he half expected to see the tall man there again standing over him. There was no one there. The gully was deserted. Nearby he could hear a stonechat calling, its metallic voice an eerie echo of the sound of Gartnait's hammer, and the distant slithering cascade of scree in the wake of his passing. Nothing else. He raised himself up and peered round carefully before climbing slowly up to the top of the rocks and looking behind him. There was no sign of the village. It was out of sight behind the shoulder of the hill and the heather and rocks were empty of any signs of pursuit. And of any landmarks he recognised.

He knew that to find his way home he needed to go south-east. He glanced at the sun, though he knew already which way he should go from the lie of the distant hills.

Not until the sun had set behind the shoulder of Ben Dearg did he admit at last that he was lost. He could feel the fear crawling in the pit of his stomach. The hillside looked familiar, but he could not see the stone. He could see no sign of anything he recognised. Feeling for footholds as silently as he could amongst the blaeberries and sliding scree he crept up to the rim of the gully and peered over the edge. The outline of the distant hills was the same as always, as were the contours of the glen below, but he could not see the cross-slab. In the distance he noticed suddenly the curl of smoke against the sky that showed the location of Brid's village and he calmed himself down with an effort. After all, he had been exploring these hills with his friends since he was old enough to slip away from the village. What would his heroes do in these circumstances? Men like Richard Hannay or Sexton Blake, Alan Breck or the Scarlet Pimpernel? He didn't have a compass but he would use his watch with the sun. With new determination he set off in what he hoped was the right direction, his back resolutely to Brid's village, hoping that whatever was happening there she would not get into any further trouble because of him.

Wraiths of mist were curling through the trees when he at last found the stone cross again. It was the copy, the one that Gartnait was working on. He rested his hand on it, touching the sharp-edged carving of the looping intricate designs with his fingertips. Gartnait had stopped halfway through incising a broken spear. He could feel the shallow punch-marks outlining the design.

In the east, the deep amethyst dusk was beginning to hover over the valley. It hid the distances from sight, wrapping the whole area in darkness.

He stepped away from the stone, looking round for the older original, the landmark which had stood on the hill for fourteen hundred years. There was no sign of it. The air was very still.

Frowning, he moved a few paces forward, overwhelmed suddenly by a strange dizziness. His head was spinning. He had been

35

running too fast. He stumbled, shaking his head from side to side, trying to rid himself of the slight buzzing in his ears. Then the moment had passed and his head cleared. Below him the mistiness had drifted away and in the distance he could see the grey stone roofs of the forge and the post office, the lights from the main street, and the shoulder of hillside above the waterfalls which hid the manse from his view, while behind him the old cross caught a last shaft of slanting light from the sun as it slid over the horizon.

3

'A-dam?' The hand on his shoulder was as light as thistledown. He started and sat up. 'Brid?'

It was the spring. The Easter vacation. Ten whole days of freedom stretched before him. Adam had come back several times in the autumn but there had been no sign of Brid or Gartnait, no trace, though he cautiously searched, of the shabby cottage or the village. Frustrated, he pored over maps and books in the library for signs of the place, but to no avail, and when the snows came to the mountains he gave up looking and concentrated, much to his father's satisfaction, on his school books.

He had also given up hoping for a message from his mother. He no longer raced to meet the postie or hid on the stairs peering through the banisters, his heart thudding with hope when there was a knock on the door.

Sometimes, at night, he cried for her, secretly, his head under the pillow to drown his stifled sobs. His father never mentioned her and he did not dare ask. He was not to know that there had been letters; four of them. Enclosed in the missives she sent to her husband, pleading for forgiveness and understanding, the lonely, frightened, desperate woman's declarations of love for her son went unread into the waste paper basket and slowly, miles away to the south, her despair of ever seeing Adam again grew greater. Once she had come on the bus and stood, hidden by a hedge, hoping to catch a glimpse of him, but her fear of being spotted by someone from the village, or worse still by her husband had been too great, and, in tears, she had caught the next bus back to Perth and then the train south. She did not know that that day Adam had been far away on the hillside, lost in dreams.

Jeannie Barron knew no more than Adam did. Her heart ached

for the boy as she saw his white face and the tell-tale red-rimmed eyes in the mornings. When school started he would cycle off while it was still dark to the bus stop in Dunkeld five miles away and there he would catch the bus to Perth, leaving his bicycle hidden behind a hedge. When he returned from the long day, his books in his satchel, it would be dark once again and there was no question of going anywhere but, after supper, to his own room. When the snows came he would stay in Perth during the week, lodging with Jeannie Barron's cousin Ella as he had done since he first went to the Academy.

'Brid!' He grinned with pleasure. 'I thought I wouldn't see you again!' He had been terrified for her after he had fled from her village, his memory of the tall, angry man and the gleaming knife-blade haunting his worse nightmares.

'A-dam, shortbread?' She sat down beside him and, reaching for his knapsack, rummaged through it hopefully. It contained his bird book and field glasses, the notebook and an apple.

He shrugged. 'No shortbread. Sorry.'

'No shortbread. Sorry,' she repeated.

'Have the apple.' He picked it out and handed it to her.

She looked at it doubtfully.

'Surely you know an apple!' He shook his head in despair and taking it back from her took a huge bite to demonstrate.

She laughed and nodded and taking it back from him followed suit, displaying her small white teeth. Like him she had grown taller in the intervening months.

'Apple good.' She nodded.

'Brid, why was that man so angry when I came to your village? Who was he?' He was trying to mime the question.

She looked at him and for a moment he thought she understood. The quick intelligence in her eyes, the sudden tension of her shoulders betrayed her, but she shook her head and smiled. 'Apple good,' she repeated.

Frustrated, he shrugged. Then he had an idea. 'I'm going to teach you some more English,' he announced suddenly. 'Then we can talk properly.'

His lessons went on all through the summer. Adam, his knapsack laden with shortbread, or scones or chocolate cake – immediately popular with Brid – met her on the long evenings and at weekends and then in the vacation. Most of the time they stayed on the southern slopes of the hillside, making no attempt to go to her village. He had pushed Brid on the subject of the man's identity, but she had changed the subject with a shrug. One thing was clear however: whoever he was, she was very afraid of him. A couple of times they visited the cottage where her mother lived, just for the summer, he discovered, so Gartnait could be near the carving, for carving the slab seemed to be his full-time occupation. In the winter it appeared he had a workshop and men to help him but there was something special about this carving, something special about this stone, so that he had to work on it in situ. Sometimes they would sit and watch him for hours and he too would join in the language lessons while he worked, his chisels, hammers, punches and polishing stones laid out neatly in a row beside him.

Brid was a very fast learner and talkative and it was not long before she had overcome the frustrations of not being able to communicate with her companion. Adam for his part had already found out from his lamentable marks in Latin and French at school that languages were not amongst his strengths. His tongue tied itself in knots around the words she tried to teach him and he could remember few of them though he loved the way she laughed till she cried when he tried. Her fluency though made it easy for her to avoid his questions when she wanted to, and eventually he gave up asking about her village and her people. Gypsies, he supposed, must be naturally secretive, and with that conclusion he had to be content.

Jeannie Barron, discovering that chocolate cake was one of the ways to make Adam happy, made them more often and the two young people grew brown together in the sun as they picnicked and paddled in the burns through the hot spell. Adam made no effort to see the boys who had once been his friends. He no longer knew or cared if they avoided him. He seldom saw his father, who himself stayed out late more often. If he had known that Thomas was spending more and more time in agonised prayer, locked alone in the kirk, he might have felt a glimmer of sympathy, he might have sensed his father's turmoil and loneliness and confusion, but he did not allow himself to think about his father at all. There were only three adults now in his life whom he trusted: Donald Ferguson, one of his science masters at school, Jeannie Barron, and Brid's mother, Gemma.

'A-dam, today we go see eagles.' Brid adored his bird book. She pored over the pages and told him the names of many of the birds in her own tongue – names he could never remember. To his surprise she couldn't write, so he had added that skill to his lessons, reassuring her when she fumbled with pencils, praising her when they found to the surprise of both of them that she could draw.

The eagles had an eyrie high on the side of Ben Dearg. To reach it they had to walk for a couple of hours, scrambling over increasingly steep rock and heather before stopping and sliding down the first of the deep corries that ran from east to west across the high moor. Halfway along, near the foot of the rockface, a torrent of brown burn water cascaded over a cliff some twenty feet or so into a circular pool before racing on down the mountainside. As they came to the edge of the cliff, several deer looked up startled and stared at them for a moment before bounding away out of sight.

Adam smiled at her. She was wearing as she always did a simple tunic, this one dyed in soft blues and greens, tied at the waist with a leather girdle in which she wore a serviceable knife. On her feet she wore sandals, not buckled like his but fastened round the ankles with long ribbon-like thongs. Her long hair she had fastened back with a silver clip. 'We gave them a fright.'

She nodded. She had reached the pool first and she stopped and waited for him. Adam fell to his knees and bent over the water, splashing it over his hot face. 'We could swim here.' He grinned at her. 'It's deep. Look.'

She looked at him doubtfully and then at the dark water. 'Swimming not allowed here.'

'Why not? You paddle in the burn. It's not that deep. I'll show you.'

Before she could stop him he had pulled his shirt over his head and kicked off his shorts. Dressed only in his underpants, he leaped into the brown water.

It was much deeper than he expected and ice cold. He swam a few strokes under water, reached the vertical rock wall on the far side, ducked into a turn and rose to the surface gasping.

'A-dam!' Brid was kneeling on the rock at the edge of the pool. She was looking furious now. She held out her hands to him. 'Come out. You must not swim.'

'Why not?' He shook his wet hair out of his eyes and struck out across the pool towards her. He was there in four strokes. 'Hey, what's wrong?'

She was pulling at his arm. 'Get out! Get out! Get out quickly!' She stamped her foot.

'What is it, Brid? What's wrong?' He levered himself out beside her. 'You're not afraid, surely?'

'A-dam! The lady in the pool. You have not paid her!' Brid was whispering angrily.

'The lady?' He stared at her. 'What are you talking about?'

'The lady. She lives in the pool. She looks after it.'

Adam looked puzzled for a moment, then light dawned. 'Like the *cailleach*, you mean? The old witch. A spirit. Brid! You don't believe that? That's wicked. That's against the Bible.' He was shocked.

She shook her head, not understanding him. Going to the knapsack which was lying on the ground in the shade of a rock, she rummaged in it until she found the greaseproof-wrapped cake. Opening the paper she drew her knife and carefully cut the wedge of cake into three. 'For A-dam. For Brid. And for the Lady.' She pointed to each slice in turn. Picking up the third piece she walked with it to the edge of the pool and climbed carefully out onto the rocks, which were slippery with spray, until she was as close as possible to the waterfall. Crumbling the cake between her fingers, slowly she dropped it piece by piece beneath the cascade, chanting some words under her breath as she did so.

When she had finished she stood still for a moment, staring round anxiously as though waiting to see if her offering had been accepted.

'Brid!' Adam was appalled.

She silenced him with an abrupt gesture, still scanning the water, then she pointed. He saw a small shadow flash past and it was gone.

'That was a trout,' he said indignantly.

She shook her head. Then in another lightning change of mood she clapped her hands and laughed. 'Trout messenger of the Lady!' she cried. She skipped back onto the bank. 'The Lady is pleased. Now we swim.' She sat down and began to unlace her sandals.

Beneath her tunic Brid was naked. She stood for a second on the rock, her body a pale contrast to her tanned arms and legs, then she leaped into the water with a splash and a delighted shriek.

Adam stood still. He caught his breath. He had seen the baby sisters of his friends sometimes without their clothes when their mothers bathed them before the fire, and he had always averted his eyes, particularly avoiding looking at the shockingly naked slit between their legs. He was still seriously intending to be a doctor, but he had never seen an older girl or a woman without clothes before, and now he had seen for a short moment when she stood untroubled on the rock this slim girl, young woman; seen her small firm breasts, the dark fuzz of hair between her legs, the provocative curve of hip and buttock before she leaped into the water.

He had never before considered how old Brid was. About his

own age, he assumed, but she was his friend, his pal. He had never thought of her for a single moment as being like the giggling girls in Pittenross or Dunkeld, but his body, to his extreme embarrassment, was reacting by itself.

He stood where he was, mortified, the water dripping in pools around his feet as Brid flung back her hair, which had come free of its clip, treading water near him. 'Come, A-dam,' she called. 'Come in. Nice.'

He smiled uncertainly, his eyes on her breasts as the water cascaded over her shoulders. Dark strands of hair plastered her back and clung to her pale skin.

'Come.' She had realised suddenly the effect she was having on him and her smile became provocative. She ran her fingers over her body, resting them for a moment on the pert nipples before sweeping them down over her hips. 'A-dam. Come.' Her voice had deepened. It held command. He hesitated for only a moment longer.

The cold water brought him sharply to his senses. Spluttering, he struck out for the far side of the pool, dodged round her and ducked under the waterfall itself. The noise was deafening. He was totally enveloped in the icy torrent, encircled by it, deafened by it, stunned by it. He trod water immediately under the fall and raised his face, feeling the power of it thundering over him. It was choking him, stifling him, drowning him. Abruptly he lowered his head, ducking out of it, gasping desperately to regain his breath.

Brid swam over to him in alarm. 'A-dam? Are you all right?' She touched his arm, her fingers cold.

He pulled away and felt the firmness of her naked thigh against his underneath the water. He reacted as though he had been burned. With a yell he turned away and flailed towards the side of the pool. Pulling himself up onto the rock he lay there for a moment on his back, trying to catch his breath.

She was right behind him. 'A-dam?' She knelt over him, the water dripping from her breasts. 'A-dam, what is wrong? Did the water go in you?' She had one hand on his shoulder, the other on his belly, gentle, concerned. 'Poor A-dam. You went under the falling water. Only the Lady goes there. She was cross with you.'

He opened his eyes. 'There is no lady, Brid,' he gasped. 'Saying there is, is evil. Wicked. You will go to hell if you believe such things.'

'Hell?' She was kneeling beside him, looking puzzled now, her long wet hair modestly shrouding her breasts.

'Hell. Hades. Inferno.' Adam was sounding increasingly desperate. 'Brid, you have heard of Our Lord? Of Jesus?'

'Oh, Jesus.' She smiled. 'Columcille talked of Jesus. Broichan does not like that. Brude, the king, he likes Jesus.'

'The king?' Adam was frowning at this torrent of strange names. The sun was in his eyes now as he lay back on the baking rock, Brid a black silhouette above him. 'You mean King George?'

'King Brude,' she said firmly. 'The Lady punish you, A-dam. She make water go in you. You must give her a present. Say sorry.'

'I am not going to say sorry to a heathen spirit!' he said hotly. He struggled to sit up, but she pushed him back, surprisingly strong. 'A-dam, say sorry or she make you die.'

She had learned the word die when they had found a stag, its neck broken, at the foot of a cliff. To his surprise she had cried for it, her hands gently caressing the rough red-brown fur on its nose as it expired, its head in her arms. She was anything but gentle now.

'She can't make me die.' A shiver sent goosepimples over his skin.

She nodded, her face transformed with such fury he felt a tremor of fear run through him. 'She can. I serve the Lady, I know about her. I will kill you if she asks me to. She is very cross. You went in her special place. You must give her your piece of cake.'

Adam stared at her in horror. 'I will not!'

'You give her your piece of cake or she will make you die.'

'Brid! You're mad!' He wondered for a split second as he said it if it were true. She was frightening him. There was a strange uncompromising look in her eyes which he had never seen before. A piece of cake was not going to appease some spirit in the water even if it did exist, which of course it didn't. He tried to sit up again and this time she let him. She rose gracefully to her feet and stood before him. 'A-dam, please. Give her a present.' Her voice had assumed a new, deep resonance. 'Anything. Give her your watch.' She had never seen a watch before and was enchanted by it.

'I will not.' He tried to smile. 'I'd rather she had the cake.'

'Then give her cake.' She was firm. She folded her arms.

His eyes had strayed to her breasts and he brought them back to her face with difficulty. 'All right, if it makes you happy, I'll throw away the piece of cake.'

'Not throw away, A-dam. Give it to the Lady.' She was implacable.

'Brid –'

'Give it, A-dam, or I will let her kill you.' The authority in her voice made him stare at her in awe. From one moment to the next it seemed she had changed from a provocative child-woman to a raging virago, to someone with the authority of one of his teachers at school. Shaking his head, shocked and uncomfortable, he squatted down and meekly reached into his knapsack. He brought out the two remaining slices of cake and taking one he walked across to the pool. She watched in silence as he moved out to the place where she had stood and solemnly broke up the cake and let it fall through his fingers into the water.

'There. Satisfied?' He felt cheated; he had been looking forward to the cake. And he also felt guilty and afraid. Thanks to Brid he had made a sacrifice to some pagan gypsy god and in so doing endangered his immortal soul. He sat down on the rocks at the edge of the pool and wrapping his arms around his spindly shins he sank his chin on his knees.

She glanced at him. 'A-dam?' The anger had gone from her voice. This time it was soft. Hesitant. 'A-dam? Why you cross?'

'I'm not cross.' He refused to look at her.

'The Lady happy now. She eat her cake.'

He shuffled round slightly so that his back was towards her.

There was a small sigh. Then he heard the faint rustle of paper and looked round.

'A-dam eat Brid's cake.' The last piece was being offered to him.

'I don't want it.' Crossly he turned away from her again.

'Please, A-dam.' She sounded so mournful he was suddenly sorry. He turned. 'I'll have a little bit, then.' He said it as though he were doing her a favour. He reached out and broke off the end of the slice from the piece lying in the paper cradled between her palms.

'We share.' She smiled. Sitting down on the rock beside him she broke the remains of the slice in two. Cramming her piece into her mouth she ate it with gusto. The sunlight was playing over her skin, warming it, soothing away the goosepimples where the wind had touched it with cold fingers. Adam looked away, concentrating as hard as he could on the cake in his mouth, pressing the soft sweetness against his teeth with his tongue, savouring the buttery crumbs.

'Good?' Brid smiled at him. Where the ends of her hair had dried they rose wispy round her shoulders.

'Good.' He nodded. He lay back on the rock, putting his arm across his eyes to shade them from the sun. 'We'd better get dressed

44

and go on if we want to see the eagles.' In spite of his words he didn't want to move; he wanted to stay there with this beautiful naked girl forever.

She was sitting staring out across the water, lost in thought. 'We see eagles tomorrow,' she said at last. It had been very hard to teach her what tomorrow meant. And yesterday. 'We stay here and swim.'

He nodded sleepily. 'That's good.'

She was looking at him now, half smiling. He was tanned from the sun. The scars on his back from his father's whipping had faded. He was a slightly built boy, slim, handsome, his shoulders beginning to broaden as he matured. Leaning towards him she put a gentle hand on his chest. He went rigid; she was bending over him now, her hair still cold and damp, trailing provocatively over his nipples, down towards his belly.

'A-dam?' Her voice was soft. Gently she pulled his arm away from his eyes and he looked up startled into her face, which was only a few inches from his.

She smiled, her hands running lightly over his shoulders, down his chest towards his stomach.

He caught at her wrist. 'Brid, don't.'

'A-dam,' she whispered. She wriggled free. 'A-dam shut eyes.'

He stared up at her, paralysed, gazing into the depths of her silvery eyes. He had to move. He had to get up and go home. For a moment his father's furious face flashed before him and he felt a bolt of fear transfix him. But he wanted to stay. More than anything in the world he wanted to stay exactly where he was.

'A-dam shut eyes,' she whispered again. She smiled and her grey irises were darkening now, growing deep and mysterious as she put her finger to his lips. Unable to move he shut his eyes and held his breath.

Her kiss was as light as thistledown on his lips. It tasted of cool clear mountain water and of chocolate and it sent a spasm of intense delight shooting through his whole body.

'Nice, A-dam?' she said softly. Her hands were on his chest now, playing with his nipples. His senses were beginning to spin. He didn't know whether to concentrate on his mouth or his chest or on other parts of his body as he felt her lean lower over him, her skin cold and clean from the pool touching his to fire. Her hands had moved down now, gently pulling at his underpants. He opened his mouth to protest and found her mouth there on his, her tongue fluttering provocatively between his teeth. He could not push her away. Suddenly he was overwhelmed by feelings he could not control. With a groan he pulled her face closer to his, returning her kisses, wriggling out from under her so he could throw himself across her and slide between her open legs. 'Brid!' he groaned.

His hands were on her breasts and she gasped as he kneaded them harder and harder. 'Brid!'

The moment of ecstasy which shot through him as he entered her left him exhausted and gasping for breath. For a while she lay still, gazing past him at the brilliant blue of the sky, then in one quick movement she had wriggled from under him and rose gracefully to her feet. She stood staring down at him thoughtfully as he turned to look sleepily up at her, and for a moment, as she held him trapped in her gaze, he felt a wave of fear. The surge of power coming from her was like a physical blow.

'That was good, A-dam. Nice. Now A-dam mine. Forever!' Their eyes seemed locked together, and Adam's fear threatened to lurch into panic. His pulse was racing, his lungs frozen on a trapped breath. Then the moment was over. She looked away and laughed. 'A-dam tired!'

She took two skipping steps to the edge of the pool and dived in.

Adam shut his eyes. His heart was thundering in his chest and he felt completely spent.

He was roused by a shower of ice-cold water full in the face. 'A-dam sleeps!' Her laughter was impish. She was standing over him, dripping, her hands still cupped. He could see the setting sun behind her, surrounding her in a glittering halo of red-gold, and for the first time he realised how long they had been there. He sat up slowly as she sank onto her knees beside him.

'A-dam happy?' He could feel her vitality and excitement, and something else, something wild and still, inexplicably, frightening.

He nodded. He was tongue-tied.

She leaned over him and in yet another lightning mood-shift reached for the knapsack. 'Brid hungry.' She rummaged through notebook, bird book and binoculars and shook her head dolefully. 'No cake.'

He laughed and the spell was broken at last. 'No cake. Your fault. You threw it in the water.'

Jumping to his feet he ran to the pool and threw himself in, feeling the water, gloriously cold and clean, blotting out the terror and self-loathing which was lurking somewhere at the edges of his mind. He swam the length of the pool as hard as he could, and when he struck out back across it he saw that Brid had got dressed.

46

Wringing out her hair with her hands she had fixed it on top of her head with her sliver clip. When he reached the edge she had completed the change from the sultry, demanding woman back into a hungry child. 'We go to Mama. She gives us bannocks.'

Adam nodded. 'We'd better hurry. It's growing dark.' Now that she was fully clothed the fear was receding and shame and embarrassment were edging forward in his mind. He did not want her to see him naked. He wanted her to turn away as he climbed out of the water, but she stood looking down at him, not moving.

'Hurry, A-dam.'

'I'm coming.' Crossly he began to haul himself out of the water.

But she wasn't looking at him any longer. Her eyes were on the distant glen where the mist was creeping up amongst the trees. 'Hurry, A-dam,' she said again. 'We go now.'

He had not meant to stay all night. He had intended to find his way home in the dark, but Brid's mother's fireside was warm and he was tired. Several times he dozed, leaning back against the rough wall of their house, then at last he slept. Brid smiled at her mother and shrugged and laughed and they pulled a cover over him and left him. Curling up on their own bed of cut heather covered in fleeces they turned their backs to the doorway and slept soundly.

He awoke suddenly. The cottage was cold, the fire smoored beneath its peats, the stone behind his back wet with condensation. He sat still, stiff and uncomfortable, listening to the absolute silence. Brid and her mother were still asleep but something had awoken him. Cautiously he pushed back the woollen blanket they had put over him and he climbed to his feet. He picked his way towards the doorway and pushed aside the leather curtain which at this time of year was its only protection and stepped out into the cold white mist of dawn.

Tiptoeing across to the burn he knelt and was splashing water over his face when behind him he heard the chink of metal on stone. He turned, pushing his dripping hair back from his face, and squinted around him. Seconds later grey shapes appeared at the periphery of his vision and he saw two men leading horses towards the cottage. He stayed where he was, suddenly afraid. One of them was Gartnait, he was fairly sure. The other – he leaned forward, screwing up his eyes, and then almost gasped out loud as he recognised the tall lean figure of the man who had threatened him in Brid's village. Desperate to find a hiding place, he glanced round. There was nothing to conceal him but the mist.

'Brid? Mother? Are you awake?' Gartnait's voice was shockingly loud in the silence. Though he could not speak it, Adam had picked up enough of their language to follow what was being said. 'We have a guest.'

He could not see the cottage but moments later he heard a scuffle and then Brid's mother's voice, flustered, as she uttered words of greeting, the words almost identical to those she had once used to Adam. 'Honoured brother, you are welcome to our house and hearth. Sit. Here. I will bring food.'

Brother was the extra word, a word that Adam knew. He frowned. Was it a general term or did it really mean that the man was Brid's uncle? If so, why on earth had she not said so?

'Broichan is here to see my carving, Mother.' Gartnait's voice was as always strong, easy to hear. 'Where is my sister?'

'She is coming. She is bringing bannocks and ale for our guest.'

Adam could imagine their consternation, wondering what would happen if he were still there, and then their relief when they realised that he had gone.

He had to move. At any second the mist could disappear, shredded by a morning wind or sucked up by the sun as soon as it rose over the mountains. He saw a shadow appear and then vanish again: Gartnait, leading the horses to tether them to the tree they called the look-out pine.

Cautiously Adam rose to his feet. He took a step away from the burn onto the fine grass which grew lush in the spray from the rocks. If he could reach the shelter of the trees he could disappear up the corrie and be gone before the day came.

He took another step. Then he froze. A voice, strong, deep, sounded so close to him he thought the man was standing next to him.

'The king still entertains the Christians at Craig Phádraig. He has commanded that we put up the cross throughout his kingdom to appease the Jesus God. He believes Columcille has power to defeat mine!'

'Then surely, Uncle, he is very wrong.' Gartnait's voice came in snatches. There was a shift in the whiteness and for an instant Adam could see the two men standing before the cottage. He tried to wish himself invisible as he saw Broichan's back turned towards him.

'Indeed, he is wrong. I have raised storms to splinter trees at his feet, to sink his boat, to kill his horse.' Broichan sucked his breath in through his teeth. 'He calls on his own god to compete with mine and the king, to appease him in the name of hospitality, bids me stay my hand. So be it. For now. Once he is no longer beneath the king's roof tree, I shall swat him like a fly.' He smote his thigh with the flat of his hand and Adam jumped. The man had only to move a fraction of an inch and he would see him.

A drift of mist strayed near them, barely more than a haze in the growing light. It was enough. Adam took two and then three swift steps towards the trees, holding his breath. There was a clump of whin near him. He reached it and crouched down in relief as the voices floated towards him again.

'You must cut the cross on the reverse of the sacred stone, Gartnait. Show me your designs and I will choose. It will do no harm and it will please the king and his visitors. Later we will serve our gods and show that they are stronger when I split the mountains with the force of my anger! And little Brid here shall help me.' He held out his hand to touch Brid's cheek.

From his hiding place Adam could see her now. He held his breath, his skin crawling as he saw the man's hand linger on her face with long clawed fingers. She had one of the silver plates Gartnait had engraved for his mother and was offering their visitor something from it. He accepted and Adam saw him bring it to his mouth. For a moment he stood staring at the silent tableau in front of him, then the mist drifted back and he could see no more. Without hesitating, he sprinted silently for the trees, dived amongst them, and set off as fast as he could up the hill.

The stone was touched with the first rays of the sun. Breathless as he reached it, Adam realised suddenly that he had left behind his knapsack with his precious books and binoculars. He cursed himself, but he knew it would have to wait. Brid would take care of them. Walking slowly round the stone he could feel the sunlight warm on his shoulders as for a moment he stopped to finger the intricate carvings. This was his stone. On one side were the strange symbols and figures of the ancient Picts, on the other the lattice and lace of the Celtic cross. Of Gartnait's newly carved stone without the cross there was no trace.

Brid had hidden the knapsack under the bed coverings as soon as she had spotted it. Calmly she had scanned the interior of the hut for tell-tale signs of Adam. If there were any her uncle would see them. He had sight beyond the sight of normal men. She was praying as hard as she could that Adam had gone; not just into the mist but from their land altogether.

49

She knew her uncle was suspicious. He did not yet trust Gartnait and showed it by his constant visits. Gartnait was too young. The role of stone carver and keeper of the gate was a sacred one, a calling as special in its way as that of priest or bard. It was a family trust Gartnait had inherited from their father when he had died two years before. It went with the knowledge bred in the blood, of how to travel to the realms of the ever young if only one should dare. To go there was forbidden to all but the initiated, but sometimes people slipped without realising it through the gate – like Adam.

She had known the first time she saw him that Adam came from beyond the stone. His strange clothes and speech set him apart. She had watched carefully to see how he travelled the road which was supposed to bring death to all but the very few who knew the way. That he was a proper man and not a spirit or a ghost she had proved to her own satisfaction. But he was young to be an initiate. He had fascinated her from the first moment she set eyes on him. And now she had made him hers. A secret smile touched her lips briefly and then disappeared. Whatever his power was, she was going to have it.

'Brid!' The impatient call from outside made her jump. With another hasty glance round she stepped outside into the mist to confront the steady gaze of her uncle.

'You look frightened, child.' He had caught her hand and pulled her to him. 'There is no need.' Putting his hand under her chin he tilted her head up so he could study her face. Meeting his eyes she looked away quickly, afraid that he could see the new woman-power which was still coursing through her veins, the power which had come from the touch of a man. She could feel his eyes probing her very soul, but after a moment he looked away from her face and turned to his sister. 'She runs wild here, Gemma.' He spoke sternly. 'She should be at her studies. There is much for her to learn if she is to serve in the holy places.' He ran his hand slowly, almost seductively, down Brid's cheek.

She took a step back out of his reach and straightened her shoulders. 'I wish to follow the way of the word, Uncle.' She looked at him steadily. Her fear had vanished, to be replaced by cool determination. 'I have already learned much from Drust, the bard at Abernethy. He has agreed to teach me all he knows.'

She saw her uncle's face suffuse with blood and instantly regretted her brave speech. 'You presume to arrange your own life!' he thundered at her.

She stood her ground. 'It is my right, Uncle, if I have the gift of memory and words.' It was her right as daughter of two ancient bardic families, one, her mother's, of royal descent, for Broichan, her uncle, was the king's foster father and his chief Druid.

There was a long silence. Gemma was nearby, jug in hand, in the doorway. She had been about to replenish her brother's ale but she, like her two children, was standing, eyes fixed on his face. She held her breath.

'Have you encouraged her in this?' Broichan looked first at Gemma and then at Gartnait.

It was the latter who spoke first. 'If it is her calling, Uncle, surely it is the gods who have encouraged her? Without their inspiration she would not have the talent to learn from Drust.' Gartnait spoke with pride and dignity.

Brid bit back a triumphant smile. She wanted to hug him but she didn't move.

Abruptly her uncle turned away. Striding to one of the logs positioned near the fire as a seat he pulled his cloak tightly around him and sat down. 'Recite,' he commanded.

Brid caught her breath and glanced at Gartnait. He nodded gravely. His sister's waywardness, the stubborn furies which frightened him, the wild, in-born power, would be contained and safely harnessed by their uncle.

She moved forward. At first she was too nervous to speak, then almost miraculously her nerves vanished. Straightening her back she raised her head and began.

Her teacher had been thorough. On the long winter evenings, by the fire, he had noticed Brid in his audience, aware of her breeding and her brain, and had painstakingly repeated the long poems and stories which were their heritage until she could recite them faultlessly. Brid's memory, as Adam had discovered, was exceedingly good. Already she had the basics of what was taught in the bardic school.

At last Broichan held up his hand. He nodded. 'Indeed your tongue must have been touched by the goddess. That is good. You shall study further.' He gazed at her for a moment seeing clearly her nascent power, her wild, untamed link to the Lady. He frowned for a moment, a shadow crossing his face. There was a hardness there, a stubbornness, a single-mindedness of spirit which until the moment was right would have to be carefully handled.

He turned back to his sister. 'Your children are both talented, Gemma, which is as well. As soon as this monk, this Columcille, has gone back to the west where he came from, we shall have to chase the Jesus god from the land. They shall help us do it.'

That way she could be used.

And contained.

And her blood, as the child of kings, could sweeten and purify the earth defiled by the man sent from the Jesus god.

4

'Adam, where have you been?'

Thomas Craig had spent the whole night searching the hill. Unshaven and exhausted, he stopped, leaning heavily on his walking stick, trying to recover his breath.

'Father!' Adam had been sitting on the sun-warmed rock, overwhelmed by sleepiness, too tired to face the long walk back to the manse. 'I'm sorry.' He scrambled to his feet, suddenly frightened. 'I –' He hesitated. 'I got lost in the mist. I thought it better to stay put –'

'You thought it better!' Thomas's fear and exhaustion were swiftly turning to anger. 'You stupid, thoughtless, arrogant boy! Does it never cross your mind that I worry about you? Did it not cross your mind that I might have a sleepless night and spend the time searching for you?' The guilt, the self-punishment with which he tormented himself endlessly, was taking more of his strength each day.

'I did not think you would notice, Father.' Adam took a step back, though his tone was defiant.

'You – you didn't think I'd notice!'

'No, Father. You haven't known whether I'm there or not for months.' Somehow Adam maintained the courage to speak. 'You haven't noticed me at all.'

He held his father's gaze. Overhead a buzzard mewed plaintively as it rode a thermal higher and higher over the hill. Neither of them looked up.

The silence stretched to one full minute, then another. Adam held his breath.

Abruptly, his father's shoulders slumped. He sat down on a rock and threw his stick down at his feet. Rubbing his hands across his cheeks he sighed and shook his head. 'I'm sorry.' He kneaded his eyes. 'I'm sorry. You're right, of course. I've behaved unforgivably.'

Adam sat down some six feet from him. He said nothing, his eyes fixed on his father's face. His fear and defiance had changed to a strangely adult compassion for this tortured man.

At last Thomas looked up. 'You should come home. Get some food.'

Adam nodded. Slowly he stood up. He was stiff and tired, and suddenly he was starving.

The sound of screams to which he woke were his own. Muffling his face in the pillow he stared out of the window at the rags of ivy which danced round the frame, tapping the glass and blowing, in green and cream streamers, in the brisk south-easterly wind.

He had eaten a huge breakfast under the watchful eye of Jeannie Barron and then on her instructions made his way upstairs. He had only meant to lie down on the bed for a minute, with his book on butterflies in his hand, but overwhelmed with exhaustion and his own frustration and confusion, he had fallen instantly asleep.

The dream had been terrifying. He had been swimming under-water. At first it was fun. His limbs moved with ease and he had been staring round, eyes wide, watching the streaming green weed and the swift-moving brown trout in the dark water. Then suddenly she was there in front of him. The hag. The ugliest face he had ever seen, grotesque, toothless, her eyes bagged, surrounded by carbuncles, her nose broad and fleshy, her hair a tangled mass of swirling watersnakes. He had opened his mouth to scream, limbs flailing desperately, and swallowed water. He was drowning, sink-ing, and all the time she was coming closer and she was laughing. And suddenly she wasn't the hag any more. Her face was Brid's face and her hair was Brid's hair and he was staring at her naked body, reaching for her breasts even as he drowned.

He sat up in bed, clutching his pillow to his chest, still fighting for air, and realised to his miserable embarrassment that he was sporting a huge erection. Swinging his legs over the edge of the bed he ran to the window and heaved the heavy sash up. Sticking out his head he gasped for air. He stayed there until his breathing had calmed and he was himself again, then he turned back into the room. He wondered if his father had heard. He was not to know that downstairs his father had closed his ears to the boy's tormented shouts, and sitting at his desk in the ground floor study had felt the hot slow tears trickle down his own cheeks.

*　　*　　*

54

The next day was the Sabbath. Adam had not wanted to go to the kirk. He had hung back on the path as the congregation had filed into the old stone building, wondering if he dared duck out of sight around the trees and run down through the kirkyard to the broad slow-moving river. Then Jeannie had come, Ken at her side, and somehow they had swept Adam inside with them and into the manse pew. Adam sat motionless, his eyes on his father's snowy-white bands as Thomas stood above him in the pulpit. The boy was shaking. If his father could not see what was going on inside him, God certainly could. Adam was terrified. His skin was clammy with guilt, his hands clutched between his knees, his scalp crawling with terror as he thought about Brid and his dreams and what he had done. And slowly at the back of his mind he began to wonder if what his mother had done had been as bad and whether she like him would go to hell.

As they stood for the hymns he found his mouth was dry and his voice came out as a thin squeak. When the service was over, his face was so white he was able to slide away pleading a headache without even the observant Jeannie questioning the truth of the matter.

Thoughts of Brid filled his every waking moment. Alternate guilt, fear and obsessive longing, which at night in bed turned to dreams of lust and in equal measure self-loathing, were with him constantly. He returned to the stone again and again, but he could not find his way back to her village or to the cottage. Frustrated and impatient he found himself sobbing out loud as he raced back and forth amongst the trees. But every time the hillside was empty save for the occasional herd of deer grazing on the lower slopes, and thwarted he had to go home to a lonely, unenthusiastic supper and a cold bed where he dreamed of her again, shame-facedly scrubbing the treacherous signs from his pyjamas with his handkerchief so that Jeannie wouldn't see when she did the washing.

Broichan sat for a long time staring down into the embers of the fire. Beside him Gemma and Brid had watched as he consulted first the streaming clouds, pink and gold from the setting sun, then the fall of the ogham sticks which he kept in a bag at his waist, and finally the deep red stone set in gold which hung from a cord around his neck. Now at last, the auguries clear, he raised his head.

'Brid.'

The two women jumped. Gartnait was not with them. He had departed earlier with his bow to hunt.

An imperious finger decorated with a carved agate ring beckoned Brid to her feet. 'It is decided. You will return to Craig Phádraig with me. We ride at dawn.'

'No!' Brid's cry of anguish echoed above the sound of water from the burn and the crackle of the dying fire, and spiralled up towards the clouds.

Broichan rose to his feet. He was taller than her by several hand-spans and his eyes were like flint. 'You will obey, Niece. Pack your belongings now, before we sleep.'

'Mama –' Brid threw an imploring look at Gemma but her mother refused to meet her eye.

'You must do as my brother says, Brid.' Gemma's voice, when she spoke at last, was shaking.

'I will not go!' Brid's face reflected livid colour from the dying sun. 'You cannot make me. I have power too.' She drew herself up to her full height and held Broichan's gaze. 'I can bind the storms, and I can ride the wind. I can hunt with the wildcat and run with the deer. I can catch and keep a man!' She veiled her gaze hastily. She must not let him read her thoughts, must not let him know about Adam.

Broichan stared at her thoughtfully. There was something like a small sardonic twitch of humour in his eyes as he held out his hand and without seeming to move caught hold of her wrist. 'So, little cat, you think you can duel with me,' he murmured. 'Such confidence, such foolishness.' He seized her chin in his other hand and forced her face close to his, his eyes boring into hers. 'Peace, little wild one. You are my servant and you will obey me.' He reached for the translucent red stone ball in its golden setting and held it for a moment before her eyes. In seconds the eyelids began to close and she became still.

'So.' Broichan pushed her towards her mother. 'Put her to bed, then pack her bag. I will take her tomorrow at first light. She shall ride in her sleep across the saddle like a bag of oats and at Craig Phádraig if she disobeys me I shall chain her by the neck like a slave.' He turned the full force of his gaze on Gemma's terrified face. 'I do not allow disobedience, Sister, from any of my family. Ever.'

Adam had finally given up all hope of seeing Brid again when he met Gartnait on the mountain. He followed Brid's brother and stood watching as he stooped and, picking up his chisel, squatted at the foot of the stone to work on a curved design. It was, Adam saw suddenly, a graceful, very realistic serpent.

'You must go back.' Gartnait spoke without looking up at him. Both he and Gemma could remember some of the English they had learned.

'Why?' Adam was suddenly tongue-tied with embarrassment.

'It is not safe. You will be seen. Brid was careless.'

'Why is it so wrong for me to be here with you?'

Gartnait glanced up at him. His tanned, weather-beaten face was dusty from the stone chippings, his strong hands callused but gentle on his tools. He leaned forward to blow at the work and rubbed at it with his thumb.

'Your father serves the gods. That is how you found the way.'

Adam frowned. 'There is only one God, Gartnait.'

The young man squinted at him and then down at his handiwork. 'The Jesus god? His followers say there is only one god. Is it he your father serves?'

'Jesus, yes.' Adam was uncomfortable. Jesus and Brid – or Brid's brother – were incompatible.

'Yet how can you believe this when all around you the gods are there? Brid told me you and she saw the Lady in the waterfall.'

Adam blushed to the roots of his hair. Surely Brid would not have told her brother what had happened between them? 'It is what we are taught. Only one God,' he repeated stubbornly.

'And yet you have been taught the way. How to walk between our world and yours.' Gartnait leaned closer to the stone again, the tip of his tongue protruding between his teeth as he concentrated on an intricate corner, lifting the hard stone with his sharpened blade as though it were a flake of mud.

'No one taught me to come here.' Adam frowned. 'I found it by myself. Though sometimes I can't find the way – I don't know why.' He was feeling more and more uncomfortable.

Gartnait sat back on his heels. He stared at Adam thoughtfully. 'That is because the way is not always open,' he said at last. 'It has to be taken when the time is right. The moon, the stars, the north wind. They must all be in the right place.' He smiled gravely and changed the subject abruptly. 'Brid likes you.'

Adam blushed again. 'I like her.' He turned slightly to stare back down the hillside. 'Where is she?' he asked as casually as he could.

'She has gone to work with our uncle. He is teaching her.'

Adam felt a sharp pang of disappointment – and fear. 'I was hoping to see her. How long will she be working for him?'

'Many years. Nineteen.' Gartnait gave another of his slow smiles. 'But I will tell her you came.' He looked up again. 'A-dam, do not go to look for her. She has gone to Craig Phádraig. You cannot find her. Do not try. And she must not try to see you either. It is not allowed. Broichan would kill her if he knew she had been with you. He will not allow anyone to travel between our worlds as you have travelled. It is only for the few. And she is not for you, A-dam.' He hesitated as though wondering whether to speak further. 'Brid is dangerous, A-dam. I who love her, say that. Do not let her hurt you.' He struggled to find the right words. 'She studies the ways of the wildcat. Her claws can kill. If you see her again she will surely, in the end, bring death. Death to you and to me and to Gemma.'

'I don't understand.' Adam's bitter disappointment was edged with fear. 'Why can't I see her? Why can't I travel here? What is so wrong?' He concentrated on the one piece of Gartnait's statement he truly understood. 'I bet you've been down to the village where I live.'

Gartnait gave a sudden snort. His eyes were humorous slits of silver and he looked for a moment very like his sister. 'I went once. Only on the hill. I do not have your courage. I did not go down.'

'Well, can I at least go and see your mother?' Adam fought back the misery which was threatening to overwhelm him. 'I want my knapsack.'

Gartnait frowned, then he nodded, relenting. 'Brid hid your things when our uncle came. I will show you. Putting down his tools he stood up, dusting his hands. He glanced at the canvas bag on Adam's shoulder and grinned. 'You have chocolate cake?' he asked mischievously.

Biting back his tears, Adam smiled back and nodded. 'And for Gemma too.'

They ate it by the fire, washed down with weak heather ale from the silver jug.

'What is Brid studying?' Adam asked at last. His precious knapsack lay at his feet.

'Poetry and music; prophecy and divination and history and genealogy,' Gartnait replied, all words, Adam realised, as Gartnait stumbled through them, miming with his hands, which he and Brid had used over their months together. 'It takes many years of study.'

'She must be clever.' He knew that already.

'She is. Very.' Gartnait frowned again. How clever Adam could not begin to know.

'When is she coming home?'

Gemma smiled. 'He is so sad his friend is missing.' She was speaking to the air above the fire.

Adam felt himself growing red once more.

'She will not come back to you, A-dam.' Gartnait spoke firmly. 'She must serve her people now. She is no longer a child. And that is for the best.'

'But she will come back to see you?' Adam could feel the cold hard kernel of misery in his stomach growing steadily larger. He looked from one to the other desperately.

Gemma leaned forward at last and with a quick glance at Gartnait she smiled. 'Poor A-dam. Perhaps she will come to see you. After the long days come, after Lughnasadh. I have told my brother he must bring her to see me then.'

And with that, not seeing Gartnait frown and shake his head, Adam had to be content.

At first he found he could put her out of his mind by concentrating on his school work, at least during the week. His days were spent in study, his evenings after the long drive and cycle home were spent in homework. Often now his father was there in the evenings, attempting to entertain his son with stories of the parish, with extra books bought in Perth and once or twice invitations to go, father and son, to meals with parishioners further up the glen.

Each weekend Adam would climb to the stone and each time he would be disappointed. No Gartnait. No Brid. In his loneliness he sat on the mountainside feeling the wind stirring his hair, his bird book and binoculars beside him, his sketchpad on his knee, and alone he would consume the cake he brought with him each time for Brid.

'So, Brid, your power is growing.' Broichan was standing behind her on the summit of a small hill overlooking the great loch out of which poured the River Ness. He had been watching her from behind an outcrop of rock, listening to the ringing incantation, watching the thrusting, bellying cloud split at her direction overhead and stream away to the north and to the south, leaving the black rocks of the hill bathed in golden sunshine.

With a start Brid lost her concentration and the clouds veered back on course. There was a sizzle of lightning, a sharp crack of thunder. Broichan laughed. 'I still out-magic you, Niece, never forget it!'

'But you don't out-magic Columcille, I hear.' Brid threw her

59

head back and laughed. She was energised by the storm, strong, invincible. 'He banished the beast you put in the loch to destroy him. The whole court has heard how he brought you close to death as a punishment for your treatment of one of your slavegirls and only saved you with his magic healing stone when you gave her up to him!' It was starting to rain. She raised her face and welcomed the feeling of ice-cold needles on her skin, missing as she did so the fury of her uncle's expression.

'You dare to speak to me of Columcille!'

'I dare!' She almost spat at him. 'You have taught me well, Uncle. My power is indeed growing!' And soon, when I have learned enough I shall go home to A-dam. She veiled her thoughts carefully from her uncle, with a little smile. She had seen Adam in her dreams and in her scrying ball of crystal and she knew that she had him in her snare. He would wait for her, forever if need be.

'Poor little cat. So confident. So foolish.' Broichan's voice was soft and velvety. Its menace brought her to her senses abruptly. 'Don't ever cheat on me, little Brid.' He held out his hand to her and against her will she found herself drawn to him. 'If you do, I shall feel obliged to give you a demonstration of my powers.' He smiled. 'Your brother, I think. My gatekeeper. His job is nearly done –'

'You wouldn't harm him!' Brid hissed at him.

'Indeed I would. My powers are unstoppable, as Columcille will discover when I recall the monster I put there to devour him.' Broichan smiled again. 'Beware, little cat. Stay obedient. Stay careful.'

He glanced up at the storm as he released her and turned away, leaving her standing where she was, her long white tunic and woollen cloak drenched to her skin. As he disappeared from sight the sky shuddered under a new bolt of lightning which hurtled past her and buried itself in the boiling, hissing waters of the loch.

The summer holidays came at last. Adam grew tanned and sturdy and once again, tentatively, he began to be friends with Mikey and Euan in the village.

He had been to kick a ball on the field behind the kirkyard with the boys after his supper and was walking back, late, up the street as the luminous dusk hung over the hills. In the distance on the west-facing side of the mountain he could see the sunlight still glowing on the dark cliffs, turning them the colour of pink damask. Where he was the shadows were dark. It was the sad time of day; the time that always filled him with melancholy. Kicking at the stones on the path he made his way reluctantly in at the gate and was brought up short by a hiss from behind him.

'A-dam! Here! I wait for you.' The piercing whisper made his heart leap with excitement. He stared round, confused. 'Brid?'

'Here. Here.'

He could see her now, crouching behind the stone wall in the shelter of a clump of rhododendron bushes. 'I wait for you at Gartnait's stone and you not come.' She was taller than last year, her hair braided, her figure fuller. She was dressed in a tunic as she always was, but this one was richer, embroidered, reaching down to her ankles, and her slim arms were adorned with gold bangles. 'Come.' She put her finger to her lips and smiled. It was the same impish grin that he remembered, though the face was more mature, the eyes less light-hearted.

With a glance at the forbidding blank windows of the manse he ducked behind the bushes out of sight and crouched beside her in the darkness under the glossy leaves.

She pressed her lips against his cheek. 'Hello, A-dam.'

'Hello, you.' He hesitated, embarrassed as he felt her hands pressing against his chest.

'Is your father there?' She was whispering and he could feel her hair tickling his face.

'I don't know.' There were no lights on in the house that he could see.

She had found his hand. Grabbing it she pulled him to his feet and they stood together, peering out across the grass. 'Come.' She gave a small tug at his wrist.

The gate could be seen from his father's study. He glanced again at the dark square windows and his courage failed him. 'This way,' he whispered. 'We'll go over the back.'

They ducked hand in hand into the shadows beneath the apple trees and ran round the house towards the regimented rows of potatoes and onions. Skirting the beds of vegetables, Adam led her to the pile of cut logs stacked against the wall, and out of sight of every window in the house save that of the empty kitchen he pulled her up to scramble over the loose stones and jump down onto the soft springy grass at the edge of the lane.

By the time they had reached the steep climb through the wood beside the burn they were both out of breath and laughing.

'Quickly, quickly, my mother will have food.' Brid's hair was slipping from its braids. Far above them the stone was still in sunlight. It was strange to stand in the shadowed valley and see the distant illumination like a spotlight. Adam stopped, looking up, and he shivered. 'I hate it when the glen gets dark before the mountain. I always want to be up there, where I can see the setting sun.'

'We go up.' She looked at him closely, her head to one side. 'You are growing big, A-dam.'

'So are you,' he retaliated. They both smiled and suddenly she had turned and set off ahead of him at the run. He was after her in a flash and had caught up with her before she had gone a dozen yards. They were in a small mossy dell, sheltered by a stand of silver birch. Somewhere out of sight Adam could hear the trickle of water from a hidden burn.

It was she who pushed against him, nuzzling his neck with her lips, she who, fumbling with his buttons, undid his shirt and pushed it off his shoulders, she who fondled and stroked his chest till he lost his breath in the back of his throat and was galvanised at last to reach for her body through the embroidered gown. With a throaty laugh she undid the girdle at her waist and with a small wriggle let the garment fall to her feet, leaving her naked in his arms, dragging at the belt which fastened his shorts.

This time they took longer, savouring one another's bodies, touching each other with gentle exploratory fingers which only gradually grew more urgent until at last Adam pushed her back and threw himself upon her, feeling his whole being expending itself between her lithe, compliant thighs.

When it was over they lay in sleepy contentment for a while. Then she slid from beneath him and climbing to her feet picked bits of moss and fern from her body, completely unembarrassed as she walked across the clearing to the stream which she found running through the rocks. Cupping the water in her palms she washed herself, then she turned. 'Now you, A-dam.'

Spent, he lay back on the grass. 'Not yet. I want to rest.'

'Now, A-dam.' He remembered the stern tone, but not in time. The double palm-load of icy water caught him full in the face.

He only caught up with her as they reached the stone. Laughing, he imprisoned her against it, a hand on either side of her shoulders, not letting her wriggle away. 'A kiss for a forfeit.'

'No, A-dam. Not here.' Suddenly she was afraid.

It was his turn to be stern. 'A kiss, Brid, or I won't let you go.'

'No, A-dam.' She tried again to wriggle free. 'Not here. We will be seen.' She was angry. Her eyes narrowed and he was astonished at the sudden change in her expression.

'Seen?' He did not release her. 'By Gartnait?'

'By the god.' She looked defiant.

'Oh, Brid.' Irritated, he released her and stepped back. 'You think there are gods everywhere. I've told you it isn't true. There is only one true God.'

'I know.' Stepping away from the stone she dusted herself off furiously. 'So *you* say. The Jesus god.' The Jesus god was powerful. His servant Columcille had several times now outwitted Broichan, to Broichan's fury. But then Broichan's strength had rallied . . . She put her uncle hastily out of her mind. There must be no possibility of him probing her thoughts and discovering Adam there. Broichan had brought her south himself, to visit her mother whilst he went on to Abernethy. There would be several long blissful days before he returned, days she intended to spend with Adam.

'Jesus won't care if we kiss here, anyway. Crosses are idolatrous.' Adam had shoved his hands into his pockets. His face was burning suddenly. He was remembering the kirk and his father's grey haggard face above him in the pulpit, the burning eyes boring down into his. He shivered as Brid reached for his hand.

The bothy was deserted. Brid did not seem worried by Gemma's absence. Quite the contrary, as it gave them more time together. Sitting down by the fire Adam waited while she brought him some heather ale, then he pulled her down beside him. 'So, tell me about your studies.'

She shook her head. 'That is not allowed.'

'Why?' He stared at her wide-eyed.

'Because it is secret. I am not permitted to say.'

'That's silly.' He leaned forward and picking up a stick poked the fire with it. A tongue of flame shot from between the peats. Standing on a stone beside it was one of Gemma's iron cooking pots. The familiar succulent smell of venison stew seeped from beneath the lid. 'Where is your mother?' He changed the subject abruptly.

Brid shrugged. 'She will come.' She glanced over her shoulder and frowned. 'She and Gartnait are near.'

Following her gaze Adam stared into the old pine trees. The red-barked trunks caught the evening light and glowed with a warm intensity, but behind them the shadows were cool and dark. He could see nothing in the heart of the wood.

Brid had risen to her feet. She was staring anxiously, her hands clasping and unclasping on the folds of her skirt. 'Something is wrong.'

Adam was watching her, catching something of her anxiety. 'Should we hide?'

She shook her head, concentrating, and he fell silent.

'My uncle,' she whispered suddenly. 'He is here in my head. There is blood! Someone is hurt. Gartnait!' She had gone very white.

He did not ask her how she knew. Nervously he moved behind her. 'What do we do?' he asked under his breath.

'Wait.' She raised her hand, gesturing him back, then she spun to face him.

'This way!' she cried. She was already running towards the trees.

They found Gartnait lying beneath one of the old pines, his head cradled on his mother's lap. His face was like chalk and his eyes were closed. The shoulder of his tunic was soaked in blood.

Gemma looked up. 'Brid?' The one word was a desperate plea.

Brid was already on her knees by her brother, her hands flying over his body, barely touching him as though feeling for his wounds.

'How is he?' Adam knelt beside her. He smiled uncertainly at Gemma and shyly reached over to pat her hand.

'A-dam. Good boy.' Gemma's face was tired, but she managed to return the smile.

'What happened?'

She shook her head. 'The tree break. Gartnait should know not to be there.' She gestured at the fallen branch with its rotten shredded broken end and near it the axe Gartnait must have been wielding when he was hit.

Brid had pulled away the blood-soaked fabric of the shirt. 'It was Broichan. He has done this to punish me.' She was tight-lipped.

'Broichan?' Gemma stared at her, shocked.

Brid looked up, her face hard. 'Broichan. Enough. I will make Gartnait better. He is hurting.' She glanced up at Adam. 'I will make my brother sleep while we clean the wound.'

He did not stop to ask her how. 'Shall I fetch some water?'

She nodded. 'Good. And moss. From the wood box under the lamp.'

'Moss?' He hesitated at the word but she was already cutting away her brother's shirt with the small knife she carried in her girdle.

Adam filled a leather bucket with cold water from the burn and found the moss as she had predicted in a small chest in the hut below a bronze candlestick. Also in the box were some small pots of ointment. He sniffed them cautiously and decided to take them all.

Brid nodded approval when he put his finds beside her. Gartnait was lying before her quietly, his face relaxed, his eyes closed. Adam watched as with neat deft fingers Brid swabbed the deep bruised cut she had exposed over Gartnait's collar bone and applied one of the ointments he had produced. Satisfied that it was properly cleansed and sealed she packed the wound with moss and while Adam held it in place deftly bandaged it with her own girdle.

She glanced up at Adam and gave a quick, worried smile of approval. 'You make good healer.'

He smiled. 'I want to be a doctor when I grow up.'

'Doctor?'

'Healer.'

She nodded. 'Good. Now, Gartnait must come back.' She put her palm flat over the unconscious young man's forehead and sat quietly, her eyes closed.

Adam watched, intrigued. 'What are you doing?' he whispered at last.

She glanced up, surprised. 'I put him to sleep so he could go away from the pain. He waited while we make it better. Now I go and tell him he can come back. The pain is not so bad, and it is better he come to home and we make him medicine to stop the hot time coming.'

'The fever, we call it,' Adam corrected her. He was impressed. He could see the young man's eyelids fluttering beneath Brid's commanding hand. It seemed to Adam only a matter of seconds before Gartnait was sitting up, staring round him groggily, and not long after that that they were making their way back towards the hut, Brid and Adam supporting him, one bent beneath each shoulder, Gemma hurrying ahead to stir up the fire and set a pot of water over the flames to heat.

Brid had, it seemed, a store of medicaments ready for just such an occasion. Adam watched as she brought a woven bag out of the hut and produced an array of small packages. Inside were numerous substances, most of which he guessed had dried herbs of various kinds.

A handful of this and a pinch of that were thrown into the steaming water. A bitter, strong smell began to flavour the air. Gartnait caught Adam's eye and smiled wryly. 'Will not taste like chocolate cake.'

Adam laughed. If the young man's sense of humour had returned he was starting to mend, in spite of the startling pallor of his face and the purple bruise which was beginning to spread down his cheekbone.

To Adam's relief the venison stew was placed back on the fire beside Brid's medicine and, thanks to Gartnait's sudden healthy hunger, it was not long before they were all eating bowls of it, sopped up with chunks of coarse bread torn from the loaf.

'Brid?' Only once her son was settled, his arm in a rough linen sling across his chest, did Gemma at last turn to her daughter. 'What has Broichan to do with this business?' Her eyes were sharp on her daughter's face.

Brid scowled. 'He threatened to hurt Gartnait.'

'Why?'

'He does not trust me. My power is too strong.'

Gemma stared at her for a moment, then she shook her head. 'That is no answer, daughter.'

'No.' Brid stuck out her chin. 'I have the power from you and from my father –'

'Your father is dead!' Gemma's voice was hard. 'His power was not strong enough, Brid. He was killed by the enemies of our people when he thought he was invincible. Nothing magic. A simple sword thrust in the dark from a raider, that was all it took to kill him.' She could not hide her scorn as she leaned forward and put her hand on Gartnait's forehead. 'You will endanger us all by mocking Broichan. My brother is the most powerful Druid in the land and you would do well not to forget it. You are being conceited and foolish in challenging him. And you are selfish. You put this boy's life at risk when you bring him here to our forbidden places.'

Adam had been following the conversation with great difficulty but as they all suddenly stared at him he looked away, embarrassed and frightened.

'A-dam has power of his own!' Brid retorted firmly. 'He is a traveller between the worlds and he is a healer –'

'He is not of our world, Brid.' Gemma's voice was very firm. 'We will give him food, then he must go. Before Broichan returns. And you must appease your uncle. You have seen the strength of his magic –'

'Mine is as strong –'

'Not strong enough!'

Adam had never seen Gemma angry before. Sitting, hugging his knees by the fire, he watched uncertainly as the two women confronted each other, their antagonism mounting. The moment of silence was intense.

And in the silence no one saw the dark shadow of Broichan materialise out of the night. Their visitor arrived so silently and so swiftly there was no possibility of escape. He was standing over them before any of them realised it and Adam could only look up and meet the furious, pale-blue eyes of Brid's uncle a few feet from him. His stomach knotted into a cold lump, and he felt the total paralysis of terror settle over him.

No one said anything for several seconds, then at last Gartnait put down his mug of ale and hauled himself painfully to his feet.

'Greetings to you, my uncle,' he said respectfully. Adam understood that much. What followed was wholly incomprehensible but Adam could follow the meaning of the gestures as clearly as though he understood every word. They did not bode well for him or for Brid.

Brid and Gemma were both very pale. They sat with downcast eyes and for all her earlier defiance, Adam could see that Brid's hands, still clutched around her beautifully decorated goblet, were shaking visibly. The man's voice grew louder. He appeared to be working himself into a furious rage.

Gartnait raised his chin. The young man's meekness vanished in a torrent of angry words. His eyes, dark and flashing, met those of his uncle and he was gesturing first at Brid and then at Adam.

The shouting match ended with such suddenness that the silence that succeeded it was shocking in its intensity. Terrified, Adam glanced from one to the other. Brid and her mother were white-faced. Gartnait beneath his defiance also looked afraid. Adam's blood seemed to have turned to ice. For a moment they all remained motionless, then Broichan stepped forward. For a long moment he stood over Adam, his eyes seeming to probe deep inside the boy's head. Adam shrank back. He could feel the strength of the man's mind inside his brain. It hurt him physically like a red-hot iron, and then suddenly it was over. Broichan spat on the ground in front of him. Then he stooped and seized Brid's wrist, hauling her to her feet. Her goblet fell from her hand. With a little cry she tried to pull back but he gripped her more tightly and dragged her away from the fire.

Adam looked from Gemma to Gartnait and back. Neither had moved a muscle. There were tears in Gemma's eyes.

'What is happening?' he cried suddenly. 'Do something. Don't let him take her.'

Gartnait shook his head. He gestured at Adam sharply to stay where he was. 'He has the right.'

'He doesn't. What's he going to do?' Adam scrambled up, bewildered.

'He takes her back to Craig Phádraig.' Gartnait shook his head. 'It is her destiny. He will not let her come back.'

'But he can't do that!' Adam was frantic. 'You can't just let him take her.'

'I can't stop him, A-dam,' Gartnait said quietly. 'It is her chosen life. And you must go. Now. You must not come back to the land beyond the north wind. Not ever.'

'What do you mean? Why not? What have I done? What's wrong with me?' Bewildered, the boy could feel tears in his own eyes.

'You live in another place, A-dam. The place beyond the stone. Beyond the mist.' Gartnait's gaze was on the retreating forms of Brid and Broichan. 'No one is supposed to go there or come from there. My uncle told me about it so that I could carve the stone. Brid followed me. She learned the way from me. She will learn about it in her studies, but it is secret. It is a secret which no man may tell. My uncle believes that we told you the way. I told him that your father is a powerful priest on your side of the stone, and that you learned the way from him, but he is still angry.'

'My father didn't teach me the way here. I found it myself.' Adam was confused. 'Or Brid shows me. What is so special? I don't understand. Why should a track through the wood be so secret?'

Gartnait frowned. 'It leads to the back of the north wind, where no man may go. Not Broichan himself, not Brid, not even me.' He sighed. 'I told you to beware my sister, A-dam. She is a daughter of the fire and her power will kill. Forget her, A-dam. She is not part of your destiny. Come, my young friend. I will walk with you.'

Adam shook his head, confused and miserable. 'No, you stay here. You shouldn't walk after your accident. And besides, you should stay with your mother –' He looked at Gemma for a moment.

She shook her head. 'Go, A-dam. You bring trouble for us, my son.' She gave a small sad smile and turning away, she disappeared inside the cottage.

Distressed, Adam hesitated. 'May I come back?' His face was burning with shame.

By the fire, Gartnait shook his head sadly as he turned back to the flames. He hoped Adam would never realise how close he had come to death that afternoon; how only his eloquence, courage and the fact that he had convinced Broichan of the power of Adam's father had saved the boy from the razor-sharp blade which, hidden in the older man's sleeve, had been destined for Adam's throat.

'Gemma?' Adam's voice was husky with misery. He had a sudden vision of his own mother crying and fighting with his father. Was he always destined to cause trouble for the people he loved?

She reappeared in the doorway and she held out her arms to him. He ran to her and she hugged him and kissed his cheek. 'No, A-dam. Never come back.' She softened the words with a gentle touch on his face, then she turned away once more and ducked inside.

5

Afew days later, to his surprise and delight, Adam found his old school friend, Robbie Andrews, waiting for him by the gate to the manse. The boy's face split into a huge grin as he punched Adam on the shoulder. 'Where have you been? I've been hanging around all afternoon.'

Adam shook his head. 'I've been up on the hill.' Mooching aimlessly around the stone. To no avail. There was no sign of Gartnait or Gemma or the cottage. He grinned back at Robbie, snapping out of his depression. Robbie, the son of the factor on the Glen Ross estate, had once been his best friend, but when Robbie's mother had died Robbie had gone to boarding school and stayed with his grandparents in Edinburgh. Robbie had, he now discovered, come to spend the summer with his father up at the factor's house on the estate.

'I've got a message for you.' Robbie glanced round conspiratorially. He was a tall thin boy with startling red hair, and at seventeen was a few months older than Adam. 'Come over here.' He ducked down out of sight of the manse's study window and led Adam back down the street and towards the river. Only when they were in the wood by the burn did he stop and find them a fallen tree trunk to sit on, out of reach of the spray from the waterfall. He reached into his pocket and produced a crumpled envelope. 'Here. It's from your mother.'

Adam stared at him. His mouth dropped open and he found he was having to fight a sudden urge to cry. It was two years, almost exactly, since his mother had left home and he had long ago given up hope of hearing from her ever again.

He put his hand out for the envelope and sat staring at it. It was her writing all right. Every thought of Brid and Gartnait fled from his brain as he turned it over and over in his hands.

'Aren't you going to open it?' Robbie was eager to know what it said.

Adam shook his head. He shoved it into his pocket and leaning forward, elbows on knees, picked up a moss-covered stone to throw towards the burn.

'She came to see my grandmother,' Robbie prompted him. 'She said she had written to you and you never bothered to answer. She said she understood that you must be very angry with her.'

'She never wrote.' Adam's voice was strangled. 'Not once.'

Robbie frowned. 'She said she did.'

There was a long silence. Adam was struggling to control his tears. When he managed to speak at last it was in a croak. 'How was she?'

'Good. She was looking very pretty.'

'Pretty?' Adam picked up on the word sharply.

Robbie nodded. 'She had a blue dress. And pearls round her neck. And her hair was kind of long and curly. Not like it used to be here.'

Adam bit his lip. The description did not fit the repressed, meek minister's wife who had been his mother. Perhaps his father was right. She had become a whore.

Miserably he stared at the narrow tumbling glitter of the water in front of him. He said nothing.

'Are you still planning to be a doctor?' Robbie threw his own stone at the water, angling it so it skittered over the rocks and disappeared over the edge into the whirling brown pools.

Adam nodded bleakly.

'Are you going to Aberdeen medical school or Edinburgh next year? Tell your father you want to go to Edinburgh. We could have some wizard fun together. It's great there, Adam. I'm going to read Classics.' The boy's face had lit up with enthusiasm. 'And I'm going to fly. They all say war is coming. If it does I want to be in the RAF.'

Adam shook his head. Talk at the Academy was all of war too. 'Then I hope they see you coming. You can't even ride a bike, if I remember, without pranging it!'

'That was a while ago, Adam. I can drive a car now! Grandfather taught me. He's got a Morris Cowley. And I've a licence to ride a motorbike. I can take you on the back!' His enthusiasm was beginning to cheer Adam up.

'What does your father say about all this?' Adam had always rather liked the factor, who used to take him and Robbie on bird-watching trips up in the hills when they were too young to go on their own.

'Och, he's fine about it. He doesn't care what we do.' He sounded just a little too casual. 'What about you, Adam? What about the minister?'

Adam grimaced. 'I can't wait to get my Highers and go.' It was true, he realised suddenly. Without Brid and her family, what had he to stay for?

It was nearly dark when Adam sat on the window seat of his attic room and took his mother's letter out of his pocket. He turned the envelope over several times and looked down at it. It had the one word *Adam* written on it. The sight of his mother's handwriting made him feel strange. First he thought he might cry; then he felt angry. He crumpled it up and threw it in his waste paper basket, overwhelmed by a feeling of lost betrayal, then as suddenly he dived on it and tore it open.

> My darling Adam,
> I have written to you several times before, but I don't know if you ever got my letters. It may be your father didn't pass them on.
> Please try and understand. I could not live with your father any more. Why need not concern you now, only believe me, I had no choice. I had to come away. I know how hurt and angry you must be with me. Please, let me explain. Your father won't let you come and see me now, but when you leave school, if you would like to, please come then. I love you so much and I miss you dreadfully.
> Your loving Mother.

Adam put down the letter. His eyes were full of tears. No, of course his father had not given him her letters. He looked at the piece of paper in his hand again. She did not say if she was alone or what she was doing. There was just an address, in Edinburgh, and those few impassioned words.

The light was on in his father's study. Pushing open the door without knocking Adam thrust the letter across the desk. 'Is it true? Did she write to me?'

Thomas stared at the letter. There was no anger in his face when he looked up at Adam, only a terrible haggard sorrow.

'And what was the sin you told me she had committed?' Adam wasn't sure where the courage had come from to allow him to speak to his father in this way.

Thomas's face darkened. 'That is not your business, boy.'

'Was it another man? Wee Mikey said she ran away with a Frenchman.' The question he had wanted to ask for so long burst out of him. 'Did she? Weren't we good enough for her?' Tears were pouring suddenly down his face.

His father stared at him without expression for several seconds, then at last he shook his head. 'I do not know, Adam, and I don't want to.' And that was all he would say.

The stone was silver in the moonlight, the old symbols showing clearly, their deep incisions darkened by lichen, their design as clear as the day they were cut. Adam stood looking at them miserably. The serpent, the crescent and the broken rod, and there, at the base, the mirror and the comb. He frowned. Gartnait had never copied the mirror on his stone. The designs had been finished last time he had seen him but that small corner of the stone was empty. He bent and touched the outline with his fingers. The mirror on his mother's dressing table, with her brush and comb, had been burned with all her other things on his father's bonfire. He had found the blackened ivory and splintered glass next to some charred pieces of brown fabric which had once been his mother's best dress.

He would see her again. Whatever she had done, she was still his mother. She wouldn't have gone if his father hadn't driven her away. Even if she had found someone else – his mind slid sideways around the thought, not able to confront it – she still loved him, her letter had said as much. And she missed him. His mind made up, he found himself smiling in the moonlight. He would go to Edinburgh next year, to study medicine as planned, and he would go and see his mother. And in the meantime he would write to her and tell her his news.

Chastened and obedient, Brid learned the names of the thirty-three kings. She learned the rituals of fire and water. She learned divination from the flight of birds, from the clouds and the stars, from the trees and the falling of the fortune sticks. She learned spells and incantations and healing. She began to learn the nature of the gods and goddesses and how to intercede with them and about the sprinkling of the blood; she learned about the soul which dwells within the body but which can fly free as a bird, to travel, to learn, and to hide and she learned how she too by dint of study and dreams and the use of sacred smoke could enter the dream and travel through the layers of time to the worlds beyond the world.

Her special study was the wildcat. She left the school as did the other women from time to time, completely alone, and followed the animals' secret trails into the hills. She studied their hunting and their killing. She studied their sleeping and their lazy washing on a hidden sunlit ledge amongst the rocks and cliffs. She studied their meeting and mating and the secret places where the she-cats raised their mewling kittens. She learned how to read the mind of the cat and then at last she began to walk in the paw prints of the creature, feeling its skin as her skin, tearing her prey, eating the sweet raw meat of hare or vole or game and licking the rich blood from her paws.

And back at the school in the evenings sometimes she spied on Adam in her dreams. Secretly she remembered the strength of his arms, the passion of his kiss, the soft boy's cheek above the newly rough man's whiskers, the deep thrust of his manhood, and she slipped from her meditation out into the plane where there is no time or place and all things are one, and she crept close to him to touch his lips with her own as he slept.

It was a few days after Adam took his final exam the following summer that he saw Brid again. She was waiting for him, as she had once before, near his house, and she dived on him as he climbed off his bicycle after a visit to Robbie to celebrate the start of the holidays.

'A-dam! A-dam! Where have you been? I have come for three days!' She threw her arms around his neck and kissed him on the mouth, then she pushed him away and punched him gently in the stomach. 'You forget Brid?'

'No.' Recovering from the shock of seeing her, his face broadened into a smile. 'No, I never forget Brid. How did you get back? What about your uncle?'

She smiled, and put her finger to her lips. 'I have persuaded him to be nice. I will tell you later.' She glanced round. 'Is it safe for me here?' She looked nervously up the street. She would never tell him the fear she had felt when she saw her first car, a black Alvis belonging to James Ferguson from Birnam, roaring along the narrow road leaving a trail of blue smoke.

Adam followed her gaze and then glanced back at the house. Behind him the manse would be empty. Jeannie Barron would have gone on the bus into Perth as she usually did on a Wednesday and his father would be visiting the cottage hospital. He nodded. 'No one will see us.' He smiled at her, still holding her hand. 'I tell you what, shall I fetch some cake?'

74

'Chocolate cake?' She looked at him archly.

'Maybe.'

She followed him nervously around the back of the house and even more hesitantly in at the back door.

'It's all right. There's no one here.'

He beckoned up the passage towards the kitchen.

'It's big. Like a castle.' She tiptoed over the flags in awe.

'No it's not.' He flung open the kitchen door and stopped in surprise. Jeannie Barron was standing at the table, up to her elbows in flour, rolling pastry.

It was too late to turn back. She had looked up and seen him. 'Well, young man. Did you have a good visit with Robbie? Did you remember to tell him to say hello from me to his grandmother –' She broke off abruptly as she saw Brid hovering behind him. 'So, who is this?'

Adam watched her eyes move quickly up and down, taking in Brid's long hair, her embroidered tunic, her soft leather skirt and her laced sandals. Her frown was so quickly hidden he wondered if he had imagined it.

'So, lassie, come in and let's be seeing you.'

Brid hesitated and Adam, turning, took her hand with a reassuring smile. 'This is Brid. Brid, this is Jeannie who makes chocolate cakes.'

Brid's face lit into a smile. 'I like chocolate cake.'

Jeannie nodded. 'I thought he couldn't have been eating them all by himself. Well, if you look in the pantry you'll find a new one I made specially for him.' She turned back to her dough. 'And what kind of a name is Brid, if I may ask?' Like Adam she had pronounced it Breed.

'It's short for Bridget,' Adam put in hastily. 'Sort of a nickname.'

'I see. And where do you come from then, lass? I don't think I've seen you before.'

'She lives in a village the other side of Ben Dearg,' Adam answered for her again. 'Her brother is the stone mason there.'

'I see. And you've no tongue in your head?' Once more the quick shrewd glance. Jeannie Barron had summed Brid up at once. A pretty tinker child, or perhaps foreign. More likely the latter in view of her silence. And besotted with young Adam, if she were any judge.

Adam had emerged from the pantry with the plate.

'Greaseproof is over there.' The floury hand waved towards the dresser. 'Then get you both from under my feet, if you please. I'm

75

here today so I can have Friday off and stay with my sister the whole weekend, and I've a lot to do before I'm away.'

Outside Brid rounded on him. 'I thought you said it would be safe. That is not your mother?'

'No. I told you. My mother's gone away.' Adam was fairly sure Jeannie would not mention the visit to his father.

'So, it is the woman who looks after the priest?'

He frowned. 'I wish you wouldn't call him a priest. It sounds so papist. I told you. He's a minister.'

'Sorry, A-dam.' She looked contrite. 'She makes nice cake.' Then, as she did so often she changed the subject, abruptly and without a second thought, dismissing Jeannie as no longer worthy of interest. 'Come. We go find Gartnait.'

They did, but not before she had pounced on Adam in the shelter of the lonely screed valley on the north side of the waterfall and laughingly begun to pull off all his clothes.

'A-dam! You are tall and big!' Her glance was deliberately provocative. She stood in front of him and slipped her tunic up over her naked breasts. 'Me too. I am big now.'

'Indeed you are.' He smiled. In the twelve months since he had last seen her, her breasts and hips had rounded and her slim child's legs had become more shapely.

They made love again and again and then after a respectful handful of cake had been given to the Lady in the waterfall they swam under the icy cascade. Afterwards they found a sheltered patch of sunlight where the wind couldn't chill them, and lay on the flat rocks to dry.

'I have studied the omens.' Brid was staring up at the sky. 'You and I will be together forever. I read the entrails of a doe before I ate her flesh as a cat. She told me so.'

'Brid!' Adam sat up. 'You are joking? That's disgusting!'

'No.' She smiled at him and pushed him back, her fingers playfully clawed as she raked them gently over his chest. 'I not joke.'

He stared up into her eyes and for an instant he was appalled by what he saw there. 'Brid –'

'Quiet, A-dam.' Her lips came down on his, and for a while he was silent, distracted from his thoughts by her hands.

When she at last lay back next to him, sated, he turned a sleepy head towards her. 'I thought you said you weren't allowed to talk about your studies?'

'I'm not.' She looked defiant.

'So you made all that stuff up? About the entrails?'

'I didn't make it up.' She sat up, her legs crossed, and looked down at him. 'Do you want me to show you?'

He looked at her and suddenly he was afraid again. The hardness he sometimes saw in her eyes was at such variance with her passion. He was confused. 'No!' He spoke sharply. 'It didn't really say you and I will be together forever?'

'It did.' She smiled, and he saw the small pink tip of her tongue flick across her lips. 'You and I make love together forever.'

He frowned. He had not thought about Brid and the future. The future contained university and medicine and a shining array of new opportunities. He wasn't at all certain yet how Brid fitted in, if at all. He shifted uncomfortably, watching her through narrowed eyes as she sat beside him, silhouetted against the brightness of the sky.

I told you to beware my sister, A-dam. She is a daughter of the fire and her power will kill. Forget her, A-dam. She is not part of your destiny.

Gartnait's words echoed in his head suddenly, and he shivered. 'You haven't told me yet why your uncle let you come back.'

'He has come to visit my brother and to see the stone. It is nearly finished.'

Adam sat up. 'You mean he's here too?'

'No. Today he rides to visit my other uncle, my father's brother . . .' She worked out the relationship on her fingers. 'Then he comes back from Abernethy in two, three days. And then I am staying here with Gemma until the snow comes. We can see each other all the time!'

She leaned over him and kissed him on the lips again.

Adam frowned. A shadow had drifted across the sun. 'Not all the time, Brid.' He raised himself onto one elbow. 'You remember I am going to be a doctor? I am going away to university in October.'

'To university? What is university?' She sat up and scowled.

'It's a place you go to study. Like school, but more difficult.' His voice rose with enthusiasm. 'Like you do with your uncle.'

'But I see you after you finish study. In the evening.' Her eyes were very intense, holding his.

He felt uncomfortable. 'No, Brid. We can't do that,' he said gently. 'I'm going to Edinburgh. It's a long way from here. I shall be staying there.'

'But you will come back? To see your father? Like I come back to see my mother and Gartnait.'

He looked away. The sun reflecting on the water made him screw up his eyes against the glare. 'Yes. I'll come back.'

He wondered if that was a lie. He never wanted to come back to the manse. Not if he could help it. But what if that meant he would never see Brid again? He looked back at her and gave her a reassuring smile. 'We've plenty of time, Brid. I don't go for weeks and weeks and weeks.' It still seemed like forever. Taking her hand he pulled her sharply so she tumbled forward into his arms. 'Let's make the most of now, shall we?' The future could take care of itself.

They never got as far as the stone, that day or the next. Adam went back to the manse and collected his camping things. He knew Jeannie probably suspected that he would not be sleeping in his small tent alone, but she said nothing, giving him a huge bag of food to keep him going while he watched the birds. Loaded with tent and sleeping bag and groundsheet, a Primus stove, saucepan, food, bird book and binoculars, he could hardly walk as he set off once more towards the hill. The weight did not matter. Brid was waiting for him, and anyway they were not going far.

They camped only a hundred yards from the falls. There, to his intense embarrassment, she gave him an intricately worked silver pendant on a chain, hanging it herself around his neck. 'For you, A-dam. Forever.'

'Brid! Men don't wear things like this!' He flinched uncomfortably as it nestled against his chest.

She laughed. 'Men in my world wear this with pride, A-dam. It is a love token.' She pulled the edges of his collar across to hide it and kissed him firmly on the lips. Before very long he had forgotten it was there.

Two evenings later, with the dark blue velvet of the sky sprinkled with pale stars, Gartnait found them.

'How long have you been here?' He looked furious.

'Not long.' Brid glared at him.

'I look for you everywhere. Everywhere!' he repeated. 'Broichan is at our mother's house. He is angry!' The emphasis he placed on the last word spoke volumes.

'I have a holiday.' Brid looked mutinous.

'Holiday?' Gartnait repeated the word puzzled. Then without waiting for elucidation he grabbed her wrist and pulled her to her feet. 'You have been here with A-dam?' His face betrayed a succession of emotions: anger; fear; suspicion. 'Brid, you have stayed here? *Here*? On the other side?'

Brid's chin rose, if anything, a little higher. But there was a touch of colour in her cheeks. 'I like it here. I saw A-dam's village; I saw his house,' she said defiantly.

'And what will you say to our uncle?'

'I will say nothing. I came to see our mother.'

Adam had not dared meet Gartnait's eye. He knew what they had done was wrong. It was his fault. He was the man. He should have said no. He should have sent her away. Only they both knew that was impossible. Even now, as he looked at Brid and saw the heightened colour in her cheeks, the silky sheen of her hair, still dishevelled from their love-making in the tent only minutes before Gartnait had appeared, and the line of her long slim tanned thigh beneath her skirt, he could feel his desire running rampant through his veins. Clenching his fists he looked away from her. 'Can't you say you couldn't find her?' he said to Gartnait.

'You want me to tell my uncle lies?' Gartnait looked at him disparagingly.

'Not lies.' It was Adam's turn to blush. 'Just say you looked everywhere.'

'He knows I looked everywhere,' Gartnait replied bitterly. 'He knows there was nowhere else to look.'

'He must not know you have come here,' Brid put in anxiously.

'Nor you, little sister.' Gartnait shook his head. 'Or he will kill us both.'

There was a moment of silence. Adam felt the small hairs stand up suddenly on the back of his neck.

Brid's huge grey eyes were fixed on her brother's. It was as if they had forgotten he was there.

Adam swallowed hard. 'Look, I know he'll be angry, but I'll explain . . .' His voice tailed away. He was remembering his previous encounters with Broichan.

Brid was very pale. 'A-dam. You stay here in your tent. I will go and see my uncle. Then I will come back.' She sounded very confident.

'But I should come with you.'

'No, you know that is not possible. Better he does not know I have ever seen you again, my A-dam.' Her voice softened suddenly as she saw his stricken face and she darted over to drop a kiss on his forehead. 'I will come back soon. You see –' she broke off abruptly and he saw her gaze pass to the edge of the clearing.

Adam craned round in sudden terror and saw to his intense relief a familiar face staring at them over the rim of the bank. His friend, Robbie, was scrambling towards them, grinning broadly, when he stopped abruptly, his whole expression frozen into fear. Adam looked round and saw that Gartnait had drawn the knife he wore habitually at his belt.

'Gartnait!' he cried, alarmed. 'He is my friend. It's all right.' The whole afternoon was turning into a hideous nightmare. 'Put it away. He's my friend.'

Reluctantly Gartnait sheathed the knife, but his face remained sullen and hostile as Robbie, after a moment's hesitation, came forward.

'Adam, you old devil, I didn't know you were going to camp.' He recognised the tent. He had one just like it and in the past the two boys had often camped side by side. He was staring first at Brid and then at Gartnait. 'Who are your friends?'

Adam frowned, reluctant to introduce them. Gartnait and Brid were a part of his own private world, his secret world, which had nothing to do with home. He repeated their names without enthusiasm. 'They were just going,' he added as the two young men bowed at one another stiffly.

Brid reached up and unself-consciously kissed Adam on the cheek. 'I will see you soon.' She smiled at him and touched his face with her hand. For a fraction of a second she clawed her fingers and he thought he heard a gentle purr. Then she and Gartnait had gone.

Robbie whistled. 'Who on earth were they?' He sat down next to Adam and stared at him hard. 'They're not from round here. What weird clothes!'

Adam was shivering. Not for the first time he realised that something about Brid frightened him intensely. 'I met them over the other side of the hill,' he said slowly. 'Gartnait is a stone carver. He travels around.'

'And the beautiful young lady?' Robbie's eyes were alight with intrigue.

Adam forced himself to smile. 'She's his sister.'

Robbie punched him on the shoulder. 'You randy old devil! How did you manage to get yourself a girlfriend like that!'

Adam flushed painfully and he felt a shock of annoyance go through him as well as fear. In spite of himself he glanced round. But they were alone in the centre of the huge bowl of the surrounding hills. 'Don't be daft. She's no one. Just someone I met.' Even as he said it he felt he was betraying her, but Brid and Gartnait and Robbie were worlds apart and he intended to keep them that way. He felt the cold weight of silver on his chest suddenly and shrugged the open neck of his shirt closed, surreptitiously fastening the button. He had no intention of letting Robbie see the pendant round his neck. As soon as he was alone he would remove it.

He stayed alone in the tent that night, but she did not return. Nor the next, and on the Saturday Adam packed up his gear and took it back to the manse.

With something like relief he put her out of his mind. Three times the following week he cycled over to Robbie's and together they planned what they would do when they got to Edinburgh. It was finally beginning to dawn on Adam that he was actually leaving, and his thoughts turned to Brid less and less often, visiting him only at night in his dreams. Her silver charm was hidden in a box in the bottom of one of his drawers.

His results arrived; his grades were excellent and his place at medical school was confirmed. Numb with shock and excitement he received the news in his father's study and stood looking down at the letter in his hand.

'Congratulations, Adam.' Thomas smiled at him. 'I am very proud of you.'

Adam was speechless for a moment. He read the letter again. There was no doubt; there it was in black and white.

'A great step,' his father went on. 'You'll make a fine doctor one day, son.'

'Thank you, Father.' At last Adam found his tongue.

In half an hour it hit him with dizzying force. He was on his way. He was going to the city. He was leaving the manse forever. He did not intend to come back, even in the vacations. He was going to be a doctor.

This time he did not give Brid a second's thought.

Broichan was waiting when Brid returned to the bothy with Gartnait, seated in front of the fire. There was no sign of Gemma.

'So, you have been trespassing beyond our world. You have lied and cheated and broken your vows!'

'No!' Brid faced him, her cheeks flaming. 'I have betrayed no one!'

'You have betrayed me. And you have betrayed your gods.' Broichan had not raised his voice. 'On your horse. We leave now for the north.'

'But I'm staying here –'

'You are staying nowhere!' Broichan stood up, towering over her. 'You have betrayed your brother and your mother. You have betrayed the blood that runs in your veins. You have betrayed your calling –'

'You have no proof of any of this! You are guessing –'

'I have proof enough. I have watched you in the fire and in the water. I have seen you lying like a drab with the boy son of the Jesus priest.' He moved towards her and Brid flinched backwards. 'Collect your bags and come now, or I shall tie you like a slave and drag you behind my horse!'

She had no choice. Trembling, Brid collected her belongings, kissed Gemma, who had been waiting silent and afraid inside the bothy, and climbed onto her pony. Somehow she managed to keep her head high, the colour still strong in her cheeks, as Broichan led the way up onto the track where his servants and his escort were waiting.

The sun had barely moved a hand's breadth across the sky when the riders crossed over into the next glen and were lost from sight.

Once back at Craig Phádraig, she settled into the routine of the seminary, avoiding Broichan as much as possible, her defiance secret, her anger against him simmering, comforting herself in the lonely evenings with the knowledge that Broichan was jealous of her power and by watching Adam from afar. When he joined Robbie for bicycle rides or hikes in the hills she could see them from the body of a skylark, high above the fields; when he lay at night in bed, dreaming of her, she knew it and crept to the window sill in the body of a village cat, purring with secret delight, and when he swam in the burn up on the hillside, relishing the last of the summer's heat, she thought herself into the slim brown body of a mountain trout and flicked her tail against his naked thighs.

It was while she was watching Adam in her quiet cell one stormy autumnal night that Broichan walked in and caught her.

'So, little cat, you have learned to spy on your lover.' Broichan's voice was a silky murmur.

Brid jumped with fear. The small room, lit only by the smoky flame of an oil lamp, was full of leaping shadows.

Watching her, Broichan smiled. 'Such a waste. You have great gifts, my niece. You could have been a priestess, a seer, a bard, who knows, even a queen.' He folded his arms under his cloak. 'But you choose to betray me. You cannot be trusted with your talents – you waste them on a village boy and sully your initiation vows. Only one thing can redeem you, little Brid. Your blood shall be given to the gods with your brother's when the time comes to dedicate the stone, so that your soul can be born again in a fresh guileless body –'

'No!' She made to stand up, her face as white as alabaster, but he raised his hand and held it in front of her.

Between his fingers, swinging at the end of a fine gold chain, was the egg-shaped polished red stone, its translucence gleaming in the light of the flame. 'Don't move, little Brid. Don't even blink your eyes. You see, I can enchant you with the magic sleep and hold you here until I need you.' He laughed softly. 'Poor little niece. So clever, but not quite clever enough.' He reached into the depths of his clothes and brought out a long-bladed knife. He held it for a moment in front of her unblinking eyes, letting the light of the flickering flame play on the gleaming blade. Gently he pressed it flat against her cheek. She did not flinch and he chuckled. 'You will remember nothing of this, little Brid. Nothing at all when you awake. You will obey me and you will stay quietly here, to await your fate.' Tucking the knife away again he leaned forward and snapped his fingers under her nose.

She jumped and stared at him, blinking. 'Uncle –'

'You work too hard, Niece.' Broichan gave a cruel laugh. 'Sleep now. I have great plans for you, my dear.'

He walked out of the small room. Behind him the flame on the lamp flickered.

The evening before he was due to go to Edinburgh Adam walked up one last time towards the stone. His trunk was packed and strapped, ready to go, in the hall. Tomorrow the carter would pick it up and take it to the station.

He was feeling a little guilty as he climbed the hillside. Overwhelmed with excitement about the future he had spared practically no thought for Brid and Gartnait at all over the last month. In his knapsack was a chocolate cake. A peace offering and perhaps a farewell.

The stone was in shadow. Panting slightly he stood as he had so often, running his fingers over the intricate designs carved on it. Below him, the hillside fell away into the velvet night. High above, on the west-facing slope, the sunlight still reflected pink onto the blackened heather and the rock. The evening was very still. He could hear no birds. Even the wind in the sparse grasses had died. He slung his bag off his shoulder and dropped it, then he stepped away from the stone. The Z-shaped cut – he thought of it as a lightning bolt, though Gartnait called it the broken spear – threw a hard narrow shadow across the smoothed surface of the granite. Beside it the carved serpent writhed unfinished, the tail only half drawn. It was the only incomplete carving on the stone. Under it the mirror looked as though someone had been scraping at it. The lichen had been rubbed away. He frowned. That was strange. As far as he knew he was the only person in the whole world, apart from Brid and Gartnait, who ever came to this lonely spot.

He walked slowly round, mentally recording each detail of the place that had meant so much to him, as though already he knew he would never come back. His plan was to leave the cake behind. He was pretty sure that Brid would not find it, but the birds and animals of the high screes would.

The sound of Brid's voice behind him made him leap out of his skin. 'A-dam! I knew you would come. I sent a message in my head to bring you here.' Suddenly she was sobbing. She threw her arms around his neck, then, uncharacteristically she drew back. 'I must come with you. My uncle plans to kill me.' The statement, so flat and unemotional, stunned him into total silence. 'He put me into a magic sleep, and he told me what he was going to do. But I have more power than him!' She let out a wild burst of laughter. 'I pretended to sleep, but I heard him. I did not make a sign. I did not move my face, but when he had gone I made my plans. I took one of his best ponies and rode in the middle of the night, and I rode until I came home.' She smiled wearily, a humourless, cold smile which chilled him. 'He plans to kill my brother too when the stone is finished. He knows now that Gartnait and I know what the stone is for. It marks the gateway to other times and to knowledge that is forbidden to all but the highest initiates, so we must both die. You see the mirror? That is the sign that from here you can see through the reflections into other worlds. That is how I have come to you. I am not going back. There is only a small part of the work left. When the serpent is finished Broichan will give orders that we are to be buried under the stone – a sacrifice to the gods.' The hardness vanished and she kneaded her fists into her eyes like a child. 'Gartnait has gone. He has gone south with my mother three days ago. He wanted me to go too, but I stayed. I waited for you.'

Adam had a strange cold feeling in the pit of his stomach. 'Brid, what are you talking about? Your mother and Gartnait would never leave you. Your uncle would never kill you. This is nonsense. All of it.'

'Nonsense?' she echoed wildly. 'Broichan is the chief priest of this land. His word is the law. Even the king would not defy him if it was over a matter of the gods.' Her eyes hardened again and he recoiled. 'A-dam, don't you see, you have to save me! I have to live in your world now. I am going to come with you. To your school in Edinburgh!'

'No!' Adam stepped back further. 'No, Brid. I'm sorry, but you can't. It's impossible.'

'Why can't I?' Her eyes were fixed on his face.

'Because you can't.' He was filled with horror at the idea.

'You can't stop me! A-dam, I have nowhere else to go.'

'Go with Gartnait and Gemma. You belong with them.'

'I can't. They have gone to the south.'

'Then you must follow them. This is nonsense. Brid, I can't take you to Edinburgh! I'm sorry.'

'But you love me, A-dam.'

'Yes . . .' He paused. 'Yes, I love you, Brid.' It was the truth, but at the same time, he realised suddenly, there was a part of him which would be quite glad never to see her again. Her angry outbursts and her possessiveness, her wild declamations, had become alarming. And at the same time there was a part of him which had already begun to separate itself from Pittenross and everything there. He softened his voice. 'Our love is for here. For the holidays. There is no place for you in Edinburgh. None at all.' He hesitated. 'Brid, women are not allowed where I'm going.' He did not like to lie but in a way it was the truth. Robbie had found them digs to share off the High Street and one of the landlady's conditions was, 'nae young women'. Sharing the digs there would be only one other, a skeleton Robbie had bagged for him from a newly qualified doctor. The story was that the skeleton, known as Knox, had been divested of its skin and flesh by the young man himself who had now headed south for London to become a dermatologist.

'Brid.' Adam took a deep breath and caught her hands gently in his own. 'You have to go back. I'm sorry. You know you aren't really in danger.' He deliberately closed his mind to the picture of Broichan with this cruel eyes, wild hair, and savage, tight-lipped mouth. 'That was all a wonderful fantasy. A game we played when we were children.' He frowned. 'Brid, there's a war about to start. I'm going to be a doctor. Please understand.' He touched her face gently. 'It's just not possible.'

'A-dam . . .' Her face was ashen. 'War does not matter to me. I will help you with the wounded. Please. I love you.' She grabbed the front of his sweater. 'If I go back I will die.'

'No, Brid.'

'A-dam. You do not understand.' She was clinging to him, her face hard.

'Brid, I do. Listen. You have to go back to find Gartnait and Gemma. Next holidays we'll meet and we'll compare notes, all right? You must understand. You cannot come with me.'

She let go of him so suddenly he staggered backwards. Through her tears her eyes were blazing. 'A-dam, I will never let you go. Never!' Her voice was almost vicious.

Adam stared at her, shocked. The skin on the back of his neck was prickling suddenly, but he managed to remain calm. 'No, Brid, I'm sorry.' He stepped away from her. 'Please, try and understand.' He could not bear the look in her eyes any longer.

He turned and began to run as fast as he could down the hillside, away from her.

6

The digs were situated up a curved stair in a narrow wynd of tall grey corbelled houses off the High Street. Adam felt an initial wave of intense claustrophobia as he surveyed his new domain, with its small hard bed, empty bookshelf and wobbly table, and then, seeing it instead through Robbie's proud eyes he shifted his point of view and saw it as a haven of independence.

Throwing his bags down on the bed, next to which lay his trunk, he raised his hands above his head and gave out an exultant shout of freedom. They were, Robbie told him gleefully, just ten yards from the nearest pub. In the corner the skeleton of Knox grinned amiably at him. Within seconds it had acquired a hat and a university scarf, the box containing Adam's gas mask was slung irreverently round its shoulders – it was only days after Chamberlain had returned from Munich and the threat of war had receded once more – and the two young men had pelted back down the stairs to sample a pint of Tennent's. It was the first time that Adam had ever been in a bar.

It was a path they were to tread many times over the next few months between the exhausting rounds of lectures; in Robbie's case they took place in the Old Quad, and in Adam's in the new buildings in Teviot Place for chemistry, anatomy and dissection, in the Botanical Gardens for botany and in the King's Buildings for zoology. After the initial strangeness of university life, and the shock of having so much freedom away from the deadening atmosphere of the manse, he took to the course like a duck to water, avidly soaking up each subject as it came, taking little time out to look for recreation. Once a week he wrote a dutiful note to his father. His mother he went to see at last.

She had changed out of all recognition. Gone was the tightly pulled-back hair, the sober dresses, the strained, pale face. When he walked hesitantly into the tea shop on Princes Street where they had agreed to meet he stood for a moment staring round, his gaze passing over the vivacious pretty woman with the swinging curly hair and fashionable hat who was sitting near him, already presiding over a teapot and a plate of cakes. Only when she stood up and held out her arms did he look into her eyes and see there the love and fear and compassion and feel the overwhelming rush of emotion which brought tears to his own eyes.

'I wrote, Adam. I wrote often, my darling.' She was holding his hand openly on the tabletop, playing obsessively with his fingers as though reassuring herself that they were all there. 'You must believe me. You do understand? It's not your father's fault. He is such a good man. He must have thought it best if you didn't get my letters.' She looked away suddenly and he saw the pain; the glint of a tear on her eyelashes. 'I wasn't good enough for him, Adam. I'm weak. I needed things . . .' She couldn't speak for a moment and busied herself pouring more tea for him, her hand shaking slightly. 'I was suffocating, Adam. I felt as though I would have died.'

He didn't know what to say. Smiling at her silently he squeezed her hand and buried his face in his cup.

She was blowing her nose on a lace-trimmed handkerchief. After a moment she looked up at him and smiled. The tears had gone. 'So. Are you going to be a good doctor?'

He grimaced. 'I hope so.' He withdrew his hand to stir some sugar into his cup. 'If I am, it's because I learned it from you. Visiting all those poor people in the parish. Hating to see them suffer. Wanting to help them.'

He looked down into his tea, distracted suddenly by a memory of a young man lying beneath a tree. Gartnait, with Brid's small hands busy tending his wound. How strange. He had not given her a thought since he had been in Edinburgh.

He looked back at his mother. Her face was sober. 'I hated all that. The visiting. I had no idea, when I married, what it entailed – being a minister's wife.' She paused, not noticing the crestfallen disillusion in her son's eyes. 'I've met someone, Adam. A good, kind, gentle, understanding man.'

Adam tensed. He didn't want to hear this.

'I hoped your father would divorce me. I was the guilty party.' She glanced at Adam and looked away again. 'That way I could marry again.' She refused to meet his eye. 'But of course he can't do that, being in the church, so, I – well, I've had to pretend.' She was staring down at her hands. Almost unwillingly Adam looked down too and saw that the narrow gold wedding band had gone. Instead she wore a ring of carved twisted silver.

'I am sorry, Adam. I will understand if you hate me for it.' She was pleading, still not looking at him.

He bit his lip. He wasn't sure how he felt. Anger. Hurt. Rejection and yes, hatred, but not for her, for the unknown man who had stolen her from them.

He cleared his throat nervously. 'Are you happy now?'

She nodded.

Again he looked away. She was happy! Had she ever really wondered how he was, imagined his loneliness, his desolation when she left? He found himself suddenly near to tears, remembering Wee Mikey's teasing. The boys in the village had been right all along. She had gone off with another man. She was, as his father said, a whore.

He stood up abruptly. 'I have to go, I'm afraid.' He schooled his voice with care.

'Adam!' She looked up at him at last, devastated.

'I'm sorry, Mother.' He didn't even know what to call her, he realised suddenly. Not Mummy. Never Mummy. Not any more.

'We will meet again, Adam? Soon?' There were tears in her eyes again.

He shrugged. 'Perhaps.' Suddenly he couldn't bear it a moment longer. Turning, he blundered out between the tables and almost ran into the street.

Jeannie Barron baked less often now. She had agreed to stay on after Adam left; the minister's needs were very meagre and the house very quiet. Her work did not take her so long, and it was cheerless without Adam there. So it was with some pleasure that she looked up at the knock on the kitchen door and saw the pretty face with its frame of long dark hair peering round at her.

'Brid, my lass. How nice to see you.' She smiled and beckoned the child in. But she wasn't a child any longer. As Brid sat down at the kitchen table and fixed Jeannie with a cold stare the woman felt a shiver of apprehension whisper over her skin. 'So, how are you? You'll be missing Adam, as we all are,' she said slowly. She turned the dough and thumped it with her fist.

'You will tell me where he is.' Brid's eyes, fixed on hers, were very hard.

Jeannie glanced up. 'Did he not tell you where he was going?' Alarm bells rang in her head.

'He tells me he is going to Edinburgh to study healing.'

'Aye, that's right.' Jeannie smiled, relaxing again. 'He's very bright is our Adam.'

'I will go too.' Brid folded her arms. Her expression had not changed. 'You will tell me how.'

'How to go to Edinburgh? That's difficult.' Jeannie was playing for time. If Adam hadn't given the girl an address to write to then he had a reason. 'It costs money, lass. You'd need to go on the bus or on the train.'

Brid looked blank.

'Why not wait until he comes home in the vacation? It's not so long. He'll be back before you know it. Besides, he hasn't written to tell us yet where he's staying.' She hoped she would be forgiven the lie. 'Edinburgh is very big, lass. Bigger than you can ever imagine. You would never find him.'

'I will ask. The people will know where the healers' school is. You will give me money.'

Jeannie shook her head. 'No, Brid. I'm sorry. I can't afford to hand out money, lass. You must find your own.'

'I will have yours.' Brid had spotted Jeannie's handbag on the dresser. Pushing back her chair she moved towards it, putting out her hand.

'No!' Jeannie had seen what was coming. Stepping away from the table she grabbed it, covering it in flour. 'No, miss! I had a feeling you were no better than you ought to be. You get out of here now. This minute, or I'll call the minister! If you want to go to Edinburgh you go your own way, but I warn you, you'll not find Adam. If he wanted you to know where he was he would have told you. So, that's an end of it, do you hear me?'

For a moment there was total silence in the room. Brid stared at her with eyes of flint and Jeannie felt a jolt of real fear. She swallowed hard. The minister was actually not in his study. She wasn't sure where he was. Visiting someone in the parish, perhaps, or in the kirk. She straightened her shoulders. Brid was only a slim wee thing. Why should she feel so afraid?

She read the fatal message in Brid's eyes for just one second before Brid put her hand to her leather belt and calmly drew her knife. She tried to run, but it was too late. The beaten and polished iron weapon caught her between the shoulderblades before she had taken more than one step and she fell awkwardly, clutching the bag to her chest as the blood slowly welled out over her pale blue cardigan. The only sound she made was a small gasp.

Brid stood still, amazed at the incredible surge of energy and excitement which had shot through her. Then, expressionless, she wrestled the bag from Jeannie's clutch and opened it, tipping the contents on the floor. She surveyed the items with interest. There was a little round mother-of-pearl powder compact, given to Jeannie by Adam's mother when she realised that the minister would not allow her to keep such a frivolity. A comb. A handkerchief. A small diary. A purse and a wallet. She ignored the wallet, which contained a large white five-pound note, not recognising it as money. The compact she took and examined. She pushed the small catch on the side and gasped as it opened to reveal a mirror. For a moment she stared at herself, rapt in wonder, then, hastily, she tucked it inside her dress. Then she reached for the purse. Inside were nine shillings, three sixpences, four pennies and a ha'penny. She hoped it was enough to go to Edinburgh.

Adam met Liza when she was drawing his corpse. Dissection fascinated him. It was meticulous, delicate and the structures of skin and muscle and organ that he uncovered were beautiful beyond anything he had ever imagined. The young men who shared his class joked and complained about the smell of formalin and messed about to cover their unease at what they were doing, but Adam was completely enchanted. They thought he was mad; a bit of a swot. Only Liza understood. She arrived one morning, a large portfolio under her arm, her bright clothes and long, flame-coloured scarf a shocking contrast to the dark walls and the sober overalls of the young men.

She smiled at them from huge, amber-coloured eyes and tossed her long auburn hair back over her shoulders. 'Do you mind if I draw your body?' She was already setting up her easel just behind Adam's elbow. Their supervisor was ostentatiously looking in the other direction. 'I won't get in your way, I promise.'

Adam was astonished. The women's dissection room was separate from the men's across the corridor. His surprise turned to irritation. She must have bribed a servitor or one of the lecturers to get in and she was a distraction. She made his colleagues, never serious at the best of times, behave in an even more silly fashion than usual. She herself though was as serious as he was, scowling with concentration as she sharpened her pencils and drew with meticulous detail the facial structures beneath the skin.

It was she who suggested that Adam have a cup of tea with her after the session. 'You take your work seriously. Much more than the other boys.' She smiled at him gravely. 'Are you planning to be a surgeon?' There was a faint accent there, attractive, lilting. He could not place it.

He shrugged. 'I've always assumed I'll be a GP. I like people. When you're a surgeon they're always asleep. Or so you hope.' He gave a slow smile. He had grown up a great deal in the first months of his new life.

She responded dazzlingly. 'In a way it's a pity. You've got wonderful hands.' She reached across the table and took one, opening it palm up and looking at it through narrowed eyes. 'Your life line is very strong.' She traced it with her fingertip. 'And look, there will be three women in your life.' She glanced up at him under her eyelashes, laughing. 'Lucky women!'

Embarrassed, he pulled his hand away, feeling the colour rising in his cheeks. 'Where did you learn to hand read?' His father would have had fifty fits.

'From my mother. I inherited my art from my father.' She pulled the sugar bowl towards her and drew patterns in the crystals with the spoon. 'I'm studying to be a portrait painter. But I need to know how the whole body works. However much you observe and notice the colour and the texture and the shadows of the skin, unless you know about the musculature and bones underneath, you're not going to get the depiction strong enough.' She paused and a shadow crossed her face. 'It's still hard for women, you know. They made an awful fuss about me wanting to come and draw your corpse this morning.'

'Did they?' He was beginning to fall under her spell. 'I expect they thought you would distract us.' He grinned. 'You did. Why didn't you go to the women's class?'

She smiled. 'I tried. They were much stricter. No outsiders. I didn't distract *you* though. You were the serious one.'

'I think I'm a serious person.' He shrugged self-deprecatingly. 'But I've one or two chums who are working very hard to reform me.'

'Good. Let me help. Do you want to come round to see my studio?'

He nodded. He was beginning to feel extremely happy.

She did not reappear in the dissecting room but it was arranged that he would go to visit her the following Saturday.

It was on the day before that he received a letter from his father telling him about Jeannie Barron's death.

The police can find no motive. It is completely senseless. Her handbag was rifled, but the blaggard left her wallet. He took her purse and her powder compact as far as we can guess. From what Ken says she used to keep them in there. They haven't found the weapon. No one saw anything or heard anything . . .

The minister's anguish poured off the page but Adam had stopped reading. He was crying like a child.

He almost didn't go to Liza's, but he had no way of getting in touch with her and in the end he was glad to get out of his rooms. Robbie's shocked anger at what had happened – he too had known Jeannie since he was a little boy – didn't help, nor did his way of dealing with it, which was to go out and get very drunk.

The studio was in an old loft overlooking the Water of Leith. Adam climbed the narrow dark stairway and knocked on the door, completely unprepared for the assault on his senses which the opening of the door provoked. The huge single room where Liza lived and worked was flooded with light from two floor-length windows. More than three-quarters of the floor space was given over to a studio, the bare boards splashed with paint, two easels in place, one with a picture, covered with a cloth, the other bearing a half-finished portrait of an old man. A large refectory table was barely visible under paints and pencils and palettes, knives and brushes and on a plate in one corner, Adam couldn't help but notice with a slight shudder, there was a sandwich liberally sprouting a rather pretty green mould.

Liza's living corner in contrast was far from spartan. The divan bed was covered in a scarlet bedspread; there were cushions and Victorian silk shawls, bright rag rugs, and an old hatstand where hung her supply of long gypsy skirts and shirts and jumpers. On the other side of the space was a small gas ring and a large chipped enamel sink. 'Home!' She welcomed him with outflung arms. 'What do you think of it?'

Adam was stunned into silence. He had never seen a place like this before, never met anyone quite like Liza. He was intrigued, and enchanted and shocked to the roots of his Presbyterian soul. She fed him hot buttered toast and jam and huge chunks of crumbly cheese and pots of strong tea and showed him her paintings, which were in themselves deeply shocking to him. They were powerful, vibrant evocations of personality, ugly in their reality, uncomfortable to look at and, he decided, rightly, probably very good indeed.

He wandered round, toast dripping jam in his hand, speechless as he turned canvas after canvas to face him. There were landscapes as well – rugged, moody landscapes which he didn't recognise, but more than anything he liked the portraits.

She looked over his shoulder at a dark stormy scene of rocky mountains and torn, tortured clouds. 'Wales,' she said. 'I'm Welsh. Or at least half of me is. My Da was Italian, but I never knew him.' She began to wind up the gramophone. 'Do you like music? I love it. Especially opera.' She slid a record out of its paper sleeve and put it on the turntable. 'Listen.'

It was another assault on his senses. He had never heard anything like it before. It was loud and sensuous and strident and wild. He could feel his blood beginning to race, emotions he never knew he possessed swirling up through him. Then the music stilled and grew sad and, overwhelmed by it all, to his intense embarrassment he found there were tears in his eyes. He couldn't control them and frantically he turned away from her to stare out of the window across the rocky stream towards the huddled buildings on the opposite bank.

Liza had noticed. Silently she followed him and took his hand. 'What is it, Adam? What's wrong?'

It all came out. Jeannie. The manse. His father. His mother. The man she lived with in sin, but who made her so very, very happy.

Liza was appalled. Quietly she held him against her shoulder as though he were a child and let him cry. The record came to an end and hissed quietly on the turntable, waiting for the needle to be lifted off. They ignored it. He could feel a quiet sense of peace and security engulfing him, slowly healing his pain. When at last Liza moved the tears were gone. And so was his embarrassment.

She put another record on, Chopin this time, and they listened to it together thoughtfully, sitting relaxed near each other but not touching, as the light faded from the sky. Later they went for a pie and mash at a pub in Leith Walk and they laughed and they chattered and he learned about her family – an eccentric mother, kindly, warm, much-loved farming grandparents, but nothing about her exotic father – and then at last he saw her home before taking the tram back to the High Street. By the time he got back to his digs he thought he was probably in love.

In the end Brid had not needed the money in the purse to go to Edinburgh. As she walked south along the road from Pittenross in the pouring rain a car pulled up beside her. 'Do you want a lift?' A woman was at the wheel.

Brid was dropped in Princes Street as it grew dark. Staring at the crowds, the cars, the trams, she turned slowly round, afraid and very lost. 'A-dam?' She murmured his name out loud against the shouts of a newsboy calling the evening edition of the paper from a stand by the side of the road. 'A-dam, where are you?'

Somehow she had to find somewhere quiet, then she could use her art to find him. As long as he had her silver pendant on him, it would be easy.

Adam did not go back to the manse for Christmas. He and Robbie packed their rucksacks and hitched a lift with one of their fellow students down to Newcastle for the winter break. They drank a lot of beer and walked some way along Hadrian's Wall and talked about the likelihood of war.

Back in Edinburgh Adam saw as much of Liza as he could, though they were both working hard. Her dedication to her art was total, he learned, and it took precedence over everything. It was just as well, as his own chosen career did not leave a lot of time spare for a social life. Much to Robbie's disgust, he was spending more and more time at his studies with only the occasional respite.

One evening he did spare for Liza. It was her birthday. Poverty stricken as usual, he agonised for a long time over what to give her, then providence pointed the way. He had been rummaging through some boxes in his untidy room and under some books and notes he found an old cigarette carton. Shaking it hopefully he heard something rattle. Brid's pendant had fallen out of the tissue paper he had wrapped it in and lay in the palm of his hand, tarnished but very beautiful. He looked down at the intricate, interwoven pattern, the tiny links in the chain, and just for a moment he felt a twinge of guilt at the idea which had leaped into his mind. He put the guilt aside at once. Brid would never know; he doubted if he would ever see her again anyway, and he had made it clear to her, hadn't he, that men did not wear such things. And the beauty and craftsmanship would appeal enormously to Liza. Smiling to himself, he set about polishing it up.

Liza held it for a long time in her hand, gazing at it. Then at last she looked up at Adam and smiled. 'It's beautiful,' she said. 'Thank you.' She leaned forward and kissed him on the lips, then she let him hang it round her neck.

It was the next day after taking Liza out to a quick lunch between lectures that Adam thought he saw Brid. Hand in hand he and Liza were walking up the Mound past the National Gallery, Liza wearing the pendant at the neck of her blouse, when Adam happened to glance across the road towards the Castle. A group of people were walking fast down the other pavement, laughing, some of the young men in uniform. The road was busy, full of traffic, and he could not see them clearly, but a figure walking slowly behind them caught his eye.

He stopped, shocked. The dark hair, the pale skin; something about the walk, the angle of the head . . .

'What is it, Adam? What's wrong?' Liza caught his arm. 'You've gone white as a sheet. What's happened?'

'Nothing.' He took a deep breath, astonished to feel how shaken he was. 'I thought I saw someone I knew from home, that's all. But it couldn't have been.'

'Are you sure?' Liza studied him for a moment and he looked away uncomfortably. Why did he sometimes get the feeling that she could read his very soul?

'No. It wasn't.' The pavement was empty now. The crowd had hurried on. The slowly moving traffic threaded its way down the hill and whoever the woman had been, he could no longer see her.

That night he dreamed about Brid. He dreamed they made love and then he dreamed that she tried to drown him in the fairy pool. He woke screaming and lay there, sweating, waiting for Robbie to come in swearing at being woken up. But Robbie, who a month before had signed up to join the RAFVR, was not there. He was three miles away fast asleep in the arms of a student nurse Adam had introduced him to only the previous day.

Adam lay staring at the ceiling for the rest of the night, watching for the meagre grey dawn to creep into the close and fight its way through his window before he got up at last and began wearily to shave with a kettleful of hot water.

He saw his first death that day. He was visiting a fellow student who had fallen down the twisting stair to his digs after imbibing several pints and broken his leg. At the end of the ward there was a young man who had been taken to the Infirmary after an accident in the factory where he was working. He had fallen into unprotected machinery and his leg had been severed just below the hip. As he left the ward, Adam lingered a moment to look at the white face on the white pillow and the young man had opened his eyes and looked straight at him. Reading the pain and terror and loneliness in the bright blue gaze Adam went across to the bed and put a gentle hand on the young man's shoulder. It was only minutes later that he realised the young man was dead. To his surprise for a while after life had gone the eyes stayed just as bright. He stood staring down, unable to take in the moment he had witnessed. Then the ward sister who had been escorting the doctor and his train of third-year students turned back and saw him. She touched Adam's arm. 'You all right?' Her smile was kind. 'It was nice of you to stay with him.' She pulled up the sheet with calm professionalism. 'On your way now, young man. Forget what you have seen.'

'I saw him die.' Sitting on the floor of Liza's studio, his arms round his legs, his chin on his knees, Adam was still trying to come to terms with it. 'And yet for a minute I couldn't see any difference. He was white, but he was white before he died. He just stopped breathing. That's all.'

She came and sat down beside him. They were listening to some Mozart. 'Perhaps his spirit was still there. It didn't want to go.' She smiled. 'You did the right thing, Adam, to be with him. It must be very frightening to die alone.'

He shook his head. 'Somehow I always saw myself as a doctor saving lives. Stepping in heroically and working miracles. I didn't think about the ones we can't save.' They were silent for a few minutes. 'War is coming, Liza. I'll be staying on as a student because they'll need doctors. Robbie will be in the RAF. What will you do?'

She shrugged. 'I want to go on painting. I'll do it as long as I can. It's my whole life. I don't want to do anything else.' She paused. 'I suppose the folks might want me to go home and help with the farm.'

'Back to Wales?'

She nodded. 'It hasn't happened yet, Adam. Perhaps it won't. Perhaps Hitler will change his mind.' She shook her head violently. 'I'm sorry. I can't bear the thought of him interfering in all our lives. I want everything to stay the same. I want to paint sunsets and flowers and happiness. I can't think about war. I won't.'

Adam gave a rueful smile. 'We won't have any choice. It's in the air everywhere. Besides,' he nodded over his shoulder at her shrouded easel, 'you never paint sunsets and flowers and happiness. You wouldn't know how.'

She let out a shout of laughter. 'Perhaps you're right.'

The first time they made love was after they had been to a concert together at the Usher Hall. As they walked through the darkened streets he put his arm round her shoulders and drew her to him.

97

'Liza –'

She put her finger to his lips to silence him and then gently kissed him. They climbed the stairs to her studio and in the soft darkness she led him across to her bed.

They spent the summer together, and by the time the new term began they were inseparable. Liza was not like Brid in any way. Her loving was warm. In spite of her sometimes acerbic manner, with Liza he felt safe and secure and welcomed. All thoughts of the manse and the unhappiness there vanished. He had found someone in whom he could confide all his fears and hopes.

All his fears but one.

He saw Brid again one Thursday at the beginning of the new university year on South Bridge, and this time he was sure it was her.

Leaving Liza on the tram with a quick wave he had just jumped off with three fellow medics, a pile of books in his arms, his white coat slung across his shoulder, on his way to a physics lecture. The young men were laughing and talking loudly, dodging between the trams and cars, ducking their heads against cold relentless sheets of rain. Shaking his wet hair out of his eyes he looked up and saw her staring at him across the street.

'A-dam –' He saw her mouth frame the word, but as before the traffic was heavy and the street was crowded and when he looked again she had gone.

He was not proud of what he did next. Instead of crossing the road to look for her he dived after his friends into the Old Quad and forged ahead, leaving the spot where he had seen her far behind.

Handing in his card to the servitor in his top hat, Adam edged into his seat in the lecture hall and found that his hands were shaking. He stared down at them, fiercely willing them into fists. What was the matter with him? Why was he so afraid? Was it that she brought memories of the manse, things he wanted to forget? Or was it guilt, that he had abandoned her so easily and put her out of his mind? Whatever it was he did not want to see her again. After all, it was a coincidence almost too big to be possible that she should be in Edinburgh. It was probably his imagination. Comforted, he sat back and gave his attention to the professor in front of him.

Liza stood back from the canvas and chewed the end of her paint brush. She glanced at her watch and smiled. A good time to stop.

The knock on the door came at exactly the right moment. She

and Adam were planning to bike over to the Royal Botanical Gardens for a picnic in the warm autumnal sunshine. The bicycles were a new idea, borrowed from friends of hers who had graduated to a three-wheeled Morgan. 'Come in. It's not locked!' She was rinsing the brush in a jar of turps and did not turn round. 'I'll be with you in two seconds, Adam. I've done a lot of work this morning. What do you think?' She turned, gesturing at the canvas and stopped short. Standing in the doorway was a strange young woman with long dark hair. 'I'm sorry,' Liza frowned, puzzled. 'I thought you were someone else.'

'You thought I was A-dam.' The girl stepped into the studio and closed the door behind her. She was dressed in an ankle-length, russet dress with a soft woollen coat over it which came to her feet. On her shoulder hung a loosely woven bag. Her eyes were as hard as flint.

'Who are you?' Liza put down her brush and rag. The skin on the back of her neck had begun to prickle. There was something about this strange young woman which made her very uncomfortable. She moved surreptitiously a little nearer to the table and groped behind her for the knife with which she had been scraping her palette.

'It does not matter who I am.' The voice was strangely monotone.

'I think it does. You are in my home. I would like to know what you want.'

'You are A-dam's girlfriend.' The voice, though still flat, held venom.

Liza's questing fingers found what she was looking for and she quietly picked up the palette knife. She stepped back again, putting the table between her and her visitor, praying that Adam would appear. Her nerves were beginning to scream. 'I am his friend, certainly,' she said cautiously. 'If you are looking for him, he'll be here soon.'

The young woman did not look round. Her eyes were fixed on Liza's face. 'I do not need you,' she said calmly. 'A-dam does not need you.' She was reaching into her bag as she spoke.

Liza gasped. She saw a blade flash as the woman raised her arm and had barely registered the knife when without thinking she threw herself down behind the table at the same moment as she heard Adam's cheerful shout from the bottom of the stairs.

'Adam!' she screamed. 'Adam, be careful!'

He found her sobbing on her knees, the palette knife still clutched in her hand, her fingers covered in thick yellow paint.

'Liza! Liza, what is it? What's wrong?' He was down beside her on his knees. 'Tell me. What happened?'

'Where is she?' Shaking, Liza managed to stand up. 'For God's sake, Adam, who was she?' She was staring round wildly. The studio was empty.

'Who? What? What happened?'

'That woman! That girl! You must have seen her?' Unaware of the paint on her hand she pushed her hair back off her face, leaving a smear of yellow across her forehead. 'She tried to kill me!'

Adam closed his eyes. He took a deep breath. Why had he thought immediately of Brid?

'Describe her,' he said. He led her to the bed and sat her down gently. Then he walked over to the door and stared down the stairs. As he had climbed them in the dark, glad to be out of the cutting wind, he had been halfway up when a cat had fled past him. He had time only to register the dark shape, the fierce green eyes, the wild fury of the claws on the worn steps, and it was gone. 'There's no other way out of here is there?'

She shook her head. 'No.'

'Then she must still be here.' He walked slowly round the studio searching every corner, every cupboard, every shadow. There was no one there.

'She was small, dark hair. Long dark-red clothes. She spoke with a funny foreign accent.'

Brid.

'What do you mean, she tried to kill you?' Adam sat down beside her.

'She pulled out a knife and threw it at me.'

'Are you sure, Liza?' His voice was gentle. 'Where is it? Where is she? I don't see how anyone could have been here. I would have seen her.' He found himself picturing the cat's eyes as it raced past him down the stairs.

'Are you telling me I'm making it up?' Liza stared at him furiously. 'Adam, for God's sake, I know if someone tried to kill me or not!'

'Then we should call the police.' His hands were shaking. He pushed them firmly into his pockets.

'Of course we should call the police. There's a potential murderer running round here. Look over there. The knife must be some-where. I saw her hurl it at me as I threw myself on the floor. She couldn't have gone to look for it. There was no time.'

But there was no knife. They looked for half an hour, combing every inch of the studio.

'So. Who is she?' Liza had cleaned off the paint and was feeling calmer.

Adam shrugged. For a moment he wondered if he should deny his suspicions, but Liza knew him too well. She had already read the dawning horror in his eyes. He sat down on her divan and felt in his pocket for his cigarettes. The pendant he had given Liza, Brid's pendant, was lying where Liza had left it, on the side table under the lamp. He could see the soft gleam of silver from where he sat.

'It sounds like Brid. She's someone I saw quite a bit of at home,' he said at last. He refused to meet her eye. 'We used to explore the hills in the holidays. Her brother was – is – a stone mason. He carves brilliantly. I think,' he hesitated, 'I think the family have rather exotic roots. They're very excitable.' He made it sound something unpleasant. 'Brid has a very short temper. She's attacked me before now.' He gave a small, uncomfortable laugh.

'And what is she doing in Edinburgh?'

'She must have followed me.' He shook his head. 'I told her it was all over. We were kids together, that was all. She was going to college up north and I was coming here. There was no future for us. None at all.' He paused for a moment, then he went on. 'But she didn't like it. She wanted to come with me. I told her no. I never expected her to follow me.'

'Had you seen her here before?'

He shook his head, but she saw the troubled look in his eyes.

'Adam?'

He shook his head again. 'I wondered if I had seen her the other day, in the distance. But then she wasn't there.' He shrugged helplessly.

'She's obviously good at disappearing acts.'

'Yes.' He shivered. 'Yes, she is.'

'And is she capable of trying to kill someone?'

Miserably he stared at the floor. 'I think perhaps she might be,' he said at last.

They did not tell the police in the end. There seemed no point.

Susan Craig was sitting in the corner of the tea room, her back to the wall.

Adam had seen her only once since their first encounter. 'I'm sorry, I haven't much time.' He sat down opposite her. 'We've a lot of studying to do at the moment.'

101

'Of course, dear. I'm so proud of you.' She had already ordered the tea. Pouring it into two cups, she pushed one towards him. 'Adam, there is something I must tell you.' She was perched uncomfortably on the edge of her chair. 'I've . . . we've, that is, my friend and I have decided to go away.' She spoke in a rush, not looking at him. 'To America.'

Adam stared at her.

She blushed uncomfortably. 'No one will know us there. We can make a new start, and with the war coming and everything . . .' Her voice trailed away again and she stared down into her cup.

Adam was silent for a minute. Different emotions whirled round his head: anger, loss, contempt – what kind of man ran away from his country when it was about to go to war?

'Adam?' She was staring at him anxiously.

He forced himself to smile. 'I hope you'll both be happy, Mother.' What else was there to say?

Two days later, Chamberlain announced that Hitler had not responded to his ultimatum and that therefore Britain was at war. Some weeks after that Robbie, already in the VR, was called up. Whether it was his decision or that of His Majesty's government Adam was not sure, but his friend's excitement at giving up the study of Latin and Greek civilisation for the patrolling of the clouds as part of the City of Edinburgh Fighter Auxiliary Squadron seemed totally unfeigned. To celebrate, he arranged a trip out to Cramond Inn for himself and his new girlfriend Jane. Adam and Liza went too.

Jane Smith-Newland had been a Classics student in Robbie's tutorial. He was besotted by her. She was tall and slim with huge brown eyes and thick soft honey-coloured hair, tied in a schoolgirl plait. Her family were English, her father already high in the ranks of the army, her mother living in the south in their big house in the Home Counties. Adam, meeting her for the first time after growing used to Robbie's usual flighty girlfriends, was fascinated by her accent, her background, her combination of reticence and the confidence which money brought her. She had beautiful clothes, a car of her own – an old Wolsey Hornet – bought for her by her parents, an almost unimagined extravagance to a penniless medical student. Lovely jewellery, and in complete contrast to all that, a genuine, deep fascination with Latin, Greek and the history of ancient civilisations, which had brought her to university instead of, as her mother and father had intended, being launched into

London society. She was like no one Adam had ever met before. He could not keep his eyes off her.

As they crept with shaded headlights down the narrow roads on the way to Cramond Liza groped for Adam's hand on the back seat. 'At least she can't follow us out here,' she whispered above the sound of the engine. She was convinced Brid was still shadowing her. Adam was not so sure. He had seen no sign of her, and it made no sense for her to be following Liza. If she wanted to see Adam why did she not find his rooms and confront him personally? Presumably if she had been following them, she knew where he lived too. At first that thought had filled him with apprehension, but soon, very soon, the worry had passed and he had convinced himself that Liza had imagined the whole episode.

'At least who can't follow you?' Jane glanced in the driving mirror and caught Adam's eye in the darkness. Her hearing was obviously very acute.

'Just an old girlfriend of Adam's,' Liza put in. 'She seems reluctant to let him go.'

'Popular man, our Adam.' Robbie chuckled. 'He's always had to fight off the ladies!'

'That's rubbish, Rob.' Adam could feel his face growing pink. He glanced at Liza and shook his head. He did not want to talk about Brid. And he did not want Robbie to know that she might have followed him to Edinburgh.

It was Jane who wouldn't let the subject drop. 'Who would have thought the strong, silent Adam Craig had a string of ladyfriends! You'll have to watch out Liza, or you'll lose him.'

The words hung in the silence for a moment as Jane changed gear and turned down Cramond Road. It was Robbie who leaped in to the rescue. Handsome in his uniform, he sat sideways on his seat, his arm behind her, fondling Jane's neck. 'I trust you're not looking to be one of those ladies, Janie. I'd hate that. I know these doctor fellows can be irresistible, but not half as irresistible as an RAF chap, surely.'

'Of course not!' She laughed lightly. 'As long as I don't hear you've been tempted by some of those gorgeous WAAFs.'

On the back seat Liza's hand tightened a little round Adam's fingers. They looked at each other in the dark. 'Robbie, be tempted by a WAAF!' Adam put in lightly. 'How could you ever imagine such a thing.' He leaned forward and punched his friend gently on the shoulder. 'Our Robbie's no time for such frivolity. After all, he's going to win the war single-handed, aren't you, old boy!'

In the front seat Robbie smiled. He looked sideways at Jane and gave a modest shrug.

On the sixteenth of October German bombers flew low over the Forth and 602 and 603 Squadrons were scrambled. Robbie's war had begun.

Brid had not expected it to be like this.

Her journey to Edinburgh had been easy. Prompted by the sixth sense inside her head she had found Liza when she first arrived with comparative ease. Then, inexplicably, she had lost her again. Her mind grew dizzy and clouded. She wandered, lost, around the city, vacant-eyed, afraid, not knowing where to go or what to do. Sometimes, asleep in a doorway or hidden in some secret place she would make the leap inside her head which would take her home to the hillside where Gartnait's cross marked the transition point into her world. But always Broichan was lurking near and, afraid, she would come back to the place where her poor cold body was huddled out of sight. There were many places in this great city where she roamed, where the veils of time were thin. Slipping into the ruins of the Abbey of the Holy Rood she had felt the coldness of the mist and known it was one of them. In the great cathedral up the High Street where she slept unnoticed in the shadows, she felt it too. Deep beneath the foundations of the church there was a sacred place, a place where the goddess would be waiting if she looked for her. But she had not been prepared for the pain and the dislocation which overwhelmed her. Time was a concept which in the silence of her dreams had not existed; she had been born to transcend it – a genetic imprint from her mother's womb – and her first teachers had been good. Quick to spot her natural ability they had taught her without caution and without initiation. They had not seen that ability without years of study might be dangerous. They did not think that this woman's mind might fly beyond the natural confines of the philosopher's cave and seek the stars. They did not remember that the longing of young eager flesh might prove stronger than the yearning for the alchemists' stone of all knowledge or the threat of retribution when the absolute laws were broken. By the time Broichan had seen the danger and recognised her power it was too late and Brid, not knowing that having broken the bounds of time there are long black distances of nothingness between the suns, was lost. She did not know that the air she breathed in the twentieth century was not the same air; she did not know that the body that carried her

104

spirit was subject to strains and pains she had not dreamed of. Curling down into the agony of adjustment, in the comparative security of the enclosed garden of an Edinburgh square, she escaped at last into sleep.

When she woke there was only one thought in her head, and that was to find Adam – and find him quickly. She would use her ancient arts again and locate him through the woman who she knew was in possession of the pendant.

'No!'

Liza lashed out in her sleep, fighting the clinging blankets. Overhead she could hear the drone of engines. Sometimes the Luftwaffe came to reconnoitre the Royal Navy units at Rosyth, sometimes the bombers were on their way to Glasgow again. They were having a lousy time. She took a deep breath and, as she groped with a shaking hand on her side table for her cigarettes and a box of matches, thanked God that so far Edinburgh had been spared. Only when she was sitting up in bed, the ashtray on her knees, did she pause to wonder what had awoken her.

She rubbed her eyes and yawned deeply. There was something unpleasant there in the back of her mind and it had no connection with the throb of aircraft propellers and the thought of the deadly load the planes were about to drop into the blackness of the Scottish night. She lay back on her pillows, drawing the smoke deeply into her lungs.

A-dam!

The word in her head was spoken with a strange foreign accent. An accent she remembered vividly. Her eyes flew open and she stared into the dark shadows of the studio. With the blackouts drawn and no light save the small glow from her cigarette end the room was completely dark. The sound had been in her own mind, and yet, somehow it seemed to come from outside her. Hastily stubbing out the cigarette she swung her feet to the floor and sat still, listening. The drumming of the engines had faded into silence now. She could hear nothing but the soft murmur of the wind in the chimney of the stove.

Every sense was alert.

She could feel it more clearly now, probing in her mind like a finger inching its way over the surface of her cerebellum.

A-dam?

'No, you bitch!' Sliding off the bed, she shook her head violently. She cannoned into a chair and swore loudly, rubbing her shin. 'No, you're not finding him through me. I'm wise to you, girl. What kind of a sneaky witch are you, anyway?' She rubbed her palms against her temples as hard as she could.

Switching on the lamp, she put a match to the gas and put on the kettle, taking comfort from the companionable hiss of the flame. The room was very cold. Pulling her scarlet shawl from the bed she wrapped it round her shoulders, shivering. It was there again, probing into her brain; she could almost feel the sharpness of the little iron-bladed knife digging the secrets of her life out of her head.

'Why me? What do you want with me?' She found she was backing across the studio, trying to move away from this horror in her mind. 'You must know where he is? What do you want with me?' It was the third time this had happened. And it was the worst. It was like hearing someone knocking, in the distance. At first it was not frightening – not even irritating. Then it would become more persistent and slowly her body's responses would begin to work. The dry mouth, the cold tight stomach, the prickling at the back of her neck, the icy shiver gripping her lungs until she could hardly breathe as the weight of someone else's mind slowly began to pull her down.

Suddenly it was too much. The empty building was too quiet around her, the echoing studio too lonely. Tearing off the shawl and her dressing gown she groped for sweater and jacket and a pair of woollen slacks. In two minutes she had let herself out of the building and was running along the path, divided from the river by old twisted railings, heading up towards the town.

Adam was woken by the hammering on his door. Fighting his way out of sleep he groped for his wrist watch, but he could see nothing. The blackout was still firmly drawn. He had no idea what time it was. Fumbling for the light switch he made his way to the door.

'You've got to let me in. That bitch gypsy girlfriend of yours is after me! She's using some kind of occult technique to get inside my head, Adam. You've got to do something about it.' Liza pushed her way past him and sat down on his bed. She was shaking.

He glanced behind her down the darkened stairwell and closing the door he turned the key. 'What happened?' In the light of the single bulb in the ceiling he had established that it was four-thirty in the morning. He ran his fingers over his scalp. He had been studying his physiology notes until one and his head felt like a pan of mashed potato. 'How did you get here, Liza?'

'I ran.' Her teeth were chattering. 'I know it was stupid. I didn't want to bring her to you, but I was scared. She was in the studio. In my head. She's mad, Adam. Completely mad.'

He sat beside her and put his arm round her shoulders. 'Tell me what happened. Slowly.'

There wasn't much to tell. How can you explain intuition? Knowing something deep inside you? Instinct – and the pain of the probing knife?

'When did you last see her?' Calmer now, Liza stood up. She pulled one of Adam's blankets off the bed and wrapped it round her shoulders. She was still wearing her coat and gloves.

He took the hint and went to light the small gas fire. 'I haven't. Not properly. I thought I saw her in the street a couple of times, then you said you'd seen her in the studio. Then nothing. Not a squeak.' He looked up at her from his position in front of the fire. 'She does know strange things – occult I suppose you could call them – and she told me she was studying things like that. But gypsies know these things anyway, don't they? They have powers, the second sight.'

'I have the second sight, Adam.' She spoke so quietly he didn't register what she had said for a moment. 'That is why she can reach me. That is why I understand what is happening.'

He stared at her. 'You don't mean it. That's ridiculous. That's evil!'

'Oh, there speaks the minister's son! I knew you'd react like that if I told you.' Her voice became bitter. 'Adam, for God's sake, I thought you had realised by now just what a bigoted, narrow upbringing you've had. Just because people don't conform to what your father allowed in his narrow-minded little world doesn't mean they're evil!'

'No, of course not.' He blushed. 'I didn't mean that –'

'Yes, you did.'

'Liza . . .' He stood up and went across to her, taking her hand. 'Don't let's quarrel, please. Whatever you think of me and my background, don't let it come between us.' He chewed the inside of his cheek thoughtfully for a moment, then he looked at her. 'I don't think Brid is evil. At least she wasn't. But she had different values from us. From you as well as from me. If she wants something –' He stopped speaking with a shrug, then he gave a deep sigh. 'I still don't see how she could have got here. She knows nothing about our way of life, nothing about our century –'

He stopped abruptly.

107

'Our century?' Liza stared at him.

He gave a small apologetic laugh. 'I know it's crazy, but sometimes . . .' He paused and the silence stretched out between them.

'Sometimes?' she prompted at last.

'Sometimes I used to imagine that when I went to see her, when I walked past the great stone on the hill where we used to meet, I was walking into the past. Literally. Her world was so different. She talked about such strange things – King Brude and St Columba, as though they were alive for her. And her way of life was so primitive in some ways. And then I would rationalise it when I went home. She lived in a tinker community and time does stand still for some of those people. Her family were wandering craftsmen, and –' He stopped again. He had been about to say 'priests'. 'I taught her English. I never knew what language it was she spoke. I don't think it was Gaelic. I don't know what the tinkers speak amongst themselves. Romany, I suppose. She learned very quickly. Her mother and her brother said she was exceptionally bright.' He shook his head. Sitting down at his desk he put his head in his hands. 'She wanted to come with me to Edinburgh. She thought she was in some danger from her family because she wanted to reject their way of life for mine. But our time together had run its course. She was already at college herself, somewhere in the north. I couldn't bring her here. I just wanted to finish it.'

And she had begun to frighten me. He didn't say it out loud.

'Were you and she lovers?' Liza looked up at him wanly. Her eyes were black-ringed with exhaustion.

He nodded.

'And she was – is – still in love with you?'

He shrugged, then he nodded again. 'I think she might be.'

'Why doesn't she find you?'

He shook his head miserably. 'I'm sure she knows where I am.'

'Then why does she keep coming to me?'

'I don't know, Liza. I wish I did.'

Back on the hillside, Brid couldn't understand why she found it so difficult to reach into A-dam's head. Perhaps it was because his father was a priest; he had learned techniques he had not told her about to keep her away. Liza was easy. She was receptive, open to the simplest probe. At least to start with. Brid stared down into the cold dark water of the well, one of the places where the veil was thin, and she shook her head, puzzled. The pictures, at first so clear and bright, had grown muddied and her mind was tired. She sat back on her heels and rubbed her eyes, shivering in the cold dawn. Above her the hump of Arthur's Seat rose against a hard green sky whilst below in the town the traffic was beginning to move. She squinted up at the clouds. The first time she had seen the planes they had filled her with terror. Flying in formation like geese coming in from the sea in winter they came closer and closer, their beating engines drumming against her ears till she fell on her face on the grass and cried, pressing her hands to her ears. But then they had passed, flying on towards the west, and slowly she had grown used to them. They never seemed to stop. She had no way of knowing the havoc they were causing over the industrial heartland of Scotland as they dropped their bombs.

She slept sometimes in the open, wrapped in blankets she had stolen; sometimes she slept on the floor at the home of a woman called Maggie, who had befriended her as they sat side by side on a bench in the park. Food she stole. Her clothes she stole – adept now at hiding herself within the circle of her magic. She did not know, and would not have cared if she had, that she had been noticed and classified by those who were interested as mentally defective, but harmless. As the war moved into its next phase there were other things to worry about than a beautiful young woman with vacant eyes who walked the streets of Edinburgh, sometimes down near the Dean Village, sometimes in the Grassmarket, watching, always watching, for someone who never came.

She tried once more, staring down into the peaty waters.

A-dam. A-dam, where are you?

But he was not there. Far away across Edinburgh in the Infirmary Adam, now a third-year student, was staring down at a man whose arm had been torn away by shrapnel and he was fighting the urge to be sick.

7

'So, what do you think?'

Liza pulled the cover off the painting and stood back triumphantly. Adam stared. He could see the face, the planes of the flesh, the huge dark brooding eyes, the ugly strong hands, the stormy, uncomfortable background, but he could not recognise himself at all. She was watching him closely and he saw her face fall. 'You don't like it.'

'It's a wonderful picture, Liza.' He tried to sound enthusiastic. 'It's just a bit modern for me.' He shrugged unhappily. 'Do I really look like that?'

'Oh you!' She stamped her foot in frustration. 'You're impossible! Yes, of course you look like that! In a way. It's a picture of you as doctor. You as a man. You as the essence of yourself.'

'I see.' Adam stared at it harder. Parts of the flesh tones had a translucent green quality which looked to him extremely unhealthy. 'I'm sorry, Liza. You know what an ignoramus I am.'

'You really are.' She sighed loudly. 'So, what am I to do with you?'

'Give me lessons in art appreciation?' He put on a rueful, chastened schoolboy look which infuriated her even more.

'I don't think I'll bother. There are a lot of people in this world who can appreciate art. You just go away and watch birds, or chop someone's leg off or something.' Folding her arms she turned away from him and went to look out of her window. Rain was lashing down the glass and a gust of wind rattled the panes. 'Go on. Go. I'm not talking to you.'

He stared at her, trying to make up his mind whether she was being serious. Then suddenly he gave up. He had better things to do with his precious time off than play silly games with her.

110

She heard the door bang and turned round in disbelief. 'Adam?'

He had gone.

She sighed. This had happened too often lately. Sometimes she wondered if they could agree on anything at all.

A-dam?

She looked up, shocked, her quarrel with Adam forgotten. It was months since she had heard the voice in her head. It was distant, questing.

'No!' She put her hands over her ears.

A-dam? Please help me.

'Go away!' Liza turned round, staring into the different corners of the studio as though she might be able to see the owner of the voice. 'Can't you see you're not wanted? Leave me alone!'

'Liza?' The voice she could hear now was strong, male and sounded very hurt. It was not Adam's. 'I hope you don't mean that, sweetheart?'

'Philip?' Her fear had vanished in a surge of relief. 'Come in!'

'Did I see your young doctor friend heading up the path as though the hounds of hell were behind him?' Philip Stevenson, some twenty years older than Liza, had been her tutor for the past two years. A tall, devastatingly attractive man with iron-grey hair and a charming crooked smile, he was the target for every female art student in the college and Liza was well aware that as the recipient of his occasional attentions she was viewed with a certain amount of resentment and jealousy by her colleagues.

'You did.'

'A row?'

'You could say so. He didn't like his portrait.'

'Young heathen.' He stood in front of the easel and stared at it in silence for several seconds. 'You've caught him very well. But maybe it isn't flattering to the young man's ego. Is he really that driven?'

'I think so.' She put her hand to her head, distracted. The voice was still there in her head.

A-dam, where are you?

It sounded sad. Lost.

Philip noticed her expression. 'What is it, sweetheart? Earache?'

She shook her head. 'You wouldn't believe me.'

'Try me.' He was still standing, arms folded, in front of the easel.

'All right. How's this.' Suddenly she was fed up with Adam and his attendant spirit. 'Adam had a gypsy girlfriend up in Perthshire. And when he came to Edinburgh he said she couldn't come too.

So guess what, she's put a spell on him. She's bewitched him and she's haunting me. She keeps talking to me inside my head and it's scaring me to death!'

The tremor in her voice was very slight, but she had his full attention at last. Turning his back on the painting he stared at her. 'You are joking, I hope.'

'No.'

'Oh, come on, Liza, it's your imagination.'

'If it is I should be in an asylum.'

'But things like that don't happen.'

'They do. But not for much longer. I have a feeling if I say goodbye to Adam, then the beautiful Brid will disappear too.'

'And do you want to say goodbye to him?' Philip viewed her thoughtfully under bushy eyebrows. 'You've been smitten with that young man since the day you met him.'

She grimaced. 'Was it that obvious?' For a moment she found herself staring at him. Compared with Adam he looked solid, dependable, and so very safe. 'Phil,' she plunged on, 'there is something else. Something terrible happened at Adam's home soon after he left. The woman who was his father's housekeeper was murdered.' She turned away. 'Horribly murdered. Stabbed to death. They never found out who did it.' She was staring at the painting again as though she could read an answer there.

He was ahead of her. 'And you think it was this girlfriend?'

She shrugged. 'She tried to kill me, Phil. She threw a knife at me. Adam doesn't believe it. There was no one here when he arrived, and she couldn't have passed him on the stairs, and we couldn't find the knife, but –' She stopped.

'Liza.' Philip took a couple of paces forward and took hold of her shoulders gently, forcing her to face him. 'Did you report it to the police?'

She shook her head.

'Why?'

'There was no point. It was only my word. Adam seemed to think I had dreamed the whole thing. But I hadn't. I know I hadn't.'

'And did you discuss with him the idea that she might have been responsible for this other woman's death?'

She shook her head again.

'Liza, sweetheart, it seems to me that if you really thought there was a completely insane young woman running around Scotland with a knife murdering people left, right and centre you would have told someone about it. You would have told Adam. You would

have told the police. You would, I hope, have told me before now.'
He drew her close to him and held her in his arms.

She tensed for a moment and then relaxed. The strange probing voice inside her head had, she realised, completely disappeared.

Phil stood for a moment staring over her head at the painting, willing himself to remain still, not to tighten his arms and scare her any more, then quietly he dropped a light kiss onto her hair. 'Come on, lass. I think some food is what is required. I suggest we leave your painting and your studio and this unhappy ghost to their own devices and go out and spend our statutory five bob a head on the best we can find at The Aperitif.'

When Adam found the note from Jane asking him to meet her at the North British for tea he nearly said no. Had he been busy he would have done so, but he had two hours off, and Liza told him she was too involved with her painting to break off to see him for such a short time. Piqued, he telephoned Jane from the Students' Union. They sat next to each other in the deep armchairs with a plate of cakes and scones and a pot of hot tea and Jane told him about her relationship with Robbie. They talked quietly, aware of the other couples around them all engaged in equally intense and quiet conversations, and they laughed a lot and he found himself, with a sharp pang of guilt at his disloyalty, comparing her gentle kindness and charm with Liza's acerbic manner and driven talent.

'Robbie's been posted down to England.' Jane poured tea for Adam and passed him a scone. He nodded wearily, barely able to keep his eyes open. He had been studying most of the night. 'It's awful,' she went on, 'I don't know how he is. I don't know what's happening. He can't even tell me where he is.'

Adam shrugged sympathetically. 'Why don't you go home? There must be things you can do down there to help, and your father can find out about Robbie for you.'

She bit her lip. 'Part of me wants to. I'm not exactly helping the war effort by studying the Classics!'

He laughed. 'Someone's got to keep the standards up, Janie. Why not you? You're too young and beautiful to get involved in the war! Anyway, they'll have you digging tatties or rolling bandages before long, never fear, so make the most of it.'

'Two of our tutors have gone. They'll probably close down the department soon.'

'So, that's the time to go.' He grimaced ruefully. 'I would miss you dreadfully.'

'Would you?' She glanced up at him under her lashes. 'I thought you had eyes for no one but Liza.'

He was silent. How could he explain how he felt about Liza? He wasn't sure himself. And if he knew, he wondered suddenly, would he want to tell Jane? He crumbled the dry scone on his plate, toying with the crumbs with his knife. There was no butter.

She raised an eyebrow. 'Well, she's in love with you,' she prompted gently.

He nodded. 'But it wouldn't be fair of me to get involved with anyone, not really involved. I'm going to have less and less time. I work every hour God sends as it is – they're going to need doctors so badly – and the load is only going to get heavier.' Was this an excuse, he wondered suddenly? No one had ever asked him to analyse his true feelings for Liza before. He did love her. He was fascinated by her. But something inside him held him back. Was it fear perhaps, after seeing what passion and commitment gone wrong had done to his parents? Or was it still a guilty memory of Brid and her desolate face as he left her for the last time? He didn't know. 'In the summer I'm going to Glasgow to do my six weeks' clinical practice and if I don't get called up, as soon as I qualify, I'll probably go down to London or back to Glasgow or somewhere where they really need people. I wouldn't be able to think about marrying or anything.'

'Then you should tell her.' Jane reached forward to top up his cup again. 'You're not being fair, Adam.' She smiled at him sadly, and after a moment he smiled back.

Brid smacked the water with the flat of her hand and swore. Where were the images? Where were A-dam, and the woman, the red-haired woman who painted the pictures? She could not see them. She could see nothing. Her head was spinning and she felt terribly cold. She looked at her hands. They were blue and shaking. Slowly she crawled backwards away from the edge of the spring and tried to stand up. The sky had gone black. There was a strange buzzing in her ears. Somewhere she could hear someone calling her name. She shook her head. It was Broichan's voice. Broichan who had vowed to kill her. But he must not follow her here. Not to A-dam's time. Not to A-dam's city. She struggled to her feet and turned away from the water. If she could find her way back to Maggie's room she would be all right. She had food in her bag; she could always buy her way in with Maggie with food or a bottle of ale, or better still some gin or at worst meths. The old woman was

114

foul-mouthed and verminous and her room was squalid. It smelled and it was cold, but it wasn't as cold as the clean sweet nights she spent on the hill when the wind cut into her very bones and she thought she would die. Slowly she began to put one foot in front of the other as she headed down towards the city.

She did not realise what was happening when she collapsed, or feel her body being lifted onto a stretcher. She did not know that she was being taken into the Infirmary. Her spirit was roaming the hill, confused, afraid, hearing only the angry shouts of Broichan in the wind and the echo of his horse's hooves in the black infinity of space.

The harassed doctor stood looking down at the still form in the hospital bed and shook his head. 'She must be in shock. Keep her warm and keep an eye on her. That's all we can do. Does anyone know who she is? Why doesn't she have an identity card?' He had a hundred other patients to see with injuries which were visible.

Brid stirred slightly, her head moving restlessly on the pillow. She could see the ward hazily through her eyelids, and the tall, ginger-haired man in his white coat, the stethoscope around his neck; she was aware of the other beds, the women lying in rows, some weeping quietly, some silent, their faces as white as the stiff cotton sheets in which they lay. But she could not react. It was as if there were a screen between her and that world; a screen of fog, deadening the sound, removing her into some limbo where now, behind her, she could see the hillside of her home, see her brother reaching out to catch hold of her hand, see behind him Broichan's followers coming ever closer.

When the nurse propped her up against the pillows and fed her something with a spoon she swallowed obediently. She did not fight them when they sponged her thin body and changed her gown, she did not react when someone came and brushed her hair or when the chaplain prayed over her to the Christian God. Nothing reached her. In the locker beside her bed her woven bag lay untouched. They had not found a name or address in the small leather purse; the pretty powder compact had no initials on it. The small rusty iron-bladed dagger roused interest, and some speculation, but was soon returned to the bag and forgotten.

'You don't mind coming with me?' Liza was sitting opposite Adam in The Aperitif in Frederick Street. 'You are sure you can spare the time?' There was a touch of sarcasm there he had not heard before.

'Of course not.' He smiled at her, trying not to think about the bill which any minute he would have to call for.

She grinned back at him, reading his thoughts and to his embarrassment he found a ten shilling note being pushed into his hand. 'Go on. I owe you. I've sold two pictures. When you're in London and established in Harley Street you can take me to the Ritz. Deal?'

He nodded with relief. 'Deal.'

The streets of Morningside were deserted, peaceful after the bustle and crowds and queues in the centre of the town. The house was grey, solid, very respectable, with ornate net curtains and a border of roses along both sides of the front path. They let themselves in and carefully shut the gate behind them before walking slowly towards the front door. A robin was singing from the pear tree on the front lawn, its throat swelling and fluttering with the ecstasy of its song. The woman who opened the door was in her forties, neat in a twin set and pearl necklace, her feet clad in brown leather brogues. Only the exotic rings on her fingers – amber and lapis and jade – hinted at her calling. She showed them into the front room which was solidly furnished with a sofa and two matching easy-chairs and a low table. On the table stood something swathed in a black cloth. Adam felt his stomach lurch with disgust. The woman had a crystal ball.

'Please sit down.' She smiled at them and picked up without comment the envelope that Liza slid across the table to her. Obviously payment was in advance. Tucking it into her pocket without opening it she sat opposite them and surveyed them with surprisingly astute eyes. 'So. I gather you are having trouble with a gypsy curse?'

Liza nodded. 'As I explained over the phone, Mrs Gardiner, I don't understand it. I can feel her wherever I am. I go to the art college, I go home to my studio, I go shopping, I go to my tutor's house . . .' She did not see Adam's sharp glance as she said that. 'Wherever I am she is there, watching me. Inside my head. It's driving me mad!'

'And you, Mr Craig, does she follow you the same way?'

The woman's eyes seemed to look into Adam's soul. He shrugged uncomfortably. 'Hardly at all. I thought I saw her once or twice. Standing near my digs in the High Street. I don't understand why she is pestering Liza like this.'

'Well, that's easy.' Mrs Gardiner crossed her legs elegantly and Adam heard the rasp of the silk-clad thighs. 'Miss Vaughan is a natural psychic. The girl finds it easy to reach her.'

'A psychic?' Adam looked at her in astonishment.

Liza grimaced. 'I told you I had second sight.'

'She obviously finds it hard to contact you, Mr Craig, so she is clinging to the one person with whom she can be sure of a link. This kind of telepathic link is very tenuous at the best of times. It is probably not a two-way thing. May I ask why you do not contact her in person and ask her to stop?'

'Because I can't find her,' Adam said desperately. 'When I thought I saw her I went to catch her but she wasn't there. I have no idea where she is staying.' His face was set grimly. He was not going to tell them he hadn't tried to find her, that the last person on earth he wanted to see was Brid. 'Liza tells me you can contact her somehow. Tell her to back off. That's the reason we've come to see you.'

'Of course.' Mrs Gardiner smiled enigmatically. 'But first, I have to ask you something.' She took a deep breath and then stopped, as though she were embarrassed suddenly. 'Mr Craig, forgive me asking you this, but I have to know. Miss Vaughan says that this young lady, Brid, is a tinker lass, a Romany. Is that right?'

Adam nodded.

'Do you have anything of hers? Did she give you a keepsake? A memento? A charm? Anything that you could have passed on to Miss Vaughan as a gift in your turn?'

Adam tensed. The pendant. But how could he admit to Liza that the gift he had given her had been Brid's? He took a deep breath and shook his head. 'Nothing.'

'I ask because if you had such an item it could be that she is using it as the link between you. It is a common practice amongst the Romany people, I understand, to maintain their power over others. Could she have given you something without your realising it? Hidden it in your belongings, perhaps?'

He bit his lip, aware that both women were looking at him hard, and for a moment he was transported back to the summer hillside and the tent by the burn. 'She gave me nothing. I'm sure of it.'

'I see.' Mrs Gardiner seemed disappointed. She shrugged and leaned forward towards the table. 'Well, all I can do is consult my ball and see what it says.' She pulled off the black cloth and Adam found himself staring down into the cloudy, sparkling crystal.

For a long time she was silent. Adam felt a sudden panic, wondering if she could see the truth in it. The feeling was replaced almost at once by self-ridicule at his own credulity and by a wild urge to laugh and he looked up, trying to catch Liza's eye. But she was staring at the ball as hard as Mrs Gardiner. He exhaled loudly and sat back on the sofa with crossed arms, distancing himself from what the two women were doing. Whatever it was, they were not going to reach Brid.

'Ah, I see her now.' Mrs Gardiner had been silent for so long Adam jumped. 'A pretty girl, with long dark hair. She is standing by a great sarsen stone. I see the carvings on it. The animals; the broken lightning bolt, the crescent. That is where she must be getting her strength to reach you. You touched it with her, perhaps. You made the link yourself.'

Adam stared at her and he felt the blood draining from his face. Liza must have told the woman about that on the telephone.

But he had never told Liza.

'Yes,' Mrs Gardiner went on. She seemed to be getting into her stride. 'I can see fog around her. She is lost. Her family are looking for her. There is a great deal of anger. I can see it crackling round the stone. I can see danger. Fear. I can hear them shouting. It is a strange language. I can't understand.' Small drops of perspiration were appearing on the woman's heavily powdered upper lip. 'They are hunting for you, Mr Craig.' She looked away from the ball suddenly, straight at him, and he saw the horror in her eyes. 'They are hunting for you. They are going to hunt you for as long as it takes to find you and then they are going to kill you.'

He thought he was going to be sick. He stared at her, conscious that beside him Liza had caught her breath in a strangled gasp. The woman's hands were shaking as she sat forward again and looked back into the crystal. He followed her gaze, unable now to look away, but the crystal appeared to have gone black. The rainbows and lights which had danced inside the quartz as the sun shone in through the net curtains had died. The room was growing dark.

Slowly she shook her head. 'I can't see any more.' She sat back and rubbed her face with her hands. 'There is one other thing I must tell you. I'm sorry, Mr Craig, but your Brid is dead. She may have been a gypsy once, but the young lady who is haunting you both has been dead for a long, long time.'

'You were lying, weren't you!' Liza turned on him the moment they were outside. Her expression was icy. 'You did give me something of hers. The pendant!'

Adam stared at her. 'How did you know it was that?'

'Apart from the fact that it's the only present you've ever given me, you mean?' She saw the colour flare in his cheeks and instantly she was sorry. He was after all a student with no money. But she persisted. 'Why, Adam? Why did you give it to me?'

118

'I wanted to give you something,' he said awkwardly. 'I wasn't going to see her again. It was very beautiful –' He paused, standing, hands in pockets, staring into space. 'Did you believe her when she said Brid was dead?'

Liza was silent for a moment. 'I don't know!'

'Poor Brid.' He took a few steps down the quiet road and then stopped again. 'She was so full of life.'

Liza had followed him. 'It's not poor Brid, Adam. She's dangerous. She's vicious. Even if she's a ghost, she's still here, for God's sake! And you can have your pendant back. Now. Today.'

When they reached the studio she went straight to the bedside table where the silver charm lay. Picking it up she handed it to Adam. 'No more presents, please.'

'Liza –'

'No, Adam.' She pursed her lips. 'I'm sorry. A girl doesn't want to hear that the gift she's been given is second-hand. And she doesn't want to know that she's been lied to. Even without the fact that I'm being pursued by a ghost that belongs to you! I'm very fond of you, Adam, I always will be, but enough is enough!' She turned away abruptly so he couldn't see the angry tears. 'Please go.'

'Liza, you're not serious? We've been through so much together . . .'

'Exactly!' She rounded on him. 'We've been through a lot, and it's Brid's fault. You deal with her! It's not my problem!'

Andrew Thomson, another fourth-year student, who intended to specialise in surgery, had taken over Robbie's digs. Like all medical students he had in July the previous year had his call-up deferred, a deferral which depended on their marks being passable and their eventual qualification. He and Adam rubbed along together fairly well, but both were working so hard now they had little time for more than the occasional drink together down Lothian Road. It was almost a surprise when Adam, exhausted after a day of ward rounds and clinical lectures, found Andrew standing staring out of the window of the small sitting room in the digs looking down at the narrow close where a small child, half dressed and shivering, was teasing a mangy dog. He turned as Adam came in. 'I thought you might be in about now, old boy.' He hesitated. 'I've got some bad news, I'm afraid.' He paused as Adam stood in the doorway. 'It's Robbie. He's been shot down.'

Adam took a deep breath. It had happened to several young men he knew. But no one close. Not yet. 'Is he badly hurt?' His voice was husky.

'I'm afraid he bought it. So sorry, old chap, I really am.'

He lay face down on his bed for a long time after Andrew had gone, as the room grew dark around him. His mind was a blank. He did not let himself remember the good times. He didn't let himself think about Robbie's father or his grandparents or Jane. The picture in his head was of the young, laughing RAF officer, the blue of his uniform setting off the blue of his eyes, excited, eager, treating war as a challenge, even a game. He had survived the posting down south, he had survived the Battle of Britain, he had written to say he was coming up on leave and would see them all in two weeks' time, and now he was gone.

It was fully dark when Andrew pushed open the door again and walked across the room to pull the blackout into place before switching on the light. 'You okay?'

Adam rolled over and put his hand across his eyes to shield them from the light. 'I think I should go and see Jane.' His voice was harsh, but he hadn't cried. His misery was lodged tight inside his chest.

Andrew lit a cigarette and stood, his back to the window, looking down at him. 'I can borrow the old Riley from my mate Jimmy Grant. I'll drive you down to her place, if you like.'

Adam swung his feet to the floor and rubbed the palms of his hands up and down his face. 'Give me a cigarette. Poor Jane. How is she going to cope with this?'

The car went slowly through the narrow border lanes, feeling its way in the dark until they reached the huge gates which led to the old peel tower. Robbie and Adam used to joke that Jane was like Rapunzel, but in her case the prisoner not of a witch, but of a wicked uncle. The Kennedys, the family with whom she was living now she had given up university, were distant cousins, but far from being a prisoner in the high tower, she was helping on their farm with enormous enjoyment.

Adam sat for a moment in the front of the Riley staring up at the dark mass of the tower. 'It's like something out of *Macbeth*.'

Andrew nodded. 'Look, I'd better be getting back. Can you find your own way tomorrow?'

'Sure.' Adam opened the door and climbed out. 'Wish me luck.'

Hauling on the bell-pull he waited in the cold wind as the small car drove away into the darkness. It was Jane who opened the door.

'Adam?' She pulled him in and closed the door behind him. Then she burst into tears.

'I wasn't expecting you,' she said as she led him into the kitchen, the only warm room in the house. 'I should have known you'd come. You're so sweet, Adam. I'm babysitting. The others have gone into Edinburgh to see the Half Past Eight Review at the King's Theatre. They're staying overnight and coming back tomorrow. They were going to cancel, to stay with me, but I wanted to be alone.' She was silent for a minute. 'Then I wished I wasn't. I'm so glad you came.'

They sat together in the kitchen for a long time. She cried a bit more and then fell silent, staring down into the mug of cocoa he had made for her as she rocked back and forth in the old chair by the range. 'You know, Robbie always talked about getting engaged,' she said at last, looking up at him with red eyes.

'Did he?' He was astonished at the flare of jealousy that went through him, and immediately bitterly ashamed.

She nodded. 'I didn't want to. I think –' She paused. 'I think I knew something would happen.' She put down her mug and stooped to pick up the black cat circling round her legs, wanting its accustomed chair. She hugged it to her. 'My parents didn't approve of him, you know. Oh, they liked him well enough but they didn't think he was right for me. Not to marry.' A tear ran down her cheek and she brushed it away. 'It's funny that he should die in England. If it had to happen he would have wanted it to be up here, defending Scotland.'

'We're all on the same side, Janie.' Adam was fighting back his own tears suddenly. He slipped out of his chair and went to put his arms around her. 'I'm glad he wasn't horribly wounded and left a cripple. Robbie couldn't have lived with that. I've seen such terrible things, Janie. You wouldn't believe. I know it isn't much comfort, but I think that if he had to be shot down, it's what he would have wanted.' He rested his head against Jane's shoulder, very conscious suddenly of the warmth of her body near his, of the clean lemon scent of her skin.

It was some time later that she stirred. He had been asleep like that, cramped in her arms for nearly an hour and she had spent that hour looking down at him, gently stroking his hair. 'Adam?' she whispered. 'I must go and check the children. Come with me.' There were two children in the house aged four and five. They adored Jane and she them.

She took his hand and led him up the draughty, narrow spiral staircase from the kitchen to the third floor where the two children slept, snugly tucked beneath their blankets. They looked down at

121

them for a minute in the light of the lamp in her hand and then quietly closed the door.

'Come.' She led him along the landing to her own room.

He hesitated as she turned on the light. 'Janie –'

'Please, Adam. I can't bear to be alone. Just hold me, that's all.'

Outside the narrow tall windows the wind buffeted the glass and moaned in the high chimneys. The children, used to the wild noises, slept soundly. Lying fully dressed beside Jane on the narrow bed under the covers Adam dozed fitfully and then found himself wide awake, staring up at the ceiling in the dark. She had slipped away into the bathroom to undress and returned wearing a high-necked cotton nightdress which came down to her feet. It was virginal, white, trimmed with broderie anglaise, and he felt to his intense shame a surge of lust at the sight of it. Restraining himself firmly he stretched out next to her, the image of Robbie lying somewhere in a wooden coffin enough to keep his thoughts sober. It was a long time before he felt her body relax into sleep and he lay listening to her gentle, even breathing as the wind battered even harder at the window.

He had at last fallen asleep in the early hours of the morning, to dream of running through the woods with Robbie, playing with home-made bows and arrows when they were very small, when something woke him suddenly. He stared into the darkness listening hard. Jane was still asleep. There was no sound in the house save for the ticking of the old longcase clock on the landing. He held his breath, wondering if he should get up and go and look at the children. Or had the Kennedys perhaps changed their minds and decided to drive back instead of staying in Edinburgh for the night, and what he had heard was their car on the gravel outside?

Jane stirred and he heard her mutter something under her breath. He put his arm over her protectively, feeling the rise and fall of her breasts beneath the blankets.

A-dam?

It was the wind in the chimney again. There was no fire in the hearth. Small wisps of old ash were sighing across the stone. Somewhere a board creaked. Adam found his mouth had gone dry.

Where are you, A-dam?

He held his breath. It was a nightmare. There was no one there. The wind had awoken him.

Jane turned towards him, half awake, her body curved cosily into the old mattress. 'What is it?'

'Nothing. Go back to sleep.' His hand was still resting over her breasts. Gently he caressed them through the blanket. She did not turn away. Her eyes closed, she snuggled closer to him. His lips touched her hair in the darkness. 'Janie? Are you awake?'

She didn't answer, but her hand had found his shoulder and then his shirtfront. Slowly she began to undo the buttons.

'Janie –'

'Sssh.'

She was warm and relaxed and soft. A fragrant haven. Almost without realising it he had pulled off his trousers and climbed in beneath the blankets, drawing them up over their heads. He was very gentle with her, conscious that this was a very special love, a love to give comfort and companionship, a love to stem their grief. He caressed her thighs lightly beneath the long nightdress, and untied the ribbons to reach her breasts with his lips, intrigued and enchanted by her modesty and her combination of eagerness and reluctance. 'Jane!' He buried his face between her breasts. 'My love!'

For a moment he thought she was going to refuse him as he drew her into his arms and began to insert his leg between hers. He was excited now – eager. Robbie was forgotten. The children along the landing were forgotten. His memory was of a lithe, supple body lying on the rocks in the sun, its legs provocatively apart, laughing teasing eyes, the bitter peaty water drying on soft pale skin.

'Brid!' He was terrified he had shouted it out loud as he drove into Jane's soft flesh, and not until it was too late did he realise the significance of the resistance he felt there. He collapsed, panting, onto her breasts, kissing her silken skin, triumphant after the surge of his own passion, unaware for a moment that she was lying very still, tears running down her cheeks. 'Jane? Janie? What's wrong?' He sat up and reached for the switch on the bedside light.

She grabbed at the blankets, pulling them up to her chin. 'Nothing. Nothing's wrong.'

'But it is. Janie. Oh my God! It was your first time!'

She sniffed. 'Everyone has to have a first time.'

'But I thought you and Robbie – oh Christ!' He swung his legs over the side of the bed and reached for his trousers.

He dressed with his back to her, then when he had lit a cigarette he came to sit on the edge of the bed beside her. 'Janie, I am so sorry!'

'Why?' She smiled at him wanly. 'It's what I wanted.'

'But –'

'Robbie and I waited, Adam. He didn't want to. It was my idea. We waited so we could do it properly on our wedding night. If we had a wedding night. There isn't going to be a wedding night. If we had made love I would have known what it was like. I would have known what he was like.' She was sobbing uncontrollably. 'I would have had that memory. So would he.'

Adam stared at her, appalled. He felt a mass of conflicting emotions: hurt that she could have used him so cynically; horror that her pain was so great she could act so out of character; disgust at himself that he could have so casually taken advantage of her unhappiness. And also something else; a knowledge that he had in some way betrayed both Liza, even if she had made it clear she no longer wanted him, and the girl he was trying to forget, the girl whose name he had cried out as he possessed this gentle, blonde woman whose trust he had violated. He stood up and went to throw his cigarette into the fireplace where it glowed red for a moment in the draught amongst the long-dead ashes. He was full of self-loathing.

'Adam, don't.' Jane sat up. Her eyes were red, but she had grown calm. 'Come back here.' She patted the bed cover.

He hesitated for a moment, then he went back and sat down beside her. He reached for her cold hand and squeezed it gently.

'We both loved him, Adam. Don't let him come between us. What we did was for Robbie. And for ourselves. A sort of exorcism of grief.' She smiled wanly. 'Don't be angry. No one need ever know what happened here tonight.'

He was looking at her with such intense concentration she found it disconcerting.

'Adam, please. It doesn't matter.'

'It does matter. It matters to me. A lot.'

She reached out and touched his face. 'Bless you.'

He jerked back out of her reach. 'Don't.'

'Adam –'

'No. I'm sorry, Jane. This matters to me a great deal. I'm not in the habit of sleeping around, especially with the girlfriends of my dead friends!' He walked back to the fireplace, trying to control the anger which had swept over him.

A-dam. Where are you?

The voice in his head was suddenly so loud he could not ignore it. He clapped his hands to his face. 'No!' His cry was so anguished Jane scrambled out of bed and ran to him. 'Adam, Adam. Please. What's wrong?'

'It's nothing.' He turned away from her. 'A headache, that's all.' He took a grip on himself with an effort and turned back to her. 'I'm sorry, Janie. I think we should both get some sleep. If you don't mind I'll go downstairs and sleep on the sofa. As soon as it's light I'll borrow Sam's motorbike and get back to town. I've a ward round at eight.'

He didn't wait for her to argue. Letting himself out of the room he ran down the spiral stairs and went into the cold living room.

Shivering, he sat on the edge of the broad stone window ledge and pulled the curtains and then the blackout aside, looking out into the dark garden. Somewhere in the distance he heard an owl call as it hunted along the hedge. He could not bring himself to think about Jane at all, his guilt was too profound. Only one worry circled now round and round inside his brain. Brid had found him, out here in the Pentland Hills, because still there in the pocket of his coat was the pendant that Liza had returned to him. He stifled his sudden urge to throw the thing out of the window into the garden. It would bring Brid here, to Jane, and that he could not allow. He suddenly needed to talk to Liza badly, but he wasn't sure if he would be able to talk to Liza again.

'It has its face to the wall in case you were wondering!' Liza grinned at Adam as he walked into her studio a few days later and stared awkwardly round. 'I won't inflict my work on you if it causes such offence.'

Adam shook his head. 'It never crossed my mind. In fact I'm flattered you painted me. When you're very famous that will be worth millions of pounds and my face will hang in some rich man's collection, and they'll all say, that's the famous Dr Craig who was such an inspiration to the artist.'

She laughed and caught his arm. 'I'm glad we're beginning to see sense at last. So. How are things?'

He hesitated uncomfortably. 'You've heard about Robbie?'

She nodded. 'I'm so sorry.'

He sighed. 'It's such a waste. It's all such a waste.' There was a moment's silence. Then he remembered why he had come. 'Liza, I've heard Brid.'

She stood very still, staring at him. 'Was it because I gave you the pendant?'

He nodded. 'It was in my pocket. I forgot about it –'

'You must do what Mrs Gardiner said, Adam. Protect yourself against her. Visualise yourself surrounded by light. Make the sign of the cross. Carry a crystal to help with the protection. Be strong. Don't let her sense you are afraid. Don't let her into your head. And get rid of the pendant!'

'I have.' Ashamed and angry at his own superstition, he had driven out to Queensferry a few mornings earlier. He had stood for a while on the quay, watching the ferry load the queue of waiting cars and cast off to chug out into the Forth. Then he had pulled the silver charm from his pocket. With a quick glance around to make sure he was unobserved he had flung it as far as he could out into the grey frothing water. For a moment he had wondered if it would refuse to sink, if he would hear a scream of protest inside his head, if Brid would somehow materialise beside him, but nothing happened. The waves slapped as steadily as before against the green weed-encrusted stones of the quay and the pendant was gone forever.

With a shiver he glanced round at the door behind him as though half expecting it to fly open and reveal Brid standing there. Liza shook her head. 'I'm glad you got rid of it. But you have to go on being careful. I thought you understood. She has the power to enter people's minds, Adam. She invades their heads. Mrs Gardiner explained all that, or weren't you listening?' She laughed suddenly, the sound bubbling up inside her as she saw Adam's face. 'Oh dear, the Presbyterian boy rebels again. Adam, my sweet love, don't you see? This girl, this Brid of yours is – was – a psychic, a witch, if you like. She had powers. You can't guard yourself against them unless you know how. They might intrude on you anywhere, at any time.' She paused, suddenly struck by the expression on his face. 'Oh dear. I see she has.' She could not for a moment hide the anguish in her eyes. She bit her lip.

'Liza –'

'No. It doesn't matter. What matters is that you know what to do. That you know how to save yourself from her. She was – is – an adept, Adam. You said she had gone to some kind of college which taught her these things?'

'I don't know what she learned there. Some of it was reciting poetry and stuff . . .'

'It was magic.'

'Liza! That's nonsense.'

'It's not nonsense! How can you be so blind! Use your head.'

'I am using my head. I'm training to be a doctor. I'm a scientist, Liza, and you tell me this girl studied magic. You'll tell me she can fly next.'

'So why did you come to tell me that you had heard her voice?'

'Because,' he hesitated. 'Because I need your help. I don't think Brid's dead. I was thinking about it. Why should we believe that woman? She's a backstreet medium. No one would take her seriously.'

Liza flushed with anger. 'I took her seriously!'

He shrugged. 'You're being too credulous, Liza,' he went on swiftly. 'I think Brid is using telepathy or something like that.'

'Telepathy! And that's not magic?'

'No, it isn't.'

Liza smiled. 'But doctors don't recognise that either, do they? All right. So, do you know how to protect yourself against telepathy?'

He shook his head.

'Do you want me to show you?'

He hesitated. 'I don't want to get involved in table turning and stuff like that, Liza.'

She tightened her lips. 'All right. We'll leave it.' She paused. 'So, what were you doing that allowed her to invade your privacy so badly?'

'Liza –'

'You keep saying that. It doesn't matter, you know. It's not as though you and I are together any more. But I thought we were still friends. It's a pity Brid doesn't realise that it's not me she has to be jealous of.' She turned away from him and went to stand by the window. It was something she often did when he was there, he realised suddenly.

'Liza, don't. Listen, I don't have to be back until two. Come out and have some lunch.'

'I don't think so, Adam.' There was a long pause. 'Adam, I think you should know I'm seeing someone else. Phil Stevenson.' It had happened so gradually she had hardly noticed at first the developing relationship. 'I thought you'd probably guessed . . .'

'Will you marry me?' Adam was still holding the bunch of red roses he had brought with him. They were awkwardly clutched in his arms as he sat beside Jane on the window seat. Sam and Elsie had made themselves absent with the children, all gardening strenuously out of sight around the corner of the tower.

Jane stared at him fondly. She laughed. 'Adam, you don't have to ask me.'

'I do.' He stared down at the roses as though he had never seen them before and then pushed them at her. It had been his first thought when he had heard of Liza's engagement to Philip. Ask Jane. Marry Jane. Show Liza you don't care.

'Here, take these. I've something else for you too.' He groped in his pocket for the small box containing the ring over which he had agonised for so long in George Street. It was a tiny star of rubies on a narrow, gold band. 'I hope it fits.'

She stared down at it, blinking back her tears. 'Adam –'

'I love you, Jane. Please. Marry me. I know I'm not qualified yet, but it won't be long.' He had forgotten his earlier protests that marriage would be impossible for him. Suddenly they didn't seem important any more. 'I won't be earning much, I know, but I'm ambitious and I work hard.' He smiled self-deprecatingly. 'I've hopes that I'll do well. I think I can convince your father that I can look after you. Perhaps if we got married after I graduate –'

'Yes.'

'Then we could look for a small flat if I do my residency at the Royal Infirmary –'

'I said yes.'

He stopped in mid-sentence. 'What?'

'I said yes, Adam. Yes. I would love to marry you.'

'You would?'

She laughed with delight. 'In a minute I shall think you don't mean it.'

'Oh, I mean it.' He scrabbled in the little velvet-lined box and extricated the ring. To his relief it fitted. 'Oh Janie, I'm so honoured.' He leaned forward and kissed her gently on the lips.

'Not honoured. Pleased. Happy,' she corrected gently. Firmly she pushed away the small flicker of doubt which was nudging at the corner of her mind.

It was strange how they didn't notice her. Brid walked swiftly, her head down, keeping to the edge of the corridors, avoiding people's eyes. The hospital smelled strange. There was death and fear and over it all a strong smell she couldn't identify. There were doctors here; healers. So Adam must be somewhere here too. But where? The passages were so long. The sounds were so strange; the clank of metal, the rolling of little wheels over the flag-stones, the starched rustle of the women who took care of people. They were kind enough. They had looked after her, but even so it didn't seem to be the sort of place people would go to get better. There were no dark places to consult the gods. There were no rooms for the distillation of herbs. There was no music. There was no peace.

She saw two young men approaching and flattened herself against the wall. Their white coats flew open as they walked, and they both had the long strange tube with metal pieces hung around their necks. Her doctor had taken his off and pressed a part of it to her chest and stuck it in his ears. It was some kind of sign of office, she supposed. They passed her without noticing her, engrossed in their conversation. One of them, had she but known it, was Andrew Thomson.

Behind her, in the ward, a doctor was standing looking down at her empty bed in confusion. 'When did you realise she had gone?'

'Only about ten minutes ago, Doctor. She was asleep. She wasn't reacting. You know how she was!' The distraught nurse was wringing her hands. 'No one could make her hear. Suddenly she sat up; she looked as though she was listening; as though she could hear something far away in the distance. I went to fetch Sister and she came and talked to her. The girl listened to her. Her face became almost intelligent. That strange vacancy had gone. Sister spoke to her very kindly and the girl seemed to understand. Then Nurse Standish came in and called Sister away and when I came to check, the girl had gone. She's taken her bag, her clothes and the charity clothes she was given. There's no sign of her.'

The doctor shook his head and shrugged. 'Well, I suppose we'd better just be thankful it releases a bed for someone who really needs it. See that it's prepared, Nurse. And you'd better ask Sister to have a word with me when she can.' He had already put the case of the strange, silent young woman with the dull grey eyes out of his mind. There were more important things to worry about.

When she grew tired of walking the corridors Brid made her way outside into the fitful sunshine. She had to find her way back to old Maggie's before it began to grow dark, and get hold of some food or a bottle to buy her way again into the shelter of the stinking room. She was still disoriented, still distanced from the world around her with its pushing crowds and noisy vehicles and crowds of uniformed men.

Always, somewhere behind her shoulder, she could sense the other world, the world from which she had come, the world which was haunting her. It came between her and everything else, distracting her, sapping her strength. She tried to push it away and sometimes she thought she had succeeded. On the open hillside, under the brilliant frosty sky, she would take deep breaths of the clean, empty air and feel something of her old vivacity and enthusiasm. She would stretch her arms above her head and shake out her hair till it crackled with energy, and begin to run down the side of the hill, jumping over the grasses, dodging outcrops of rock. Then she would remember A-dam: his serious, deep brown eyes, his strong sun-tanned hands stroking her breasts, his slow sleepy smile, and she would feel the excitement start again in the pit of her stomach and her energy would leap and soar. And then in a moment it was gone. She was back in the swirling mists, fighting unseen demons which were struggling to draw her back.

A-dam . . .

She threw back her head and cried into the darkness.

A-dam, where are you? Please. Wait for me. I love you!

PART TWO

Jane
1945–1960s

8

Often over the last year Adam had wondered if he was mad. Proposing marriage to a woman he hardly knew was not the action of a sane man. But inexorably time had moved on. He and Jane had become close and companionable, his plans had been laid, his exams taken and passed and his time at the Royal Infirmary completed as the war drew to an end. The Smith-Newlands were a terrifying prospect as parents-in-law. The announcement of the engagement had been followed by an immediate state visit from the south, but Jane's father seemed to like him, and strings had been pulled to find Adam a nice safe practice as the junior of three partners in Hertfordshire, with an income higher than he had ever dared to hope and with it a rented house, which would be ready for them when they moved in. He had watched the activities around him in a daze, hardly feeling that any of it concerned him at all, except that it meant he would leave Edinburgh. When Jane had dared to question her parents' plans and remind him that they loved Scotland and would like to live there always he had shrugged and shaken his head. 'It's kind of them to help us and I'd never get such a good chance up here – or not for ages.' He did not see her crest-fallen expression, and did not add his own, single over-riding thought: Brid would never find him in England.

The summer before he had agreed, against all common sense, to be a witness at Liza's wedding to Phil. The misery he felt as he watched her exchange vows with the man beside her was profound and totally inadmissible. As was the devastation which had overwhelmed him as he said goodbye when they set off for Wales. As she left Liza had leaned forward and whispered in his ear, 'No sign of Brid?'

He had shaken his head. 'Not a word.'

'Good.' She had put her arms round him and given him a hug. Then she had climbed after Phil onto the train.

That autumn he had heard that his mother was dead. The letter from his father was brief, without emotion. She had been killed, it appeared, in an automobile accident in Chicago. There was no mention of the man she had left Scotland with, nor of where she would be buried. Adam stared at the letter for a long time, all the old emotions of grief and anger, loss and regret resurfacing one after the other. Jane had comforted him and he had torn the letter up and then he had gone at last to Pittenross to see his father. Thomas knew no more of the circumstances of Susan Craig's life and death in America than he had told Adam in the letter. If he felt any grief he hid it totally. The two men shook hands and parted. They were not to meet again until the day before Adam's wedding. Adam did not climb the hill to visit the stone. And he did not pass a night under his father's roof.

Meryn Jones lived in a small, white-washed, stone-built cottage which lay in the shelter of a ridge of the Black Mountains, with a view of the Wye valley spread out below it in a panorama of pale shifting colours. The house was only a mile from Pen-y-Ffordd, where Liza and Phil had come to live in her old family home now that her mother had gone to live with her sister in Kent.

Liza stood for a moment staring at the house, then, half reluctantly, she moved forward to knock on the door. Meryn had lived here for as long as she could remember, certainly since she had been a child, and his reputation locally as a wizard and a magician was formidable, so much so that when she was little she had called him Merlin. If asked, all he would have admitted to was the ability to charm warts, to predict the weather, something any farmer could do as well, as he always said, and sometimes, perhaps, to give advice on ghostly happenings in the vicinity. What he did in his lonely cottage, alone, when there was nobody to watch, no one knew.

As she sat down by his fire Liza's nervousness disappeared as Meryn's kindly smile reassured her and he made himself comfortable to listen to her tale.

Beside them the logs cracked and hissed and the room filled with the aromatic scent of burning apple and oak.

'So, you want me to make you an amulet to keep your friend Adam safe from this woman who pursues him?' he ventured at last. 'You feel that although he has not heard from her in a long time, she hasn't gone away.'

Liza nodded. 'He's getting married. I think she might not like that.'

Meryn gave a grave nod. 'From what you have told me, I would agree.'

'Can you do it for me? Please?'

'I suspect I can.' His smile was gentle. 'Leave it with me, Liza, my dear. I shall think about it and come up with something suitable. Something which will give him and his bride protection from this girl and at the same time not shame their elegant home.' The smile had become distinctly mischievous. 'And neither you nor I need admit there is anything of the supernatural involved.' He took Liza's hand and held it for a moment. 'Come back in a week. I shall see what I can do for you.'

After she had gone he sat for a long time, his eyes fixed on the fire. He frowned uneasily as the pictures came, confused and strange at first, then slowly more vivid. He could see the girl with her long dark hair and her wild frightened eyes and he could see the great stone on the hillside. Behind her, in the shadows, was a power which turned the flickering apple flame to the colour of blood and roared in the chimney like a giant wind. He shivered and shook off the vision. Enough to know that Adam Craig and his new wife would face danger beyond their imagining. He stood up and walked over to the table which stood in the centre of his room. On it lay a litter of objects, amongst them a small, intensely bright crystal which he had been given when he had visited New York State to learn the ways of the Iroquois Indians. It was pretty enough in its diamond brilliance to please the eye and its protective power was profound.

'Darling, you look so pretty.' Patricia Smith-Newland, kneeling on the pink Chinese carpet, fluffed up the white silk skirt, which had been made with a careful combination of hoarded coupons and a white silk bedspread. Her daughter sat in front of her bedroom mirror, adjusting her veil. 'I can't believe it!' Suddenly there were tears running down her cheeks again, forming ugly rivulets in the pink face powder. 'It's not too late, you know, to change your mind. Daddy could make it all right if you want to stop the wedding.'

'Mummy!' Jane turned round on the narrow stool and glared at her mother. 'Please stop it! I am marrying Adam and that is that! I love him. He loves me! You should be jolly glad I've found someone so respectable.'

135

'I am, sweetheart. It's just . . .' The woman shrugged helplessly as she climbed heavily to her feet. 'Well, he's so Scottish!'

Jane stared at her mother with something like real disdain. 'All the best doctors are Scottish, Mummy. Everyone knows that.'

'And that father of his!' The hand gestures spoke volumes. 'Thomas. He's like the spectre at the feast.' She shuddered ostentatiously.

The object of her dislike was a house guest, at that very moment adjusting his snow-white bands and black gown before setting off in the car to the church where, much against his better judgement he was to help officiate at the very Church of England wedding of his son to an English lass with blonde hair so very much like the English lass who had captivated him so many years before.

'Mummy, do you mind if I'm on my own for a few minutes?' Jane smiled at her mother in what she hoped was a conciliatory way. 'Just to compose myself. You know.'

Patricia gulped. 'Of course, darling. I'll wait downstairs with the bridesmaids.' Six of them. 'I'll send Daddy up to find you in five minutes, shall I?'

The small twelfth-century Surrey church was packed on the bride's half of the aisle. The groom's side was less well represented, but Adam's friends had made a noble effort. Amongst them were Liza and Philip Stevenson. Andrew Thomson was sitting beside him now, his best man. Both were resplendent in the kilt, the only thing, Adam felt, which went even a little way to pacify his future mother-in-law's implacable dislike of all things Scots.

Climbing out of the old Bentley, which for the whole of the war had been stored in a barn at the bottom of the field near the house, Jane took her father's arm. He patted her hand. 'All right, sweetheart?'

She nodded nervously. If only she could talk to him alone; if only he had come on the long walk with her which she had tentatively suggested the evening before. Just to be with him one last time as his daughter before she became a wife. It wasn't that she didn't love Adam. She did, desperately. And yet she was afraid. It was as though there was a shadow there somewhere, where she couldn't quite see it. A shadow which frightened her. Did everyone have doubts like hers at the last moment? Did everyone want a few words of reassurance from someone, a sign that they were doing the right thing? She didn't know. But her mother had stepped in, as she always did, making sure any small moments of tenderness between father and daughter were lost in her own overpowering need to control every single member of her family. 'Don't be silly, Jane. The last thing you want is to go for a walk! You must have an early night. Conserve your strength! Heaven knows, you're going to need it! Leave the poor child alone, James.'

And so the chance had gone. She was pulling at her skirts, arranging them, vaguely wondering where the bridesmaids were when James turned her to face him. 'Remember, Janie. It's your life. Be happy.' There they were. The six small girls in a froth of pink and white and rosebuds, being shepherded along the path. 'Adam is as straight as they come, Janie. He's a fine young man. I happen to think you've made a good choice. Don't listen to anyone who says otherwise.' It was the nearest he ever came to rebellion, this quiet contradiction of the accepted view in his house. He smiled down at her with so much love and understanding she felt the tears flood into her eyes. He had understood all along. Seeing the tears he patted her hand again. 'Come on. Let's get these children fell in. Forward march!'

The service passed, for Jane, in a dream of happiness. As she stood beside her kilted husband, gazing up at the old stained-glass window, still criss-crossed with brown paper to save it from any nearby explosions, she did not believe anyone could be so lucky. All her doubts had gone. She glanced across at Adam, and feeling her gaze upon him he smiled down at her and squeezed her hand.

Mrs Adam Craig. Changing later into the soft heather tones of her suit and hat in the bedroom which was from today no longer hers, Jane tried out the name. Dr and Mrs Craig. Adam and Jane.

She turned enquiringly at the knock on the door. It was Liza. 'I wanted to bring you my present up here. I hope you don't mind.'

Marriage had not altered Liza. Her hair was still long and wild and curly, her clothes unconventional and brightly coloured, her manner relaxed and warm. For a moment Jane felt herself as gauche and naïve as she had always felt in Liza's presence. Then she remembered. She was married too. She was Mrs Adam Craig and she knew, deep inside, that that was something Liza might have once wanted to be herself. She smiled and went forward to kiss Liza's cheek. 'I was so pleased to see you and Philip had come. Really pleased. I thought Adam said Philip had been ill.'

'He was.' Liza's sparkle faded for a moment. 'But he's fine now. All he needed was to get away from the university and rest. He'd been working too hard. Professors have a surprisingly stressful life.'

Jane turned away from her to sit down in front of the mirror again. She reached for her lipstick. 'You will come and see us in St Albans, won't you, when we're settled in the new practice? We've got a lovely old house, too. Adam is terribly lucky to get the partnership. He wanted to get away from Edinburgh so badly. I couldn't quite understand that.' She glanced at Liza in the mirror and found the other woman's eyes fixed on hers. 'When he finished at the Infirmary they offered him a post, a plum post, but he didn't take it. He said he wanted to get away from Scotland.' She outlined her lips with vermilion and blotted them elegantly. 'It's funny that, though. You both wanting to leave Edinburgh so badly too. I can remember you swearing you would never go.'

'Coincidence.' Liza laughed uneasily. So Adam had not told Jane about Brid. She sat down on the bed and lay back on the shiny satin counterpane. 'Perhaps we'd all been there too long. One can, you know. I needed new ideas. Phil wanted a complete change of scene. Perhaps now the war is over we can go abroad. I would love to go to Italy. My father's family came from Tuscany somewhere. Edinburgh will still be there if we want to go back.'

'Methinks you do protest too much.' Jane put the lipstick in her handbag. She swivelled round and looked at Liza. 'You are happy – you and Phil?'

Their eyes met.

'Yes,' Liza smiled. 'Yes, we are happy. And I hope you and Adam will be too. Just don't let –' She broke off.

'Don't let?' Jane felt a small worm of unease turn in her stomach. She knew Liza had come up here to say something.

'Don't let him get too serious.' The laugh was light and unforced. 'Did you see papa Thomas? The wrath of the Scottish God is not to be courted.'

Jane smiled. She stood up and checked the seams of her nylons. 'Adam is nothing like his father.'

'No!' Liza sat up suddenly. She swung her legs to the floor, frowning. 'Don't ever go back, Jane.'

'What?'

'I mean it. Don't go back to Edinburgh. Don't ask me why.'

'You're not making any sense at all.' Jane half turned towards the door, distracted by a shout from downstairs. 'Janie! Come on. Your guests are waiting to see you off!' It was her father's voice.

'Liza?'

Liza shrugged. 'Just a feeling I have, I suppose. Intuition. Put it down to my superstitious Welsh upbringing. I just think it wouldn't be lucky. Here.' She held out her hand. In it was a small parcel wrapped in white tissue paper. 'This is for you. To bring you both luck.'

Jane took it from her and turned it over in her hands. It was surprisingly heavy. 'Shall I wait and open it with Adam?'

'If you like. As long as you take it with you.'

Liza was half a head taller than Jane. She reached forward suddenly and pulled Jane to her. 'Please be happy,' she whispered. 'Both of you.'

Jane only thought of the parcel again that night when they had checked into their hotel bedroom in the New Forest. She pulled it out of her handbag and waved it at Adam. 'Look what Liza gave me. We were having a chat, just before we left.'

'Why haven't you opened it?' Adam smiled at her. She was very pretty, his new wife, and he was extremely fond of her, and what he wanted more than anything was to take her to bed, but just at this moment she looked totally exhausted. The final parting from her mother had been harrowing and he had nearly lost his now almost legendary calm as he dragged Jane to the car with its obligatory old boot tied to the bumper and left Patricia sobbing in her husband's arms surrounded by embarrassed wedding guests and over-tired bridesmaids.

'Champagne?' Adam asked quietly. James had stowed two carefully hoarded bottles in the boot beside the matching old leather suitcases.

She nodded and began to pull at the ribbon which tied the package as Adam eased out the cork and filled the two glasses which were standing ready on the chest of drawers near the window. Outside the forest was already dark. In the grate someone had lit a fire of apple logs and the room was warm and snug.

Adam clinked glasses with her. 'Here's to us, my darling.'

'To us.' She smiled. She took a sip and put the glass down, going back to the ribbon. He watched her affectionately for a moment as she struggled with the knot then he turned away and went to stand by the window looking out into the darkness. 'Isn't it wonderful not to have to worry about blackouts any more? Look at the light flooding out amongst the trees! It seems almost extravagant.' There was no answer and he turned. 'So, what is it?'

'I'm not sure.' She was examining something in her hands. 'It's heavy and it's very pretty – some kind of ornament.'

He put down his glass and went over to her. 'Let me see.'

'There's a card with it: *From ghoulies and ghosties . . . This is to keep you both safe. Keep it with you forever. With all my love and blessings, Liza.*

Adam frowned. He held out his hand. Jane put into it a small sparkling rock crystal set in what looked like the branches of a silver tree. 'Stand it up on the bedside table. Look, it's lovely.' She clapped her hands like a child. Adam shivered. He knew exactly what it was.

You'll need to protect yourselves. Use a talisman against the Romany magic. Counter her power with your own. Mrs Gardiner's voice floated back to him from the afternoon in Morningside when he and Liza had sat before her looking at her crystal ball. Liza had thought he wasn't listening, but he was. *Use rock crystals. They've long been considered lucky charms by the Scots. Use the ancient powers of the rowan tree. Fight her. Show her it's no use tormenting you. Poor lass. She doesn't come from the same world as you. You have to show her that you can be free of her.*

The crystal sparkled in the light of the beside lamp. On the silver branches tiny rowan leaves nestled around it and here and there a bunch of minute red enamelled berries. 'She must have had it made specially.' Adam shook his head. 'I expect one of their arty friends is a silversmith but even so, it must have been expensive.' There was a lump in his throat. He guessed she had had the crystal made into an exotic ornament which would appeal instantly to Jane because otherwise he would not have had it in the house. It was superstitious rubbish. So much idiotic nonsense. Like the pendant.

Leaving it on the table he walked over to the window and pulled the curtains across with a rattle. He shivered. The last person he had wanted to think about on his wedding night was Brid.

Jane put the ornament on the mantelpiece in the sitting room of their new home in St Albans. It was very pretty, but somehow out of place between the austere gilt carriage clock which her uncle Frederick had given them as a wedding present and the three white leaping horses which she had brought with her from the shelf in her bedroom at home. On the wall nearby were some of her books. Jane had always been a great reader and in the first months in St Albans it was only her books which saved her from total misery.

She wasn't sure how she had seen her life as a doctor's wife, but certainly not one of unending boredom and loneliness. The practice was a busy one; it had its own secretary and she was helped by Sarah Harding, the wife of the senior partner. Sarah, invariably dressed in immaculately cut skirts and cashmere twinsets or tailored silk shirts, her nails neatly manicured, her jewellery discreet, was cast in the same mould as Patricia Smith-Newland. But she was also hard-working and violently protective of her husband; she had long ago got the measure of his roving eye and fiercely headed off any threat, real or potential, to her marriage. She could have made Jane's life wonderful, or miserable. She chose to do the latter. She did not invite her to help in any way, she did not arrange for her to meet people or to take part in the activities of the women's institute or the mother's union or the practice whatsoever. She actively discouraged Jane from appearing at any social function – 'Perhaps when you know us all a little better, dear.' When Jane timidly asked Adam what she could do he shrugged and told her she should be pleased. It would give her a chance to follow her own interests. He had no idea what was going on.

At one of the partnership meetings Robert Harding had a quiet word with him. 'Only when she's ready, of course, old boy. But it would be nice if Jane would join in sometimes. I know it's a bit strange for her, so we won't rush it. But it looks a bit, you know, stand-offish!'

'I want to, Adam! I hate spending all day on my own in the house!' Her wail of anguish when he broached the subject with her shook him. 'Sarah keeps telling me I'm not needed!'

'She's only concerned in case you feel shy.'

'Oh no, Adam. I don't think so!' Her vehemence was so uncharacteristic he reeled back. 'That woman hates me. I can't think what I've done to make her feel like that, but she does. She doesn't want me doing anything at all.'

What neither of them knew was that after Adam's initial interview, when he had returned to introduce the members of the partnership to his fiancée, Robert Harding had commented to his wife later, 'What an exceptionally nice young woman. Pretty, too. She should bring some life into the place. Give you older ladies a run for your money, what!' He had not noticed Sarah's expression, neither the hurt nor the anger, nor the final rigid setting of her jaw.

The discovery that she was pregnant filled Jane with complete and utter joy. She had suspected it for some time, but when at last she mentioned it to Adam, and he confirmed it, she could not contain herself. The first person she had to tell was her mother.

Patricia's response was predictable, implying that Jane could not under any circumstances cope with pregnancy or baby without her mother close at hand. But her father, who had overheard the far end of the conversation, grabbed the telephone receiver and whooped down it. 'Tally ho, Janie. Brilliant! I'm so pleased, sweetheart. Wonderful. When?' In ten short words he had restored her confidence, her happiness and all her optimism. And amongst all the joy she hugged to herself was one small gleeful thought: Dr and Mrs Harding were childless.

Calum James Craig was born in September 1946. He had honey-coloured hair like his mother, brilliant blue eyes and enormous charm. Adam was besotted by him.

'He's got your features, my boy.' James Smith-Newland looked down into the wooden crib and gave the baby his little finger to hold. It had been a while before his wife had been persuaded to stop handing out gratuitous advice and go downstairs to supervise the kitchen arrangements instead. Jane was asleep, worn out by the visitors who had come to wish them well. Only Sarah Harding was conspicuous by her absence.

Adam smiled adoringly at his sleeping wife and then joined his father-in-law by the crib. 'I hoped he would look like Janie.'

'He does. He's got her colouring.'

Adam seemed to have aged far more than the few months since James had last seen him. He had also put on a little weight, but that was good; it suited him and gave him a certain gravitas which was useful in a young doctor. He was popular with his patients, or so Janie said, and they were, if not comfortably off, at least not on the breadline.

'Are you whispering about me?' Jane opened her eyes and stared at them drowsily.

Adam smiled. He went over and dropped a kiss on her forehead. 'Whatever gave you that idea, my love?'

'Because you're a couple of old gossips.'

'We're a doting father and grandfather!' James came to sit on the edge of her bed. 'And if you begrudge us that, young woman, it's too bad! Now, there's another visitor downstairs for you. Your friend Liza, from Wales. Shall I send her up whilst Adam and I go and find some sherry to pacify your mother?'

'Liza?' Jane glanced at Adam. 'Did you know she was coming?'

Adam shrugged. 'She said she might look in on her way to London. You don't mind do you? I should have told you.'

'Yes, you should.' For a moment Jane frowned. Then she relaxed. There was no need any more to feel jealous of Liza. She nodded and smiled. 'I'm glad she's here.'

'Good. I'll tell her to come and view the son and heir.' James stood up. He patted her again. 'Don't let her tire you out, my love.'

Liza picked Calum out of his crib and brought him to cuddle on the end of Jane's bed. 'He's gorgeous! So gorgeous. Oh Jane, I swore I didn't want any children, but I think I'm going to change my mind!' She kissed the small cheek and hugged him tighter, then she leaned forward and pushed him into Jane's arms. 'Go on, how can you bear to leave him in that lonely little bed. He needs his mummy.'

Jane's arms tightened round him. She frowned. 'My mother said he ought to get used to being on his own. I'm to feed him every four hours and not pick him up between.'

Liza stared at her. 'What if he's hungry! He's so tiny! Oh, Janie. You can't. Take no notice of her. I'm sure Adam would tell you I'm right.'

Jane nuzzled the baby and he whimpered, searching for her breast. 'I'm not supposed to.' She was tense. Uncertain.

'I have never heard such rubbish in my whole life.' Liza jumped off the bed and going to the door, turned the key. 'I should send your mother home!'

'You're so good for Jane.' Adam had walked down to the bottom of the long walled garden behind the house with Liza. The air was soft with the mellow autumn sun. 'She doesn't stand up for herself. Her mother has bullied her resistance out of her. I think that's the problem with Sarah too. She reminds Jane too much of Patricia, and instead of standing up for herself she crumbles if Sarah so much as looks at her. I know why she came to Edinburgh to study now. It was about as far as she could get from home.'

'It must have taken a lot of courage to tell her parents she wanted to go away to university.'

'James was on her side. He's a real brick.'

Liza smiled. 'Picking up all the English expressions, I see. So, how does the good doctor like the Home Counties?'

Adam hesitated. 'I'm not sure I fit, to be honest. I miss the hills. I miss the country. This garden is all I see of mother nature for days on end. I sometimes go out to the countryside to see a patient, but mostly I'm working in the town. Robert and John, our other partner, keep the well-heeled patients for themselves. I was taken on to do the less lucrative side of the practice.'

'That stinks!'

'I have to start somewhere. Don't forget James helped me buy into the partnership. I couldn't have done it on my own. If I had had my way I would have settled down a million miles from Patricia – St Albans is at least a bit of a way. As you know Jane wanted to stay in Edinburgh. Before her mother started organising our lives!' He was standing, hands in pockets, staring down at a pale pink rose. 'You know why I couldn't stay there. She was there. Even if I couldn't see her or hear her, she was there.'

Neither of them had to state who 'she' was.

'I was so afraid she would latch onto Jane. She begrudged me visiting you, imagine what she would do if she found out I was going to get married.'

'But you never told Jane?'

He shook his head. 'Why worry her?'

'You've never seen Brid since you came to England?'

'No. Perhaps your magic charm has worked.' He knew Liza had noticed it. Patricia had too. 'Why don't you move that hideous geegaw!' was her comment. 'It does lower the tone of the room, Jane darling. I know that arty friend of yours gave it to you, but really . . .'

'You've been safe, Liza?' He broke off the rose suddenly and handed it to her. 'At one point I wondered if she might follow you to Wales.'

She shook her head. 'I'm sure she lost interest in me long ago. After all, I'm married to someone else. I hardly ever see you. What reason could she have for hating me, still?'

They both stared down in silence at the soft pink petals of the flower in her hand.

'None,' he said after a minute.

Once or twice Brid had seen Adam as she gazed into the pool on the hillside. He looked older; bigger; more solid. And she saw with him a woman. Not the woman Liza but another, a weak, pretty woman with honey-coloured hair and blue eyes. A woman who was not right for him. The last time she saw the woman she had a belly. She was near her time. Brid's eyes narrowed with anger. A-dam's child.

She had made her way once to Liza's studio and climbed the stairs. There was a padlock on the door and she could tell the place was empty. So, the Liza woman had gone too. She had stood looking down the narrow staircase. A tortoiseshell comb had lodged in a crack in the old deal of the steps. Some of its teeth were broken and between them there were one or two long red hairs. Stooping, she had picked it up and smiled. She had seen combs like these before; the woman Liza always wore them. She had wrapped it carefully in her scarf and put it into her bag.

On Midsummer's Day Brid went back to the room off the Grassmarket where she and Maggie, maintaining their grudging friendship, had found lodgings, to find Maggie lying unconscious on the floor. She stared at her for a moment, shocked by the sight of the woman, angry that Maggie was not there for her when she needed her. Then she remembered that she was a healer. It was necessary to bring Maggie back to health and she would do everything in her power to ensure that that happened. Unemotionally and carefully she nursed the old woman for four days until, finding tucked in her filthy clothes a piece of paper with the address of her much talked about but never seen daughter, the daughter who could help make her better, she sallied forth to find her.

Catriona had long ago lost patience with Maggie and her drinking, but with a sigh she gave Brid money to buy milk and bread and electric lightbulbs.

It was Brid who found warm blankets; who watched over her like a hawk as the old woman grew stronger than she had been for many years. It was Brid who went back to Catriona's to collect clothes, some of them for herself, some of them for Maggie, and books and records for the old gramophone which Maggie had found in an empty room in the tall house in which they lived. She would sit for hours listening to the nocturnes of Chopin, rocking back and forth, tears in her eyes, and she would beg Brid for the money to buy a bottle, but Brid never weakened. So when she returned one evening from an expedition onto the hill to collect herbs and found Maggie dead, she could not believe her eyes. She touched her face and took her hand, trying to coax the poor tired spirit back into the cold, worn-out flesh, and then she sat and cried.

Two days after the burial Catriona returned home from a day at the bank where she worked to find Brid on her doorstep in a state of trance from which she could not awaken her. She called her doctor and within hours Brid had been admitted to the Craighouse in Morningside.

In the border world to which she had retreated Brid flitted amongst the shadows, aware of Broichan stalking angrily around the stone. His power had grown. She could feel the tentacles of energy reaching out, touching her spirit, drawing her back and, frightened, she dodged back into the darkness. There was another figure there too now, a shadow she did not recognise, tentative,

145

exploring, his power as yet undeveloped but very real, a challenge to Broichan. She felt him questing inside her head, gently searching. Afraid, she shrouded her thoughts and withdrew into the silence. She could see her body lying propped in the small room in the hospital. It looked empty, drained of life. From time to time a nurse would go in and do things to her, otherwise she was left more or less alone. Catriona visited her once a week, and had she known it phoned every day to see how she was. But she was lost in between the worlds again, her life force drained by the shock of Maggie's desertion.

Liza's daughter, Juliette, was born on October the thirty-first 1947. Halloween. Adam and Jane came to Hay-on-Wye for the christening at St Mary's and stood as her godparents while Calum gurgled happily in the back of the church.

Pen-y-Ffordd, the old farmhouse high up in the Black Mountains, where they all adjourned afterwards to wet the baby's head, had stone walls two feet thick and small square windows which had let in a surprising amount of light once the insides of the rooms had been painted white. Round the back there were two large old barns, his and hers, which Philip and Liza used as their studios. Retired from his teaching, Philip had reverted to what had always been one of his first loves, painting landscape, which he did enormously successfully whilst her portraits were now increasingly full length or bigger and her prices, according to her proud husband, matched. 'We don't have to live here, you know,' he confided to Jane. 'We could get a bigger place, but we love the mountains so much. And Liza feels safe here. Brid could never find her, even if she wanted to.'

'Brid?' Jane turned from Calum's pram and stared at him. 'Who is Brid?

His mouth fell open. 'Don't you know?'

Jane shook her head. 'Should I?'

He shrugged. 'You had better ask Liza.'

She did. Minutes later, in the kitchen, Calum in her arms.

Liza turned from the sink where she had been rinsing mugs and looked at her for a moment, then she shrugged. She reached for a towel. 'I couldn't believe Adam hadn't told you,' she said.

Jane listened in silence, her eyes on Liza's face. When she had finished the story at last Jane shook her head. 'No,' she said firmly. 'You can't seriously expect me to believe all that. Oh no, Liza. That's too much. You're making it up. Why? Why would you want to frighten me with a story like that? Is it because of Adam and me?

Is that it? Are you jealous of us or something?' She clutched the baby more tightly.

'Ask Adam if you don't believe me.' Liza was tight-lipped. She turned away sharply. 'And no, Jane, I'm not jealous. Not one bit. I have everything I want here.'

There was a short uncomfortable silence, then Jane put out her hand to touch Liza's. 'I'm sorry. I didn't mean that. I know you're not jealous.'

'Good.' Liza went back to the sink and turned the taps full on, watching the water splashing down the drain. 'Don't believe me about Brid if you don't want to. I just hope you don't find out about her the hard way.'

Catriona stared at Brid's face intently. There had been a movement there. The eyes had for a moment focused on hers, she was sure of it. The strange vacancy which had been her only expression for weeks had lessened. Dr Freemantle, the psychiatrist, had visited her several times. He had recognised her from her stay in the Infirmary and was fascinated by Catriona's description of Brid as an animated, intelligent young woman. 'It must be a brain disorder. Perhaps an injury as a child? Some kind of state which is affected by shock.'

The energy came back in waves, small currents through her veins, pathways of light through the fog which separated her from the people around her as, slowly, she managed to drag herself back into her body.

Catriona drove her home two weeks after she had first seen the movement in Brid's eyes, and Brid understood that she could stay at the flat in Royal Circus until she felt fully recovered.

Liza was painting in her barn, standing before the easel, surveying the portrait of Aneurin Bevan which she was working on for a gallery in Cardiff, a commission of which she was intensely proud, acknowledging as it did her swift rise to fame as a portraitist. In spite of her baby, nearly a year old now, she managed to put in several hours a day at the easel, and her output was increasing steadily.

As so often happened when she had been painting for a long time she was exhausted, and her brain, so engaged as she worked, had slipped into neutral as she stood back to rest her arm. Nevertheless, the movement by the door caught her eye and she turned round to look. 'Phil? Is that you?'

147

It had been an impression, no more, but the slim figure, the long dark hair, the presence, was unmistakable. Her heart thudding with fear, she ran to the door and flung it open, staring out. The path through the orchard to the house was empty. There was no sign of anyone. A robin was sitting, singing, on the branch of an old lichen-covered apple tree near her. Surely if someone had passed close to him he would have flown away?

She said nothing to Philip and after a while she forgot the incident. Until next time. On this occasion she was playing with Juliette on the bed in the long, low-ceilinged bedroom in the attic of the house which she and Philip shared. It was pouring with rain outside and after she had finished feeding Juliette in the kitchen she had brought her upstairs to change her, then stayed for a while, singing lullabies to the little girl, reluctant to put her down in her cot in her own little room to sleep. The room was warm and cheerful as it always was, the bed covered in the same silk throw which she had used in her studio in Dean Village. One moment she was singing, the next she had stopped. She was listening intently, aware of a presence in the room near her. She could feel the skin on the back of her neck prickling with sudden cold. Juliette stopped looking at her with those intense, loving deep-blue eyes. Her gaze refocused on something immediately behind her mother. Liza felt her mouth go dry. She held her breath, then slowly, she turned.

There was nothing there.

Standing up, Liza grabbed the baby and clutched her to her chest. Her heart was thudding so much she was sure Juliette would feel it as she fled across the room and out onto the landing. Downstairs in the kitchen she began to laugh. How stupid. There wasn't a chance in hell that Brid could have found her. She did not notice until later, her tortoiseshell comb lying on the carpet near her dressing table, though she remembered putting it away.

Later that day she climbed the hill to visit Meryn. His house was empty, the door locked. She grimaced and turned back.

The night was dark, the wind swirling through the trees. At his feet the water poured over the rocks and sucked down into the whirlpool of dead leaves and green weed. She was there, waiting. Adam paused, looking down, his heart in his mouth. He knew he was going to have to climb down. Somewhere there the pendant lay, deep in a crevice under the rock, guarded by the hag with her small sharp knife. He could feel the wet rock slipping under his fingers; he could smell the strange electric smell of the water as it poured

148

down round him. There was no escape. Inexorably he was being pulled towards the whirlpool. Already he could feel himself drowning, feel the reaching, clinging cold fingers of the woman who waited for him there.

'Brid, no!'

His scream was so loud it woke him up and he lay staring up at the ceiling, shaking, the bedclothes soaked in sweat.

Beside him Jane kept her eyes tight shut. She was terrified. It was the third time in as many weeks that he had awoken her shouting Brid's name; Brid, whom he had explained away when Jane questioned him months before, after the christening, as an old girlfriend who had become a nightmare.

Adam wasn't sure when he had begun to be so afraid. It was after they had gone to Hay for Juliette's christening. It was as if talking about Brid again had conjured her in some way. Coming back to the house he had had a sudden strange feeling that she was there in the building, waiting for him. His terror was total. He stood there, completely paralysed for a moment, unable to breathe, unable to move, feeling the sweat starting underneath his stiff collar. Then sanity had returned. The feeling had left him as swiftly as it had come and he had walked into the living room and thrown the keys down on the table with a sigh of relief. Only then had he allowed himself the comfort of walking across to Liza's crystal and touching the cold glittering surface for just a second with his fingertip. That same day he had moved it up to their bedroom and told Jane the whole story.

Liza seated her guest at the table and put a large cup of milky coffee in front of her whilst Calum, oblivious of the fact that he had arrived at his destination and been lifted from the car, slept on. Jane stared round the kitchen. The white-washed walls and low-beamed ceiling with the heavy iron saucepans hanging from hooks along the beams had been almost hidden since she had last been here by dozens of paintings and collages, and arrangements of the pretty hand-thrown pottery on the open shelves. On the huge scrubbed table a few early daffodils, picked in the orchard that morning, were opening from tight buds in a Royal Worcester cream jug with a missing handle.

'So, why hasn't Adam come with you both?'

Jane smiled. 'Work, of course. They never seem to be able to spare him at the practice. I don't know if he'll ever get a holiday at this rate.'

149

'Then you must insist.' Liza glanced at her. 'Everything is all right between you, Janie?' There was an awkward pause. It was nearly a year since they had seen each other, since the almost-row over Brid, and so much had happened in between. 'I was so sorry to hear about the baby.'

Three months before, to her utter devastation, Jane had lost the baby she was expecting in the fourth month of her pregnancy. When Adam had rung Liza to tell her he had broken down and sobbed.

Jane nodded without looking up. 'It's fine. He just gets so tired and I get so fed up with the situation. It hasn't improved you know. That cow is still making my life a misery.' Sarah Harding's open hostility had, after the miscarriage, been replaced by a constant stream of sympathy; she was forever offering to help with Calum, almost every day turning up at the house or phoning with advice and interfering on a scale which eclipsed anything Patricia had ever achieved; it was driving Jane to distraction.

'Adam should say something.'

'Or I should.' Jane sighed. 'The trouble is I don't want to make things awkward for Adam. And I think one of the other partners is considering leaving, which would put Adam in line for promotion in a manner of speaking. He doesn't want to lose out on that. And there is something else.' Picking up the spoon from her saucer she fiddled with it for a moment. She glanced up. 'Do you remember at the christening you told me about Brid? I didn't believe you and I was very rude.' She looked away, embarrassed at the memory. 'Well, he's been having nightmares about her. He's brought the amulet you gave us into our bedroom.'

'Do you think he's seen her?' Liza could feel the skin on the back of her neck prickling suddenly. 'How could she find him?'

How had she found *her*?

'I don't know. There must be loads of ways she could discover where he is. He's a doctor after all. She could reach him through the medical school. They know where he is. Or she could get a private detective or someone.'

'Jane.' Liza bit her lip. She had been about to say, 'She wouldn't work like that. She's not real.' But that wasn't true, was it? Brid had been – and was – very real.

Jane glanced up and her face was suddenly naked in its misery. 'Did he love her very much, Liza?'

Liza stared at her, dumbfounded. 'No! Whatever Adam felt for her once, it was over long before he met you. Before he met me.

The last person in the world he would want to see would be Brid, I promise you.'

She shuddered. So, this was the reason Jane had taken it into her head suddenly to brave the cold March winds and drive across country to the Welsh borders. Liza stood up and coming round the table, put her arm round her shoulders. 'Adam would rather meet the devil himself than Brid.' She smiled gravely. 'In fact, from some of the things he told me, he was under the impression at one time that she was the daughter of the devil at the very least. He never seemed to be very sure where she came from but she really scared him. She really scared me.' She paused. She had been so certain they were safe. So confident. But now . . . 'I'm sure she can't find us. Any of us. She might be looking,' – she was looking – 'but she won't succeed. And now, I'm going to lay the table for lunch, then we'll round up Philip from his studio and see if Juliette is awake yet and not think about Brid any more.'

She turned away to open the dresser drawer and rummage for knives and forks, aware that Jane was studying her closely.

She hoped her worried expression did not give her away.

Adam had finished the last of his house calls by about midday and had just walked through the front door when the phone rang. He sighed. He had been looking forward to a glass of whisky before the cold lunch which was waiting for him in the kitchen. Picking up the receiver he glanced out of the window. 'Dr Craig here.' It had stopped raining at last. But the infernal east wind was still blowing. Half his patients were down with chest complaints because of it and the other half were racked with rheumatism.

'Adam? It's Jane. I just thought I'd see how you are.'

His face softened into a smile. 'I'm well. So, how are you and Calum? And Liza and Phil?'

'We're all fine. It's lovely here. Oh, Adam, can't you come? Just for the weekend? Please.'

Adam sighed. He was missing her so much. The house was very quiet without her and the little boy, and although the nagging worry for their safety had gone it had been replaced by a whole new set of anxieties about them being so far away.

'Adam, are you there?' Jane's voice on the phone was filling him with longing.

Suddenly he had made the decision. The practice could spare him for a day or two. They owed him enough holiday. Somehow he would arrange it.

'I'll see if I can come, darling, all right? I really will try, I promise.' His voice was buoyant. 'Tell Liza to make some of that wonderful beef stew she cooked when we came to the christening last year. I'm starving to death here without my wife to feed me. I'll be there on Saturday. I promise.'

And he was, driving through the early hours of the morning to arrive at the farm in time for breakfast.

Calum threw himself on his father with a squeal of excitement. 'Daddy come see the lambs!'

'So. I thought this was a painting farm.' Adam kissed Jane and then Liza. With Philip he shook hands, passing over in the same gesture a bottle of malt whisky. 'Where do the sheep come from?'

'The field next door. They're gambolling in the sunshine.' Philip smiled. 'Go with him, Adam. He's been looking forward to showing you all week.'

Adam swung his son up into his arms. 'Right, young man, which way?'

Jane followed them outside. 'How did you manage to pacify the powers-that-be at home?'

'I pointed out that I hadn't had a proper holiday since I joined the practice.'

'And that mattered to them?'

'I doubt it.' Adam shrugged. 'Let's not talk about them. How are Liza and Phil?'

'Fine.'

It was the next day before Adam had a chance to talk to Liza on her own. He slipped out of the house and followed Liza to her barn. He closed the door behind him firmly. 'What is it? Are you and Jane getting on all right? I can see you're worried sick about something. What has gone wrong?'

'She's back. Inside my head.' Liza threw down her brush and turned to him. 'And from what Jane says you've been having nightmares about her too. I don't know what to do.'

Adam stared at her aghast. He did not have to be told who she meant. 'Dear God!' He sat down abruptly on an old cane chair near the table. 'Tell me what's happened.'

She told him about the occasions she had thought she saw Brid, then about the comb. 'It was an especially pretty one. One of a pair. I lost the other.' She shrugged. 'I hardly noticed at first. But it moved. It was moving round the room. I had put it away in the dressing table drawer.' She stroked back her long hair distractedly. 'But it was on my bedside table in the morning. I thought I'd done

152

it myself. Of course I did. Then it happened again. Then the next day when I was holding it, it began to get hot.' She shook her head slowly. 'I couldn't believe it. I dropped it. When I picked it up again of course it was quite cold. So I put it away in a drawer . . .' She was, he realised suddenly, wearing a ribbon to hold back her hair. 'Then this morning I found it under my pillow.' She heaved a deep shaky sigh. 'I've seen her, Adam. In here. And then she was standing in the doorway to the kitchen. Not really her. A ghost. A wraith. I don't know. Just a shadow. Then she had gone, but it was enough. She's found me. She's watching me. I don't know why. You and I are not together, so why is she following me?'

Adam bit his lip. His face had gone white. 'Would you like me to send your crystal back?'

She shook her head. 'We have a neighbour. Meryn Jones. He knows about these things.' She gave a watery smile. 'They reckon locally that he's a wizard. He made the crystal tree for you. He says she's following me because I'm more psychic than you. She finds it easy to get inside my head. I'm the only contact she has with you –'

'And you let Jane and Calum come here!' Adam stood up. He was suddenly furiously angry. 'Knowing that girl had found out where you live, you asked Jane and Calum here, under your roof?'

'I didn't ask them, Adam! Jane asked herself. And she came because she was worried about Brid, too. What am I supposed to do?' Liza faced him. 'Am I going to be haunted for the rest of my life by that female because once I was in love with you?' There was a long silence. She shrugged. 'Sorry. Tactless. Forget it. Anyway, we're both happily married. But Brid does not seem to have understood that we have moved on.' She continued more quietly, 'She should not be my problem, Adam. And certainly not Phil's. Or Jane's, come to that.'

'Jesus Christ.' Adam sat down again. He put his head in his hands. 'What does your friend Meryn say we should do?'

'He's been away. He only came back last night. I've rung him and explained. You and I are going to have to go and see him tomorrow.'

'Not Jane?'

'Not Jane. Not yet. Let's you and I deal with this ourselves.'

They drove up the mountain the following morning, heading up the narrow pitch, where the hedges met overhead, turning the lane into a tunnel of black-laced hawthorn, not yet showing more than tiny shoots of green and pearly buds, with hazel catkins trailing gold dust across the roof of Adam's car.

Outside Meryn's house Adam stood for a moment staring out across the woods and fields towards the distant mountains.

'Makes you realise how much you miss Scotland?' Liza put her arm through his. She was shivering in the wind.

He nodded. 'The hills get in your blood.'

'You'll go back one day.'

He followed her towards the low door which had already opened. The man who was standing just inside was nothing like Adam had expected. He was tall, dark-haired, perhaps in his forties. The lean, lined face was weather-beaten, not aged as Adam had thought it would be, and the eyes, far from being vague and mystical were piercing blue and very shrewd. He stood back to usher them in and they found themselves in the single room, half kitchen, half living room, which took up the whole of the ground floor of the cottage. Adam stared round and he felt a sudden shiver of distaste. Bunches of herbs hung from the ceiling, filling the room with strong exotic scents which were somehow far from being of a culinary nature. On shelves near the window, he could see rows of stones and crystals. There were several bookcases, stuffed to overflowing with books and magazines. On a dark shelf near the cooking range he noticed a sheep's skull pushed back behind some brown glass jars. The atmosphere of the room was strange. It seemed very still.

Liza however seemed undeterred. To his surprise she flung her arms round their host and kissed him on both cheeks. 'Meryn, this is my friend Adam.'

Meryn turned to him and gravely proffered a hand. 'Dr Craig.' There appeared to be a twinkle in the blue eyes but it was gone in an instant. Adam had the feeling that Mr Jones had sized him up within seconds of their arrival and he had a sudden vision of himself as he must appear to the other man. A reserved, studious, Presbyterian doctor, sceptical in the face of Welsh feyness and superstition. He wondered how Liza had described him. As if reading his thoughts she turned back to him and caught his hand. 'Adam, I told Meryn all about you and Brid when he made the amulet for you. He knows you don't like this sort of thing.' She waved her hand to encompass the room and its contents, including, but Adam was not sure whether or not it was intentional, their host.

He flushed a little, embarrassed. 'I'm sorry if my scepticism is unwelcome here. I am learning.' He paused. 'I know most of the problem is Liza's at the moment, but I've had dreams recently –

nightmares.' He shivered and glanced at Meryn who was watching him in silence. 'I'm afraid for Liza.' He floundered on uncomfortably. 'And I'm afraid for my wife and son. I don't know why this has happened!'

Meryn said nothing. He continued to watch Adam with unblinking eyes.

Adam shoved his hands deep into his trouser pockets. He was growing more and more unhappy with the man's silence. 'She seems to be a ghost, but I don't know if she's alive or dead.'

'Sit down, Dr Craig,' Meryn spoke at last, as though he had heard nothing that Adam had said. He went to stand in front of the window as Adam found himself a place on the old sofa next to Liza. Adam glanced sideways at her but she was staring straight ahead, her eyes seemingly fixed in space. He looked down at his feet and grimaced, feeling like a small boy summoned to the study of his headmaster as Meryn turned to look down the hillside towards the distant Wye valley. 'The girl, who, for our purposes we shall consider very much alive, has been using something of Liza's to establish a contact.' He spoke in the soft lilting tones of the Welsh mountains. 'Liza thinks it may be the comb she lost in Edinburgh before she moved and its pair, here, has been moving about by itself, perhaps under some kind of psychic influence. A comb is a real possibility. It is not the comb itself so much as the hairs which may have been attached to it which are used to make contact. It is a very simple technique. One used by adepts the world over.'

Adam found his mouth had gone dry.

'Unfortunately the fact that this girl has established a link in this way means that Liza is going to have ongoing problems unless we can sever the connection. Have you, Dr Craig –' he swung round and fixed Adam once more with his piercing gaze – 'any reason to think she may have anything of yours?' He waited only a second and answered for Adam, giving him no time to think. 'I assume that she doesn't, or she would have been able to reach you.'

'If my nightmares are anything to go by I think she has reached me.' Adam's voice was hoarse. He cleared his throat loudly, trying to dispel the intense silence which clung to the room like a pall. 'I've never been very, what you might call, psychic. I'm a scientist.' He gave an apologetic grin. 'From the very start it was Liza she seemed to be able to talk to. To reach. I don't know how she does it.' He grasped suddenly at straws. 'Brid is a healer. Like you.' He smiled and hoped suddenly that he hadn't sounded patronising. 'Such people have certain abilities, I know.'

155

'We all have such abilities, Dr Craig,' Meryn answered soberly. 'Even you, did you but know it.' He walked across to the empty hearth and stood with his back to it looking down at Adam with intense concentration. 'Liza tells me you have used the amulet, that you have placed it in your bedroom. Was this because you felt it gave you and your wife further protection, or was it a gesture of crazy superstition which you regretted but did anyway for reasons you could not quite fathom?' His eyes held Adam's and at last he smiled. 'I see it was the latter. No matter. Ritual even without substance can still work and even a feeling such as that one is a start. You see I cannot help you unless you are prepared to take my advice.'

'He will take your advice,' Liza put in at last. 'I shall see to it myself.'

Meryn shook his head. 'It must be more than that, girl. He has to be more than willing. He has to be strong. He has to believe.'

'And what if he can't?' It was Adam who spoke.

'Then, I don't know that I can help.'

Adam swallowed. In spite of himself he felt a frisson of cold run across his shoulders. 'I don't see why we're all still so afraid of her.'

'Because she tried to kill me once, that's why.' Liza stood up and walked up and down the floor with small, agitated steps. 'Because you're afraid she'll try and kill Jane. And the reason you think that is because you can't be sure she hasn't killed before. I always suspected she killed your father's housekeeper. She's a gypsy, for God's sake. They are passionate people. They have vendettas. They put curses on people.'

Adam bit his lip. He was trying to rationalise his thoughts. 'Look, I do believe she has the power to get inside our heads. She's telepathic. She has the power to worry me. To frighten me, if you like. So I should be able to believe that you have just as strong a talent as she has. And that Mr Jones can tell me what to do. So, shut up, Liza. Let me answer for myself.'

Liza looked up at the ceiling as if invoking divine aid. 'Right. Good. So be it.'

Meryn gave a small humourless smile. 'If you fight hard enough between yourselves perhaps she'll sense it. Then she'll leave Liza out of it anyway.'

'I'm sorry. We're not fighting.' Liza sat down next to Adam again. 'I think I'm a bit agitated by all this.'

'Right. Well that's the first thing. Don't be. You have to learn to stay calm. To stay centred. You have to learn to control your thoughts and be master of your own brain. You have to learn to exclude outside influences. You have to learn to protect yourself. You know all this, Liza. You inherited your psychic powers from your mother. Surely she must have taught you something about it when you were a child. She knew how to draw a circle of protection around herself.'

'I've tried.' Liza bit her lip. 'It doesn't seem to work with Brid.'

'Because it's the first time you've ever come up against this sort of thing, that's why. You're letting yourself be panicked. Stay calm. That's all you need to do. Surround yourself with a wall of light. This Brid is a creature of the darkness.' He had seen her in his meditations more than once now, Brid and the man who hunted her.

'She told me once she came from the people who lived beyond the north wind,' Adam put in slowly. 'That's how she saw herself. Wild. Untamed. Free.'

Meryn stared at him.

'Does all that mean something to you?' Liza asked quickly.

Slowly Meryn shook his head. 'Probably not,' he said thoughtfully. 'Probably coincidence. Now, Dr Craig. Let's try and sort you out. You are going to have to learn to use your imagination. You are going to have to picture things with your mind's eye so strongly and so well that they become real. And you're going to have to do this for your wife and your son as well. You are going to have to learn to build walls around yourself and your family to keep this girl out and you're going to have to make them so strong that whatever she does she can't break through your defences.'

It was after Adam and Liza had gone that Meryn went to his bookcase and rifled through the volumes there. The old copy of Herodotus lay on its side, the pages loose, discoloured with age. He picked it up lovingly and thumbed through it to find the passage. The people of the north wind. Surely the reference he remembered was in there somewhere.

Some time later he sat before the fire and prepared himself for meditation. There was much he was going to have to remember, much he was going to have to study, before he could take on Brid and the shadowy figure who followed her.

9

Brid was standing on the top of Arthur's Seat, staring south towards the Pentland Hills. In her pocket was a cotton scarf, in which was wrapped the comb still entwined with the few precious hairs. Where were they, A-dam and his Liza? She knew they were not together, but why could she not reach them any more? Her strength was failing and with it her health. She was thin and weak, her hair was ragged and had lost its shine, and her eyes were dark-ringed and haunted.

'He is there. To the south. Somewhere to the south.'

And so was the other man, the man from Adam's time whose questing mind had encountered hers in the darkness of her dreams.

Two people standing near her on the summit turned and seeing the girl talking to herself, wild-eyed, they moved away and began the descent towards the Salisbury Crags, leaving her quite alone.

A-dam!

Throwing her arms up into the air she faced the north wind and called out his name. 'A-dam, where are you?'

There were tears on her cheeks.

'A-dam, my A-dam, I need you!'

Slowly she turned in a complete circle, calling his name again and again. But there was no answer.

Sometimes she went to stand at the bottom of the stair which had led to Adam's digs just to feel that she was somehow nearer to him. The entry was dark and scruffy and a bit smelly but she didn't mind. It was where he had been. The dizzy spells were becoming more frequent now and sometimes her other life, the life on the far side of the stone, was breaking through the veil which separated her from the past. They were waiting for her there, Broichan and his followers, waiting to kill her.

She leaned back against the grey stone of the building and closed her eyes for a minute. When she opened them there was a young man standing in front of her. He looked concerned. 'I say, are you all right?'

She smiled groggily. 'I think so. Just tired.'

'I've seen you here before, haven't I? Are you looking for someone?'

She nodded. 'For A-dam Craig. He used to live here, but he is gone.'

'Adam Craig?' The young man smiled cheerfully. 'Oh he's long gone, I'm afraid. My brother used to room with him. That's how I got these digs. Adam's got a practice down in England now. I can probably find his address if you want.'

'You know where he is?' The transformation in her face was miraculous. Suddenly she was glowing with happiness.

'Sure. Come on up and I'll have a look.' Jimmie Thomson led the way up the narrow stair and fumbled for a key. The rooms were dark and crowded with heavy old furniture. They had, did she but know it, not changed one bit since Adam had left them. Jimmie walked over to the desk and rummaged for a scruffy address book. He found it and flipped through the pages, half of which were loose. 'Here you are. It's St Albans. He bought into the practice there after he married, so the chances are he's still there.' He grinned at her. 'Do you want me to write it down for you?'

She shook her head. 'There is no need. I shall remember.' She paused, staring round the room. There were things of A-dam's still here, she could sense them: a book, a picture on the wall, and on the narrow shelf above the fire – she tensed and moved towards it. 'This. This is A-dam's.' The small copper cufflink was half hidden behind a candlestick.

'You're right.' He wondered how on earth she had seen it. She must have the eyesight of a hawk. 'I found it down the back of the old armchair after he left. I always meant to post it to him, but I never got round to it.'

'It is no matter. I will take it.' She had already tucked it into her bag. She turned away. In the doorway she paused and stared at him for a moment. 'What is married?'

He frowned. 'What is married?' he echoed, puzzled. 'You know. Taking a wife. Living with someone. He's got kids too, now, I gather. Or at least one, and another on the way.'

'I see.' Her face had somehow dimmed. She stared at him for a moment longer, then disappeared down the stairs and into the street.

Jimmie stood silent for a second and bit his lip, looking at the doorway. He felt a momentary qualm. Perhaps he shouldn't have given her the address. He walked over to the door and without quite knowing why he turned the key. No, that was silly. Besides, the chances were that Adam had long ago moved on.

'I need to go here.' Brid had written down the address herself in her careful looped writing. She showed it to Catriona as soon as she came in.

Catriona felt a sudden leap of elation – she was weary of her unexpected and so very dependent guest. She thought hard. 'St Albans is down near London, I think. Why on earth do you want to go there?'

'A-dam is there.' Even without the cufflink she could find him now, but this way was easier.

'Adam?' Brid had never mentioned him before. She scanned Brid's face and saw the fleeting emotions – longing, anger, fear, misery. 'Is he someone very special?'

Brid nodded. 'My friend.'

'I see.' Catriona shrugged. 'After we've had supper I'll have a look at the map and see if I can find it.'

'Now. I want to know now.'

'Why? If you want to write to him . . .'

'I will go there.'

'Brid. It's a very long way. You'd need to go on the train to London which is hundreds of miles and then you'd need to get another train. And you can't go and see someone without letting them know you're coming. Do you have his telephone number?'

Brid shook her head. A-dam would know she was coming to find him.

'Then we'll ring up directory enquiries and ask. As you have his address they'll tell you his number and you can phone him. Easy.' She smiled. Taking the paper from Brid's hand she went across to the desk and picked up the receiver. 'So, what is his surname?'

'His surname?'

'His second name. He must have one. Adam who?'

'A-dam Craig. He is a doctor.'

'I see.' She looked at Brid for a moment, then she nodded. 'Right. Here goes.'

Brid waited. She had long ago grown accustomed to Catriona's telephone and had even plucked up the courage to answer it once or twice when she was alone in the flat. There seemed nothing strange in being able to talk to someone many miles away; in fact it was a distinct improvement on the way she was used to, which sometimes could be less than effective. It explained why people in Adam's world did not seem to understand the way her people could reach each other just by thought. They had worked out a better way. In only a few minutes Catriona was passing her the receiver.

Brid took it, her hand shaking, and listened to the ringing sound. Then there was a click and a ping and a woman's voice sounded in her ear. 'Hello? This is Jane Craig, can I help you?'

Brid frowned. 'A-dam?' she said softly. 'I want to speak to A-dam.'

'I'm sorry, Adam's on a call at the moment. Can I help?' The voice was light and friendly. 'Are you a patient?'

'I want to speak to A-dam.'

She heard a sigh, felt the barely concealed impatience. 'I'm sorry, if you want to speak to him you'll have to ring back tomorrow. He's out at a confinement and I've no idea when he'll be back.'

'He is not there.' Gently Brid laid the receiver back into its cradle. 'I will go there.'

Catriona sighed. 'We'll find out about the trains tomorrow. It's a very long journey, Brid. It will take all day.'

'I do not mind. I will go. Now.'

'You can't go now. There are no trains in the middle of the night.' She did not know if it were true, but she had to deflect that burning determination somehow. It frightened her. 'Tomorrow I shall come with you to the station and make sure you get the right ticket and help you onto the train, all right?' She put a gentle hand over Brid's. 'It's quite an adventure, my dear. It's a very long way. You have to get it right.' She met Brid's eye and for a moment felt a quick breath of fear.

There was pure venom in her gaze. Then the expression on the girl's face changed and she relaxed. 'All right. Tomorrow. I go to A-dam tomorrow.'

That night, as Catriona lay in bed trying to sleep she had heard the girl rummaging about in the living room. Silently she had climbed out of bed and padded over to her door. Instead of accosting Brid and asking her what she thought she was doing, she had quietly turned the key in her lock and stood, her shoulders against the door, shaking with fright.

Catriona drove Brid to Waverley Station, paid for her ticket, gave her five pounds for the onward journey, wherever it led, and saw her onto the train. She felt a moment's compassion when she saw the terror on Brid's face as they walked close to a huge, steaming engine, and then again as she saw the girl into a corner seat in a second class carriage, but as she stood and waved on the platform as the train pulled out she found her emotion was one of pure relief.

It wasn't until three days later that she noticed the silver paper-knife, which she had thought was hidden beneath the sea of papers on her desk, had gone.

Adam climbed into the Riley, his black bag on the seat beside him, a list of the calls he had to make on the pad next to it. He glanced down at it as his foot toyed with the accelerator, warming the engine. *A-dam*, Jane had said. She had mimicked it exactly and the sound of the word had filled him with apprehension. If Brid had his phone number, she probably had his address. She didn't need telepathy any more. She had found him. His hands were sticky on the wheel and he sat still for a moment, resting his head back against the top of the seat, breathing slowly and deeply. 'What did she say, exactly?' he had asked, panic-stricken.

'Nothing. Just, "I want to speak to A-dam". I told her she'd have to ring back today.'

'If she does, tell her I'm out. Tell her I've gone away.'

'Adam!' Jane had given her sweet gentle laugh. She was pregnant again at last, and it suited her. She had never looked so radiant or so serene. 'I can't do that. For goodness' sake. Who was it?'

He had taken a deep breath. 'It sounds as if it might have been Brid,' he had said slowly. 'She's the only person to call me A-dam like that.'

Jane had stared at him, her eyes wide. 'Oh Adam, darling. But I thought all that was finished?' He had only ever told her a little about his trip to Meryn with Liza, determined to protect her, not sure how much she would believe. 'It can't be her. And even if it is what on earth is she going to do? You're married now. You're a father. Please God, you're about to be a father again . . .' Let it be all right this time. 'You're a doctor, not a schoolboy!' She had put her hands on his shoulders and given him a quick kiss on the cheek. 'Oh my darling, don't worry. I won't let her put any spells on you, I promise. If she rings again, I'll say you've gone away to be a doctor to the Eskimos. How's that?'

162

He had laughed in spite of himself. 'That's fine. Perfect. Good idea.'

Then he had put the thought of her out of his head. But now, this morning, he was suddenly not so sure. He glanced into the driving mirror at the quiet street behind him. It was bathed in sunlight. There was no one in sight. With a sigh of relief he engaged gear and let off the handbrake. His first call was going to take him the other side of town.

On the train, Brid dozed. The sound of the wheels pounding over the tracks soothed her. At first she had looked out of the window, watching the scenery, staring in wonder at the glorious blue of the sea as they steamed south. She held herself rigid with fear as the sound of the wheels changed as they rumbled over the Berwick Bridge, high in the air, then on into England; as they drew nearer and nearer to Adam she slept again. She did not eat or leave her seat and the compartment stayed empty. She did not think about the future. She had no idea how she would get to him. Catriona had talked of another train, another station. She would not think about it now. Her head was growing light. Here, on the train, away from the land she knew, the veil was thinning and she was holding on with all her strength to some kind of reality, fighting back the demons. As they drew into King's Cross she knew she had lost. Her eyes were fixed, her pulse rate was almost nil, her skin cold as ice. She heard the noise of the station, but she did not move. She was staring into the eyes of Broichan, her uncle.

Patricia stared round the sitting room, and nodded contentedly. Jane had made it very nice. It was comfortable, lived in without being untidy, Calum's toys were neatly put away and the day before she had moved the mess of medical magazines into Adam's study. She adjusted a cushion slightly and went to twitch the curtain back another inch. The new house, in a pretty suburban street, had a bigger garden than the old one. The house itself had been built in the 1920s and was very different from their former home, but she knew Jane loved it already because it was their very own. Patricia smiled. It wasn't as elegant as the old house, of course, and sadly it did not have the cachet of the old Georgian street, but at least it was theirs.

Jane was in the kitchen making them a cup of tea and Calum was resting. The house was peaceful at last. Patricia sighed. The little boy was indeed a handful these days. Perhaps if she lay down for a while, before he woke up again? It was a pity she couldn't stay longer, to help Jane in these last months before the baby was born, but it really was so exhausting . . .

Climbing the stairs she paused to catch her breath, staring in at the open door of Jane and Adam's bedroom. It was full of sunshine, a pretty, feminine room with nice pictures and elegant ornaments. She stepped in for a moment, looking round and nodding. If nothing else, she had instilled good taste into her daughter. Almost as she thought it, her eye caught the ornate little enamelled and silver tree standing on the table beside the bed. The brilliant crystal on it caught the sunshine, throwing rainbows onto the wall on the opposite side of the room. It was a vulgar little thing, completely out of keeping with the rest of the furnishings. She frowned. It had been given them by that dreadful, blowzy artist woman who had once gone out with Adam. Walking over to the bed she picked up the amulet tree and looked at it. It wasn't even well made.

'Mother! What are you doing?' Jane's voice in the doorway made Patricia jump.

'Nothing, dear. I was just thinking how much nicer the room would look without this – thing – beside the bed. It's completely out of keeping.'

'Put it down, Mother. Please. It is a lucky charm.' Jane was exhausted. Patricia had come to stay ostensibly to allow Jane to rest. In reality she had made twice as much work. Like now, when Jane would have loved to put her own feet up while Calum slept and yet was making tea to bring up to her mother's room.

'Superstitious nonsense! Couldn't you get rid of it, dear? Give it to a jumble sale or something. I'm sure someone would like it –'

'I like it, Mother.' Jane put down the cup on her dressing table and held out her hand. 'Please give it to me.'

'You don't have to be defensive, dear. I'm sure Adam wouldn't even miss it . . .' Patricia was turning to replace it on the bedside table when the amulet seemed to slip from her hands. She made a clutch at it as it fell and the crystal came away in her hand. The small tree caught on the edge of the table and lay bent and twisted on the carpet at her feet, two of its tiny enamels ripped free.

'Mother!' Jane stared at it in horror. 'What have you done?'

'I'm sorry. It slipped.'

'Oh, yes. It slipped.' Jane blinked back sudden tears of fury and exhaustion. She went down on her knees and picked up the little pieces, staring down at them in sorrow. 'This meant so much to Adam.'

'Then it's time his taste improved!' Patricia's voice was tart. She was completely unrepentant. 'I should throw the pieces away, dear. Adam will never notice. Now, I think I shall take my rest otherwise I shall still be tired when dear little Calum wakes up.'

Jane stared after her in disbelief, then she shrugged. Carefully she put the broken pieces in a drawer. She had already resolved to take them to the jeweller and have the ornament repaired.

The mental hospital contacted Catriona from the address they found in Brid's bag. Guiltily she shook her head as she sat in the flat in Royal Circus. 'She was a down-and-out my mother befriended and I took her in for a while after my mother died, but she wasn't normal. To be honest I was a bit afraid of her. I was glad when she left. No, I don't know her name. Just Brid. That's what she called herself. I thought perhaps she was a tinker from up north somewhere. But I know nothing about her family or if she had any . . .' She looked down at the telephone number scribbled on the piece of paper on the blotter on her desk. Brid had not bothered to take it with her. Dr Adam Craig. No, she would not give them that name, nor would she mention the knife. She had no wish to get involved.

The treatment had affected her memory in some way. There were huge black holes inside her head where there should be memories. She was sitting now in the large bland common room of the mental hospital in front of a table strewn with balls of knitting wool. She was supposed to be sorting them out but they kept moving around, randomly organising themselves into patterns which had nothing to do with the neat baskets she was supposed to be packing them into. She gazed round vaguely, taking in the bright patterned curtains on the windows, the other inmates sitting like her drugged and half comatose on the metal-framed chairs with sagging canvas seats. Her blue cotton dress was ill-fitting and uncomfortable, stiff from so many washes, and her hair was dull and unkempt, held back from her face by an elastic band. How had she come to be here? She could not understand anything.

The kindly doctor, with his wire-rimmed spectacles and white coat, seemed to want to be her friend when he had time. She enjoyed talking to him. He was intelligent and treated her as though she were interesting and educated and sane. She had learned this word sane. You had to be sane to get out of the place in which she found herself. But she did not know where it was she came from or where she was going to, and that seemed to be a problem from which there was no escape. 'If we just knew you had someone to take you in, Brid, my dear.' He smiled and she found herself gazing as she so often did at the fascinating flash of gold from the tooth at the corner of his smile. 'But if there is no one then we must be sure, mustn't we, that you can take care of yourself.'

Time passed so swiftly in here, in the institutionalised world in which they lived. It was all the same to her. That was one of the things which fascinated him. She had no concept of time.

At night, sometimes, after they had been round to check she was asleep, she would take Jeannie Barron's pretty compact out of her bag and open it, staring down into the little mirror, stilling the small movements of her hands until the reflections stopped dancing and swaying and her eyes were led down and down past her own shadowy face into infinite depths of blackness. At first she saw nothing and she wondered why she did it, then one day she saw a shadowy figure, for a second, no more, and she began to remember. Somehow she knew she must not let anyone see her do it. And she must not mention it to Dr Sadler. If she did, she sensed, he would say he was disappointed in her and things might start to go wrong again. So, quietly, she practised in secret and slowly the pictures grew more clear.

At first she thought they were dreams. She was a cat. A beautiful, glossy, striped cat with huge golden eyes, and she could roam at will through gardens and over walls and fences, climb trees, and scale creepers to look in through people's windows. Then, one day, she found earth under her fingernails when she woke in the morning and she lay in bed, hugging the flat, hard hospital pillow and staring up at the ceiling, a small triumphant smile on her lips. She had found A-dam. In her dream she had seen him in his garden. In her dream she had walked out from the shadows and, cat-like, had pressed herself against his legs, and in her dream he had stooped and touched her head and stroked her shoulders, and run his hand down her soft, silky flank.

She sat up and swung her legs over the side of the bed. In the locker was her old, woven bag. She pulled it out and opened it. Inside, hidden in the lining, was her own small rusty iron knife and the much prettier and more deadly silver paperknife she had stolen from Catriona. Besides that the bag held only the compact and a few other small possessions, including the tortoiseshell comb. She brought it out and sat on the bed with it in her hands, looking at it. Her own hair, though faded and tangled, was still jet black.

The hair twisted in the comb was red-gold. Wrapped up in a handkerchief at the bottom of the bag was the small copper cufflink.

Jane stooped wearily to pick one of Adam's shirts out of her washing basket. Her mother, thank God, had gone at last, otherwise she would have been there calling at her to be careful, not to strain herself, but not actually offering to help, as she had done every day of her visit. It was a bright cold windy day. Shaking the shirt out she glanced round proudly, taking in the pear tree, the rose beds, the sandpit which Adam had made for Calum, and contentedly she smiled as she reached to peg the shirt on the line. At once the fine white cotton filled and danced and she stooped to find another peg to hold it secure.

The cat seemed to come out of nowhere. One moment she was peacefully hanging out her husband's shirts, and the next she was falling, the warm furry body mixed up with her feet, then clinging to her shoulder with its claws, then gone. It took her several minutes to get over the shock, kneeling, gasping, on the grass, winded and frightened.

When she at last climbed to her feet and turned to go back indoors there was a sudden, sharp nagging pain in her stomach.

The pain took her again suddenly in the middle of the night. She woke up with a gasp, and beside her Adam groaned. 'Jane? What is it? What time is it?'

'Adam, help me!'

It was only five months, five months pregnant after the last miscarriage, and now she could feel the hot blood beginning to flow. 'Adam!' Her scream of terror and misery brought him to his feet in seconds and, with a sickening certainty that this had been her last chance to have another baby, he began to tend to his wife.

It was dawn before she was at last settled back to sleep, heavily sedated in the pretty back bedroom which they had made their own. Walking wearily down to his new study Adam drew back the curtains and pulled the French doors open. The early spring morning was fresh and cold, the grass on the back lawn heavy with dew. Nearby a blackbird was singing its heart out to the background of the dawn chorus from the neighbouring gardens. There were tears in his eyes as he stood there. Poor Jane. And poor baby. Why had it happened? He had studied every book to give her the best of treatment. He had consulted the most experienced gynaecologists. He had put her under the care of Roger Cohen, reputed to be amongst the leaders in the field of antenatal studies, who had written copious papers on the care of women prone to miscarry. He had said all was going well when they went for her check up only a week before. So what had happened?

He went over to the cupboard behind his desk and pulled out a three-quarter-empty bottle of Laphroaig. Pouring two fingers into a glass he tipped it down his throat, neat. It burned satisfactorily and he had another.

He tensed as he heard a baby cry and then realised that the sound came from an upstairs window next door.

When he had realised what was happening he had rung Robert Harding. He had come at once, with Sarah who had against all Adam's protests insisted on dressing a peevish, fretful Calum before taking him away to sleep at their house. Jane still didn't know he had gone. Robert had only left when it was all over. He had been a tower of strength. 'Take the time to be with her, old boy. Don't worry. I'll cover for you. Take all the time you need.'

Adam sat down on the leather-covered sofa near the wall and stared out of the open window, deaf to the birds. Under his breath he was cursing his father's God. Why? Why did He let it happen? Why, when there were so many unwanted children in the world, would He let Jane lose this so much wanted, so treasured little girl? Tears spilled over onto his cheeks and he sat, the glass held slackly in his fingers between his knees, letting them flow unchecked as the light grew stronger and it began to grow less cold.

Not until he had finished the bottle did he stagger to his feet and slowly climb the staircase to see how she was. She was lying on her side, her face very white, her eyes closed. 'Jane?' he whispered. 'Are you awake?' She did not move. He sat down heavily on the side of the bed and gazed at her miserably. 'Janie, my darling, I'm so sorry. We tried everything, you know we did . . .' His gaze fell on the side table and he frowned. Liza's amulet was not in its accustomed place next to the lamp. He looked round the room. It wasn't on the dressing table or on the shelf of small china ornaments. It wasn't on the bookcase or on the table near the door where only the afternoon before Jane had lovingly placed a small vase of daffodils. 'Jane,' he said quietly. His whole body had tensed as though someone near him had drawn their fingernails down a window pane. 'Jane, darling. Where is Liza's amulet?'

She groaned a little and buried her face deeper in the pillow.

'Jane!' His voice was louder now. He stood up and walked round to her side of the bed. 'I'm sorry, darling. But I must know. Where is Liza's amulet?'

'What?' The white face she turned to him was reddened down one cheek from the pressure of the pillow. Her eyes were swollen, bleary from the drugs he and Robert had given her.

'Sweetheart, I'm sorry.' He knelt beside her and dropped a kiss on her cheek. 'Just tell me where it is and I'll let you sleep.'

'Liza?' She frowned. 'Where's Liza?'

'Where is her amulet, Jane?' He repeated the request more loudly. 'Please. I have to know.' He shivered violently.

'Adam, the baby –' Suddenly the tears were welling up in her eyes.

'I know, my darling, and I'm so sorry.' Suddenly he thumped his fists on the bedcover. 'Please, Jane, just tell me. Where is it?'

'I took it to be mended. It got knocked over and the little silver branches were bent. The crystal broke off –'

'Hell and damnation!' Adam stood up and slapped his forehead. 'She did it. Brid! She's murdered our baby.' He let out a deep groan. 'Oh, Jane why? Why didn't you tell me? Why did you let it out of the house? You knew! You knew how important it was that it stayed here.'

'Mummy said it was superstitious nonsense.' She was crying now. 'She dropped it. I think she did it on purpose. She never liked it. Oh, Adam!' Suddenly she was sobbing bitterly. She threw herself back onto the pillows. 'I didn't think it mattered to take it out – just for a short time – while it was mended. It's so long since you've mentioned Brid. It can't have been her. It can't. It was an accident. The cat. No one would do that to someone else. Oh, Adam, please.'

He turned back to her at last and went to kneel by the bed. Taking her hand he pressed it to his lips. 'I'm sorry, darling. I shouldn't have upset you like this. No, of course it wasn't her. You go back to sleep. It was just not meant to be, that's all. And we have one gorgeous, handsome wee boy so we already have the perfect family.'

In the garden later he lit himself a cigarette and stood staring down at a bed of bright blue squill. The little flowers cheered him. They were so tough in the face of the icy wind and the showers of sleet which had chased away the early beauty of the spring morning.

A-dam?

He shook his head slightly and drew deeply on the cigarette.

A-dam, where are you?

Straightening, he looked round, his stomach clenching in sudden denial. He pinched out the cigarette and threw it down on the grass.

Breathe slowly and deeply. Calm yourself and draw a circle round yourself in your mind. Put an imaginary mirror between yourself and the girl and throw her thoughts back in her face. If you are in the kitchen use salt to make a ring on the floor . . . He could hear the firm Welsh voice in his head, see Liza's face suddenly watching him, a half-smile on her lips as she saw him fight with his scepticism.

'You bitch!' He was speaking out loud suddenly. 'You small-minded evil gypsy bitch with your curses and your spells. Get out of our lives! Do you hear me? Get out!'

I love you, A-dam!

She was more distant now, fractured, like the wireless when he listened in the evening and there was a thunder storm near.

'NO!' His shout was audible two gardens away where a neighbour was cutting white heather for a bowl in the hall. She looked up but mercifully did not recognise the voice of her sober-mannered, elegant doctor.

Adam turned his back on the garden and went into the house. He closed the French doors, bolted them and shut the curtains with a rattle, then he went into the kitchen and put the kettle on the gas. He would take Jane a cup of tea and then go round and fetch Calum before she found out that he had gone to the Hardings.

She was sitting on the bed wrapped in a dressing gown. 'Who were you shouting at?' She smiled at him wearily. Her face was wan.

'No one. I burned myself on the kettle.' He set the tray down carefully.

'Oh Adam, you should take care. Where's Calum?'

He took a deep breath. 'Sarah took him home last night. We thought it best. He was getting frightened, poor little lad.'

'I see.' She pursed her lips. 'And when is Sarah bringing him back?'

'I was going to go and fetch him now. That is if you want him home. I'm sure they'd keep him if –'

'No! I want him here. With us.' Suddenly she was crying again.

'All right, darling, but I'll have to leave you on your own.' He put a cup of tea on the bedside table next to her. 'Here, climb back into bed, and stay here warm and safe. I'll be less than half an hour.'

She nodded. 'I'll be all right. Just get him, Adam. Please.'

He let himself out and looked up and down the street. It was deserted as it always was on a weekday afternoon. It was cold and the children had gone in from their play to have their tea and do

170

their homework. A strong wind had got up and was bending the trees and hedges before it in the front gardens, shaking the elegant wrought-iron sign on the house next door. Adam shivered. He strode over to the Riley, which was parked neatly against the kerb. Groping in his pocket for his car keys, he glanced over his shoulder.

A figure had appeared at the corner of the street in the distance. He straightened up, staring at it. It was a woman and from her silhouette it looked as though she had long hair. He was clutching the keys so tightly in his hand he felt the skin of his palm abrade and bleed under the pressure, but he took no notice. For a moment he was unable to move, then he unlocked the car quickly and dived in. He slammed the door shut, surrounded by the usual comforting smell of leather and oil and old cigarette smoke, and with a shaking hand inserted the key into the ignition. He glanced into the driver's mirror. There was no sign of her. Pulling away from the kerb he swung the car out into the empty street and put his foot on the accelerator.

A few yards down the road he stepped on the brake and screeched to a halt. He couldn't leave Jane on her own. He would have to go back. Shaking, he turned in the seat and began to reverse slowly to stop outside his front door once more. What, after all, could Brid do to him? She was a slip of a thing. Slim. Delicate. He couldn't quite remember now, how she had looked, but she couldn't harm him. Not face to face. He turned off the engine and opened the door. Climbing out he squared his shoulders and turned towards the end of the road where he had seen the woman. There was no sign of her. He looked carefully up and down, scanning hedges and front gardens, the few parked cars, the broad, tree-planted pavement. Nothing. The street was empty. Had she gone into another house?

He gave the road one final scrutiny and then turned back to the car. He wasn't going to be more than half an hour at most, and the doors of his house were locked.

Inside the house Jane slept on. She hugged her pillow miserably in her sleep, feeling the ache in her heart and the soreness in her belly, blacking them out with uncomfortable dreams. She could see Adam standing in the garden. It was dark out there and stormy moonlight was streaming through the trees. Near him there was some kind of an animal. She stiffened in her sleep, watching, wanting to call out to him but afraid to draw attention to herself. Perhaps it hadn't seen him. Perhaps it would go away. It stepped away from the bushes a little and she saw what it was. A cat. A huge striped cat with low-set feral ears and, as it turned and looked straight at her, she saw that it had blood dripping from its fangs. 'Adam!' Her call died in her throat. She fought against sleep, knowing it was a dream, yet unable to wake up. 'Adam, be careful. Come in, quickly.' But her voice wouldn't work. No sound came.

And then, as she watched, the cat walked out into the full moonlight. It went up to Adam and leaned against his legs, purring. It had washed off the blood with soft silver paws and he looked down and smiled. He bent to stroke it and only then did she wake up. She was shaking violently and she knew she was going to be sick. She staggered out of bed and through to the bathroom, kneeling on the cold linoleum to vomit again and again down the lavatory. When she had finished she was drenched with sweat and shivering all over. She went to the door. 'Adam?'

But of course he had gone out. Gone to collect Calum from the Hardings. Clutching her dressing gown around her she walked over to the window and stared out. The sunlight had gone. A strong gusty wind was tossing the branches of the pear tree on the back lawn, rustling last year's dead leaves from their resting place at the foot of the old wall. She was feeling very wobbly still and she propped herself up against the window sill for a minute, feeling the chill from the glass cooling her hot forehead.

The cat was watching her from the shadow of the wall. She caught her breath in shock, as her eyes met the intense golden stare. For a moment they looked at each other without either of them moving. It was a striped cat, with snow-white paws, bigger than usual, she thought in terror, as she stood mesmerised by its gaze, transfixed by the intense feeling of hatred which seemed to come from the animal. Neither moved for several seconds, then Jane at last tore her eyes away. She ought to throw something at it. Horrible creature, threatening to scratch up her seedlings, tripping her up, perhaps causing her to lose her baby. Fighting back her tears she glanced round looking for something to throw. Then she looked back. The cat had gone.

'She can't cope, Liza.' Adam was sitting at his desk, the phone in his hand, a cup of coffee rapidly growing cold in front of him. He ran his fingers through his hair distractedly. 'She won't hear of the Hardings having him, or her mother, and yet he's wearing her out.' Physically Jane was still very weak, drained by the events of the last few weeks, but by now she should have been improving.

Psychologically she seemed to be handling the loss of the baby better than he had dared hope. She was sad and sometimes weepy but that was to be expected. She was taking comfort from the little boy and yet she was terrified for his safety; obsessed by the thought that something was going to happen to him; obsessed with the cat which had attacked her. She refused to let him leave the windows open. She panicked if he opened the French doors here in his study and at night she insisted they close both windows and curtains, something they had never done in all their time together. The amulet had been retrieved from the jeweller and was back in place beside their bed.

'Let Calum come to me, Adam.' Liza's voice the other end of the line was eager. 'I'd love to have him, you know I would. And she wouldn't object to him coming here, would she? He can play with Juliette and see the lambs again. And he would be safe, I promise. I'd look after him.' And keep him from Brid. The unspoken sentence hung in the air.

There was a long silence. 'Are you sure? All she needs is some time to recuperate. I don't think she would mind him coming to you.' He closed his eyes with relief. At Liza's Calum would be away from the house – and near Meryn. 'You're a saint, Liza. You're sure Phil won't mind?' He listened to her assurances for several seconds, smiling, before he put the phone down and exhaled loudly.

Liza arrived to collect Calum in a brand new Morris Traveller. Her glorious long red hair had been cut fashionably short, and she was wearing a stunningly elegant dress. 'Liza, what's happened to you?' Adam was really shocked. This was not his Liza. It was a stranger.

She let out a peal of laughter. 'Must move with the times. My sitters expect me to look up to the mark.' She giggled with the old Liza throaty cynicism. 'They don't see me at home, don't forget. I usually go to them. To Rome and Paris. You should see me!' She twirled round, showing them the spin of her skirt. 'Then I go back to Wales. This gets put in the cupboard and I dive into old trousers and thick woollen jumpers and I paint and paint and paint in the barn until it's time to come out again and go and find another victim!' She pulled Juliette to her and dropped a kiss on the little girl's golden head. 'Phil and Julie won't talk to me when I'm being posh. They don't recognise me, do you, darling?' She patted the little girl's nose and sent her back to play with a delighted Calum.

Adam smiled. He had been watching Jane's face, and seen the longing as she stared at Liza's lovely dress. That at least was one

173

thing he could do for her. Suddenly he had had an idea. He would take her to Paris, or to London. And he would spend some money on her. He cursed himself for not thinking about it earlier. It was always Jane who had the ideas, Jane who booked their holidays – somewhere where there was plenty of sand and sea for Calum. It had never occurred to him, as he slept in a deckchair, exhausted by his work, or built sandcastles or romped in the waves with Calum, that she might be bored and restless and longing for the bright lights of the town. That was it. They would have a holiday whilst Calum and Juliette played together in the safety of the Welsh border hills. Then perhaps they could all forget the striped cat with the slanting eyes and, protected by the amulet, put the unspoken thought of Brid behind them. For good.

In the hospital Brid sat quietly, her eyes fixed on interminable distances. At first she had fought the psychiatric staff, but they gave her drugs and she lost track of the long circling ribbons of time inside her head. Again she fought the men and women who tended her. Again they strapped her down and plunged needles into her arm. Time froze. Weeks. Months. Years – she did not know or care. Her abilities dulled and shrank and she withered like a flower in frost. But in the end she woke. Memories returned. She focused on Adam and saw him in her mind. This time she would be more careful.

She had upset Adam. He knew she had frightened the woman Jane and he blamed her for the death of his baby. Stupid. He was not so clever. The baby was already weak and failing in the woman's womb. If it had been strong it would have clung to life. She thought about it again and again. If she chose to destroy Jane one day she would have to be much more clever. More subtle. Adam must not know. And in the meantime somehow she must get close to him again. Make him love her again. He could not resist the cat. Slowly between the drugged sleeps in the hospital which wanted to trap her spirit and tie her down, she would slip free of her body and visit the garden. There she was sure she could make him forget Jane and the weakling dead baby and turn back to her for comfort and love.

10

Visiting Liza and Phil and Juliette had become a regular activity. Every summer now they had done it for more than ten years. Sometimes Adam would go too, and sometimes Calum would go on his own on the train, but more usually Jane would pack her son into the car and they would set off together for the west.

Adam enjoyed being left alone at home. Without Jane the pressure was off. He could relax, smoke the odd pipe, go down to the pub, without her looking at him reproachfully, and then when she came back, leaving their son in Wales for the summer holidays, they would go off together for a break before Adam came back to settle to his work again. And it was in the summer, when the others had gone and left him on his own, that he dared to let the cat into the house.

Calum and Jane regarded their drive across England as an adventure. Neither of them would acknowledge it, but they found Adam a stifling influence sometimes. He was too strict, too ambitious for Calum as the years passed, pushing the boy ever harder at his school work. 'One day you'll be a doctor like me, my son,' he'd say with a smile, and Calum would nod and agree. At first it was a joke to both of them. Neither knew nor cared where Calum's talents lay; it didn't matter. The boy was clever, his exam results were always good. But slowly the game had hardened into a pattern. The pressure had subtly increased and changed into total seriousness, and Calum's true feelings were, his mother sometimes thought, completely ignored whenever the subject was discussed, with the boy too conscious of his father's ambitions for him to stand up for himself. She had tried talking to him about it, but he smiled at her in the lovely gentle way he had, pushing his hair back out of his eyes, and he said, 'Don't worry, Mum, I won't let him push me into anything I don't want him to.' And with that she had to be content, sure that she would be able to tell if he were seriously unhappy. He was not like Adam. And as far as she could tell he was not like her either. There was an echo of her beloved father who had died four years ago, in her son, but only an echo. Where the rest of the quiet confident charm and the shy mannerisms originated she would never be able to guess.

There had been no more pregnancies. As the months had turned to years she gave up hoping for the miracle that would give Calum a brother or a sister and instead turned more and more of her attention to her son.

This particular summer, when Calum was due to choose which A levels he was going to study, she was determined that he and she should have a serious talk.

It was harder than she had anticipated to get him on his own. From the first moment that they had arrived at Pen-y-Ffordd he and Juliette had been off together for every moment of the day, leaping on two of the old rusty bicycles which had been rescued from a neighbour's barn, doused in oil and pressed into service to get them into Hay or up into the hills.

'Calum?' Jane put her hand on his handlebars as the two of them pushed their parcels of sandwiches into the basket on Juliette's bike. 'I haven't seen you at all this holidays.' They were already two weeks into their six-week stay.

'Oh, Mum.' He gave her the winning smile which never failed to melt her heart. 'Come on. You see me every day of the year. This is the hols. I only see Julie for a few weeks . . .'

Shrugging, she stood back. 'All right. But this evening, can we talk? Please.'

He gave a quick frown. 'There's nothing wrong, is there?'

'No, there's nothing wrong, I just want to discuss something with you.' Away from your father. Away from home. Did she have to spell it out for him? She smiled. 'Go on, both of you. Have a lovely day and I'll see you this evening.'

'But Aunt Jane, we were going to a party.' Juliette flung her long golden hair back across her shoulders. She was wearing a pale blue shirt and tightly belted jeans.

'And so you shall, Julie. I heard your father say he would drive you.' Jane managed to stop herself sighing. 'All I want is half an hour with Calum and then he is all yours.' She watched them cycle up the steep pitch and heard their ringing laughter as they disappeared round the bend and out of sight beneath the green canopy of overhanging hedges.

Walking slowly back towards the farmhouse she paused to lean on the orchard gate. Was part of the weight in her heart because she was a little jealous? They were so carefree, these children today. When she was their age the horizon had been black with the shadows of threatening war. Not that that had stopped her going to parties. It was Adam whose childhood seemed to have been the most bleak and lonely. He never talked about it much, but always in his stories there was the looming gloominess of the manse and his strict, humourless father.

The old man was in his early seventies now, still living in the manse, still alone. After the murder of his housekeeper he had employed no one else to look after him. They had never been to visit him, not once, in all the years they had been married, in spite of Jane's pleas and Calum's curiosity to see his father's home and meet his grandfather. Since the wedding they had seen the old man only once when he had made the journey south to be present at Calum's christening. He had stayed one night, his sober, black and unsmiling demeanour not endearing him to the guests at the party after the ceremony, and then he had asked Adam to drive him to the station. Father and son, out of sight of Jane, had spoken barely a word. They shook hands on the platform and Adam had not waited to see his father board the train.

'Penny for them.' Liza had wandered out into the sunshine and come to stand beside Jane at the gate.

Jane jumped. 'I was miles away.'

'Worrying about your old man?'

'No.' Jane smiled. 'That's one thing I don't have to do, thank God. No, I was worrying about Calum.'

'He seems fine to me.'

'He is. I just wonder sometimes if Adam isn't too strict with him. You know, it's strange. He hated his own father so much for his strictness, and yet there's more than a little of that dreadful straight-laced side to him as well.'

'There is?' Liza's eyes twinkled. 'Then he must have changed a lot!'

Jane frowned. She still hated references to Liza's and Adam's past together. 'Only in some ways. Adam is so set on Calum becoming a doctor, too.'

'And doesn't he want to?'

'That's it. I don't know. I have a feeling deep inside that he only says he does to please his father; that what he would really like is something quite different, but I don't know what. He doesn't confide in me about the future.'

'He's so young, Jane. Does he have to make up his mind yet?'

'You know he does. He has to choose his A level subjects.' Jane shook her head crossly. She hated hearing herself being so fussy.

Liza laughed. 'Forget it for the holiday. Let the children have some fun without thinking about the future.'

A stray breeze had found its way down from the dark shoulder of the mountain and into the orchard, stirring the leaves on the trees. Liza shivered. 'Come on in and have a cup of coffee, then let's find Phil and see if he'd like to come into Brecon with us.'

Calum and Juliette had hidden their bicycles in some bracken near the road and struck off on foot across the hillside, their sandwiches in a bag on Calum's shoulder. The hot sun was beating down on their heads as they walked and they headed instinctively for the distant trees where a narrow valley cut up into the hillside, its steep sides bordering a tumbling brook of ice-cold mountain water.

'What does your mum want?' Juliette turned to him, dancing at his side like an eager child.

He shrugged and glanced heavenwards. 'She's worrying as usual. She's got it into her head that I don't really want to be a doctor. That I'm only saying I do to please Dad.'

'And are you?' She turned cornflower-blue eyes on him, squinting in the sunlight.

He shrugged again. 'Dunno. Maybe. I've got to be something.'

'Don't you care?'

'I expect so. I don't want to think about it yet. Dad is always so serious. He never lets up. You'd think he could find time to come down here with us for a week or so in the summer, wouldn't you? But no, he'd rather be at home on his own. That's how much he cares about us.' He kicked viciously at a stone on the narrow sheep path through the mountain grass.

'He's very fond of you, Calum.' She was serious for a moment, sensing the hurt behind his words. 'That's not why he doesn't come. I expect he has to work so hard because he is a doctor. They don't seem to have many holidays and days off. Our doctor in Hay is always there. I don't think he ever goes away. I bet Uncle Adam would rather be here with you if he could.'

'Maybe.' Calum's mouth turned down in a pout. 'Then perhaps

I don't want to be a doctor. I don't want to work all the time without ever having a day off. That's no fun.'

'No, it isn't!' She caught his hand. 'Come on. Enough serious talk. Forget your father. Forget everything. I'll race you to the *nant* over there and we'll have our sandwiches out of the sun.'

They had a favourite spot near a small pool where the nut-brown water lay deep at the foot of a cascade. The rocks near it were covered in sun-warmed moss and they sat there, dangling their feet in the water which was freezing cold. 'Are you going to swim?' Juliette turned to him as they stared down at their reflections.

He nodded. 'You?'

She grinned. 'The perfect way to work up an appetite.' Under her jeans and shirt she was wearing a tiny blue nylon bra and matching pants, her slim figure a pale contrast to her tanned hands, arms and face. Calum smiled. 'I like the bikini.'

'It's not!'

'Well, near enough.' He had had the foresight to wear swimming trunks under his own jeans. Cautiously he slid into the water, gasping at the coldness. 'Come on in.'

'You won't splash me?' She smiled conquettishly.

'Only a little.' He had his father's eyes with their long dark lashes. 'And only if you are longer than two minutes getting in!' He struck out with one or two strokes across the small pool and his feet found the rock bottom almost at once. Balancing on the slippery weed he stood up and turned to face her. 'I'm counting! One!'

'No!' She shrieked and put one toe in the water.

'Two.'

'It's so cold!'

'Three.' He put his hand in the water and curved it into a scoop.

'No, Calum, no! I'm coming!' She held her breath and slid down the mossy rock. The coldness of the water took her breath away and she was gasping as she waded and then swam towards him.

'Well done!' His eyes were sparkling. 'Did you know the water made your bra go all transparent?'

She clapped her hands over her breasts. 'Calum, you beast!'

'Take it off. Go on. You might as well.' He reached forward to flick a strand of her long hair off her shoulder. 'Why not? No one is going to see.'

'You will.' Her indignation was only half serious.

'I've seen you naked before.'

'When?' She was indignant.

'Loads of times. When you were in the bath as a baby.'

179

'We shared a bath, so I saw you too.'

'In the sandpit behind the barn.'

'I was only three.'

'When I walked into the bathroom last summer and you were painting your toenails . . .'

'All right, all right!' She had blushed scarlet. 'But I'm not taking it off now.' She fell back onto the water and kicked her feet up and down, showering him with spray.

'No!' Laughing, he dived for her toes. 'I could have it off you!'

'You mustn't.'

Her voice rose to a shriek as she tried to find her feet and failed, going under. She rose choking and Calum stood up, concerned. 'Are you all right? I'm sorry.' He put his arm round her shoulders. As she coughed and spluttered his fingers strayed lightly to the fastening on her bra. By the time she realised what he was doing it was too late. With a shout of triumph he had snatched it away from her clutching arms and danced out of reach.

For a moment her face registered dismay then slowly she began to laugh. She stretched her arms above her head, and arched her back thrusting her small, dripping breasts at him, then slowly she reached for her pants and began to edge them down. 'Go on. If I do it, you must too.'

'Me?' For a moment he hesitated, aware of what the waist-high water concealed.

'Go on.' She was naked now, still laughing.

In one movement he swept off his own pants and swinging them round his head he hurled them at the rocks and began to wade towards her, his eyes on hers. Gently he drew her to him and their bodies touched, their cold skin taking fire as their lips met. Without a word they waded to the bank and there he drew her down on the grass with him, his hands on her shoulders, then on her breasts, his lips everywhere as she caught him to her in return.

On the far side of the pool the shadows stirred. The figure of a woman seemed to hover for a moment near the water, then it was gone.

Half an hour later, they were sitting side by side on the shingle which skirted the pool. They were both cold, their skin pimpled from the chilled water and they pressed together for warmth, but neither wanted to go and fetch their clothes. Calum linked his arms around her body and buried his face in her straggly hair. His teeth were chattering. 'That was fantastic.'

She nodded. 'I knew it would be.'

'You knew?' He drew back slightly so that he could see her face.

'I've often thought about it. Haven't you?'

He gave a small laugh. 'I suppose I have. Yes.'

'You and me. It was meant to be. I always knew I would marry you.'

He hugged her. 'Me too.' He was silent for a moment, gazing into the depth of the pool which was rippled now only by the trickle of water sliding down the black rocks from the open mountainside above them. 'Except sometimes I think of you as my sister.'

She giggled. 'Incest. That makes it more wicked.'

'And you like being wicked?'

She threw herself back suddenly. 'Do you have to ask?' She put her hand over her eyes and gave a deep sigh of animal content. 'We mustn't tell the olds of course. It will have to be our secret until you've taken your exams. Can you wait until the holidays each time?'

He stared down at her body. The pale skin was shivering, and her lips were going blue. Suddenly he laughed. 'I can wait. But there won't be a holiday if you get pneumonia and die. Come on. Let's get dressed and run to get warm. Don't forget there are weeks and weeks before the end of this holidays before we have to think of the next.'

Jane glanced at her son as they strolled together down the orchard. He had already changed for the party and she eyed his slim tall figure in the clean jeans and white shirt with approval. Something had changed in him. He was more confident, more grown up than she had thought. 'I don't want to spoil the holidays by worrying for weeks.' She suddenly felt nervous; at a disadvantage. 'I just wanted to talk to you for a few minutes about the future and then we'll forget it till we get home.'

He was as tall as her now, she realised. In fact, perhaps half an inch taller.

He had stopped beside her and she found he was holding her gaze, a faintly amused expression somewhere in his eyes. 'It's about your exams, Calum,' she floundered on. 'I don't want you to feel that your father is forcing you to choose something you don't really want to do. He has always been so single-minded for you. I suspect sometimes he doesn't realise what he is doing. He has such a strong perception of what he wants himself . . .' She stopped as he put his arm round her shoulders.

'Mummy, I shan't let him railroad me into anything I don't want.'

He gave her that beautiful smile which always made her go weak at the knees with love and protectiveness. 'Give me a little credit for strength of character, will you? I'm choosing sciences because, at the moment, I do want to go into medicine. I don't think I shall want to go into general practice like Dad. I think I'd like to do research, or specialise in something, but for the time being I am sure that science is what I want, all right? Now, forget it. Don't worry. Have a lovely time with Liza for the summer and let Julie and me get out of your hair and explore the mountains and go to the parties she's arranged, so that in September we can all get back to work refreshed!' He gave her a quick kiss on the cheek and turned away.

She watched him lope back across the orchard and saw in the distance the bright flash of Juliette's hair as she appeared from behind the house. She had been waiting for him and already Liza had the car engine running to drop them down the hill into town. Slowly she shook her head. He had handled her very well, really. She ought to be proud of him. So why was she still feeling so uneasy?

With a sigh Adam shut his notebooks and his diary and sat back in his leather-upholstered chair. His study was feeling stuffy and rather dusty. It was two weeks since Jane and Calum had gone and his first guilty euphoria at having the house to himself had worn off to be replaced by a sense of ennui which was very unlike him. He leaned forward, putting his elbows on the clean, meticulously-positioned blotter and rested his forehead on his fingertips, gently massaging his temples.

Tucked into the top drawer of his desk was a letter from his father. Thomas Craig wrote only once a year, on Adam's birthday, enclosing always a ten shilling note 'to buy himself something', an incongruous present, Adam always thought with a wry shake of the head, from one reasonably well off adult man to another, who was now, let's face it, over forty – just. It did however keep the space between them impersonal and distanced as ever. Thomas's present for his grandson was the same. Ten shillings on every birthday. Nothing at Christmas.

The arrival of a letter this morning, out of sequence, was a shock. For the whole day Adam had carried it around in his pocket, not wanting to open it, knowing already in some part of himself what it would say. Then this evening, before he sat down to bring his records up to date, as he did meticulously every evening, he had pulled the white envelope out of his pocket and stared at it. His father's handwriting, in its accustomed blue ink, was as firm as ever but the contents were as he suspected, indicative of a weakening.

I thought it best to tell you the news as soon as I knew myself. I have a cancer which is not worth the operation. There is no need for you or Jane to bother yourselves with me. My affairs are in order, my will, of which you are the sole beneficiary, is lodged with James and Donaldson in Perth. God bless you, my son, and your wife, and Calum.
Yr affectionate father, Thomas Craig.

Adam bit his lip. He wasn't sure how he felt. He read the letter twice, then put it in the drawer, turning the small key but leaving it as always in the lock, and went back to his work. It was two hours later that he had closed his books and sat back to think. Should he go to Scotland? His mind wouldn't register. His father didn't say what kind of cancer, how far advanced, what he intended to do for his care, whether he was going to remain at the manse, whether he was going to retire. There was so much unsaid in the letter! He sighed angrily and then caught himself sternly. He was angry with his father for being ill. For being about to die. For making a plea, however inadvertently, for Adam's attention, and that, in Adam's eyes, made him every bit as cold a fish as his father had been to him. He found himself wishing suddenly that Jane were there. She would know what to do. She would put her arms round him and hug him in that warm motherly way she had, and make him feel cared for and safe and strong. Strong enough to deal with anything the world threw at him, even his father.

With another sigh he leaned across the desk and was drawing the telephone towards him when he heard the small scratch at the window. He put down the receiver and swivelled his chair to face the garden with a smile. 'There you are, puss. I thought you'd deserted me.' Levering himself to his feet he walked across to the French doors and unlocked them. The tabby cat trotted in past him, brushing against his legs as it did so and jumped on a chair. He smiled. 'So, puss. Where have you been?' It usually came when Jane was away. It seemed to sense her hostility and never appeared when she was there. He had asked tentatively several times during their marriage whether they could keep a cat or a dog – he still remembered with wistful love the puppy he had had for such a short time as a boy, which Jeannie had taken in, but Jane had shaken her head.

He stooped and touched the cat's head gently. It looked up at him and then, standing on its back legs it pawed his chest, rubbing its head under his chin. He smiled and scooped it into his arms. 'So, sweetheart, what am I going to do about my old father, you tell me that. Should I go up to Pittenross?' He carried it back to the window and stood staring out across the lawn. The cat stiffened. It appeared to be listening. 'I haven't been to Scotland for so long,' he went on quietly. 'I wanted to put it all behind me. The manse, the kirk. But I suppose I'll have to face it one day. Perhaps that's best. To face one's nightmares.' He was running his fingers up and down the warm silky spine. The cat began to purr. 'That's what my psychiatrist friends would tell me, I expect. Dig deep and see what hidden traumas there are in my life! Dr Freud would have a lot to say, I suspect, about my relationship with my mother and father.' His hand moved up to the cat's ears and he scratched gently at the animal's ruff and then bent his head to drop a kiss on the top of its head. 'Come on. I'd better ring my Janie. Hey, why did you do that!' He let the cat fall suddenly from his arms as it lashed out and raked at his face with razor-sharp claws. He put his hand to his cheek and his fingers came away dripping blood. 'You little devil. Get out! Go on, buzz off! I was going to fetch you some milk after my call!' He turned away from the door, dabbing frantically with his handkerchief as the blood poured down his face, staining his stiff white collar and blue striped shirt. 'Hell and damnation!' He hurried to the door of his study and ran upstairs, trying to stem the flow before it ruined his shirt altogether. Tearing it off, he flung it into the wash basin and ran the cold tap. By the time he had patched his face with sticking plaster, changed into a casual shirt and sweater and poured himself a stiff whisky it was beginning to grow dark. He wandered back into his study and stood for a moment looking out of the open French doors across the garden, sniffing the night-time scent of stock and roses. Then he turned back towards the desk and picked up the phone.

Jane drew up in the deserted street and turned off the engine. She was stiff and exhausted after the long drive and for a moment she sat where she was, looking at the house. The windows were in darkness. She had thought long and hard after Adam's call two nights before, and then she had made her decision. 'I can't let him go up to Scotland on his own. If I drive back, can I leave Calum with you, Liza?'

'Of course you can!' Liza had hugged her. 'You know you don't even have to ask. Leave him as long as you like. The whole holidays if you want. I know the children love it. They always get on so well and you've done it often enough before. It will give you and Adam some well deserved time alone again.'

She had rung Adam back twice to tell him her decision but he was out on calls so in the end she had decided to surprise him, driving through the night to avoid traffic and arriving home at four-thirty in the morning. She climbed slowly out of the car and stretched, breathing in the sweet smell of suburban gardens, so different from the cool wild air of the Welsh hills, then she dived into the car and pulled out her suitcase and her hold-all. Slamming the door and locking it she made her way up the path and reached into the pocket of her jacket for her keys.

The house was all dark inside and she put a hand out to the hall light switch, closing the door silently behind her.

The steps of the staircase creaked beneath her weight as she tiptoed up. Their bedroom door was open and she went in, reaching to switch on the small lamp on the tall chest of drawers just inside the door. Adam was fast asleep, and as her eyes adjusted to the sudden light she realised that there was a second head on the pillow beside his, a woman's, her long dark hair fanned across the sheet.

'Adam!' Her anguished shriek woke him with a start and he sat up, still half asleep.

Jane caught at the back of the chair near her, shaking. She was weak with shock. There was no woman.

'What, in the name of God, are you doing, giving me a fright like that!' Adam threw his legs over the side of the bed and reached for his dressing gown. He was naked. He never slept naked when she was in the twin bed next to him. They had bought the beds after Jane's miscarriage when, for a time, her pain and restlessness and misery had driven Adam away and somehow they had never brought the old double bed back into the room. It was something she had often regretted. She watched as he pulled on his robe and knotted it round his waist.

There was a livid red scratch across his cheek and his hair was rumpled like Calum's. 'What on earth are you doing here in the middle of the night? Is something wrong?'

'I thought I'd give you a surprise.' She grimaced, kicking off her shoes. 'I thought you'd be pleased to see me. I didn't want you to have to go to Scotland on your own.'

'I am pleased to see you.' He came and put his arms round her and kissed her cheek, thanking God silently that she would never

185

know how, sleepily, he had welcomed the cat into his bed, not wondering how it had got back into the house or if it would attack him again, but instead feeling the sensuous softness of its fur as it slid down under the sheet and nestled against his loins. Nor would she ever know about the violently erotic dream from which she had woken him. The dream about Brid.

Brid sat up in bed with a start, her body cold and shaking. A-dam. She had been with him. In his bed. She closed her eyes and took a deep slow breath, trying to steady the thundering in her chest and pulses. Around her the other women in the dormitory were asleep. She could hear their breathing, their silence, their groans and their sobs. She had come back to her body too fast and it had shaken her badly. She sat up, pushing the hair off her face and hugged her knees miserably. It had been so good. As good as she remembered. When he welcomed her, like that, she could overcome the strange emanations from the amulet beside his bed which for so long had held her back inside her dreams and kept her away from the house where he lived. He had held her to him and stroked her shoulders and murmured lovingly as his lips sought hers in the darkness beneath the sheet.

Then the bitch woman had arrived. Not the one with red-gold hair – his Liza. The other one. Jane. The woman with hair the colour of old dead grass who smelled of soap like the stuff they used in the hospital, the mother of A-dam's son. Looking up at the ceiling above her bed she felt her fingers curl into claws. That woman did not make A-dam happy. She did not look after him. She went away without him and left him alone in a house which in her view was without colour or warmth or beauty.

Sometimes out of curiosity she had reached out over the years to Liza, questing, still resenting her, needing to know if she were still a threat. But Liza was strong. Far stronger than A-dam. And most of the time she was shielded by a blinding force field which repelled and weakened and Brid withdrew. It was not worth the expenditure of energy it would take to pierce the shield. One day, she promised herself, she would deal with Liza, the woman who had taken A-dam from her. But not now. Now she preferred to concentrate on A-dam himself or, when Liza had forgotten her shield, to peer at her from the darkness and amuse herself with silent threats and promises and spy, thoughtfully, on A-dam's child and the girl who was now his lover.

At the end of the dormitory a door opened and she saw the light of a torch shining into the dark cavern between the beds. Silently she slid down under her blankets and shut her eyes. If they found you awake they would bring the needle and put it in your arm and then you would sleep for a long, long time, only to wake confused and dry-mouthed without having dreamed or travelled or even rested. And days would turn into weeks and weeks into months and years again without you knowing they had gone. She had learned a long time ago to play quiet and asleep a lot of the time, in this strange world in which she had been ensnared.

Footsteps progressed slowly up the ward. She could hear the soft jingle of the keys at the woman's belt and as she drew closer she could smell the odd carrion smell on her breath. She shuddered and squeezed her eyes more tightly closed. The nurses in this strange place were afraid of her. They did not like her. And she did not like them. But this one, Deborah Wilkins, she especially hated. The woman sensed something of Brid's otherness, her spirit which could never be entirely captured, and her resentment had turned to sadistic persecution.

The footsteps stopped at the end of her bed and the woman walked towards her. Brid held her breath. For a moment there was total silence, then Nurse Wilkins turned away and resumed her hourly patrol of the regimented beds.

The next day was one of those when Brid went into Dr Furness's office and sat talking to him while they drank a cup of tea. She liked this other doctor who seemed to be in charge of the place in which she lived. She trusted him. He was wise and gentle and she didn't mind that he wrote down the things she said to him. Gradually, as her confidence in him grew stronger and her loneliness amongst the other inmates became greater, she confided in him more often.

'So, Brid, my dear. Did you go travelling again last night?' Dr Furness smiled up at her as he opened the now bulging file with her name on the front. He had seen her psyche strengthen and grow as the effects of the drugs wore off and he was pleased. Here was a patient who responded well to a psychotherapeutic approach.

She nodded shyly. 'I went to see A-dam at his house.'

'This is Dr Craig?' He glanced back through the pages of small neat black writing.

She nodded. 'The woman was away still and I went to him. To his bed. He was pleased to see me. But then . . .' She shook her head mournfully. For a while she was silent, sipping her tea, then she reached for the slice of chocolate cake which he had brought in for her. He smiled indulgently as she sank her teeth into it. It was several long minutes before he decided he had better prompt her again. 'Then what happened?' he asked.

'His woman, Jane, came back. It was still night-time and we were asleep. She let herself into the house and came upstairs quietly, so she caught me.'

'I see.' He frowned. 'And what did she say when she found you in bed with her husband?'

'She was not pleased. She screamed.'

'And what did you do?'

'I ran away from the room and then I came back to my bed here.'

'And how long had you been away do you think?'

She took another bite of cake, then she shrugged. 'Time is not the same here and there. When I woke up the horse-face nurse came in. She looked at me with her torch and I pretended to be asleep.' She chewed for a moment. 'Did you ask her to make sure I was there?'

He smiled. 'I worry about you, my dear. Sometimes I wonder if you could get into trouble on your travels.'

'If there is trouble I come back to my bed. My cord is a strong one.'

He nodded. 'We've decided this is your astral cord, yes?' He made a note. 'I would very much like to see you when you do this travelling. I haven't met anyone yet who does it as you do and who can talk about it.'

'Why not?' She frowned. 'It is very easy. Especially when things are not very nice where you are. You can go away. I do not like this place.' She turned a look of such abject misery on him that he was for a moment quite shaken. 'I want to go to A-dam's house to live. He would want me to, I know it.'

Dr Furness kept to himself the guess that Dr Craig, if he existed at all, would almost certainly not want this beautiful, wild and completely insane young woman visiting him.

'Tell me more about Dr Craig's house, my dear. It interests me to hear about it.' He picked up his pen again. In his file there was an address which he had looked up for a Dr Adam Craig. It would be interesting to go and see the man, he had decided, see the house which this strange young woman claimed to visit in her dreams, and ask him if he knew a dark-haired lustful beauty who, after more than ten years in a mental hospital in north London, still looked not a day over twenty-one.

He had asked her once why she didn't want to go home. She had sat for a long time in silence and then shaken her head. 'They will kill me if I go back.'

'Kill you? Why?'

'Because I left. Because I came here, to your world. Because of A-dam.'

'And your people are Romanies?' He had asked her before, and she did not seem to recognise the word.

She shook her head again. 'I have told you, I come from the people of the north wind.'

He wrote it down again and circled the phrase with his pen. It sounded wild, romantic and vague. Just like her. He had mentioned her claim at home and to his astonishment his Classics student son had reacted at once. 'That is what Herodotus called the Celts.'

He reached into his desk drawer and pulled out an atlas, borrowed this time from his daughter. 'Do you recognise places on maps?' he asked casually.

Brid shrugged.

He opened the book at the map of Great Britain and pushed it across towards her. 'Do you see? England Scotland and Wales. You told me you were in Edinburgh.' He stabbed the map. 'There. You see?'

She stared at it blankly and shook her head. 'Catriona showed me one of these. It did not have Craig Phádraig on it. I saw Abernethy where my uncle sometimes went and the village where A-dam lived.'

'So, you lived in Scotland. Was that all your life? From a small girl?'

She nodded doubtfully.

'And you wandered round the mountains, you said.'

She nodded again.

'And you were at college?'

'Like A-dam. Yes.'

He shook his head. 'But where are your parents, Brid? Your brother? Your uncle? Why do they not try to find you?'

'I do not want them to find me. Broichan will kill me.' She could see him sometimes, shouting. He was still trying to reach her, hammering against the strange veil which separated them, like the glass in the hospital windows, calling at her to come to him. She had broken the sacred *geas*, the taboo which forbade the traversing of the worlds, and the punishment was death. She leaned across the desk and closed his atlas. 'Why do you not let me go to A-dam? Why must I stay here? I do not like this place.'

189

'I know, Brid. It's very hard.' It was all there in her records. She had been committed after being found wandering in London. There had been a few notes on her life in Edinburgh – admission to the Royal Infirmary, one to a mental hospital in Morningside and before that nothing.

He closed the file. 'I have to go, Brid, my dear. We'll talk again. Now, I want you to be good. Shouting and threatening the nurses does not help, you know. If you want to leave here, you have to prove to us that you can behave and look after yourself.'

She wandered out into the garden later. There she felt safe. The others didn't seem to like the trees and the flowers. Perhaps she should tell Dr Furness about the trees and flowers in A-dam's garden. They were beautiful.

Ivor Furness did not realise until he was almost there that his journey to his second cousin's wedding that weekend in Harpenden would take him through St Albans and almost down the street where Dr Adam Craig lived. The address which he had found in the medical directory was engraved on his heart – the suburban house in the quiet street with the flowering cherry outside and the coloured glass in the front door which were described so fondly by Brid. 'A detour. Only a moment,' he told his surprised family as he swung his car out of the main road.

And there it was. The cherry tree, the blossom gone now and the leaves green and heavy with summer. The door with its inset panes of stained glass depicting an Art Nouveau white lily just as she had described it. Of course that did not prove anything. She might have been there before, as a child or as a young woman. She might have seen photographs.

Leaving his family in the car he walked up the path, raised his hand to the doorbell and rang.

It was the next door neighbour who told him that Dr and Mrs Craig were in Scotland.

'I told you not to come.' Thomas Craig opened the front door and stood barring the way into the shadowy hall. The house behind him smelled faintly of TCP.

'I had to see how you were, Father.' Adam resisted the sudden childlike urge to turn and run away. 'Jane and I were worried by your letter.'

'There was no reason to worry. Everything is under control.' The old man pushed his chin forward slightly and scowled. Then unexpectedly he relented and stepped back. 'Well, now you're here, you'd best come in, I suppose.'

The house was spotless and tidy, his study the only room which looked even remotely lived in.

'I thought he was going to send us away again,' Jane whispered as they stood in the cold kitchen looking round. 'And I'm almost sorry he didn't. The hotel would have been better than this morgue.'

Adam shuddered. 'This is where Jeannie died.' He looked down as though expecting to see the bloodstains still on the floor. His voice broke and Jane put her hand gently on his arm.

'There's no sense in thinking about it.' She sighed, and reaching for the kettle she glanced round. 'The range isn't lit. Is there an electric ring or something? I can't think how your father could have stayed here alone after it happened.'

'There is a cooker in the pantry there.' Thomas appeared behind them. In the sunlight streaming in through the windows Adam saw for the first time how grey and drawn his father's face was. 'I never light the range.' He walked over and pulled the back door open, allowing more light to flood the dark kitchen. 'I stayed here, young woman, because it was my home and my parish. Where else was I to go? Going would not bring Mrs Barron back.'

He watched Jane carry the kettle through into the pantry and put it on the Baby Belling she found next to the meat safe.

'How long will you be staying?'

Jane gave him a faint smile. 'Only as long as you would like us to, Father-in-law. We just wanted to make sure you were all right.'

'I'm fine.' He frowned. 'As you see.' He turned away to the door. 'When you've made the tea, bring it through to my study and we'll have a wee bit talk before you both go on your way.'

Jane gave a small chuckle. 'I think that can be counted as a success, don't you?'

Adam picked up the tray and followed Jane back down the passage to his father's study. 'I thought maybe Jane and I could stay here a night, Father?' he said as he laid the tray on Thomas's desk. 'You must have room in this big house. We won't put you to any trouble. In fact we'll take you out to a meal this evening at the hotel, what do you think of that?'

They were given the room that had been his parents'. It was cold, impersonal, the cupboards empty, the dressing table bare. Thomas now slept in Adam's old room. But they could not persuade him to go with them to the hotel and it was alone that they sat down in the restaurant that evening and ordered cold salmon and new potatoes and peas accompanied by a fairly nice and very expensive bottle of wine.

'It must be strange, coming back after all this time.' Jane had been watching her husband's face as he stared out of the window at the slow broad sweep of the river at the end of the lawn.

'I beg your pardon?' He dragged himself back from his thoughts with an effort and nodded. 'It is. We should have brought Calum.'

It was something she had also been thinking, but it was too late now. She shook her head slowly. 'So, are you going to take me up to see your famous Picts' stone with its weird carvings? I jolly well hope so.' She reached forward for the bottle and topped up both their glasses. 'You are going to, Adam, aren't you?'

He shook his head. 'I don't know. It's quite a climb. I was young and fit in those days.'

'We'll take a picnic. I can't believe your father will miss us if we take ourselves off for a few hours. He really is a curmudgeonly old soul, isn't he! How long has he got, has he told you?'

He shook his head. 'Not long, I think. He's got a drawer full of painkillers in his desk and another lot in the bathroom and they're hefty ones. Poor Dad. I wouldn't have wished this on him for anything.'

They left the manse in the late morning, leaving Thomas to walk stiffly over to the kirk. On Adam's shoulder was a bag full of food and a bottle of white wine bought the night before from the hotel bar. He led the way across the river and up the steep path beneath the overhanging trees and shrubs, and within minutes was very out of breath. 'This path wasn't so steep in the old days, I'm sure it wasn't.'

Jane laughed. 'So, aren't you sorry you didn't join the squash club when I did?' She danced a few steps ahead of him and then slowed again. 'This is so beautiful, Adam. I can't imagine anyone being lucky enough to live here all the time.'

'It didn't seem lucky at the time. I was miserable after Mother went.'

They stopped and stood looking down into the steep ravine where the river hurtled down the hillside in cascades of cold rainbow spray in the deflected sunlight of the overhanging trees. The roar of the water was deafening.

'Come on. This way.' Catching his breath he strode on ahead of her, following the path with difficulty in places, ducking beneath the pale green lichen which hung from the trees in ragged curtains.

Once they were on the open hillside he stopped, panting again. 'Up there. See?'

Jane followed his pointing hand and saw the stone silhouetted against the sky on the top of the ridge. 'It's certainly imposing.'

They were both panting when they reached it. Throwing the bag down on the ground, Adam bent over and touched his toes with a groan. 'I've got a stitch! My God, I'm unfit. So, what do you think of it?'

'Weird.' Jane walked over and traced the patterns of the designs with her fingertip. 'And it's hundreds of years old, you say?'

'More than a thousand.' He smiled. 'The Picts had this amazing reputation for being magicians and Druids and stuff. They really caught my imagination. And this is a spooky place. The mist was always playing round the top of this ridge when I was young. I was an impressionable boy, on my own, prepared to believe in anything. And then I met Brid and . . .' He paused, staring away down the hillside towards the valley.

'And?' Jane prompted.

'And I used to follow her into what felt like another world. It was like some strange, wonderful adventure with me as the hero.' He sat down on a rocky outcrop a few feet from her and went on staring into the distance. 'I felt very bad when I left her and went to Edinburgh.' He paused. He was trying very hard to put the image of Brid out of his head. It was a seductive, erotic image, an image linked to his dreams, linked in some way to the beautiful vicious cat he had befriended; it was an image which at the same time filled him with dread.

There was a long silence as they both stood watching a circling hawk. Suddenly it closed its wings and stooped out of sight into the high corrie and they were left in the intense silence of the heat. Behind them the summit of the mountain was a blaze of heather.

'So, tell me what it means.' She was standing again, her hand on the stone.

Don't touch. Leave it alone.

For a moment he thought he had spoken out loud, but she didn't move. Her hands were still tracing the deeply incised symbols, the Z rod, the crescent moon, the serpent, the mirror.

'It's a message to those who come after.'

'And what does it say?'

'It says this is a special place.'

Behind them, in the valley, the mist was creeping closer.

*   *   *

Liza was leaning on the orchard gate in the dusk, watching the bats swooping above the apple trees. She gave a deep sigh of contentment. From where she stood she could see the lights on in Philip's barn. He had come in to have supper with her and the children, and then, almost before it was finished had gone out again, that particular intense preoccupied expression on his face which meant, though he might have been sitting at the table with them in the flesh, that his spirit had still been standing in front of the huge canvas of an abstract landscape on which he was working in the barn. He had slipped back there without a word, almost unnoticed, and he would be there all night, perhaps crawling into bed as it grew light, perhaps still painting when next morning she carried a cup of coffee over to the barn. He painted with an intensity which sometimes frightened her. When she had gently suggested that he slow up, that there was all the time in the world, he shook his head. 'I can't. I've wasted too much time. All those years teaching and running a department when I should have been painting. I can't slow up, Liza, there's too much to be done and too little time left.'

Her most recent portrait had been crated and shipped to Paris over six weeks ago now, and her studio was empty of work in progress. She pictured it as she stood in the dusk. It was swept and the paints and empty canvasses neatly stacked. She fished in the pocket of her cotton sweater for a pack of cigarettes and lit one, smelling the fragrant tobacco on the cool night air. This was the best time, when she was pregnant with a picture, waiting. She sketched all the time of course, and painted small things, watercolours, but the big formal portraits, the attempts to capture and lay bare a man or a woman's soul, that was something which needed to be thought about and developed, sometimes over months. She was fortunate. She could pick and choose amongst the people who wanted her to paint them. She could read up about them and talk to them and then when she was ready begin on her preliminary sketches.

A slight breeze had risen from nowhere, whispering amongst the apple trees, stirring the seeding grasses. It was almost dark, but her eyes could pick out the silhouettes of the low hills on the far side of the valley where the occasional bright light moving across the landscape showed a car following the winding road alongside the Wye or turning up into the network of narrow lanes which threaded the dark countryside.

She shuddered suddenly and throwing down her cigarette

ground it into the earth with her heel. The children had gone for a walk after supper, strolling up across the fields behind the house. She turned, her back against the mossy gate, and tried to see into the darkness of the slope behind the house, listening for their voices. Somewhere in the distance an owl hooted.

Dreamily she began to walk back towards the house but halfway there she stopped. She would go into her studio and look round. It was almost there, the urge to start painting. In some part of her mind she had already selected the woman whom Juliette would describe as her victim; she was an elderly French poet, a woman of enormous learning and wisdom with a craggy, lived-in face which displayed a quite staggering beauty and the most piercing lovely eyes of anyone Liza had seen for a very long time. She turned and walked with sudden determination towards the studio and put her hand to the door. To her surprise it was open. She hesitated. Had she left it like that? She doubted it. Usually she locked it, but now while there was no painting in progress perhaps she had let her usual concentration slip. Or perhaps Philip had come over to borrow something – he often did, lifting without shame her most expensive pigments or a precious sketch book as the fury with which he worked consumed him.

She pushed open the door and looked into the cavernous darkness. Parts of the barn roof had been removed and replaced by glass to give her the north-facing light she needed. Even in the dark there was a luminosity about the interior of the building. She stared round as her hand reached for the light switches and it was then she heard a stifled giggle. She froze, every sense alert. For a moment there was silence, then she heard a murmur coming from the far corner where her old sofa, covered by a brilliantly-coloured kelim, stood back against the wall. Suddenly knowing what she was going to find she smacked her hand down the bank of light switches, throwing the barn into brilliant light.

Calum and Juliette were lying together naked on the sofa. Beside them on the floor was a half-full bottle of white wine. Next to it, another, empty and on its side, showed that their consumption in the relatively short time since supper had been rapid. For a moment neither of them moved, then they leaped from the sofa. Juliette grabbed at the kelim, holding it in front of her, her face set in a defiant scowl whilst Calum after a frantic search had grabbed his jeans, and with his back to Liza dragged them on and hauled up the zip. When he turned round his face was scarlet. 'Aunt Liza, I can explain.'

'I don't think anything needs explaining, thank you, Calum.'

Her first blinding fury that they had somehow desecrated her work place was being replaced in quick succession by anguish that the children had shown so plainly that they were no longer children, sympathy with their embarrassment which said more eloquently than any words that they were, terror at what Philip would say, horror at the thought of having to explain to Adam and Jane and a terrible urge to laugh at their pathetic, frightened-rabbit expressions.

'You won't tell Father?' Calum's plea as he reached for his shirt broke into her racing thoughts. 'Please. He'd kill me.'

She shook her head. 'He wouldn't do that, Calum.' She took a deep breath and reached for her cigarettes again. 'I think you'd better give me some of that wine while I think how I should react.' Her brain was racing.

I've been young.

Damn it, I made love on this same sofa to his father!

Yes, but they are only children.

Supposing she gets pregnant.

We'd cope.

We always do.

'Mum.' Juliette had somehow managed with complete dignity to slip on her panties and the huge man's shirt she had taken to wearing. She poured her mother a glass of wine and then one for herself. Apart from her bright eyes and the slight flush on her cheeks, which Liza suspected came from her interlude with Calum rather than too much wine, she appeared quite calm. 'I'm sorry. We shouldn't have used your studio.' She had focused unerringly on the most – and the least – important thing. 'Don't worry about us. We were careful. And besides, we are going to get married.' She smiled beatifically. 'You mustn't tell Daddy, or Calum's parents, because they wouldn't understand. But you do, don't you?'

Artfully managed, Liza thought. As she sipped her wine she found her mind was a cheerful blank. 'I'll have to decide what to do,' she said at last. 'I'll have to think.'

Juliette's face broke into a brilliant smile. Her mother always said that when she was about to cave in, but needed to save face. She dropped a kiss on Liza's head. 'You're a darling. I knew you'd understand. Aunt Jane is such a fuddy-duddy she would probably have kittens.' She caught Calum's hand and pulled him close. 'Uncle Adam would understand, I know it. You and he were lovers, weren't you?' Her eyes sparkled even more.

'Julie, that's an outrageous suggestion.' Liza wondered if she was blushing. She was suddenly wishing she hadn't turned on all the lights, they threw such a pitiless, hard illumination on the scene.

'Calum and I always thought you were. We used to discuss it, didn't we, Cal? We thought it meant we were nearly brother and sister and that was nice when we were children. But it would be incestuous now, wouldn't it!' She poured herself some more wine. She was drinking it too fast. 'So we are lovers instead! It's perfect. It brings everything full circle, especially if Cal goes to Edinburgh to read medicine like Uncle Adam.'

A sudden draught found its way through the open door and Liza felt her skin icing over. 'Julie –'

'No, Mum, don't be stuffy. It's all perfect.' The girl took another gulp from the glass and twirled round in a little dance, her long slender legs barely concealed by the dangling shirt-tails.

There were no shadows in the barn now. Every corner, every huge oak beam in the roof was clearly visible. Liza glanced round. Was it the mention of Adam that had done it? Or the scent of lust and wine and the warm summer night . . .

Suddenly Meryn's voice was echoing in her ears. *It's you she will go for, Liza. She has targeted you and she is still there, in the dark. I'm afraid that she thinks you took him away from her, and I don't think she is the kind of woman who will forgive. Keep yourself protected. Never let her catch you unawares. However many years have passed, however much water has gone under the bridge, never turn your back on the shadows. One day she will find you again.*

'Let's go to the house.' Liza put down the glass. 'Get dressed, Julie, before your father sees you. Quickly. I want to shut the barn up. Look at all the moths coming in.'

Don't let them see you're afraid. Don't let *her* see you're afraid. Remember the circle of protection, and throw it round these children that you love so much. She wouldn't harm them, surely – not Adam's son – but protect them all the same.

She could feel the eyes watching them now, even pinpoint where they were coming from. She spun round towards the door and stared, expecting to see the dark hair, the wild grey eyes, the hand with the wicked gleam of a blade. There was no one there. Outside the owl was hooting again and the night was still. It was as they were trooping outside and she had turned to switch off the lights and pull the door closed that she momentarily felt the cold whisper of silky fur against her bare leg.

197

11

Thomas Craig died six months after Adam and Jane's visit to Pittenross. Independent and strong to the last, overseeing his flock and taking services until only days before the end, he had died, sitting grimly alone in the back of his own kirk, to be found by a complete stranger who had entered the building, guide book in hand, in search of the medieval painting which hung on the wall near the door. His body had been cold.

Adam, Jane and Calum travelled north for the sad business of arranging the funeral and deciding what to do with his belongings. The church had already decided to sell the manse: too large, too old, too expensive to run.

Standing looking down at his father's grave in the kirkyard he had known all his life, on the day before they travelled back down to England, Adam felt enormous sadness and regret. It had all been such a waste. There had been so much unhappiness. So much striving. So much bitter anger in his father's life. And for what? Had he found the peace and the reward he had so unforgivingly sought? Was there an afterlife out there, waiting with recompense or retribution, or would his father's restless, furious spirit continue to stride around the village and the house he had called home? He felt himself shudder at the thought.

Jane reached for Adam's hand. 'Are you all right?'

He shrugged. 'It makes it all look rather pointless, doesn't it? What a life.'

'He did what he thought was right. That's all any of us can do.'

'And died a very lonely man.'

'He had his God, Adam.'

A cruel God with no forgiveness or kindness in him. The unspoken thought hovered between them for a moment, then

Adam shrugged and turned his back on the grave. 'Come on. Let's go down to the hotel and have a drink.' He shivered. 'Thank heaven I need never come back to this miserable place!'

If he gave a thought to his own childhood memories or to Brid, there was no sign of it.

Once back in St Albans they settled down again to the usual routine. But things had changed. Adam was more remote, more intolerant, and alone at night in their bedroom Jane found him often far too tired to make love. His patience with Calum too had grown thin, so when his son announced to his astonished parents his intention of marrying Juliette there was an immediate and violent reaction.

'I have never heard such nonsense in my whole life!' Adam stared at his son in complete disbelief. 'No! I don't care what you say, you are not going to marry her!' His face was white. 'For heaven's sake, boy, you are about to take your exams! You are still at school! You can't think about marriage for ten years yet! Tell him, Jane!' He turned on his wife who was standing by his study window, her back to them, staring out into the wintry garden.

'I told you, Dad, we'll wait until next summer. We will both have left school by then.'

'Then you go to university.'

Calum took a deep breath. 'I'm going to take a year out, Dad, do some travelling, see something of the world. That's the point. Julie feels the same. We've been at school forever. We don't need any more work for a bit. Liza doesn't mind.'

'Aunt Liza, to you young man.' The response was automatic.

'She's not my aunt,' Calum retorted. 'And she hates being called it. She says it makes her feel old. I call them Liza and Phil. And if you weren't so antediluvian you'd let Julie call you by your name. It's crazy to insist on Aunty and Uncle as though you were old fossils and we were six!' The colour in his cheeks was flaming. 'Anyway, I don't know why we're talking about this. It's not for ages. Don't worry about the stupid exams. I'm not going to fail them.'

He stormed out of the room slamming the door behind him, and Jane and Adam were left listening to racing feet on the stairs and then the crash of his bedroom door.

Adam ran his hand across his brow distractedly. 'Where have we gone wrong?'

Jane bit back the rueful smile which was trying to escape. 'We haven't gone wrong, Adam.' She walked over and put her arm round his shoulders. 'Don't worry. He won't let anything get in the way of his exams. It's nerves. The whole thing is an elaborate cover so we won't see how much he's worrying. Don't rise to it, Adam. We've known about Julie and him for ages. They were bound to fall in love. They're sensible kids; they won't do anything silly.'

'He does want to go to medical school?' Adam had shrunk away from her touch.

'Of course he does.' She straightened, trying not to mind his rejection and dropped a light quick kiss on the top of his head. His hair, as wild and curly as ever, showed no signs of thinning but there were wiry grey hairs showing now amongst the brown. She walked back to the window with a shiver. 'I wish there was some sign of spring. I've seen the snowdrops, but this wind is endless.' As she spoke a fresh gust hurled itself against the window and rattled it in its frame. 'There's a cat out there. Poor thing. It must be frozen.'

'A cat?' Adam sat up and spun round in his chair. 'Where?'

She gave a rueful smile. 'No, not your vicious friend. It's black. Look.' She turned towards him and frowned. 'Adam, what is it?' She could see as he played with the fountain pen that his hands were shaking.

'It's nothing.'

'Don't be silly. It must be something. Is it Calum? Oh, for goodness' sake, don't let him upset you like this!'

Adam closed his eyes. Your vicious friend, she had said. If she only knew. He bit his lip, desperately trying to steady himself as he thought back to the last time he had seen the cat, when Jane had gone to stay with her mother in Godalming a few weeks ago.

He had been at home in the morning, writing up his notes, and at lunchtime he had stood up at last, stretched and walked out into the garden to take some deep breaths of fresh air to clear his head. Right on cue, as if it had known he was alone, the cat had jumped down from a low, snow-covered branch of the apple tree and run to him, purring. He had picked it up and brought it in, giving it a saucer of milk under the table in the kitchen. But it had ignored the milk and running to the door had shot through it and up the stairs, straight to the bedroom.

'Puss?' He had stood in the kitchen for a moment or two, half of him already knowing where it had gone. Then slowly he had followed it into the hall and stood at the bottom of the stairs, looking up. 'Puss?' His voice sounded querulous, even to him, in the empty house. 'Puss, where are you?' Silence. He had stayed where he was at the bottom of the stairs, his hand on the flat, white-painted newel post staring up. Half of him had already known that this was the moment of truth. He could not face the reality of what was happening – he did not even understand it. All he knew then was that if he went up he would re-enter the strange world of his dreams and he would be lost. He could remember looking down at his watch: ten past one. He had a surgery at three-thirty.

Walking slowly up the stairs he had felt a strange, sick excitement beginning to build in his stomach. Almost without realising it, he reached for his tie and begun to loosen it. On the landing he stood for a moment, listening, then he had walked over the thick grey carpet towards the door of the bedroom which he and Jane had shared for so many years. It had been standing wide, to let the pale winter sunshine from the window play across the landing. He walked slowly in and closed the door behind him.

She had been sitting on his bed. Behind her the amulet tree lay on the carpet in a dozen pieces.

'You little witch.' He said it without rancour as, almost automaton-like, he'd begun to get undressed. As he had slid down inside the bed, feeling the sheets cold against his hot naked skin, he had closed his eyes and waited for her to slip down under the sheets next to him. He hadn't opened his eyes again until much later. When he had sat up at last and groped for his shirt, the light had already begun to fade from the sky. The room had been empty.

Ivor Furness was standing looking down at her bed, stroking his chin with his left hand, whilst his right held the thick file of notes. She had gone to lie down on her bed after lunch saying she was feeling tired, so the nurse had reported. When they tried to wake her at half past two when she was late for her remedial art class, they had failed to do so. After shaking her and shouting, and calling for help one of the staff had come to fetch Ivor, who was sitting in front of the old typewriter in his office.

'Why didn't you come for me at once?' He leaped up and grabbed her file. 'I have given orders that she is not to be woken when this happens!'

'You can't wake her!' Deborah Wilkins, the nurse on duty, sniffed angrily and glared at his back as he swept down the corridor in front of her. 'Nothing short of a bomb!'

He ignored her, pushing through the heavy doors into the long dormitory and striding to Brid's bed.

201

'So, my dear. You are away at the end of your silver cord, are you?' He stood looking down at her, half expecting to see it. She was lying on her back, her arms crossed on her breasts, looking for all the world like an alabaster figure on a cathedral tomb. And alabaster was the word. He rested the back of his hand gently against her cheek. It was ice cold. Behind him Nurse Wilkins stood looking down at the girl, a frown on her heavy face. Ivor could feel her dislike and disapproval like a tangible cloud around her. He turned. 'Thank you, Nurse Wilkins. I'll look after her now. Please get on with your duties.'

The woman shot him a look of intense dislike which he failed totally to see. He was bending over Brid, his fingers lightly seeking for a pulse in her wrist. For a moment he thought there wasn't one and he felt a shot of alarm run through him, then he found it, so light it was no more than the tiniest flutter. He reached for his stethoscope and began to unbutton her blue dress. 'All systems on minimum,' he murmured to himself. He tucked the stethoscope into his pocket and stood back, watching her. 'Brid?' He said her name softly, although he could imagine there was nothing subtle about the way Deborah Wilkins had tried to wake her. There was, as he had expected, no response. 'So, where are you, Brid? Are you with your handsome Dr Craig?' He thought back to his visit to the quiet suburban street with the pretty detached house where Dr Craig – a Dr Craig – lived with his family. Did he ever see this beautiful witch woman in his dreams? Did he even guess what a strange hold he had on her fantasy life? One of these days he and Dr Craig were going to have to meet.

He realised suddenly with a start that she was staring up at him. 'Dr Furness?'

'Hello, Brid.' He smiled down at her. 'So, my dear. Where have you been?' Almost automatically he had reached for her wrist, but he didn't have to feel for the pulse to know it was racing; he could see the colour flooding back into her cheeks, sense the vibrancy, see the satisfied curve to her lips. To his embarrassment he felt a sudden surge of desire himself, and what was worse, she noticed. She gave him a sleepy smile and turned her hand over to grasp his. 'I have been to see A-dam.'

'And was he pleased?' He took a firm grip on himself.

'Oh, yes, he was pleased. His bitch wife was not there.' She pulled herself up onto her elbow so her long hair cascaded over one shoulder. How the devil did she manage to look so seductive in her horrible regulation dress? He realised he had not rebuttoned it for her after listening to her heart and breathing and found himself staring at the shadowy vee above her breasts.

'We made love.' Her voice deepened. 'It was very good.'

I'll bet it was. He almost said it out loud, but stopped himself in time. 'Brid, my dear. You are late for your class. You'd better get up and brush your hair and go down to the recreation room.' He was holding her notes across his chest like a shield. 'I have some phone calls to make.'

There was no answer from Adam Craig's private house so he rang the surgery. The stern voice on the other end of the line said Dr Craig was seeing a patient and could not be disturbed. Ivor smiled. If he ever retired into private practice he would have a gorgon like that in the office to fend off interfering colleagues. Leaving his name and number he rang off and pulling open a drawer in a filing cabinet he put away Brid's notes.

In his study Adam sat watching his cup of tea grow cold. Jane was next door watching television. On his desk the pile of paperwork he had brought back from the surgery confronted him reproachfully. He had so far managed to ignore it today, but as he sat forward to switch on the desk lamp he saw the note Emma Souls, their new receptionist, had clipped to his diary at the end of surgery: *Please ring Dr Furness as soon as possible. URGENT.* Below it was a London phone number. He frowned. The stupid woman should have told him it was urgent. She should have pointed it out to him at the end of the consultation, not left it for him to find next time he looked at his diary. Furness. It was not a name he knew. He unclipped the piece of paper and studied it, then he pulled the telephone towards him and began to dial.

'Dr Furness?' He swivelled his chair to look out at the garden.

'I'm sorry, Dr Furness has gone home.' The voice was expressionless, bored.

Adam frowned. He reached for a pencil and began to doodle on the pad by his elbow. 'I see. This is Dr Adam Craig. I have a message to ring him urgently. Is there another number where I can reach him?'

There was a moment of silence whilst the voice the other end went into consultation with a second, more distant and shriller companion. Then she came back. 'I'm sorry, Dr Craig. Dr Furness has not left a contact number for this weekend. Could you call him again on Monday?'

Adam put the phone down with a shrug. Outside in the light

thrown from the window he could see the sleety rain was beginning to turn to snow. The lawn was already white. He hoped the cat was somewhere safe and warm.

Jane turned the television off as soon as Adam had left the room. Ten minutes later she was still staring at the blank screen. Supper had been a total disaster. The three of them had sat in silence picking at their food and as soon as they had finished Calum had flounced off upstairs, banging his bedroom door behind him as usual. She sighed miserably. Life with two touchy men was not the ideal she had dreamed of once. Standing up with a groan she walked to the door and pulled it open. The house was totally silent. Even the usual beat of pop music from Calum's bedroom was missing. She wandered into the kitchen and stared distastefully at the pile of dirty dishes in the sink. From Monday to Friday she had a daily woman who came in to clean the house, but at the weekend and on Friday night she did all the housework herself, and that included the washing up unless she could trap Calum or Adam in the kitchen long enough to persuade them to help her. One of the things her mother had drummed into her was that you never left a pile of dirty washing-up until morning. That way you never had to face a filthy kitchen first thing when your defences were at their lowest. She stood staring at the saucepans and plates for a full thirty seconds, then she turned and walked out, shutting the door behind her.

Slowly she climbed the stairs and went into her bedroom. Pulling the curtains she switched on the lamps on her dressing table and stared round. The pink shades gave the room a pretty, warm feel and she felt suddenly more at home and relaxed. Next to her bed there was, on the small cupboard, a pile of new novels. She sat down on the bed and pulled them towards her. Iris Murdoch and Margaret Drabble, and for sheer romantic indulgence Mary Stewart's latest. This was her own small comfort, writers with whom she could curl up over the weekend whilst Adam went out on call or played golf with the Hardings, something she could not bring herself to do. She kicked off her shoes and hauled her legs up onto the bed, lounging against the pillows and the small lace cushions which decorated the pale pink cover. Adam's bed, identically made up stood, unruffled, the statutory two feet from hers with between them the small bedside table on which stood his lamp and his books – in his case a volume on natural history and a thriller by Raymond Chandler. She glanced at it as she made herself comfortable, and then she froze. The silver amulet tree was missing. She glanced round the room. Her dressing table, Adam's tallboy, the bookshelf, the window sill. There was nowhere else it could be. When had she last seen it? She racked her brains, frowning. Mrs Freeling cleaned the bedroom on a Wednesday. If by any chance she broke something – it had only happened twice in all the time she had been working for the Craigs, she had at once made a tearful confession. So that was not it. Perhaps she had moved it. Or Adam had. She frowned. She had been so tired last night and the night before she probably would not have noticed if the bed itself had been missing. So, when had it gone? For a moment she contemplated getting up and going downstairs to ask Adam if he knew where it was, but she changed her mind. She was tired, and her books beckoned. She would ask him later, when he came to bed.

She had read for nearly an hour when she looked up again, distracted by the pins and needles in her foot. Putting down the book she stretched and yawned and looked at her watch. It was after nine. She frowned. There had been no sound in the house. No pop music, no phone calls, no footsteps on the stairs. Standing up she went to the door and pulling it open she listened. Calum's room totally silent. Tiptoeing on stockinged feet across the landing she went to the door and listened, then she raised her hand and tapped. 'Calum? Calum, darling, can I come in?' There was no reply. She frowned. He was probably asleep. Carefully she turned the handle and pushed the door open. The room was in darkness. She knew he wasn't there even before she had turned on the light. She surveyed the room with dismay. His books were where he had left them on his desk, a folder of chemistry notes lying open on the bed. There was a half-eaten apple, brown and disgusting on the desk, a glass empty but for the dregs of ginger beer in the bottom. She looked round, her heart sinking. His rucksack, always stashed on the cupboard, was missing, as was the anorak from the back of the door.

'He's gone to Wales.' She stood in the doorway of Adam's study. 'He must have hitched.'

'Don't be silly. He can't have.' Adam stood up.

'He has. He's gone to see Juliette.' She bit back the urge to cry. 'He'll be all right, won't he? He's a sensible boy.' She was trying very hard to convince herself.

'He's not all right.' Adam closed his eyes for a moment in sheer frustration. He took a deep breath. 'And I'm not at all sure that's where he's gone. Good God, he's got school on Monday. He can't just hop off and go to Wales for the weekend! He's probably gone off to see one of his friends. If you ring round you'll track him down, you'll see.'

'He'd hate me to ring his friends.' Miserably she went to the chair by the electric fire and sat down. 'We've handled this very badly, Adam.'

'You mean I have.'

'No. We have. We should have been more understanding. They're so young. We were young once too, Adam.'

He gave a grim smile. 'We didn't put our exams at risk.'

'He's not doing that. He's no fool. We must give him the benefit of the doubt.'

'You'd better ring Liza and warn her in case he has gone there.' Adam frowned. 'And if he has she'd better drive him straight to the station and put him on the train back home. The stupid boy. I knew something like this would happen. You should have kept a better eye on what was going on down there.'

'I should?' She raised an eyebrow, trying to ignore the spurt of anger which invariably hit her when Adam accused her of something she thought was his fault. 'I don't seem to remember you thinking it was anything other than a good thing.'

'To leave an impressionable young man in a house with all those bohemian women?' He scowled.

'There are only two women in that house, Adam, and Philip seems to cope with them all right.'

'Philip is so old he can't see an inch in front of his nose,' Adam said tetchily. 'You should have known what would happen.'

My fault. She bit her lip to suppress the internal wail. My fault. Everything is always my fault.

Wearily she stood up. 'I'll go and ring Liza, then.' Why didn't he ring? He was sitting there with the telephone in front of him on the blotter as though he had just been making a call when she came in. He didn't reply and she walked slowly towards the door. 'Adam?'

He looked up.

'What happened to the amulet tree?'

'Nothing, why?' He looked away and she was astonished to realise that she could see guilt and embarrassment written all over him, in the angle of his shoulders, the way he shifted his gaze uncomfortably away from hers, even the slight colour which rose to his neck and face.

'Adam, what on earth has happened to it?'

'I broke it.'

'You broke it?'

He nodded. Brid had broken it. But how could she when she was nothing but a dream? No, he must have knocked the ornament over and trodden on it in his sleep. When he woke he had collected the small snapped pieces of silver and the crystal and put them together, wrapped in one of his handkerchiefs, into the back of the bottom drawer of his tall boy. It had not occurred to him to tell Jane or to take it to the jewellers to see if it could be mended, and sitting looking up at his wife's serious, worried expression and her short sensible hair with the few wisps of grey appearing at her temples he knew why. He no longer wanted to protect himself against Brid. He wanted to dream about her. He wanted to lock himself upstairs in the empty house when Jane was away and fantasise about Brid's young supple body and her silky hair and her warm firm lips.

He swallowed hard and ran his hand across his face. 'It's stupid of me. I forgot all about it. I must have knocked it off when I was dressing in a hurry and stood on it by mistake. I'll take it with me tomorrow on the way to the surgery and get it mended.'

She smiled. 'Good. I miss seeing it there on the bedside table.' She was watching his face intently. 'It always makes me feel safe.'

'I know.' He nodded vehemently. 'I know, Jane. I know.'

But he also knew now with a strange inner certainty that last time it had been broken it had lost most of its protective power. That was why Brid had found them. That was how she had managed to overcome all his defences. Now it had been broken again it was useless. He would take it to the jewellers when he had time if it kept Jane happy, but it would do no good. It was no longer strong enough to act as a safeguard against anything. Not now that Brid had gained entry to his home.

Calum stood shivering outside the phonebox in Hay. Broad Street was deserted. From where he stood he could see the butcher shop across the road and a solicitors' office locked and in darkness; in the distance the low hills were silhouetted against a cold, lightening sky. He glanced up the street past the clock tower hopefully. It was twenty minutes since he had rung Liza and confessed where he was and she had said she would come and fetch him. He could tell from her voice that she had been expecting the call. He wrapped his arms round himself and stamped his feet to try and bring back the circulation. It was still dark and the town was very quiet. He could see one or two lights appearing in upstairs windows now, and as he watched a milk lorry tumbled down the street and around the corner in the distance. He could smell sweet woodsmoke on the air and in the distance the cold aromatic tang of the Black Mountains.

When the old Land-Rover finally rattled down the street and stopped near him he was nearly dead from cold and exhaustion. Liza took one look at him and drove them down the hill, parking the car in a narrow cobbled street outside a small café. It was shut but there were lights on behind the blind in the window. The door opened to her knock. 'A couple of stranded starving travellers, Eleri, can we come in and have a cup of tea?' she asked the plump, red-faced woman who opened it. With the blast of warmth from the doorway came the almost overpowering smell of newly baked bread.

'Course you can, sweetheart.' The woman stood back and ushered them into the café. It was dark there, the counter empty. The light and smells came through a door at the back where the kitchen was all warmth and bustle. The woman reached for the lights and switched them on. 'I'm opening soon anyway for the boys from the town. Come by here, near the radiator, and I'll get you breakfast.'

'Thanks, Liza.' Calum gave her a rueful smile. 'I'm sorry to put you to so much trouble.' He leaned across and put his hands on the radiator to try to thaw them out. 'It took four different lifts to get here.'

'Which is not bad, considering,' Liza commented tartly, 'that you left home after nine and that you were travelling across country all night and that you have exams at school any moment.'

His smile grew more sheepish. 'Mummy has been talking to you, then.'

'Of course. She was frantic.'

'She knows I'll be all right.'

'She doesn't know anything of the sort, Calum. There are such things as notes you know, or don't they teach you to write at that expensive school your father sends you to?'

'I know. I'm sorry.' He looked about six.

'Eleri, you're a saint.' Liza looked up as a large earthenware pot was unceremoniously plonked on the table, with cups, saucers, milk, and a huge basin of sugar.

'That's what they all say.' The woman smiled contentedly. 'So, what do you say to bacon and eggs and all the trimmings?'

Liza glanced at Calum. 'Yes please. I think this young man is about to die of hunger.'

'I can see he is.' Eleri gave Calum an affectionate punch on the shoulder. 'Won't be long.'

'She's nice.' Calum watched as the woman disappeared back into her kitchen.

'She is.' Liza reached for the teapot. 'So, are you going to tell me what this is all about?'

He shrugged. 'Dad.'

'What's he done now?'

'He won't hear of me and Julie getting married.'

Liza suppressed a sigh. 'Why on earth did the subject even come up, Calum? I told you there is no question of you getting married until you are older.'

'And we won't. We're going to wait until after the exams. Julie agrees –'

'Julie agrees?' Liza sat forward and fixed him with an eagle glare. 'Calum Craig, you and my daughter are not getting married for years yet, do you hear me? You are both much too young. You have your whole lives ahead of you. I am not going to let you spoil them by rushing into something as serious as marriage when you still haven't even made up your minds what you want to do in life.'

'We both know what we want to do.' Calum set his jaw. 'I'm going to be a doctor, like Dad, and Julie wants to paint.'

'And both those things require years of training, Calum. Years of living on practically nothing as students. Years of hard grind!' She took a deep breath and counted silently to ten. 'Believe me, Calum, we are saying this for your own good. After all, who should know better than Adam and me just how hard it is? He is a doctor and I am a painter and we both had to study and work for years and years and years to get where we are.'

Calum reached for his tea and gulped some of it down, scalding his throat. 'But you and he were together. You had each other. You were lovers, before he ever met Mummy.'

'Maybe we were, maybe we weren't.' She fixed him with an eagle eye. 'That is not at issue. What is, is that you are only seventeen, Julie is only sixteen, and you are children!' She reached into the pocket of her coat and pulled out a packet of cigarettes. Opening it she concentrated on withdrawing one, tapping it for a moment on the table, finding a box of matches and selecting one. Striking it she lit the cigarette and at last drew on it deeply. Only then did she look at him again. 'Please, Calum. I'm not trying to separate you. I know how much you love each other. Just believe me, it would be a disaster if you and Julie got married too soon.'

Their food arrived and she stubbed out the cigarette. Watching Calum tuck into his plate of eggs and bacon and fried bread she felt an overwhelming fondness for him. She tipped her own bacon and bread onto his plate and watched him eat that as well. Only when he had finished every scrap, wiping the last piece of toast around the greasy plate did she speak again. 'You can come back to the farm for a few hours. Then you must get back. Phil is driving across to Cardiff this afternoon. I'm going to get him to put you on the fast train to Paddington and then you can find your way home from there. Agreed?'

He looked up and nodded at her reluctantly. 'Agreed.'

'I'm glad to hear it.' Feeling in her pocket for money she found none. She turned towards the brightly lit doorway. 'Eleri, can I settle up next week?' she called.

'Course you can, sweetheart.' The voice from the depths of the kitchen was comfortingly matter-of-fact.

'Good, then we're on our way.' She caught Calum's hand as he stood up and squeezed it. 'I know it all seems complete hell, love. Just stick it out. It will all come right in the end, I promise.'

Julie was waiting for them in the kitchen. She threw herself at Calum and clung to his neck. 'You idiot! I love you!'

Liza shook her head. 'You have until two,' she said threateningly, 'and until then you behave yourselves!' She turned and walked out of the room to tell Philip, working on his own in his studio, that he would have a passenger on the way to Cardiff.

It was on the way back in that she stopped, shivering inside her jacket, to watch for a minute the play of light through the clouds across the valley. It was a view she never tired of watching, the shadows racing across the green and brown and grey of the country, the successive rays of sunlight pinpointing and highlighting a village here, a church spire there on the far side of the valley and the occasional glint from the River Wye itself as it wound its way across the landscape. A cloud crossed the sun and the grass around her grew momentarily dark.

Liza . . .

She shook her head and rammed her hands deep into her pockets. The bitch had started using her name now. She was questing again, searching, but for what? Adam so rarely came here. Surely by now she knew where he was, or was she expecting Liza to show her the way to find him? She looked up suddenly and took a deep breath. Of course, it was Calum. She was following Calum. But why? Why was she interested in Adam's son?

Turning, she walked back into the house. 'Julie? Calum?' she called. She glanced round the kitchen. It was empty.

'Julie?' She ran to the foot of the stairs and looked up. There was no sound from the bedrooms but she ran up anyway and threw open Julie's door. The room was empty, the bed still unmade, the floor a tip. She gave a rueful smile. If Julie had thought the beloved was coming she would have tidied up!

'Julie? Calum?' She walked down again to the kitchen and stood staring out of the window. They could be anywhere, but the best bet was a walk across the frosted fields. She would have to wait until they returned and in the meantime she would ring Meryn.

He was waiting for her at the door of his cottage. His face broke into a smile as he saw her. 'It's always good to see you, Liza, but not for emergencies. What has happened?'

She followed him in and sat down on the sofa by his blazing fire, holding her hands out gratefully to the warmth. 'The same old thing. She's getting into my head again.'

'The trouble is she too is on a learning path.' He squatted opposite the fire and hooked a small stool forward to support his weight. Behind him his table was piled high with papers and books. 'As fast as we learn to protect you from her, so she learns ways to get round the protection.' He studied her for a moment. 'The amulet is no longer working.'

She stared at him in horror. 'How do you know?'

'I know.' He looked at her seriously for a moment. 'Sometimes – just sometimes – I can reach into the head of your mysterious Brid. There is much that is strange about her. For long periods she is not there. Not anywhere.' He paused, frowning. 'It is as though she is asleep or in a coma. Then she stirs. Her energy increases and I can sense her.'

'How?' Liza was staring at him. A rash of small goosepimples ran across her forearms and she shivered.

He smiled. 'I have my own ways of doing these things. Of tracking her, seeing where she goes. Of seeing who it is who is following her through the expanses of darkness where sometimes she hides.'

'But can't you stop her?'

The anguish in Liza's voice made him grimace. 'I too am learning, Liza. There is much here I don't understand. But don't despair.

211

I am as strong as she is, in my way. Now, you are worried about Adam's son.'

She nodded. It was clear her mind was easier to read than Brid's.

He shook his head thoughtfully. 'It is possible she has focused on him now. She is jealous; possessive. It may be that he is in her way. All I can suggest is that you teach the boy how to protect himself as you do. She cannot harm you, and she cannot get inside your head unless you let her. Tell him the same.'

She nodded. 'I will. I'll tell him.'

Meryn sat forward, his elbows on his knees. 'How is his wife? She is in far more danger than either you or the doctor, or I think her son. If Brid decides to remove the opposition, it is she who would be the prime target.'

Liza shrugged then she shook her head slowly. 'I don't know. I don't think Jane really believes all this stuff. I relied on the amulet protecting her, but if as you say it doesn't work any more she needs help. It's strange. Such long intervals go by when nothing happens. As you say, it's as though Brid has gone away. She's lost interest. I feel secure and forget about her, then suddenly there she is again, inside my head, as insidious as ever.'

There was a long pause as he stared thoughtfully into the fire. 'You know, it may be that where she is, she has no sense of time. A year or a minute are the same to her. What about Adam? Does he have the same experience of her?'

She was silent for a moment. 'I don't know. It's a long time since we talked about it.'

She remembered the last conversation, months ago, when he had told her brusquely to forget it; that Brid was someone from the past; nothing more than a memory and not a very happy one at that. The idea that she was, or ever had been, a danger, was completely ludicrous. Hanging up the phone incredulously after that conversation Liza had sat perfectly still for several minutes then, thoughtfully, she had walked back to her studio where she had picked up a brush and stood for a further half an hour in front of the current painting. Adam had changed. He had sounded defensive and angry and guilty all at once.

He had not sounded like himself at all.

When she had gone Meryn sat for a long time staring into the embers of the fire. His body relaxed, his eyes unfocused, he searched lightly in his mind. It was not Brid whom he sought but the other, the one who pursued her. There was power there, intelligence, enormous learning. Once or twice he had come close, sensed the piercing gaze, felt the energy of the man's anger – it was a man, of that he was sure – and he had needed all his own resources to stay firm. He had a good idea who it was he was dealing with and the knowledge terrified and excited him.

A bright orange flame shot up the chimney from the ashes and he felt his attention quicken. His nerves tightened and he made himself relax. 'Come on, my friend. Let's see you. You and I need to talk.' He didn't know if he said it out loud. It didn't matter. A pathway was opening up between the planes of existence and there, in the shadows, Broichan was waiting for him.

Ivor Furness had been standing at the window of his office lost in thought, his thighs resting comfortably against the warmth of the radiator as he planned the next chapter of his book on the hospital care of the mentally ill during his coffee break, when he spotted Brid outside in the hospital grounds. He moved his position slightly so he could keep her in view, an easy task against the white sprinkle of snow which had fallen only that morning and stubbornly refused to melt. She was wearing an ugly brown cardigan over her blue dress and her ordinary indoor sandals, but she did not look as though she were feeling the cold. On the contrary she looked as though she were relishing it. He could see from where he stood that her cheeks glowed, and her hair, whipping round her head in the light vicious wind, seemed to have a life of its own. She was walking confidently, her shoulders back, not huddled into her cardigan for warmth and she was walking with purpose rather than strolling as he would have expected of someone who, in their break between activities and in a garden icebound by winter and surrounded by a high wall, had nowhere to go.

She was walking away from him now, still in full view heading towards the leafless trees round the perimeter wall. Suddenly he frowned. He had a mental picture of her shinning up the wall and dropping out of sight into the road outside. Grabbing his jacket from the coatstand by the office door he let himself out into the corridor and headed for the stairs.

Outside he stared round. His office looked out over the west-facing gardens and he should be able from here to see where she had gone. He strode out across the grass, conscious that his foot-marks in the thin snow left irregular green patches with every step he took. Drawing near to the high red-brick wall he paused and looked round carefully. There was no sign of her that he could see, nor was there a trace of her footprints. He scouted round carefully and then walked a few yards further on. There was a robin sitting on the bare branch of a cherry tree near the wall, its chest feathers puffed as it sang its heart out and he watched it for a minute, conscious that he had been listening to its song as he walked across the grass. If someone had been there, scrambling over the wall, it would have flown away, indeed as he drew a few steps closer it stopped singing, cocked its head at him suspiciously and in a second was gone. He stopped, and stared round again, feeling suddenly rather foolish, though his head felt immeasurably better after his sojourn in the fresh air. Where the devil was she? And then suddenly he saw her only a few yards away standing watching him from the shelter of a tall holly tree.

'Dr Furness. You were following me.' She put her head slightly to one side, a little like the robin, he thought suddenly.

'I'm afraid I was.' He smiled at her. 'I was worried you might be cold without a coat.'

'I'm not cold. I like the snow. It makes me feel free.'

Why did she always manage to make him feel guilty, where none of the other patients did?

'You don't get on with any of the other women, do you, Brid?'

She did not deign to answer. Instead she turned towards the building behind them, surveying its Edwardian towers and red-brick solidity. 'This is not a happy house. I would like to live somewhere else.'

'I know, Brid, and one day soon you will, I promise.'

She turned to face him and he found himself held by the silver-grey of her eyes. 'When?'

'As soon as you are well enough.'

'I am not ill.'

'Well, no.'

'Then why am I here? It is like prison.' He was wrong about the other women. Some of them she did like, and some of them talked to her. They all agreed this was a prison and when she enquired were happy to tell her what a prison was.

'Brid, it is just that you find it hard to manage in the outside world.'

'No, I do not find it hard. I am all right. Because I am sleepy it does not mean I am not all right. Everybody sleeps. And because I go on my travels to see A-dam, that does not mean I am not all right either. In my country all the people who have studied as I have studied can do it.'

'I believe you, Brid. And I will help you.' He held out his hand to her. 'But now, it is cold. Let's go back inside.'

'I am not cold.' He could feel the steely strength under her charm. It was something she was usually careful to hide from him, though in front of the nurses whom he suspected she despised, it showed more often than she probably realised.

'Well, I am.' He began to walk slowly towards the hospital. 'Stay out here if you wish, but I'm going in.'

Brid watched him go, then she turned in her tracks. As she headed across the grass once more she was smiling.

The shed stood against the high perimeter wall, its door hanging off on a broken hinge. Once upon a time the groundsmen at the hospital had used it for keeping mowers and gardening equipment, but for a long time now it had stood empty and forgotten, hidden by a clump of laurel bushes. It was dark inside, but it was out of the wind and the snow and the walls, though gaping in places where the boards had slipped, gave plenty of warmth and above all privacy. She had found a pile of old sacks in the back, and various bits of discarded gardening equipment, including a pair of rusty shears. These she had hidden above the door in case she found a use for them. The sacks she had folded and piled so that she could sit comfortably, well back from the door but still able to see out of it. From that angle the hospital building was completely hidden and all she could see was a vista of grass, a few leafless trees and some cheerless beds of shrubs. But it was wonderful compared with the sterile horror of the wards and recreation rooms in the hospital, and it was above all silent but for the gentle sound of the wind in the tree branches and the laurel leaves nearby. She knelt down and pulled at a board in the side of the wall. Behind it was another piece of wood on which with the aid of the rusty blade from the shears she had carved some symbols: a crescent moon, a broken spear, a mirror and a comb. They were her map and her key. Propping it up near her she sat down on the pile of sacks and closed her eyes. It was strange that here, in this small hut of all places on the vast hospital estate she should sense power. Deep under the ground there was water, not the sluggish water in metal pipes which she felt everywhere around her in this strange world, but living water from the depths of the earth, welling up through the sand and the clay and the gravel until it burst into an under-ground cavern of some kind far below her feet. With a succession of deep breaths she closed her eyes and pictured the water. It was cold and vibrant, like the water of the streams on the mountains at home, and she could feel its energy surging through her blood.

*   *   *

Calum was sheepish and exhausted in equal measure when he at last arrived home in the early hours of Monday morning and it wasn't until the evening, whilst Adam was still tied up in a late surgery, that Jane asked him what had happened.

He shrugged evasively. 'Liza was okay about it. She's not as fussy as you and Dad.'

'Perhaps she's not. It doesn't mean she's not worried. She wants Juliette to do well too, you know.'

'I'm not going to stop her.'

'Not as long as you're both careful, no.' She looked down at her hands. A doctor's wife and she found it difficult to talk to her own son about contraception.

'Mummy –' He had taken a deep breath and then stopped.

'Yes?'

'Liza talked to me about something. It was all a bit odd.' He glanced away from her, clearly embarrassed, and she gave an inward sigh of relief. So Liza had spoken to them. That was good.

'She said it was something to do with her and Dad, from their student days.'

Jane frowned. 'What do you mean?'

'Someone called Brid?'

'Brid?' she echoed, surprised. 'Why did she talk to you about her?'

'It sounded really far out, Mum. She said this woman was haunting her, and that she thought she was trying to get to Dad through me and that I had to learn to protect myself with all sorts of psychic stuff. I tell you, it was really weird.'

The silver amulet tree: still broken, it was in the drawer of Adam's desk, she had seen it there only yesterday when she was looking for the phone number of the pathology lab at St Thomas's for him. He had obviously forgotten it.

'Do you know about this?' Calum's voice sharpened. 'Who was she?'

Jane shook her head. She was overwhelmed by a sudden sense of betrayal. 'She was a gypsy girl your father knew when he was a boy.' She paused, remembering suddenly the spread of black hair on his pillow. 'He and Liza got it fixed in their heads that she had put a gypsy curse on them. Years go by and we don't hear anything about her, and then something reminds your father or Liza and suddenly they get all superstitious again and start making signs against the evil eye all over the place. Take no notice, Calum.'

Calum was watching his mother through narrowed eyes, able

to read her with no trouble at all. 'You're worried about her too.'

She shook her head. 'Not really. No one truly believes in that sort of stuff. It's superstition. Complete nonsense.'

'It certainly is. For God's sake, Mum, you don't seriously think Dad believes it? I can imagine Liza getting all sucked up in that sort of thing, and Julie, she's really into all that sort of weird stuff – vibes –' he waved his arms above his head and fluttered his hands – 'but not Dad. He's a doctor!'

'And science knows it all.' Jane smiled faintly.

'Well of course it does. We're civilised now. I sometimes think Julie's a bit nuts.' His fond smile contradicted the words immediately. 'But she'll come round.'

Jane raised an eyebrow. 'You mustn't try to change her, Calum. That would be a disastrous start to a relationship. Just as she mustn't try to change you. I know you love each other, but you could be chalk and cheese.'

Calum laughed. 'Rubbish.' He flung his arms round her and whirled her round till she was breathless. 'Silly old Mum! You wait and see. We'll have the happiest marriage ever!'

Jane was sitting companionably in Adam's study, sewing, when he at last got round to telephoning Ivor Furness again. 'I can't think what the man wanted so urgently. He hasn't rung back.' He sat with the receiver to his ear. 'I'll try once more and then I'd better get back to the surgery.'

Jane sat back and broke off a thread. She patted her handiwork and held it at arm's length to admire it before reaching down into her basket for another reel of cotton. 'Do you want me to leave? Is it confidential?'

He shrugged, listening to the line ringing the other end. 'I've no idea. It must be about some patient or the other, I suppose.' He paused as the phone was picked up the other end.

'Dr Furness? This is Adam Craig. I understand you have been trying to reach me?'

There was a moment of silence. Adam was not to know that Ivor Furness had stood up and edged round the desk, carefully looping the telephone flex over the piles of books and folders on his blotter in order to stare out of the window. It was a reflex action as though trying to make sure that Brid was outside. She wasn't. He wasn't sure where she was but he always had the strange feeling that she knew what he was doing and worse, that she knew all the time what he was thinking.

'I wanted to talk to you about one of our patients, Dr Craig. Her name is Brid.'

Adam stood for a moment, stunned into silence, then he sat down slowly and put his elbow on the desk, instinctively turning a little away from Jane as she glanced up at him.

'We have the woman here as an in-patient, and she claims to know you – or at least she claims to know a Dr Adam Craig. I don't have a full name for her, but she is young – early twenties I should say – attractive, long dark hair.'

'Early twenties you say?' Adam felt a rush of relief. He hadn't realised he was holding his breath. 'I knew someone of that name once, or a name like it.' Perhaps he had misheard. 'But the age is wrong. She would have been in her forties I should say, by now.'

Attractive. Long dark hair. Brid.

'So, you don't know her?'

Slowly Adam shook his head. 'No. I'm afraid not.'

'What did he want to know?' Jane asked as he hung up. In spite of his obvious relief, his face was ashen.

He shrugged. 'Oh, a patient they are trying to identify. For some reason she had my name.'

'And you didn't know who it was?'

'No. Never come across her.'

'Perhaps there is another Dr Craig.'

He nodded. 'Perhaps there is.'

He sat for a moment looking at her. Dear, sweet, comfortable Jane who was always there for him, always supportive, always cheerful no matter how tired or irritable he got. He loved her so much, and yet . . . He bit his lip, wondering suddenly how long it had been since they had last made love. That was the trouble with the twin beds, you didn't roll into each other's arms by accident. You didn't find one another embracing for comfort, for warmth, for security, or even just because the dip in the middle of the bed precipitated you, in memory of earlier, more passionate encounters, into each other's orbit. You just went to bed, too tired sometimes to stand up a moment longer, just glad that the day was over, and crashed out without a thought for the other human being on the far side of the bedside table.

The thought of the bedside table made him glance down at his desk drawer. He really must take the amulet to be mended. He pushed the memory of Brid's dark hair, her passionate lips, out of his head. When he looked up, his eyes focused on the wall in front of him, his brain had started to work again.

A girl in her twenties. Young enough to be Brid's daughter. But not his. Surely not.

He glanced at Jane again and then slowly standing up he tore the page with Dr Furness's number off his pad and put it into his pocket. He went over to her and stooped to drop a kiss on the top of her head. 'I'm off, darling. I've got a late surgery this evening, so don't wait supper. I'll grab a sandwich when I get back.'

Jane sat where she was for several minutes after she heard the front door bang behind him, then she put down her sewing and stood up. She went over to his desk and looked down at the pad. Every instinct screamed at her that something was wrong. She had seen the sudden stillness of his body as he spoke to Dr Furness, the whiteness of the knuckles on the black telephone receiver, the defensive posture as he turned away from her as though by doing so he could blank out her presence in the small room. This had not been an impersonal call about a patient. This was something that had touched him deeply.

Twenty-five. If he and Brid had had a child she would be twenty-five. Adam sat in his office at the surgery, staring at the packet of notes referring to his first patient. Outside the waiting room was full. He could hear a rasping cough going on and on in the background. A daughter? A daughter by Brid? His brain kept returning to the thought of his bed at home, to the dreams, the fantasies, when she came to him and tormented him with her beauty and her passion. He reached for the telephone – he would call Dr Furness back, perhaps go and see the young woman – then he pushed it away again to the very edge of the desk. That would be madness.

Madness.

Why was the girl in a mental hospital at all?

Because she was the child of a different world, out of time, out of place? But why was she called Brid?

He shook his head slowly and began to pull the wadded notes out of their envelope. Now was not the time to think about her.

'I think Julie is going to fail her exams, Mum.' In the kitchen Calum was eating the final portion of shepherd's pie out of the dish as she cleared the table.

'Calum, that was your father's!'

'He won't eat it. You know he won't. He's always too tired when he comes in. I mean it, Mum. She says you don't need exams to be an artist.'

Jane sighed. She went back to her place and sat down opposite him. 'Does Liza know how she feels?'

Calum shrugged. 'I don't think so. Julie doesn't care. She's going to travel round the world. She's going to paint and swim and explore for a year or two before she settles down.'

'I see.' She knew what was coming.

'I think that's a brilliant idea. After all, one can always go to university afterwards. Loads of people take a year before they go up.'

'Provided they have brilliant exam results.'

'Oh yeah, of course.' He shrugged again. 'That goes without saying.'

'Does it, Calum?' She fixed him with a gaze of such intensity that he looked away.

'Don't let her distract you too much, Calum. Julie is a bit of a tomboy, darling. I know you love her, and I'm sure you can both settle down fine, but she's wild. She doesn't know what it is to have a vocation like you.'

'Have I?'

'Yes, Calum. You have.' Where was Adam when she needed him? 'Just get your exams first, then you can do a bit of travelling.' It was only three months until his A levels. Please God let him get through those.

She washed the dishes and dried up. It was her contribution to the exam effort. It allowed him to disappear upstairs and turn on his radio or put on some records full blast and, according to him, revise. Some nights a friend would come over and they would work – that was what they called it – together. Other nights he would go over to Roger's house, or to Paul's or Mark's and a reciprocal arrangement was entered into. Every night, after school before revision, Julie rang and they would talk in whispers for what seemed like hours. She had learned now to bring supper forward. It interrupted the flow, put a damper on the endless exchanges of endearments and plans.

Pulling off her rubber gloves she hung them on the side of the sink and sighed. A few more months and he would be gone. Off to travel, off to university, off to his new life as a grown man. Then what would she do? She had thought about it a lot. Cook and housekeeper for Adam; was that her destiny for the rest of her life, with occasional coffee mornings with Sarah Harding, whose no doubt well-meaning interference was still sometimes more than she could bear, as the only relief to the monotony? It was depressing. As depressing as when she sat down at her dressing table and stared at her reflection, noting the newly appearing wrinkles, the sagging at her jaw line, the expression of exhausted defeat on her face. She could see her own mother's face when she looked in the mirror and the thought didn't please her. Her mother had been a good-looking woman, and a strong character, busy and bossy. She thought back to when she was a child and her father had more and more often taken refuge on the golf course. Adam did that now. Was that because she and her mother were destined to follow parallel paths of duty and sacrifice and, in her case, terminal boredom?

She turned off the lights and made her way upstairs. The noise from Calum's room was less boisterous than usual. She could hear the mournful notes of a Bob Dylan ballad echoing sadly down the landing as she pushed open her bedroom door and went in.

Walking over to her dressing table, she picked up a hair brush and glanced in the mirror at the reflection of the bed. A woman was sitting there watching her, a young woman in a blue, ill-fitting dress. A young woman with beautiful long dark hair and silver-grey eyes.

With a cry Jane swung round. 'Where did you come from? Who the devil are you?' Her heart was thundering in her chest and she had to bite back the scream that was rising in her throat.

The young woman had not moved. 'I come to see A-dam.' She had a strange accent, pronouncing his name as if it were foreign and exotic.

'You came to see my husband,' Jane accentuated the word possessively, 'and you wait for him sitting on his bed?'

'Of course.' The grey eyes narrowed provocatively. 'You are no use to A-dam. He loves me. He has always loved me.'

Brid. You are Brid!

She wasn't sure if she had said the words out loud. This was a dream. It had to be a dream. If she counted to ten she would wake up. She swallowed, strengthening her grip on the brush. 'Look, young lady, I don't know why you want to see Adam, but you can come back in the daytime when he is at home. I want you to leave now.'

The young woman smiled. 'I have come often to visit A-dam in his bed. I make love to him. I make him cry out with pleasure.' She ran her hand suggestively over her thigh. 'He does not love you any more.' She licked her lips. 'Why did you take him away from his Liza? He loved her.'

'He loved me!' Jane heard herself cry out indignantly. 'That is enough. You little hussy, go away! Do you hear? Go away! I don't know who you are or what you're doing here, but you must go away. Now!'

The young woman stood up slowly, uncurling from her position on the bed with a cat-like grace which made Jane stiffen. It's a dream. I know it's a dream. Then why can't I wake up? 'Get out!'

Brid shook her head. 'I don't think so. I don't like you.' She stepped towards Jane, as she did so feeling inside the embroidered bag Jane had noticed she wore across her shoulders. As Jane watched, horrified, the young woman brought out a small silver knife.

'Oh no!' Dropping the brush, Jane whirled round and grabbed the first thing that came to hand on her dressing table – a metal nail file. Out of the corner of her eye she saw Brid coming, knife upraised. Panic-stricken, she turned and lunged back at her, catching the young woman's shoulder with the sharp blade.

Brid let out a screech. With a hiss of pain she shot past Jane and out of the door.

'Mum?' Calum had flung open his door and hurled himself along the landing. 'Mum, what on earth is the matter? Where did that cat come from? Oh Mum, it scratched you!' He stood in the doorway, his eyes round with horror. In the interval between changing one record for the next he had heard the commotion and the scream through his bedroom door.

Jane sat down heavily on the dressing table stool. She was shaking like a leaf. Blood dripped from a long narrow scratch on her forearm.

'I'll get the first aid stuff.' Calum ran back to his room and returned within seconds. 'It's not a bad scratch.' He dabbed at it with some Dettol. 'Here, let me find a dressing.' As a potential doctor, he had all the right things neatly locked in a cupboard in his room. Jane doubted if there were any other first aid things in the house – doctors' families did not often fare well in that department. Trying to steady herself she was looking at the bed. There was no crease on the cover where the woman had sat. The only sign that she had been there was the long angry scratch on her own arm.

'You did see the cat?' She smiled shakily at Calum.

'Of course I saw it.'

'It was real?'

'Mum?' He put his hand on her forehead professionally. 'I think you're in shock.'

She gave a weak smile and shook her head. 'No. Just a bit shaken, that's all. You didn't see a woman up here?'

'A woman?' Now she knew he thought she had gone mad.

'No, of course not. I'm sorry, darling. The truth is I fell asleep and I was dreaming, then this wretched cat came in and gave me a fright.' She took a grip on herself with an effort.

It wasn't until Calum had gone back to his maths books that she went downstairs again. She searched the house and checked that all the doors and windows were locked. They were, as she had known they would be at this time of night. Then she went to Adam's study and opened the bottom drawer in his desk. She took out the broken amulet tree, still in its paper wrapping, and carried the pieces upstairs. Broken or not it was going back on the table between their beds.

It was evening when Nurse Wilkins rang Ivor Furness with the information that Brid was once more in some sort of coma. If she was in a coma, perhaps she was travelling.

'It was when I checked that she was asleep, Doctor. Her eyes were open and she was smiling.' Deborah Wilkins turned and followed him as he strode towards the ward and waited for her to unlock the door. 'She is in bed now, and seems to be asleep, but I still cannot wake her.'

Brid was indeed in bed. He could see the hump of her shoulder beneath the sheet, the spread of her hair on the pillow.

He hesitated. Supposing she was not yet back in her body? Then he shook his head. For goodness' sake, he was being a credulous fool. In his own private study of this strange, enigmatic woman he must not at any point allow himself to be led to believe her passionate explanation of her exploits.

'Brid!' Gently he shook her shoulder. Deborah Wilkins pursed her lips as she stood behind him.

'Brid, wake up.' He was almost whispering.

For a moment he thought she was not going to respond, then slowly she opened her eyes and stared at him. It took several seconds for him to see recognition there, then she smiled. 'Dr Furness?'

'Hello, Brid.' He turned. 'Thank you, Nurse. You may go.'

Nurse Wilkins stared at him and for a moment he saw the hostility in her gaze, then she turned and flounced down the ward where most of the other patients were already asleep. He waited until she had closed the door at the end behind her, then he turned back to Brid. 'Do you remember we said we would talk about your visits to Dr Craig?'

She nodded. He saw the slyness in her eyes as she turned over onto her back to look at him. He also saw her wince. 'What is it, Brid? Are you hurt?'

For a moment he thought she was going to deny it, then he saw the slight shrug. 'My shoulder hurts.'

'May I see?' He paused, watching for a nod of agreement, then gently he folded back the sheet. She was still fully clothed, and her dress was stained with blood. 'Brid, you've cut yourself.' Folding back the dress at the neck he saw the deep stab wound with a sense of complete unreality. 'We'll have to clean that up, it looks deep.' He glanced at her face. 'How did it happen?'

He expected her to prevaricate so it was with amazement that he heard her proclaim without any hesitation, 'It was A-dam's woman. Jane. She stabbed me with the little knife she had on her table.' She snorted with derision. 'A stupid little weapon; something for children. But she stopped me. I would have killed her. She is no good for A-dam. No good at all. He needs me there.'

Ivor Furness took a deep breath. This woman had been locked in her ward. She had been nowhere, certainly not miles away in St Albans.

Once he had left her to the not-too-gentle attentions of Deborah Wilkins to patch up her wound and get her ready for bed he went to his office and switching on the light he closed the door, sat down at his desk and reached for the phone. When his conversation with Jane Craig was over he sat for a long time staring at the empty blotter in front of him, trying to make sense of what he had just heard. Every part of his rational mind was rejecting the evidence of his own eyes. It was not possible. Not under any circumstances or in any way was it possible that Jane Craig could have stabbed Brid with her nail file. Nor that Brid could have turned into a cat. 'You suckle a young Devil in the shape of a Tabby Cat.' From somewhere in the depths of his memory the words from Congreve floated suddenly into his head. He shuddered and then he frowned. He had not asked her about the cat. For a moment he hesitated, then he stood up.

The ward was once more in darkness, but she was awake, lying with her hair spread on the pillow round her, a pad of lint taped across her shoulder, her eyes staring up at the ceiling.

'How is your shoulder?'

'Better. But Nurse Wilkins is not a good healer. She is too rough.'

Ivor nodded. He suppressed a sudden thought that he would not like to be in Deborah's shoes if she antagonised Brid too much. He reached up to draw the curtain halfway round them, and then sat down on the chair next to her. 'So, I wanted to ask you some more about how you do your travelling,' he said softly. 'Are you feeling tired, or can we talk a bit?' It was refreshing that she seemed to enjoy talking to him, and to have no reservations about sharing her thoughts, in fact, seemed very proud of them.

She smiled, and propped herself up onto her elbow. 'All right. I am not tired. When I come back from travelling I am full of life. What does Nurse Wilkins call it? Energy.' She smiled enigmatically. 'You want to know how I do it?'

He laughed quietly. 'Indeed I do. From my point of view you are performing a miracle.' Her look of satisfaction was so feline he could almost hear her purr. He shivered. It reminded him what he had come to ask her. 'Brid, do you ever pretend you are a cat?'

Her eyes sparkled. 'Of course. But it is not pretend. I change to a cat to move quickly. Cats are sacred to my family. We use their power, their knowledge. It was the first thing I learned under Broichan when I was still a child. You believe me, that I can change the shape of my body?'

There was a light in her eyes again, a mocking glint which pulled him up short. 'I don't know what to believe, Brid.'

She nodded. 'I have listened to a lot of people since I came to your world,' she went on, suddenly very serious. 'You no longer know how to do these things. You do not believe in them. It is called by you shape-shifting: entering the body of another creature. Borrowing its power and its knowledge. Using its memories, its strength. Using it to hide and travel and watch. In my country the people expect that what you would call a Druid will know how – and I was training as a poet and a Druid.'

'A Druid!' Now he had heard it all. 'You are a Druid?'

'Of course.' She lay back against the pillow with a sigh.

Hiding a smile, he resisted the urge to reach forward and push the hair back from her face. 'Brid, if you don't mind my asking, how old are you?' It had been asked often before of course, with no coherent answer.

As before, she shrugged. 'I cannot remember.'

It seemed to him that her memory was selective in the extreme. He decided to be brutal. 'Dr Craig thinks you must be about forty.'

'Dr Craig?' Her eyes lit up. 'You have spoken to A-dam?'

It was his turn to shrug. 'I don't know if it was the right one. As I said he told me he had known a Brid once, but that she would be about forty by now, and you are not nearly that old, are you?' He glanced at her. To his surprise she showed no indignation. The significance of what he had said did not seem to strike her. Instead she persisted in asking about Adam Craig. 'He is the same one. He knew me. He will come and see me now he knows where I am. He will.'

He shook his head. 'I don't know, Brid.' Nothing seemed to make sense. It didn't add up. With a sigh he stood up. 'One day soon you must show me how you do your travelling, Brid. But not now. You're tired. You must sleep. We'll talk again tomorrow.' He paused, expecting her to argue.

She merely smiled, and turned away from him.

He waited only a moment, then he tiptoed away.

Later that evening, Adam Craig rang. The two men talked for twenty minutes. When they at last hung up they had agreed to meet as soon as possible. In the meantime Ivor Furness would go up to central London the very next morning and visit Foyles, and there he would buy a copy of every book he could find on the study of the occult and on the Druids.

The following evening, as he stood in the station, several books in his briefcase, waiting for the train to take him back to the northern suburbs, he glanced down at his copy of the *Evening News*. The headline on page two was succinct: *Hospital Nurse Found Murdered. Mental Patient on the Run*. He closed his eyes. Please God, no.

12

'I'm sorry, officer. I don't think I can help you any more than that.' Adam's hands were clenched on his lap behind his desk. 'As I told you, the Brid I knew before the war was the same age as me.' He paused, aware of the policeman taking in his greying hair, his worn, tired face, the reading glasses lying before him on the blotter. 'It couldn't be the same person.'

'And you are sure you haven't seen her?' Inspector Thomas seemed more than a little suspicious. The connection with Dr Adam Craig was too specific. He had already spoken to Mrs Craig and she too had seemed to be holding something back.

Adam shook his head. 'I can only assume, as I told Dr Furness and as I've told you, that this Brid is my Brid's daughter. But I can assure you that she has not come here.' He could not meet the other man's eye.

'Why is it, Dr Craig, that I have the feeling you are not telling me everything?' Thomas sighed. 'I'm sure you would not wish to protect someone as dangerous as this. We have issued a warning to the public not to approach her if she is seen.'

'I will let you know if I see her. I promise.' Taking a deep breath Adam stood up, hoping the man would take it as a sign that the interview was at an end. They had been talking for over an hour.

There was a long pause as Inspector Thomas scrutinised his face, then at last he levered himself out of his chair with a sigh. 'Very well then, doctor. Please let me know if you think of anything else. I may need to come and talk to you again, but in the meantime, I'm sure I don't have to repeat the warning to be careful. Dr Furness seems convinced that she will be making her way here.'

Adam waited for the anonymous black car to pull away from the gate before ringing Ivor Furness.

'Did you show her your records? Mention the cat business?'

'I'm surprised you need to ask.' Ivor had all his private notes on Brid in a briefcase before him at that very moment. Of one thing he was sure. They would not remain in his filing cabinet at the hospital. These were confidential patient notes. Besides, he would never be able to hold up his head in public again if it ever got out that he had begun to half believe some of her stories about shape-shifting and time travel. 'Look, old boy, I know I don't have to tell you, but be careful. She seems to have ways and means. And she is dangerous. No question of that.'

'And you are sure,' Adam was staring out at the garden, half expecting to see the cat at any moment, 'that you don't know where she is?'

'Absolutely sure.' Ivor clicked his briefcase shut. 'She has completely disappeared.'

She was exultant for a long time after killing Deborah Wilkins. Her triumph at ridding herself of the woman with her petty cruelties and her inferior mind and the surge of energy from the flowing blood had combined to give her the strength to leave the hospital – to draw a cloak of invisibility around herself and walk through the gates as they opened to let in a delivery van, to walk up the road and around the corner and out of sight. The only thing she had with her was her bag. In it, still, the paperknife, the comb, the compact and Adam's single cufflink. She walked for a long time, aware that when people started to notice her she would be recognised by the ugly dress she was wearing. She had to find other clothes, and in the event it was easy. She saw a complete selection dancing in the wind on someone's washing line. The house was empty, the garden pretty and secluded. She chose a dress, a lace petticoat, underclothes and two woollen jumpers, one to wear, one to carry over her arm. She buried the blue dress and coarse regulation underwear in the garden's compost heap, said a little prayer of thanks and blessing to the owner and let herself out of the gate. No one saw her, and the theft was not reported until the next day, by which time Brid was many miles away.

Her energies had been kept up by her anger and frustration in the hospital. Now, as the initial relief and excitement wore off, she began to flag. Twice she stopped to rest and the second time she felt a strange buzzing inside her brain which filled her with foreboding. She staggered to her feet. She had to find somewhere safe to hide, somewhere where she could take stock, somewhere where she could fight off the demons which crowded to overwhelm her, Broichan at their head. And she was not going to allow it to happen in public again. She had at last learned her lesson. When strangers found you in a trance, they took you to hospital, and if the hospital could not understand what had happened to you and if they could not find a way of fitting you in, with families and addresses and people to speak for you, they treated you as mad. They were very primitive in their approach to the human mind, these colleagues of A-dam's. They had no understanding of the way things worked. They dismissed the sacred arts as imagination although, she suspected, Ivor Furness was beginning to understand.

She was sad to have left him. She liked the man with his kindness and his attempts at understanding. She had felt safe with him. But Deborah Wilkins had spoiled all that with her constant unkindness and, on that last day, with her anger and her threat to stab Brid again with the needle that brought the black sleep. She narrowed her eyes slightly at the memory, but already it was fading. The woman had been of no importance, as long ago Jeannie Barron had been of no importance, and she would not be given the status of one who is remembered.

Forcing herself to move on Brid turned the street corner and saw ahead of her a bus standing stationary at a stop. She walked across to it and climbed aboard. It was empty, the driver and conductor leaning against a wall having a quiet cigarette in the pleasant spring sunshine as they waited for the appointed time of departure. She climbed the stairs and made her way to the very front. Then she wrapped herself again in nothingness – one of the simplest tricks they had been taught at Craig Phádraig. As the bus filled up and the driver took his place at the wheel she was left undisturbed. The front seats, usually the most popular, were for some reason not favoured on this occasion and she was left alone. When she stood up and walked the length of the bus and down the stairs ready to get off, the conductor had still not collected her fare. If any of the passengers had been asked they would probably have said, yes, they did vaguely remember a woman sitting in the front, but they could not describe her and did not notice when she left.

She decided to get off when the bus turned out of the busy streets and set off into the country, its destination a village some ten miles north of London. As she stood on the platform the bus drew up at a lonely stop. She jumped off and within seconds the bus had moved on, the driver wondering why he had bothered to stop at all as there was no one waiting and no one had rung the bell.

She stood for a moment staring round and then headed for a gate leading into a field. The grass rose gently ahead of her in the evening light and she walked with a lighter step, happy now she was away from the claustrophobic streets. There were black-and-white cows grazing in the field but they ignored her as she made her way between them, only one or two raising their heads to watch the slight, shadowy figure slip past.

To leave the field she climbed a stile and found herself in a small wood. It was growing cold now and soon it would be dark. She wasn't afraid of the cold. If necessary she would go and huddle up with the cows; they would keep her warm and understand why she had need of them, but she wanted more than warmth. She wanted somewhere where she could think and meditate alone, somewhere where she could reinforce her intention of staying in the time and place where she wanted to be, and where she could fight off Broichan's pursuit.

She found it in a small shelter built by some children the preceding summer under the spreading arms of a centuries-old oak tree. She stood for a while in silence, feeling the tree, sensing its energies, asking for its strength and its favour, and then, satisfied, she ducked inside the shelter. The children had left nothing but a huge pile of dried leaves, gathered for their game, nested in and musty from the small animals of the wood, but insulating, nevertheless. There was also an old saucepan, a broken chair and a kettle.

She went back to the animals' drinking trough for water and lit a fire with ease, taking enormous pleasure in using the simple skills like making a strike-a-light from a rusty iron nail and a stone, breaking up the chair for firewood, heaping up the bedding ready for the night, and then gathering shoots and roots for soup, all things which, insulated in the claustrophobic hospital atmosphere where everything was done for her, she had not practised for so long. With the warm gruel inside her and the darkness of the trees wrapping itself around her like a blanket she sat down near her small fire and composed herself to go home.

Broichan, as she had sensed, was not there. She did not pause to wonder why, did not sense that other man, the man from A-dam's time, who was also questing for her uncle. Behind her closed lids she searched the pathways of her brain and then, reassured, she made the leap deep inside herself which would bring her to the Scottish mountainside where so many years before she had abandoned the life she knew for the love of a twentieth-century schoolboy.

The cottage was abandoned. There was no sign of her mother or Gartnait, and no new message carved on the stones. She stood for a long time by the great cross-slab, staring out across the mountainside, feeling the wind in her hair and breathing deeply of the cold spicy air beneath the old pines. Inside her head she was calling – cautiously in case Broichan heard – knowing her mother would hear her.

But no one came. The silence of the echoing hills was immense.

Frightened, she laid her hands upon the stone, trying to feel its power. But the energy had gone. The earth was sleeping. And she was trapped once more at home in the Scottish hills.

In the small wood in Hertfordshire the fire burned low and went out. The kettle fell sideways into the ash and almost at once a few leaves blew over it, half hiding it from view. If there ever had been anyone there to watch the badgers creep out of their sett and trot purposefully down the path towards the field they had long ago gone, and left the wood deserted.

Jane was staring down at the bowl of muesli in front of her with fixed concentration. The silence at the table was broken only by the singing of a thrush high in a tree in the garden, the sound resonating through the open dining room window as Adam turned the pages of his *Times* with a rustle. Jane glanced at Calum. The Hardings had sent a good luck card which he had opened and thrown down next to his plate in what looked like despair. He had eaten nothing and was on his second cup of coffee, an open maths textbook beside him on the table; for once Adam had not said a word about reading books at meal times. Jane had suggested an egg, or toast or oatcakes and honey, to no avail; Calum's pasty white colouring reinforced his angry outburst that if she forced him to eat he would throw up all over his plate.

Adam closed the paper at last and folded it with a sigh. He glanced at his son and grimaced. 'Okay, old chap? Shall we go?' He had promised to drive Adam to school during the exams, so he needn't worry about missing the bus.

Calum nodded. He stood up, hesitated, and bolted from the room.

'Poor kid.' His father shook his head. 'I've never seen him so wound up before.'

'He's no need to worry. Dr Passmore said he'd sail through them.' Jane stood up too and began to stack the plates as the phone rang. Adam went to take it in the study. Two minutes later he reappeared. 'It's for Calum. It's Julie. I suppose she wants to wish him luck. I wish the girl would let him alone just for these couple of weeks.'

He went to call his son out of the lavatory where Calum had been standing wondering if he was going to be sick. Watching the boy disappear into the study, Adam shook his head. Grouchily he picked up the newspaper and began to fold it even smaller, ready to put it into his case, though he knew he wouldn't look at it all day and that Jane resented having to wait until he got home to read it. 'Come on, Calum,' he called over his shoulder.

There was a pause. When Calum reappeared he looked stunned.

'What is it?' Jane glanced up as he walked through the door, and she saw his face. 'What's happened?'

'It's Julie.' Calum flung himself down in a chair and put his head in his hands.

'What's wrong with Julie?' Jane glanced at her husband.

Calum shook his head. Looking up he forced himself to look at his father. 'She's pregnant.'

'What?' Adam's shock was palpable.

'Julie's pregnant.' The boy's hands were shaking.

'And she chooses today to tell you? Half an hour before you start the most important exams of your life?' Adam was incredulous.

'She forgot about my exams, Dad. She hadn't given them a thought.' Calum rubbed his face miserably with the heels of his hands. 'Oh Shit! Shit, shit, shit!' He was on the point of tears.

Jane glanced at Adam. Taking a deep breath she walked over to Calum and put her arm round his shoulders. 'As you say, shit,' she said firmly, the word far more shocking coming from her. 'But there is no point in worrying about it today. Go to school, Calum, and concentrate on the exams. That is the most important thing at this moment.' She squeezed his shoulders tightly as he opened his mouth to protest. 'Oh yes it is. Julie can wait. Does Liza know? I'll talk to her later. Please, darling. Don't let this put you off. Whatever happens, whatever you and Julie decide to do, you need your exams behind you, you know that. Put her out of your mind for now. I know it's hard. It's complete hell, but we'll work something out, you know we will. I'm just so glad you told us.' She knew he hadn't meant to. He had blurted it out without thinking and for that she mouthed a small prayer of gratitude. 'Go on, sweetheart. Get your things. Adam, is the car ready?' They were both sitting there as if pole-axed and she had to galvanise them into action.

As Calum stood up and walked out of the room she caught Adam's arm. 'Don't you dare give him a hard time on the way to school, do you hear? Whatever you think, *whatever you think*! Don't take it out on him!'

Adam shook his head. 'I'm not a complete idiot, Janie.' He ruffled her hair unexpectedly and then gave a small defeated shrug. 'That minx. I've known all along she was bad for him. Stupid, stupid girl. And to ring today of all days! How selfish can you get?'

'I'll phone Liza. We'll sort something out.' She reached up and gave him a kiss. 'Go on, drive him to school. And send him off feeling really good about himself, okay?'

She sat down at the uncleared table after they had gone and reached for the coffee pot; there was enough for a cup of black. Sipping it she stared out of the window at the lawn. The thrush had stopped singing and had come down to its favourite perch on a large stone near the rose beds where it was hammering a snail. She winced instinctively as she watched the single-minded manner in which it smashed its way into the shell to find the soft body inside.

There wouldn't be an abortion, of course. After all, the kids had already declared their plan of marrying one day. It wasn't such a disaster. As long as Calum got his grades he could go to university as planned and Julie would have to go with him. It wasn't ideal, of course it wasn't, but it wasn't as if Adam and Philip couldn't afford to subsidise them. She took another sip of coffee. She didn't see why there should be any problem over it at all, really. Except for Adam.

Wearily she stood up and walked into the study. Sitting down in Adam's swivel chair she pulled the phone towards her and dialled the farm. Liza picked it up on the third ring which meant she was in the kitchen. The Stevensons had never bothered to put in extensions anywhere else.

'He's told you?' She sounded quite cheerful.

'He told us. How is she?'

'Being sick.'

'Poor Julie.' Jane could not quite keep the coolness out of her voice.

Liza heard it. 'Jane, I know. We feel the same. But it's not as if they hadn't planned to get married one day. Oh, I know they're a bit young, but these days I suppose it's all about being young.'

'That's as may be, Liza.' Jane took a deep breath to steady herself. 'But today was Calum's first maths A level exam. Julie rang him five minutes before he was due to leave. The boy went off to school in a state of total shock. Do you not think she could have timed it a bit better?'

There was a moment's silence. 'God, I'm sorry, Jane, I really am.

Listen, tell him not to worry about it. Everything will work out all right. Somehow. And let me talk to Adam tonight.' There was an infinitesimal pause. 'I bet he made a fuss?'

Jane did not need to answer.

'Yes, I thought so. He doesn't think Julie is intellectual enough for his precious son, does he? I'll deal with him. And tell Calum I'm so sorry about the exams, I didn't realise they had started. Wish him lots of luck from us and tell him we're rooting for him.'

Jane went back to the breakfast table and picked up her cup. Absent-mindedly she reached for the paper which in his hurry Adam had left for once by his plate. Unfolding it she glanced at the front page and then turned inside to find the news. The item was so small Adam must have missed it in his first quick look through the paper. She nearly did. *The hunt for the missing mental patient, known only as Brid, a suspect in the Wilkins murder mystery, switched yesterday to the Home Counties when a woman, thought to answer the description of the missing patient, was spotted near St Albans. Nurse Deborah Wilkins was found three months ago, stabbed through the heart in the grounds of the institution in north London where Brid had been an in-patient for several years. Psychiatrist Dr Ivor Furness reiterated his warning that she should not be approached if seen.*

Jane realised suddenly that she was holding her breath. It had to be a coincidence. Perhaps it wasn't her at all? She stared out into the garden again, her eyes going automatically to the stone. The thrush had gone, leaving a scattering of translucent pieces of shell as the only traces that the snail had ever existed.

Adam had not yet called in his first patient when she rang. 'Did he get to school all right?' She had resisted the urge to lock the garden door.

'He was there in plenty of time. I think it was better once he was with his friends.' Adam had been sitting at his desk, staring into space.

'And you didn't give him a hard time?'

'Of course I didn't.' There was a touch of irritation in his voice.

'I spoke to Liza.'

'And what does she think?'

'Same as us. Though I suspect beneath it all she's quite pleased in a way.'

'Pleased?' Adam's voice registered total disbelief. 'For God's sake, what does the woman think she's doing, being pleased?'

'She's going to ring you this evening.' For once Jane was glad they were going to have one of their private conversations which

234

made her feel left out and jealous. This one she could well do without. 'Adam, listen.' She changed the subject suddenly. 'I don't know if you saw it in the paper this morning, but the police think Brid has been spotted near here.'

There was a long moment of silence, then the one word, 'What?'

'I'm sorry, Adam, but I thought I'd better warn you. I'm surprised the police haven't been in touch.' For that split second he had sounded afraid. 'Be careful, darling.' Jane was clutching the phone receiver as though her life depended on it.

'And you. You'd better lock the windows, Janie.'

The amulet tree, dented and broken as it was after it was rescued by Jane, had been left on the table between their beds, the crystal at its foot. Mrs Freeling had twice moved it, and once suggested it be thrown away, but stubbornly Jane had replaced it and now the woman dusted it and put it back, trying to hide it behind the lamp as though its very presence offended her in the otherwise immaculate room. Jane went upstairs and sat down on the bed after she had closed the French windows. She reached across and picked it up. She wasn't sure why it still reassured her. It was stupid and superstitious to think a small broken piece of silver and enamel and crystal could protect her from Brid. But then it was stupid and superstitious to think that Brid could get inside her house the way she did. For several minutes she sat staring at the ornament in her hands, then gently she put it down again, this time ostentatiously at the front of the table.

'How was the exam?'

Calum had come home on the bus and gone straight to the fridge, where he helped himself to a large wedge of cheese.

'Not too bad, I suppose. I cocked up one or two things. Stupid things.' He reached for a bottle of orange and poured himself a glass. 'I suppose I'd better go up and revise for the next one.'

'Not for a minute, Calum.' Jane was standing between him and the door. 'I think we should talk about Julie.'

He shrugged. 'What's there to talk about? I suppose we'll have to get married.'

'That doesn't sound very enthusiastic.' She tried to keep her voice neutral. 'It's not so long ago that you were fighting with your father over your decision to marry as soon as possible.'

Calum scowled. 'I know. I do still want to marry her. It's just that I wanted to live a little before we settled down.'

'And she got pregnant after you told her all this?'

'No, of course not. She wouldn't do it deliberately. That would be blackmail. Julie would never do something like that. No, it happened that weekend when I kind of ran away. You know, after the row with Dad?' He let out a great sigh.

'I hope you're not saying it's your father's fault.'

'No.' He shuffled his feet.

'So, you don't want to get married.' She kept her voice carefully even.

He shrugged. 'I'll have to. I can't let Julie down.'

'No, I don't think you can.'

'It won't be that bad.' He sounded hopeful suddenly. 'She's a great laugh. And I do love her. I'll get some kind of job . . .'

'No.' Jane folded her arms. 'No, you don't have to do that. You must still go to university, Calum. We'll find the money somehow to make it work. We'll find you a little flat or something up in Edinburgh. Don't worry about that.'

Weeks passed and there was no further news of Brid. After the first few days, Jane began to leave the windows open again. She and Adam did not discuss her – Adam's thoughts on the subject were strictly private, as had been his conversation with Liza that day – and Jane wanted to put Brid as far out of her mind as possible. Their attention was fully taken up with Calum and Juliette in any case.

Calum had passed his exams, but nothing would persuade him to agree to go up to university the following autumn.

'Loads of people take a year out, Dad,' he had said after the quiet wedding in the church at Hay that July.

Adam had surveyed his son's colourful wedding outfit and that of his by now obviously pregnant daughter-in-law with distaste and retreated to the far side of the farm kitchen, where he had knocked back two large whiskies in quick succession. 'Not if they are going to study medicine, Calum,' he said through tight lips. 'Not if you care about your career. You are going to be studying for five years at least, perhaps more if you specialise.'

'All the more reason to have a break and enjoy himself!' Julie caught hold of Adam's hand and squeezed it. 'Stop being such a grump, Uncle Adam!'

Adam could feel himself growing increasingly angry. This child, this pretty, silly child had distracted his son so easily. Why couldn't Calum be strong like he was? After all, he had turned his back on Brid to go and study.

The thought of Brid made him even more cross. Where was she, this child woman who looked so like his Brid? Why had they heard nothing? Had she really murdered a nurse and run away or was she being made into a scapegoat? After that one reported sighting of her near St Albans there had been no further word. She had disappeared into thin air, as had the cat. He had seen no sign of it for months and he had to admit he missed it. God, he missed it! If there was a slight frisson in the air as he thought about it, he did not notice.

'Penny for them.'

He realised suddenly that Liza was standing in front of him. She was looking particularly lovely in a dress of cornflower blue with, when they were in church, a large cartwheel straw hat which had been deposited on their return to the farm over the fruit bowl on the dresser.

'What did you say?'

'Penny for them. But I know what you are thinking: why did that wretched child seduce my Calum away from his great career – right?'

He gave a reluctant smile. 'Something like that.'

'She didn't, you know. It must have been fifty-fifty. And she's not going to hold him back. She is tremendously proud of him.'

'Even though she stopped him getting the grades he needed?'

'Oh Adam!' She was infuriated. 'You don't know he would have got As. As it is he did very well. He's got his place in medical school. For goodness' sake, stop being such a fussy old thing. That's it, you know,' she giggled. 'You're getting old!'

'Am I?' Adam was standing in front of the mirror in the attic bedroom later. 'Am I getting old?'

'Of course not.' Jane was already in bed. She was wearing a white cotton nightdress trimmed with broderie anglaise like the one she had worn on their wedding night and to Adam, as he turned round and caught sight of her, she looked suddenly ethereally beautiful.

'What is it? Why are you staring at me like that?' She smiled at him.

'Christ, I fancy you, woman!' It was a long time since he had made love to her, a long time since he had felt any attraction to her at all and here he was overcome by a sudden wave of something very like lust. He walked over and sat down next to her. Gently he put his hand up and pulled at the ribbon which held the neck of the nightdress closed. 'I think I must have had too much to drink.'

'Why do you think that? Because suddenly you've remembered you've got a wife?' She put her hands on his shoulders and pulled him forward so she could kiss him. 'They'll be happy, Adam, I know they will.'

He shook his head and put his finger to her lips. 'Let's not talk about them any more. They've chosen their path. They must follow it.' God, I sound more and more like my father every day, he thought to himself suddenly. It was not a happy thought. He pulled her closer. 'It's not just the young who can be happy,' he murmured. Behind the lust there was a sudden moment of guilt. 'Time for you and me, now. Why don't we go away somewhere? Just the two of us.' He pushed the nightgown off her shoulders and down to her waist. Her breasts were still firm, her stomach flat. He dropped his mouth to a nipple and took it gently between his teeth, hearing her quick gasp of pleasure as he did so. Urgently he pushed her back on the pillows, fumbling with his trouser zip, feeling her hands caressing his face, his hair, his shoulders, going to his shirt buttons and then to his own chest. 'Oh Adam.' Her breathless murmur urged him on. 'Yes, yes, please!'

The growl behind them from the window was very quiet but they both heard it and froze. For a minute neither of them moved, then very slowly Adam sat up and turned to face the sound. For a moment he could see nothing. The room was dark save for the shaded lamp on the table in the corner. It was so hot in the attic room under the roof that they had left the window wide open to catch the slightest breeze from the fragrant night outside. Two moths circled the lamp dizzily, otherwise nothing in the room moved. Holding his breath he stared into the shadowy darkness, aware that behind him Jane was frantically trying to pull her nightdress back over her breasts without drawing attention to her movements.

Very slowly Adam stood up. He pulled his trousers into place and zipping them up he took a step away from the bed. The room was full of the honey smell of the night. Above the line of the hill outside and the right-angle of the roof with its huge Welsh slates he could just see the glow of the rising moon. Behind him Jane pushed herself back into the pillows, her eyes straining to see beyond Adam as he took another silent step forward. The room was eerily quiet. Even the noises of the night seemed to have died away. The owl had drifted off across the hill into the next valley and the younger wedding guests who had stayed, their sleeping

238

bags lined up in Liza's large barn, had finally fallen asleep, their snores contained by the thick stone walls.

'Adam?' Jane's whisper was almost soundless.

He waved his hand at her behind his back and took another step towards the door. He was reaching out towards the light switch when they heard it again, a throaty growl from somewhere very close in the room.

'Oh God,' Jane pulled the sheets and blankets up to her face. 'What is it?'

Adam grabbed at the switch and flicked on the light, then he turned, his back against the door, and surveyed the room which was now bathed in pink from the small lamp hanging from the beam. Bed. Cupboard. One rush-seated chair, a pretty woven mat on the broad oak boards and a small table with a Victorian mirror on it which served as a dressing table. Besides that there were their two suitcases, both lying open on the floor, Jane's neat, an improvised chest of drawers, the lid sitting propped up against the wall, his own with the lid back on the floor, clothes and shoes lying scattered out of it and around it in cheerful disarray. The cat was lying in the middle of his clothes, regarding him from brilliant golden eyes.

'Adam, it's her!' Jane's strangled cry was cut off short by his angry gesture.

'We don't know that. Think,' he murmured. 'Can it have got in here from the roof? Or from the house earlier? Is it Liza's?' He realised suddenly that he was shaking like a leaf.

'Of course it's not Liza's.' Jane's whisper rose into an hysterical hiss. 'Don't you recognise it? It's her.'

'If it's her, Jane, it's not real.' He forced himself to move a step closer. The cat remained motionless except for the very tip of its tail which began to move almost imperceptibly from side to side. 'It is a projection of her imagination.'

'Hers or ours?' Jane slid over to the far side of the bed and knelt there, a pillow clutched against her chest. The cat ignored her. Its eyes were fixed on Adam's face. 'It looks bloody real to me.' Her voice was shaking.

'Brid?' Adam spoke to the animal hesitantly. 'Brid, is that you? Please, show yourself so we can talk.'

Behind him Jane smothered a burst of hysterical laughter in the pillow. 'Now I've heard everything. "Brid?"' She mimicked his voice. '"Show yourself, my darling. I like you better with long black hair."'

239

Languidly, the cat turned its head and stared at her. She shrank back against the pillows.

'What the hell are you trying to do?' Adam turned on her. 'For God's sake, Jane, don't be so stupid! Come on, puss.' He squatted down and held out his hand to the cat. 'Come on. Come and talk to me.'

The cat walked over to him and, purring, rubbed its head against his hand. 'It's just a cat, Jane. A stray off the mountain.' He breathed a sigh of relief and laughed. 'We are so silly. You know it really had me scared! I thought she was genuinely capable of turning herself into a cat! It will be my turn for the funny farm at this rate.' He rubbed the cat behind the ears and stooping, scooped it up into his arms.

'Don't bring it near me!' Jane slid off the far side of the bed and walked over to the window. She peered out into the darkness. 'I expect it jumped from the slates out there. Look. It's not so far. Stick it outside again and let's get some sleep, shall we?' Her voice was tense and frightened.

'I can't put it out there, Jane. It's too high.' He walked across to her and peered out beside her. The cat shifted in his arms uncomfortably and then made a sudden leap for the bed.

Adam laughed. 'It knows where the warm comfortable spot is.'

'I bet it does.' She spoke under her breath. 'Please, Adam. Get rid of it.'

'It's not doing any harm –'

'Get rid of it! Either you do or I'm going to spend the night somewhere else.'

He sighed. 'Okay, hang on. I'll carry it downstairs and put it out from the kitchen.' He bent to pick it up but the cat was too quick for him. Hissing, it dived under his arm and leaped straight for Jane's throat. With a scream she fell back against the wall, trying desperately to protect herself. Lunging after it Adam found himself with a handful of fur, then it was gone.

Behind them the door flew open. Liza appeared, followed by Philip. 'What on earth . . .' They fell silent as they looked into the room. 'Sweet Jesus, what happened?' Philip strode in past his wife and stared round. Jane was kneeling in the corner, her white night-dress covered in blood. She was sobbing hysterically.

'Jane? Jane, what is it? What happened. Dear God, Adam, what happened?' Liza grabbed the cover off the bed and wrapped it round the other woman's shoulders. Jane was shaking uncontrollably.

'It was a cat.' For a moment Adam seemed too stunned to move.

'A cat?' Philip turned round and stared at him.

'Not just any cat!' Jane screamed. 'It was that sodding Brid!'

Liza looked up at Adam. Her face was white. 'Where did it go?'

Adam shrugged. 'Out of the window, I suppose. I don't know.'

'Come downstairs, both of you.' Liza helped Jane to her feet. 'Phil, close the window.' She drew Jane out of the room. 'Come on. It's all right. I'm going to bathe those scratches. Did you bring your doctor's bag with you, Adam? Go back to bed –' She realised suddenly that two more doors had opened on the landing and terrified wedding guests were peering out. 'It's nothing to worry about. I'm afraid one of the farm cats got into the house. Everything's all right now. It's all under control.'

Half an hour later, cleaned up and daubed in antiseptic and attired in one of Liza's bright cotton kimonos, Jane was sitting with the other three at the kitchen table sipping hot milk. Her face was still very white.

'It was probably a feral cat,' Phil said at last. 'I know you three have an obsession about this woman, and dear old Meryn has been egging you on, but it's just not on, is it? I mean, is it! For goodness' sake! You're talking witches and familiars and things. No, no, no. I won't have it! I'm really sorry the damn thing jumped in through your window, and I'll have a look round the barns tomorrow with a shotgun. We can't have an animal like that attacking people. In fact it sounds more like a wildcat than a feral, though I've never heard of them round here. I didn't think there were any left in this part of the country.'

'There aren't.' Liza shivered. 'It was too much for her. We were all here together and enjoying ourselves and she wanted to be here too. With Adam.'

'Great. It sounds as though I'm the next on her murder list.' Jane folded her arms across her chest protectively. 'Anyone who comes between her and Adam.'

'Poor Nurse Wilkins didn't.'

'I think she did. I think she tried to stop her escaping.'

'I think there are two Brids.' Liza stood up and went to fetch the kettle. She poured some hot water into her mug to warm the drink, thinking back over what Meryn had told her. 'I think there is the real one, the one who can be locked up in a hospital. And I think there is this other one, the one she can think herself into. I think all of us have the capability of living in our imaginations. It's just she has had the opportunity of practising so much that she can do it for real. She can think herself somewhere else.'

241

'And disguise herself as a cat?' Phil looked at her pityingly.

'Why not?'

'Because it's dotty, woman, that's why not.' Phil got up and went to the cupboard. He stooped and pulled out a bottle of brandy. 'Anyone want a drop of this in their milk? I certainly do.' He poured some into Adam's mug and then his own. 'At least the kids didn't wake up. It's been a big day for them, and it would have been terrible to spoil it. I suggest we all go to bed and forget this ever happened. I'm prepared to bet good money that we don't see that animal again. And if we do, I shall shoot it.'

'Aunt Jane?' Juliette was sitting on a hay bale in the courtyard outside the farmhouse later that morning. 'Will you teach me how to knit?'

Jane stared at her in astonishment and then she burst out laughing. 'I thought you young things regarded knitting as really square!'

Juliette smiled. 'I want to make some things for the baby.'

'Of course.' Jane felt a sudden rush of warmth towards her new daughter-in-law. In spite of the healthy bump which was appearing beneath Juliette's long sweater the girl looked so frail out here in the brilliant sunshine. Jane reached across and squeezed Juliette's hand. 'Of course I'll teach you. I'd love to.'

She was feeling better this morning. The ugly scratches were safely concealed beneath the soft cotton of her shirt and in the bright daylight she found it hard to imagine the previous night's attack had occurred. Philip had kept his word and searched all the outbuildings, his shotgun under his arm in spite of Liza's objections, but there had been no sign of a cat, feral or otherwise, and after an hour he had given up.

'When you're back from your honeymoon, I'll come down for a few days and teach you. I'm sure your mother knows, though, doesn't she?'

Juliette shook her head. 'I've asked her. She swears she doesn't. Anyway, she's left-handed, she can never teach me anything. She does it all backwards.' Juliette laughed. Then she glanced at Jane again. 'You are happy for us, aren't you, Aunt Jane? I'd hate it if you weren't.'

'I'm very happy, sweetheart.'

'And you don't mind us going away after the baby is born?'

Calum had only sprung this part of their plan on her two days before. Once the baby was safely there and he had got his driving licence, they were going to buy an old van and drive off across

Europe heading east. 'Don't tell Dad. Not yet. I'll do it in my own time!' Calum's sheepish plea did not have to be repeated. She did not have the courage to tell Adam and never would. Calum for once would have to face his father himself.

'I do mind a bit, if I'm honest.' Jane squeezed her hand again. 'My first grandchild is pretty special. I can't bear to think I won't see him growing up.'

'Or her.'

'Or her.'

'You will.' Juliette reached across and planted a kiss on her cheek. 'We'll send you photos from everywhere and we won't be gone that long. Once we're back we won't get the chance to go away again for years and years and years. Don't begrudge us this one adventure, Aunt Jane, please.'

Jane found herself smiling in spite of the heartache. How could she possibly resent their going? They would be free, free of responsibility in spite of the baby, free of rules and work and respectability. Free of all the things she and Adam had so carefully surrounded themselves with over the years to turn themselves into clones of his father and her mother in spite of their best efforts to avoid it. She shivered.

Juliette had closed her eyes and was sitting in the warm sunshine, basking like a plump little animal with her big tummy securely clasped beneath her hands. Their honeymoon was going to start tonight. They were going up onto the mountain to Meryn's house which he had lent them for a week to be alone together. Jane wasn't sure where he was going. Liza had been vague, but she suspected he was going walkabout over the hills in order to give the two young people a chance to have some time in peace. She hadn't met Meryn, but he seemed to feature in Liza's conversation a great deal. A surrogate father, perhaps, as well as some kind of weird spiritual mentor.

Jane shivered again and looked round puzzled. The courtyard was warm and out of the wind. There was no reason to feel cold. But it wasn't a physical cold. She had a sudden feeling that there was someone watching her. She glanced round again, this time more carefully, her skin prickling with sudden foreboding. The cat? Phil swore he had checked everywhere, but a cat could hide with ease round here in the outbuildings, in the hedges, in the long grass.

'Julie.' She spoke very softly.

Julie didn't appear to hear. She was sitting, her head back, her eyes closed, enjoying the sunshine.

'Julie, let's go inside.' The farmhouse was a hundred yards away. She could see that the kitchen door was half open. Liza was inside talking to some of the lingering guests from the party the night before. Phil and Adam had driven down the hill on some mysterious errand and her son, overwhelmed by the excitement of his own wedding day was, it appeared, still asleep.

'Julie!' Her voice sharpened. 'Please, we have to go inside.'

'Why?' Juliette opened her eyes. 'What on earth for? What's wrong?'

Jane shook her head. 'I'm not sure anything is wrong, sweetheart, I just want to go inside the house for a while, that's all. Please.'

'Aren't you feeling well?' Julie sat forward, but still made no attempt to stand up.

'I'll explain when we're in there.' Casually Jane stood up. For some reason she didn't want to be seen to be running. She didn't want her – it – to know she was scared, and above all she didn't want to provoke a chase. 'Come. Quickly.' The urgency of her voice as she held out her hand was reinforced by the strength with which she gripped Julie's wrist and pulled her to her feet.

Juliette gave up arguing. She followed Jane across the courtyard. Jane's shoulders were hunched, as though she expected any moment something to land squarely on her back. She could feel her skin crawling with fear, her hand clammy around Julie's fingers. They were almost there when she heard the anxious clucking of the hens from their run nearby. 'It's probably a fox, Aunt Jane. Let me go and see.' Julie stopped.

'No!' Jane caught her hand again. 'No, please. Come inside. I'll ask someone else to go and see to the hens. Please, Julie.'

Julie gave her a sideways glance but she obeyed and in seconds they were inside the kitchen and Jane had closed the door. She leaned against it, aware suddenly that she was shaking like a leaf.

Liza was standing at the kitchen sink, filling the kettle. 'The others have gone off for a walk on the mountain,' she said over her shoulder. She turned. 'What is it? What's wrong?' she asked sharply.

'It's there.' Jane took a deep breath and went over to sit down at the table. 'In the courtyard.'

'Dear God!' Liza paled. 'Are you sure?'

'What is it? What is there?' Juliette looked from one to the other of them, suddenly frightened.

'It's a wildcat, darling.' Liza frowned at Jane in a manner which clearly said, don't tell her the truth – whatever the truth was. 'It

244

got into the house last night and attacked your Aunt Jane. It was awful. The poor thing must have come down off the mountain and got lost.'

'A wildcat? You mean a real wildcat, not just one of the barn cats?'

'I mean a real wildcat.' Liza's voice was dry.

'Aunt Jane,' Juliette turned to her, all sympathy. 'Did it hurt you?'

Jane nodded. 'I'm all right. I just didn't want to meet it again face to face unless I absolutely had to, and I certainly didn't want it scratching you.'

'As soon as the men come back, we'll get them to have a look around. Until then, I think you should both stay inside.' Liza walked over to the window and shut it with a bang.

'What about the others, on their walk?' Juliette frowned anxiously.

'They'll be all right. There are four of them, and I don't think it will attack them in broad daylight on the hillside. I think for some reason it's hanging round the house.'

'It's probably hungry. Why don't we put some cat food out?' Juliette had already stood up and headed for the cupboard.

'No!' Jane and Liza spoke simultaneously. To her surprise they both seemed to greet the idea with wry amusement. 'No, darling. We won't feed it. I don't above all want to encourage it,' Liza said at last. 'Let's just stay inside and wait. The men won't be long.'

When their car drew up in the courtyard it was Liza who slipped out of the house and ran towards them. 'Jane thinks she's seen it again. In the courtyard.'

She turned and scanned behind her, looking at the open shed doors, the long grass in the corners, the walls. There were a hundred places it could hide.

'Perhaps I should go and look for her,' Adam said slowly. 'She won't hurt me.'

'Wait, I'll get the gun.' Philip closed the car door and headed for the house.

'No!' Adam shook his head. 'No. You can't shoot her. Leave it to me. You all go inside.'

He watched them go, closing the door behind them, and then slowly he turned round. He walked towards the orchard gate, his hands in his pockets, a tall slim man, his hair greying, his handsome face tanned by the Welsh sunshine after the pallor of six months' hard work in the practice without a break.

'Brid?' His voice was sharp. 'Is that you?' He leaned on the gate and sighed. 'Brid, come on. If it's you, show yourself and let's talk. Now.'

There was no reply, but suddenly in the silence he felt himself shiver.

Brid had wakened as the sun rose above the mountains. She stared round; her heart sank. She had hoped that in her sleep her strength would return and she would find herself again securely in Adam's time. But it had not happened. Slowly she resigned herself to what must be. With food and sleep in her old summer home by the burn and with hours of study and meditation each day beneath the sun and beneath the stars she began to feel her power coming back. It was hard though, because she could feel Broichan prowling near. When he did she played the role of the mountain cat, treading on soft soundless paws across the heather, crouching down in the gulleys and scree out of his sight, climbing high into the swaying pines and peering down from the rough red branches with their spiny needles. Sometimes he came as a man, sometimes he too took on a disguise. Now he was a stag, proudly bearing a head of royal points, now an eagle soaring over the stone, searching the ground with eyesight which would pick up a cowering ant and once or twice, as if he guessed her disguise, he came as a fine, glossy-coated king cat, calling beneath the trees, its nose raised to trace her female scent.

But each time she hid and waited and each time he went away. And then at last with the turning of the moon she found the time when the power returned to the great stone, as her own brother's carving had shown that it would, and she put her hands upon the symbols and felt the surge of energies rush through her, giving her the strength to go wherever she wanted, and she wanted to go where A-dam was.

Thus it was she had found herself once more seated beneath an oak. The tree was in full leaf, the ground beneath it cushioned with long seeding grasses, and in front of her the hillside stretched away towards the Wye Valley in the sunset. For a moment she did not move, then she stretched and flexed her legs and realised that she had brought with her the body of a cat. Inwardly she smiled. That did not matter. It was easier to spy as a cat; easier to creep into houses and into beds; easier to find A-dam, who must have come to see his Liza at last. When she leaped from the wall of the yard onto the low roof of the old stone farmhouse and ran easily up the heavy moss-covered stone slates she already knew which bedroom he slept in. She had not expected to find him with Jane.

Opening the gate Adam let himself into the orchard and walked slowly down the steeply sloping path beneath the old apple trees. It was cooler down there, out of the sun and the air was fragrant with the scent of wild roses. He could hear the breeze rustling through the grasses and, in the distance, the crooning of a dove. He wasn't sure if he expected to see a cat or a woman. He wasn't sure of anything any more.

He found himself thinking back suddenly to the last time he had talked to Ivor Furness. The man's stories about Brid – if it was Brid – had been quite astonishing. He had described how she had gone into a deep trance every so often, and how he was convinced the trance was self-induced, and that during the trance she left her body in some way and could assume other shapes at will, shapes which could be seen by others, and he had questioned Adam closely about his house, comparing Adam's answers with transcripts he had made of her descriptions.

The trouble was neither of them could be sure that at some point over the years she had not visited the house and been given entry by Jane or Calum or Mrs Freeling, or one of the receptionists from the surgery – the possibilities were endless. And then there was the possibility that in some way she was using telepathy to make them think they had seen a cat. Or seen her. Adam had found himself unable to mention the curiously erotic dreams he had experienced after letting the cat into the house to sleep in his bed when Jane was away, and he rather wished suddenly he had been more open with the man. He had liked Furness. For all his weird hypotheses he was a genuine and intelligent practitioner with whom he would have liked to talk much more. Perhaps when they went back to St Albans he would contact the man again and go and see him.

He paused suddenly, aware that there had been a movement under the trees in the distance. Narrowing his eyes to see better he ignored the quite irrational bolt of fear that had shot up his spine and slowly he began to move in that direction. He could see nothing now, but over to his right a blackbird shot up from the undergrowth pinking its alarm, and he could hear the piercing chitter of a wren that had also been disturbed. His skin was prickling anxiously as he moved, more cautiously now, in the direction of the noise.

A-dam . . .

It was a long time since he had heard that plaintive voice in his

247

head. He clenched his fists in his pockets and forced himself to go on walking, pushing his way through the long grass now he was no longer on the path.

A-dam . . .

He stopped. He couldn't see her. The light was dim beneath the gnarled old trees with their curtains of ivy and lichen. She could be anywhere. He realised suddenly that he was no longer looking for a cat, he was scanning the shadows for a slim young woman with long dark hair.

He moved on a few paces and stopped. He could see her. A shadow, no more, behind the trees.

'Brid?' His voice came out in a croak. 'Brid, is that you?'

He frowned, squinting into the shade of the old tree at the far end of the orchard. It was larger than the others, and the grass there was shorter for some reason. 'Brid?' He couldn't see her now. Where he had thought he saw the shape of a woman there was only flecked dancing sunlight as the breeze played with the apple boughs.

Behind him the gate creaked. Jane stood for a moment as she let herself into the orchard, her hand on the warm, lichen-covered wood. She was watching her husband intently. He had stopped in the dappled shade and was staring round as though to try and see something in the distance. She followed the direction of his glance and then began to move slowly forward. Under her arm was Philip's shotgun.

Her sandals trod almost silently on the path, her skirt brushing through the grasses with a sound no louder than that of the wind. Adam did not hear her. He walked forward a few paces and stopped again, still staring. He could sense that there was something there, just out of sight. The birds had stopped singing, and then he heard once more the sudden alarm cry of the blackbird from the under-growth. Was it calling because of him or because it had spotted something else out there in the shadows by the hedge? He moved on slowly and behind him Jane drew closer. When she saw him stop again she paused and raised the gun to her shoulder. Adam did not hear the click as she cocked it. He had spotted her now. A figure – a woman, standing beneath the old tree.

'Brid?'

She couldn't have heard him. His voice had come out as a croak, but she turned and just for an instant he saw her face before the ear-splitting bang erupted from right behind him.

There was a scream. For a moment he wasn't sure what had

happened. He spun round and found his wife standing beside him. 'I got it!' She was laughing hysterically. 'I got it! The bloody thing! Serve it right!' In her hands the barrel of the gun was still smoking.

Adam stood for a moment, transfixed with shock, then he turned and raced for the trees. 'Brid?' He reached the spot were he had seen the figure and he stopped, looking round wildly. 'Brid?' There was a patch of blood on the moss under the tree. Kneeling, he touched it with a finger.

He turned to Jane who had followed him, the gun outstretched in front of her as though ready to shoot again. 'Be careful, it will be dangerous if I've only wounded it,' she called. She stopped beside him. 'Where is it?'

'It?' Adam looked up at her from his knees. He was shaking. 'It? You shot at a woman, for Christ's sake!'

'A woman?' Jane laughed again. 'Don't be so silly. It was a cat. It was a vicious wildcat, Adam. I'm sorry. I wouldn't have wanted to hurt it, but it attacked me. It could have killed me! It was dangerous, Adam!'

'It was a woman.' He stared round blindly, still on his knees. 'I saw her.'

Jane looked down at him, her face set. 'It wasn't her, Adam. I saw it clearly. It was a cat. It must have run into the undergrowth.' She was scrutinising the hedge. 'We'll have to be careful. It's wounded now. It will be more vicious than ever if it's cornered.' She lowered the heavy gun and put a hand on his shoulder. 'I wouldn't have shot a person, Adam, you know that. You must have imagined you saw her.'

He was climbing to his feet, still looking round in every direction. 'Are you sure?' He rounded on her suddenly. 'Are you sure you wouldn't have shot her? You're jealous of her, you always have been!'

'Adam!' She looked at him, aghast.

But he had turned and was striding away from her back towards the house.

13

They barely spoke on the way home. Adam drove fast and viciously, pushing the car as though it were an enemy, his face set in hard, uncompromising lines. From time to time Jane looked at him as she sat beside him but she did not speak. It seemed to her that they had said all they were ever going to say to one another in the attic bedroom at the farm after she had shot at the cat. After he had found the blood on the grass Adam had spent hours searching the orchard, and then the surrounding countryside, staying out until long after it was dark. The next morning he had gone out again as soon as it was light but not before he and Jane had had the worst quarrel of their long marriage.

'Adam, I'm sorry,' she had cried at last. 'What else can I say? I was afraid. I hate her.' That last sentence had come out as a long wailing cry before she threw herself down on the bed and buried her face in the pillows. They both knew they were not talking about a cat.

Adam had looked down at her, his face set, then abruptly he had turned on his heel and left the bedroom. When he had returned, Jane was asleep.

Liza did not query their decision to go back to St Albans early. The atmosphere between the two had become unbearable and Adam was beyond reason. 'You can't blame her,' she said to him in a whisper as they stood for a moment outside the kitchen door after supper. 'For God's sake, Adam, she was viciously attacked.'

'Jane might have killed her!' Adam was fumbling in a crumpled packet for a cigarette. 'She might be badly hurt.'

'We know she's not, Adam.' She tried to keep her voice even. 'We would have found something –' A cat? A woman? '– if she was badly hurt. She's run off somewhere into the woods. She'll be fine.' She tried to lighten her comment with a smile. 'Here I am as bad as you calling her "she". We don't know it was a she. It might just have been a wildcat. That's all. Or a feral cat from the farm up the pitch. We don't know it was Brid, Adam. How can we? How could it have been? That's totally ludicrous and we both know it.'

'Do we?' He turned and fixed her with an angry stare. 'Do we know anything at all?'

They had not discussed it again, and the following day the Craigs had packed their belongings, left a note for Calum and Juliette and left the farm. 'Drive carefully.' Liza had reached up to kiss Adam on the cheek. 'It will all turn out all right, you'll see.'

'Will it?' He gave her a peck in return. 'I wonder.'

It was late when they turned into their street and drew up outside the house. Adam switched off the engine and sat for a moment, staring out of the windscreen. Then he reached to open the car door, stiff after the long drive.

'Wait.' Jane's voice was husky.

'What is it?' He turned and looked at her.

'Please, don't let's go on like this. I've said I'm sorry. Adam, the house is going to be so empty without Calum, please, don't let us quarrel.'

'I have no intention of quarrelling.' Adam hauled himself out of the car. 'As far as I'm concerned the matter is finished.' He went round to the rear of the car and opened the boot. 'Give me a hand with the cases and let's get inside. That drive seems to get longer each time we do it.' He pulled out a suitcase and a canvas grip and turned to walk up the path. Jane was following him with another case when he stopped in his tracks. Something had moved in the window upstairs.

'There's someone in the house!'

'What?' Jane stared wildly at the building, scanning the windows. Everything seemed as it should. 'Burglars, you mean?' Her voice had dropped to a whisper. She could feel her heart banging somewhere under her ribs.

He shrugged. Dropping the cases he moved on quietly, feeling in his pocket for his keys.

'Be careful, Adam.' Jane ran after him. 'Shouldn't we call the police?'

He shook his head. 'Stay behind me.' The front door was locked and the windows appeared as they had left them. There was no outward sign that there was anything wrong but he could feel a strange prickling at the back of his neck, the feeling that they were being watched.

'Jane,' he swung round on her, 'go back to the car. Lock yourself inside.'

'Why?' She was staring round wildly. 'I'm not leaving you. I'll go next door and ring the police –'

'Go to the car.' He caught her arm and spun her round. 'Do as I say.'

And then she understood. 'You think she's there. You think it's your girlfriend. Your cat friend! She's beaten us home, is that it?' Suddenly she was almost hysterical. 'That's it. Send Jane back to the car to sit out in the road all night, just so long as Brid is comfortable. No thank you!' She snatched the house keys out of his hand and pushed past him. 'No, Adam. This has gone far enough. I am not standing outside my own house whilst you pet your little friend inside and make sure she's comfortable.' Sobbing she ran up the path and with a shaking hand she put the key into the lock.

A pile of post sat on the hall table. Sarah must have come in to water the plants even though Jane had told her not to bother. She stopped. There was a strange smell in the house, a musky animal scent which made her feel suddenly very sick. She turned to Adam, her anger turning to fear. 'She's here!' she whispered.

He nodded. 'I wanted you to stay in the car because it's safe,' he murmured. 'Please, Janie. Go outside.'

He had moved past her and quietly he tiptoed down the hall towards his study door. 'Go. Please,' he hissed over his shoulder. He pushed the door gently. The whole house was silent.

Jane did not move. She was staring after him, her mouth dry with fear. It was dusky in the study from the half-drawn curtains, and she could smell the heat. The sun had been beating on the glass windows all day and only in the evening had it gone round the side of the house leaving the room in the curtained shade.

In front of her Adam pushed the door open a little further and took a step over the threshold. 'Brid?' His voice was gentle. 'Are you there?'

There was no sound and after a pause he took another step into the room. 'Oh dear God!' He threw the door back against the wall.

'What is it?' Jane followed him and stopped in the doorway.

The woman slumped onto the hearth rug had a small brass watering can still clutched in her hand. Nearby a pale pink cyclamen lay amidst the broken shards of its pot, its leaves and flowers already wilted and dying.

'Sarah?' Jane let out a sob. 'Oh no! Is she . . . ?'

'Yes.' Adam didn't need to go any nearer to see the woman had been dead for several hours. 'You'd better call the police, Jane.' He knelt down on the rug but he didn't touch her. He could already see the vicious cuts across the woman's face and throat and the brown patches beneath her where her blood had soaked into the rug. 'And then one of us is going to have to tell Robert.'

The house was empty. There had been no trace of any intruder, no sign of a window or door being forced; nothing had been stolen. The police noted that Jane had been attacked by some sort of cat during her stay in Wales but it was put down as being no more than a coincidence. They made the connection with the Brid who had escaped, the Brid who might be following Adam, but could take their investigation no further. Her trail had long ago gone cold. The verdict at the inquest was left open, but two days after it appeared in the paper Ivor Furness rang Adam.

'May I come over? There are things we ought to talk about.' He had seen the report and Adam's name had caught his eye. 'It was her, wasn't it,' he said soberly as they all sat outside in the evening sun.

Adam nodded. 'I think it must have been.'

'You and I are both doctors. Men of science. Sane. And you, Mrs Craig,' Ivor turned a warm smile on his hostess. 'Sane. Educated. Twentieth-century woman. None of us believes that a human being can turn itself into a cat, right?'

They all nodded.

'Nor can she, for we are talking about a she, visit places as some kind of other being, whilst leaving her body in bed, or wherever.' He was slowly packing the bowl of his pipe with tobacco. 'You did not, I take it, mention any of our suspicions to the police?'

Adam shook his head. 'It did not seem appropriate. They naturally thought of the Brid who escaped from hospital, but there was no evidence, nothing. They found no prints other than our own.'

'I told them about the cat,' Jane put in sharply. 'I told them I had been attacked.'

'And they thought it of no relevance as it had happened miles away. Quite.' Ivor nodded slowly. 'I am afraid we will always get that response. You are sure in your own minds, however, that this killing was done by Brid?'

Adam nodded slowly. He sighed. 'I don't understand it. Why would she do it? Poor Sarah, what had she done to make Brid

253

angry?' He shook his head in bewilderment. He and Jane had discussed moving house. At first it had seemed imperative. Now, they weren't so sure. Poor Sarah had left no ghost and Brid would follow them wherever they went.

'Robert is completely devastated. She was everything to him. They had no other family apart from each other.' Jane found herself sobbing suddenly, her antagonism towards Sarah forgotten. She reached out for Adam's hand.

Ivor frowned. He struck a match and held it while the flame steadied. 'I am so sorry for you both, as well as that poor woman and her husband. What a mess. As the focus for Brid's attention you are in an unenviable position.' The match went out and he stared at it for a moment before tossing it over the wall of the terrace onto the rose bed. 'Brid does not have the social restraints of a normal person,' he went on thoughtfully, speaking half to himself. 'She is an attractive woman and is undoubtedly very charming when she wants to be, but there is a psychopathic person-ality there. She acts as she feels at the moment without conscience or remorse, and her background appears to have taught her the use of unrestrained violence. Fascinating.' He shook his head again and withdrew another match from his matchbox. 'The question is, did she come here in person, for real, or was it merely a visit in her dream state?' He looked from one to the other for a moment before striking the match and holding it over the bowl of his pipe. 'And if in a dream state, where was she – the corporeal Brid – as it were? And if she can murder while she is in fact elsewhere, how can you two protect yourselves from her in the future?'

There was a long silence. Ivor was staring across the garden, his gaze fixed unseeing on Adam's cherished roses. 'I wish I'd had the chance to investigate her more while she was in hospital.'

'I wish you had, too.' Adam spoke with feeling. He had reached out to take Jane's hand as he saw the implication of the other man's statement sinking in.

Jane had gone very white. 'She would never hurt Adam. It is me she wants to kill. Do you think she saw poor Sarah and thought she was me?' She bit her lip, trying to keep her panic under control.

Ivor shrugged. 'I would have thought a woman with powers such as we are presupposing would be able to distinguish between two different people. Oh, my dear, I'm sorry.' He stood up suddenly and put his arm round Jane's shoulders. 'I am not being reassuring.'

At the unexpected show of sympathy and warmth she felt tears well into her eyes again. 'I'm so scared.'

'Of course you are.' He glanced at Adam, surprised that he was not supporting his wife, but Adam was lost in thought.

'Dr Craig!' His voice was sharper than he intended. 'We discussed Brid as she was as a girl. Did she show signs of abstraction then? Did she seem violent? Irrational?'

Adam nodded slowly. 'Oh yes. She had a temper.' He pictured her suddenly standing by the waterfall, her naked body silhouetted against the rock. 'And I thought, even as a somewhat naïve school-boy, that she was irrational in her approach to life.'

'But you never suspected that she had come from another place?'

'Another planet, you mean?' Adam gave a humourless laugh.

'Another age.'

'No.' He shook his head vehemently. 'No, that never occurred to me. Brid was real enough, believe me. There was nothing ghostly about that young lady.' He gave a deep sigh. 'I cannot believe that you and I are having this conversation! There must be a rational explanation for what Brid has done. It seems to me that there is a sleight of hand going on here. She makes us believe she is in two places at once, and we in our credulity –' without realising it, he looked at Jane for a moment – 'fall for it. We assume the extraordi-nary and look for mystery when the ordinary would do. She seems to move around quickly. Perhaps she is just good at getting lifts. You assume she was in a hospital bed while she was somewhere else. Perhaps she had slipped out, leaving pillows or something in bed to look as though she were still there. After all she found it easy enough to leave after Nurse Wilkins was murdered. By coincidence a cat came into this house once or twice at a relevant moment. A cat attacked my wife in Wales. On neither occasion was there proof that it was anything other than a real cat.' Was he being disingenuous? He paused for a moment uncomfortably. 'To make the assumption that Brid and the cat are the same and that she is capable of time travel and remanifesting herself in different places is to my mind ludicrous. It just isn't possible. The only doubt is whether this person is my Brid or a lookalike, possibly her daughter, or, maybe,' he looked up suddenly, 'two people, mother and daugh-ter, engaged on the same quest.'

'A quest to murder me,' Jane said softly. She was shivering in spite of the warmth of the summer afternoon.

Neither man spoke.

'It had not occurred to me that she might be two people,' Ivor said at last. 'Mother and daughter. That is plausible.' His relief at having a new idea around which to rearrange his thoughts was palpable.

'Brid's mother didn't look like her.' Adam went on with a shake of his head. 'She was a nice woman. Kind.'

'And her father?'

'Dead when I knew her. Her uncle was a complete madman though. That would explain where she got the violent streak.' He stood up and wandered onto the grass, absent-mindedly snapping off the dead head of a rose as he did so. 'They will catch her?'

'Of course.' Ivor shrugged. 'But until then, you should not lower your guard.' He looked at Jane. 'Either of you.'

The fever burned her body as she lay in the cottage by the burn, but she fought it, crawling once each day to the water to slake her thirst and wash the sour sweat from her face and neck. She had packed the shot wounds above her breast with herbs, and the flesh had stayed free of infection after she had cut the ragged edges of skin away with her knife. For a long time she had not known what had happened. She had ricocheted away from the orchard in Wales in deep shock, finding herself first on the mountainside and then seconds later in Adam's house. She had not known until she drew the knife that she was once more in a human body and she had no knowledge of why she had stabbed the woman who had found her in his study and who had asked if she could help. All she remembered was a sudden blinding rage that someone should stand in her way. For several seconds she had stood over the collapsing woman, staring down at her, puzzled, as she lay dying on the carpet. Then, suddenly, she had felt the surge of energy and excitement which came with the blood and without warning she was upstairs in the house, looking out of the window watching eagerly as A-dam's car drew up outside, then in an instant she was back in the glen, the wind cooling her burning flesh and tearing at her clothes.

For the first time in a long time she wept. She was alone and afraid and the pain beneath her collarbone was intense. Sometimes, in her delirium, she called for her mother or for Gartnait; more often she called for A-dam. But he never came. Day succeeded day and slowly she grew weaker. She had almost lost her strength entirely when, lying by the burn to scoop the soft brown water into her mouth she noticed the scraped nest bowl of a plover amongst the heather stems. In it were two speckled eggs, still warm from the mother. She took them and broke them into her mouth, feeling the rich yolks running down her throat. Lying still, her head in her arms, she felt the sun's rays on her back and she gave thanks to the hen bird whose eggs had given her strength. Later she sucked the sour juice from blaeberries and sat for a while, staring down into the sparkling water. When she crawled back into the cottage at dusk she slept without fever, knowing she would soon be recovered, and in her dream Adam came to find her at last and put his hand upon her head and declared her fever gone. And in her dream she smiled, and rubbed her face against his hand.

The moon had waxed and waned twice before she felt strong enough to go to the stone and look for the gateway to Adam's time. Her energies were still low and her concentration feeble, but as the nights grew longer and the air chill and damp, she found herself longing more and more to be with him. He had never come to her again, beyond that first night when she had dreamed about him and she knew in her heart it had been no more than a dream.

She stood for a while beside the stone, her hand caressing gently the carvings her brother had made with such care. A crisp frosting of palest green lichen had crawled into some of the deeper cuts in the granite and she scratched at it with her fingernail. It did not matter. It did not diminish the power. That came from beneath the ground, welling and ebbing up like a tide in the ancient rocks beneath her feet. And now, with the new moon a slim sickle in the sky she could feel the tide gathering. Its strength would carry her down the years to Adam's time.

As the sun set behind the mountains she watched her shadow lengthen across the ground, then slowly she turned towards the east and raised her arms above her head. Her eyes were closed as she went within and felt her strength grow.

Adam was sitting at his desk in his study. For a moment he did not sense her there in front of him and she looked round, breathless and triumphant. He was alone. The room was empty. She watched him for a moment, her love spilling out towards him, then slowly she held out her hands.

A-dam!

As he looked up, startled, she felt the atmosphere in the room curdle and separate around her. It grew suddenly very cold.

'Brid?' Adam's voice echoed after her as she found herself once more on the hillside, on her knees beside the stone, tears pouring down her face.

She tried again the following night. This time he was in his garden. She watched him from the shelter of the old pear tree, her heart aching with longing as he pottered about in the flower bed and then walked slowly back towards the house.

'Adam!' The woman's voice from his study window cut through

the silence like a knife and Brid found herself shaking violently. For a moment she hung on, her nails digging into the mossy bark of the tree, and then she was gone, back to the hillside where the darkness had already fallen and the moon was obscured by rushing cloud. Back in the cottage she hugged her knees and rocked back and forth in her misery. What was wrong? Why couldn't she stay with A-dam? Why couldn't she focus? She needed his love to hold her, and with that woman always there, his love was not strong enough.

She knew it must be that she was too weak. She made herself a hunting knife and some snares and caught rabbits and birds for her pot. She sought out herbs and infused them in rainwater in the sunlight to increase her strength and then she tried again.

This time A-dam was in Scotland, too. She felt her heart leap with excitement as she recognised the mountains and knew that he was very near. Then he turned to face her and she saw with a cry of horror that A-dam was old. His face was lined and coarsened and his hair, still wild and curly, was white as the snow on the high peaks in winter. It was the wrong time.

No!

Her cry of anguish as she moved towards him startled him visibly. He stared at her and she saw the recognition in his eyes, but already he was fading, and the rush of cold wind on her face and the stone beneath her desperate hands once again told her that she had lost him.

'Time. I must study time. I must find him when he is young.' Her hands shaking, she made her way back to the hut and felt over the door for the strike-a-light to fire the wood and kindling she had left stacked in the dry near her stone fireplace. Holding her hands out to the warmth she breathed slowly and deeply, trying to concentrate her mind. She remembered her training – when you return from travel you eat to regain strength and re-establish your roots in the ground. Reaching above her into the darkness she found the capercaillie meat, hung from the roof beams where the thin slices she had carved from the carcass had dried in the smoke of the fire, and she chewed on it, feeling the flavour grow rich and nourishing in her mouth. In her head she was working out the position of the stars and of the moon and remembering the lessons of her Uncle Broichan.

When she again made the leap into time A-dam was young once more, but he was holding his wife in his arms and Brid, watching, knew that he must be freed from these people who clung to him and held him from her and stopped him reaching out to touch her as she hovered hear him. When she stood next by the stone she had her knife in her belt and an amulet at her throat. This time she would not fail.

She knew by the stars she was in the right time. The place too was correct, though the windows of the house had been painted and the door was shut. Standing in the garden she crept forwards and looked into his study from the flower bed outside. At first she thought the room was empty, then she saw that Adam was standing near the door. Facing him was his son, and behind the young man was a woman. Brid stiffened as she watched, her senses quivering. In the woman's arms was a baby.

'You cannot take that child out of the country. It would be complete madness!' Adam was shouting now. 'Good God Almighty, Calum, have you no sense at all! Please, think. She is only a few months old! Have you any idea at all of the diseases you will find in these places! Have you any idea how many adults die on the hippy trail? Do you know what hepatitis can do? Or typhoid or cholera?' He turned round and walked over to the window, smacking his fist against the palm of his hand. His face was working with anger and grief. 'And what about your career?' He swung round without looking out. 'Have you no interest at all in going to university any more?'

'Cool it, Dad.' Calum put a protective arm round Julie. 'You'll upset the baby. Look, you knew this is what we planned to do. Of course I'll go to university. When I come back. What's the hurry? There's all the time in the world, okay? And as for Beth catching diseases, that's rubbish. She's had her vaccinations and stuff, and she'll be fine. Loads of babies go off with their parents; loads of babies get born on the way. That's what's natural.'

'She will be all right, Uncle Adam.' Julie's voice was very quiet. 'You mustn't be so stuffy. And you can't stop us!'

'No!' Adam threw himself down on the chair behind his desk. 'No, I haven't been able to stop Calum doing anything, have I, since you entered his life? Have you any idea how much damage you have done? His exams, his ambitions, his future.' He ran his fingers through his hair. 'And now you take that innocent child –'

'Dad, that's enough!' Calum's voice rang through the room. 'You can't talk to Julie like that.'

'Yes I can!' Adam's face was white with anger. 'Isn't it bad enough to know the mother of my grandchild smokes pot –'

x

259

'I haven't touched any –'

'No? You think I don't know what the stuff smells like!'

'Julie, I think we should go.' Calum reached for the door handle. 'I'm sorry, Dad. I really am. I thought you and I would one day be able to have a sensible conversation, but as it is, I doubt if it will ever happen. So I don't think there is any point in continuing this discussion or any other. Tell Mum I'm sorry we missed her. We'll be in touch with her when we come back from Nepal.'

'Calum –'

'No, Dad. That's enough. And I think you can forget the career in medicine. You're right. I don't have what it takes. I'm not sure if I'll bother to do anything at all. Why don't I just behave like the layabout you obviously think I am!' Calum ushered Julie past him into the hall. 'Don't bother to see us out.' With one last furious look at his father he slammed the door.

'I won't!' Adam bellowed after him. 'And don't bother to come back, I never want to see any of you again!'

He sat where he was without moving. He was shaking like a leaf. For a long time he stayed, staring down at the blotter on his desk, then slowly he reached for his handkerchief and blew his nose. When he stood up and walked over to the window again, of long habit seeking the comfort of looking at his roses, his eyes were full of tears.

Outside the window Brid watched him in silence. She wanted to reach out and touch him, but the glass was in the way. Stepping forward she put her hands up against the pane, near his face, trying to reach him, but he didn't see her. For a moment he stayed where he was, then he turned away. Slowly he walked to the door and went out into the hall.

The front door was open. On the step a small teddy bear lay face down amongst the scatter of dead leaves. Stooping, he picked it up, then quietly he closed the door and walked back towards his study.

In the car little Beth was screaming. Julie clutched at her, trying to rock her to sleep. 'Quiet, quiet, please, please be quiet. Drive slowly Calum, there's no need to go so fast. Calum, please!'

'He's so stupid!' Calum changed gear and turned onto the A1. 'He is so damn stubborn and old fashioned. And as for accusing you of smoking pot!'

'I did once.' Julie buried her face in the baby's hair. 'I did once, when I was staying there and you came back late. I felt so lonely and unwanted, and your father was so sniffy towards me, I went up to the bathroom and had a joint – '

'You did what?' Calum turned and stared at her in shock. 'Julie!'

'I know, I'm sorry. Calum, for Christ's sake, watch the road!' She closed her eyes and sighed with relief as Calum pulled the car back on course, narrowly missing a white van which came racing out of the darkness of the straight road, horn blaring. On either side of them the tall poplars rose, black sentinels in the darkness, flashing by as Calum increased his speed. It was beginning to rain again and the windscreen of the old Mini smeared beneath the wipers. 'Come on, Calum, let's forget your father. I'm fed up with him always there, always criticising me. Let's go. Let's just go. We could be in France by tomorrow. Let's drive towards the sun, and never come back!'

Calum turned towards her and grinned. 'You're right. Life is for living. We'll go back and get our gear together and tell Max we want the van he offered us. We'll get shot of all this hassle.' He groped for her hand and squeezed it. 'Beth, baby, you are going to have one incredible childhood!'

Brid, standing in the garden, watched in despair as Adam sat at his desk weeping. She pressed her hands against the window again, then went to the French doors, and knocked. Still he didn't seem to hear her. Her hands on the glass made no sound and she beat against them harder.

A-dam! A-dam!

Her cry was caught up on the wind and whisked away without him hearing her.

A-dam, let me in!

What was wrong? Why couldn't she make him hear? Sobbing with frustration she stepped away from the glass doors. It was his son's fault, his son and that stupid insipid child his son called wife. They made A-dam unhappy. He wasted his love and emotion on them when he could be with her. Her desperation and fury focused suddenly on them, the two young people with their baby in the silly little blue car who had gone away laughing to leave her A-dam crying and alone.

When she found herself out on the road in the rain she did not understand for a moment what had happened. A car sped past her, hooting and she jumped back out of its way. Then she realised where she was and she smiled. The Mini was going more slowly, but still, when she stepped out in front of it and raised her hands to curse the man and woman whose faces she saw momentarily as white screaming shapes in the blackness, it spun and skidded round four times before spinning off the road and into the ditch, where it lay with its wheels in the air, the only sound the hissing of steam and the thin high-pitched wail of a baby crying.

PART THREE

Liza
1960s-1980s

14

'You should have made Adam come with you.'

Standing in the pouring rain, Liza and Jane were the last two left standing by the grave. At their feet the gaping hole which contained two coffins side by side was overshadowed by the huge heap of flowers, chrysanthemums and Michaelmas daisies mixed with the more exotic lilies and roses. 'He'll never forgive himself for not being here,' Liza added.

'I don't understand him.' Jane was sobbing uncontrollably. 'He's like a madman.'

In his anguish and fury and pain Adam had sworn never again to have anything to do with Liza or Phil or the tiny child who had been pulled so miraculously alive from the mangled wreck which had taken the lives of her two young parents; his fury with Julie had turned to rage against her mother.

Under the yew trees near them Phil waited, his huge umbrella giving shelter to the baby in the crook of his arm. Beth stared up at the bright striped umbrella, watching the drops of rain hanging like diamonds round the rim and snuggled wide-eyed into her nest of blankets, unaware of the tragedy which had befallen her. Beside him Jane's mother, leaning heavily on a walking stick and dressed all in black, stood sniffling into a wet handkerchief.

The rest of the mourners huddled together at the lych gate, then slowly, driven on by the rain they climbed back into the line of cars which had been parked, wheels in the hedge, down the narrow lane outside the old mountain church where Julie, in a fit of romantic gloom, inspired by a summer of reading Keats, had told her mother she wanted to be buried. Calum had never as far as Jane knew thought for a single moment about his own death – the only thing she knew was that he would want to be with his Julie and as far away from his father as possible. The two hearses had already gone.

Adam had refused to come. He did not even want to talk about it. When the police had brought little Beth back to Jane he had not looked at the child at all, and the next morning he had told her to get rid of it, as though the baby were an unwanted pet. It had in any case taken Liza only four hours to drive across from Wales. It was a foregone conclusion that Beth would go back with her. Jane had gone too.

'If only they hadn't had that row!' Jane was sobbing uncontrollably. 'If only I'd come back sooner, before they left.'

'You mustn't blame yourself for that.' Liza put her arm round the other woman's shoulders. It was the sixth time she had said it in as many hours. 'Janie, you know your being there would have made no difference; you know how stubborn Adam is. And Calum was like him.' She stopped and stared down at the coffins, unable to speak for a moment for her own grief. 'It was what was supposed to be, for some reason.' She gave a deep sobbing sigh and closed her eyes.

'Liza, darling. Janie.' Phil had walked forward silently, his red-and-white umbrella an incongruous splash of colour in the sombre greens and browns of the old churchyard beneath its backdrop of dark, mist-shrouded mountains. 'Come away. Look, little Beth and Patricia are getting cold. Let's go back to the farm.'

Jane shook her head. 'I don't want to leave him.' Tears were pouring down her face. 'It's so cold and lonely up here.'

'It's a beautiful place, Janie my love. You'll be glad one day he's got such a lovely spot to lie.' Phil pushed the baby into her arms, holding the umbrella higher to give her shelter. 'Here, take your little granddaughter. She wants to go home to the warm. This is not the place for her.'

Gently he ushered the three women away from the graveside along the narrow path towards the gate where only their own car remained. Behind them the two grave-diggers moved discreetly forward and reached for their shovels.

In St Albans Adam sat unmoving at his desk. He had not washed or shaved since Jane had gone, getting up now and then only to make himself a cup of tea or climb the stairs, painfully slowly, to lie on his bed, staring up at the ceiling. Sleep had evaded him completely. Robert Harding had looked in every day, avoiding as he always did the room where his own wife had died in this doomed house, and on the morning of the funeral had come himself and made Adam some breakfast. Adam left it untouched, thanking him with barely civil indifference.

Twice the police had come, the first time to say that a witness had been found who had seen in the brief second before the crash a woman step out in front of his son's car, and the second to say they could find no trace of that woman but would go on hoping she might come forward. The sergeant who spoke to him, his helmet resting on his knees uncomfortably in Adam's study, was hoping the news would help. 'It sounds as though by his action in avoiding her, your son saved her life,' he said. 'It was very brave.'

'It was stupid.' Adam stared dully ahead of him.

'Nevertheless, courageous,' the policeman replied firmly. He stood up. 'I will let you know, Dr Craig, if we hear anything further.'

When he had let the man out of the front door Adam stood for a long time where he was in the hall, staring into space, then slowly he turned and walked through to the kitchen. Opening the back door he walked into the wet, cold garden and stepped out onto the grass.

A-dam . . .

She was waiting for him by the roses.

'Brid?'

Dazed with lack of sleep and misery he let her lead him back into the house and up the stairs. In the bedroom he found himself lying down on the bed, his head swimming with exhaustion and, at last, he found himself shutting his eyes, barely aware of the weight on the bed next to him, of the hand gently caressing his hair, of the lips brushing his face as he sank deeper and deeper into oblivion.

Shaking her head, Jane put the phone down. 'He's still not answering.'

'Let him be.' Liza pressed a cup of hot tea into her hand. 'You know as well as I do that there are times when Adam needs to be alone. Don't worry. He'll be all right.'

Privately she had her doubts about that. The sight of Adam's grief and anger had shaken her badly, as had his furious rejection of her and the baby, his own grandchild. Jane hadn't been there when Adam had spoken to her, his rage spilling out like venom, his face red, the veins in his neck throbbing dangerously. If he had never met her, Liza, it seemed, her child would never have killed his son. It was irrational and cruel. It was the first time she had recognised his father's recalcitrance in Adam, and remembered his descriptions of the old man's stubbornness as he fought on his knees with his stern unforgiving God and turned his back on the woman he had loved so much.

Checking that little Beth was fast asleep, Liza slipped on a jacket and letting herself out of the house, she walked slowly over to the orchard gate. It was already growing dark. The air was sweet with the scents of wet grass and leaves and the gentle smell of the mountain thyme. Patricia had been driven back to Surrey, the last of the funeral guests had gone and the house was quiet. Jane was lying on the sofa in the living room near the fire, her eyes closed, whilst Phil had withdrawn to the kitchen with a sudden urge to tidy up. She knew that sign. He was overwhelmed, unable to contain his grief except by working all night until sheer fatigue numbed his pain. He would start with the washing up, then tidy the house for her, then move out, when he could bear to be alone, to the studio and probably stay over there for days. She was different. She could not bear to be indoors. She found comfort in nature, relying on the mountains and the great immensity of the sky to put her own problems in perspective and soothe her with their peace.

It was beginning to drizzle again. She listened to the patter of raindrops on the leaves as she leaned on the gate. It was strange, but she felt closer to Adam now than she had at any time during their long relationship. She wished he had come to the funeral. If she had been his wife she would have insisted; would have forced him out of that awful, stiff, lonely, empty house where a woman had been murdered and made him come down to see his son buried. That way he would have come to terms with what had happened. That way he would have been forced to take his little granddaughter in his arms and let her heart-breakingly beautiful little smile melt all that ice in his heart.

She shivered, picturing Adam sitting in his study, staring at the desk in front of him. Then she tensed. In the picture with him she could see Brid, a Brid she remembered only too well, young, wild-haired, beautiful, a Brid who had put her arms around him and was nuzzling into his neck, a Brid who suddenly stiffened like a cat who has sensed an enemy close by and looked up, and, it seemed to Liza, looked straight into her own eyes. Just for a second she saw the venom and the triumph there, then the picture disappeared and she was once more staring out into the rain.

For several minutes she stood without moving, cold with shock, then she turned and made her way swiftly back to the house.

Jane was sitting in the armchair by the fire when Liza walked in. 'Did you say the crash was caused by a woman walking out in front of them?' Liza asked abruptly. She squatted down in front of the smouldering logs and held out her hands to their warmth.

Jane nodded. 'She never came forward,' she replied without opening her eyes.

Liza took a deep breath, then she lapsed into silence. There was no point in saying to Jane that she thought Brid had killed their children, that Brid had done it cynically and cruelly in order to get Adam to herself. That sounded like the height of paranoia. Besides, Brid hadn't got Adam to herself. Jane and she were still alive. And so was little Beth.

'Ring Adam again.' Liza had settled on the hearth rug, her arms wrapped around her knees. 'See if you can persuade him to come. I can't bear to think of him alone.'

'He won't come.' Jane shook her head. 'You know he won't. He can't cope with it. He's better on his own.'

'No one is better on their own, Jane,' Liza whispered. 'Can I ring him if you won't?'

The other woman opened her eyes. 'You think you can persuade him when I can't? You think you could have made him come, don't you?' She gave a small sad smile. 'Perhaps you could. Perhaps you should have been the one to marry him, I don't know. None of it really matters now, does it?' She hauled herself to her feet. 'Ring him if you want to, I don't mind.'

Without another word she went over to the door and let herself out into the corridor. Liza, sitting without moving near the fire, heard the slow drag of her footsteps as she went upstairs and then the bang of her bedroom door.

For a long time she didn't move, then she reached up to the table for the phone and dialled the number.

It rang and rang without answer as though in an empty house. In the end she gave up and gently replaced the receiver. She wondered if the picture she saw suddenly in her head of Adam lying naked in bed with a dark head on his chest was real or just her own worst imaginings.

Two weeks later, Liza drove Jane back to St Albans. Little Beth was in her carrycot on the back seat as they drove up the road and pulled to a halt outside the house.

'You'd better go in first.' Liza turned to Jane. 'Make sure it's all right for me to bring Beth in.'

'Of course it's all right.' Jane pushed open the door. 'I've never heard such nonsense. He'll be fine when he sees her.'

In the past fortnight they had only managed to speak to Adam twice. Once Jane had caught him at the surgery when she had rung there in complete despair of ever getting hold of him, and once Liza, ringing late in the evening had caught him when he was on night call. Both women were comforted that he had at least gone back to work. Both, for different reasons, had reservations about his dull, unresponsive voice and insistence that Jane should not go home.

Liza peered through the windscreen as Jane walked up the path, searching in her handbag for her keys. It was a bright cold windy day and her hair was blowing across her face and round her head in a pale blonde nimbus which Adam once would have found irresistible.

Liza saw her push the key in the lock. The door didn't open. Jane pushed at it, and wriggled the key, then she took it out and looked at it, then tried it again. She tried a second key on the ring, then the first for the third time, then she pushed open the letter box and called.

Liza glanced over into the back seat. Beth was fast asleep. Opening the door she climbed out. She ran up the path. 'What's wrong?'

'I think he's bolted the door.'

'Can you get round the back?'

Jane frowned. She glanced at the neighbouring house, then nodded. 'Wait here. I'll see if I can get in through the kitchen.'

'Do you want me to come?'

For a moment Jane hesitated, then she shook her head. 'No, you wait here. If I get in I'll come and open the door.' She glanced at the car. 'We can't leave her alone, Liza.'

The path led between the garages of the two houses past the dustbins and followed a black slatted board fence, to a small gate which led into the garden. The gate was open and Jane went in. The French doors to Adam's study were shut, but the door into the kitchen was ajar and she made for it, her stomach knotting with anxiety.

The house was very quiet. Holding her breath she tiptoed in and stopped. There was no sign of anyone having been in there lately. No dirty plates, no food. The cooker was cold and the table was covered in a fine layer of dust.

But there was someone there. She could feel it. Someone who shouldn't be there. She stood where she was listening with every ounce of attention then slowly she crept across the floor and peered round the door. The hall was empty. She knew she should turn and run; she should call Liza, call the police, but she couldn't move.

Somewhere in the distance she could hear a clock ticking in the silence. Swallowing, she tiptoed across the floor and plucking up every ounce of courage she possessed she pushed open Adam's study door. The room was empty. On the desk a full cup of tea sat untouched, a brown sour skim on its surface. Cautiously she peered into each of the downstairs rooms then she turned to look up the stairs. She could hear nothing. It was almost as though someone up there was listening to her in their turn.

'Adam?' It came out as a whisper.

Slowly she began to climb.

Her hand on the bedroom door, she paused for a minute, then cautiously she pushed it open. The curtains were half drawn and the room was in semi-darkness. There was a small stir in the air, a slight frisson by the bed, a feeling as though between one moment and the next someone had been there and then not been there. She took a step inside the door.

Adam lay fast asleep on the bed. Apart from a trailing sheet he was naked.

'Adam? Adam!' Jane stepped forward and shook him by the shoulder. 'Adam! Wake up!'

There was no response.

'Adam!' Her voice rose in panic.

Outside, Liza shivered. She glanced behind her at the empty street and then, as Jane had done, stooped and raising the flap of the letterbox, peered through. The hall was dark, and she could see a scattering of post on the mat. The air smelled dusty and stale. The house was very silent. She lowered the flap and stood up again, inhaling deep breaths of cold air. In the distance she saw a small red post van turn the corner. It drove down the street slowly and stopped about four doors down. She saw the postman climb out with a parcel, walk up a path, ring a doorbell, have a cheery word with the person who opened the door and then climb back in his van. In less than a minute it was out of sight and the road was again empty. She felt incredibly lonely. She glanced at her watch. Jane had been gone only a few minutes. It seemed like hours.

She thought she heard a wail from the car and turning she ran back down the path, but Beth, when she looked in, was fast asleep. She wished she could lock the car, but Jane had taken the keys with her and she didn't dare push down all the knobs. She locked three of them and then, leaving one so she could reach Beth if she had to, she walked back up the path and crouching, raised the flap

of the letterbox. 'Jane?' she called softly. 'Adam? Are you there?'
Jane should have been there by now. If she hadn't been able to get
in surely she would have come straight back. She glanced at her
watch again and then, making up her mind she turned and ran
towards the side of the neighbour's garden where Jane had disappeared. At the corner she paused once, giving a final glance at
the car with the sleeping baby, then she dived into the damp,
narrow pathway. 'Jane? Where are you? Jane?' She ran up the
steps from the wet lawn onto the terrace and pushed the kitchen
door open fully. 'Jane, where are you?'

There was no one there and she ran on into the hall. The front
door was still closed and she went to it, drawing back the bolt and
unlatching it to let in the fresh damp air. The car was where she
had left it and there was no one around that she could see. She
stood for a minute, torn between going to make sure that Beth was
all right and looking for Jane.

'Jane!' She shouted at the top of her voice this time. 'Jane, where
are you?'

Adam's study was empty, as was the sitting room. Glancing round
she came back to the hall and, her throat tight with apprehension
she took the stairs two at a time.

'Jane!'

Pushing open the bedroom door she took in the scene at a glance.
'Jane? Is he all right? What's wrong with him?' Her hands were on
Jane's shoulders.

'I don't know.' Jane's voice was strangely flat. Her face was
pasty-white. 'I can't wake him.'

Liza pushed her towards the door. 'Go and ring Robert. Quickly.'
She went over to the bed and put a hand on Adam's forehead.
'Adam? Adam, can you hear me?' Please God let him not have
taken an overdose. He was warm, and relaxed. His eyes when she
carefully lifted a lid appeared normal. She could see no sign of any
pill bottles on the bedside table. She caught his hand and rubbed it
hard between her own. 'Adam! Come on, wake up! Adam!' She
looked up at Jane as she reappeared in the doorway. 'Did you get
through?'

Jane nodded.

'How long will he be?'

'Not long. He's coming straight from the surgery. Has he – he
hasn't taken something?' Jane was shaking violently. 'I can't lose
them both, Liza.'

'You're not going to lose him. I think he's going to be all right.'

Liza was still chafing Adam's hand. She pulled the bedcover up and over him. Then she went to the window and glanced down, appalled to find that she had forgotten all about the baby.

'Go down, Jane, and bring Beth in. I had to leave her on her own. I'll stay with Adam.' She sounded stronger than she felt. 'Please, I hated leaving her out there but I didn't dare bring her in until I knew what was going on in here.'

Jane hesitated, then slowly she walked out of the room. From the window Liza saw her reappear outside a few seconds later, walk down the path to the car and open the door.

Turning to the figure on the bed Liza put her hand on his forehead again. 'Adam!' she said sharply. 'Adam, can you hear me? Has Brid been here with you?'

She hoped Jane hadn't noticed the tell-tale red marks on his neck, the small sharp marks of a woman's teeth on his shoulder, or the scratches on his chest. Undoubtedly Robert would.

He arrived moments later and she waited downstairs while Jane took him up to the bedroom. When Jane came down she had put on a record of Chopin nocturnes and was turning her attention to the fire.

'He's waking up.' Jane threw herself down in the chair. 'Robert doesn't think he's taken anything. It was just exhaustion. He seems very confused. He's just checking his blood pressure to be on the safe side.'

Liza sat back on her heels, a lump of coal in her hand. She came straight to the point. 'That amulet I gave you all those years ago. Where is it?'

Jane looked vague. 'By my bed, I think. In the cupboard. I don't know. Why? It doesn't work any more, I told you. Does it matter?' Frowning she went over and looked down into the carrycot. Beth stirred and opened her huge blue eyes. Waving her arms around she began to whimper.

'I don't know if it matters but I could try taking it back to Meryn. Get him to take a look at it when he comes back. There must be something we can do to keep you both safe.'

'So you think Brid was here too.' Stooping, Jane lifted Beth from her blankets. 'What is she, Liza?' she wailed suddenly. 'A ghost? Some kind of devil?' She clutched the baby to her. 'Why won't she leave us alone?'

It grew easier as time passed. He turned to her whenever he was lonely and he was lonely often. She had watched when he had sent Liza and the baby away and she had watched when he packed his things and moved from the bedroom with his wife and the silly, dented amulet with no more power than a child's toy, into the room which had been for visitors. His son's old room was locked. Neither he nor Jane went in there any more.

Jane wept every night in her lonely bed and grew thin and pale and nervous. When Adam was at the surgery she would sometimes ring the farm in Wales for quick guilty words with Liza and later, when she learned to talk, with little Beth who knew about her granny in St Albans but did not remember ever having seen her. Brid did not care what she did. At the moment she was not interested in Adam's wife.

She had learned how to tease him; how to hide when he came upstairs after a silent dinner with Jane, how to wait until he had changed from his doctor's suit with its dark colours and neat striped tie into a dressing gown, or better still in the warmth of the bedroom, nothing at all. Then she would sprawl on the bed, her dark hair spread across the pillow, sometimes wearing her long green gown, sometimes naked, her arms beckoning him away from his book and under the sheets, where she would caress and lick and kiss until with a groan half of guilt and half of ecstasy he would abandon himself to her every wile. Once or twice she took him with her, out of his body into a dream world where he could fly and run and leap naked across the heather, reaching out to keep hold of her hand before falling, inextricably twined together on the grass beside the pool where they had first made love.

Lying alone in what had once been their bedroom Jane could hear him sometimes cry out in the night, and thinking it was misery she cried too, but then she realised the sound was one of anguished, grudging pleasure, and she buried her face in the pillow and allowed it to absorb her desperate tears.

Once she tried to win him back.

She cooked his favourite meal and put on a dress she knew he liked and daubed her wrists and neck with perfume. His face brightened when he saw her. 'You look happier, Janie,' he said. 'I'm glad.'

He ate the meal, if not with relish at least with more enthusiasm than usual and answered her questions about the practice and Robert and her tentative suggestion that they might consider going on holiday next year. He listened and nodded and smiled at her and for a moment she allowed herself to feel hopeful. Carefully she avoided the topic of Liza and Beth – which she knew would bring fury and recrimination – and focused instead on a future where he and she could travel and look forward, not back.

For once when she cleared the dishes he stayed where he was and talked to her while she put the kettle on for tea and when she rather coyly produced a box of chocolates he took one and smiled and touched her hand. Her excitement growing, she squeezed his shoulder and allowed her fingers to trail across the back of his neck. He stiffened for a moment then relaxed and smiled again. He took her hand. 'I haven't been much help to you, Janie, over the last couple of years. I'm sorry.'

She smiled back. 'It doesn't matter. As long as we're there for each other now.'

She thought he was going to reach up and kiss her, and her heart leaped with excitement, but with another squeeze of his hand he leaned back in his chair. 'What happened to that tea?'

'It's coming.' Hiding her disappointment she turned away and busied herself with the pot and caddy. 'Shall we go out later?' she said, not looking at him. 'It's a lovely evening. We could go up to the abbey or walk in the park.'

'That might be nice.' Noncommittal.

'Here.' She passed him his cup. 'Or we could take a drink out into the garden. What would you like to do?'

'Just sit here for a while and enjoy my tea.' He was growing restless though, she could sense it.

She could feel herself becoming uneasy. She mustn't rush him, she knew that, but she longed so much for him to turn to her, to put his arms around her and make love to her. Putting her own cup down she went to sit next to him. 'Adam –'

'Wait! Did you hear something?' Adam straightened suddenly. 'Listen!'

'There's nothing to hear.' She found she was frightened. There was a tightening in her chest as she listened. 'Why should there be anything there? Come on, let's go out,' she stood up and caught his hand, 'please, Adam.'

But it was there, outside the open window. The sound of scraping, and then, suddenly a rustle of ivy and from the silence outside a low, threatening growl.

'Adam, please. Let's go. Don't wait.'

'It's only a cat –'

'It's not only a cat!' Her voice rose to a shriek. 'You know it's not only a cat! Adam, please, listen to me. You can't stay and let her do this to you. You can't!'

She was clinging to him as he stood up and walked towards the window.

The cat stood for a moment on the sill, its ears flattened, its eyes a blaze of orange, then it leaped lightly down into the room, its tail swishing viciously.

'Adam,' she shrank back. 'Adam, don't let her hurt me.'

'Go, Janie. Please, go.' He put a gentle hand on the animal's head and immediately it raised its face towards him and pressed against his legs.

Jane backed away with a sob. 'Adam! Please.'

'Go, Jane!' His voice was harsh. For a second he hesitated, glancing at her, then, slowly, he turned and walked towards the door, the cat stalking stiff-legged beside him. In a moment they had gone and the door closed behind them.

Jane subsided onto the chair, tears pouring down her face. She sat there until it grew dark, then at last she reached for the phone and dialled Liza's number.

Liza glanced at her watch. The train was as usual late. She had been standing on the platform at Newport for what seemed like hours, having drained a second cup of revolting British Railways coffee and read the paper from beginning to end. Jane's call the previous night had been hysterical and so desperate Liza had nearly offered to get into the car and drive to St Albans on the spot, but good sense had prevailed, together with the fact that little Beth, now three years old and attending a kindergarten in Hay had a feverish cold and wouldn't let her out of her sight. This morning she was better and the little girl had agreed to stay with Grandpa Phil provided she was allowed to paint in his studio. Liza was fairly sure that the doting grandpa did not mind nearly as much as he made out. It was too bad if he did. She was going to meet Jane off the fast train from Paddington and then take her out to lunch on the way back to the farm so that she could find out exactly what had been happening.

The train pulled in at last and when she saw Jane's wan face the moment she climbed off, dragging her small suitcase behind her as though it weighed ten tons, her heart sank. Jane looked desperately ill and unhappy. Taking the case out of her hand she led the way to the car and then threaded her way out of Newport's morning traffic towards the mountain road. 'Tell me what happened.' She glanced at the woman beside her.

Jane shrugged. 'It's Brid. She's there every night. He's moved into the spare room with her.'

Liza bit her lip, trying not to let her shock show. 'Are you sure?'

'Oh yes, I'm sure.' The voice was very bitter. 'He's bewitched.'

Liza braked and changed gear as she swung the car onto the Abergavenny road. 'Does he know where you are?'

'No. He's forbidden me ever to see you or Phil and little Beth. I'm not even allowed to talk to him about you all. He still blames you for Calum's death. He's sour and twisted and I think he's going mad.' Suddenly she dissolved into tears again. 'Liza, I think I'm going mad too. I don't know what to do.'

Liza reached over just for a second and touched Jane's hands as they lay locked together in her lap. 'We'll stop in a minute and I'll buy you a drink. Then when we've got some food inside you we'll go home. You're going to stay with us for as long as you like and get to know your granddaughter and you're going to put that silly silly man out of your head. You are not going mad. It sounds as though he might be, but we'll deal with that.' She frowned as she turned into the narrow gate of the white-painted stone-built pub on the edge of the road. Inside she knew they would find a discreet landlord, a roaring fire and delicious home-cooked food. She didn't want Beth seeing Jane until all her tears were spent.

Several days later it was Liza who drew up outside the Craigs' gate in St Albans. The lights were on and she could see Adam's Rover parked in the drive. She was exhausted; her initial fury and indignation at Adam's insensitivity and selfishness had abated slightly as the car ate up the long miles across England and been replaced by a feeling of unease.

Taking a deep breath, she unlatched the car door and climbed out. She kept her finger on the bell for several seconds before letting the echo die away into silence. No one came.

In the back garden the winter grass was uncut and Adam's pride and joy, his roses, were a sprawl of untrimmed branches and dead flowers. The kitchen door was open.

Stepping inside she stood and looked round. There were unwashed plates in the sink. The kettle was, when she put a hand gently on its flank, slightly warm. There was a smell coming from the unemptied rubbish bin. She tiptoed across the floor and carefully pulling open the door, she listened.

'Adam?' Her voice sounded hollow and nervous as she stood at the bottom of the stairs and peered up. She held her breath and listened. The silence in the house had suddenly changed quality. It seemed alert as though someone or something were listening in return. She shivered, wishing she had had the chance to see Meryn before she came back to Hertfordshire, but he was away and had been for a long, long time.

'Adam!' She spoke more loudly this time. 'Where are you? It's Liza. For goodness' sake! I've driven a long way. The least you could do is answer your door.'

Again silence. Then she thought she heard a sound upstairs.

'Adam!' Not giving herself time to think she put a foot on the staircase and peered up. 'Adam? Are you all right?'

At the top she paused and looked round. The door to Adam and Jane's bedroom was open. It was deserted as she had guessed it would be, the twin beds meticulously made, the dressing table bare, the curtains half drawn though it was still daylight.

'Adam!' She withdrew into the hall and, resolutely not looking at the closed door of what had been Calum's bedroom, headed for the spare room.

'Adam!' She knocked loudly.

The silence behind the door was palpable.

'Adam, I know you're there.' She tried the handle. The door opened and she stared in.

Adam was lying on the bed, his arm across his eyes. He was fully dressed, though his shirt was open.

'Adam?' She spoke sharply, her voice edged with fear. 'Adam, are you all right?' Hurrying to the bed she looked down at him. His shirt had been torn open. She could see two of the buttons lying on the carpet, and a small hole ripped into the cotton where another had failed to pull clear of its button hole. There were scratches on his chest.

'Adam!' She grabbed his wrist and felt for his pulse.

He seemed to be breathing normally, but when she shook him she could get no response. His eyes stayed closed and his head lolled to one side on the pillow. 'Adam, what's wrong?' She put her hands on his shoulders and shook him, then she headed for the bathroom and came back with a toothmug full of cold water.

As she threw it into his face his eyes flew open and he stared at her without recognition. 'Adam, are you all right?' She sat on the bed next to him. 'It's me, Liza.'

He looked at her, dazed, for several seconds, then slowly he sat up and swung his legs out of the bed. Sitting there he put his head in his hands and rubbed his face hard. Then at last he looked up at her with some semblance of attention.

'Adam, for God's sake, what's the matter with you?' She stood

278

up and looked down at him. 'I've been knocking and shouting for hours.'

'Liza?' His voice was croaky. 'Did I ask you to come?' The edge in his voice was not entirely hostile. There was genuine confusion.

'No, of course you didn't ask me, but we need to talk. This quarrel has gone on long enough. It's ludicrous.'

He was recovering fast. 'I don't remember thinking it was ludicrous. Your daughter was responsible for Calum's death –'

'That is crap, Adam, and you know it!' Liza turned on him. 'What has happened to your wits? You know as well as I do that they were in love, they were happy, they had everything to live for.' Her voice cracked and she brushed an angry fist across her eyes. 'Look, I did not come here to talk about the children. I came to talk about Jane. And about Brid.'

Adam went white. 'There is nothing to discuss. My wife has run off, and what I do and what friends I have are none of your business.'

'I think they are. So Brid is a friend now, is she? Do you make a habit of having psychopathic, murderous ghosts as your friends?'

Adam's face suffused a deep red. He stood up. 'Out.' He pointed to the door.

'No. I've just arrived. You might be able to terrorise your wife, but you can't terrorise me, Adam Craig. You are mad, do you realise that?' She folded her arms across her chest and stuck out her chin aggressively. 'So, where is she? Or are we still imagining she isn't real?'

'Oh she's real enough.' Adam smiled.

'Real enough to scratch you, certainly.' She looked meaningfully at his chest.

He glanced down and put his hand on the scratches. 'I was pruning the roses.'

'I don't think so. More likely you've had a visitor in your bed.'

'Don't, Liza. Just go away. I'm sorry you've had a wasted journey, but there is nothing for you here. Go home.'

'No. I'm not going until you talk some sense. We'll go downstairs and discuss this.'

'There is nothing to discuss.'

'I think there is. Whether you like it or not we have a little granddaughter who is going to grow up wondering why her grandparents don't talk to each other. Are you going to let her grow up thinking her grandfather is mad?'

'Get out, Liza.' His voice had gone suddenly very quiet.

279

'No. Not until I've had my say. This has gone on long enough.'

'Liza. There is nothing to say. Please leave my house.' He turned and pulling off his ruined shirt, reached for a sweater from the chair in the corner. His back too, she saw, was covered in thin scratches. She felt suddenly very sick.

'Adam. Please come down.'

'Go now.' She saw him glance beyond her at the door and she felt a cold shiver run down her back.

'I am going to talk to you first.'

'I don't think so. Please leave.'

There was a slight sound behind her from the landing and, her heart lurching in sudden fright, Liza turned. Standing in the doorway was Brid, her hair a dark shining frame around her shoulders, her eyes the colour of old silver. She was wearing a long blue dress which almost reached the floor. Below the hem her feet were bare.

A-dam, make her go away.

Although she didn't appear to have spoken aloud Liza heard the words clearly in her head.

'Please leave, Liza, for your own sake.'

But Brid was in the doorway.

Liza clenched her fists. Protection. Remember the psychic protection Meryn had taught her. 'I have come here to talk to you, Adam. Please ask your friend to go away until we have finished.'

'You go, Liza.'

'Not until we have finished.' She hoped she looked braver than she felt. Taking a deep breath she stepped towards Adam and put her hand on his arm. 'Send her away.'

'I can't.'

'Yes you can.' She raised her chin. 'Make her go away.'

Brid moved closer. She didn't appear to walk, it was just that one moment she was in the doorway and the next she was standing only four feet away from Liza and Liza could see the small knife clutched in her hand.

'Adam, are you going to let her stick that thing in me?' She tried desperately to control her voice, pushing down the waves of panic which were sweeping over her.

'Brid, please.' Adam suddenly sounded firmer. 'I want you to go away. Just for five minutes. Then you can come back. Otherwise, Adam will be cross.' For the first time he looked at the girl and Liza saw her grow pale. For a moment she thought she looked less distinct, as though she were nothing more than a shadow, then Brid turned and left the room.

'You are a fool, Liza. I can't control her. She could have killed you.'

'But she didn't.' Liza took a deep breath. 'So, what the hell is going on here? Does she live here now?'

'Liza, listen to me.' He seemed to have regained his composure. Ignoring her questions he took a deep breath. 'There is too much separating us now. I do not wish to see you here, or anywhere else for that matter. And if my wife is with you, you can take her away as well. That is all I have to say. Now, please go before Brid returns, or I will not be responsible for what happens.'

'Adam –'

'I mean it, Liza.'

'You are out of your mind.' It was true, she realised suddenly. The expression behind his eyes was vacant, wild. It was as though another voice were speaking through him. Suddenly afraid, she took a step away from him. 'Adam,' she tried one last time. 'Please. Come with me. Let us at least talk. Outside, in the garden.' If she could get him away from the house, perhaps he would be himself again. 'Just listen to me for a few minutes.'

'Go, now.' He gave her one last hostile look then he turned away from her and walked towards the window. When she glanced at the doorway she saw Brid standing there, the knife in her hand.

'All right.' She bit her lip. 'I'll go. Call off your bodyguard.'

Brid smiled. She moved towards him and Liza felt the cold shiver of the air as the woman walked past her. With a triumphant smile Brid put her hand on Adam's chest and pushed up against him, her head under his chin. His arm came around her shoulders and he looked at Liza over the dark head.

'Go.'

'I'm going.' Liza felt a wave of nausea rise in her throat. Without another glance she turned and ran down the stairs. Letting herself out of the front door she ran down the path and climbed into her car. Then she sat, her head resting on the rim of the steering wheel, shaking like a leaf. Behind her the curtains of the upstairs room closed. The light did not go on behind them.

'Jane, you have to stay. You can't go back to him.' Liza put her hands on Jane's shoulders. 'I mean it. You won't be safe there. He's gone mad.'

'I have to go back. It's my home. He's my husband.' Jane sat down abruptly. She had been asleep when Liza finally drove home in the early hours of the morning, but the sound of the car turning into the gate had woken her from a light, troubled sleep. Neither Phil nor Beth seemed to have heard her.

Jane poked the fire into life and curled up on the sofa. 'I am not going to allow that, that . . .' Words failed her for a moment. 'That harpy to steal my husband. She's not even real!'

'She's real enough.' Liza cupped her hands around a mug of hot tea and subsided onto a cushion, warming herself before the flames. 'And I don't have to tell you how dangerous she is.'

'So, are you telling me never to go home again? To abandon Adam to her? To let her have everything?'

Liza, staring deep into the fire, did not answer for a moment. 'No, I don't mean that. I just think we have to work something out. We have to be sure what we're doing. She's dangerous, Janie. At least you're safe here.'

'Am I?' Jane hauled a cushion onto her knee and hugged it defensively. 'I seem to remember none of us was safe here. It was in the same bedroom I'm in now that she attacked me and gave me these scars.' She pointed at her shoulder.

Liza fell silent. 'I wish Meryn were here,' she said at last. 'He helped us before.'

'Where is he?'

Liza shrugged. 'They say he's gone to Scotland. The house is closed up. He's done it before – disappeared for long periods, then come back again as though he'd never been away. It didn't matter then. He was there when I needed him.' Her eyes filled suddenly with tears. He didn't even know that Julie was dead.

'Liza, I'm sorry.'

Liza shook her head. 'Take no notice of me. I'm exhausted.'

'And I'm being incredibly selfish making you stay up to talk to me when you've driven for about ten hours without stopping, and all for my sake.' Jane stood up, full of resolve. 'Listen, go to bed. We'll talk in the morning.' Crouching, she put her arms round Liza suddenly and hugged her. 'You're a true friend. Don't let Adam come between us.'

'He won't.' Liza rose wearily to her feet. 'Somehow we'll defeat Brid, Jane, I promise. We'll get Adam back for you. Somehow.'

15

Meryn was standing in the shelter of the trees looking out towards the stone. The decision to come here had been made high in the Andes where the air was thin and the barriers between the planes were paper fine. He stared round and nodded with satisfaction. He had been right to come to Scotland now. The high peaks in the distance were covered in a fresh layer of snow, blinding white against the intense azure of the sky, and the air crackled with cold energy. Thoughtfully he waited, his eyes on the serpent picked out in glittering frost amongst the other engravings on the face of the slab. Broichan was near. He could feel the coiled energy, the intelligence, the power of the rage and frustration and the absolute danger of the man.

He waited unmoving, drawing a cloak of darkness around him, letting the silence of the mountains sink into his very bones. Near him a squirrel sat stripping the scales from a pine cone oblivious of the man standing unmoving in the shadows of the trees. Suddenly it sat up. It remained completely still for a second, then dropping the cone it raced up into the top branches with a sharp cough of alarm, leaving a flurry of tiny tracks and the fluffed up snow where its tail had for a moment flicked along the ground. Meryn tensed. He could feel him closer now. Broichan knew he was there. He could sense the man's suspicion, feel the strength of his vigilance and the gathering fury of his displeasure.

Imperceptibly he shifted his gaze towards the mirror on the stone. Was that the key to Brid's dexterity with time?

There was a distant rumble of thunder and he frowned. The sky was cloudless. Then he understood. Broichan had sent a warning shot across his bows as his attention wavered. He smiled quietly to himself as he walked out of the trees and onto the rocky plateau to stand near the stone. 'One to you, my friend,' he muttered under his breath. 'I must learn not to look away. You are not to be trusted, not for one minute.'

Meryn . . .

He stiffened. The voice came from far away, but it was not from the past, it was from home. Someone needed him in Wales. Liza.

Lying in bed savouring the warmth under the blankets Liza stretched and smiled to herself. It would be frosty outside and the air would be fresh and cold and rich as milk. In a minute she would get up and have a bath and dress, then she would make breakfast for herself and Jane. She reached for the little clock by her bed and squinted at it. It had gone ten, but after the long two-way drive yesterday and the incredibly late night she was prepared to treat herself to a lie-in. She snuggled down again, her eyes on the bright blue of the sky above the trees outside. Phil had got up hours ago, no doubt, and by now would be ensconced in his studio. She had been careful not to wake him when she at last climbed into bed in the early hours of the morning, but he must have realised how late it was when she came in.

He would have taken Beth to play school before he started work. His job this week – they took turns. After he had collected her at lunchtime he would probably stay in the studio till dark, and it would be their turn to look after her while they planned what to do next. She closed her eyes to focus better on what they should do. Adam was obviously under some sort of spell. He had acted like a man bewitched – not at all his usual rational self – and spells could be broken.

Ten minutes later she realised that she could not lie there another second. All her tension and worry had returned. Getting up, she ran a bath; the water would soak away some of her exhaustion which, now she had left her bed, returned in full measure.

It was not until she had run downstairs to the kitchen and opened the back door that she realised her car had gone from the yard. She stared for a moment, then she turned back inside and ran back upstairs.

'Jane?' She knocked on the spare room door and then threw it open. Jane's clothes, her bag, her shoes, had all gone.

Phil was standing in front of his easel lost in thought when she burst into his studio. Beside him the cooker timer, set to remind him to leave to fetch Beth home from school, ticked loudly on his bench.

'Phil? Where's Jane?'

He turned to her thoughtfully, and it was a moment before he focused and registered her question. 'I don't know. Why?'

'She's gone. She's taken my car, her things, everything.'

'She's probably gone home then.'

'She can't have. Phil, I saw her last night – no, it was this morning. Only a few hours ago. We talked. She can't go back to Adam, not yet.'

Phil walked over and put his arms around her. 'What is it? What happened yesterday? I thought it couldn't be good if you'd come straight back.'

She told him and he listened without interruption. Only when she had finished did he ask, 'Did you tell Jane all this?'

She nodded.

He shook his head. 'She shouldn't have gone back to him. Perhaps she hasn't. Are you sure she didn't leave a note?'

She hadn't looked. When she found it, all it said was: *I'll leave the car at the station. Sorry. Jane.* It wasn't until ten o'clock that night that she heard from Jane again. She was already in bed when the phone rang and, grabbing her dressing gown, she ran downstairs to the cold kitchen. Beth had long been asleep. There was no sign of Phil. He must still be out in the studio.

'I'm sorry I ran away.' She could hear from her voice that Jane had been crying. 'I lay awake for hours thinking about what you'd told me, then I realised I was never going to fall asleep so I just got up and left. I wanted to talk to him.' There was a long pause.

'What is it, Janie? What's happened?'

'I thought if I caught him at the surgery I could speak to him without the risk of her being there. I thought I could persuade him to see sense. But it wasn't any good. He wouldn't listen. He was rude to me in front of the receptionist. He walked out and drove home and when I got here he was already upstairs, and the door is locked. I wish I hadn't come.'

'Oh, Janie, I'm so sorry.' Liza shivered. She moved to the full length of the phone cord which just allowed her to switch on the lamp on the dresser. Outside it was raining. She could hear the spatter of raindrops against the window.

'He's here. Upstairs. With her.' Jane let out a small sob. 'Liza, he doesn't want me any more.'

'Come back, Janie. Come back here. We want you.' The warmth in Liza's voice was genuine. 'Listen, don't stay there.' She had been going to say that it wasn't safe, but she bit back the words. What was the point in frightening Jane further?

'I'll come in the morning, maybe . . .'

'Jane, you must.'

'I can't just leave without trying again.' Her voice faded briefly, as though she had turned away from the receiver. 'Hold on. I can hear footsteps. I think he's coming downstairs. I'll call you back tomorrow.'

'Jane, don't hang up –'

But it was too late. The phone had been slammed down.

Liza stood for a moment looking at the receiver in her own hand, then slowly she replaced it on the rest. She was trying to picture the scene at the far end of the line.

'Adam.' Jane smiled in relief. 'Are you all right?'

He stared at her in silence for a full minute and she realised suddenly that he wasn't focusing. His gaze was going straight through her as though she weren't there.

'Adam?' she repeated, more timidly this time. 'Can you hear me?'

He looked as though he were asleep.

'Adam?' Cautiously she stepped forward and put her hand on his arm. 'Adam, darling, can you hear me?'

She glanced behind him at the door. The house was very quiet. All she could hear was the roar of the wind in the branches of the pear tree outside the window. 'Adam, let's go into the kitchen. It's warmer in there.'

He followed her obediently and quietly she shut the door and turned the key. Closing her eyes she took a deep breath.

'There. Why not sit down while I put the kettle on?' She busied herself at the tap, watching him out of the corner of her eye. He was still gazing into space, his actions those of a sleepwalker.

Having switched on the kettle she sat down at the kitchen table next to him and took his hand. It was ice cold. Chafing it gently she smiled at him. 'Perhaps we should put on the fire next door? It's cold enough to snow, you know. There was a frost up at the farm last night.' She bit her lip. She shouldn't have mentioned the farm. But perhaps if she talked about Liza's visit it would trigger some sort of reaction in him. 'Adam, Liza was very upset by what happened here last night.'

He said nothing. His eyes were still fixed on the middle distance.

'It was dreadful to make her drive all the way back to Wales. She was exhausted.'

He was listening, she realised suddenly. His eyes had re-focused and his attention had sharpened. She breathed a sigh of relief. 'Adam, we have to talk about what's happened. I'm not sure I understand –' She broke off as he stood up abruptly, pushing the chair over onto the floor behind him.

'Brid?' He was looking at the door.

Jane went white. She looked at the door too. The handle was moving gently up and down.

'Adam, don't let her in. You have to talk to me.' She caught at his hand but he pushed it away.

'Brid? Is that you?' Striding quickly across the room he unlocked the door and pulled it open. The hallway was empty.

Jane moved behind the table. 'Is it her?'

Adam peered up the stairs.

'Don't go, Adam.' She was afraid. 'Don't go up there.'

Adam shook his head. 'I have to, Jane. If you don't like it, you go.'

'But this is my home, Adam.' Her fear changed at last to anger. 'I'm not going to leave! I've been hurt too. I've lost a son too. You're not alone. But I face up to it. I'm coping with reality, not losing myself in a web of fantasy and perversion! If anyone is going, it should be you. You're mad! Go on, get out!' She was crying now, her voice almost hoarse from shouting.

Adam turned away from her and walked out into the hall. 'Do what you like.' His voice had lost its power suddenly. Slowly, he began to climb the stairs.

Jane spent the night locked in the kitchen. The next morning she waited until she heard Adam stirring, then she went and stood behind the door, her hand on the key. He was bound to come down for breakfast. When he did so she would let him in, slam the door shut behind him and lock it.

But he didn't come in. She heard his footsteps on the stairs; they moved across the hall to the front door. She heard it open, felt the draught sweep in under the kitchen door around her feet, and then she heard it bang again. Moments later she heard the distant sound of the car engine in the drive.

She stood where she was, holding her breath, listening. The house was totally silent.

It was half an hour before she plucked up the courage to look out into the hall. It was dark. The dull wet morning allowed very little light to seep through the small window beside the front entrance and the sitting room and study doors were closed. Her heart was thundering in her ears as she tiptoed to the foot of the stairs and looked up. Her spurt of anger the night before had been short-lived. It had been replaced by self-pity, by fear and by indignation in quick succession as she huddled at the table in the cold room, warming herself now and again by turning on the electric cooker and leaving the oven door open, an action which gave her a perverse pleasure in that she knew how furious Adam would be if he learned of such a blatant waste of money and heat.

One by one she pushed open the ground floor doors and peered into each room in turn. All were empty. Then at last she plucked up courage to climb the stairs.

It was the first time she had been in Calum's room for many weeks. Once a month she would go in there to dust and vacuum, to sit on his bed and have a little cry, to touch his things and try to make the resolution to do something about it all, to resist making it into a shrine; then she would blow her nose and stand up and go out and close the door, thankfully to try and put it out of her mind for a while longer. She stood for a moment, looking round. No one had been in there, she was sure. Everything was exactly as it had been. There was no one else to go in there, apart from Adam. Mrs Freeling had left after the murder, too scared, she said, to stay in the house, and they had never had the heart to replace her. And now there was no need. With just her and Adam there was very little to do in the way of housework and she could get through what there was in no time at all.

She went into their bedroom next – the room she now slept in alone. It was empty, the beds neatly made. Her eyes went automatically to the bedside table and suddenly she froze. The broken amulet which she had put defiantly back in its place had gone.

She knew it didn't work any more; she knew there was no point in it, but it was all she had to cling to. Frantically she ran to the table and stared down between the two beds. Kneeling, she looked under the bed covers, beneath the pillows and then over the rest of the room. There was no sign of it anywhere.

'Oh, please God, let it be here!' She looked again, throwing open drawers and cupboards, then spread her search wider to take in the bathroom and Calum's room, where she had not looked inside the cupboards for months. In her panic she forgot to be sad, throwing football boots and a cricket bat out onto the carpet as she rummaged in the depths. But it was no use. Only then, at last, did she pluck up courage to go to the door of the spare room and rest her ear against the wood, listening. Inside there was total silence. Taking a deep breath she put her hand on the handle and turned it.

The room was in chaos. The bed was unmade and frowsty, the

sheets strewn across the floor. A pile of Adam's unwashed clothes lay spilling from a chair and there were streaks of dried blood upon the pillow.

Jane felt sick. There was a feral smell in the air which made the small hairs on the back of her neck stand on end, but there was no sign of Brid or of any cat.

Then she saw the amulet. It was lying on the floor, half covered by the trailing sheet. Stooping, she reached for it with a sigh of relief, then she gasped with horror. It had been snapped and twisted again beyond recognition, the rest of the branches broken off, the small coloured enamels crushed as if with a hammer. The crystal had gone. Carefully she gathered up all the broken pieces and looked down at them through a haze of tears. What use would it be to her now? Turning, she walked out of the room, closing the door behind her. Carrying it through to her own bedroom she sat down on the bed and laid the pieces on the clean fresh bedspread. The fury with which they had been torn apart was clear in every twisted fragment. 'Oh Adam,' she found herself sobbing the words out loud. 'What have you let her do to you?'

It was a long time before she pulled herself together and stood up. Half an hour later, she was in the waiting room at the surgery.

'I'm sorry, Mrs Craig.' The face of Doreen Chambers, the new receptionist, was a picture of anxiety and embarrassment. 'Dr Craig says he is too busy to see you.'

They both glanced round at the empty room. The last patient had walked out of the door minutes before.

'I see.' Jane straightened her shoulders. 'Doreen, would you be so kind as to step into the back office for a moment. I should hate you to get into trouble.' She smiled, a small brittle lift of the mouth which left Doreen even more nervous.

'I shouldn't, Mrs Craig.'

'I think you should, if you value your job.' Jane was amazed at the strength she was finding to stand up to the woman. In the past the receptionist staff at the practice had filled her with terror.

For a moment Doreen hesitated, then with a little shrug she went through to the back office, shutting the door behind her.

Jane walked to Adam's door and opened it without ceremony. 'I want to talk to you.'

He was standing behind his desk shuffling papers into his brief-case. Startled, he looked up at her and for a moment her resolve wavered. His face was haggard and ill, his eyes red with lack of sleep.

'I am not prepared to be made a fool of in my own house.'

She closed the door behind her, aware that Doreen would have reappeared from the office and be standing at the receptionist's counter, listening. 'If you want to live with another woman, I suggest you find a real one.' Her voice dropped to a hiss. 'Or go to Scotland and live with Brid there, in her mud hut or stone circle or wherever she lives when she's at home, but don't ever,' she paused, taking a deep breath, 'don't ever bring her back to our house again.'

'I don't bring her, Janie.' His voice was weary. He dropped the briefcase on the desk and throwing himself down into his chair he closed his eyes with exhaustion. 'I have never invited her there. She comes.'

'Then tell her to go.'

'Do you think I haven't tried?'

'You got rid of her before.'

'By running away. Do you want me to do that again? I can't get away from her, Jane. You know that as well as I do. Somehow she is able to follow me. She came to Wales, remember? She found us in St Albans. She would find me anywhere.'

'She doesn't come here.'

'Because she knows I am working here. She respects the fact that I am a doctor. She knows I would be angry if she came between me and my work.'

'But you're not angry when she comes between you and your wife!'

'That's different.'

'How, pray?' Her voice was icy.

He looked up and she saw naked despair in his eyes. 'Because of Calum. Calum is coming between us, Jane. I don't know why. I don't want it to happen, but it is. You and I. We shouldn't still be alive. You stand there, and you remind me of him –' He put his hands over his face and to her dismay she saw tears trickling from between his fingers.

Speechless, she just stared at him, then slowly she stepped back towards the door. 'Does it never occur to you that I might be broken-hearted and lonely too?'

He shrugged. 'You seem to be able to cope.'

'*Seem*, Adam. You forget that I have lost two of you. Calum is dead because of an accident. He did not choose to go. You have made that choice. And what is more,' she hesitated, almost afraid to say the words, 'you seem to be enjoying a wonderful relationship with the woman who killed your son.'

There was a long silence. It was Adam's turn to stare at her in shocked disbelief. 'Don't say that,' he choked at last. 'Don't say such a thing. How low can you stoop! How can you, Jane!'

'Easily if it's true. Has it never occurred to you who the mysterious woman was who stepped out in front of the car – the woman who disappeared and was never traced?'

'It was not Brid!' His voice was harsh with passion.

'No?' She was fighting tears. 'Well there's no point in asking her, is there? No doubt, amongst all her other talents, she is a first-class liar. Adam, how can you defend her? You know she's a murderess!'

'We don't know!' He was crying openly. 'With me she is gentle and loving and sweet. She knows how to please a man. She can soothe me, and make my headaches better, she can relax me and she listens when I talk.'

'And I do none of that?' The pain in her voice was palpable. 'Adam, this is me, Jane. Remember?' She stared at him for a long minute. 'Obviously not. Obviously the years I have given to you were a complete waste when you would rather I had not been there.'

'No, Jane, please, don't say that.' He focused on her suddenly. 'I do love you, Janie.'

'But clearly not enough.' Her voice was full of hurt. 'I just ask you one thing, Adam, please. Don't do it in our house. Ask her to go somewhere else to seduce you, not my home.'

She walked out blindly into the reception area. She did not even see Doreen as she found her way outside. Only when she reached her car did she allow her pride to waver. It was a long time before she put the key in the ignition and pulled out of the car park.

From the window of his consulting room Adam watched her go.

'Leave him, Jane.' Liza, standing by the phone in her kitchen, was staring out at the pouring rain. 'Please, just leave him. Come here.' She was biting her nail as she talked, aware that every part of her body was tense with anxiety. 'Look, it doesn't have to be forever, just while he is under this spell. For your own sake, Jane.'

But it was no use as she knew it wouldn't be. She pictured Jane immured in that dark, soulless house, locking herself in her lonely bedroom at night whilst Adam frolicked with – with what? A succubus? A ghost? A witch?

'Not Jane again?' Phil walked in from the studio and shook the rain from his shoulders like a dog shaking its coat to find her standing, lost in thought, by the phone. 'She caused enough trouble, leaving your car in Newport! I don't know why you keep ringing her. She's a grown woman. She has to make her own decisions. Perhaps she's a masochist. She likes being humiliated by that bastard.' He ran the tap and washed his hands. 'Where's Beth?'

'Playing next door.' Liza shrugged. 'I'm sure it's not safe for her there, Phil. Brid is dangerous. She can kill.'

The door opened and Beth appeared, pushing a doll's pram in which she had tucked a small toy rabbit. Liza bent and picked the little girl up, giving her a huge kiss. 'You'd think she'd want to be here. To see Beth.'

'Liza.' Phil sat down at the table and pulled the pile of unopened post towards him. The small red post van winding up the hills did not get to the farm until nearly lunchtime. 'Liza, has it ever crossed your mind that we don't want to draw attention to ourselves? Remember when that cat followed them here? It was never seen or heard of again once they had gone back to St Albans. We don't want to put ourselves, or,' he hesitated and reached over to put a gentle hand on the back of the little girl's hair for a minute, 'little Beth here at risk.'

Liza met his gaze over the child's head. 'You don't think she'd hurt Beth!'

He shrugged. 'Just give the phone a rest, love. Jane knows where we are. She knows there is always a bed for her if she wants one and she knows our number so she can call us if she's in trouble. Leave it at that, all right?' He put his arm round his wife's shoulder and gave them both a bear hug which made Beth shriek with delight.

It was two days later that Liza decided to take the longer route back from shopping in Hay. She had loaded the car with supplies, called in at one of the book shops to have a quick look at her favourite corner, bought two books she couldn't resist, hidden them under her shopping, knowing how Phil would tease her that the house would collapse if she bought any more, bought some wine and picked up the papers from Grants, then slotting Beth back into the car she set off up over the hill. The road, climbing out of the woods and fields, led after a few miles out onto the mountain, where the sky swooped low over the soft green and grey of rocks and grass, dotted with grazing ponies and sheep. At the end of the narrow track which led to Meryn's cottage she stopped the car and thought for a minute.

'Go home.' Beth put a small hand on Liza's arm. 'Go home, Granny Liza.'

Liza smiled. 'In a minute. I just want to see if Meryn has come home.' She wasn't sure why she had this strange feeling that she should turn up the track. There was no sign of smoke from the chimneys out of sight behind the stand of pine trees, no fresh tyre-marks on the grass, but suddenly she had an overwhelming urge to see. Climbing out of the car she opened the heavy old gate and climbing back in she turned up the drive.

The door was open and in one of the windows she could see a huge pot of geraniums. Meryn was writing at the old pine table in the centre of the room when she and Beth put their heads round the door.

'So, this is the little one.' He kissed Liza and then squatted down to take Beth's small hand in his own huge one.

'You know what happened to Julie and Calum?' Liza suddenly found she had tears in her eyes.

'I know.' He stood up again and reaching into a bowl of fruit he took a shiny red apple and gave it to the child, then he led Liza to the settle by the fire.

'Where have you been?' Liza looked up at him. His face was even browner than she remembered, and his brilliant blue eyes were brighter than ever. She found herself wondering as she did every time she saw him how old he was, and she decided as she always did that he could be anything between fifty and a hundred. He squatted down on the stool before the fire and reaching out threw on a couple of logs. Beth, chewing on her apple, came to stand just behind him. He did not turn, treating her like a small animal which must overcome its shyness in its own time before friendship and trust can be established.

He ignored Liza's second question, concentrating instead on the first. 'There is a reason these things happen, Liza.' He was staring into the fire. 'It may be hard to bear, harder to understand, but you must not be sad forever. You will see them again. You know that.'

With a sniff Liza nodded. 'I suppose I do.'

He turned and fixed her with his intense gaze. 'Suppose?'

'It's difficult. I still miss her so much.'

'Be strong, Liza.' He sounded very stern. 'Now, what have you done about the woman, Brid?'

'You think she is a woman, then?'

'Oh yes, she's a woman.' He gave a grave smile.

'She broke the amulet. Or Adam did. Jane has the pieces, but she doesn't think it works any more.'

'Then it doesn't work. A talisman has only as much power as it is given. You must make her another.'

'Me?'

He nodded. 'Jane doesn't understand what we are dealing with here the way you do. Brid is a powerful, highly trained practitioner of the black arts. They were not black when she learned them, but her perceptions have been blunted and changed by her lust and her fear of the man who pursues her, and she has lost her judgement and honesty. You have to fight her with her own weapons or she will win.'

'What do I do? Phil is frightened she will turn her attention here.' She nodded towards the little girl who was still standing behind him, her eyes fixed on his face.

Meryn reached out a gentle hand to the child. She stepped forward into the circle of his arm and leaned against him trustingly, sucking her thumb.

Meryn nodded thoughtfully. 'He is right to be worried, but I think at the moment there is no need for that worry to be for Beth. Adam has rejected the child, you say? Then she is no danger to Brid. She is not a distraction or a rival for his affections. You will monitor the situation, but I feel at the moment there is nothing to fear.' He looked up at Beth and she returned his smile with a trusting kiss before offering him a bite of her apple.

'So. Should I make a new amulet for Jane, and take it to her?' Liza was concentrating on what he was saying, trying to put out of her mind the thought that Julie and Calum had spent their honeymoon in this house – two weeks out of their so-short lives together. 'How?'

He nodded. 'Take rowan wood, bind it into a cross with red thread and imbue it with protection and power. It is a symbol Brid will recognise and respect.'

'How do I imbue it with power?' Liza shook her head.

He laughed out loud. 'You are wondering with a part of your mind if the old man has finally gone doolally! Are we talking magic and spells? Is he wizard or witch or lunatic?'

'You know I'm not thinking that.' Liza was indignant. 'I wouldn't have come to you for help if I'd wondered that. I just wonder if I can do it. I have no training in these things. I visualise Brid as having learned it all from some great occultist, like a Dennis Wheatley villain. She can turn herself into a cat, Meryn!'

He fixed his gaze on her again unsurprised. 'But there is still no reason to be afraid. Calm, strength and a belief in the power of protection is all that is needed. If Jane is a Christian then her protection will come from Christ. But you will help it. I will tell you what to do.'

She waited until Phil was asleep and snoring before checking on Beth and then creeping downstairs and pulling on her wellington boots which were waiting by the back door. There was a part of her which was embarrassed and sceptical. Another part was afraid. Another felt enormously excited and empowered.

She had located the tree in daylight. It stood a little apart from the others, behind the orchard out in the field above the edge of the drop to the *nant* which raced over the rocks and through the valley towards the meadows which bordered the Wye in the distance. In the silence she could hear the water as it poured into the waterfalls and cascades down in the damp mossy shadows beneath the trees. Up here, in the open, the moonlight was like day. A white frost had already settled over the grass.

Pushing her hands deep into her pockets she felt for her knife. It was one of her grandmother's silver fruit knives, small and brilliantly polished and wickedly sharp and pointed. The perfect knife for performing a magical act. Quietly she pushed open the orchard gate and let herself in under the huge old apple trees, glancing nervously into the black moonshadows. It hadn't occurred to her before that Brid might sense what she was doing, but now, in the dark, in the silence of the night she could feel a small but persistent worm of fear somewhere deep inside her. She glanced behind her at the house. It was in total darkness. Phil had been painting late and had come in, opened himself a can of tomato soup, heated it, drunk it from a mug and gone to bed all within the span of ten minutes. She didn't mind. She knew what it was like when the creative urge was upon one. She resented stopping for a single moment when she was painting, and used to go on for hours after she was too tired almost to hold the brush. She frowned. It was a long time since she had painted anything. Bringing up a small child had seen to that.

Turning her back on the house she looked into the trees again. The night was so still she could have heard a leaf drop, but even the sounds of nature seemed to have died away. There was no breath of wind, no snap of breaking twigs down in the valley as a small animal made its way along the tracks in the undergrowth, no distant hoot of a hunting owl.

Silently she pulled the gate closed behind her and began to make her way through the orchard. Every sense was alert. She could feel the frost as it crisped the moss on the north side of the tree trunks, she could smell the lichen as it combined with the ice crystals, she could hear the tinkling snap of the frozen blades of grass beneath her feet.

Six counties away, in Hertfordshire, Brid, asleep in the curve of Adam's arm, stirred, sensing the moonlight outside the window.

Forcing her fear to the back of her mind Liza walked on steadily, her eyes searching the shadows, alert for any sound. None came. She reached the gate at the far end of the orchard and began to climb over it, feeling the soles of her rubber boots slip on the icy rungs. Jumping into the field she stopped and held her breath. It was empty as far as the eye could see, the sheep already taken down to the shelter of the lower meadows, out of the mountain winds. She could see the rowan tree now, standing on its own, a small graceful shape in the moonlight, the thin branches casting a network of webbed shadow over the pale ground.

'Ask permission,' Meryn had said. 'Explain why you need her help. Make the cutting of the twigs a sacred act.'

Swallowing, she walked across the grass, feeling very exposed without the shelter of the orchard. Out here, on the hillside, she could be seen from fifty miles away across the valley, a tiny dark speck in her green jacket on the frost-white hillside. Behind her a trail of dark footprints marked her passing. In front the ground was sparkling. She glanced up at the moon. It hung low over the hill in front of her, every hill and valley on its surface seemingly visible to the naked eye. She could feel its power.

Ten feet from the tree she stopped. She groped in her pocket for the knife and drew it out. The blade flashed in the moonlight and she thought she felt the tree flinch. 'Explain,' Meryn had said. 'Explain why you want her strength and protection, and ask. If you snap a branch or a twig out of malice or ignorance or even necessity, the tree goes into shock. She withdraws her essence. You want her to allow you to take some of her strength, so you must explain and ask permission. And thank her afterwards.'

Liza stood looking at the tree. She bit her lip, ignoring the sudden treacherous whisper of twentieth-century logic and cynicism which had re-emerged to ask her what she thought she was doing outside at midnight under the full moon talking to a tree.

'Please,' she pushed away her doubts and moved a few steps

closer. 'Please, I need two of your small twigs to make a cross. It's to give protection to my friend. I don't want to hurt you. I need your life force and your strength.' Her voice sounded very thin in the silence of the night. She paused, wondering how she would know if the tree had agreed.

'Please, may I come and take the wood?' She stepped closer, within touching distance now of some of the branches.

There was no response.

Clutching the knife, she became acutely aware that the blade was glittering in the moonlight like a surgeon's scalpel. 'It won't hurt. It's very sharp. Please, can I have a sign?' Meryn hadn't told her to say that, but it seemed right, somehow.

She waited, staring up into the branches.

From the edge of the wood a ghostly shape detached itself from amongst the trees and swooped low across the field towards her. She watched, holding her breath. Part of her was aware that it was a barn owl, but in the deep, inner recesses of her mind, which understood the buried mythic traditions of the soul that are beyond rationality, she knew that this was a sign. The owl settled on the rowan tree and sat looking down at her. It didn't seem afraid. For a moment she didn't dare move, afraid of scaring it away, then slowly she raised the knife. Taking the tip of the branch in her cold fingers she cut two small twigs from it. Slipping the knife into her pocket she groped for the red thread which she had cut earlier from a skein of old embroidery silk inherited, like the knife, from her grandmother. It was difficult to knot the silk, her fingers were numb with cold and she couldn't see properly for all the brightness of the moonlight, but she managed it at last and held up the small cross, aware that the owl was still there, watching her with detached interest and absolutely no fear. 'Thank you,' she said out loud. 'This is to protect and bless my friend Jane, giving her your strength and your love and your safety.' She held it out towards the owl. It didn't move.

Not quite sure what to do next, she reached up and touched the tree. 'I'm grateful,' she said softly. 'Can I come and talk to you again in daylight?' There was no response, and slowly she turned away.

'I don't believe I said that!' The cynical mutter under her breath escaped in spite of herself. Behind her the owl took off on silent wings and skimmed across the field and down the valley. When she turned again, on the edge of the orchard, to look back towards the rowan tree, there was no sign of the bird.

Slipping the cross into her pocket she headed for the gate and the shadow of the apple trees, which were dark after the brilliance of the frosty fields. Suddenly, she felt confident again.

Brid sat up. The curtains were only half drawn and she could see the moon above the dark roof of the house across the road. She frowned. Something had awakened her. There was a feeling of danger in the air – a shiver on the surface of the night. She looked down at Adam. He groaned and turned away, sensing the moonlight behind his closed eyelids and burying his face in the pillow. Slipping from the bed she walked across to the window and stood looking out, her long dark hair clinging round her naked shoulders. She was listening.

Her hand on the cross, Liza walked through the sleeping apple trees, hearing the frost crunch beneath her boots. She was careless now, her attention fixed on the house and the warmth of the kitchen waiting for her. She didn't notice the cat's eyes, staring at her from the shadows, or hear the stealthy tread of its paws.

'Brid, come back to bed.'

Adam's voice, heavy with sleep, reached her as she flexed her claws. She glanced over her shoulder, confused, already sensing the raw power, as yet undirected, coming from the woman's pocket. Spirit of rowan is red and lively; normally she counted it her ally. She could fight it, but already she was feeling uncentred, pulled in two directions, losing focus. In a moment she was gone from the moonlit orchard and back in the bedroom of a quiet, tree-lined city street. Around her the moonlight sang in the darkness and Adam raised himself on his elbow. 'Brid? Come back to bed. You'll catch cold over there. Why have you opened the window?' He sounded querulous and old. For a moment she glanced back over her shoulder towards the ice-bright orchard, then with a shrug she slipped in between the sheets, hearing Adam gasp with pleasure as she pressed her cold body against his warm flesh.

By the gate Liza stopped and looked round. For a fraction of a second she had sensed the movement in the shadows, smelled the feral breath of the hunting cat, and she clutched the cross more tightly and brought it to her breast. 'Go away, Brid,' she muttered under her breath. 'There is no room for you here. Go back to where you came from.'

There was no reply. In Adam's bed Brid flexed her fingers against his chest and he winced as a fine line of blood welled up on the spot above his heart.

'Bitch!' He caught her hand.

She gave a quiet, throaty laugh. She would deal with the woman later.

16

Liza put the cross, carefully wrapped in tissue, in a small box and silently sliding out the top drawer of her dressing table she tucked the box into the back under an unused packet of stockings. Behind her Phil was asleep. He had pulled the blankets and sheets over himself and wrapped them round him in a cocoon. Smiling, she undressed and pulled on her nightshirt, then she walked over to the bed. 'Phil,' she only wanted to wake him enough to be able to extricate some of the blankets. 'Move over. Let me in.'

He groaned and turned over, taking the sheets with him.

'Phil!' She caught the end of a blanket and pulled.

He opened an eye. 'Whatisit?' His voice was almost incoherent with sleep.

'Let me in.'

For a moment she thought he had gone back to sleep, then with another groan he rolled over and made room for her. 'My God woman, you're cold!' He was awake now. 'Where on earth have you been?'

'Dancing under the moon!' She snuggled up against him, grateful for the warmth.

'Wow!' He put his arms round her. 'Then why on earth did you put this dreadful flannel thing on. Come on, off with it!'

'No!' Half laughing, she pulled away. 'Phil, it's late and we're both tired!'

'It's late and we're both wide awake!' He buried his face in her breasts. 'Mmm, you smell all fresh and wild and frosty. Next time you go dancing in the moonlight, call me and we'll both go.'

She lay awake a long time after he had gone back to sleep, her body warm and satisfied as she lay naked under the blankets next to him. From time to time her eyes strayed in the darkness to the black outline of the dressing table where, she could have sworn, a gentle red glow came from the top drawer. Smiling at her own foolishness she let her thoughts stray to Adam and she wondered where he was now, and if he was with Jane or Brid. Somehow she knew it was the latter and she frowned. If it were her husband being seduced by that she-devil she would go in and fight.

The next morning she rang Jane as soon as Phil had disappeared into the studio. Near her Beth was playing with her toy rabbit, intent on stuffing its fat paws into a tiny doll's jumper. In half an hour Liza was going to drive her down the hill to her little play school, then she would go on into Hay to the post office.

The phone rang on and on. Liza frowned. She hung up and went over to the table to finish her cup of coffee. It was early for either of them to have gone out. These days Adam usually left the house just before nine for the five-minute drive to the surgery, and Jane would not go out until she did the shopping much later, if she went out at all. Lately, Liza knew, she had been staying in the house more and more.

Draining her cup she picked up the phone again. She hung on five minutes this time, but still there was no reply. Glancing at her wrist watch she knew she ought to be leaving with Beth. Instead she found the telephone directory and looked up the number of Adam's practice. There the phone was picked up instantly.

'I wonder if I could speak to Dr Craig. It's Liza Stevenson.'

'He's in with a patient, I'm afraid.' The voice was crisp and efficient. 'Would you like to speak to Dr Harding?'

Liza was about to say no when she changed her mind. Seconds later she was connected. 'I am sorry to bother you, Robert, only I haven't been able to get in touch with Jane Craig for several days – there's no reply from home at all, and I was a bit worried. Are things all right there, do you know?'

There was a slight pause. 'Have you not spoken to Adam?'

'He's busy.' She said it more crisply than she intended.

'I see.' He hesitated. 'I believe that Jane came into the office a few days ago, and as far as I know everything was all right then. Adam certainly looks very tired. I think he is under a great deal of strain, to be honest.' They had known each other on and off over the years, well enough for him to confide in her, and after Julie and Calum had died Robert had been a tower of strength to both families. Even so, he was guarded.

She had no such reservations. 'There is something wrong, Robert. Terribly wrong. Will you do me a great favour? Will you check on

Jane today sometime – even if it's over the phone. I'm really worried about her.' She hesitated. 'And Robert, please, don't tell Adam I rang.'

Jane rang her at lunchtime. 'I've had Robert Harding on the phone.' She sounded depressed, her normally attractive voice heavy and dull. 'He said you were worried.'

'I couldn't get an answer from the phone.'

'I had taken a sleeping pill. I can't sleep these days. Robert got them for me.'

'He didn't say.'

'No, of course he didn't. I'm his patient.' She gave a low ironic laugh. 'As the cause of my problems is my husband, he probably thought he'd better honour patient confidentiality.' She sighed. 'Don't worry about me, Liza.'

'You know I do. Listen.' Liza paused. 'Is anyone there with you?'

'No. Who would be?' There was a moment of silence. 'Oh, the cat woman. No, she's never here when Adam's at work. I expect she goes back to whatever swamp she crawls out of to rest until the sun goes down.'

'Oh, Jane.' Liza frowned. 'Listen, I've put something in the post for you. Another amulet. One I made specially. I went to see Meryn. He's back, and he knows all the recent developments. He said that if I did this for you it will work. She won't be able to touch you. You must keep it with you all the time. All the time, Jane. And you must protect yourself. Do you remember, how we showed you before?'

'It doesn't work though, does it? What is the point of me being protected if she can walk off with my husband?'

'We'll work on Adam next.' Liza frowned in exasperation. 'Come on, Jane. You've got to help. Between us we can get rid of her, I'm sure we can. Listen, will you come down here, soon? Beth wants to see her Granny Jane.'

There was a sob from the other end of the line. 'I want to, Liza. But I can't leave him. She's sapping his life blood. He's shrivelling away before my eyes, and he won't listen to me. I can't talk to him any more.'

'Then don't try.'

'He might listen to you, Liza. He's always respected you.' There was a long silence.

'You know he doesn't want to see me, Jane. He made it quite clear the last time I visited.'

'I think he'd see you. Without Beth. It hurts him to think about Beth. He remembers Calum as a little boy and he can't cope with the idea of him having been a father himself. Please, Liza. Will you come?'

Liza chewed her lip. 'I'll talk it over with Phil. He's working at the moment, and he might not want to be left with Beth.' Her skin crawled at the idea of going back to that cold, unwelcoming house with its locked doors and hidden grief, and at the thought of crossing swords with Brid.

'Two days. That's all I can spare.' Phil shook his head. 'And only if you absolutely insist. I don't like the thought of you going to that mad house one bit.'

'Nor do I, but what else can I do? I've got to help them.' She was pushing sweaters into her overnight bag. 'You are sure you'll cope without me?'

He grinned suddenly. 'Of course we will, bossy boots. Beth can look after me. If we get snowed up we'll look after each other and go tobogganing on a tea tray every day. But I can't spare more than that, Liza.' He was serious suddenly as he pulled her to him and kissed her. 'I've got to work now that my famous rich wife has decided to take a sabbatical from her equally famous clients and wear an apron instead. My paintings don't rake in the lolly like yours, my love.'

She snuggled against him for a moment. 'Maybe not, but they are a million times better. The awful part about portrait painting is that one always wonders how much the subject is paying for his or her own vanity rather than one's skill!'

'Modesty as well. What more could a man ask?' He dropped another kiss on her head. 'Take care, my love, won't you?' He couldn't hide the worry in his voice.

'Of course I will. Promise.'

She thought about that promise again and again as she drove east. She had called in at Meryn's cottage on her way back towards Hay, but he had been out and as she scanned the hillside behind his garden there had been no sign of him. Not seeing him filled her with panic. She had wanted his advice and his blessing. Without it she felt exposed.

This time there was no car outside the house in St Albans as she turned into the quiet road. The front garden was neat once more, the house appeared quite normal, the curtains all open, the windows catching in the fitful winter sunlight. Ringing the doorbell she waited, her shoulders hunched against the brisk easterly wind.

There was no reply. Ringing again she frowned and looked at

her watch. Jane knew she was coming, and she was just about on time. Someone – Jane – should have been there to meet her. Ringing it a third time she was about to walk round when, stepping back and looking up to survey the front of the house, she caught sight of a face at an upstairs window.

'Jane!' She waved her hand. 'Let me in.'

The face stared down at her for a minute, then abruptly it disappeared from view. Liza turned back to the door.

'I'm sorry, I was asleep.' Jane was still in her dressing gown, her hair tousled and unwashed, her face crumpled.

Liza frowned. 'Well, at least you heard me in the end.' She spoke more harshly than she meant to, but the sight of Jane's despair repelled her. 'Come on, let's get you up and dressed, then you can make me a cup of coffee.' She suspected Jane's need was greater than her own, but at least it was a reason for Jane to stir herself. Half an hour later they were sitting in the study, the French windows open onto the small terrace, allowing the fresh wind to stir the curtains and clear the stale cigarette smoke from the room. 'I'm sorry, the place is a mess.' Jane seemed half asleep still in spite of the large mug of black coffee in her hand. Under her sweater she was wearing the rowan cross, suspended on a fine gold chain around her neck.

'Don't you have a cleaner any more?' Liza was looking round the room. Even Adam's desk had a layer of dust over it.

Jane shrugged and shook her head. 'I didn't bother after Mrs Freeling left. No cleaner would stay after the murder, and now Calum's gone . . .' Her voice trailed away uncertainly.

'You decided to stay in this house, Jane.' Liza was bracing. 'Once that decision was made surely you decided to make the best of it. You can't "never clean again" because of what happened, Janie.'

'I know.' Jane huddled her hands round the mug, her shoulders slumped. 'It's all my fault and I have done the garden.'

'It is not your fault at all!' Liza's indignation was strenuous. 'For God's sake! Nothing that has happened here has been your fault.'

'Adam says it has. If I hadn't spoiled Calum so much –'

'Oh no! I'm not wearing that. The bastard! Where is Adam?'

'At work.'

'And how is he managing to work in this state? He can't be doing his patients any good.'

'His patients all adore him whatever he does.' She shrugged.

'They won't if he kills them.' Liza was swiftly running out of patience. 'Come on, Jane, snap out of it. Let's try and clean this place up and get a meal ready for Adam when he comes home. Then I can talk to him once he's eaten.' She paused. 'I take it Madam isn't here during the day?'

Jane shook her head. 'She disappears when he leaves.'

'Disappears?'

'I've never seen her go out of the door.' Jane gave a hard brittle laugh. 'I expect she dematerialises, or flies up the chimney on her broomstick. But she'll be here when Adam gets back. Waiting for him up there in the bedroom.' She shuddered.

Liza studied her face, her impatience giving way to sympathy. She couldn't imagine how it must feel to be in Jane's position – to lose a husband to another woman was one thing, to lose him to a ghost was quite another. If Brid was a ghost. She shook her head in despair and then putting down her mug she stood up. 'Come on. Let's set to and get the house straight.'

'In two hours?' Jane hadn't moved.

'In two hours we can do an awful lot.'

By the time Adam put his key into the front door lock the sitting room was vacuumed and tidied, there were fresh flowers on the table, and Liza had a beef casserole simmering on the cooker. She had even put on a record of one of Adam's favourite pieces, the Elgar violin concerto. Jane was changed, her hair washed and brushed, her face made up.

The two women were in the sitting room when they heard the front door open. Liza smiled encouragingly at Jane and nodded.

'Adam,' Jane called. Her voice was steady. 'Come in and have a sherry. We have a visitor.'

Adam appeared in the doorway, his black leather bag still in his hand. At the sight of Liza his face darkened. 'I don't remember asking you to come.' He put the case down with a thud.

'No.' Liza stepped in before Jane could say anything. She moved across to him and gave him a kiss on the cheek, shocked by how tired and emaciated he looked. 'I asked myself as I had to be over this way. I wanted to see you both.'

'And it didn't occur to you that we might not want to see you?' He threw himself down on the sofa and accepted the glass of sherry that Jane handed to him.

'No, it didn't. Neither did it occur to me that you might have become surly, rude and inhospitable!' she retorted sharply. 'Never mind, your wife more than makes up for your shortcomings.'

'Liza has cooked us supper,' Jane put in defensively 'It's really kind of her after her long drive.'

'She'd have to cook it if she's hungry. I don't remember you cooking lately.' He took a large gulp of sherry, emptying the tiny glass. Standing up he went over and picking up the decanter he poured himself a second dose.

'I had no one to cook for,' Jane snapped back. 'You were too busy upstairs to come down and eat.'

'Let's not argue!' Liza interposed herself between them. 'Why don't we just have a nice quiet meal?' She glanced at Jane, aware that she was listening suddenly, her head cocked sideways as though she could hear something upstairs. Clutching her glass a little more tightly Liza smiled determinedly at Adam. 'Come on, let's go into the kitchen. The stew must be cooked by now.'

'I'll go upstairs and wash.' Adam put his glass down.

'No!' Jane's voice rose into a cry of anguish. 'Don't go upstairs.' She looked from him to Liza and back. 'The meal will spoil,' she finished lamely, 'and that would be such a shame,' she added.

There was a moment's electric silence, then Adam shrugged. 'All right. Let's eat straightaway.' He stalked ahead of them out of the room and across the hall without so much as glancing at the staircase. Jane looked up as she followed him and so did Liza. Was there a flicker of movement up there? She didn't know, but she felt an unpleasant shiver play across her shoulders as she glanced up towards the darkened landing.

They sat down and Jane lifted the lid from the casserole, releasing a waft of spicy steam. 'That smells wonderful.' She smiled at Liza gratefully. 'Doesn't it, Adam?'

Adam nodded. He rested his elbows on the table and propped his head in his hands. His exhaustion was unmistakable.

Jane ladled a helping of meat and carrots and mushrooms in rich gravy and a dollop of mashed potatoes onto a plate and pushed it in front of him. 'That should make you feel better,' she said quietly. 'It will make a new man of you.'

'Something you no doubt profoundly wish would happen.' Adam leaned back in his chair.

'That is not what she meant and you know it!' Liza put in firmly. 'Just eat, you two. Don't waste all my efforts at cooking you a nice meal.' She took a mouthful of stew herself and sat solemnly chewing, her eyes on her plate. For a moment she thought Adam was going to stand up and go without even sampling the food, but at last he picked up his fork. He toyed with the potato and beef for a few minutes and at last lifted a forkful to his mouth. Liza sighed with relief. He seemed to enjoy it, and began to chew on a second.

The crash from upstairs had them all staring at the ceiling.

'Don't go!' Jane's fork clattered to her plate. 'Please, Adam, don't go up.'

He frowned, staring at the ceiling. 'Something must have fallen over . . .'

'It doesn't matter, Adam. Go on eating.' Liza smiled at him as persuasively as she knew how. She hoped neither of them could see how her skin was crawling with fear. Somehow she forced herself to take another mouthful. 'One always gets strange noises in old houses, what with beams expanding and contracting.'

'This isn't an old house.' Jane's voice was strangely dull again. She had put down her knife and fork. Liza could see her hands were shaking.

A-dam!

The distant cry was audible to all three of them. Jane put her hands to her ears. 'Don't go. Please, don't go.' Her plea came out as a sob, but Adam was already pushing back his chair.

'Adam!' Liza stood up and bent over him. 'Don't even think about going up there! If you do, you're a fool!'

'Get out of the way, Liza.' He pushed her aside and stood up.

'Adam, think what you're doing!' She caught his arm. 'Protect yourself, fight it, remember what she is!'

'And what is she?' He rounded on her abruptly and she took a step back, astonished at his sudden viciousness. 'I'll tell you what she is. A beautiful, warm, loving person, who cares about me deeply, who sympathises because I've lost my only son, who under-stands what I've been through when other people only think about themselves! That's what she is!'

'Adam, that's not fair!' Jane cried. 'You know it's not.'

'And what is more it isn't true,' Liza put in. 'She isn't even real, Adam!'

'No?' He gave a strange half-smile. 'She feels real, believe me; she acts real, she sounds real.'

'So, if she's real, why doesn't she come downstairs and join us for supper in a civilised fashion?' Liza tried to steady her voice. She stepped away from Adam. 'Go on, call her. Tell her to come and eat with us.'

'Don't be stupid.'

'Why is it stupid? I can't see any reason why she can't do it.' She was standing between him and the door. 'Go on, give her a shout.' She raised her chin defiantly. 'After all, we all know her, don't we?'

He stepped away from the table. 'Please move out of my way, Liza.'

'Adam!' Jane ran to him and caught his arm.

He shook her off. 'Believe me, you don't want her to come down here.'

'But we do, Adam.' Liza moved in front of him again. 'We want to see her. We want to speak to her. We want to ask her what it is she's doing here, breaking up a family home! We want to ask her,' she narrowed her eyes, 'what she was doing in the middle of the road in the rain in front of the car containing my daughter and your son!'

'No!' Adam screamed at her. 'No, that's not true. You stupid, stupid, ignorant woman! That was not Brid!'

'No?' She stood her ground. 'Then ask her!'

'I don't have to ask her. She would never do anything to hurt me. She is good and beautiful and kind.'

'Rubbish! She's a harpy. No, Adam, stay here!' She caught at him again as he started to move. 'Think! For God's sake, wake up!'

He pushed her out of his way. 'Go home, Liza. You are not welcome here!' Striding towards the door he pulled it open. 'You are interfering in things you don't understand.' Stepping into the hall he slammed the door behind him and they heard his footsteps running up the stairs.

Jane threw herself back into her chair and burst into tears. 'You see! What am I to do? She's bewitched him.'

'I'm going after him.'

'No!' Jane's voice rose to a shriek. 'You can't do that! She's dangerous, Liza. She's killed people.'

'She won't kill me!' Liza's temper was rapidly reaching boiling point. 'You stay here!'

Dragging open the door without giving herself time to think she raced up the stairs after Adam and along the landing to the spare room. She expected him to have locked himself in, but as she threw herself at the handle the door flew open easily. Adam was standing by the bed, his shirt already half off, with Brid, completely unclothed, clinging round his neck. They both looked round as Liza stopped in the doorway. Brid smiled. She made no effort to cover herself, nor did she move away from Adam.

'Out!' Adam put his hands on Brid's buttocks and pulled her against him. He turned away from Liza. 'Go on, out, or have you become a voyeur in your old age?' His words were deliberately cruel. He nuzzled against Brid's hair, holding her closer.

308

'You stupid idiot!' Liza couldn't believe her eyes. 'Have you no shame? No sense?'

'None.' He was smiling down into Brid's eyes, and Liza could swear she heard her purring like a satisfied cat.

'Poor Jane.' The disgust in Liza's voice was undiluted.

'Yes, poor Jane. Leave her alone, Liza.' He wasn't even looking at her, his face still buried in the lustrous long hair.

Suddenly Liza couldn't bear it any more. She turned and ran out of the room, slamming the door as hard as she could behind her. Hurling herself across the landing she ran into the bathroom. She had barely reached it before she was violently sick.

Running the cold tap she splashed water over her face and hands. She was shaking like a leaf. 'Liza?' She could hear Jane's voice, timidly calling from the bottom of the stairs. 'Liza, are you all right?'

'I'm all right.' Somehow she forced herself to answer. 'I'm coming.' Blowing her nose on a piece of lavatory paper she took a deep breath and opened the door. There was silence from the spare room. Running down the stairs she passed Jane in the hall and went back into the kitchen. 'Please, can you make me some coffee?' She flung herself down on a chair.

'What happened?' Jane's face was white but her hands were steady as she reached for the kettle and filled it under the tap.

'She's in there with him.'

'We knew that.' Jane's voice was completely flat.

'But with him. Really with him.' Liza looked up and pushed her hair back from her forehead. 'I'm sorry, Jane. I didn't realise. I thought . . .' She broke off and shook her head. 'I don't know what I thought.'

'They're having sex,' Jane said unemotionally. 'I hear them every night. Why do you think I need sleeping pills? He can't keep his hands off her. He is completely obsessed. He doesn't eat. He doesn't sleep much, I shouldn't think.' She gave a bitter laugh. 'He just comes in and goes upstairs and screws. And Robert Harding asks me what is wrong. With me.'

'Let's go. Now. Come back to Pen-y-Ffordd. You can't stay here.'

'I have to stay here. This is my home. There's nowhere else. Since Mummy moved into the sheltered housing, I can't go to her.'

'And you wouldn't want to anyway! But this isn't a home, Jane. It is a prison. And you know you will always have a home with us. Always. Leave him. For goodness' sake, how can you let him humiliate you like this?' She stood up. 'Go on, get some things. We'll leave now. I'll go up and get my bag.'

Jane shook her head. 'I haven't enough energy to fight it any more, Liza.'

'No, but I have. I'm not leaving without you.' She could feel her rage and indignation and her own humiliation bubbling up inside her. Turning she ran back into the hall and took the stairs two at a time.

Jane had put her in Calum's old bedroom as the spare room was occupied and she threw open the door, feeling the same pang of terrible sorrow and regret she had felt the first time she went in there. His things were still so very much a part of him. Jane had moved nothing. Her case was lying on the bed. She had not unpacked. Scooping up her coat she turned to the door. Adam was standing there, wearing a dressing gown. His hair was ruffled on end and his face was a picture of fury.

'What exactly are you doing in here?'

'Collecting my things. I'm leaving.'

'You had no business in this room.'

'Well, as you can see, I'm not staying.'

'You killed my son.'

'Crap! If anyone killed him, it was Brid! Ask her. Go on, ask her what she did.'

'Don't say such a thing!' His face was contorted with rage. 'Get out of my house, Liza, and don't ever come back here. Don't dare to set foot in my son's room again. You and your daughter, you murdered him. Without you, he would still be alive!'

'You know that's not true, Adam,' she shouted. 'Calum loved Julie. I lost her too, you know. Beth lost her parents! Can't you understand what happened? It was no one's fault except the woman who stepped out in front of them on that wet road. It was Brid's doing, and yet you go on allowing her to come here to seduce you! Get rid of her, Adam. Send her away. She's evil. She's a monster.'

A shadow moved behind Adam on the landing. Liza stepped back. 'Don't let her come near me, Adam. I won't be responsible for what I might do.' She had already noticed the kukri on Calum's bedroom wall, a much-loved trophy from a school adventure trip to India. In two steps she was beside it and had the handle in her hand. She turned, brandishing the razor-sharp blade in front of her. 'Get her out of here, Adam.'

The animal snarl from the shadows was vicious. Adam smiled. 'Don't be a fool, Liza. You can't kill her. Jane tried it and it didn't work.'

'It'll work for me.' She waved the knife menacingly in front of her. 'Order her off.'

She couldn't see her, but she could smell the animal fear and lust in the air, and suddenly she could hear it again, a low growl from the doorway behind Adam.

'You go, Liza.' Adam did not seem to be reacting naturally. She wondered for a moment if he were sleep-walking – or in some sort of hypnotic trance. 'We don't want you here.'

'Adam!' Her voice was harsh. 'It's me you're talking to. Liza!'

'I know who I'm talking to.' Again he gave a strange smile. 'An intruder. We don't want you here. Can't you see?' He beckoned behind him and Brid stepped forward into the circle of his arm, tall, slim, beautiful, her dark hair over her shoulders, her body wrapped in a pale sheet.

Her steady grey eyes met Liza's defiantly. 'Why do you want to take A-dam away from me?' Her voice was low and musical. 'You have another man now.' She rested her head for a moment against Adam's shoulder. 'I am the one he has always loved.'

'No, Brid.' Liza steadied her voice with difficulty. 'You are not the one he loves. He loves his wife. He loved his son. What did you do to his son, Brid?'

'Liza!' Adam's furious voice cut her short.

'No, let her answer, Adam. What did you do to his son?'

'A-dam has no son. He does not love anyone but me.'

'He did have, though. Don't you remember? A son, and a daughter-in-law and a little baby granddaughter, in a car –'

'I do not remember. It is not important.' Brid had begun to move her lips gently, pressing against him seductively. She reached up and touched his face. 'Make her go away, A-dam.'

'Please, Liza.' Adam's voice was very quiet.

'If you don't go away and leave us, I will take away your man.' Brid's eyes narrowed, cat-like, as she looked at Liza from the security of Adam's arms. She had sensed the rowan cross as soon as Jane put it on. It circled the woman with fire and kept her safe, and this woman too had the strength of the light wrapped around her. But she was vulnerable in other ways. 'You try and take Adam away from me and I take your Phil away from you.'

Liza went cold. The circle of her protection wavered. 'Don't you threaten me.' She paused. 'How do you know my husband's name?'

'I know everything.' She was holding Liza's gaze relentlessly, never blinking. 'Go.'

'I'm not going without Adam. I want him to come with me.'

'You are a fool, then.' Brid looked her up and down disdainfully. 'And I will curse you. I will make you suffer. I will not let you take my A-dam.'

'Liza, I warned you!' Adam tightened his arms round Brid's shoulders. 'Don't antagonise her any more!'

'Then for God's sake, come to your senses!'

Brid shook her head. 'She will not listen to you, my A-dam.' She raised her hand and pointed at Liza. 'I curse you, A-dam's woman. I curse you to lose the man you love as you would curse me to lose mine.'

Liza shrank back. She could feel cold, poisonous air suddenly round her, swirling outside her imagined shield. 'All right. I'll go. But I'm not coming out of here until you move.' To her horror she found she was shaking like a leaf. She glared at Adam, who was still standing in the doorway. 'Go on, take her back into your room and I'll go.' Desperately she tried to straighten her shoulders. Don't let her see the fear. Don't let her realise how badly she had been frightened.

Brid was smiling, a long, slow, supercilious smile. Without seeming to move she left Adam's arms and crossed the hallway. 'Come, A-dam.'

Adam followed Brid to the door of the spare room. There he turned. 'Don't ever come back.'

'I won't. So she can take away her curse!' Liza's mouth had gone dry.

Brid smiled over her shoulder. 'It is too late. The curse will stay.'

'Adam . . .' But Liza's call fell on deaf ears. Adam had gone.

She stood for a moment after he had closed the door, unable to move. She was literally frozen to the spot. 'May God protect you, Adam,' she whispered. 'God protect us all.'

'I can't leave him.' Jane shook her head in defeat. 'Something awful will happen if I go.'

'Something awful will happen if you stay.' Liza already had her bag over her shoulder. 'I'll wait for you in the car.' She walked to the door. 'I mean it, Jane. I'm not staying in this house a moment longer. I'll give you ten minutes.'

Outside it was already dark. She walked down the short drive, past Adam's car and out of the gate. There, in the quiet street, she unlocked the old Triumph and, throwing her bag onto the back seat, she climbed in. She was still shaking. Glancing at her wrist watch she noted the time.

312

The curtains in the upstairs window were not quite drawn and she could see the light shining out through the narrow crack in the pale-blue chintz. There was no sign of movement. She glanced at her watch again. Only two minutes had passed. She wanted to go. She wanted to be at home with Phil and Beth, far away from this horrible house with its evil occupant. One minute more. Oh God, keep them safe. Don't let anything happen to Phil or Beth.

Come on, Jane. Come on.

She closed her eyes and began to count softly under her breath. After twenty-five she stopped and opened her eyes again. She glanced up at the window with the blue curtains. It had gone dark.

Jane. Where are you?

She was biting her lip. Should she get out and have one more go at persuading her? But she had tried. Surely she had tried.

Another five minutes had passed. Only two to go. She put her hand on the ignition key, her eyes on her watch seeing each second tick by on the luminous dial.

The front door remained firmly closed. She wasn't coming. With a sigh Liza started the engine.

Two stops for black coffee at lorry drivers' cafés and she managed to do the drive in under four hours. Turning up the long narrow lane off the Talgarth road she slowed the car, engaged first gear and put it at the pitch which led up to the farm. To her surprise the lights were all on. With an uncomfortable feeling of foreboding she pulled into the yard, switched off the engine and sat still for a minute, listening to it ticking in the cold air; then, stiff and exhausted, she got out and made her way to the house.

The kitchen door opened and a woman appeared, her anxious face clearly illuminated in the yard light.

'Jenny? What are you doing here?' Liza felt a cold lurch of terror deep in her stomach at the sight of her neighbour. 'Where's Phil?'

Jenny shrugged. 'I hoped that you were him. He went out a couple of hours ago. There was a phone call from Harry Evans up at Bryn Glas. He said there were some school children lost up on the mountain. They were getting a search party together. Phil rang me to come and sit with Beth and he went.' She shrugged. 'I rang Eleri an hour ago to see if there was any news and she said she didn't know anything about any children and Harry was asleep in bed. Oh, Liza, love, I didn't know what to make of it. I don't know if it was some kind of practical joke, or what. I didn't know what to do. I couldn't leave Beth. I didn't know whether I should ring the police?'

Liza stood where she was. Her whole body had gone completely numb. She stared out into the darkness behind the barns at the great black shoulder of the mountain lying asleep under the stars.

Brid.

'Shall I ring the police, or what?' She realised suddenly that Jenny was still talking.

'I don't know. Yes, I suppose so.' Panic was sweeping over her in waves. 'I'll come in and have a word with Eleri myself. When did Phil get the phone call?'

She was shaking so much she could scarcely lift the phone. This time it was Harry who answered. 'Strange kind of a joke, Liza. I wonder if he misheard, or dreamed it or something?' The deep voice was reassuring. 'Look, if he turns up here I'll ring you. Perhaps you'd better have a word with the police, just in case he's gone off the road. It's icy up here. Don't worry, he'll turn up.'

The police were polite, reassuring and not inclined to take action for the time being. Liza slammed down the phone. 'They are not going to do anything. They don't care. He's not been gone long enough, apparently. How long do you have to be?' She turned towards the door. 'Please, Jenny, will you stay a bit longer? I'm going up there myself.'

'Are you sure? Do you want me to call Ken?'

'No.' Liza shook her head, pulling on her rubber boots and reaching for a jacket and scarf. 'No, I'll find him. He can only have gone up on the mountain road. He might have gone to Meryn or he might have driven on over the pass into Hay.' Or he might have skidded and come off the road at any one of a number of places on the single track, some of which had sheer drops on one side.

The car was still warm and welcoming. Slamming the door she gunned the engine and backed round, nosing out onto the lane again and turning up the hill.

Meryn's house was deserted. She stood in the garden outside, staring in dismay at the lean-to shed where he kept his car. It was empty. The chimney was cold and the living room, when she peered through the windows with their open curtains, had a deserted, unlived-in air.

'Oh Meryn!' Standing outside she burst into tears like a disappointed child. She had been relying on him, she realised suddenly, for comfort and advice and strength.

'Phil!' Her shout seemed to echo across vast distances under the stars and lose itself on the side of the mountain. There was no reply.

She drove slowly, the main beam of her headlights picking up the twists and turns in the road. Ice sparkled over the gravelled tarmac, and she realised that in places where the skim of tar had been renewed and the ice was glassy smooth she could see the faint traces of another car ahead of her. 'Phil?' She braked a little, feeling the wheels slide on a corner as the headlights picked up the huddled shapes of some dozen wild ponies, standing with their backs to the wind, their long shaggy coats covered in mud as they watched her pass with uncurious eyes.

The car engine laboured and she glanced in sudden terror at the petrol gauge. It showed the tank still a quarter full. She was nearing the top of the pass. Once there she could pull off onto a broad lay-by and view the countryside in the moonlight.

Standing beside the car she could see the road ahead, a silver ribbon running up and down along the side of the hill almost as far as the eye could see, only here and there disappearing into a dip or behind an outcrop of rock. Forcing herself to be calm she let her eye travel slowly and carefully over each inch of the distant view, cursing herself for not bringing the binoculars from the peg by the back door.

It was almost as light as day up here. Behind her, in the fold of the valley where the trees grew thick on either side of the brook, it was pitch dark. Somewhere down there, behind her, she could hear an owl calling, and in the distance the occasional conversational bleat from a sheep. They were huddled now down on the lower fields of the farm at the bottom of the mountain, but the sound carried up onto the hills where the summer grazing led up to the foot of the high black cliffs which were the haunt of buzzard and kite.

The low growl from somewhere in the shadows of the rocks at the edge of the lay-by made her spin round, her eyes desperately trying to penetrate the darkness. Her heart was thumping audibly beneath her ribs. She turned a full circle trying to pinpoint the spot from which the sound had come, but she could hear nothing now in the immensity of the silence. Carefully she edged back towards the open door of the car and then in an instant she saw it. The cat was standing there in front of her – large, tabby markings, its ears set low and flat on the broad sweep of its forehead, its eyes glowing almost red in the moonlight, its lips curled back to reveal its teeth. Liza turned and dived into the car, slamming the lock down as hard as she could. Breathing hard she looked in the mirror, then craned round to see where it was. It was no longer there, but she thought she saw, just for a second, the figure of a woman standing in the shadow of the rocks.

'You bitch!'

Starting the engine, Liza manoeuvred the car round with shaking hands until the headlights were shining full on the spot where she had seen the figure. There was nothing there but a small stunted thorn tree, its trunk twisted and bent by the wind.

She drove slowly right across the shoulder of the hill where the road clung to the solid ground between soft mountain mires with ice-rimmed waterholes and gorse-strewn grass, then followed it carefully, winding downwards towards the treeline. There, almost by the cattle grid, she saw the skid marks leading off the road and over into a small ravine. Pulling the car up she muttered a breathless prayer before forcing herself to open the door and climb out.

The mountainside remained silent.

Slipping and sliding she ran across the icy road onto the grass and began to make her way down the almost vertical hillside to where a small brook burbled along towards the forestry.

Phil's old Land-Rover had pitched bonnet first into the brook. At first she hadn't recognised it, a patch of darker shadow in the deep shadows of the small valley. Then she saw the familiar outline of the vehicle, unfamiliar in its position.

'Phil?' Her voice sounded so small in the echoing quiet of the mountains. 'Phil, are you all right?'

She knew he wasn't. She had known from the moment she had set out from the house half an hour before, but still she had hoped. Still she fought the door open and pulled at his hand; still she felt for a pulse in the ice-cold wrist; tried to ease the angle of the bruised, battered face. Still she fetched a blanket and wrapped it around him as tenderly as if he had been a sleeping child. Then she sat down on the frozen grass beside the Land-Rover and cried.

She was discovered two hours later by a farmer driving up towards Capel-y-fin in the early hours of the morning after a drinking session with a friend at Glasbury. He was brought to a halt by Liza's car standing in the middle of the road, the driver's door still open, the lights by now dim.

Only faintly aware that in her dreams she had slid from Adam's warm bed and walked for a while on a cold, frost-covered mountain, Brid pressed her icy body against his warm one and heard his sharp, shocked intake of breath as one of pleasure. Closing her eyes she allowed herself to become one with her happiness, breathing in the scent of his skin, tasting its salt with the tip of her tongue. He groaned in his sleep and turned away from her abruptly, reaching instead for his pillow and dragging it under his head. She sat up, angry at his rejection, her eyes narrowing in the dark. She fed on his strength; if he withheld it she could not stay with him. Without him she was lost. She glanced round into the darkness and at once sensed the prowling shadows. They were so close. Broichan had not given up. He was waiting for her at the boundaries of time.

Neither Jane nor Adam came to the funeral. On the phone when Liza had rung them Jane was sympathetic but distant.

Adam would not speak to her at all.

17

T he pain of the loss did not lessen but as time passed it grew more bearable. No one ever questioned Phil's skid on the ice and Liza had no proof – and never would have – that a beautiful young woman from a distant age had appeared on the road in front of him, just as she had in front of the car that carried Julie and Calum – the arbitrary, vicious act of an obsessed and violent spirit lost somehow in the corridors of time.

Those first years after Phil's death were unbelievably busy. She had to start work almost at once – neither of them had had the temperament or the inclination to save. Phil had been the one earning the money while she brought up Beth. That had been the agreement, and she had been surprised at how easily she had been able to put her career on hold. She was equally surprised at how relieved she was to have to start painting again – it helped to distract her from her loss – and how easily the commissions began to pour in. It was difficult to balance the needs of a lively youngster with the peace and space she needed to work, but she had managed it with the help of kind neighbours and tolerant sitters.

Beth's beauty as a small child and her sunny temperament had helped. As had the ease with which she had fitted into the way of life which evolved round them, the startling peace and silence of the Welsh countryside alternating with glamorous and bustling visits around Europe as Liza's already brilliant reputation flourished.

It had been a lonely life, though. At first Liza did not know how she would survive without Phil. Every corner of the house seemed empty without him, every action she performed seemed meaningless. Without the small girl to look after she would have lost the will to live. But Beth was there for her all the time, the small arms creeping round her neck, the comforting kisses, the first lisped words which, Liza guiltily remembered seemed to have been, 'Don't cry, Granny Liza,' as the little fingers wiped away her tears.

Meryn had been there too. For the first time ever he came down the hill and she found him one day sitting in her kitchen. His philosophy was simple. Phil had gone nowhere. He was still there with them, watching over them, expecting them to show him they could cope. He taught Liza how to talk to Phil, how to ask his advice and listen deep inside herself for his answers. He taught her that Phil would not want her to waste her life in tears, or let Beth's childhood be full of unhappy memories. And he taught her at last to let Phil go, to allow him to move on so that his memory no longer filled the house, to visit the grave next to those of their daughter and her husband on the sun-warmed hillside with joy, not sadness, not every week but occasionally when there was a special memory she wanted to share. He also taught her to ring-fence their lives against Brid. There would be no more visitations at the farm from wildcats or from vengeful, jealous spirits. Then when he felt she was strong enough again to stand on her own he came less and less to the farm and, one day, when she turned off the lane to his cottage, she found him gone, the chimney cold, and realised that once more he had left her to manage alone.

There were even, in the end, other men over the years. Not many and not seriously, except for one, an Italian count, an author, who lived in an ancient, half-ruined castle in the hills behind Fiesole whose portrait she had painted one glorious, never-to-be-forgotten summer. She had come near to marrying him but even with him, something held her back. It was not that her feelings were not strong enough. Without any sense of disloyalty to Phil she had allowed herself to adore him and would happily have spent the rest of her days at his side, but some inner sense of preservation stopped her. She did not want, now, to belong to someone as Michele would want her to belong to him. She was her own person. And she was her art. They were too independent and too precious and he had not understood. It was a long time now since she had been to the beautiful castello amongst the olive trees.

From the very beginning Beth went with her on her painting trips, staying in hotel rooms, lying by swimming pools, whilst Liza sat in front of her easel with her latest celebrity sitter. If they stayed in the sitter's house, as they had with Michele, that was better. It was more fun and the child had more freedom to wander around. From very young she had got into the habit of taking her own sketch pad and her colouring chalks. Later she had graduated to paints, but she never did portraits. That was Liza's department. Instead she had concentrated on landscape, studying the differences of the places they went: the South of France, Italy, Switzerland. As the years went by, book after book of neat, meticulous sketches piled up at home in her small bedroom at the farm. She did O Level art, then A Level, then went to St Martin's, and once or twice a year she and Liza met up with Granny Jane, who seemed twenty years older than Liza who was technically her granny too, although she always thought of her now just as Liza, and sometimes, secretly, in her innermost fantasies, as her mother.

She knew she had a grandfather who was a doctor in St Albans, but he was never mentioned by either woman when they were together, and when she asked Liza about him she was greeted with a shrug and a look of intense sadness which put her off any further enquiries. She sort of knew there was Another Woman. It sounded Victorian and romantic and very sad, and it accounted for Granny Jane's white hair and wrinkled, sunken face, but Liza never talked about her, which was strange because in every other department Liza was very modern and broad-minded and you could talk to her about anything. And considering there were so many vital gaps in Beth's life – her parents, Grandfather Phil whom she didn't really remember apart from a pair of huge huggy arms – she didn't think one could afford to waste a perfectly serviceable grandfather. She was intrigued.

The last time the three women had met was at Christmas, when Liza had delivered a painting to a flat in Eaton Terrace. She and Beth had arranged to meet Jane at Harvey Nichols and the three of them ensconced themselves at a table near the window in the restaurant. Liza stared at Jane for a moment, unable to hide her shock at how the other woman had aged. She said nothing until Beth had disappeared to find the loo, then she reached across the table and touched Jane's hand.

'Why do you stay after all this time?'

Jane shrugged. 'Someone has to look after him. He drinks, you know.'

Horrified, Liza stared at her. 'Adam?'

'Who else? She has sucked him dry. There is nothing left. He works one day a week, and that is only because Robert can't think of a way of getting rid of him. He's only got to make one more mistake and he's out. They've got another partner now, so he wouldn't be missed.'

'Oh, Jane. What a mess.' Liza's eyes filled with tears. 'When I look back he had so much promise. So much enthusiasm.'

Jane nodded. 'I'm winning, you know. Just by being there.' She gave a strange smile. 'She can't stand me being in the house. I still have the rowan cross, that's probably why I'm still alive! She can't understand why I am still there. She tried to kill me again the other day.'

Liza stared at her in horror. 'What happened?' she breathed.

Jane shrugged almost nonchalantly. 'I'm always careful. I know what she's like. I don't turn my back. Usually she's not there when Adam's out. The day he goes to the surgery I can go upstairs. I clean their room. It's pitiful. An old man's room. I was carrying the Hoover downstairs and she pushed me. I saw her out of the corner of my eye. She hasn't changed, you know. Still all that long hair which keeps him so besotted. I can't think what she sees in him. He's like a raddled old man!' Her voice took on a tone of extreme disgust. 'If I wasn't there he wouldn't eat or have clean clothes, or someone to throw away his bottles. As it is he knows I won't let him go to the surgery if he's drunk. He did it once. It was nearly the end. That was when Robert said there had to be a new partner. No one stays in the same practice for forty years any more, you know, they all move around. When Robert retires, Adam will have to as well.' She reached for the gin and tonic she had ordered as soon as they sat down at the table. 'Beth is looking very pretty,' she added abruptly.

'She is.' Liza nodded, glad to change the subject. She was watching Jane's hand, which was shaking as it gripped the glass. 'Don't say anything in front of her. She has this romantic image of Adam – I don't know where it's come from!'

'From you.' Jane fixed her with a disconcertingly steady eye. 'You always were besotted with him. But you had the sense to stay out of reach once you knew you couldn't win.' They were both silent for a moment, thinking of Phil. Jane snapped out of her reverie and smiled as she saw Beth making her way between the tables towards them. She had indeed grown up to be very pretty, with her father's dark hair and her mother's delicate features. She was a little plump perhaps, but she turned heads. Her vivacity and charm ensured that.

For the rest of the lunch Liza and Beth regaled Jane with stories of their latest trip which had been to New York, where Liza had painted the wife of a Wall Street tycoon and then amused herself by agreeing to paint a portrait of his favourite dog.

'And now,' Liza went on, 'Beth has a commission to illustrate a book about our mountains. So, when I go to Italy next month, she is staying behind at the farm to start her first serious job. You've heard of Giles Campbell, the travel writer?'

Jane smiled and shook her head. 'My dears, I've heard of nobody. Tell me.' She looked at Beth expectantly.

Liza noticed that she had hardly touched her food and frowned, but she said nothing. She turned to Beth. 'Go on, you'd better confess.'

Beth blushed. 'All right. So I fancy him desperately! So what? He's married, but everyone knows his wife is a terrible flirt. In fact they say she's had several affairs. Poor Giles! I don't know why he puts up with it! Don't listen to Liza, Granny Jane. She teases me about him like mad and it's not fair. She introduced us, after all. She practically threw me at him.'

'Rubbish.' Liza smiled comfortably. 'When Hibberds published a book about my painting I used to go up to their London office sometimes. Bob Cassie introduced me to Giles at a party and he and I talked because he was writing a history of the Black Mountains. What was more natural than that I should ask him to come and stay?'

'She fancied him herself, Granny,' Beth put in pertly.

'I did not!' Liza laughed. 'Or at least not in any serious way. He's thirty years younger than me –'

'Which makes him perfect for me! And while the cat's away, the mouse shall play, with a bit of luck.'

'You be careful, dear.' Jane gave a gentle smile. 'You don't want to get hurt.'

'I won't!'

When at last they stood up to go, Liza put her arm round Jane's thin shoulders. 'One day will you come to the farm to see us? Please. Surely Adam can spare you for a few days?'

'He wouldn't notice if I wasn't there at all.' Jane met her gaze steadily. 'I don't think I'll come, Liza. You and Beth are happy. And safe. Let's leave it that way.'

'What did she mean, safe?' Beth asked the moment they had waved Jane off in her taxi to St Pancras Station.

Liza shrugged. 'I don't think she wants us to know how bad Adam is. It's terrible when someone drinks.'

'But he wouldn't come. He hates me.'

'He does not hate you, sweetheart.' Liza frowned crossly. 'I don't know where you've got this idea from. He is a very unhappy man, that's all. You would remind him of Calum.'

'And my mother.'

'And your mother.' She nodded with a little sad smile.

'So.' Beth took a deep breath. 'He's not violent, is he? He doesn't beat up Granny Jane or anything like that?'

'No, sweetheart, he doesn't do anything like that.' Liza sighed. She had never mentioned Brid to Beth and had no intention of doing so now. After all, what was there to mention? An old man's obsession? A ghost story going back fifty years? She did not let herself think about a murder on a mountain road on a frosty winter's night.

As Adam drank, so his life force diminished, sucked dry by Brid's insatiable demands. He grew weaker and as he did so, so did she.

'I did warn him.' Robert was standing in the sitting room, his back to the fire, looking down at Jane who was seated on the sofa. Adam had not yet come back to the house and as far as she knew they had the place to themselves. Today was one of the days she had gone upstairs to the spare room, changed the sheets, put flowers on the small dressing table, opened the window wide to let in the cold damp afternoon air and defiantly made the sign of the cross above the bed.

'He wasn't exactly drunk, but I could smell the drink on his breath ten feet away. God knows what his patients thought. I'm sorry, Jane, but it reflects on the practice.'

She nodded wearily. 'I will speak to him, Robert.'

'You have to, because there won't be another chance. If it happens again, that's it. We'll have to ask him to resign.' He looked round the room and lowered his voice. 'How are you coping, my dear?'

She smiled. 'All the better for knowing you are there, Robert. I don't think I could do it on my own.' She wasn't sure how much he knew; how much anyone, except Liza, knew. After all, Brid was never seen outside the house. To outward appearances they were just an ordinary, rather worn-out couple who had perhaps seen too much of each other over the years and grown bored with their marriage. No one knew they slept apart. Quite a few people, she suspected, must know that Adam drank.

She was sitting on her own in front of the Six o'Clock News when Adam came home at last. She heard the door bang and waited to hear him run up the stairs. For once he didn't. He walked slowly into the sitting room and stood looking down at her. His face was grey with fatigue. 'Did Robert come to see you?'

She nodded.

'He told you what happened?'

'He gave me a rough idea. What possessed you to go to work like that? You are a fool, Adam.' She spoke without any particular rancour. It was merely a statement.

'Have you any idea of the strain I'm under?' He sat down abruptly on the edge of a chair and brought his hands up to his face, rubbing wearily against the rasp of an unshaven chin. 'I don't know what to do.'

She stared at him. 'If you're tired perhaps we could go away on holiday somewhere. We haven't had a break for years. I know Robert would give you the time off.' Only too gladly, she suspected. She did not expect him to agree. He never had in the past.

'It would be nice.' He threw himself back against the cushions with a sigh. 'I don't know how to get rid of her, Janie.' His voice broke. 'I'm so tired! I just want her to go away.'

Jane stared at him in amazement. 'How long have you felt like this?' she whispered at last.

He shrugged. 'I don't know. Months. Years. When she's here I can't think. I can't eat. I can't do anything. I know how much I've hurt you. I just don't seem to be able to function as a normal human being. I can see myself throwing away my career, what's left of it, my reputation, my home – you. I've hurt you so much.' There were tears in his eyes. 'Help me, Janie.'

Jane stood up. 'Do you mean it?' She felt suddenly strong again. Walking over to him she leaned down towards him and put her hands on his shoulders. Kissing him on the top of his head she smiled. 'Leave it to me.'

'Jane –' As she walked resolutely towards the door he called to her in sudden panic. 'Be careful. What are you going to do?'

'Just have a word upstairs. You wait here. Then, my darling, you and I are going out for a meal!' She ran up the stairs two at a time, her heart singing with joy and relief. At last! She had waited for so long for this moment! She couldn't believe that he had seen sense; that he had come back to her. She wasn't afraid. Adam's love was all she needed. She remembered Liza's warnings over the years and her instructions on how to protect herself, and, round her neck she wore the little cross that Liza had made for her. She wasn't sure why she had kept it all these years, together with the crushed fragments of the amulet tree; she didn't believe that Liza had some particular hotline to a guardian angel somewhere up there in the sky, but the thought of having the crumpled pieces in her pocket gave her just that little bit of strength she needed to walk into the spare room, flinging the door back against the wall, to confront Brid.

The room was empty.

She looked round, feeling cheated. There was no sign of her. The room was just as she had left it earlier that afternoon, with the bed still made, the window slightly open onto the damp cold darkness, the curtains drawn right back against the wall. It felt empty and . . . spare.

She hesitated in the doorway for a moment, not quite believing what she saw, then she turned and closing the door behind her she ran back down the stairs. 'She's not there.'

'No.'

'You knew?' Suddenly she was furious. 'You mean she's gone. That's why you've decided to come back to reality.'

'No. But she doesn't come unless I'm here, does she? Otherwise, what would be the point? By the time I got upstairs she would be there.'

Jane stared at him. 'All right then. Come on. You come up with me. Call her and tell her it's over.'

'I can't.'

'Yes, you can. Here. This will give you the strength.' She held the small wooden cross with its red thread out to him. He took it and stared at it, then suddenly he burst into laughter. 'Why do I have a feeling that I know who gave you this?'

'Yes, it was Liza. It will keep you safe.'

'You think so?' He threw the cross towards the hearth. Too light to go any distance, it fell at his feet. 'Nothing can keep me safe, Jane. Nothing. Brid is stronger than any of us. There is no fighting her.'

'Rubbish!' She leaned forward and caught his hand. 'Come on, let's go upstairs and finish this.'

'No, Jane. Let's just go out for the evening.' He drew her to him. 'Please, my darling. I want to get out of this house.'

'So do I, but I don't want to be afraid to come back, Adam.' Tugging his hand, she dragged him to the door. 'Come on. It will only take a minute. Then you'll be free.'

Pausing, she released his hand for a second and ran back to pick up the cross. The slim gold chain had become tangled in it and as she pulled at it gently to free the catch, the cross, brittle with age, broke and crumbled in her hand. She stared at it in shock. 'My cross!' Tiny fragments of red silk clung to her fingers. 'Adam, my cross!'

He looked down at it and shook his head. 'You don't really think that has kept you safe from her, Jane? If she had wanted to hurt you she would have done it by now.' He sighed.

She looked down at the small fragments of twig in her hand then, reluctantly, she let them fall to the carpet and dusted her palms together. 'Come on then. Let's go up.'

Slowly he followed her up the stairs. She paused on the landing. She had left the spare room door open, she was sure of it. Open to let the cool damp draught sweep through the house. Now it was closed, and she could smell the hot feral smell that always seemed to follow Brid whenever she was there. She saw Adam hesitate and she took his arm and gave it a squeeze. 'You can do it. Just tell her it's over. Tell her to go.'

'She won't go, Janie.'

'She will if you're strong enough.' She reached up and kissed his cheek. 'Between us we can do it. Then we'll go out and celebrate!'

He looked down at her doubtfully. She had let go of his arm, and he was conscious of the place where her fingers had been. It felt cold.

'Go on,' she whispered. She felt naked without the cross. Firmly she pushed the feeling away. All she had to do was be there for Adam. He would deal with Brid.

Reluctantly he stepped forward and put his hand on the door knob. 'Are you sure about this?' he said over his shoulder.

'Yes.' She gave him a little push. 'Go on.'

Slowly he turned the handle and pushed open the door. Brid was standing just inside the room. She was wearing a long green dress, and her hair was clipped back in a silver filigree pin carved in the shape of a leaping salmon. She was looking straight at him and yet he had the feeling that she did not see him at all.

A-dam . . .

The words appeared to come to him from a great distance.

A-dam, why are you cross with me?

'It's time for you to go.' Jane's voice seemed suddenly very loud beside him. 'Adam doesn't want you any more. We want you to leave our house.'

Brid was still looking towards Adam and he had the strong impression that she hadn't heard Jane's words. She took a step forwards, and Jane, in spite of herself stepped back.

A-dam, I love you. Where are you, A-dam?

She moved closer and Jane moved back once again. She was out on the landing again now. She should have kept the fragments of the cross. In her pocket they would have given her strength. 'Go away, Brid!' Her voice was still strong. 'Adam, say something! Make her go away.'

'I'm sorry, Brid.' Adam had turned to look at his wife. He smiled, then he looked at Brid again. 'You must go. I'm tired.'

Brid looked towards him and she seemed to focus on his face for the first time. *Tired?* She spoke at him, and Jane realised suddenly that her words seemed to come from somewhere far away, inside her own head, not from the woman's lips at all.

Poor A-dam. Brid will make you better. She moved towards Adam, her hands outstretched.

'No!' Jane cried. 'Don't touch him. Go away!'

Brid spun round, seeming to see her for the first time, and she frowned. 'You are not good for him,' she said almost gently. 'You must go. Not me.' Her eyes widened suddenly as she saw that the cross had gone; the small cross with its vibrating pulses of protective light was no longer at Jane's throat.

She stepped forward past Adam and out onto the landing.

'Adam!' Jane's voice became shrill with fear. 'Tell her!'

Go away. A-dam does not want you.

The hand Brid stretched out towards Jane barely seemed to move, but it made contact violently with Jane's chest. One moment Jane was standing on the landing, the next she had stepped backwards into space and was falling down the stairs.

There was a small sharp cry as she fell, the thud of her body as she landed, and then complete silence.

'Jane!' Adam screamed. 'Jane, are you all right?'

She has gone. Brid smiled at him. *Come, my love.* She reached out to take his hand.

Adam pushed past her and ran to the top of the stairs. 'Jane? Jane! Oh my God, Jane, are you all right?' He leaped down two steps at a time.

Without touching her he could see that she was dead. Her neck was twisted, her head at a strange angle against the wall.

'Jane?' It was a whisper. He knelt beside her and felt under her ear. But he knew it was no use. She was dead. Jane was dead.

For a moment he stayed where he was, staring down at her in disbelief, then he felt a gentle touch on his shoulder. Brid had followed him downstairs.

A-dam, come upstairs. I love you, A-dam.

He stood up. He was shaking violently. Turning he stared at Brid for several seconds, unable even to speak. 'Do you realise what you have done?' he said at last, his voice strangled. 'You stupid, vicious, despicable little cow!'

Brid looked down and shrugged. 'Come to bed, A-dam,' she said without emotion. 'Do not worry about her. She was not good for you. You love me.'

'Not any more.' His voice had gone suddenly very quiet. 'Get out of my house!'

'A-dam, I love you. I want to make love.' She came to him and rested her head against his shoulder. A new strength enveloped her, an energy snatched from the dying woman. It felt good. 'Please, A-dam. It will be good now she is not there. We will have the house all by ourselves.'

Adam pulled away from her violently. 'Get out,' he hissed. 'Get out, get out, get out!' His voice had risen to a shout. 'You bitch! You murdering little whore! You Jezebel! Hellcat! Get out. I never want to see you again!'

'A-dam.' She stepped away from him, puzzled. 'A-dam, why are you cross?'

'Because you have killed one of the only people I ever really loved, that is why I am cross.' Suddenly his anger had gone. Tears began to run down his face. Throwing himself down on his knees again he cradled Jane's head against his chest. A small trickle of blood had found its way from the corner of her mouth and as he turned her face towards him it smeared his shirt. 'Jane!' He sobbed her name out loud. 'Jane, my darling, I'm so sorry. Oh my God, how am I going to live with this?'

Brid stepped away from him, staring down, a puzzled frown on her face. 'I will come back again,' she said in a small hurt voice. 'A-dam is cross with Brid.'

He ignored her. He had taken one of Jane's hands and was chafing it desperately as though trying to bring some warmth back into her body.

A-dam, I love you.

The words were only faint now in his head. He did not look up.

Beth found Liza sitting by the telephone in the dark. 'What is it? What's wrong?' She switched on the light. 'Liza, what's happened? It's freezing in here.'

'What?' Liza looked up and stared at her.

'Liza?' Beth stooped and put her arms around Liza's shoulders. 'Come on. You've been crying. What's wrong?'

'It's your Granny Jane.' Liza groped in her jeans pocket for a tissue and wiped her eyes with it. 'She's dead.'

Beth stepped back in shock. 'Granny Jane? But she's not old!' It was a cry of protest. 'What happened?'

Liza shrugged. 'That was Robert Harding, your grandfather's partner, on the phone. It appears she fell downstairs and broke her neck.' She broke into sobs again.

'And how is Grandfather?' Beth was stunned.

Liza shrugged. 'Not good. Drunk.' She shook her head miserably. 'Robert doesn't know what to do. He's seen to the police and everything, but he wants me to go. There is no one else.'

'You can't go.' Beth caught her hand. 'Liza, I need you here.' She was not sure why, but she was suddenly afraid.

Liza shrugged. 'I have no choice, Beth. Adam has no one left now.'

Except Brid.

She did not say the words out loud, but they seemed to hang in the air around her.

As she had done so often over the years, Liza sat in her car in front of the house looking up at the first floor windows for a while before climbing out. She shivered. The house looked strangely blank, as though the heart had gone out of it. The front garden was untidy. Someone had chucked a Coke can over the hedge and no one had bothered to remove it. It was already rusting as it lay on the grass in full view of the path. With a sigh she walked up to the front and rang the bell. There was no reply.

When eventually she walked around to the back and peered into the windows she could see Adam sitting at his desk. His head was buried in his arms and he appeared to be asleep. She banged on the window.

'Adam!'

He did not stir.

'Adam! Let me in.'

The kitchen door was unlocked and she walked in. Pausing to glance round she went on through into the study.

'Adam!'

He was snoring.

'Adam, for goodness' sake, wake up.' She shook his shoulder hard. He groaned and shrugged her off and went back to sleep.

While he slept she rounded up the empty bottles. He must have moved back into the bedroom he had shared with Jane and slept in her bed the night before. Wrinkling her nose, Liza extricated the small flat whisky bottle from beneath the pillow, threw it into the corner with the others and stripped the sheets. At least when he woke up he would find the room clean and ordered and the rest of the house hoovered and neat as Jane would have kept it. She left the spare room – the room Adam had shared with Brid – till last. Taking a deep breath she flung open the door and looked inside. The room was a wreck. The bedclothes and curtains had been shredded, the wallpaper was hanging off in strips and one of the panes in the window had been broken. Staring round, she shook her head in despair.

'So, what do you think?' Adam, awake at last, had come upstairs behind her and was standing looking over her shoulder. He smelled stale and unwashed.

'I don't know what to think.' She turned and looked at him. 'Beyond the fact that you need a bath and a change of clothes and then probably a square meal. Drinking like this doesn't help, Adam, you know that.'

'Don't you want to know what happened?' His eyes were red and swollen.

'If you want to tell me.'

He walked past her and stood in the doorway looking round. 'I told her to go.'

'Brid?'

'Who else?'

'And has she?'

He shrugged. 'I suppose so.'

'After she wrecked this room?'

'As you see.' He went over and sat on the bed with a groan. 'She killed her.' Tears were pouring down his face. He made no attempt to stem them.

Liza walked across and sat down beside him. 'Brid killed Jane?'

He nodded. 'I wanted to finish it. I wanted to give Janie some happiness at last. She deserved it. She still loved me, Liza, after all I had done to her. She still loved me. She stuck by me.' He paused.

Liza waited for him to go on. He struggled for a moment with his words then, taking a deep breath he continued: 'She wouldn't listen. She – she – just sort of pushed Janie down the stairs!' He wiped his nose on the sleeve of his sweater. 'She landed so awkwardly. I knew she couldn't be alive, but I talked to her. I begged her to stay with me. I begged . . .' He hauled the torn pillow into his arms and stifled his tears in it. 'The cross. The little cross you gave her. It had kept her safe. She gave it to me and I threw it back at her. It fell to pieces. She gave it to me to keep me safe and I destroyed it!'

Liza gripped his shoulder.

He sniffed. 'I told Brid to go back to whatever hell she came from. She's mad. She's got no feelings. She's some kind of fiend!'

'What did you tell the police?'

'What could I say? That I had been sleeping with a woman who had escaped from a mental home and who knifed people all over the place and who I had allowed to kill my wife?' He hurled the pillow across the room suddenly. 'What could I say? That I was as mad as she was? That she had bewitched me so that I couldn't break free of her? That she still looked as if she were eighteen even though I had known her most of my life? That every time I set eyes on her I couldn't stop myself from wanting her so much?'

He turned and looked at Liza through bleary eyes. 'Jane stood by me through all that. When I think how much I hurt her. When I think what I did to her! I can't live with myself, Liza. I can't!'

'You have to, Adam.' Liza's voice was very gentle. 'That, I'm afraid will be your hell.' She sighed, then she repeated her question. 'What did you tell the police?'

'That she fell. It was true. Robert sorted it all out.'

'And has Brid gone for good?'

He shrugged.

She bit her lip thoughtfully. 'Come on, Adam. Please, go and have a bath. You'll feel better. I'll go and rustle something up for supper. Then when you've had something to eat we'd better decide what to do.' She put her hand on his shoulder again. 'What about the funeral?' she asked gently.

He shrugged. 'There has to be an inquest. Robert is looking after it all.'

'Robert?'

'There isn't anyone else, Liza.' He turned his back on her and walked out of the room. 'I have no family. I have no friends. And now I have no wife.'

Adam bathed and put on clean clothes as she heated some soup from the freezer, then he came down to the kitchen and made himself some instant coffee while she cut up the bread. He looked at her sheepishly. 'I don't deserve your kindness, Liza.'

'Of course you do. We're old friends, remember?' She put the plate on the table and, walking over, gave him a hug. He smelled a great deal better. 'Some soup will make you feel stronger, then we'll decide what to do. I think after the funeral you should come home with me to Wales for a bit. You do have family, Adam. Beth and I are your family.'

On the way to the house she had stopped off and bought a bunch of freesias in a small shop on the corner. She lifted them from the counter and going over to the sink, ran some water into a glass. Putting the flowers into it she set it on the middle of the kitchen table; their scent seemed to fill the room.

'You can get through this, Adam,' she said slowly as she began to stir the soup again. 'It will take courage, but you've got plenty of that.'

'Have I?' He sat down, nursing the mug of coffee between his hands.

'We both know you have.'

'I don't want to come to Wales.' He looked up at her suddenly. 'I don't want to know Beth. She's better off without me in her life, and so are you.'

'Don't be silly, Adam.'

'No. I've thought about this, Liza, in my more sane moments.' He gave a sheepish half-grin. 'I should like very much for you to stay for the funeral, then I want you to go back to Wales and forget I ever existed. Brid is a vicious, murderous, amoral parasite. She hasn't gone; she's biding her time. I have a feeling that she will follow me wherever I go for the rest of my days. I shall fight her, if I have the strength, but I don't want to think, ever, that I have brought her with me, to hunt you or that child down. Let me do this last thing for you, Liza. Keep Beth safe. Forget me.'

'I will never forget you, Adam.'

He smiled sadly. 'Perhaps not, but you can damp down the memories.' He looked up again. 'Did Brid kill Phil?' It was the first time he had ever asked her about the accident.

She hesitated. 'I will never know for sure. He skidded off the mountain road.'

There was a long silence.

'Don't put Beth at risk too, Liza. You've seen what the bitch can do.'

Liza sighed. 'We'll see. Perhaps she'll never come back.'

'Perhaps.'

He drank some soup and ate a piece of bread, then he went back into his study. When Liza glanced in later he was sitting, staring at the wall.

Twice in the night she looked in on him, asleep in Jane's bed. He seemed peaceful enough, though she found herself wondering if, in his dreams, he was somewhere far away on the Scottish mountainside.

Liza begged Adam to allow Jane to be buried in Wales beside Calum and Julie and Phil, but he was adamant. There would be no burial. There would be no country grave. And Beth was not to come. The funeral was pitiful. Although there were quite a lot of people there for the church service, only Robert Harding, Adam and Liza went with the coffin to the crematorium. Patricia, in the Surrey old people's home where she had spent the last year, was too frail and too confused to take in what had happened. She sent flowers, and then only days later rang up and asked to speak to Jane.

Once the coffin had disappeared, with the full inexorable horror, behind the curtain in the crematorium chapel, Adam turned away and walked steadfastly out of the door. He stood for a moment in the rain looking up at the sky, his face set, then he headed towards the car. They had travelled together in Robert Harding's Volvo and he stopped beside it, his expression closed, looking neither to left nor right as the other two, with exchanged glances, hurried after him.

'I hope you are going to come home with me for tea,' Robert said firmly. 'I know you said there was to be no official get together, and everyone else has respected that and gone, but you can't go back to an empty house on your own. I want you and Liza to come back at least for a while.'

Adam did not answer. He seemed to have withdrawn within himself as he climbed into the front seat beside Robert, his collar pulled up around his ears, the cold rain still dripping from his hair.

'Thank you.' Liza answered for him. 'We should like that very much.' She glanced at Adam's profile and was not reassured. His expression was shuttered and bleak.

That night he drank a whole bottle of whisky and sank into oblivion on the sofa in front of the blank television screen. Liza covered him with a rug, threw away the empty bottle which had fallen from his hand onto the carpet, and turned off the light. Slowly, with a heavy heart, she made her way up the stairs.

The thought which was haunting her was that she had to stay, at least another few days.

Before supper she had rung Beth. It was like a breath of fresh air to speak to her, and to imagine her in the untidy kitchen at home, the house smelling of newly made bread – Beth's latest craze – and spicy woodsmoke from the fire in the living room. Another of the old apple trees had fallen in the autumn gales and they were burning it slowly, branch by branch, savouring the wonderful rich smell which lingered in the old stone of the hearth.

'You're not lonely, darling?' Liza had asked.

'Of course not. I'm working on my sketches.' Beth was bubbling with excitement. She had taken over Phil's studio when she got the commission to illustrate Giles's book and tactfully and with as little upset as possible she had gone about changing it so much Liza would never have recognised it. She was delighted. It kept the place alive and vibrant. There was no need to retain Phil's studio as a mausoleum to keep him in her heart. He would always be there somewhere.

'How are they going?'

'Well.' There was a small hesitation the other end of the line. 'Actually Giles is coming up for a few days. We thought it might be easier to visit places together and discuss it all up here.'

'I see.' Liza took a deep breath. 'Is his wife coming too?'

'No.' It was almost too pat. 'You know very well she's a town girl. She's much too busy with her own affairs, according to Giles,' there was a suppressed giggle the other end of the line, 'and she hates the mountains. He says she would die if she moved more than a few hundred yards from Chelsea.'

'And she doesn't mind if her husband spends time in the mountains with a very attractive young lady like you?'

There was another giggle. 'Actually, she was far more worried about my attractive sexy grandmother being here. She was relieved when she heard you were away! No, that's not true. I don't honestly think they get on. Truly. Oh, Liza!' There was a quick horrified pause. 'How awful of me to be laughing and everything. How was it? Was it grim? How is poor Grandfather coping?'

'He's okay.' Liza did not elaborate. 'I think I ought to stay a bit longer though, just to be here while he finds his feet. Can you manage on your own? Can I trust you with the beautiful Giles?'

There was a snort the other end of the line. 'He and I have a working relationship, that's all. And I would do nothing to jeopardise that, believe me!'

Later, in the bedroom which had been Calum's, Liza took off her skirt with a sigh. She stood for a moment, staring at herself in the mirror. Attractive, sexy grandmother, eh! She had to admit she rather liked the description. She smoothed down her petticoat across her flat stomach and neat hips and smiled.

The sound behind her was so faint she hardly heard it. She tensed and turned, staring at the closed door. There it was again, a quiet scratching on the woodwork. She frowned. It sounded like a mouse. Reaching for her dressing gown she pulled it on and knotted it around her waist defensively then she tiptoed to the door and put her hand on the knob. Pulling the door open she peered out.

There was no one there. The landing was dark and the house silent. She listened for a second, then slowly she closed the door. Momentarily she stood there frowning, then she turned away to continue getting undressed.

When she went downstairs next morning she found the sofa empty. The French doors were open and the room was full of the scent of wet garden. She walked over to the doors and stood looking out. Adam was standing in the middle of the lawn in the rain, soaked to the skin. He caught sight of her and raised a hand in greeting. His face was pale and drawn and he looked a hundred years old, she thought with a sudden pang of compassion.

'I thought the rain might cure my hangover.' He walked towards her, and she realised his feet were bare, squelching on the wet grass.

She smiled. 'And did it?'

'It helped. I'll go up and bath and shave, then I'll feel better. I'm sorry about the whisky.' He looked like a sheepish, small boy.

'So am I.' She reached up and kissed him on the cheek. 'Go on, then, get dressed and I'll make us some coffee.'

In her explorations of St Albans she had found a wonderful coffee shop in the centre of the town and had them grind her some specially. The scent of it filled the house, and she hoped made it feel a little more welcoming. That and the flowers were really all she could do. The gap Jane had left was too big, too empty and too raw.

'Liza!' Adam was standing in the doorway. His face was ashen and there was a small object in his hand. 'Did you put this on my bed?'

She felt her heart sink even before she stepped forward to see what he was holding. 'No, Adam, I didn't put anything on your bed,' she said gently as she took it from him.

It was a small, exquisitely carved figure of a naked woman.

'Is it ivory?' She turned it over. It was ice cold.

He nodded. 'I suppose so.' He walked over to the window and stared out into the garden. A robin was standing on the brick parapet which bounded the small terrace.

'I know what I would do with it,' she said softly.

'I'm going to burn it.' He was decisive. 'Is that what you think I should do?'

'I was going to tell you to bury it,' Liza said. She smiled. 'Perhaps that is less final. But you are right. Burn it. That will show her.'

Their eyes met. 'You always did think she was a witch, didn't you?' He took the figure from her and headed for the back door.

She followed him. 'Something like that.'

She watched as he gathered some twigs and leaves which had blown into the garage where they had stayed dry. He managed to start a blaze with his cigarette lighter. For a while they watched it flare and spark, then when the fire was really hot he dropped the little figure on it. For a while she thought it wasn't going to burn, then at last it blackened and disappeared.

She glanced up at his face, which was tight with pain. 'I wondered if it was going to scream.'

He nodded. 'I don't suppose it will be the last message I get.'

'Where do you suppose she is now?'

He shrugged. 'Who knows? And who cares, as long as she stays there and doesn't come near this house ever again.'

18

The bed was hard and cold. Brid stirred uncomfortably and groped for her pillow. She found coarse linen and the dry stems of heather which dug into her face.

'So, you are awake.' The language was familiar, lilting. 'My little traveller returns. And where have you been, little cat? Are you going to tell me?'

She clung to sleep. The voice was strange, threatening, from another time, another place.

Broichan . . .

Her eyes flew open and she sat up, dizzy with sleep.

A-dam . . .

Where was he? Why did he not want her any more? What had she done to make him angry?

She could smell the bitter-sweet scent of a fire, and on it cooking meat. Her mouth watered suddenly. How long had she been asleep? Or had she travelled through time as Broichan had taught her? Wherever she had been she was hungry and stiff. Trying to swing her legs over the side of the bed she stopped suddenly, fear coursing through her stomach. There were chains around her ankles. She stared round into the shadows of the room and saw him sitting by the door. He smiled at her, his eyes like quicksilver in the wrinkled face.

'*No!*' She shook her head pitifully.

'You misused your powers, Brid. You did not honour your oath to let the sky fall and the waves rise up over your head if you betrayed the trust which was put in you.' He stood up slowly. 'I have put you under the *geas* and now you must pay the price of your betrayal.'

With a small cry of fear she threw herself back onto the bed and dragged the coarse pillow over her face, willing herself away. She did not have to look for the place where the veil was thin. It was thin wherever she looked. When Broichan reached her and stood staring down at the girl, lying on the bed, she was already gone, her body comatose, her eyes blank, her pupils dilated and still. He smiled. He would continue to keep her alive, causing her to be fed, dripping milk and wine and pulped meat juices down her throat, sponging her face and hands, turning her body to keep it supple and one day, before her soul returned so he could kill her and give her wholly to the gods, he would follow her into the other world, the world where A-dam lived, and see what it was that had captured her soul.

Liza sighed. She picked up yet another bottle, which was still a third full and, shaking her head at the waste, poured the rest of the whisky down the sink. Adam did not stir. Sometimes now his sleep was too deep for dreams, too deep even to snore. He lay as though dead, and all she could do was put a pillow under his head and cover him with a blanket.

It was time she went home, she knew that. What was there to stay for? When he was sober Adam was his old charming self, gently humorous, rising above his grief, making the effort to entertain her, showing his affection with the courteous, old-fashioned mannerisms which had always endeared him to her. Then she thought she could talk him round; she thought maybe there was a future for them together if she could take him back with her to Wales and feed him and cajole him and wean him from the drink. They would stroll together in the park, or walk down Fishpool Street, or visit the Abbey, listening sometimes to the choir practising, or the organ as the sound rose and swelled beneath the ancient roof. Then they would go back and he would sit and talk to her while she cooked for him and together they would laugh and remember sometimes the old days in Edinburgh, and she would postpone opening a bottle of wine as long as possible. But he grew irritated if she left it too long, and he would become more and more edgy. Sometimes the wine was enough. Other times it was just the start.

She knew the moment Brid returned. She had managed to get him upstairs before he passed out and she had levered him onto the bed and taken off his shoes. Covering him with a blanket she turned away and stopped dead. There was a presence in the room, a slight change in the atmosphere, almost too small to detect, but her sixth sense had kicked in at the back of her brain and she felt the small hairs on her arms prickle in warning.

She looked round. The room was very still. Adam lay slumped, his head on the pillow, his mouth slightly open. He muttered something and, smacking his lips, he half turned over, his arm flying out so that he knocked over the lamp on the bedside table. It fell with a crash and a pop as the bulb exploded, plunging the room into darkness.

Liza held her breath. She strained her eyes, gradually getting used to the faint leak of light round the door from the landing. Carefully, not turning, she backed towards the door, aware that nearby someone else seemed to be holding their breath as well.

Reaching the door she dragged it open with relief and stepped outside. She glanced back. Was that a shadow standing by the bed? She wasn't sure. 'Be careful, Adam,' she whispered. 'God bless,' and slowly and quietly she pulled the door closed.

Downstairs, she turned on the TV in the kitchen and put on the kettle, but however much noise she managed to make as she set out a cup and saucer for herself, and started on the washing-up, she knew she was still listening to the silence upstairs.

That night she slept on the sofa in the sitting room and she kept the light on. At dawn she got up and walked for an hour through the rainwashed streets before coming back to a still-silent house.

She left it until lunchtime, then she went upstairs. Adam was still asleep and as far as she could tell he was as she had left him. There was no indentation of another head on the pillow, no scent of a woman on the sheets, but even so she wondered who had picked up the spilled blue Michaelmas daisies which had been scattered under the broken lamp and put them back in their little vase. Perhaps it was Adam.

She rang Beth at teatime. 'So, how are things in the Wild West?' She thought she could hear music in the background.

'Fine.' She could hear the amusement in Beth's voice. 'Giles is here and today we drove around taking photos. He wants me to do some pen and ink sketches and there are going to be about sixty major watercolours to illustrate the book, plus they want one of them for the jacket.' She sounded delirious with happiness. 'We thought we'd drive over to Brecon for dinner tonight, then tomorrow we might go up into mid-Wales for some really wild scenery.'

Liza heard a giggle and some off-stage comment from the background. She smiled wistfully. 'You are being sensible, Beth. Remember, whatever he says about it, he is married,' she said sternly. 'I don't want you to be hurt, darling.'

'Of course I'll remember! Giles would never hurt me. So, how is Grandfather?' Beth's voice changed, becoming slightly prim.

'Not very good I'm afraid.'

'Oh, Liza.' Beth sounded genuinely sad. 'What are you going to do?'

'I don't know. I can't stay here forever, however much you might like me to!' She laughed at the not very convincing denial the other end. 'Oh, I will stay another few days, but I don't think there is any point. He doesn't seem to want to fight the drink, and he doesn't want to come back with me, and he doesn't seem to care about his job. As far as Robert is concerned I think he'd rather Adam never went back to the practice at all. And let's face it, he's just about retirement age. To be honest I don't know what to do. I can't stay here and nursemaid him.'

'Nor would I want you to.' The voice in the doorway behind her made Liza jump guiltily. 'Must go, Beth! Take care, my darling.' She hung up and swung round. 'So, you're up at last.'

He looked dreadful. 'I'm so sorry, Liza.' He rubbed his face wearily. 'That is the last time, I promise.' He did not mention Brid.

The trouble was, as always she believed him.

For three more days they walked and talked and he ate her meals and his colour began to improve. Once they made love on the sofa downstairs in the sitting room, a gentle, retrospective, dreamy coming together which left them both, strangely, near to tears.

'Adam, I do want you to come back with me.' Liza lay in his arms, gently stroking his chest, her head cushioned on his shoulder. 'My darling, we could be happy in Wales.'

He gave her a quick hug. 'No we couldn't. It wouldn't work, Liza. If we had thought it would work we would have married years ago.' He smiled ruefully. 'I love you. I think I have always loved you. But you and I are chalk and cheese. And if I came to you, Brid would follow us and Beth would be in danger too. We can't risk that happening. Ever. Let it rest, my love. Dreams and memories. That must be enough for both of us.'

That night Adam got drunk again; violently and viciously drunk, and Brid reappeared. Liza was never sure which happened first.

She was sitting at the small dressing table she had improvised in her bedroom from Calum's desk and a mirror she had rescued from the attic. It was a long time since she had made love to someone and she was staring at her reflection, wondering if the warm, happy glow that she could feel inside her showed. She felt no disloyalty to Phil. He of all people would have understood.

Adam's shout brought her to her feet with a start, her hair brush clattering down onto the table top.

'You bitch! You murdering, vicious bitch! Get out of my house! Do you hear me? Get out!' There was a loud crash and the sound of breaking glass.

'Adam?' She hurried to the top of the stairs. 'Adam, where are you?' Her heart in her mouth, she ran down and headed for his study. 'Adam, what's wrong?'

Brid was standing near him, holding out her hands. One of them was bleeding. *A-dam, I love you.* She was looking her most beautiful, her long hair brushed loose about her shoulders, her gown of softly textured checks of moss green and violet and the browns and golds of autumn falling in graceful gathers around her legs, a silver necklet at her throat. *A-dam, what is wrong?* Her eyes were on his. She did not seem to have noticed Liza in the doorway.

'Get out!' Adam was swaying slightly. He reached onto his desk and picked up a heavy marble ashtray. 'If you don't get out of here I am going to kill you once and for all, you murdering bitch!'

'He means it,' Liza said from the doorway. 'You have to go. Can't you see? Your hold on him is over.' She stepped into the room, her heart thumping with fear. 'Do as he says. Leave him alone.'

Brid turned. She seemed to focus on Liza for the first time. Her eyes narrowed. 'You!' She said the one word with such venom that Liza recoiled. 'I showed you what would happen if you came near my A-dam. Your man died.'

Liza went cold.

'I kill you too!' The eyes were hypnotic. Liza found herself unable to look away. 'I kill you and I kill the child of A-dam's child. Then A-dam is left for me!'

Behind her Adam raised the ashtray. 'Bitch!' He only seemed capable of saying the one word.

Brid moved as he struck at her, and the blow caught her sideways across the temple. Reeling back, she spat at him once and then leaped at his throat.

'Adam!' Liza's scream was cut short as Adam grabbed at the whisky bottle he had left on the floor beside his desk. He swung it at the spot where Brid had been standing but it met only space before it smashed into a thousand pieces on the marble mantelpiece and fell into the empty hearth.

Sobbing with shock and fear Liza stared round the room. 'Where is she?'

'Did I kill her?' Adam staggered back a few paces and propped himself up against the desk. He was panting.

'I don't know. I don't think so.' Liza's legs gave way and she sat down abruptly on the sofa by the window. 'Dear God, where did she come from?'

'Hell, where else?'

'And where has she gone?' Her eyes were scanning the room fearfully.

'Back there.' Adam began to laugh. 'Isn't she beautiful? Did you see her? With her lovely hair and her huge eyes and her wiles and her temptations!' Suddenly he was crying. He held his arms out piteously to Liza.

Standing up shakily she went over to him and cradled his head against her chest. 'She admitted that she killed Phil,' she said tonelessly.

'I heard.'

'And Calum and Julie.'

'Yes.'

'And she threatened to kill me and the child of your child. She meant Beth, Adam.'

There was a long silence.

'Adam, I have to go. You know that, don't you?' Liza was holding his hand gently. 'I don't think there is any point in me staying here.'

He nodded. 'You're right. You must go. That's what I want. I'll be all right.'

'Are you sure?'

He nodded vigorously. 'And what is more I never want you to come here again, Liza. This house is finished. I'll sell up. There's nothing for me here now, anyway. Don't think I don't know what Robert Harding thinks of me. He'd be really glad to have me out of that partnership.'

'Where would you go?' There was no point in denying anything he had said.

'I don't know. Maybe travel a bit? See the world?'

She sat without moving for several minutes, watching him miserably. He had subsided, after a final shrug, into a deep reverie of such sadness she found her heart was physically hurting as she stared at him.

'Adam –' She didn't know what to say.

He forced himself to smile. 'It will be all right. In the end. I'll come through. I come from tough stock, Liza, remember?'

'I remember. Listen, I have to go back to Beth, but I will come and see you. Often.'

'There's no point. I won't be here.'

'You might. You have to be somewhere. I'll come and see you wherever you are. The more exotic the better. You know me. I love travel. If you settle in Tahiti or Tibet or Tijuana – I'll be there.'

He managed to smile. 'You're in danger of sounding like a very poor pop song.'

She smiled back. An hour later, after one tight desperate hug, she left.

Brid had been in the orchard before and that time someone had shot her.

She shook her head as the blood dripped into her eyes. That woman, Jane, had died. Now she would remove the others. Two women had dogged A-dam's life and kept him from her; and now there was a third. The child of A-dam's child.

She walked slowly up through the orchard, only half aware how unsteady she was on her feet. It was dark and the grass was wet. She padded lightly, keeping to the shelter of the trees, climbing the gate and crossing the gravel yard with soft silent steps. In the corner a large shiny car was parked beside the old Land-Rover that Beth used as her own. Brid eyed it for a moment and then moved on. She had to find the child and kill her.

Inside Beth was kneeling before the fire in the living room with a toasting fork. On the plate beside her was a pile of toasted bread – her own home-made – which Giles was spreading with melting yellow butter. They were laughing.

'I'm sure this is plenty. We're both fat enough as it is!' She pushed her long hair out of her eyes with the back of her arm. Her face was shiny and hot from the fire and she could feel a trickle of sweat running down between her breasts.

Giles kept looking at the deep vee in her jumper which revealed Beth's pronounced cleavage. 'You're right. If we eat all this we won't have any energy left,' he commented. He laid down his knife. He was a stocky, attractive man of medium height with a square face framed by floppy, golden-blond hair. His bushy blond eyebrows and eyelashes framed eyes of a deep limpid blue.

'Energy for what?' Her attempt at artful coquetry was spoiled by the dollop of butter on the end of her nose.

'Looking at photos,' he said firmly. He leaned forward and took the fork out of her hand. 'Enough, sweetheart.' He edged closer and licked the end of her nose. 'Delicious.'

'Giles, what about your wife?' She said it helplessly, as though knowing there was no point. The words had become like a mantra, something to repeat again and again to distract her from her thoughts, but they no longer worked. Her thoughts were totally and completely taken up with him.

He grinned. 'I've told you. Idina and I have an open marriage. She doesn't mind, my darling, as long as I leave her to do her own thing in London.' He hooked a finger into the top of her jumper and pulled her towards him so that he could kiss her buttery lips. 'You taste gorgeous.'

'And fat.'

'You are not fat, Beth. You are curvaceous. Which is gorgeous. I have never understood what men saw in Twiggy. I like a woman I can get my hands on.' He pushed her back onto the hearth rug and kissed her again.

An ice-cold draught coming under the door suddenly sent the flames shooting up the chimney and stirred the ash in the hearth.

'What on earth is that?' Beth turned her head to look at the fire. 'Is there a window open somewhere?'

'If there is I'm not going to look.' Giles pushed her hair off her face gently and kissed each eyelid. 'But there is a storm getting up outside. All the more cosy in here. Now, are you going to eat this toast?' He reached for a piece and held it to her mouth.

She lunged forward and took a small bite. 'Bliss.'

'I'm fattening you up for my pleasure!' He bit the other side of the toast.

'Sounds disgustingly decadent. Don't tell Liza. She's a modern woman.'

'And a gorgeous one. You can see it runs in the family. You can be as feminist as you like, my darling, as long as it doesn't involve slimming or wearing dungarees.' He pulled away and took another, more man-sized, bite of toast. 'This is heaven.'

Beth frowned. Her attention was suddenly on the fire again. 'There is a terrific draught coming from somewhere. I'd better go and check if a window has come open, I don't want it tearing off its hinges. Listen to the trees out there.' She jumped lightly to her feet and smiled down at him. 'Don't finish all the toast while I'm gone.'

Opening the sitting room door she peered out into the dark hall. It was cold out there. She closed the door behind her to preserve the heat in the sitting room before she padded over the flagstones in her socks in the dark.

The kitchen was freezing. The door into the yard had blown open and was banging back and forth against the wall. Stepping out into the wet she wrestled with it for a moment before she was able to pull it closed and slide the bolt in place. Her feet and her hair were soaked, but the sudden calm in the kitchen was almost shocking after the roar of the wind.

'Beth, are you all right?' Giles had followed her into the hall. 'What's happened?'

She turned towards him at the very second the cat launched itself at her from the dresser. With a scream she fell back, her hands trying frantically to protect her face from the flailing claws.

'Giles!' Her shriek of agony turned into a sob and then to silence as she collapsed onto the floor. Giles kicked out at the cat, missed, and then picking up the nearest thing to hand took a swipe at it with the frying pan which had been left on the table. The cat yowled and fled past him into the darkness of the hall.

'Beth! Beth, my darling, are you all right?' On his knees beside her Giles pulled her hands gently from her face. 'Dear God, are your eyes all right? Beth, can you see?'

She stared up at him in silence, paralysed with shock, then slowly she tried to sit up. 'I think so. I'm all right. My face . . .' She stared at her hands, which were covered in blood.

'I think they're just scratches. By some miracle you turned away as it jumped. It was going for your face, but it missed. Mostly.' He pushed her hair gently, a mirror gesture of the one he had made earlier, exposing a long livid gash down her temple and cheek to her jaw line. 'Can you sit here, on the chair, then I can look properly? Is there a first aid box? Perhaps I should drive you to the hospital?'

When she was at last settled by the fire, the scratch dressed, at her insistence, with Hypercal, two arnica tablets under her tongue for shock, and her reassurance that she had had all the jabs she needed in her life, thank you very much, Giles went searching for the cat, with the poker.

He found no trace of it.

'I don't understand it. I have searched every single nook and cranny.' He sat down beside her on the sofa and took a deep breath to steady himself. The shock was beginning to kick in. 'How is it feeling?'

'Okay.' She grinned shakily. 'I hope it doesn't mar my beauty.' She gave an ironic little laugh. 'I don't understand it. Cats usually like me.'

'That wasn't any ordinary cat. I saw it clearly. It was much bigger. It was a wildcat. The sort they have in Scotland. I didn't think they had them in Wales.' He took her hands. 'And as for your beauty,' he leaned forward and kissed her nose, 'nothing could mar that.' He peered at her closely. 'I think your homeopathic mumbo-jumbo stuff has done the trick. It's already healing. A couple of days and you won't know it was there. Pity really,' he smiled roguishly, 'it makes you look rather elegantly rakish.'

She smiled wanly, then she shivered. 'Where is it, Giles? It scares me. It must be hiding somewhere in the house.'

'I've searched everywhere, Beth. It must have run out of the door . . .'

'It didn't. It attacked me after I shut the door.' She huddled into the corner of the sofa, trembling. 'All my life I've felt safe here, and now –'

'Now you still feel safe. Listen, whatever it was, it's gone.' He thought for a minute. 'I tell you what. Why not ask your nice neighbours up at Bryn Glas to bring a couple of those vicious sheep dogs of theirs down and let them run through the house? They would find it, wouldn't they, if it was still here?'

She sat up eagerly. 'That's a brilliant idea. I'll ring Jenny now.' At the door she stopped suddenly. 'Come with me?'

He followed her.

Jenny arrived twenty minutes later in the old truck, with two Border collies and the family retriever. 'Twm, Dai and Bertie will find it if it's still here,' she said cheerfully, the dogs milling round her ankles in the yard. 'What on earth happened?'

They explained and she frowned. 'You know, that's extraordinary. I remember when poor Mrs Craig was attacked by a wildcat up here, oh years ago it was. She was quite badly hurt. It came through the bedroom window. You ask your grandma. Frightening, it was. They always reckoned she shot it. I was very impressed, but Dr Craig was furious with her. I wonder if there are a couple of those big cats one hears about escaped from somewhere breeding up here? Shall I just let the dogs in the house?' She looked doubtful.

'Please. Will they search?'

'Bertie will and the others will follow him. Bertie, seek,' she commanded. The retriever glanced at her pointing hand and with a sharp bark of excitement streaked off into the house. She sighed. 'He's such a mut. He never waits to find out what he's supposed to be looking for!'

Beth laughed. 'Come in, Jenny. Have a cup of tea or something while we wait.'

'I think we ought to follow them, dear. Your faith in their good behaviour is touchingly naïve.' Jenny gave a cheerful laugh. 'Perhaps tea later would be nice.'

The dogs found nothing. A wild scramble round the house including a chase through the attics raised nothing more alarming than a cloud of dust. Then Bertie stopped, outside Beth's bedroom. He raised his nose, pointing, and the line of hackles rose along his back. The other two dogs lined up behind him expectantly.

'Oh, God.' Beth looked at Giles. He had brought the poker with him. Leaning forward he pushed open the door.

The dogs hesitated.

'Go seek,' Jenny said quietly. Bertie turned and gave her a reproachful stare. Then he sat down.

'Keep back.' Giles gripped the poker tightly and tiptoed to the doorway. 'I can't see anything,' he whispered. He took another step forward.

'My bed!' Beth squealed suddenly. 'Look at my bed!' As though released by her voice from a spell all three dogs bounded into the room. They clustered around the bed sniffing, but none of them went near it. Their tails, Jenny noticed quietly, were clamped between their legs. She felt a pang of fear. Her dogs were not afraid of any animal that she had ever seen. They followed into the room cautiously and stood looking down. The beautiful patchwork quilt had been torn into shreds.

'Look!' Beth picked up the remains of the quilt. Under it the sheets and blankets had been torn as well. 'Why?' she whispered.

'I think it went out of this window.' Giles noticed suddenly that the stay had come loose and the casement had swung shut in the wind. 'Do you see? It must have knocked over the flowers as it jumped out.' He rubbed his palm over the latch and looked at it. 'Blood, and a couple of black hairs.'

He pulled the window tight shut and secured it. 'Well, at least we know it's well and truly gone.' He smiled at Jenny. 'I think with your permission a biscuit each for your intrepid trio.' He glanced at Beth. 'Are you coming downstairs?'

She was staring down at the bed. 'I keep thinking it could have done that to my face.'

'You'd best go down to the surgery and have those scratches checked, love.' Jenny reached to push back Beth's hair. 'You were very, very lucky.'

'We were so happy, having such a lovely evening, and then that happens . . .' Beth shuddered violently. 'It's like some sort of evil omen, coming out of the dark.'

In the kitchen Jenny snapped her fingers at the three dogs and they lay down under the table. 'Listen. Can I suggest something? I wouldn't worry your grandmother about this if I were you. I have a feeling it would upset her – she might feel she can't go away again and leave you.' She gave a small half-glance at Giles. 'I dare say you wouldn't want that either.'

Beth gave her a gentle punch on the shoulder. She managed to raise a smile. 'You are not making insinuations, are you, Aunty Jenny?'

'No I am not! It's just I thought your grandma doesn't need any more worries, does she?'

'No, she doesn't.' Beth looked thoughtful for a moment. 'No, you're right.'

'So, mum's the word?'

Beth nodded. 'Mum's the word.' She shuddered again in spite of herself as she looked towards the window. Outside, there in the dark, there was a dangerous animal hiding. She pictured the shredded quilt on her bed. Why had it done that? Why pick her room out of all those in the house? And why set out to destroy her bed?

Beth and Giles had returned to the sitting room after Jenny and her dogs had left. The pile of toast was untouched on the hearth, the fire a bed of ash. Beth looked at Giles. 'I can't believe all that happened.'

He shook his head. 'Neither can I.' He leaned forward to throw on some logs and put his arm round her. 'Poor darling. I do wish you would go and see the doctor.'

'I told you, I don't want to. I don't need a doctor.' She leaned against him. 'How long can you stay, Giles?'

'I don't know.' He shrugged. 'I ought to go back. I've got to work on the manuscript.'

'Stay till Liza gets home. Please.'

He touched her cheek gently. 'I would stay forever if I could.'

Giles had gone to the kitchen to fetch a bottle of wine and two glasses when the phone rang.

Beth had followed him. 'Perhaps that's Liza.' She picked it up and turned to watch as he began to draw the cork.

'I need to speak to Giles.' The voice on the other end was female and icily impersonal.

Beth handed him the receiver in silence. With a glance at her Giles took it. During the conversation which followed he grew more and more agitated. Beth, sitting at the kitchen table, watched him, her heart sinking.

'I take it that was Idina,' she said when at last he hung up. Her voice was husky with fear. She had picked up the gist of what was being said.

'Beth –' He was ashen.

'You are not going!' She could feel the tears welling up inside her like a tide. 'Not yet. Not till Liza gets home. You promised!'

'Beth darling, I have to. She's threatening to take an overdose.'

'You can't. You can't leave me alone. I won't let you. She doesn't mean it!'

'Beth!' He was standing in front of her. 'I wouldn't go if it wasn't important, you know that.'

'I'm important!'

'Yes, you are. You are the most important thing in my life. But Idina needs me.' He took a deep breath. 'She's done it before, Beth.'

'But I need you, Giles! Supposing it comes back! Supposing it attacks me again?' She stared at him in sudden real terror. 'You're not going now?' Her voice slid up the scale in panic as he turned and began to collect his scattered belongings.

He stopped and came over to her, his face anguished. This was the hardest thing he had ever had to do. 'Please, darling Beth, don't make it even more difficult for me. I have no choice. I hate to leave you, but you will be safe. I'll go and fetch Jenny and her dogs. They'll come back if I ask. Keep all the doors and windows locked until daylight. I shall ring you the moment I get there, I promise. The thing is, I can't leave Idina on her own when she gets like this. If she's busy with another man she doesn't care. But he's dumped her.' He shook his head miserably. 'I know it's emotional blackmail but I am her husband, Beth. I feel responsible for her. I am still very fond of her.' He shrugged and put his hands gently up to her injured face. 'You're strong, Beth. You're a survivor. That's why I love you. And you've got your art. Idina has nothing. And I promise I shall come back. Somehow I shall sort things out with her and I shall come back.'

'You love me, but you're still very fond of her!' Beth retorted.

'That sounds like you want to have your cake and eat it to me!' She watched as, slowly and methodically, he collected up luggage and carried it out to the car whilst she sat unmoving at the kitchen table.

'Giles – please!' She followed him out at last. Standing looking helplessly at his car she started sobbing again.

'No, Beth.' He pushed the last case in and closed the hatchback door. His patience was wearing thin. 'I'll go and get Jenny –'

'Don't bother!' Beth ran inside, her unhappiness and fear suddenly turning to fury. 'You haven't got everything, have you! I think you'd better take these as well!' She raced round blindly, scooping up all their carefully worked notes and photos and sketches and the lists of headings, topics and chapters, bundling them together. Frantic with anger and misery, she hurled them at him across the muddy yard.

He stared down at them, almost dazed by what she had done, then he looked up at her in sudden cold rage. 'You're being selfish and childish, Beth!' he shouted. Then he sighed. 'Perhaps it's as well I found out now, before it's too late!' Climbing furiously into the car he reversed it round, running over one of her nicest sketches, and drove out of the yard.

She stared after him in disbelief, the cat completely forgotten as she heard the sound of his engine die away in the distance. Why had she been so stupid? She knew about Idina. She had known the score before she asked Giles here. But if she had been unreasonable, so had he.

Only then, as the rain began to fall again in huge, slow drops did some modicum of self-preservation at last kick in. She found a torch and went round the yard resolutely picking up all the papers and, shuffling them together, bundled them into a wet heap on the kitchen table before she slammed the door shut and threw the bolts across. Then she returned to the living room and flung herself down on the sofa to cry.

It was dark when Liza drove up the pitch at last and pulled into the yard. Only Beth's car was there and she wondered if they were out. The kitchen light was on though, and when she pushed the back door it was bolted.

'Beth? Giles?'

Beth opened the door alone. She threw her arms round Liza's neck. 'He's gone!' She had been crying so much her face was puffy and her eyes red.

'What happened? You didn't have a row?'

'Sort of.' Beth sniffed. 'It was so lovely. We were working on the book. Photographing. I was doing sketches. We had planned great chunks of it. He was going to stay until next week. Then his wife rang.' Tears welled up again and she groped in her jeans pocket for a tissue.

Liza sighed. She took Beth's hand and led her into the sitting room. It was in almost total darkness. One table lamp was glowing in the corner. Beth had been sitting on a cushion in front of the embers of the fire. Liza snapped on a couple more lights and threw a log on the fire. 'Didn't I tell you not to forget he was married?' she said sternly.

'He said they had an arrangement.'

'Oh, please!' Liza threw a glance up at the heavens. 'Sweetheart. Never believe a man when he says he has an arrangement with his wife, and never believe him when he says she doesn't understand him. That probably means she understands him only too well. So what happened? She summoned him back, I gather?'

Beth nodded. 'She threatened to kill herself if he didn't go back.'

'I see.'

'And I hurled all my sketches at him.' Beth burst into tears again.

'Oh, Beth.' Liza threw herself back against the cushions and closed her eyes. 'What am I going to do with you?'

'I'm sorry.' Beth looked so young and helpless, sitting on her cushion, her arms wrapped round her knees, the tears pouring down her face, that Liza wanted to cry with her.

'I'll give him a ring in the morning,' she said firmly.

'No!'

'Beth, this is a business arrangement. There is a lot of money involved, and a contract. You can't just cry and scream and throw your notes at him. You have to behave like an adult and so must he!' Liza made herself sound a lot sterner than she felt. 'If I don't ring him then you must. There is no room in this job for a prima donna, or for him to seduce you, the bastard. You both have to learn to be professional. And for future reference, as a rule, that means not going to bed with your business associates.'

'Just like you didn't go to bed with Michele.'

'That was different.'

'How?'

'It was. Just believe me, Beth. For one thing he wasn't married!

351

And for another he wasn't my only source of income, my first and most important job and my contact and recommendation, with any luck, to many jobs to come.'

She frowned suddenly as Beth looked up and gazed into the fire. 'What on earth have you done to your face?'

'Nothing.' Beth dropped her head into her arms again hastily.

'Show me?' Liza slid off the sofa and knelt beside her. 'My God, Beth, what happened? He didn't –'

'No, he didn't. How could you even think it!'

'Then what was it?' The sudden knife of panic in her stomach was reflected in the sharpness of Liza's voice. 'Tell me, Beth!'

'It was a cat.' Her voice was muffled in her knees.

'Oh, no.' Liza shook her head. 'Oh, please God, no.' She hauled herself back onto the sofa in silence.

So the fact that Liza had left Adam alone had not been enough for her. Brid had come to Wales anyway. Perhaps it was just a warning, or had her vindictiveness reached new depths? Julie, Calum, Phil, Jane. There were only two people left in Adam's life. Herself and Beth, the child of Adam's child . . .

Liza shuddered.

She checked every door and window that night, and searched the house herself after Beth had at last gone to bed, and before she climbed wearily into her own bed she unlocked the cupboard which contained Phil's gun and propped it up in the corner of the bedroom near her. Under her pillow she put a kitchen knife and she slept with the light on.

The phone call from Robert Cassie came at ten past nine. 'Liza, what's been going on? Giles says he can't work with your grand-daughter.'

'Of course he can – or he could if he kept his knickers on,' Liza retorted sharply. She had had a restless night and was feeling lousy. 'Tell him to be a bit more professional. Beth is distraught. He can't play with her like that. It's disgraceful. Just tell him to keep away. They've done all that needs to be done for now.' She had been looking at the notes and pictures and was impressed by the professionalism which had come through in spite of the streaks of mud and the occasional torn sketch. 'It will be all right. They will calm down.'

'I wish I shared your optimism!'

'Trust me.' Liza smiled. She had had an idea in the night which filled her with excitement.

It was a long time before the phone was picked up. '*Pronto?*'

'Michele? It is me. Liza!' She held her breath. 'Can Beth and I come out to see you?'

The *terrazza* was just as she remembered it. The crumbling white stone threaded with sweet-scented thyme and oregano seemed to merge with the hillside as though the old castle was growing from the very core of the mountain itself. Liza gave a deep sigh of contentment. She caught Michele's eye. 'You are a very nice man.'

'So I was always trying to convince you.' He smiled. 'When are you going to tell me the truth?'

'The truth?' She reached forward from the low chair and picked up her glass of wine.

'The truth.'

He was a tall man, his hair as thick as she remembered it, but now completely white. The tanned face was if anything a little more wrinkled, the eyes a little brighter, otherwise he had not changed. She still felt an intense pang of physical longing every time she set eyes on him. It was ridiculous, she kept telling herself, at her age, to lust after a man the way she was doing. It lacked dignity and it lacked style. But still she found herself wanting to reach forward and run her fingers over the silky hairs on his tanned arm as it rested on the edge of the table near her. He smiled. 'Yes, I know you have come to get Beth away from some unsuitable man, and to let her relax and unwind and compose herself, and – what were the other words you used?' He chuckled. 'But I don't think that was why you came at all. I remember my Liza. It is not like her to be afraid and she would not be afraid of an importunate author. After all she is not afraid of me!'

She laughed. 'As observant as ever.'

'So. The truth.'

'Michele, I would tell you the truth if I thought there was the smallest chance of you believing it. But as it is, I don't think you would.' She could see Beth, wandering in the gardens below them. The pale straw hat she was wearing bobbed up and down amongst the trees and then stopped. She saw the flash of white as the sketch book was opened and knew she was settled, at least for a while.

'Try me.' His voice was stern.

'All right. I'll tell you. I'm afraid. For Beth and for me.'

He listened without interrupting, once leaning forward to take the wine bottle from its bucket of ice to refill her glass, then sitting back in his chair, his whole body relaxed. Behind his dark glasses his eyes were an enigma.

353

When she had finished he said nothing for a moment, then slowly he sat up and leaned forward, his elbows on the wooden table.

'Did you ever go to a priest for advice?'

She shook her head. 'That's not Adam's way. And it's not mine.'

'And your friend, Meryn?'

'I don't know where he is.' She hesitated. 'Do you believe me?'

'Why should I not? I am old enough to have seen many strange things in my life. After all,' his face broke into a smile, 'my beautiful Liza has come back to me.'

'Flatterer.'

He acknowledged the remark with a slight nod of his head. Then he leaned forward again. 'I am intrigued by this. In some ways it is a lovely story. A young girl, driven by love, pursues a man through the years. It shows a depth of devotion we might all envy.'

'It shows madness, Michele. Single-minded, obsessive madness.' Liza's voice was sharp. 'Do you know how many people she has killed?'

He shrugged. 'Ah, I did not say she was not dangerous.' He paused thoughtfully. 'How do you know she will not follow you to Italy?'

'I don't. I am hoping she won't.'

'And you still have not told Beth why the cat attacked her?'

'No. I don't want to frighten her. I was eighteen when Brid first attacked me, Michele. I can't believe it! She has hunted me for nearly half a century!'

'But she has not killed you. For some reason she has let you live, or you are protected and she cannot harm you. Which?' He removed his glasses and fixed her with a piercing stare. 'We must work this out. It is important. Do you still love Adam?' He kept his voice carefully neutral.

She smiled. 'In a way, I will always love him. Yes.'

'But not enough to live with him?'

'No. We are very different people. We could never live together.'

'I wonder if that is it, then. She knows you are no threat. On the other hand she killed, you think, your husband as well as your daughter. That was to punish you? There could have been no other reason?'

'No.' She looked away to hide her sudden tears.

'Liza.' He put his hand on hers gently.

'I know. I'm sorry.' She sniffed. 'Will you give me some more wine?' She held out her glass with a shaky hand. 'So, you do believe me?'

'I told you so.'

'And are we safe here?'

There was a pause. 'I believe so. After all, why would she pursue you when she has her Adam all to herself now? Surely that is all she wanted.' He was silent for a long time, then slowly he drew her to him. 'Liza. I think the time has come for us to get married.'

For a moment she tensed, then slowly she relaxed. She looked up, the tears still in her eyes. 'Do you mean it?'

His arms tightened round her. 'I mean it, *carissima*. I have never meant anything more in my whole life.'

She gave a little sigh. 'I would feel safe here.'

'You would be safe.' He held her at arm's length and smiled. 'I wouldn't stifle you, Liza. I wouldn't stop you painting. All I have to offer is adoration. Think about it at least, please?'

A-dam?

Her voice was growing weak.

A-dam?

Endlessly she searched the rooms, but they were empty. The furniture had gone. Only dust remained on the floors. Silently drifting up the stairs she wandered from room to room yet again. The room she had shared with Adam, the room he had shared with his wife, the boy's room, even that was empty, the walls stripped of posters and pictures and books.

A-dam? I need you.

Her strength was going without Adam to sustain her. Soon she would have to return to the mountains where her sleeping body lay, captive in another time. There was no link now, no means of searching for him. No energy to do anything beyond roaming endlessly round the empty house in St Albans where the new season's roses were hanging unpruned and uncared for on the spindly bushes. Soon the new owners would move in. They planned extensive renovations. They were going to knock walls through, change window frames, turn the garage into a playroom, put a conversion in the attic. They were going to take a bulldozer to the garden, put in a pond, take out the old pear tree and the roses. They did not care that two women had died in the house. They were not superstitious; it did not cross their minds that there might be ghosts.

Brid watched them from the window as they walked around the garden discussing in loud voices what they would do to A-dam's beloved flower beds. If they saw the cat lurking in the shrubs it did

355

not worry them. A good sprinkling of pepper dust would soon see it off.

So, Brid, are you awake?

Broichan's voice came to her from the distance, muffled as if with sea mist. *It is time to come back to us, Brid. Your time for travelling is over. See, I have your brother here waiting for you.*

'Gartnait?' She opened her eyes. 'Gartnait, are you here too?'

Where was she? The pavement was wet and cold. Someone was standing over her. 'It's one of those hippies. Drugged, I wouldn't wonder.' The woman in a plastic raincoat, with a shopping trolley on wheels, sniffed and passed her by. The next person threw a few pennies at her, which rattled onto the paving and lay scattered round her in a semi-circle. She was crying now.

'Gartnait?'

'What did she say? Foreign, I shouldn't wonder. Better fetch the police.'

They came, they went away. No one did anything. As it grew cold and dark she huddled smaller into the shadows, praying for her cat self to come so she could hide and hunt and curl up somewhere in the shelter.

Brid, there is no point in hiding any more. Come back.

She could feel him tugging at her. The chain around her ankle bit tightly and she moaned with fear. Adam would save her if he knew. Where was he? Why had he left his house? Why had it all changed?

Brid, you disobeyed the rules of the priesthood. You disobeyed the gods. They are angry, Brid. You were too clever. You used their gifts for your own lust. You must go before them and atone.

Stand up. Move, get away from these people. She knew what interfering people did. They took you to a mental hospital, where you were locked up and made to wear silly clothes and eat horrible food. They kept you where you could not see the sun or the moon; where you could not wash your limbs in the soft brown waters of a mountain stream, or the hot steaming baths of A-dam's house. Instead you were kept like a slave. She could feel the chain now. Broichan's chain, around her ankle, holding her, stopping her from fleeing. When she went back to her bed in his hall she would die by his hand, a sacrifice to the gods who were affronted by her behaviour. There was nowhere for her to go. No one to look after her. She had to stand up. She had to move.

She wasn't sure how she reached the orchard. One moment she was in the wet St Albans street, the next she was standing leaning against the old lichen-covered gate, her fingers stiff with cold as they rested on the top rail. The farmhouse was in darkness. She frowned. Her green gown was wet and thin. She was shivering violently. Closing her eyes for a second she tried to imagine herself inside the warm sleek cat skin, feel herself looking out of narrowed feline eyes, listening with acute, sharp, pointed ears. Her fingers flexed on the gate and tried to become claws, but nothing happened. A splinter of old wood ran up under her nail and startled by the pain she looked down to see a spot of blood stain the pale lichen. She pulled off some moss and packed it round her finger, then she walked slowly towards the house.

Carefully she walked all round it, peering in at the windows. Already she knew there was no one at home. There were two cars in the garage but it was padlocked shut. She did not sense they were near. Certainly A-dam was not there. Nor had he been.

Huddling into one of the old barns, she pulled a sack around her shoulders and sat down to listen to the rain on the roof slates. Broichan could not reach her here. Neither could the interfering people of St Albans who wanted to take her somewhere and give her soup. Here she could rest until morning, then she would begin her search. Somehow she would find her A-dam again, if it took her all eternity.

PART FOUR

Beth
Early 1990s

19

Robert Cassie sat back and stared round The Granary with immense satisfaction. He had just consumed his third cup of coffee and his second slice of delicious carrot cake and he was fairly sure he had won. He brought his attention back to Beth with a smile. 'You know it is not every illustrator I would drive a hundred and fifty miles to see.'

'I know.' She smiled back. 'But then it is not every illustrator you would dare put such a proposition to. You know Giles and I do not get on.'

'But you are a winning team.' Their book, *The Magic of the Black Mountains*, had sold 30,000 copies in hardback and reprinted three times within the first three months. Getting them to finish it had been a triumph for Robert's diplomatic powers, which were considerable but had never before or since been tested to such limits.

'Listen, Robert, I said I would think about it, and I will. You are offering me a lot of money.' She allowed her eye to stray for a moment down to the file of papers lying on the red-patterned oil cloth which covered the round table between them. The working title *These are My Mountains: the Beauty and Mystery of the Scottish Highlands* was printed in black italics across the cover. Somehow seeing it like that made it seem a *fait accompli* – a psychological ploy for which she gave him full marks for effort.

The door opened and three hikers came in, their faces reddened by the wind, their boots grating on the flagstones. They stood before the blackboard menu rubbing their hands and blowing on them, comforted and cheered by the warmth and the smell of cooking.

'Does Giles know you are asking me to do the illustrations?' She looked at Robert quizzically.

'Of course. He knows you are essential. Without your pictures

361

the book wouldn't work. Giles needs the money, Beth. He is desperate to do it.' He looked at her under beetling eyebrows and grimaced. 'I shouldn't tell you that, but I think you should take it into account before you turn the whole thing down out of hand.' He was fairly sure she wasn't going to turn it down, but he couldn't count completely on her agreement until she had signed something. Perhaps it was time to change the subject. 'Tell me, how is the gorgeous countess?'

Beth giggled. 'She doesn't like being called that at all. She is very left wing, my grandmother.'

'She must miss Wales.'

'Of course she does. She found it very hard to sell the farm. In fact I don't think she would have if she hadn't been able to buy Meryn's cottage for me. She knows she can come any time. And they do in the summer. When it gets too hot for her over there and she longs for a bit of mist and Welsh rain.'

'And she must miss you, too.'

Beth gave a wistful little shrug. 'Of course. But I visit often. And she and I are working girls. She goes and paints people all over the world still, and I have my moments!'

'Like this one, when a London publisher comes and grovels at your feet and sparing no expense, takes you out for carrot cake and coffee.'

'Were you shocked I wouldn't come to London?'

He grinned. 'Shocked but not surprised. You're playing hard to get.' His grin broadened. 'I know you and Giles have problems. And I do know you hate coming to London. You're a country girl through and through, aren't you?'

'I am. And I'm a Welsh girl, Robert. I know nothing about the Scottish mountains.'

'You could learn. And you may have been brought up in Wales, but one of your grandfathers was a Scot, wasn't he? Wouldn't you like to find out about your ancestors on your father's side of the family? And you would love the mountains up there. I guarantee that you couldn't fail to fall under their spell.'

'You're believing your own publicity already!' She smacked his wrist. Sitting back in her chair she allowed her eyes to close for a moment. Her brain was whirling. She had not seen Giles for three years.

They had tried to be just friends, but it hadn't worked. Sex got in the way. And Idina. And love. Hers. Then they had blazing rows. Even so, she had done the work. Her sketches and paintings had been brilliant. But on each occasion when they had had to meet to discuss the book she had insisted that it should be in London, so that they could meet at the neutral offices of Hibberds in the West End, and there they had been carefully and ostentatiously polite. Two or three times he had criticised her drawings and she had flounced out of the meetings. Twice she had told Giles his captions were crap and Robert had had to retrieve him from the pub across the road, but they had managed to finish the book in the end and, as she vowed never again to go to London, had been photographed together, smiling, at the launch party in Hay and again on the top of Hay Bluff. It was there that Beth had told him, between clenched teeth as she pretended to smile at the stunning view across what felt like the whole world, to take a running jump over the edge of the steep hillside. Neither of them had ever referred again to their idyllic few days together in the old farmhouse, or to the attack by the wildcat which had, in the end, left a slight scar down the side of Beth's face beneath the sweep of her long curly hair, or to the unbelievable hurt she had felt at his abandonment of her.

She leaned back in her chair to gaze at the log fire burning in the hearth nearby. The place was filling up and she found herself having to raise her voice a little to make herself heard. 'Why is Giles so hard up? He made a packet out of the book.'

'I don't think that's our business, Beth. He just said he was.' Robert, with a glance at the neighbouring table, put on a carefully neutral voice. 'The point is, I'm sure you and he could work well together again. It would be a new project, in a new place. He would behave.'

'Did he say so?'

He nodded, then stood up. 'I'm going to fetch myself a beer. Can I get you something?'

She shook her head; and watched as he threaded his way through the crowded room to the queue at the counter. Half of her was tempted by the offer of the commission, but the other half, the half which was in charge of her self-preservation and her self-esteem, said: No. Don't do it. Don't get involved. If she didn't care it wouldn't matter. But she did still care, that was the trouble.

After Giles there had been no one else. No one serious, that is. And she suspected there never would be. Giles was the first man she had fallen in love with and, stupid though it seemed, it looked as though he would be the last.

She watched Robert returning to her, carefully making his way between the crowded tables. It had felt like a good idea to suggest they meet here when she had spoken to him on the phone. Although it was filling up fast now, early in the day the place was quiet and warm and comfortable, perfect for coffee and a meeting of this sort. But he had, it was now beginning to dawn on her, driven one hundred and fifty miles for this cup of coffee. It would hardly be hospitable to send him back without lunch. Perhaps she should even offer to put him up for the night, too.

In the end she suggested they take a walk along the Wye, then she drove him to the Radnor Arms for a late lunch. When their discussions were finally and impassably over, she dropped him back at his car so he could start back for London. There had been a slight hesitation, she thought when she offered to take him up to the cottage, but in the end he had declined. There were meetings all tomorrow he couldn't miss, he said sadly. She did not enquire if one of them was with Giles.

She parked by the standing stone as she often did on the way home and stood for a few minutes looking out across the steeply sloping hillside towards the Wye valley and the Radnor forest beyond. It was a peaceful place when there were no other cars parked there, a place, she sometimes thought, where one could feel the heart of the mountains beating with a slow, gentle reassuring rhythm. The clouds had drawn back a little and there was a watery sun appearing low in the west, throwing etiolated shadows across the hills. The air smelled cool and fresh and sweet. It was a long time since she had allowed herself to think about Giles. Damn Robert! He had presented her with a dilemma she didn't want to have to face.

Realising she was cold she turned back to the car and climbed in. It wasn't far down the narrow winding pitch to the track which led to Ty Mawr. It was extraordinary the way she had come to own the cottage. Almost the same day that Liza had told her she had finally agreed to marry Michele and had offered her the farmhouse – too big, too rambling, too expensive to run, too many memories – Meryn had walked in and sat down at the kitchen table and told them he was going to give up the cottage. 'I'm so seldom here. It fills me with sorrow, but I don't see any alternative.'

They still did not know where he went; the address of his solicitors was in Cardiff, but he had asked a ridiculously low price and given Beth his blessing and told Liza, quietly in private, that she would be safe there.

Beth's old car bucketed over the rough track – she was going to have to do something about both car and track soon – and came to a halt outside the cottage. A small blue Peugeot she didn't recognise was parked there and she stared at it for a moment with a sudden illogical rush of excitement. Had Giles come to persuade her himself?

Getting out of her own car she looked at it, puzzled, then she stared round. The house was locked and there was no sign of anyone there.

'Hello?'

She walked round the back to Meryn's small herb garden – too long a wilderness during his extended absences and not much better looked after by an owner who preferred to sketch the plants rather than weed them. An old man was standing there, hands in pockets, looking up towards the cloud-wreathed top of the hill behind the cottage.

'Hello?' She stopped, puzzled. 'Can I help you?'

He turned. He was tall, white-haired, perhaps in his mid-seventies, a strikingly handsome man. She recognised him at once. The portrait of her grandfather as a young man had hung in Liza's studio; she had had many offers to buy it but had always resolutely refused to sell. Almost cruel in its brutal reality it had fascinated and terrified Beth for as long as she could remember.

'Beth?' The old man had a strong voice, but something in his manner worried her. 'I'm Adam Craig.'

She smiled uncertainly, thrown by such a formal introduction, then she moved forward. 'Grandfather.' She reached up to kiss his cheek.

'I came looking for your grandmother. I went to the farmhouse.'

'She sold it.' Beth hesitated. 'You knew she had remarried?'

He nodded abruptly. 'The people at the farmhouse told me. They also told me you were up here alone.'

'I like being alone.' She had not intended to sound so defensive. 'I have my work.' She felt uncomfortable and wasn't sure what to do. This, after all, was the man who had refused to see her for almost all her life, who blamed her, or so she had always suspected though she could never guess why he should do so, for his son's, her father's, death. 'Will you come inside? I could make you some tea or coffee.' He was an alcoholic, she remembered that much about him. Shortly after Liza's last visit to him in St Albans a few years before, he had sold the house and disappeared. No one had heard from him since. She remembered how hurt Liza had been.

He sighed. 'Thank you, lass. I should like that.' She could detect the Scots accent now. Faint, but definitely there.

He followed her into the house and stood looking round. She had brought a few of her favourite things up from the farmhouse: the small black oak Welsh dresser, two Windsor chairs which had stood in the kitchen, her own bed, some antique tables, a chest of drawers. The rest of the stuff had been sold or gone with Liza to Italy. She had made her studio in an old byre at the back of the cottage: as a family they were obviously destined to be barn painters.

'Please, sit down.' She filled the kettle and put it on the Rayburn. 'I've been down in Hay. The publisher of the book I illustrated came up from London today to discuss doing another one.'

'You're a painter too, like your grandmother?' He seemed surprised.

She nodded. Ducking outside the back door she gathered an armful of blocks from the pile stacked up against the wall of the byre. Coming back in she threw them into the fireplace and knelt to build them into a pyramid over a fire-lighter.

'I don't think I even know where you're living these days?' she said as lightly as she could. He was still standing in the middle of the floor, staring round.

'I went back to Scotland, where I was born and brought up.'

'Really?' She swivelled on her heels and looked up at him. 'How long have you been there?'

He shrugged. 'A couple of years. I went to America after I sold the house in St Albans. I travelled around a lot. Then I went to Scotland – to Pittenross.' He paused thoughtfully. 'I visited the minister when I was there and he told me about a cottage for sale up on the hill and in the end I bought it.'

'I've never been to Scotland.' The kettle had begun to whistle. She reached for the pot, warming on the back of the stove, and spooned in some tea. 'But strangely enough this morning I was asked if I would go there to do some work.'

'It's very beautiful.' He sat down at last. 'Is Liza happy?' The abruptness of the question startled her.

'Yes.' She glanced at him. 'She's very happy.'

'And she still paints her portraits?'

'Of course. She could never stop that.'

'Does she come over at all?'

Beth nodded. 'Several times a year. They go and stay at an old manor house hotel down in the next village for three or four weeks each time they come.'

'And you say you're not lonely up here?'

She shook her head vehemently. 'I love my own company.'

'No boyfriend?' His eyes were suddenly piercing.

'From time to time.' She paused, a sudden lump in her throat. 'Nothing serious. Nothing at the moment.' She found she didn't resent his questions; perhaps a grandfather had the right to ask them.

He nodded. 'And the chap who used to live here. Meryn. What happened to him?' She looked up from pouring the tea. There had been a subtle change in the tone of the question. Where the rest had been casual this one, amongst them all, mattered to him.

She shook her head. 'I am sorry. I don't know. He used to come and go. I haven't seen him since I moved in.'

'But you have his address?'

She shook her head again. 'I don't. Only that of his solicitor in Cardiff.' She hesitated. 'Was it important?'

He shrugged his shoulders and stood up again, pacing restlessly up and down the carpet. 'Your grandmother, Liza, had a lot of time for the chap. He seems to have been very wise.'

'He was lovely. My parents spent their honeymoon in this cottage, you know. I like that. It seems to bring them closer, somehow.' She passed him a cup and offered him some sugar. 'When I was little I used to call him Merlin. I thought he was a wizard.'

Adam looked at her hard. 'And was he?'

'I don't know. He was a man of mystery. I've no idea what he did for a living. If anything. He dropped the price of the cottage by half when he heard I wanted to buy it. It was almost a present. I had the feeling that maybe he went to live abroad. I wondered sometimes if he was in love with Granny Liza, but I never found out.'

'Will you give me the name and address of his solicitors?' He put the cup down untouched and strode to the window. 'Maybe I can reach him that way.'

'Why did you want to speak to him?' She felt saddened suddenly. He hadn't come to see her at all.

He shook his head. 'I thought maybe he could help me with something, that's all. Not important.' He didn't meet her eye. 'I'd like your grandmother's phone number too, if you think she wouldn't mind.'

'Of course she wouldn't. She was desperately sad when you left St Albans without telling her where you'd gone.'

'I did that for a reason. She knew why.' He sat down again, sipping his tea. He was staring into the fire abstractedly and didn't seem to notice when she sat down opposite him, but after a moment he said, 'You look like Liza. She was very beautiful when she was young.'

'She still is.' Beth was Liza's greatest fan. She smiled at him. 'And I'll take that as a great compliment. Thank you.'

He almost smiled. 'She is all right?'

'She's fine.' Beth paused. 'Why don't I ring her now? She'd love to hear from you.'

'No!' He stood up, agitated. 'No, I don't want to make the connection. Not from here.'

'Why not? Grandfather, what's wrong?'

His manner had suddenly changed and his hand, as he put down his cup, suddenly trembled so that it rattled in the saucer. 'I have to go.'

'Grandfather. Please. Stay. You can stay here. I have a spare room . . .'

'No! I have to go. I shouldn't have come.' He looked round distractedly. 'Tell your grandmother to be careful.'

'I will. Grandfather, what's wrong? Is it something to do with Liza? Please, let me ring her.'

'No.' He shook his head. 'I shouldn't have come,' he repeated. 'Forget you saw me. Don't tell her I was here.'

'But I must.'

'No. No. Say nothing.'

He made suddenly for the door and pulled it open, ducking out into the dusk. 'I'm sorry. I shouldn't have come. I'm sorry. It was a mistake.' He was muttering under his breath.

'Then at least give me your address. Your phone number . . .'

'No.' He groped in his pocket for his car keys. 'This was stupid. Selfish. Idiotic! No. Don't let her come after me. Just forget I was here.'

He climbed into his car and shut the door with a slam. As she stood, watching helplessly, he started the engine and backed the car round to face the track. For a moment she thought he was going to drive off without a word, but he wound down the window as he started to let in the clutch. 'God bless you, Beth, my dear. I wish I'd known you. I was a stubborn, silly old man, but I had my reasons for staying away, believe me. Just forget you saw me now.'

And he had gone, pushing the car along the track far faster than was sensible. She winced as she saw it ground on a ridge, then he was out of sight.

She walked back into the house slowly and shut the door behind her. He had left a strange atmosphere behind him. She frowned, and then did something she had never done before. She turned and bolted the door. Then she reached for the phone.

'Michele? *Come stai*? Can I speak to Liza please?'

His answer was long, affectionate, detailed and negative.

She gave a small sad laugh. 'Does she often go off on her own like that with no number or anything?'

She was apparently painting a family of wine growers somewhere in the Abruzzi.

'It was part of our agreement, *carissima*, so she would not feel trapped and owned by her terrible chauvinist husband.' He sighed, only half humorously.

'But I need her.' She did not mean it to sound quite so desperate.

'So do I, Beth.' Suddenly he picked up on the tone of her voice. 'What is wrong? Is it something I can help with? Do you want me to come over?'

She smiled, her eyes filling with tears. 'No. Bless you, Michele, but no. There's nothing wrong. Just silly female stuff.'

Like intuition. And loneliness. And fear.

It was later, after she had made herself a boiled egg and toast and had sat down with a mug of hot chocolate to watch a Jane Austen dramatisation on the television, that she remembered Liza telling her that Pittenross was in the mountains.

These are my mountains . . .

She murmured the phrase to herself, her eyes glued to the drawing room of a beautiful Georgian house in Hampshire with its complement of elegant guests engaged in dextrous verbal sparring, a distraction from her whirling thoughts. Adam Craig had intrigued, unsettled and – a little – frightened her. She could not get him out of her head. What was it he had really come to say to her? Or rather to Meryn, for he hadn't meant to come to see Beth at all, that much was clear. And what was he afraid of?

She puzzled over it for most of the evening, when she wasn't thinking about Robert Cassie's offer. Then the two came together with sudden blinding inevitability.

She could not make up her mind about Robert's offer unless she had been to Scotland herself and assessed its potential as a subject for her talents. After all, she did not have to see Giles again to do it. She need not even tell him she was going. And if she was there anyway, surely she would be able to locate Adam Craig's cottage and find out why he was so afraid of renewing his contact with his family. Over the years he had been an enigmatic stranger in her life. A grandfather who did not want to know her. A man who had, Liza had confessed, been her lover. A doctor. A brilliant, competent, intelligent man who had become an alcoholic and who had suddenly disappeared off the face of the earth. And now, having come all the way to Wales to find Meryn, he had run away again. There was no other word for it; he had fled. And Beth wanted to know why.

The hotel was Scottish baronial – a cross between St Pancras Station and Inveraray Castle with a touch of the Taj Mahal thrown in. Beth stared open-mouthed as her taxi pulled round the bend in the drive. Then she found herself smiling. It was the most amazing, wonderful outrageous piece of architecture she had ever seen. The taxi pulled up on the gravel near the front door and she climbed out to be greeted by four dogs pouring out of the front door, tails wagging.

'Beth?' The short, plump sandy-haired man who followed the dogs held out his arms in welcome. 'Giles told me to expect you about now. Welcome to Loch Dubh. This is my wife, Patti.'

An equally plump woman had followed him out. Dressed in blue jeans and a thick Fair Isle sweater, she had long white-blonde hair barely contained in a fat disorganised plait. She gave Beth a hug as though she had known her for years. 'Giles is coming later if you say he can. He is contrite and abject and swears to be good. Isn't that what he said to say?' she threw over her shoulder at her husband.

He guffawed. 'If you believe that, you'll believe anything!' He swooped on Beth's cases. 'I've been ordered to give you the best room, the best food, anything you want. Your wish is our command. The place is fairly empty at the moment, so to be honest, we can wait on your every whim till you are sick of us, so say so if you want to be alone!' His eyes twinkled irresistibly. 'You may also borrow my car. Giles said to hire you one and he would pay, but I'll relieve the old bugger of that expense at least. We don't need two most of the time, so it's yours whenever you need it. Come in, let me show you where everything is.'

She wasn't entirely sure how she had got to Scotland so quickly; a phone call to Robert Cassie, a toing and froing of cautious messages with Giles, who, it appeared, did have to know all about her visit, and it was all fixed. Giles, she discovered, had known Dave and Patti Andrews when they lived in London. They would look after her. They were, she suspected very quickly, one of the reasons Giles had chosen to centre the book on this particular area.

Her bedroom was huge. The black oak four-poster looked big enough to sleep four and the view was of green rolling gardens, hillside and heather, leading down to the small loch from which the hotel took its name and beyond it the hills.

'And your bathroom is in here.' Dave threw open another door and revealed a room almost as big again, in the centre of which stood a vast bath with four clawed feet. 'Don't be alarmed by the colour of the water. It's peat not rust!' he said cheerfully. 'Bar's open as soon as you want to come down and then just treat it all as home.' With a grin he withdrew, leaving her to get her breath back and unpack.

She did not bargain on finding Giles downstairs waiting for her. At the sight of her face he raised his hands in mock surrender. 'Don't shoot, please.'

He had lost weight since she had seen him last, and was looking even more handsome than she remembered. She stamped sternly on the leap of excitement and longing which took her completely unawares and concentrated instead on a fierce frown. 'I didn't think you were coming up here yet.'

'I wasn't. But I needed to talk to you. Please. Just about the book. We have to do it. Did Robert tell you the kind of advance they are going to pay?'

'He told me.' She kept her voice as even as possible. 'Where is Idina?'

'In London.' He frowned. 'Please, Beth. Can we talk as friends and colleagues? No strings.'

Somehow she managed it.

With a tight rein on her emotions she forced herself to concentrate on the folder of notes Giles produced as they sat down in the hotel's cosy sitting room whilst Patti and Dave cooked supper. They weren't alone. Nearby there were other guests: a couple of middle-aged women were giggling over some photographs on the sofa, and an elderly man who had earlier walked the moors with a gun was dozing over a tumbler of the local malt.

'You see? The local history is wonderful. We follow the same format as *The Black Mountains* exactly. Some history, some legend. Local birds and animals. Start with the geology. And there are some fabulous castles here, both nineteenth-century baronial and the real thing. And ruinous ruins!' His enthusiasm was as usual infectious and she felt her own excitement rising. 'You can base yourself here if you want to, as long and as often as you wish. Did Dave tell you? He always has rooms free even in high season, and for a friend he won't charge.'

'He's never going to grow rich on that philosophy.' She was leafing through Giles's notes.

'He's been rich. He didn't like it!' Giles grinned at her. 'Didn't they tell you their story? They came up here to live out a dream.'

'And did it come true?' She glanced up at him. For a moment he met her eye and she felt the spark leap between them. Hastily she looked away.

'Do dreams ever come true?' he replied quietly. 'I think they're very happy here. Perhaps that is enough to ask.'

She ignored the message he was trying to convey. 'They certainly look it,' she said briskly. 'It's strange, but though I don't know Scotland at all, my grandfather was born and brought up less than an hour's drive from here.' She was gabbling too fast and she knew it, as she told him the story – as much as she knew – of Adam's childhood and his life, anything to keep from talking about themselves. It was with something like relief that she looked up as Patti came in, her face shiny with heat from the kitchen, and announced that dinner was ready.

The guests climbed to their feet.

'You must meet my grandfather,' Beth said quietly as they went into the dining room behind the two women guests. It had occurred to her suddenly that Giles was an excuse to visit him – her grandfather must know a lot about local history – and also that she would be less afraid if Giles was with her. What she was afraid of she was not quite sure. The old man had been brusque and even a little strange, not intimidating in any way; but there was something in the air around him which had made her skin prickle with tension.

They talked for a long time, then at last she stood up. Giles was still drinking his coffee. 'I'm going up now,' she announced firmly. It was a moment part of her had been dreading. 'I'll see you in the morning.'

He looked up and gave her a lop-sided, contrite grin. 'Are you absolutely sure you want to sleep alone?'

It was said half jokingly, and so quietly no one else in the room could hear, but even so she glanced round, embarrassed. 'Giles, you promised!'

'Sorry.' He raised his hands again.

She glared at him and turned away. 'I will see you in the morning,' she repeated firmly. 'And maybe we'll give Grandfather a ring and go and see him then.'

Up in her room, she tried to phone Liza. Michele still had had no word, and she hung up miserably. She wanted to talk to Liza very much indeed.

The following day Giles and Beth borrowed the promised car, which turned out to be an aged red Porsche. 'All that remains of my career as a money trader in the City.' Dave looked from Giles to Beth and then handed her the keys. 'If you want to know how to lose ten years of bonuses and most of your hair, buy a Highland hotel the size of a railway station and find after you've bought it that it's falling down the hillside at the rate of several inches a year! Take care of her and be warned, she can still go quite fast.'

She could indeed, once Beth had plucked up courage to change out of second gear. They drove through brilliant sunshine and breathtaking views of mountains and glens and intense blue lochs, winding across country towards the east until at last they turned off the main road to climb the narrow road towards Pittenross.

The first person she asked in the narrow village street, with its scent of woodsmoke and wet pine needles, directed them to the new manse, a small, concrete bungalow in a neat development of recently built houses on the outskirts of the village. Leaving Giles in the car, his nose buried in the Ordnance Survey map, Beth knocked on the door and it was answered after a few minutes' delay by a pretty woman in a tracksuit. The minister was out, it appeared, but when Beth explained the nature of their visit her face cleared. 'You're Dr Craig's granddaughter? My dear, I am so pleased to see you!' The woman's warmth and kindness shone out. 'He seems such a lonely man, and he's not on the phone up there, which worries us. I'm Moira Maclaren, by the way, the minister's wife.' If she thought it odd that Beth had lost her grandfather's address she did not say so.

Her directions were detailed and fairly lengthy. Beth found out why when she set the Porsche at the network of steep lanes and tracks which led to the cottage, which rejoiced in the name of Shieling House. As they drew up outside, and climbed out of the car, she sniffed ruefully at the smell of burning rubber.

Her heart was in her mouth as they walked up to the front door and rang the bell. She could hear it pealing somewhere at the back but there was no reply and there was no car outside. The place seemed deserted and she found suddenly that she was overwhelmed with relief. She had a sneaking feeling that her welcome when she finally made contact with her grandfather would be less than ecstatic.

Slowly they walked around the building. The house was built of grey weathered stone with blistered white paint on the window frames and door. It was quite small, barely more than a cottage, as he had said. Behind it, bounded by low walls of dry stone, was a small garden. Here someone had made an effort. There were signs that vegetables had been recently dug and there were several neatly pruned rose bushes. Beth smiled. She remembered Liza saying that Adam adored his roses more than anything else in the world.

To their surprise the back door was standing ajar and she pushed it tentatively. 'Grandfather? Are you there?'

There was no response. Beth peered cautiously round it. 'I don't know whether we should go in,' she whispered uncertainly.

'I think we should.' Giles was immediately behind her. Too close. She could feel him breathing down her neck and she desperately wanted to reach out and touch him. 'You need to check he hasn't been taken ill or something,' he went on. As if he sensed what she was feeling he reached out and touched her shoulder lightly, then he drew back. 'And as his nearest living relative, if not his only one, from what you said, you have every right to go in.'

She glanced at him and nodded. Plucking up courage she led the way inside. Giles strode into the kitchen after her.

The kitchen was large, almost as big, she discovered on looking round the further door, as the living room, the only other room on the ground floor. Both were comfortably furnished with sturdy furniture. In the middle of the living room was a large table. On it was a typewriter and piles of papers and books. There were books all over the place, overflowing the shelves which had been put up on the end wall of the room, on the furniture, piled on the floor and all over the kitchen, mixed up with bread and milk and rancid butter and half-drunk mugs of coffee and tea.

'Grandfather?' Beth stood at the bottom of the short flight of stairs and looked up. The house felt empty, but it was with slight trepidation that she tiptoed up the modern, open-tread staircase onto the small landing. Off it opened two bedrooms and a bathroom. There was no one there either. Only one bedroom contained a bed, the other held boxes and storage cartons, and more furniture piled to the ceiling. Her grandfather's bedroom was untidy, the double bed unmade, heaps of books overflowing here as downstairs. Intrigued, she picked a couple up: *Pagan Celtic Britain* and *In Search of the Picts*.

Downstairs she found Giles intent on looking through the books on the table. The topics were the same. The Picts and the Celts of

Scotland, the Druids and early Scottish history, and with them books on every form of occultism and magic. Amazed and a little shocked Beth glanced through some of them. Was her grandfather writing a book? He had made copious notes both in his small, neat, but barely legible handwriting, and on the typewriter. Beside it she found, neatly stacked, lists of references and dates and what looked like recipes for magic potions. At least now she could guess why he had wanted to see Meryn.

'My God, Beth, look at this!' Giles pulled another pile of books towards them. This time they were in German, but their illustrations, of devils and fiends of every description engaged in acts which were graphic to say the least, left no doubt as to their subject. 'Is your grandfather writing a book on German erotica?' He laughed incredulously.

'He can't be!' Beth pushed them aside and pulled another pile of books forward. Dion Fortune's *Psychic Self Defence* and various books on the art of High Magic were muddled into a heap with two volumes on the mythology of cats.

She frowned. Cats? Something stirred uncomfortably at the back of her mind; both she and Granny Jane had been attacked by cats. She shivered and stepped away from the table uneasily, looking round. 'Oh God, Giles. We shouldn't be here.'

'Of course we should. This is fascinating, Beth.' Giles had hooked a chair up to the table and was engrossed. 'He's got the most amazing library here, you know. It must be worth a fortune.'

'He's got a crystal ball!' Beth had found it, wrapped in black velvet, on a shelf in the corner. 'And look at this. Runes. Tarot cards. Stones and feathers, oh, and a skull!'

'Human?' Giles looked up at last.

'No, you idiot! Some kind of bird with a huge beak.'

'Raven.' Giles had come to stand immediately behind her. 'He is into some seriously interesting stuff, Beth. All these Pictish symbol stones for example. You are going to have to paint one or two of them for the book.' He leaned close to her, pointing at the huge tome open before him on the table; she could smell his aftershave. 'Everyone knows about the Celtic crosses and the interlaced designs the Celts were so good at in their carving, you'll have to do one of those too, of course, but the Picts did these incredible strong drawings in the stone as well. Carving doesn't seem the right word. There is so much power in them. I've read a bit about them. There are so many theories about what they were: messages, clan totems, signposts, magic; gravestones. You get these animals and birds.

Symbols. There's one here.' He pointed at it, his arm brushing hers. She did not move away. 'He's photographed it from every angle, and he's copied the symbols on it – you see? There is a serpent there. And a Z rod. And a mirror. And the crescent moon with that sort of v-shaped thing. And then the Celtic cross on the back, but only half finished, which is interesting because it shows that the Pictish symbols came first, and the cross was an afterthought –' he broke off. 'Beth, there's someone coming!'

They had both heard the car engine. Guiltily they glanced at one another. It was too late to hide or go outside. Whoever it was would have seen their own car outside the front door.

When the door opened they were standing side by side by the table. A short, sandy-haired middle-aged man dressed in a thick sweater and a jacket strode in. He smiled and held out his hand. 'I'm Ken Maclaren, the minister down in Pittenross. I understand from my wife that you are Adam Craig's relatives?'

Beth stepped forward. 'I'm his granddaughter, Beth. We've been looking for him.'

Maclaren shrugged. 'He goes off on his own sometimes. I've been coming up each day to keep an eye on him and I have to say my wife and I have been a bit worried about him.' He looked down at the table uncomfortably. 'You have found his books, I see.'

'We certainly have.' Giles studied the man's face. 'His father was one of your predecessors, I understand?'

Maclaren nodded. 'A fine man, Thomas Craig. Very much respected in the neighbourhood and I like Adam enormously. He and I have been friends ever since he came back to this part of the world, but I have to say I am concerned.' He looked at Beth intently for a few seconds. 'My dear, he didn't tell me he had any relatives. I understood he was alone in the world.'

Beth shrugged. 'I have only met him very recently. Before that I hadn't seen him since I was a baby. I believe he was very unhappy after my grandmother died, and went away. No one knew where he was.'

Maclaren nodded. 'He does seem a very solitary man. He goes out each day at dawn, sometimes earlier, and wanders round in the hills. When he is here he is studying his books.' He stopped talking and sighed. 'And I am really not at all happy about some of the things he is doing up here. I should perhaps not say this to a stranger, but you are a relative, and the situation is dire. He is engaged in some very dangerous experiments.' He looked from Beth to Giles and back. 'I am not sure as to what he is trying to do.

376

He occasionally discusses some of his interests with me – where he thinks I can advise on spiritual practices, for instance – but I think some of what he does is not only a danger to his immortal soul but also an immediate danger to his life.'

Beth stared at him. 'What on earth is he doing?'

'It's black magic, isn't it,' Giles put in. He glanced down at the books on the table.

'I think he is trying to conjure spirits, yes. I think he is also involved in witchcraft. I am sorry to have to tell you this, but I am afraid for him. And on top of everything else, I don't know where he is. The house is not usually this . . .' he looked round, searching for a word, 'squalid. He forgets to clean it. But he doesn't let food go bad like this. I don't think he's been back for several days.'

Beth and Giles exchanged glances again and Giles reached out to give her shoulder a reassuring squeeze. 'Perhaps he's gone away somewhere? After all, his car is not here. If he had gone off walking in the hills and had a fall or something, surely it would still be here?'

'But he left the door unlocked,' Beth said quietly. 'He wouldn't have done that if he had gone off for several days.'

'Oh, he might,' Maclaren put in. 'That is typical, I'm afraid. He says no one used to lock doors and I can't convince him that crime has come to the glens, although not as much, I have to say, as it has elsewhere in the country.' He hesitated. 'I think he leaves the door unlocked deliberately. I think he is hoping someone might come.'

'Someone in particular, you mean?' Giles enquired. He was opening Adam's notebooks one by one and leafing through them.

The minister nodded. 'Last time he and I talked about his leaving the door open he said as much. He said "she" might recognise it as a sign that he wanted her to come home to him. I take it he didn't mean you?' He looked at Beth and gave her a small wry smile.

She shook her head. She liked this man with his pale blue eyes and thick-lensed glasses. He was sympathetic and caring, and she could feel a strength in him which reassured her. 'I doubt it. He didn't, to be honest, even give me his address. I got the strong impression he did not want anyone coming up here. When he came to find me it was my grandmother – my other grandmother, my mother's mother – he wanted to see, not me. But she lives abroad now so he went away.' And he wanted to see someone else. Meryn. Merlin the wizard.

'We're staying at the Loch Dubh hotel,' Giles put in. 'Beth and

I are collaborating on a book' – he glared at her, daring her to deny it – 'and she suggested Dr Craig might be able to help me with my research into Scottish history. We thought it gave us a good excuse to come and see him.' He paused. 'He seems to be especially interested in the symbol stones which I want her to draw for me.'

Maclaren nodded. 'That one,' he indicated the stone Adam had photographed, 'is very close to here. You walk up the hillside and over the ridge behind this house. It is a bit of an obsession with him, you're right. I wondered if it had anything to do with his father. There were quite a lot of notes about that stone in the old man's handwriting, which came to me in the parish papers. In his day it was regarded as heathen and in some way spiritually polluting. Thomas Craig had a very fundamentalist faith, and a very unforgiving one. He wanted it torn down.'

'But that's ridiculous. It's an ancient monument!'

He nodded. 'Different ages see things very differently. There is a signpost to it now, and a notice about it.' He paused thoughtfully. 'I wonder if it is your grandmother he is expecting?'

'He's not getting senile, is he?' Giles put in suddenly.

'No.'

'No!'

The minister and Beth spoke simultaneously.

'No,' the minister went on. 'I think he is a man with a quest. I only wish he had chosen other ways to pursue it, because the way he is going about it he is playing with hell fire, and although he is far from senile, I do think his sanity is at stake.'

They pulled off the road halfway back to the hotel and sat watching the stormy sunset. Giles had bought a tin of shortbread when they stopped to fill up with petrol and he pulled off the lid, offering Beth a piece as he scrabbled in the glove compartment for his notebook. 'Just near here there's a wonderful waterfall, if I remember. I'm not sure if there's time to go and see before it gets too dark.' He glanced at her. 'You're worrying yourself sick about him, aren't you?'

She nodded. 'None of it makes any sense.'

'You're going to have to try and speak to Liza again. There must be some way her husband can reach her in emergencies, surely.'

She shrugged. 'Mr Maclaren frightened me. He was really worried.' She reached for the door handle suddenly. 'I need to walk. Let's try and find your waterfall. After all I've got to have some variety in my drawings. Perhaps this one can be by moonlight.'

The track was hard to see in the twilight, but they followed it carefully with the help of a small pocket torch. It led through lichen-draped trees and over steep rocks, climbing almost vertically up the hillside.

Beth stopped to rub her foot after her shoe had slipped on a loose piece of scree and Giles waited for her. 'Are you all right?' He waved his hand vaguely towards the misty distance. 'I can hear the falls. Listen.'

They stood listening to the rush of water, and the whisper of the wind in the larch. The western sky was still bright with the setting sun, but in front of them the hillside was dark. Beth shivered. She desperately wanted Giles to put his arm round her. 'Is it far? It's getting dark very quickly.'

'Not according to the map. It's a tourist spot. A series of wonderful falls. It must be fairly close. And look. Here comes the moon.'

The silver light flooded through the trees suddenly and they both saw the glint of reflections where the water cascaded down the hillside. Scrambling on up the steep track they found themselves on a sort of natural platform, looking down into the dark cavernous pool beneath the fall.

Beth shuddered. 'It looks very sinister down there.'

'Look up,' Giles breathed. 'That's where the beauty is.' Streams of pure silver seemed to be pouring down the black face of the rock, threaded here and there by the delicate silhouettes of the trees which clung to the precipitous cracks. The noise was deafening. Giles looked down at Beth, then at last he put his arm round her shoulders. He murmured something to her but she couldn't hear him. She reached up to hear better and he mistook the gesture. His lips on hers were warm and firm, his arms reassuring. She knew she should pull away; she should break free. But in a moment she was lost. They clung together, locked in one another's embrace as the moon sailed higher over the mountainside, sending its light down into the depths of the pool below and turning it to liquid fire.

It was a long time before Beth remembered her resolutions and a little shakily pushed him away. 'We shouldn't have done that.'

'No.' He grinned. 'I'm glad we did.'

'But Giles, what about Idina?'

He sighed. 'Beth, our marriage is over. We've tried. God knows I've tried, but we don't have anything in common any more. And she realises it at last, too. She is a town girl and I'm country. It's as simple as that. No, it's more than that. I bore her. And it's a long time since I loved her. Since before you and I ever met, Beth.

I tried to tell you, but I suppose I can't blame you for not believing me.' He hesitated. 'The threats to kill herself –' He paused again and shrugged. 'I've discovered they don't mean anything. They are dramatic and they call me to heel very effectively. But she's the one who has been straying. I've been faithful.' He paused. 'To you. Please, believe me, we're not hurting her.'

'Giles, I want to believe you –' she broke off. 'What was that?' All her senses were suddenly alert.

'What?' He stared at the trees and rocks around them.

'I'm sure I saw something – there, in the shadows.' She felt a sudden wave of real fear. 'Giles, let's go. Let's get back to the car.'

He glanced at her in astonishment. 'But it's lovely here, Beth. There's no one about. And if there is it doesn't matter. They're not interested in us.' She had stepped away from him and he followed her. 'I want to kiss you again. And I need to take some pictures.' He had his camera slung over his shoulder.

She looked round again, trying to see into the shadows. 'No. There's something watching us.'

'Something?' He put his arm round her again, this time protectively. 'Where?'

'I don't know. I can feel it. Please, let's go.'

She caught his hand and dragged him towards the track.

'No, Beth. Wait. You've let all that talk about your grandfather and black magic spook you. Just a couple of photos.' He disengaged himself from her grip and reached for the camera. Focusing carefully he stepped out to the edge of the rock platform, angling the lens towards the shining water. 'There. Lovely. And again. That's beautiful. Don't you want to make any sketches, take any notes?'

She shook her head. 'Let's come again in daylight. Please, Giles, I want to go.' The skin on the back of her neck was crawling. The silvered beauty of the woods and the water had become suddenly very threatening. This is panic, she thought suddenly. Panic in the true meaning of the word. Fear before Pan, the god of beautiful and wild places. She bit her lip. Or was Giles right? Was it Adam's books which had frightened her, not the glorious wild beauty of a moonlit burn?

She did not see the narrowed eyes watching her from the shelter of an overhanging rock, or hear the rasp of claws, the sound hidden by the immensity of the rush of falling water.

Broichan was still there waiting, but she had grown clever. She did not return to her bed where he stood watching over her sleeping form. She hovered nearby, unseen even by him, and slowly her strength was returning. She stood near the stone, tracing its carving with her finger, seeing the moss and the old dry lichen of centuries encrusted in the drawings her brother had made and she smiled. No one now could read the code but her. No one could follow the secrets it proclaimed. The mirror on the stone was all but obliterated. When she wanted to see into the reflections of time she stared into the tiny mother-of-pearl mirror in the compact in her old woven bag.

She wandered the hills. Sometimes she returned to Hertfordshire and drifted through the house where once a long time ago A-dam had lived. There were strangers there now, and she did not like them, but she did not touch them. They were nothing. Not worth her notice any more than was the family who lived in Liza's old house in the Welsh hills.

A-dam was thinking of her again. She could feel him. She could feel his energy questing for hers, but still she could not see him.

When the child of A-dam's child came to Scotland she had felt it at once in her blood. The tie was there, and the girl was very near. Brid grew stronger.

Broichan sensed it too. He left the hut where Brid lay sleeping and went to his own. There he could scry in the smoke and the water, watching the girl, Beth, with her cloud of dark hair, knowing she would lead him eventually to Adam, the man who had broken the sacred laws, and to Brid. He sharpened his knives and stared out of his hut at the moon and knew that other people in other times watched the same moon and he felt a shiver run across his shoulders.

In the shadows he could sense again the other one, the man from Adam's age who had followed him for so long. The Welshman was growing stronger and more adept all the time. Broichan frowned to himself. He would have to beware. The Welshman's power was special and his own was not as strong as it had been. But he could renew it. Once the pathways through the other worlds which Brid had opened and which had allowed this man through were safely closed again and her wild, dangerous search through parallel centuries brought to a halt he, Broichan, would reclaim the strength of his race. Then he would ensure the safety of his world with the sacrifice of blood.

20

The cottage was empty. Standing on the windy Welsh hillside Meryn stared round, puzzled. He was needed. He had heard voices calling. Broichan was prowling angrily through the shadows and his threats had reached out to the farthest corners of the planet. Beth was in danger, he was sure of it, but where was she? He stood for a moment, staring down across the valley, watching the trail of sun and shadow illuminate the landscape, hearing the distant cry of a buzzard wheeling somewhere in the eye of the sun. In the distance, across the water meadows and the Wye he could see the hillside rising steeply against the afternoon sky. It was misty there. Rain was coming from the north. So was something else. A voice, out of the dark. The landscape was calling him.

Climbing back into his car he sat for a moment. On the seat next to him a pile of old books, culled from the storehouse where he had left his library, contained all the information he had needed. One of them in particular, an old Victorian guide book, lay open before him. He glanced at it and frowned. Then he knew what he must do. Driving fast, he headed down the lane, round the corner at the bottom, and took the next lane down, diving between high hedges, some of which met overhead turning it into a narrow tunnel, his long strong fingers steady on the wheel as he skidded over loose gravel and bits of shale spilled from the sheer banks, heading for the river and the Glasbury bridge.

The church was open and Meryn let himself into the dim, cold nave. In his hand was the old guide book, his finger marking the page which described St Meilig's Cross on Bryn-yr-Hydd Common, a place where the fairies were said to dance on Midsummer's Eve. He paused, glancing down at the woodcut showing the cross. It had no Pictish symbols, of course, and the date they gave was around

AD650, a hundred years later than St Columba, but St Meilig had been born in Clydeside, the son of Caw of Pictland. So this Welsh abbot, whose cross had once stood on the common high above Llowes, had been a Pict. Had he inherited any of the knowledge of the Picts? Did he, in his hidden Welsh abbey, still know the secret places in the landscape where the fabric of time was thin and man could come nearer to his God?

The cross was there, at the west end of the aisle. It was huge, grey and heavy, but somehow without the majesty and power which it would have had when it stood under the open sky. Now, like so many ancient stones, its beauty and its historical interest had made it a target, to be garnered in and protected from weather and vandal and even time itself, and in the act of bringing it inside it had been in effect castrated and short-circuited and turned into a bland exhibit for the curious to gape at and move on and forget.

He walked over to it, thinking about Broichan's stone on the hills of Scotland. That stone was still a wild, living part of the landscape, linked into the circuits of the earth. It contained power in its own right, as well as the power which the carvings on it had instilled. Raising his hands he rested them flat on this great stone for a minute, to feel if anything of its power was still there. It was cold and crudely carved, tamed by the still, silent atmosphere of the church, but somewhere under his palms there was a slight throb, deep within the stone. He nodded in satisfaction. The silence in the church was oppressive, suddenly. He could hear nothing from the village outside, or from the main road beyond the hedge where the traffic between Hereford and Brecon sped on its way along the broad Wye valley. He ran his fingertips lightly over the stone face of the cross. Yes, he could feel it again now. He had awoken the stone from its sleep. He smiled, emptying his mind of everything but the sensation. For a few seconds it seemed to get stronger, then behind him he heard the clatter of the latch being raised on the door. He stepped back angrily. As the door opened noise and light and movement seemed to flood back into the church. The strange unearthly silence had gone.

He waited, arms folded patiently as the visitors pottered around, burying themselves in the guide book, staring up at ceiling and windows, chatting to each other loudly. Then they came to stand beside him near the cross, examining the old green-painted hand plough which for some reason stood there between the pews. The atmosphere had lifted. If he had been about to make any contact with the stone or its makers, it was too late. With a small, polite smile he turned and left the church.

Outside he stopped for a moment, taking deep breaths of the cold air.

He waited ten minutes to see if they would come out of the church and go away, but there was still no sign of them, and then another car drew up and three old ladies climbed out. Silently he cursed. He turned back to his own car. The fog had come down whilst he was in the church. It was dank and murky now and suddenly cold, but he had to go to a place of power. He paused for a moment to glance at his map, reminding himself where the footpath was, and drove out onto the road.

Parking alongside an old barn, he could see a fingerpost pointing away across a stile beside the barn and up a track. He surveyed the field beyond, which sloped up into the mist with here and there a tree showing as a shadowy silhouette in the distance. The place was deserted.

It was becoming colder and more damp. Rain trickled down into his collar and he shivered as he climbed over the stile, wondering suddenly if this was sensible. He was after all not as young as he used to be, and what he was about to undertake was dangerous in the extreme. He paused, staring round, listening, feeling the distances in the silence. He was right. Close to here was a trackway into the past.

Resolutely he plodded on, his hands deep in his pockets, his eyes on the muddy path in front of him. Behind him the mist closed in, drifted away, then closed back again. He could hear nothing of the road in the distance. Only the sound of the wind and the silence impinged on his consciousness. He was very close now. He could feel the pull of the earth. He paused, allowing himself to feel the pulses beating beneath his feet. The cross had stood near here, on the summit of a small hill, its shaft driven into the web of veins which carried the life force of the ages. From here he could find Broichan and Brid, and Beth and Liza and Adam Craig and, if necessary, he could project himself into the very heart of Scotland.

Beth and Giles were enjoying dinner in the dining room at Loch Dubh when Dave appeared in the doorway. 'Beth? Sorry to interrupt.' They had notes and sketches spread on the table between the knives and forks and plates of delicately pink salmon. 'Phone one for you I'm afraid. Ken Maclaren?'

384

Beth stood up. 'That's the minister. Oh God, I wonder what's happened.'

Dave waved her towards his office. 'Take it in there, it'll save you going upstairs.'

Giles followed her and stood by the door as she picked up the receiver. 'Miss Craig? I thought you should know. Your grandfather has come home. I saw him this afternoon just after you had left.' Ken hesitated. 'He seems very agitated. Upset and angry. I know it's a lot to ask, but I think maybe it would be a good thing if you could come over.'

'Now? This evening?' Adrenaline shot through her stomach. She glanced at Giles, white-faced. He was watching her anxiously. 'I don't know if there is anything I can do. I hardly know him, and I don't think I'd be a help in any way.'

'Please, Beth. I really think somebody needs to talk to him and he won't listen to me.'

She had grabbed a pencil and was drawing frantic small rings and swirls on Dave's neat blotter. 'Are you sure?'

'I'm sure. Just come and speak to him. Reassure him that there is someone there for him. Warn him that what he's doing is dangerous. Please.' The voice at the other end of the line had the calm strength of someone who is used to getting their own way.

'What could I say?' She put down the phone and looked at Giles miserably.

'You could have said no.' He frowned at her. 'If you go I am coming with you.'

'It's silly, but I'm scared.'

'You don't have to do it, Beth.' Giles put his hands on her shoulders. 'You really don't. Just ring Maclaren back and say you can't come. Or I will. He is using emotional blackmail and that is so unfair.'

'But he's right. Grandfather is all alone. Perhaps he is frightened too. He would never have come to Wales if he hadn't needed some kind of help.'

He sighed. 'Then ring Liza again. Perhaps she's home by now. She's the one who should speak to him, not you.'

Beth hesitated. It was a nice idea. A comforting one. But then she shook her head. 'No, she's miles away. What can she do anyway? If anyone is going to go, it had better be me. We don't know there's anything wrong at all. Perhaps he's just confused. Or ill.'

Or conjuring up some sort of devil there in the mountains in his lonely house.

They left twenty minutes later. Dave had made them a thermos of coffee and a packet of rare-beef sandwiches, spread with rich butter and grainy mustard. 'Instead of supper. I can't have my guests starving to death. It's bad for my reputation.' He had looked at them both carefully as he gave Beth the keys to the Porsche. 'Just how much whisky did you drink this evening before dinner?'

She smiled reassuringly. 'Not enough to register, Dave, I promise. I'm okay, honestly.'

He shrugged. 'I hope so. I don't want to lose my last perk!'

'You won't.'

She drove fast but carefully through the dark winding lanes, very aware that Giles, seated beside her, was unusually silent. The headlights cut swathes across the countryside at every bend, lighting heather and bracken, rock and water with the same narrow, pitiless beam. They drove mile after mile without passing another car and then at last turned down onto the A9. 'Nearly there.' She risked a glance.

'Go more slowly. There's no hurry.'

'The sooner we get there, the sooner we can go back.' Her knuckles were white on the steering wheel. She swung the car off the main road again towards the east. A spattering of raindrops hit the windscreen and she realised that the moon had disappeared behind black streaming cloud. 'What time is it?'

'Just after nine. Is Maclaren going to meet us there?'

She nodded, her eyes glued to the hairpin bends in the road. Larch and pine clung to the steep banks on either side of the tarmac and the headlights flung skyward as the car began to climb steeply.

When they drew up at last there was no sign of the minister's car. Beth parked beside Adam's blue Peugeot and turned off the engine. There were no lights visible in the house.

Giles peered through the streaked windscreen. 'Are you sure you understood him correctly? Perhaps we should have gone straight to the manse.'

She shook her head. Her stomach was turning over with apprehension. Groping for the door handle she climbed out and stood still for a moment, breathing deep lungfuls of the sweet, cold air. 'No. He said here. Shieling House.'

She hesitated, and Giles followed her. He put his arm round her shoulders and kissed the top of her head. 'It'll be okay. Maclaren will be on his way. I don't expect he thought we'd get here so quickly.' He gripped her hand firmly and led the way round the back.

Light poured from the kitchen windows and almost immediately they saw Adam standing at the kitchen table, looking down at something lying in front of him. Beth glanced at Giles. 'Shall I knock?'

He nodded.

Adam looked up startled at the sound, then slowly he walked over to the door and pulled it open. 'So, young woman. Ken told me you'd been here.' He did not smile. 'You'd best come in. You and your young man.' He peered at Giles. 'You're fools, both of you.'

'We wanted to be sure you were all right,' Beth said quietly as Adam closed the door behind them. She glanced round the kitchen nervously. It seemed much as it had been when they had left it earlier, but there was a kettle on the hob this time and Adam had laid out a mug and a jar of instant coffee on the table amongst his books.

'I'm all right.' He stood still, staring at them.

'We came yesterday because I was worried. The door was unlocked and it looked as though you'd been away for some time.' The plate of mouldy food had, she realised suddenly, disappeared from the draining board. She suspected Ken Maclaren had thrown it out before he went home.

'And you needed to interfere.' He said it quite mildly. 'Beth, my dear. I didn't want you to come up here for a very good reason. I am not so old and doddery I can't look after myself. I'm perfectly compos mentis. I was trying to protect you.' He sighed deeply. 'But now you're here I suppose I had better tell you the whole story.' He picked up the coffee jar and lifted two more mugs from the hooks on the dresser. 'I've sent Ken home. He warned me he had rung you. He's a pleasant enough young man, but a lightweight when it comes to what I am doing here. He does not understand. It is better he stays out of it.'

'And what are you doing, Doctor?' Giles spoke at last.

Adam cocked an eyebrow in his direction. A flash of amusement sparked in the brown eyes as he stirred hot water into the coffee. 'Dr Jekyll or Dr Frankenstein? I can see the way your mind is working, young man – what did you say your name was? – no, I'm not conjuring monsters.' He paused, the spoon dripping on the table, and stared for a moment into space. 'Or perhaps I am. Who knows?'

Turning, he led the way to his living room and threw himself down on the sofa. With a glance at Giles, Beth followed him. Giles picked up the two remaining mugs.

The three sat for a minute or two in silence, illuminated by the soft glow of one single desk lamp in the corner. Outside, the wind had increased and they all heard the splatter of raindrops against the window.

Adam roused himself and looked at Beth. 'I don't suppose Liza told you much about me,' he began slowly. 'Why should she? I was never a grandfather to you.'

Beth shrugged. 'She told me a bit.'

He nodded slowly. 'Did she ever tell you about Brid?'

Beth glanced at Giles. 'I don't think so,' she said cautiously.

He sighed. There was a long pause then he began to speak. The room was totally silent save for the sound of the wind soughing round the eaves of the old slate roof and the quiet, almost monotonous sound of his voice. 'When my Jane died, I cursed Brid. I sent her back to whatever hell she came from. She killed your father, my Calum –' His voice broke and he looked away, his hand over his eyes. He took a deep breath and then he went on. 'She killed Phil Stevenson. She killed your mother.'

The silence in the room lengthened. Beth was watching him, speechless with horror, her eyes riveted to his face. She had gone cold all over.

At length, when he had finished his story, Adam stood up. He walked over to the window and stared out into the dark. 'I turned my back on her. I wouldn't listen to her pleas. I cursed her again and again.' He was silent, gazing through his reflection into the darkness. 'I went to America and travelled around. I drank a lot.'

Beth stared unseeing at the half-full bottle of Laphroaig in the corner on the desk.

'Then I went south to Brazil. To Peru. To Bolivia. I thought I could forget her, but she came with me, in my head. Everywhere I went I could hear her calling me: *A-dam.*' He mimicked Brid's voice. 'She was pleading with me. If I did not let her back into my life, Broichan would kill her.' He fell silent again.

Giles and Beth were watching him in silence.

'One day they picked me up on the streets in La Paz. To this day I don't know what I was doing there. I had been beaten and robbed, but I was still alive. A Scots priest took me in.' He gave a tight laugh. 'A Catholic priest. My father in all his Presbyterian narrow-mindedness no doubt turned in his grave, but the man was a real Christian. He taught me what Christianity should be. Full of compassion and forgiveness and love. When I recovered I worked for a couple of years with him in his mission. In some ways I still barely knew who I was. I knew my name. I still had my passport. It appeared that I had been carrying it in a bodybelt and the robbers didn't find it. But that was about all I knew. The embassy tried to trace my family and my address, but of course I had sold the house and had no family left.' He did not notice the hurt on Beth's face and went on, his eyes focused at some distant point in his memory. 'Then Brid came back. I began to hear her voice again, more and more strongly. Broichan was so close. She was terrified of him. I knew I had to return. Father John lent me the money to fly back to the UK.' He paused again. 'When I arrived in England my memory started to come back in dribs and drabs. I found some friends. I found Robert Harding, my former partner. I found my solicitor. I found my bank. I found I had plenty of money after all. I sent Father John back the money for the fare, plus a lot more for his mission. I floated around a bit, not really knowing where to go. I couldn't get Brid out of my head. Still I could hear her calling me, begging. So I came back to Scotland.' There was another long silence. Then he went on, 'I had forgotten so much. Everything.' He shrugged. 'But slowly it all returned. The deaths. The murders. But whatever she did, however angry I was with her, I began to realise that she had done it for love of me. She came from a world where people thought differently. She didn't realise how evil and wicked she had been.' He paused, as if considering for a moment. Then he shook his head. 'I have to forgive her. That is the Christian thing to do. I have to release her. Save her from Broichan. But now I can't find her.' He walked back to the chair by the wood-burning stove and threw himself onto it.

'When I was a young boy and I first met Brid, she was the most exciting thing I had ever seen. Exotic. Beautiful. I thought she was a tinker. That's what we called gypsies in Scotland. But she wasn't, of course.'

He closed his eyes and rested his head against the back of the chair. Beth studied him. He had a handsome, strong face, his weather-beaten colouring a contrast to his shock of unruly white hair. He was tall and wiry, his hands, clutching the arms of the chair, the strong hands of a working man rather than those of a doctor. 'I still want her, Beth.' His cry was tormented. 'In spite of all she has done I still seem to be obsessed by her! I am trying to call her back to me, but suddenly there is silence.'

'What is she?' Beth's voice was no more than a whisper.

He shrugged. 'Broichan was the Chief Druid and foster father to

King Brude. He was the man who opposed St Columba when he came from Iona on his mission to convert the Picts. By all accounts he was a very powerful magician.'

Beth glanced at Giles. He was frowning. 'Are you saying that this – this Broichan – is some sort of ghost? That he is haunting Brid as she is haunting you?' he asked at last.

'And who *is* Brid?' Beth put in under her breath.

'Brid is the daughter of Broichan's sister.' Adam had not opened his eyes.

'Then,' Giles hesitated, choosing his words with care, 'you are saying that Brid is a ghost, too.'

'No!' Adam sat upright, his eyes flashing with anger. 'No, she is not a ghost! How could she be a ghost?'

They glanced at each other. 'Then who is she?' Giles persisted.

'She is a Pictish princess; she was training to be a bard and a Druidess. She went to their equivalent of a college to learn. The training lasts nineteen years, but she gave up.' He paused, lost in thought for a moment. 'She broke the sacred oath. She ran away to follow me and Broichan cursed her.' He was staring into the middle distance, his eyes fixed as he recited the facts as though ticking them off against some list in his head. 'I have studied the books and worked it out. Her clothes were so exotic, her speech so strange – all I could think when I was a child was that she was from the Romany people, and I went on to think of her like that. A wild, glamorous gypsy girl. But she was far more than that. She had power and knowledge. Dangerous power and knowledge.'

Giles glanced at Beth and grimaced. He brought his forefinger to his temple quickly and made a small screwing motion. Beth frowned. It had occurred to her too, to wonder if her grandfather was sane. She cleared her throat. 'Are you saying that these people, this college, still exists?'

'Everything still exists, Beth. In parallel dimensions with ours. Do you remember your *Four Quartets*? That wonderful quote about time? You should look it up.'

She bit her lip and shrugged. 'And Brid can travel between these dimensions?'

He nodded, still staring into the distance. 'She was destined, I think, to be a bard. She has a phenomenal memory. But she also has the gift of the sight, and she learned to shape-shift. Furness spotted that. He could not believe it.'

'Furness?' Giles had picked up his coffee at last. He glanced at Beth.

'Furness was the psychiatrist who took care of her when she was ill.' Adam turned to face him suddenly. 'You think I'm mad, don't you? I don't blame you. Why should you believe me? It is incredible. She can turn herself into a cat.' He stood up and paced up and down for a minute. 'It's all there, in the books.' He waved his arm towards the table. 'You study the animal and meditate with it, then you leave your body in a trance state and become one with it. You can be whatever you choose: an eagle, a horse, a salmon, a snake – what is it, girl?' He had noticed suddenly the chalk-white face of his granddaughter, heard her gasp.

Beth bit her lip. 'I was attacked by a cat. At home. At Pen-y-Ffordd. Our neighbour told me that Granny Jane had been attacked there once too . . .' Her voice trailed away.

Adam was silent. Then he shook his head. 'Why can't I find her?' His voice was anguished.

'You don't really think it was her?' Giles was incredulous.

Beth frowned. Half of her was afraid, half, like him, sceptical. 'You sound as though you've studied this shape-shifting.' She kept her voice steady, realising she was not very far from the edge of hysteria. 'Have you tried it, Grandfather?'

He shook his head. 'I have not yet learned to be single-minded enough. My technique is weak. But I have to learn. I have to find her. I have to know that none of it was her fault. That she was driven by that fiend, Broichan. That she is no danger any more to Liza or to you, Beth. I have to know that because I need her.'

'And what if Broichan is waiting for you?' Beth wasn't sure where to look. She couldn't believe she was having this conversation.

He looked across at her, his face sad. 'You think this is a huge joke, don't you, Beth? Ask your grandmother. She will tell you. Expand your small, literal mind and use your imagination if you cannot use your brain. I am surprised, brought up with her, that you don't have more vision.'

Beth looked away, cut by his scorn. 'I am broad-minded,' she said defensively. 'It's just that I haven't ever considered that any of this stuff could be real before.'

'You have heard of Einstein?'

'Yes, of course. I –'

'You have heard of quantum physics?'

'I don't see –'

'No. You don't. But that doesn't mean it doesn't exist. One of the failings of the modern era is to rely on reductionism as the

391

ultimate proof that anything exists. My profession of course is particularly susceptible to this, and rightly. I was trained in an empirical science.' He threw himself back down into his chair. 'But we have made the mistake of ignoring anything we cannot explain by our own criteria and dismissing any phenomena which are not susceptible to so-called scientific experiment and proof, as not existing at all. It is so arrogant.' He leaned forward and thumped the table with his fist. 'This is, I am glad to say, slowly changing.' He waved his hand once again, this time at the books and magazines strewn across the table. 'If you consult these there is a wonderful mixture of science and hokum. New Age hope, vision, and yes, rubbish, and true exciting experimental science combined at last with philosophy and observation of things which cannot be rationally explained.' He was silent for a moment, then he went on, slowly, as though talking to a not very intelligent child. 'I have seen a woman who lived during the time of Columba, that is in the sixth century AD, walking about as solid and real as you or you,' he nodded at Giles, who was trying hard to hide his amused scepticism. 'I have spoken to her, touched her, and yes, I have slept with her. I am not mad. I am not delusional, although you, young man, clearly still think so. And I am not, as our friend Ken Maclaren thinks, in cahoots with the devil.' He stood up again abruptly. 'Today I was in Edinburgh, consulting the university library, and I am very tired. I would like to go to bed. So, if you will both excuse me, I should like you to leave now. I don't see any reason for you to come again. I do not enjoy being mocked.'

As soon as they were in the car Giles let out a loud whistle. He smacked his hand down on the dashboard. 'Nutty as a fruit cake!'

Beth gave a small smile, half agreeing with him, half puzzled. 'I wish I could be sure.'

'You don't believe him!'

She shrugged. 'Giles. Please, not now.' She closed her eyes. Then she reached for the door handle. 'Listen, I'm exhausted. Will you drive?'

'Of course.' He stretched out and touched her cheek. For a moment they looked at each other in the darkness and Giles, overwhelmed by the feelings of love and protectiveness which flooded through him, leaned across and kissed her gently on the lips. 'I'm sorry, Beth. This isn't really funny, is it? That old man is probably a danger to himself. Come on. I'll drive us back to the hotel.' He climbed out and walked round the back of the car.

Beth didn't move for a moment. Her worry about Adam had fleetingly been swept away by Giles's kiss. She closed her eyes, hugging herself quietly in the warm darkness of the car. Then reluctantly she reached for the handle and opening her door she climbed out into the cold wind. The lights in the cottage behind them had already gone out. The night was very silent.

She shivered. 'Poor Grandfather.'

The growl from the hedge of rhododendrons behind her was so quiet she wondered if it was her imagination. She stopped, her hand on the car door, the hairs on the back of her neck prickling with sudden warning.

'Giles!'

He had walked round to her side of the car and was standing very close to her. 'What is it?' She could feel his warmth, his solidity.

'Listen.' She held her breath. 'Oh my God! Listen.'

'Beth, you mustn't let all this get to you.' He put his arm round her shoulders and pulled her against him. 'It's the wind. Come on, get in. Let's get back before the rain starts again.'

This time the growl was louder and he heard it too. They froze.

'Oh God, Giles. It's her!'

He swallowed, his eyes raking the darkness. 'Get in, quick,' he whispered. He pushed her back down into the driving seat. 'And shut the door.'

'But what about you?'

'I'll go round the other side. It's all right. It's some kind of animal, that's all. Probably a badger or a hedgehog or something.' He closed the door softly after her, pushing it shut with a click and turned to face the bushes. He could see nothing. The wind had increased sharply and all he could hear was its passage across trees and heather and grass and then the flap of the heavy rhododendron leaves.

His back to the car, he began to edge round towards the passenger door again.

Beth leaned across the seats and pushed it open a few inches. 'Get in, Giles!'

He scanned the darkness, feeling ridiculously vulnerable as he crept round the back of the Porsche. There was something there. He could feel its eyes, watching him. Whatever had made that noise had been far, far bigger than a hedgehog. Sweat broke out across his forehead as he felt the tail lights of the car pressing against the backs of his legs.

He launched himself at the door as the creature sprang. He saw eyes, teeth, and smelled the stink of its breath as he threw himself head first into the car and landed across his seat, half in Beth's lap.

'Shut the door! For Christ's sake, shut the door!' He pulled his legs in after him, sobbing. It had got him. His arm felt like fire.

Beth had leaned across him and was desperately pulling at the handle. 'It's your foot. Bring in your foot! I can't shut it!'

She saw the blaze of the eyes and felt the creature's hatred like a physical blow through the glass of the window, only a few inches from her face, then it was gone.

'Oh, Giles!' She was shaking like a leaf as he tried to straighten up. 'Are you all right?'

He disentangled himself from brake and gear lever and sat up in the seat, holding his elbow in his other hand. His fingers were sticky with blood.

'Drive! Quickly, Beth, drive!' He was trembling violently. 'It was a cat. I saw it. Let's get out of here.'

She started the engine, engaged gear and let out the clutch. The car stalled. 'Oh Christ!'

'Calm down.' He took a deep breath himself. 'It can't get us in here. Just drive slowly. Let's get away –'

'What about Grandfather?'

'What about him? He can take care of himself. Didn't he even say he had slept with the creature!' He gasped with pain as the car jerked forward again. 'Just get us out of here, sweetheart. Please.'

In the quiet of his austere bedroom Adam looked out of the window into the darkness. He had turned out the lights and gone up as soon as his unwelcome guests had disappeared and within minutes he had forgotten all about them. He opened the window and leaned out, resting his elbows on the cold stone of the sill, breathing the soft night air, which was sweet with heather and mountain thyme and wet, peaty earth. His window looked out from the back of the house, across the small garden with its newly turned rose beds, towards the rise of the hillside. Over the ridge, which he could see black against the wind-shredded clouds with their backdrop of stars, was the hillside where Gartnait's stone stood, displaying its array of enigmatic symbols.

Turning into the room with a sigh he pulled up a chair and sat down, staring out into the night. He was too tired for ritual; tonight he would just dream, launching himself out onto the wind in his imagination until, if he was lucky, sleep took him and erased the memories of death and fear and left him only with the beauty, the silver-grey eyes, the laughing red mouth, the darkly lustrous, silken hair.

21

Earlier that day Idina Campbell had been to Peter Jones. The four carrier bags with their distinctive green and white stripes lay discarded on the elegant Regency sofa in the drawing room. She had dropped them there when she came in, losing interest in her purchases almost as soon as they were made. Fretfully she had made her way into Giles's study and looked round. The floor as always was covered with books and maps, the desk a sea of papers, old half-drunk mugs of coffee, overflowing ashtrays and sticky notes to himself stuck over the phone, the wall, the filing cabinet and the computer – sometimes she wondered how he could see the screen at all. She would have been astonished to know that every inch of the chaos and muddle in Giles's room represented meticulous filing to him. He could lay his hand on any paper or letter within seconds – well, more or less – and knew where just about every book in his extensive travel library was. As long as Idina didn't touch anything.

She shuddered. Her husband's room was so different from the rest of the house, so alien to everything that she liked and aimed for she wondered sometimes how she could live with him another minute. It was such a relief when he was away. She thought for a moment about Damien Fitzgerald, her latest protégé; he was everything Giles was not. A society photographer who had entrée everywhere that mattered, he kept his creativity and his talent carefully confined and organised. She had seen his study and dark room only the day before. It had been in that dark room that Damien had turned to her with perfect timing and gently but masterfully put his beautifully manicured hands on the shoulders of her shantung suit and pulled her towards him for a kiss. The kiss had shot a message through her system which dear old Giles with his dutiful fumbling had failed to convey for years.

She stared round thoughtfully. On the top of Giles's desk were some sketches of a Celtic cross and others of a castle. She sighed. Giles and his latest obsession. The book. The book he was going to do with Beth Craig. She sat down on the chair near his desk, first lifting a pile of magazines and papers and throwing them to the ground. There was nothing in here that would betray him, of course. All Giles's dreams and fantasies about Beth were where Idina would never find them, in his head. That little bitch had set her cap at Giles the first time she had met him. With a shudder she pictured Beth's wild dark curling hair, her Bohemian, don't-care clothes, the paint under her fingernails, and her equally dreadful grandmother, the countess. Well, they could be seen off with no difficulty again as they had been seen off before. If that was what she wanted. Idina smiled to herself and went back to contemplating the delightful prospect of whether or not she should have an affair with Damien. Damien or Giles.

If she flew up to Scotland now, today, that would shake Giles and his floozy up a bit. Spoil their fun. And she could still be back in time for Damien's party. That would be amusing. Idina stood up purposefully. Amusement was, after all, what life was all about.

Accident and Emergency. Fourteen stitches. Painkillers. The police.

It was dawn before Beth turned the Porsche wearily into its place outside the doors of the hotel and climbed out. She stood for a second taking deep breaths of the cold, pure air and then went round to help Giles. He was very white, his torn blood-stained jacket slung round his shoulders, his left arm heavily bandaged and in a sling.

Patti met them on the steps. 'Oh my God, what happened?' She was already dressed in jeans and a heavy sweater, her hair pulled back from her face in a perky knot. Breakfast for her energetic hill-walking guests started very early. 'You haven't crashed Dave's car?'

Giles managed a grin. 'No. No damage to anything important. Just me.'

'Oh Giles!' She caught his good arm and squeezed it. 'You know I didn't mean that! What happened? Did you have a fall?'

'He was attacked by some kind of wildcat. Near my grandfather's house,' Beth put in. 'We've spent most of the night in the hospital. And with the police.' Trying, she wasn't quite sure why, to persuade them not to go hunting for the animal with high-powered rifles.

She was pushing her way in through the front door when Patti put her hand on her arm. 'Listen, you two.' She lowered her voice.

'Idina arrived last night, after you left. I thought you ought to know. She insisted I put her in your room, Giles, and of course she wanted to know where you were.' She glanced from one to the other and registered their shocked faces. 'Dave and I said that Beth had been summoned because her grandfather was ill and you went with her, Giles, to help drive. I don't know whether we did right, but we didn't know you'd be out all night! She stayed up until after midnight, waiting for you. She was awfully cross.' This was, even by Patti's standards, an understatement.

'Oh shit!' Giles closed his eyes, swaying slightly. 'That's all I need.'

Beth relinquished her hold on Giles's arm. 'You'd better go up and explain,' she said bleakly.

'Beth –'

'No, Giles, there's no point in talking about it. Just go.'

She followed Patti into the kitchen and sat down at the table, exhausted. 'I can't believe it. Not after everything we've been through last night. Why did she come?' She was near to tears. She had sworn she wouldn't let herself fall in love with him again. She had determined to be so strong. And it had worked. Almost.

Patti shrugged diplomatically. 'You look as though you could do with some good strong coffee and a huge cooked breakfast. How does that sound?'

Beth hesitated, automatically assuming she could eat nothing, then she realised suddenly that she was ravenous and that the wonderful smells coming from two plates being carried into the dining room had made her mouth water.

'Can I have it in here with you?'

'If you don't mind me rushing about like a mad flea. She won't give him up easily, you know.' She paused looking down at Beth.

For a moment Beth was confused. How did Patti know about Brid? Then she realised that she was talking about Idina again and she slumped back in her chair, allowing exhaustion and depression to sweep over her.

'I'm sorry, love.' Patti put the coffee down in front of her. 'But I've known Idina for years. I like her very much but there is no hiding the fact that she is a very possessive woman. Dave and I have always wondered how much she really loves Giles. I suspect not all that much. But he is one of her possessions. She will fight to the death to keep him.'

'Is that why she's come up here. Because of me?'

'You bet. Nothing would drag her out of Chelsea otherwise. Specially not Scotland. She's never bothered to come here before.'

Patti was breaking eggs into a bowl. 'Now tell me about this cat. It must have been terrifying. And how was your grandfather?'

'Odd.' She had an overwhelming urge to tell Patti everything that had happened, but something stopped her. She did not want Adam ridiculed any more, and she needed time to think. The cat attack had terrified them both. It was too violent and too sudden – and too specific – to be a coincidence.

She was coming out of her bathroom after breakfast, hair washed, bathed, wrapped in a towel, her thoughts still relentlessly and miserably whirling from Giles and Idina to her grandfather and back, when the phone rang.

'Beth, I'm at Heathrow. Michele says you've been trying to reach me. What's wrong?' Liza's voice was sharp. 'Something's happened, hasn't it? What are you doing in Scotland? Shall I take the shuttle to Edinburgh and come?'

How could Beth have forgotten her grandmother's intuition?

'Sweetheart? Can you hear me? Are you all right?' Liza went on, her voice so clear she might have been in the same room.

Beth threw her towel on the bed and sat down, the telephone receiver in her hand. 'Oh thank God! Liza, you are not going to believe what's been going on.'

During her recital Liza was totally silent. Only when at last Beth paused to draw breath did Liza speak.

'Never mind the ifs and buts, Beth.' Far away in the busy arrivals lounge in Terminal 2 Liza had gone completely cold. 'If Adam is looking for a way to raise Brid from the dead, or conjure her up or something, I take it very seriously indeed. That cat was no coincidence. Don't go near your grandfather again, do you understand me? If she is back, she won't let anyone close to him. She won't hesitate to kill again. And you are probably her prime target as the only member of his family left. Listen, I'm catching the first plane and I'm coming up there. I mean it, Beth. Don't go near him again until I come.'

Beth sat still for several minutes after she had hung up, trying to take in what she had heard, then at last she lay back on the bed. Her mind was still racing in spite of her exhaustion. Adam and Brid. Giles and Idina. The cat with its vicious claws and snarling teeth. Closing her eyes she felt warm slow tears beginning to slide down her cheeks and miserably she turned her face into the pillow.

She was awoken from an uneasy doze by Giles creeping into the room, his finger to his lips. He had showered and changed out of his blood-stained clothes but he was still looking very white and strained. 'Idina's gone out for a walk. To cool off.' He sat down on the bed. 'Oh Christ, Beth, what are we going to do?'

She glanced at him as he eased his painful arm in the sling. 'What does she want?'

He grimaced. 'She thinks I'm having an affair with you.'

Beth was silent. She didn't know what to say.

I love you so much it hurts.

I wish I was having an affair with you.

What good would that do? The only night he had spent with her in Scotland had been in the Accident and Emergency department of a hospital.

Not very romantic.

Idina was his wife and he must still love her or he would have divorced her by now.

She levered herself up onto her elbow. 'What did you tell her?' Her voice was husky.

He shrugged. 'She wanted to know about my injury. But we didn't really talk. She was too angry.'

Beth sighed. She pushed her hair out of her eyes. 'Liza has just rung. She has flown into Heathrow from Florence. I told her what happened. She is coming straight on here.'

Don't go near your grandfather . . . She won't hesitate to kill again.

Liza's words echoed suddenly again in her head. 'She said it's all true about Brid.'

There was a moment of shocked silence. Giles shook his head wearily. 'I don't suppose you're joking?'

'No.' She closed her eyes. 'No, Giles, I'm not. I wish I was.' She looked at him and suddenly her hands were shaking. 'Liza said Brid wouldn't hesitate to kill me.'

'She can't mean it.' Giles shivered. 'My darling, I won't let anything happen to you.'

'How can you stop it with Idina here?' She sat up and wrapped her arms round her knees. 'You'd better go and let me get dressed,' she added bleakly. 'Liza will be here soon. Then she and I can concentrate on what to do about Adam.'

'Beth.' He sounded very stern. 'I am here for you.' Suddenly he leaned forward to kiss her. She closed her eyes. She should move away. She should leap out of bed and run. She should not let this go any further.

Their kiss lasted a long time. Then slowly he drew back. 'I love you.'

She shook her head. 'You can't love two people, Giles. Not if they're going to be happy. You have to decide between us.' She slid out of the bed and picked up her clothes. 'I'll see you downstairs.'

He hesitated, then he got to his feet. 'Idina and I don't get on any more –'

'Don't tell me. Tell her. Go on down, Giles.' She sounded so calm; inside she was screaming at him: Tell her; tell her you love me! Get rid of her if she makes you unhappy! She forced herself to smile. 'Please. Go.'

Only after he had closed the door behind him did she let herself cry again.

In his meditation Meryn frowned. The threads he was trying to gather between his fingers had grown tangled. Distress and fear and blood clouded the images, and his touch grew less sure. He was needed. The time had come to withdraw from his searches of the pathways of time. The one he sought was waiting in the shadows, waiting for a passage to open to allow him to travel freely down the centuries. He had to be stopped. But first there were matters to address in this existence: not on a dark, mist-shrouded area of common on a Welsh hillside but on the lonely Scottish mountain where the story had begun and where the energies were coalescing for a battle which would end only in death.

When Beth walked at last into the library where guests were encouraged to congregate before meals for a drink, Giles was already there. He looked strained as he stood up and beckoned her over to the sofa by the fireplace. No one else was there yet and they had the room to themselves.

He reached forward and touched her hand. 'Beth, I love you. I'm going to ask Idina for a divorce. Right now. While she's up here.' He paced up and down on the threadbare Persian carpet. 'She's playing games with us and if she wants a showdown, she's going to get one.'

'Giles –'

'I need you. I've always loved you, since I first met you.'

'But I don't think you mean it, Giles.' Beth spoke very gently. 'We've said all this before, remember? In Wales. You can't live without Idina. We both know that in an ideal world you could have us both and we'd both be happy, but we all know it is not an ideal world. We would all end up miserable.'

'I don't love Idina. It's you I can't live without.'

'You can.' She bit her lip. 'And I don't think we can work together. I'm sorry.'

401

'Beth! What is it?' He looked up angrily as Dave put his head round the door to tell Beth there was a call for her.

It was Ken Maclaren again. 'I am so sorry to bother you,' he said when Beth picked up the phone, 'but Dr Craig has gone up into the hills somewhere and the weather is deteriorating badly. I don't know if I should call the police – what do you think?'

She stared out of the window. The early-morning watery sunshine had disappeared and now it was raining hard. She could no longer see the distant mountains, and smoky cloud was drifting up across the lawns below the house.

'Why do you think he's in trouble?'

'The door was wide open. The kettle had boiled dry. His post was lying on the table half open; he hadn't taken his coat or his stick.'

Beth took a deep breath. 'Listen, I'm waiting for my grandmother to come.'

Don't go near your grandfather . . .

'She's on her way. You do what you think best, then when she arrives we'll come over.'

When she returned to the library Idina was there, standing next to Giles, her hand resting possessively on his good arm. She was dressed in a shocking-pink wool dress and black tights. Her figure was pencil slim, her hair immaculate, her make-up porcelain-brittle.

She greeted Beth with a tight smile and a double kiss in the air a good three inches from Beth's cheeks. 'Mmm. How are you, sweetie? I hear you and Giles are going to be doing another book?'

Beth was for an instant intensely aware of her own less than svelte curves, clothed in bog-standard navy jeans and heavy cream sweater, a silk scarf knotted round her hair, and immediately put the image out of her head as being too depressing to live with. She smiled bravely. 'I don't know about that, Idina. It very much depends.' She glanced at Giles, who was concentrating on his drink, his knuckles white on the glass. 'How's London?'

'Better than this.' Idina looked at the window and shuddered.

'I can't think why you came,' Beth couldn't resist saying.

'We won't be here long, sweetie, I assure you.' Idina gave an icy smile. 'Just as soon as Giles has finished up here we're going on to visit some friends in Edinburgh.'

'I told you, Idina, I am staying.' Giles's voice was harsh. 'Beth and I are working on our book.' He glanced at Beth. 'What did Maclaren want? Is everything all right?'

'Grandfather has gone missing again. I said we'd go over as soon as Liza arrives.' Beth went over to the bar to order a whisky from George. The glass safely in her hand, she turned back to Idina, trying hard to contain her misery and resentment as she stared at the woman's elegant figure. 'He lives near Dunkeld.'

'I see.' Idina raised an eyebrow. 'Well, I fail to see why Giles needs to go with you.'

'He doesn't need to.' Beth smiled wearily. Then she couldn't resist adding, 'But he might choose to.'

When Liza finally appeared late that afternoon she looked exhausted. Beth who had been watching from the library window, ran down the steps and enveloped her in a huge hug.

'It's been awful, I can't tell you! Oh God, I'm so glad you're here!' She pushed Liza away so she could see her properly and felt a pang of remorse. 'You look tired. I'm sorry. Perhaps I shouldn't have told you –'

'Don't be so silly!' Liza said crisply. 'All I need is a cup of tea. And I need to know exactly what is happening.' She was as slim and young-looking as ever, her fashionably cut hair showing only a few white threads amongst the auburn.

It took an hour for her to charm Dave and Patti, find her room, change, have her cup of tea and be ready for Beth to drive her over to Adam's house.

There was no sign of Giles or Idina as Beth went into the office for Dave's car keys. 'Will you tell him where I've gone?'

'Don't worry.' He winked. 'If it's any consolation they are not having a good time. You can hear the shouting down the corridor. Amongst other things, Idina doesn't like the Scots rain. She must be afraid her frock will shrink.' He gave a snort of laughter.

'Dave!' Beth pretended to be shocked. 'I'll ring you when I know what we're doing, but don't worry if you don't hear tonight. Adam isn't on the phone, and I suspect we'll stay over there. We'll play it by ear.'

'Do I gather you and Giles are an item again?' Liza leaned back in the deep leather passenger seat of the Porsche and closed her eyes as Beth turned out of the drive. It was already dark.

'Hardly, with Idina here.'

'Would you like to be?'

'There's no point in thinking about it. He's still very married in case you hadn't noticed. She's the one in the pink dress.'

'Silly woman!' Liza sighed. 'Poor darling. Life and love are never easy, are they?'

Beth glanced at her profile, illuminated by the dashboard lights. 'Everything is all right with Michele?'

'Yes, darling, everything is very all right with Michele.' Liza's eyes were still shut.

They stopped outside the Maclarens' bungalow at last, after a slow journey through heavy rain, and ran up the path to where Ken waited in the open doorway.

'Come away in and get warm and dry for a minute, then I'll drive us all up the hill,' he said after introductions had been made.

'Did you speak to the police?' Beth asked anxiously.

He nodded. 'They have been up to Shieling House. They said there was no sign of the animal that attacked your friend, and they could see no tracks, but the rain has been so heavy, and my car or theirs, or the postie, or anyone else, might have obliterated them. There was still no sign of Dr Craig.' He shook his head. 'I'm worried. I know he thinks he knows the hills, but it's a long time since he lived up here, and he's not a young man. And the weather is appalling.'

They climbed into the minister's old four-wheel drive and Beth, sitting beside him, peering out of the windscreen at the twin beams of the lights which reflected rivulets of mud pouring down the track, thanked heaven she had not had to drive the Porsche up here in the dark.

When they finally arrived Beth stared round nervously. She was wishing desperately that Giles was with them. Ken Maclaren had produced a large torch and the bright beam lit up the dripping bushes and the flattened grass in a wide arc as he swept it around. Beth held her breath, listening, but she could hear nothing but the sound of the wind and the rain.

They ran round the side of the house and Ken used his own key to Adam's back door. He slammed the door shut behind them and scrabbled for the light switch.

'It doesn't help to think that wretched cat might be lurking somewhere around,' he said soberly.

Beth and Liza exchanged glances.

'It doesn't look as though he's been back,' Beth said slowly. 'Nothing has changed from last night.'

They walked through into the living room. Beth went over and pulled the curtains closed with a shiver. 'I can't help wondering if there is someone, or something out there watching,' she said quietly.

Liza grimaced. 'I think it's a fair bet that there is. Go and check upstairs, sweetheart. Make sure the old reprobate isn't asleep in his bed.'

404

Beth took a deep breath. She made for the staircase. Even with the lights on she could feel her fear returning, every nerve jangling as she climbed, her eyes frantically searching as she stepped onto the landing and looked at the open door of Adam's room.

It was very quiet up here. Suddenly she could no longer hear the subdued voices below her where Liza and Ken were standing at the table looking down at Adam's books.

Icy trickles of panic were creeping over her skin as she took first one step then another towards the darkened shadows ahead of her.

You have made my A-dam unhappy . . .

The voice was suddenly there, inside her own head. Beth clutched at the top of the banisters. Her mouth went dry.

I do not like people who make my A-dam unhappy . . .

'Oh God!' Her whisper sounded loud in the silence of the landing. She turned and fled downstairs.

'Beth, what is it?' Liza, peering at her over the top of her spectacles, had seen her white face.

'It's nothing. I just felt –'

'You felt what? Did you see something? He's not there, is he?'

She shook her head. 'I'm sorry. I didn't look.' She sat down at the table and put her head in her hands.

Ken looked from one to the other. 'I'll go,' he said. He took the stairs two at a time and they heard his footsteps stride across the landing, followed by the snap of a light switch.

'I heard a voice. Inside my head. Was it Brid?' Beth looked desperately at Liza.

Upstairs they heard Ken retrace his steps and repeat the manoeuvre in the bathroom and the other bedroom, then he reappeared on the stairs. 'He's not there. There's no sign of him.' He smiled at Beth. 'My dear, I'm not surprised you're worried. That cat could have got in when the door was open, but to be honest I doubt if it would. They are very shy beasts. It is unusual if not unheard of for them to hang around human habitation as far as I know. The police were very puzzled. They assumed you must have cornered it in some way and it felt threatened. I doubt we'll ever see it again.'

Liza looked at Beth and frowned. The meaning of the expression was clear. Not in front of the minister. If Giles had initially found Adam's story impossible to believe, how much more so would a man of the cloth?

'What are we going to do? He can't stay out all night in this weather.' Beth was trying hard to get a grip on herself.

Ken shook his head. 'I think I'd better ring the police again. Discuss it with them. I don't know if we should suggest a search party? The thing that worries me so much is that his car is still here. But on the other hand we don't know someone didn't come and collect him.'

'He would never have left the door open like that,' Liza put in. 'He might be old but there is nothing wrong with his memory. Is there?' She turned to Beth.

Beth shook her head. 'He seemed all there to me.' She sighed. 'How would a search party know where to look? He could be anywhere if he has gone out into the hills.'

'And he wouldn't. Not without his coat. He's a sensible man,' Liza added.

Beth raised an eyebrow. 'Why didn't he have a phone here? Surely he could afford it.'

'I've asked him that.' Ken sighed. 'That, I'm afraid, was sheer stubbornness. He was very sharp with me and said there was no one he wanted to talk to on a phone and that he was perfectly capable of looking after himself. I asked him what would happen if he had a fall or something and he said if he had a fall it was his own damn silly fault and he would take the consequences.'

Liza smiled. 'That's my Adam.'

'Not very helpful though, in these circumstances.'

'No.' Liza hesitated. 'Mr Maclaren, can I ask, were there any signs that Adam was drinking heavily?' She too had spotted the whisky bottle on the side. The level of alcohol in it, Beth had already noticed, did not seem to have moved.

Ken shook his head. 'He told me he had been an alcoholic as near as makes no difference and he said he had it controlled. I've certainly never seen him drink.'

'Liza!' Beth's eyes had strayed down to the books on the table and she realised suddenly that they had been rearranged since she had been there last. Several were lying open, others had bookmarks and one, on the top of the pile, had been marked in red ink. 'Look!' It was entitled *Psychic Self Defence*. She pushed it over the table.

Liza drew it to her and lowered her glasses from her hair onto her nose. She studied it for several minutes.

Ken frowned. 'I deplore the content of most of those books.'

'They consist mostly of history,' Liza retorted. 'And philosophy. They contain a great deal of wisdom.' She went on reading.

'They contain evil. Black magic. Witchcraft.'

'Rubbish.' Liza pushed her glasses back onto her hair. 'Listen, young man, why don't you go and make us all a cup of coffee

406

whilst I look through some of these? They may give me some idea of where he is.' The briskness of her tone told Beth that she was thoroughly irritated.

She watched as Ken made his way out of the room. 'What is it? What have you seen?'

'Look.' Liza pushed the book across the table at her. 'You spotted it. Read it.'

Beth sat down. Slowly she flipped through the book, reading the passages which had been marked and underlined in red:

It is a well known fact that if an occultist, functioning out of the body, meets with unpleasantness on the astral plane, or if his subtle body is seen, and struck or shot at, the physical body will show the marks.

And again, further down the page:

The artificial elemental is constructed by forming a clear-cut image in the imagination of the creature it is intended to create, ensouling it with something of the corresponding aspect of one's own being and then invoking into it the natural force. This method can be used for good as well as evil . . .

Was Liza suggesting that that was how Brid made the cat? Or did she actually turn herself into it? Or had she somehow gone inside the body of a real cat? Beth looked up at Liza. 'You believe all this stuff, don't you?'

'Yes, Beth, I believe all this stuff. Look at this. And this. And this.' Book after book on Celtic magic had been marked in red. The sections were all on shape-shifting and out of body experience, pathworking. 'He's been trying it. Or he's been planning to try it. And it's all linked to that stone.' She threw the sketch on the table in front of Beth. 'Do you see? He's been working out what these symbols mean.'

'Giles knows about those.'

'I doubt it.' Liza frowned. 'He might think he does, but I think Adam has worked out some totally different system. You see how he's annotated this book?'

'The carving of a mirror. He's ringed that.

'*Brid's mark*, it says. *The sign of a Druidess or female magician, able to transcend ''reality''. These stones are signposts; they direct the way through parallel worlds, not to places in our own.*

A man that looks on glass
On it may stay his eye;
Or if he pleases through it pass
And then the heaven espy.

407

She hesitated, squinting at the tiny scribbled writing: *Into the past or the future. Place where the veil is thin.* She looked up at Liza. 'Veil?'

'Between the planes.' Liza smiled. 'Esoteric stuff again. He is implying that that is where Brid comes and goes between our time and hers.'

Beth shook her head. 'I'm sorry. I just can't get my head round this stuff. I'm not being obstructive, but it sounds like some kind of fantasy world.'

'There is often truth behind fantasy, Beth.' Liza smiled. 'Read your Jung. Don't worry about it for now. Let us just assume that that is what Adam believes. Has he gone to the signpost?'

'The standing stone thing? Ken Maclaren says it isn't far from here. You walk up the ridge behind the house, apparently. He said Grandfather had been obsessed with the stone.' She paused. 'You think he's gone up there? In the dark?'

'It wouldn't have been dark when he went.'

They stared at each other.

'Beth, darling. I don't know if it has occurred to you but tonight is Halloween. That is one of the nights when the veil, if you will allow me to use that term again, is thin. It is traditionally supposed to be easier for spirits to pass between their world and ours on a night like this. Supposing he has chosen tonight to try and go and look for Brid?'

'But why should he want to look for her if she keeps chasing him? If she was here, as a cat? If I could hear her, just now?'

Liza bit her lip. She shook her head and shrugged, then she sat down again, and rested her head on her hands. 'I don't know what to think. I just can't get this vision out of my head, of him up there on the open mountainside, in the pouring rain, perhaps taken ill, perhaps too tired to come home, perhaps injured or lost.'

'You think we should go and look for him don't you?'

'Yes, I do.'

They both glanced up as Ken reappeared with a tray of coffee mugs. Sliding it onto the table amongst the books he sighed. He had heard her last comment. 'I think we should look for him too. Drink this whilst I ring Moira. We'll stop off at the manse and collect torches, and some of my camping stuff and survival equipment.'

Beth looked at Liza doubtfully. The thought of going out in the dark terrified her. 'Do you think you should wait here –'

'No.' Liza glared at her. She was indignant. 'I'm probably fitter than you, and this young man, and his wife as well. I walk miles each day in Tuscany and I have lived in the hills all my life. If you think a bit of wind and rain are going to put me off, you are very mistaken.'

But they put me off, Beth thought miserably. And so does the thought that out there somewhere there is a vicious female magician fourteen hundred years old and spoiling for a fight, or a wildcat bent on slitting my throat. And the fact that it is Halloween. But she said nothing.

'We've both got strong shoes and good coats,' Liza went on. 'Beth, I know what you're thinking but I'm guessing that she won't be there.' She glared at Ken again, challenging him to ask who they were talking about. 'If Adam has gone into her time, then she will be there with him. If he is ill or injured she will want us to find him. Believe me, whatever else she does or doesn't do, she loves him.'

Beth did not see, luckily, the surreptitious crossing of her fingers under the table as she spoke.

'If you go after her, I am going to get a divorce.' Idina had screamed the words after him as Giles climbed into the car and sat for a moment staring up at his wife, who was standing in the hotel doorway, sheltering from the streaming rain. Lightning lit the front of the hotel for a fraction of a second then all was darkness again except for the small square of light seeping round her slim figure from the lamps in the hall behind her. He shook his head. 'I have just spent three hours telling you that that is what I want.' He sighed. 'I'm sorry. I have to go.' He paused for only a second. 'Didn't you say Damien is waiting for you, to take you to a party, Idina?' The look he gave her was one of complete contempt. 'I'd say that was more important than waiting to see if an old man has died in a storm, wouldn't you?' Without looking at her again he backed out his borrowed car – from one of the waitresses this time – and turned it towards the drive, wincing at the sharp pain in his elbow. When he glanced in the mirror he saw her still standing there in the rain, watching him drive away.

He reached Shieling House as Liza and Beth were getting into the minister's car. 'Giles?' Beth stared at him, her face alive with hope. 'Where is Idina? What's happened?'

'Idina is going back to London,' Giles commented tersely. 'For good. I am here to stay. Wherever you want me, my darling.' He put his arms out and gave her a quick hug.

Beth looked up at him. She smiled incredulously, then she reached up and kissed him on the cheek. 'Oh Giles – '

'Come on, you two.' Ken pushed his wet hair out of his eyes. He grinned at them. 'If a celebration is in order, I suggest we do it later.'

They stopped at the manse. Moira was ready for them with thermoses of hot soup and two rucksacks, one large, one small, and all the torches she had been able to find. She was already dressed in stout walking shoes with a thick quilted jacket and scarf. Ken frowned at her, worried. 'Are you sure you want to come?'

'How could I not?' She reached up to kiss him, standing on her toes. 'I'm very fond of old Dr Craig. And don't worry. I phoned and told the police the situation. If we run into any kind of problem they'll come out or call Mountain Rescue for us.'

They parked the car in a lay-by at the foot of a hillside path. A sign, slightly askew amongst the brambles, pointed up the hill indicating that the footpath led up to the Symbol Stone one and a half miles away. Somewhere out of sight to their right Beth could hear the rushing of the mountain stream, as it cascaded down the hillside through its ravine of rocks. On either side of them the trees, clinging to the steep path, were festooned with dripping lichen. Her feet were slipping on the wet rock, and the roar of the wind in her ears blocked out everything but the rush of water. The footpath followed the bed of the stream fairly closely, climbing the ravine between the trees, winding round rocky outcrops, swiftly growing steeper and steeper until in places the footholds were almost like a staircase amongst the entwined tree roots. The water was deafening as the burn, swollen by the storm, hurled itself down over waterfalls and cataracts. When Ken, leading the way, turned off his torch for a moment they could still see the luminous foaming white in the darkness and feel the trembling of the ground beneath their feet. Lightning flickered between the trees and Beth shivered. She glanced up at Ken's back in its shiny waterproof and heavy rucksack to where he was shining his torch along the path until the beam of light grew feeble between the serried trunks. He had handed out the torches, spare batteries, and woollen scarves before they set off and had tried very hard and without success to persuade Liza to stay behind in the car.

Every nerve tense and alert, Beth plodded on, every now and then glancing back to see that Liza was still there beside Moira, aware that Liza, at nearly seventy, was not kidding when she said she was fitter than any of them.

Giles, stumbling on the scree, hurried to catch her up and she felt his hand take hers. She glanced at him and smiled. She felt safer with him there. Behind them Moira, her own small rucksack loaded with coffee and sandwiches, stumbled on the steep path. They waited for her and Liza, their torches bright on the slippery rock. 'Okay?' Giles felt his words being drowned in the roar of the water nearby. Moira looked up and smiled. She nodded. 'Okay.'

There was a sudden rush of wind, stronger than the rest, and Beth stumbled on a loose piece of scree. They were coming up out of the treeline now, and it was getting colder. Ken stopped. He turned and waited for them. 'Everyone all right? It's a bit further, I'm afraid, and it gets quite a bit steeper. Shall we take a breather?' He turned off his torch to save the batteries and they stood together for a moment.

'What happens if he's there?' Liza asked, raising her voice against the scream of the wind.

'If we need help getting him down we ring the police.'

She nodded, staggering against him as another gust of wind caught her.

'We'd better get on,' he bellowed, trying to make himself heard. 'I don't like the way the weather is deteriorating. And we don't want to get chilled. Come on.'

They walked closer together now, their torches illuminating a faint path through the rocks and heather, the bright circles of light blocking out their night vision so that when Beth looked up into the teeth of the wind and sleet she could see nothing at all. She stumbled and almost fell.

Liza caught her arm. 'Are you all right?'

Beth shook her head. Her fear was growing. There was something out there watching them, she could feel it strongly now. She saw Liza's eyes on her face, and she saw her grandmother smile reassuringly. She wanted to cry out, but the words wouldn't come. Already Ken was moving on without them and all she wanted to do was to catch him up.

'Not far,' Liza mouthed. 'Keep going.'

Beth shrugged herself deeper into her coat and forced herself to move on, Giles close beside her. Whatever it was out there wasn't coming any closer. It was pacing them.

It was Liza who stopped next. She bent over and caught her breath. 'Sorry. Stitch. We're going a mite too fast even for me!'

Ken waited, his eyes going out at last into the darkness beyond their small circle of light.

Then at last Liza felt it. She straightened and looked round. 'There's someone here.'

'What?' Ken stared round. 'Where?'

She turned off her torch, and gestured for the others to do the same. 'I can feel someone watching us.'

'Adam?'

She shook her head.

'I'll shout –'

'No!' She clutched at his arm. 'No, don't. We don't know who or what it is.' She turned round slowly, staring out into the dark. 'Whoever it is doesn't want us to know he or she is here.'

'How do you know?' Ken spoke close to her ear.

She shrugged. 'Women's intuition. Instinct. It's not Adam.'

'Is it Brid?' Beth huddled closer to them, feeling an icy shiver running across her shoulders. Giles had put his good arm around her.

'I don't think so. Don't ask me why. How far is it to the stone?'

Ken stared round. 'It's easier to see where we are with the torches off. Between the clouds there, against the stars see, that's the high peak of Ben Dearg in the distance. I think we're fairly close to the cross. We're lucky there is a path up here now. Not so long ago no one came up here at all.'

'Except Adam,' Beth put in quietly.

Liza was frowning. 'You called it a cross!' She pulled at Ken's coat. 'We're not going to find a cross! We are looking for a Pictish symbol stone.'

He nodded. 'That's right. There is a Celtic cross on the front and Pictish symbols on the back.' He smiled at her cheerfully. 'Not long, I promise, and you'll see for yourself.' He turned swiftly as a flicker of lightning lit up the horizon. 'I hope that's not the heathen Picts in action. When St Columba came to Inverness to convert King Brude his Druid conjured up a storm to frighten him away. Or at least he tried to. I have a feeling it didn't work, because Christ's power was so much greater.'

'That was Broichan,' Beth said slowly. She was wiping the rainwater out of her eyes.

'That's right. Broichan.' Ken looked at her in surprise. 'You've been studying your grandfather's books, I see.' He turned and led the way on upward and after a glance at each other in the dark, Liza and Beth switched on their torches and followed him.

As they climbed higher the storm grew worse. Lightning flashed around the mountain peaks in the distance, then began slowly to travel towards them and now at last they could hear the thunder rumbling round the hills. Beth bit down on her fear, forcing herself to plod onwards. Whatever was watching them was still there, she was certain of it, and as she caught sight of Liza looking quickly over her shoulder beside her she knew her grandmother was feeling the same.

Liza reached out and took her hand. 'Not far, sweetheart. He'll be there. I can feel it.'

Ahead of them Ken stopped again. He was flashing his torch around on the track in front of him. 'The path's gone. I can't see it. This wretched sleet is obliterating everything.' Ahead the heather and grass stretched in all directions, as far as his beam of light reached. Beyond that there was darkness.

Beth shivered and this time Ken noticed. 'We'll find it, don't worry.'

'What if we don't?' She was staring round, flashing her own torch into the distance. 'What if Grandfather couldn't find his way either? It's getting colder. Supposing he's lost? Supposing we are all lost?'

'We're not lost, Beth.' Liza's voice was still strong. 'Don't worry. We're close, I am sure we are.'

Ken took a few paces ahead and stopped again. He shone his torch up into the rain and then he gave a cry of triumph. 'I can see it. There!'

The huge stone slab, black with rain, reared up ahead of them like a great jagged tooth, illuminated by the flickering lightning, and even from where they stood they could see at once that there was someone or something huddled at its foot.

Alone in the darkness Brid stared round. She did not know where she was. She could feel the wind, hear the rain on the leaves of the trees, hear the thunder, but she was lost. Lightning flickered and she felt a charge of energy but in a second it had gone and she was left in the long dark night once more. A-dam was there somewhere. She had heard him calling her. Desperately she fought to reach him but she couldn't.

She could feel Broichan close. He was hunting her, his skills far greater than hers, his strength unabated. When he caught her he would kill her and he would kill A-dam.

There was someone else there too; the Welsh stranger who followed Broichan through the layers of time. He was drawing closer.

She turned round slowly, feeling the wind lift her hair, sensing the darkness. If the storm came closer she would feel stronger. Her body, the body which lay in the bed as Broichan's prisoner, was growing weaker by the day.

For him to kill her body without the soul would mean nothing.

So he kept it alive by employing the best healers to wash it and feed it and give it broth and milk and wine until her spirit returned from searching between the ages. When she returned to that bed it would be to die at Broichan's hands.

Her brain was fuzzy. It would not think properly. Nothing stayed in her mind save the one imperative, to find A-dam and be one with him. And now he had gone again. He was not in his house, not in his car, nowhere that she could find him, and somewhere out there, somewhere close, other people were hunting too. People who would take him from her, just as he had learned to come back to her at the stone.

She waited for the lightning to flash again, breathing in its energy, feeling the strength return. A-dam was close. If she could get to him she would take him into the shadows with her and then they could be together forever without bodies to shackle them.

She smiled to herself. There was another source of energy, of course. One which would revitalise her completely, at once. The shedding of living blood required no skill. It required no initiation, no special Druid learning. She had discovered for herself in the act of killing that the energy released by death would come to her. And close, near the stone, she could sense now the people who wanted to take A-dam from her. It was as her knife appeared in her hand that her wandering mind realised who they were, the two who had come between her and A-dam for a very long time. The woman Liza and the child of A-dam's child, Beth.

It was right that they should die to give her and A-dam life.

'Is he still alive?' The five figures huddling over him shone their torches down at Adam, and saw his white face, his soaked clothes, his closed eyes, felt his freezing skin. Ken pressed beneath the old man's ear, seeking for a pulse, and he looked up, shaking the rain from his eyes. 'I've got one. He's alive. But only just.'

He was tearing off his own jacket when Liza put her hand on his arm. 'There's no point in you dying of cold too, Ken. You need it.'

He stared at her and then he nodded. He lowered the rucksack to the ground and tore it open. 'Help me wrap him up. Here, Beth,' he groped frantically in his pocket, his fingers wet with rain, 'take the phone, ring the police. We're going to need help getting him out of here.'

She took it from him as he, Moira and Giles worked on Adam in the light from the two torches which Liza held aloft. From the rucksack came chemical heatpacks which Ken tucked inside

Adam's shirt and jacket at armpit and groin, then they wrapped him in the deceptively frail foil survival blanket, their fingers slipping in the cold rain, fixing the cocoon around him with its sticky tapes, then finally Ken reached for the bright orange survival bag.

As they hurried to make him warm, Beth, with her back to the wind, fumbled with the tiny buttons on the phone, her frozen fingers slipping as she tried to dial.

'I can't get a signal.' Panicking, she tried again, moving further away from them. 'Ken, I can't get through!' She turned round slowly and moved further, wondering if the stone itself was interfering with the reception.

Preoccupied in their small intense circle of torchlight the others did not hear her. The wind was trying to wrestle the bag out of their hands, and Adam was a dead weight between them, his head falling back helplessly, his eyes still closed.

In the trees Brid watched, the knife steady in her hand. Adam was ill. She reached out for him in the darkness.

A-dam, what is wrong? A-dam, come to me.

There was no reply. She was not strong enough.

Her eyes narrowed. Beth was moving closer to the trees.

'Hello?' Beth had dialled and was trying to hear if there was a ringing tone against the roar of the wind. 'Hello? Help us, please! We've found him at the cross. He's unconscious. He's desperately ill. Hello, can anyone hear me?'

Behind her Ken and Giles had at last managed to push Adam's feet into the bag. Slowly and painfully they eased it up his cold body. Liza was chafing his hands, trying to warm them as she tucked them into the silver foil. Carefully they propped him with his back against the stone, letting it shelter him from the worst of the sleet and wind as they knelt round him.

At last Giles looked up. 'Beth? Have you got through?' He stared out into the rain. 'Beth, where are you?' His voice rose sharply.

Ken looked up. 'What's wrong?'

'Where is she? I can't see her!'

Ken climbed to his feet and flashed his torch towards the trees. Liza and Moira were still holding Adam, their arms around his shoulders. 'Stay there. Don't move,' he instructed. He stared round, narrowing his eyes against the rain, shivering. He shone the torchlight in a huge circle, cursing the fact that the batteries were failing. He ought to go back to the rucksack and replace them, but he did not want to change them until the last possible minute. 'Beth, where are you?'

The Scots pines were grouped on the side of the ridge. Frowning, he stared at Giles. Why couldn't they see her torch? Had hers failed?

'Beth?' Giles bellowed with all his strength, but the wind snatched the word from his lips and shredded it long before anyone could have heard it. He glanced back at Liza. She had both her arms round Adam, rocking him gently, willing warmth back into his frozen, wet body. Anxiously he stared round again and took a few steps nearer the trees. 'Beth!'

Ken followed him. Now that he was standing up again and could feel the full force of the wind he was suddenly very tired. He stopped. He should never have allowed them all to come up here. He should have left it to the professionals. But every time he had been here before the weather had been gentle, the path easy to see, the views stunningly clear on every side. He had not realised how steep the path was, or how rugged the ground. Beth could have tripped and fallen, or lost herself in the trees. She could have slipped into a boggy mire or fallen over one of the cliffs which sliced the countryside into its stunningly rugged profile.

'Beth!' He was growing hoarse and he could feel the chill penetrating his body to the bone.

And then he saw her. The smallest flash from the torch, its beam weak, over by the trees. She had her hand to her ear – still trying to make herself heard on the mobile against the raging wind.

'Beth!' He pointed at her, his torch picking up at last her pale green jacket and her white face being lashed by her hair. Giles strode towards her. He had nearly reached her when they heard the growl from the trees.

She lowered the phone and stared in the direction of the noise. 'Did you hear that?'

'Come away. Slowly.' He held out his hand towards her, directing the beam of the torch into the pines. 'It can't be the same one. It can't!'

'It is. It's Brid. She's come for Adam.' She was breathing heavily, the phone clutched in her hand. 'Oh God, where is she? I can't see!'

Giles stretched forward and caught her elbow. 'This way. Away from the trees. Don't run.'

The torch beam was failing. He glanced back. Ken was standing waiting for them, his torch pointed in their direction. Behind him at the stone Liza and Moira were still cradling Adam, oblivious to what was going on. They had nothing to protect themselves with, beyond the heavy torch with its rubber casing.

'Ken!' Beth called softly. 'Help us!' As she and Giles walked cautiously towards him she heard another snarl and she saw Ken look round. He had heard it. 'Ken, be careful. It's not a real cat.' Her eyes were straining into the trees. 'If you know any really good prayers I think you should say them now.' Her voice was shaking violently.

'What do you mean not a real cat?' The wind was whipping the words from his mouth.

Slowly and steadily Giles was drawing her away from the trees.

'I mean it is a woman. Some kind of an evil magician. Please don't doubt me. Just use whatever power you have as a priest to send her away.' Beth's voice rose hysterically. 'She's going to attack us. She's done it before. She wants to kill me!'

Giles's arm tightened round her. 'Come on. Let's get back to the others quickly. I won't let her touch you.'

The growl came again, closer, although he could see nothing in the fading beam. 'Come on. Quick!' He broke into a run, pulling her with him, jumping across the rough ground, running over heather and tussocks of bog cotton, followed closely by Ken.

Behind them the cat leaped from the trees.

Beth let out a scream.

Whirling, Giles pushed her behind him and faced the animal as it flew at them. Freeing his arm from the sling in one quick movement, Giles thrust the torch as hard as he could into the animal's face with both hands, hearing the crunch of bone, followed by its yowl of pain.

The cat disappeared.

Shaking, his hands slippery with rain and blood, Giles stared round in the dark. The torch had gone out and he waited, breathing hard, listening with every ounce of concentration he possessed. Where was it? Had he killed it?

Suddenly a light reappeared over to his left. 'Giles?' Beth's voice was very shaky. 'Are you all right?' She shone the light towards him and then beyond him at the trees. Standing near the pines they both saw, for a fraction of a second, the figure of a woman. She had her hands to her face. As the light hit her she stared up at them and as she moved her fingers they saw the blood pouring from her forehead beneath the long dark hair, the frightened, pain-filled eyes, her mouth open in agony; then Beth's torch flickered and died.

'Sweet Jesus!' Ken was staring at the spot where they had seen her. 'Oh my God, what have you done?'

'He's saved our lives. Maybe.' Beth caught Giles's hand and held it tightly for a moment. 'Come on. Quickly. Don't wait. Let's get back to the others.'

'But the woman . . .' Ken was staring over his shoulder.

'Leave her!' Beth was once more verging on being hysterical. 'Come back to Liza, *please*!'

It was as they were making their way back towards the stone that Ken staggered suddenly backwards.

'What's wrong? Are you okay?' Giles waited for him anxiously.

'Fine, just a stitch.' Ken could feel the sweat breaking out on his forehead. There was an agonising pain in his chest and down his left arm.

'Ken?' Beth was there now, her face close to his. 'Come on, what's wrong? Can you make it back to the stone?' A flash of lightning illuminated his white face for a second and she could see the agony in his eyes.

'I'm okay. Just let me rest a minute.' The pain in his chest was getting worse. He couldn't catch his breath.

'We're nearly there, old chap.' Giles's arm was round him now. 'Only a few more steps.' He glanced behind them into the darkness, but there was no sign of any movement.

Step by step he led Ken onwards, half carrying, half pushing him, terrified he was going to collapse, with Beth close behind them glancing in terror every few seconds over her shoulder.

Ken closed his eyes. 'I'm sorry. I don't know what's wrong with me.' He tried to smile. The irony that Liza was at least twenty-five years his senior had not escaped him. He was gritting his teeth against the pain. Trying to hide it, he closed his eyes for a moment.

'You've been fantastic.' Beth squeezed his arm. 'Just breathe slowly and steadily. You'll catch your breath.' Her eyes scanned the black shadows between the trees behind them. 'The worst is over. Once we reach the stone we can decide what to do.'

They staggered back towards the stone, and Giles lowered Ken gently down beside Adam.

'What's wrong?' Moira's voice was shrill.

'Nothing.' Ken forced himself to smile. 'A silly stitch, that's all. I'll be all right in a minute. Giles. In the rucksack. New torch batteries.'

With a worried glance at him, Giles threw himself down on his knees beside Liza and started rummaging in the rucksack with shaking hands. 'A wildcat attacked us.' He glanced at her, holding her gaze for a moment, then he looked down at Adam. 'Is he holding his own?'

'Only just.' Liza was staring at him in horror. 'Are you both all right?' She shone her own torch at him and saw the blood. 'Oh my God. She's hurt you.'

'Only a scratch. Most of it is hers. I injured her pretty badly.' Giles found the batteries and started to rip them from their packets. 'Keep watch.' He shook the rain out of his eyes. 'It was a cat that attacked us, but then I saw a woman. Was that Brid?'

'Of course it was Brid.' Beth had knelt down beside them. She was staring out into the darkness, holding her dead torch in front of her like a baton. 'She's a witch. A magician. Liza was right. And she's a killer.'

Giles slotted the new batteries into his torch with shaking hands and switched it on. He trained it on Adam and reached into the sleeping bag to check his pulse again. 'It's still very weak. Beth, the phone – did you get through all right?'

She stared round, stricken. 'Where is it? Oh no, I must have dropped it when the cat attacked us! Oh God, I'm sorry! What are we going to do?' She was staring round frantically.

He bit his lip firmly. 'It doesn't matter as long as you got through.'

'I don't know. I don't know if I got through. There didn't seem to be a signal and it was crackling, and the wind and rain were so noisy I couldn't hear if anyone spoke. Oh Giles, I'm sorry, I'll go and look for it.'

'You can't.' Liza was adamant. 'You can't possibly go back out there, not while that creature is still lurking around, and the phone will be ruined anyway if it's been exposed to the rain. There's no point in looking.'

Giles stood up. 'I'm afraid there is. It's Adam's only hope.' He glanced out into the darkness. 'I'll go. You all stay here.'

'You'll never spot it, Giles. Not in all the wet heather and mud.' Liza appealed. 'Don't be silly.'

'I've got to try.' He gave her a grave smile. 'Don't worry. I'll keep my eyes skinned. I've got a good torch this time. I'll find it.'

The three women watched as he retraced the route they had taken earlier, flashing the torch all round, onto the ground in front of him, then again into the trees ahead. Beside them Ken lay back in Moira's arms, his teeth clenched against the pain.

'I'm such a fool.' Beth dropped to her knees beside Liza. 'Oh God, this is awful.' She glanced over her shoulder. 'We wouldn't see her if she crept up in the dark, would we?'

'No.' Liza was cradling Adam against her shoulder. 'No, we wouldn't.'

'It's my fault. If I hadn't dropped the phone . . .'

'Beth, you didn't do it on purpose. No one is blaming you.' Liza switched off her own torch with a shiver. 'We'd better preserve the batteries and let our eyes get used to the dark. We've a better chance of spotting her that way.' She was remembering Meryn, thinking of his strength, surrounding them all in her mind with a wall of impenetrable light.

Huddling together, from time to time they caught sight of Giles's torch beam in the distance, methodically raking the ground as he drew further and further away towards the pines. Every now and then he swung it up into the air, drawing a quick sweep around him as though to check that there was no one there.

'Will she attack us again?' Beth huddled closer.

Liza shook her head. 'I don't know.' She put her hand gently on Adam's forehead. 'Where is he, Beth? If he has gone into her time, why isn't she there with him? Why is she still here?'

Beth stared at the old man's face. His eyes were closed, his skin, wet with sleet, pale. There was no sign of inward struggle. His expression was serene. 'You think he has transported himself into another time?' She was speaking quietly so that Ken and Moira couldn't hear.

Liza nodded. 'I think he probably has, but maybe he got it wrong. Maybe he has gone to the wrong place or the wrong time. Oh, Beth, how do we know?' She stared out to where Giles's torch had temporarily disappeared. 'Maybe Brid could tell us if she wasn't so intent on killing us.'

'I can't see him.' Beth too was searching for the sight of the distant torch beam. Her voice rose in panic. 'Liza, I can't see him!'

Liza tensed, staring round.

A-dam. Where is A-dam?

She was hearing the words somewhere in the back of her skull.

'I still can't see him!' Beth had risen to her knees.

'Wait.' Liza put her hand on Beth's arm. 'Listen.'

'What is it?'

'I heard a voice. Her voice.'

'Brid's?' Beth whispered the name. Both women listened, trying to tune out the sound of wind and rain.

A-dam!

'There.' Liza clutched at Beth again. 'Did you hear it?'

The figure was barely visible in the periphery of her vision. She shook her head, trying to rid herself of the rain in her face and stared again. Yes, there, on the edge of darkness, a darker figure, barely more than a shadow, the long hair and cloak part of the rain itself. She swallowed. 'Brid?' she called. She felt Beth stiffen in terror. 'Brid, we have lost Adam too. Help us to find him.' She held her breath. Was the shadow drifting closer? 'Please. He's lost. We all love him. Help us find him.'

The figure was definitely closer now. The terrified women could make out the details of her cloak, see the silver brooch which fastened it, the sweep of her hair under the hood now, her white face with its regular, pale features, a vivid, raw, blood-stained scar above her nose, the expressionless eyes and the rigid set to the mouth. She did not seem to be looking either at them or at Adam, but rather between them on the ground.

A-dam!

Her mouth didn't move.

A-dam, I love you!

She was standing about twenty feet from them, her eyes now fixed on Beth's face.

'We all love him, Brid.' Liza tried to keep her voice steady. She held her breath as the figure drifted closer.

Then, without warning, it launched itself at them and they both at the same moment saw the vicious, long-bladed knife in her hand. Beth screamed as she pulled Liza out of Brid's path and found her eyes only inches away from the blazing fury of the fixed gaze. Desperately she raised her arm again to try to save herself. She was fending off the knife once more when she heard a voice from beside her.

'In the name of Christ, go!' Ken was sitting up, his hand shaking as he made the sign of the cross.

Brid hesitated. The knife still clutched in her hand, she paused in her attack.

'It's okay. I'm here!' Giles had seen it all. He raced the last few yards towards them and, gasping for breath, he reached out towards Brid. 'Leave them alone, you hell-hag!' He was trying to grasp her knife. The torch arced up into the air and fell to the ground nose-down in a clump of tangled, wet heather, and he found himself flailing about in the dark.

A-dam!

Her pitiful scream tore through their heads.

A-dam, save me. I love you!

He felt the sharp bite of metal on his palm and he swore, desperately trying to wrestle it from her, but he was already exhausted. He couldn't catch his breath.

A-dam!

Beth had climbed to her feet. She groped for the torch and shone it wildly in the direction of the struggle.

'In the name of Christ, go!' Ken was sobbing with pain.

Giles and Brid were circling, their feet slipping on the wet ground. In the torchlight and intermittent lightning Beth could see the flash of the blade. Behind her Liza rose to her knees, Adam still cradled in her arms. 'Beth, no!'

'I've got to help him.' Beth crept closer to the fighting pair, the heavy torch raised high, ready to bring it down on Brid's head if she could get close enough. She could hear Giles's frantic, breathless gasps, see the knife only inches from his face. She was almost there when, with a deafening roar of engines and a whirlwind of spinning darkness, a helicopter swung in over the shoulder of the hill and hovered twenty feet above the cross-slab, flooding the area with light.

With a scream Brid dropped her knife and looked up, her hair and cloak streaming in the down-draught.

When Giles and Beth looked again, she had gone.

22

By tacit agreement neither Giles nor Beth mentioned their knife wounds when the helicopter lowered the doctor to the ground. It was obvious it could not take them all and it had been equally obvious that Liza and Ken should be the ones to go with Adam. Liza's indomitable spirit had not flagged, but the whiteness of her face and the shakiness with which she had at last stood up had alarmed Beth.

As they stood watching the machine rise into the air and swing away towards the south, Giles put his arm round her shoulders. 'I'm sure Brid has gone,' he murmured. 'Courage?' he grinned at her.

'Courage,' she agreed. She knew it was not what she felt.

Without delay they set off, turning their backs on the cross-slab with its enigmatic carvings, every nerve tensed, each waiting in spite of what they had said, for a growl from the trees, or a glint of a knife in the dark. Ahead of them Moira plodded determinedly on, not allowing herself to think about the white, strained look on her husband's face as the doctor listened to his heart or the way he had reached out to take her hand as the stretcher had lifted him from the ground.

'Are you okay?' Giles caught her up and then stopped and waited for Beth, trying to catch his breath. His arm was back in the sling, he had a sharp pain under his ribs and his left shoulder seemed to have gone numb.

Beth wiped the rain from her face. 'Can we rest a minute? Are you sure this is the right way?' There was no sign of movement behind them. If they could get into the trees at least they could have something at their backs, anything other than this vast expanse of heather and scree and blackness.

They reached the treeline at last, where the path dipped dizzyingly downward into the larch and spruce which clung to the hillside in the narrow ravine. There they managed to find the moss-covered trunk of a fallen tree where they could sit, their backs to a solid boulder, and fight to recover their breath.

Moira grinned at them shakily. 'I've been up here dozens of times. Don't worry. It's easy, even in the dark. Shall I go first?' Her hair had whipped free of her scarf and framed her face in a tangled mass of rain-glossed curls.

Giles swept the beam of the hand-held halogen spotlight, which the doctor from the helicopter had given him, around them and nodded. 'Once we reach the burn we can follow it down. It should be easy then, shouldn't it?' He gave them a determined smile. 'Keep your chins up.'

Slowly they retraced their steps, stopping frequently to regain their breath. Once Beth looked at Giles and reached out to touch his arm. 'Are you okay?'

'Sure.' He nodded. He looked up at the sky. Lightning was still flickering amongst the clouds, although he thought the thunder had abated. The storm was drifting north. 'I'm fine.' He breathed a silent prayer: *Give us the strength to get back. We can't do it on our own. And, please, keep that witch away from us.* He thought he could make out the path now, in the heather; a streak of darker mud and rock, where on summer days a steady stream of visitors would make their way along the signposted path towards the cross-slab on the hill.

He wasn't sure what made him turn suddenly. An instinct he hadn't known he possessed gripped him so strongly that already as he whirled round he had raised the lamp clubwise in his fist. In a split second he saw Brid so close behind them he should have heard her – would have heard her if she had made any sound at all – and he knocked the knife from her hand.

She stopped and he saw her waver. She shook her head slightly as though puzzled, then before their eyes she began to fade. In a moment she had gone.

'Giles!' Beth cried out. 'Are you all right?'

'In the name of Jesus!' Moira tumbled up beside them, her feet slipping on the muddy rocks. 'Say that if she comes again: "In the name of Jesus!"' She swung her torch round. 'Where's the lamp? What happened to the lamp?' Her voice rose hysterically.

'I dropped it.' Giles was gasping heavily. 'It must have gone out.' His hands were shaking. 'Oh God, I hope it's not broken!'

Brid had been close enough for him to be able to see the jagged bruising on her forehead, and those strange unseeing eyes, fixed not on him but on Beth behind him. He swung Ken's rucksack off his shoulders. Swallowing his fear he searched the rough canvas with cold frantic fingers, looking for another torch. He found, rattling round at the bottom, an old Swiss Army knife. Slipping it into his pocket he went back to feeling for the torch. His fingers closed over a heavy square shape and he drew it out and glanced down at it. A pen flare kit. Why in God's name hadn't Ken remembered these flares when they thought the phone call had not got through?

'Giles!' Moira's strangled gasp brought him to his feet abruptly, his heart thundering with terror.

Brid was there again, only a few feet from them.

Beth's scream was cut off by Moira's voice. Her confidence and her faith were strong. She was very calm. 'In the name of Jesus go, woman. Leave us alone. Go away.' She stepped forward and put her hand out towards Brid.

'Moira, be careful!' Giles's shout had no effect. Moira stepped forward again.

Brid's attention was suddenly full on her. She narrowed her eyes. She had not touched the priest; his power was no doubt as strong as Broichan's, though she had not felt it, but this was the priest's woman. She was of no importance. She had no power. And she was in the way. The silver knife was back in her hand. With a faint smile she raised it and struck.

Moira's piercing scream was cut off short as the blood spurted from her throat.

A surge of power shot through Brid and with the dripping knife in her hand, she turned her attention once more towards Beth.

Paralysed by shock, Giles stood between Moira's body and Beth. The flare gun was still in his hand. Somehow he had freed his arm from the sling again. With fingers almost too weak to move, he tore off the launcher and screwed it with shaking hands into one of the flares, his eyes never leaving Brid's face. She had taken a step closer and he could see the look of wild exultation in her eyes. He pulled the flare off the clip and began to push back the spring.

'Giles, help me!' Beth had picked up a flat piece of rock and was holding it in front of her. She was beyond fear.

Brid smiled, her eyes still fixed unswervingly on Beth. She raised her hand and they both saw the glint of metal from the knife's blade, still streaked with Moira's blood, as she began to move.

425

The spring was too hard. Desperately Giles pushed it back with his thumb. His hands were slippery with sweat, his strength gone. It was their only chance. With one last effort he had it back full. He pointed the flare straight at Brid and let go.

The burning ball of magnesium caught Brid full in the chest. For a moment they saw her, her clothes in flames, her face a mask of fear and pain, then she had gone.

The blackness once the flare had died was total.

'She was going to kill me.' Beth closed her eyes. She felt as though she was going to be sick. 'You saved my life. Oh God, Moira!'

She glanced round in terror. She couldn't see her. Panic-stricken she groped around for the dropped torch. When at last she found it, she ran a few steps back to where Moira was lying huddled on the path. 'Moira, are you all right?' The light beam fell on her and Beth could see the blood soaking through her clothes, pooling on the wet rock, seeping into the grass. There was no doubt that she was dead. 'Giles!' Beth's shout came out as a whisper. Suddenly she was crying.

'Christ. What do we do now?' Giles stood looking down. 'Oh Beth.' He knelt beside Moira and took her cold hand, feeling hopelessly for a pulse. There was none.

He glanced up into the rain. 'Poor Moira.' He took a deep breath. Then he looked round again. 'I'd better go and see what's happened to Brid.' Forcing himself to stand up he took a step forward. Then another. His legs were shaking so much he could hardly move.

Moira's torch in his hands, he walked slowly back up the track till he reached the spot where the burned branches and scorched grass showed where the flare had landed. He searched round with the help of the torch, shining it over the edge of the rocks, down into the water, up amongst the lichen-draped spruce, into the rocks. There was no sign of Brid.

'She's not here. There's no trace of her. She's gone. Back to wherever it is she came from.' He went back to Beth. 'Are you all right, darling?'

She was leaning against the rock, her face white in the torchlight, tears pouring down her cheeks. Slowly she opened her eyes. She took a long, deep shuddering breath. 'Are you sure she's gone?' She was trembling violently.

He nodded. 'There's no trace of anything. No clothing. Nothing. If she had been burned by that flare she would have been unconscious or screaming. Believe me, she has gone.' He put his hands on her shoulders and gave them a hard, reassuring squeeze. 'At least for now.'

Adam had nearly made the mistake again.

Each time he had found himself out of his body, his shock and surprise that the technique had worked, and then his subsequent elation and sense of triumph, had been so great he had rebounded straight back into it again and lain there, his heart thudding against his ribs, wondering if he were going to have a heart attack.

At first he had treated Brid as a spirit, a ghost who could be conjured from the dead, and he had wasted precious months practising from ancient texts on necromancy. Then his brain had kicked in. She was a priestess. An initiate of one of the most powerful magical traditions the Western world has ever known. She was not dead. And she was not undead in the vampire sense. She was a time traveller and still very much alive!

The technique had taken a long time to perfect. Different books gave different instructions. None of them gave enough. He suspected many of them, especially the ones he categorised as Celtic California, had been written by people who had never tried it themselves at all. But he had persisted in his studies. If Brid could do it, so could he. Using modern terms and techniques, self-hypnosis was the key to the intentional out of body experience; creative visualisation with a bit of magic thrown in. But he had studied reproductions of Grimoires as well. And John Dee. And Crowley. And Castenada. And finally he had done it. He had found himself poised somewhere near his bedroom ceiling and for the first time stared down at his body, seemingly asleep on his bed. He had learned cautiously to move – drift, really – and then to explore the house room by room. Finally he had plucked up courage to go out and drift around above the garden. One thing terrified him still. In all the literature, fiction and putative fact, there was a silver cord – the link which remained between body and soul, the lifeline by which the traveller could find his way back to his body. He did not appear to have one, or if he did, he could not see it.

There was more to learn of course. He needed to be able to travel vast distances, and he needed to be able to travel in time. And still he did not see how Brid could bring with her on her travels a solid, real body.

This, he suspected, was where the stone with its mirrored sign came in. It was the gateway, the place where the parallel planes somehow interconnected. Perhaps all standing stones marked gateways such as that. By tradition the countryside was full of such sacred places. Water-courses, fords, crossroads, special venerable trees, unusual rocks, hills. They were numerous and well documented. He remembered the time when as a student he had allowed himself to be lured down to the Eildon Hills by Liza to the place where Thomas of Ercildoune had slipped into Elfin Land and stayed there lost for seven years. Try as they might they had not found the exact place!

The first time he tried it up by the symbol stone he had risen from his body, but the old panic had set in. The second time he had drifted quietly in a mood of solemn practise round the stand of Scots pine, and had gone a little way down the burn, following the water, but not too close. To get back to his body he had only to form the intention and there he was. It seemed simple. Too simple.

Halloween was a time when traditionally the veil was thin. It was a shame the weather was so foul, but needs must. He could not wait another year. Carefully he had made his preparations, rehearsed his words, and set out for the stone. His mind had been so totally on the journey to come he had not noticed that he had failed to latch the door properly behind him. Nor had he noticed the prowling cat still waiting in his drive, obsessive, blind, fixated on revenge and hate, trapped in his time as surely as was the victim she waited for, yet not seeing the very man she yearned for and sought so hard.

He was aching in every limb when he reached the stone, and shivering violently, but his excitement was intense. Some part of him, still the highly-trained doctor and twentieth-century man, noted that he would probably die of hypothermia and that he was undoubtedly out of his mind. The rest of him was determined to press on. He sat down, leaning with his back against the stone, and fixed his mind on Brid's time. On Gartnait and Gemma, and Broichan. Above all on Brid, as he had first known her, young and carefree and wild. It should be easy. After all, he had been there before.

'He's in a coma.' Liza glanced up as Beth and Giles made their way into the intensive care side-ward and stood looking down at the still body on the bed in front of them. At his side the steady electronic beep of the life support machine was the only sound in the room. Adam had been transferred to Edinburgh in the early hours of the morning.

'Will he be all right?' Beth asked quietly. She stepped forward and put her hand on the old man's thin white fingers.

Liza shrugged. 'No one knows. They can't find anything wrong now that his temperature has stabilised. He's just not there.'

'And you can't tell them where he is?' Beth gave a rueful glance at Giles.

Liza shook her head. 'Hardly! But I've asked them to see if they can get hold of Ivor Furness. He took care of Brid many years ago when they had her in a psychiatric hospital in North London somewhere. I remember Adam saying he was the only person who had worked out what might be happening. He had actually watched Brid go into a coma and out of her body and then come back. She murdered one of his nurses.'

Beth shuddered. 'Murder seems to come very easily to her, doesn't it.'

She and Giles had spent hours with the police when they had eventually staggered down off the mountain and directed the search party back to where Moira's body lay, covered by Giles's jacket. By unspoken agreement they let the police assume that they had been attacked by someone lying in wait in the trees. The only thing which the police found hard to understand was that Moira's murderer was a woman. She had, they assumed, fled under cover of the explosion of the flare. They were still waiting at Ken's bedside to tell him of his wife's death when he was sufficiently recovered from what was thought to be an angina attack.

Liza stood up wearily and stretched. 'I don't suppose she was killed.'

Beth shook her head. 'I don't know. She just vanished. Completely. No trace.'

Liza looked back at Adam. 'Perhaps by now she has found him?' She touched his forehead gently.

Behind them the door of the ward opened and closed again softly. No one turned round. Their eyes were fixed on Adam's face.

The figure behind them was hazy, almost transparent, as it drifted towards the bed. Her clothes were torn and blackened, the knife sheathed at her girdle. Her gaze was fixed on Adam as he lay motionless on the white sheets.

A-dam.

Liza frowned. It was the merest whisper, somewhere in the back of her head. In the hot room with its relentless hum of air conditioning and electronics, Liza felt a slight draught brush against her skin. She looked up. 'Beth!' The fear in her voice made Beth jump. 'She's here.'

'She can't be.' Beth backed away from the bed, staring round.

Giles put his good arm round her and pulled her against him. 'We shouldn't have come. We've brought her with us.'

'We can't have.' Beth shook her head. 'Oh God, I hate this. Grandfather!' She looked at him helplessly. 'Please, come back.'

'He can't hear you, Beth.' Giles was looking at a spot a few feet from the bed, near Liza. He could feel the hairs on the back of his neck standing on end. 'She's there. Look.'

The two women stared at the place he was pointing at, and first one and then the other saw her – no more than a faint shadow. Liza stood up and backed away. She was conjuring up the protective light, visualising it around them all, but it wasn't working.

A-dam, come back to Brid. I love you, A-dam . . .

'He hasn't found her, then.' Beth's voice was very sad.

At the sound of it, Brid looked up. She half turned and before their eyes her shadow seemed to become stronger. She looked straight at Beth and her hand went to her girdle, freeing the dagger from its leather sheath.

'No!' Beth backed away, clutching at Giles's arm.

'Not again.' He pushed her behind him. 'Why can't the bitch leave you alone?'

'Go away, Beth,' Liza said quietly.

'But what about you?'

'Don't worry about me. Just go. Take her away, Giles. I'll follow. She won't hurt Adam. And don't call a nurse. She doesn't like nurses.'

Leave A-dam, child of A-dam's child!

The voice seemed to echo through all their heads as Brid launched herself across the small room, the knife raised.

A stand holding a plasma drip hurtled sideways against the sink and toppled over. One of the visitors' chairs was pushed against the bedside table and suddenly an alarm rang. The door flew open and a nurse appeared, behind her a doctor. As they stared, startled, into the room there was a vicious growl.

'It's a cat!' The doctor gave an astonished cry as, with a shriek of rage the cornered animal shot past him out of the door.

'Leave it, see to the patient!' The doctor shouted as another alarm went off in the corridor. The ward seemed to be filled with the sound of running feet.

In his bed Adam slept on oblivious. Where he was it was cold and raining, but he had spotted the warmth of a fire down by the edge of the stream outside Gemma's hut.

* * *

The tea shop was small and crowded. It smelled of warm bread and cake and was extremely cosy. Seated at the little round table Liza and Beth and Giles looked round at the other customers – mainly ladies who had finished their shopping and were carefully shepherding treasured carrier bags full of trophies from a hard afternoon's spending. There were one or two men – exhausted and stressed – but all were cheerful and relaxed in the warmth. Every now and then the shop door would open and they could glimpse outside the dark evening, the wet pavement, with its reflections of street lights and the hiss of car tyres on the road.

Liza picked up her cup and drank from it thankfully. 'I couldn't believe it when they accused us of smuggling a cat into the ward!'

'How else, logically, could it have got there?' Giles was piling cream and jam on to a fat, crumbling home-baked scone. He felt as though he had only just stopped shaking. Glancing at the two women he knew they felt the same.

Liza rubbed her face with her hands. She had just phoned home again. She wanted Michele there beside her in Edinburgh. Except Michele didn't come. Her phone calls to him had gone unanswered and their *donna delle pulizie* had said she did not know when he would return from Rome.

'I wish I knew how to contact Meryn,' she went on, shaking her head in frustration. 'He would know what to do. Listen, I want you two to go back to Adam's house.' She reached over and poured herself another cup of tea, noting grimly that her hands were still trembling. 'Two reasons. I want you to be there in case . . .' She hesitated. 'In case Adam is there – up there, by the stone. All alone.' She glanced at them both. 'You understand, don't you? If he managed it, to travel out of his body, and is trapped somehow.' She shrugged. 'I can't bear to think of him all alone. I don't know which is him, the man in the hospital bed or the man travelling somewhere out there amongst the stars. And the other reason is that if Brid is going to hang around Adam here in the hospital, you'll be safer there, well away from her. Out of her reach.'

In the street outside, Brid moved closer to the window. She could see them through the condensation-streaked glass. She remembered Edinburgh, this street, even perhaps this café from when Adam was young and a student and she had been befriended by an old woman called Maggie.

People hurrying through the rain to catch their buses and find

431

their way home barely noticed the shadowy dark figure on the edge of the patch of light which spilled from the window. Without realising why, they parted and moved round her, leaving her alone in her circle of dark stillness, then they moved on, part of the noise and the bustle of the early evening rush.

Brid smiled to herself. The woman Beth had taken refuge inside the café, but she would have to come out soon. She would have to go away on her own and leave this big man who seemed to follow her everywhere. And then she would kill her. Then she could make the blood flow; the blood of the child of A-dam's child would be rich and strong and full of energy and be perfect for saving A-dam's life.

The wind was lashing round Shieling House, making the windows rattle. Draughts played across the floor and Beth, huddling in front of the stove, was shivering violently. The place was damp and cold, and there was a strange atmosphere of fear and anger in the air.

'She's been here.' Beth looked round the room after they finally got the wood-burning stove lit. 'I can feel her. It's like a poison.'

Giles followed her glance. He could feel nothing but the rather stale, unlived-in feeling of a house that has been shut up for several days without any heating on.

'I don't think so.' He grinned at her. 'Let's not worry about Brid. She'll be in Edinburgh with Adam if she's anywhere.'

She glanced at him doubtfully. If only she was as certain as he was. She changed the subject. 'Giles, when are you going back to London to sort it out with Idina?' She didn't look at him. 'You can't just pretend she doesn't exist any more.'

'Why not? She's pretended I don't exist often enough.' He was leafing through one of Adam's books at the table. In the pool of light beneath the desk lamp the drawings of the symbols were stark. He glanced up as somewhere nearby there was a sudden sliding noise followed by a crash. 'It's all right, it'll be a slate from the roof,' he said reassuringly. He had seen the immediate terror on her face.

When his phone rang they both looked at it for a moment, then Giles picked it up. Beth watched him anxiously.

'You gathered what that was about.' Giles came over to her and put his hand on her shoulder after he switched the phone off. 'It was Ken. He's home and he wants to talk about Moira.'

Beth bit her lip. 'Poor man. Giles, I'm not sure I'm ready for that. I would cry and make things worse.'

Giles nodded. 'Listen, I think I should go down and see him.

432

Would you mind? Will you be all right on your own up here for an hour or two?'

She wanted to say yes, I do mind, she wanted to scream at him don't leave me, but she shrugged and forced a smile. 'No, of course I don't mind. Poor Ken. It must be so awful for him. You go. But come back before it gets dark. Please.'

Giles turned to the door and reached for his coat. 'Lock up after me. I won't be long, I promise. And I'll leave you the phone.'

She stared at the door after he had gone. The wind seemed to be stronger than ever now, screaming in the eaves, roaring across the hillside like a train. Shivering, she threw some more logs into the stove and went to stand looking down at the book Giles had been studying. It showed a series of rather beautiful stylised Celtic animals and symbols. She stared down at one, a comb and a mirror. Adam had ringed the mirror and scribbled in pencil: *Denotes female burial spot or clan totem.* Next to it was another rough note – *Mirror used in fortune-telling; scrying; necromancy; magic; signifies one world and its mirror image.* Then he had drawn five ornate question marks.

'I wish I knew about this stuff. I wish I could help Grandfather.' She turned the page. Listening. For what, she wasn't quite sure. The wind? Voices? The sound of ghostly hoof beats in the dark? Brid?

She shivered and suddenly making up her mind, she walked to the back door and pulled it open, staring outside. There was an icy sharpness to the wind, a fresh clean bite against her face which indicated snow, but the afternoon was empty. There was no one out there.

She tensed. Behind her, in the house, Giles's phone was ringing. She turned and ran back inside, the door banging behind her. As she reached out for the phone, it stopped. She shrugged. Suddenly she didn't want to talk to anyone anyway.

Brid felt the pain as though it were in her own chest. She tensed and fought it, not knowing for a moment where she was. She could not focus. She was distracted. Part of her had been on the hillside near the house, watching the child of A-dam's child standing out there in the garden, her hair blowing in the wind, the other part was with A-dam in the hospital, unseen as doctors and nurses crowded round the bed.

The flat line had appeared on the screen at three p.m. to the accompaniment of a shrill alarm. Frantically they were trying to resuscitate him. Brid wept quietly in the corner, Beth for the moment forgotten. Where was A-dam? Why had he left his body? Surely he would not have risked going back to look for her in a place where Broichan waited at her bedside.

'He's gone.' The voice by the bed was sober.

'One more try.' The doctor had picked up the paddles. 'Stand back, everyone.'

As Adam's body arced on the bed and the ECG picked up the faintest beat once more, he leaned against the hill-top tree which had supported him as he began to fall and put his hand to his chest, surprised at the agonising pain which had shot through him.

He closed his eyes and tried to breathe calmly. Now was not the time to dive back into his body. Things were getting too exciting. He had seen Gemma come out of her hut to stand by the fire. She was older than he remembered, her hair white now, and her face lined, and she was talking to Gartnait in quick, frightened tones. Adam drifted closer. He called out to them but they did not seem to hear him. Gartnait looked smarter than Adam had ever seen him. Gone was the dusty tunic and leggings. Instead he was wearing an embroidered cloak fastened with a silver brooch, leather thongs criss-crossed his calves and at his waist hung a serviceable-looking sword. They were speaking their own language but he found he could understand them easily.

'He intends to sacrifice her to the gods. If I do not rescue her, she will die and so probably will we. Don't you understand, Mother? We have to act!'

Brid! They were talking about Brid.

'He is waiting beside her day and night. The moment she re-enters her body he will seize her and then she will die up here, by my stone. I marked it with her symbol and by doing so I ordered her death with my own hand.'

Gemma shook her head. 'She will not return. She is not so foolish.'

'She has grown weak. She is no longer rational, Mother. I'm sorry, but she was not sufficiently trained. She was a fool. A besotted fool.' He smacked his fist into the palm of his hand. 'If I could only reach her, out there in the land of dreams, before she tries to come back.'

'No, Gartnait!'

'What else can I do? Do we sit and watch Broichan lead her to her death?'

'If you go to the other world, you may not find her. You may be lost too.'

He turned and stared down into the fire. 'I shall consult the omens. If I watch the birds I shall know whether to fly with them after Brid into the sunset or turn my back on her and fly towards the dawn.'

'Gartnait!' Adam stepped forward and stood above him on the bank.

Gartnait did not turn.

'Gartnait, I am here, in your time. I came to find Brid!'

It was Gemma who turned and faced him, her face alert like a dog scenting a rabbit. 'There is someone there!'

'Gemma! Can you see me?' Adam stepped forward.

'Who is it?' Gartnait turned and looked straight at Adam, and through him. He frowned. 'Is it Broichan?'

She shook her head. 'I don't think so. Beware, my son. We are not alone.'

'Gemma! Gartnait! Please, it's me.' Adam stepped down nearer to them and stood by the fire. The flames dipped and flared a warning and he saw Gemma watch it, wide-eyed, as though listening to its message.

'Take care. Take care.' She put her hand on Gartnait's arm. 'Broichan is near and he has spies everywhere. Go. Quickly.'

He looked down at her as though trying to read the message in her eyes, then he nodded. 'I go, Mother. Let your gods go with me.' He leaped onto the bank where a few seconds before Adam had been standing and he began to run towards the stone.

'Gemma. You can see me, can't you?' Adam moved closer to her. 'Please!' He was desperate.

She paused as she was about to go back inside her hut and looked round again, shaking her head as though trying to rid herself of the sound of his voice. Then at last she stopped. 'A-dam, is that you? I cannot see you, boy, nor can I help you. Go back to your own people, A-dam. Brid is lost. She is no longer with us. She followed you into your time and she is under Broichan's *geas*, his curse. She is lost to us all, A-dam. Lost.'

She paused for a moment, as though listening for his reply, then she turned and ducked back into the hut.

Adam stared after her, then down at his own body. Boy, she had called him. To himself he looked as he had looked when he sat down at the foot of the stone in his own century, an old man in a worn waxed jacket with under it two thick Shetland sweaters and a shirt; an old man, with drawn, wrinkled skin and wiry hands and wild white hair.

Turning he scrambled out of the hollow and hurried after Gartnait. He had to reach the stone before him. He had to make himself understood. He had to travel back with him, then they could search for Brid together.

The stone was wreathed in mist. Panting, he slid down a gully and climbed up the other side. In front of him, hurrying away from him into the darkness, he could see a figure. 'Gartnait!' he shouted. 'Wait!' The figure did not hesitate; it moved on, swiftly, skirting a soft boggy area of ground and then leaping up over some rocks. 'Gartnait!' Adam could feel his chest tightening. He was beginning to gasp. He was forced to stop for a moment, doubled up, trying to regain his breath. When he straightened he could barely see the figure in the distance. He hurried on, and then as he came to the top of the last outcrop before the pine wood he halted again. He could see Gartnait now, his sword catching a stray ray of light escaping between the low-lying clouds. It would soon be dusk.

Adam stiffened. There was a movement near him, in the rough heather moorland to his right. Someone else was following Gartnait to the stone. Adam went cold. He dropped to one knee to make himself less visible and craned round, trying to pinpoint the movement again. Perhaps it was a stag, or a fox in the heather. It was a man. He saw him now, clearly. He was obviously following Gartnait, bending low, hiding, ducking between pieces of cover as he drew closer to his quarry. 'Gartnait!' Adam's warning was only a whisper. What could he do? Crawling now, he made his way laboriously towards the stone, as quietly as he could.

Gartnait reached the small plateau where the stone stood and touched it with his hands, tracing the carvings lovingly, obviously remembering each and every one, the hard work of months in the open with his precious tools. He stooped and Adam saw him put his hand on the carving of the mirror – Brid's sign, the sign of a priestess who could summon the power to travel to other planes of existence. Then he stood up again and raised his hands above his head. He was staring up, Adam realised suddenly, at a skein of birds flying low over the hillside towards the westering sun, studying their flight. It was the sign. The birds had told him to follow his sister towards the light.

For a moment he stood there, and Adam watched him carefully. Gartnait seemed lost in thought, his eyes closed, his face still. He put his hands, palms flat, against the stone, and he had gone. Adam gasped. Where Gartnait had stood there was another man – a tall man with wild hair and a long black robe which blew against his

436

legs in the wind: Broichan. In an instant, he too had gone, following Gartnait out of sight.

'Oh my God!' Adam sat down, his hand pressed against his mouth. He stared round, checking there had been no one with Broichan. As far as he could see the hillside was empty. He glanced over his shoulder. If only he could speak to Gemma, tell her what had happened. But it was no use. She could not hear him. There was only one option. He had to try and go back. He had to rejoin his body, lying still by the stone but in another time, and see if he could see Gartnait there. Cautiously he stood up and made his way across the grass and scree towards the great finger of stone where it pointed up towards the sky.

As he laid his hands gently on its surface as he had seen Gartnait do, he had no way of knowing that his body, the vehicle of his dreaming, questing mind, had gone.

'How long has he been like this?' Ivor Furness was standing at the foot of Adam's bed.

Ivor had aged well. He was still a distinguished-looking man, balding now, but slim and well muscled. He went to Adam's side and bent over him, examining eye reflexes, feeling his hands, his pulse. 'He looks the same as Brid did when she was comatose.' He turned to pick up a briefcase and produced a well-worn file of notes, a private file he had felt justified in taking from the hospital when he retired. 'I've asked to see the EEGs. There was a fascinating anomaly about Brid's readings which at the time were put down as just that, an anomaly, but which I privately thought might be because of –' he shrugged and flashed Liza a charming smile, '– her rather odd origins, which, you understand, I did not share with my colleagues. They would have had me locked up as well! I had a theory that the brain readings might show the activity of a part of the brain which had not before been noticed, or at least not measured.'

'Dr Furness, what I don't understand is how, if Brid's body was in bed, and demonstrably there, in front of you, how could it also have been elsewhere? Adam didn't imagine her in his bed. The people who saw her, whom she attacked, didn't imagine it.'

'How indeed?' Ivor Furness was studying Adam's chart. 'And where is the good Dr Craig now, I wonder?' He stood looking down at Adam, chewing the inside of his cheek thoughtfully. 'And does it matter that you have moved him?'

Liza stared at him aghast. 'What do you mean?'

Furness shrugged. 'Just that I have often found myself wondering about the infinities of time and space. If one can wander through time and space at will, does it matter where one has left one's body?

That is, if one intends to return to it. And if the body dies, where does the spirit, the soul, whatever we term the life force that has left it, go? Does it go, as it were, further out into yet another dimension, or is it condemned to wander forever, like a ghost, between worlds looking for the host flesh?'

'That sounds awful.' Liza shuddered. She reached out and took Adam's hand. She sighed deeply. 'Poor love. She's made his life hell on earth. And when at last he wanted her, she wasn't there.'

'Perhaps he's found her now.' Furness stared thoughtfully down at Adam's face. 'I wish there was a way we could know for sure.'

They both looked up as a nurse walked into the room, checked on Adam, and walked out again, closing the door behind her.

Liza sighed. 'You've worried me now. I thought he would somehow know what we had done, but what if he has gone back to the stone, looking for his body, and it isn't there? What if he doesn't know where it is? But we couldn't have left him there. He would have died.' She stood up and walked over to the window, staring down. 'I wonder if some of the people whom modern medicine categorise as being in a coma are actually trapped, not able to return to their bodies because they have been moved to hospital and their spirit cannot find them?' She turned and looked at him. 'I'm going to have to go back to the stone.'

Furness shrugged. 'And do what? Leave a message?'

'I don't know!' She was angry. 'But I can't just leave it, can I? What happens if he needs to go back there? Is the hospital going to let him be taken up a mountain in November on the offchance that his soul might pop back into his body?'

Ivor Furness shook his head sadly. 'You know they are not.'

'Then what happens? Is he condemned to wander forever?'

'You and he were very close, weren't you?' Furness walked over to her and gently touched her shoulder. 'Perhaps he will come and find you. I'm afraid nothing else can be done. All you can do is wait. Unless,' he stopped and gazed down at Adam.

'Unless what?'

'Unless, somehow, we *can* get him there in person.'

The mist was very heavy. Broichan moved cautiously after Brid's brother, through the trees and down the steep track. The air was thick and hard to breathe, the path strangely formless beneath his soft-soled sandals.

Gartnait was striding out fearlessly, his sword in his hand, sliding now and then on the mud, oblivious to the shadowy figure behind him, his eyes searching the murky distances between the trees. 'Brid!' His voice was strangely flat in the mist. It didn't carry and for the first time the younger man felt the prickle of fear across his shoulderblades. He stopped and glanced round, listening. There was someone nearby. The sound of the water seemed to come from a long way away, though he could see the flash of white from the torrents as they poured over the black rocks close beside him. He clutched his sword more tightly, lifting the blade slightly as he turned completely round. He did not see the figure in the shadows.

Broichan had long ago learned the art of invisibility, but Gartnait sensed he was there. So be it. He would have to deal with his uncle one day, but now he had just one aim: to find Brid and bring her home and then somehow to liberate her totally from Broichan's *geas*, and from her imprisonment.

At the foot of the hill he stopped. He had no way of knowing where to go. *Brid.* He called her in his head. *Where are you, little sister?*

There was no answer. All he could hear was the moaning of the wind in the trees behind him.

When his mind touched hers, it was only for a moment. He felt her anger and her fear and her pain. She had lost her A-dam; she did not know where he was, and she blamed another for it. She was hunting again with her knife, searching for blood to try to find her love and take away the anguish which surrounded him. And just as instantly Gartnait knew who it was Brid hunted. It was the child of A-dam's child, A-dam's only family by blood, the only person who could hold him in his own time and come between him and Brid.

The mist drew closer round him. She had gone.

Brid . . .

His call was lost in the whirling endlessness of space.

The first Beth knew of her visitor was the flare of headlights across the living room ceiling as a car headed up the track towards the house and turned into the drive. She woke with a start and found herself sitting in the chair by the stove, her heart thumping, not knowing for a moment what had disturbed her. Then she heard a car door slam. She sat up. Giles was back. Thank God! She moved over to the window and stared out. A thick white mist was drifting across the garden. She could see nothing. Then she heard slow footsteps moving towards the house. It wasn't Giles. She held her breath, staring at the tall thin bent figure making its way up the path.

Stepping away from the window and tiptoeing to the door she waited, listening. There was a long silence, then at last she heard a firm knocking and then a shout. 'Beth? Beth, my dear, are you there?'

She tensed. She did not at first recognise the voice.

'Beth, it's Meryn!'

'Meryn?' She breathed the name in utter disbelief. 'Meryn! Wait, wait! I'm coming!'

She reached for the bolts with shaking hands and dragging them back, pulled open the door. 'Meryn? How did you know? Oh, I'm so glad to see you!' She flung her arms round his neck. 'I've been so scared! Where have you been? How did you know I was here?'

If he noticed that she had rebolted the door top and bottom behind him he made no sign as he walked over to the stove and automatically bent down to throw in a couple of logs as if it were his own house. Then he turned to her. He looked just the same, perhaps a little more tanned, a little older. His eyes still had the same deep, all-seeing quality which she remembered being so fascinated by when she was a child. 'I came because I could sense you needed me, but Beth, you must realise I am only human.' He smiled at her gently. 'Not Merlin!'

She bit her lip, half embarrassed. 'Got to be Merlin. Only Merlin can help us.'

She sat down on the edge of the sofa and started telling him everything that had happened, wondering every now and then if he already knew, but determined to tell him anyway. 'I've been so afraid. She's here, in the mountains, and nothing can keep her away. I don't even know if she can get in here.'

He sat for a full minute without speaking as she fell silent, watching his face. Then at last he shook his head. 'I sense nothing beyond her fear. I suspect she is as frightened of you as you are of her.' No point in telling her the truth, not yet. He leaned back against the cushions. 'Beth, I am going to have to teach you, as I taught your grandmother, some basic facts about life and death.' His eyes twinkled for a moment. 'As well as some techniques for dealing with them. You must not be afraid. Brid is, or was, an ordinary human being. She doesn't appear to be a very nice one, but we don't know what may have happened to her in her life to have moulded and twisted her, just as we might not know what has influenced any unhappy criminal or unbalanced person we meet in the course of so-called everyday life. She has learned, in her turn, techniques which enable her to travel around in a rather, to

441

us, alarming fashion. She comes, if your grandfather is to be believed, from a culture where such things were not only believed in, but practised. An extraordinarily sophisticated culture by all accounts, which we in our self-proclaimed wisdom belittle as barbaric – though no more so than many present day people – and which we, because we cannot by and large do some of the things they could do, dismiss as superstitious and credulous. You and I know differently.' He turned back to the open doors of the stove and stooping, picked up the poker. The smouldering logs burst into flame. 'Brid went to college for years to learn all she knows. Perhaps she didn't finish the course, but she is very, very knowledgeable, of that you can be sure. I am no Druid,' he gave another smile, 'whatever your grandmother says. But perhaps I am a descendant of Druids, or at least of a school of healers and mystics which goes back many centuries. I have studied all over the world, written books, sat at the feet of teachers and watched and listened – above all listened.' He sat down on the chair opposite her. 'You look surprised.'

'We didn't know. Liza didn't know you wrote books.'

'Why should she?' He was silent for a moment. 'Your friend Giles is going to spend the night with Ken Maclaren. Don't ask me how I know, or how he knows you will be safe. That is part of the mystery.' He smiled again. 'But we have to have the time together alone to plan your instruction. You have to try to learn in a night what would normally take months or years. You must suspend that small niggling core of disbelief which I sense still there in the centre of your brain, take your brain out of the equation altogether, and learn to listen to your intuition. You need to learn to protect yourself from Brid and her companions if there are any. You need to be able to communicate with her. You need to be able to fend off the cat in her. You need to be able to secure your family from harm and, perhaps, you will learn to try to guide your grandfather home. A tall order for,' he glanced at the watch on his wrist, 'perhaps seven hours.'

Beth grimaced. 'Why so little time?'

'Because I have to go tomorrow. I know Liza likes to think of me as disappearing in a puff of smoke up there on Penny Beacon, to hide between the worlds for months or years on end. I'm afraid it is much more mundane. I am booked on a jumbo jet from London to New York.' He gave a small chuckle. 'Also, I think you are right. I think Brid has formed a link with you and you are in great danger. There may not be a lot of time before she makes her next attack.

So,' he sat forward and rubbed his hands together, 'as you do not, I suspect, have the trained memory of a bard who can recite for days or weeks on end without repeating him or herself once, I suggest you fetch a notebook and pencil and that traditional over-seer of all-night study, a large cup of black coffee, and we will start now.'

He did not tell her that before he went back to New York he too had a battle to fight. His was with Broichan alone.

Dawn came slowly, a murky paleness behind the windows, muffled by the mist which had grown thicker as the light came, but they worked on without noticing.

He gave her no time to be afraid, no time to doubt her own ability. Each time she thought she would collapse with exhaustion he called her back to wakefulness. When he had finished he stood up and smiled down at her. 'You are ready, Beth.'

She stood up too and looked down into the fire. Her head was swimming and she felt exhausted but at the same time curiously exhilarated. 'Are you sure?'

He smiled. 'Now, what did I say? Confidence! Beth, my dear, I have a plane to catch. You will be all right. You have a natural instinct for this or I would not have been able to teach you so quickly. You can thank Liza for that, I suspect. You have inherited her intuition. The scepticism you inherited from your grandfather has held you back, but now, as he has, you have learned that there is more in heaven and earth than ever you dreamed of, and that it is very real. But that you can keep control. Be brave, my Beth. I shall be with you in spirit, remember that whenever you need me.' He stooped and kissed her on the cheek. 'Oh, and Beth,' it was an afterthought, 'don't let Giles sap your energy, my dear.' He touched the side of his nose with a twinkle in his eye. 'Just for now, concentrate on what must be done.'

She stood in the doorway staring after him for a long time as his car disappeared down the track, then with a shiver she went back inside and shut the door. Her notebook, packed with scribbled advice, diagrams and information lay on the sofa where she had been sitting for most of the night. The room felt suddenly very empty and lonely.

She hadn't had time to assimilate what had happened, and feel confident that she had fully absorbed all he had tried to teach her in those few intensive hours of learning. She built up the fire in the stove and then began slowly to climb the stairs. A hot bath, and breakfast would help to take the ache out of her bones, and then she would go to bed for a few hours to try to restore her strength before the battle, for battle there was going to be, Meryn seemed certain of that, and she agreed with him. She could feel it in the air, like a distant storm, a tension, a frisson in the energy field around her body – she knew how to describe it now – a congealing of emotion in the planes where, somewhere, Adam and Brid circled one another but did not meet.

You can wait for Brid to find you, or you can go to her.

Meryn's instructions had been calm, almost matter-of-fact.

I think her soul is fragmented. One part of her hunts Adam, another wants to destroy anyone who she thinks gets in her way. That is you. It is up to you, Beth, to retrieve him, and to deal with her.

I can't do it! Lying in the bath she had been overwhelmed with panic. Meryn had made it sound easy – almost commonplace. Climb a mountain in the dark, find a time gate, go through, collect your grandfather, kill his psychotic ghost lover, then come back and live happily ever after! No problem!

'Beth!' The voice in her ear was gentle. 'Beth, my darling.' The lips were very warm on hers. Beth stretched and opened her eyes. The room was murky, the daylight outside obscured by mist.

'Giles?' She had been far away in her dreams, climbing the dark ridge near the stone. In the distance she could see her grandfather waiting. He had seen her and was holding out his arms towards her, desperately.

'I'm back. My God it's cold out there! It's starting to snow. Ken insisted I stay all night. I tried to ring but the phone wasn't switched on. I'm so sorry, I couldn't get away. But I left as soon as I could. I couldn't leave you up here on your own any longer.'

Beth sat up and reached for the switch on the bedside lamp. She picked up her watch and stared at it. It was nearly midday. 'How is he?' she asked groggily. Giles was sitting on her bed. There were ice crystals in his hair.

'Miserable, of course, and very lonely. Losing Moira has shaken his faith.'

'Poor man.'

She swung her legs out of the bed and reached for her dressing gown. 'Giles, I missed you.' She threw herself into his arms. 'Oh God, I've missed you.' She didn't mention Meryn. Suddenly she was wondering if Meryn had been real.

'And I missed you.' He held her tightly. 'What is it, Beth? What's wrong? Have you heard anything from Liza?'

She shook her head. 'Nothing. I'm just feeling a bit vulnerable.'

She couldn't remember any of it. The words had gone. Everything Meryn had told her had gone.

Shivering, she slid to her feet and groped for her slippers. 'Oh God, I want to go home. To Wales.'

'Why don't we? We don't have to be here, Beth.' Giles caught her hand. 'You know that, don't you? We could leave today. Well, tomorrow. Why don't we? Why don't we just go? Your grandfather is in good hands. We're not doing anyone any good waiting here.'

Concentrate on what must be done . . .

'Sweetheart, I love you. You do believe me now, don't you?' He was looking at her earnestly. 'I'm getting a divorce. I mean it. And I'm not going back to London.'

'Do you mean it?'

'I mean it. Listen, Idina won't contest the divorce. I know her. She's bored with me and there is someone else now, thank God, to distract her. Damien is rich and famous – right up her street. I want to spend the rest of my life with you, my darling.'

Don't let him sap your energy . . .

Beth stared at him, then slowly she reached up and kissed him on the lips. 'We'll go home soon. But first there is something I have to do. Later. After we've had a meal.'

They ate and then, at his insistence, they went upstairs to rest. She shouldn't do it, she knew. She should be on her way, but surely half an hour could make no difference now?

It's up to you, Beth. . . Meryn's last words came back to her again suddenly . . . *Don't let him sap your energy. . . concentrate on what must be done . . .*

He made love to her eagerly, his kisses tender, his hands first gentle, then rough with desire, and she lay still for a long time after he fell asleep, in the circle of his arms, safe, not wanting to move, not wanting to leave him ever again until at last she too fell asleep.

When she woke the room was dark. With a sense of shock she gently eased away from him and slid from the bed. She dressed quickly, pulling on two extra sweaters, then stooping quickly over him to drop one last kiss on his forehead she turned and made her way out onto the landing.

Downstairs, she dared to turn on the light and look at the clock. It was after six. The whole afternoon had gone. Frantic with hurry she pulled on her jacket and boots and picked up his car keys from the table. For a moment she hesitated, staring at the warm red glow from the stove. It represented at this moment all that was safe and solid in her life.

You need to be able to secure your family from harm . . . you must try to guide your grandfather home.

She had no option. She had to go.

Scribbling Giles a quick note, she let herself out into the ice-cold wind. She stood for a moment on the path, then she turned and gently pulled the door shut behind her.

Giles's car was standing by the front door of the house. Glancing up at the darkened bedroom window she reached to unlock the door and threw her notebook, map and shoulderbag into the passenger seat. Gathering her jacket round her with a shiver she was about to get in when she heard a quiet growl.

She stared round in horror, then dived into the car head-first and slammed the door. Behind her in the house Giles slept on.

Peering through the windscreen, she slotted the key into the ignition. There was no sign of any movement. The track was a darker shade of white beyond the shadowy tree and beyond that there was a uniform wall of fog. Was it her imagination, or was the car still slightly warm from Giles's drive back from Pittenross?

Where is A-dam?

The voice in her head was very clear. Her hand fell away from the ignition key.

Where is A-dam?

She stared round, frightened. Surely Brid could not be here, in the car? It was her overwrought imagination. She took a deep breath, forcing herself to breathe slowly, and deliberately put her hand on the key again. She turned it.

The engine misfired.

She gunned the accelerator, feeling sweat break out on the palms of her hands, and glanced up at the window, praying Giles would not wake up. She could not take him with her. This was something she had to do alone. This time the engine did not even turn over. It was dead. 'No, please.' She smacked the steering wheel with her hands. 'Please, go, you stupid, bloody car!' She tried a third time.

Why have you hurt A-dam? A-dam hates you.

The voice had a slight echo as though it were coming from a long way away, and yet she could hear it clearly – it was as though she were listening to a stereo whose batteries were dying.

A-dam hates you!

She battened her mind against Brid. Even the smallest thought would allow her a foothold inside Beth's head. That could not happen. She had to keep focused, keep her circle of protection intact and strong. If she were sufficiently concentrated then she could not fail. Her life and Adam's depended on her. 'Leave me alone!' This was not the time or place. She had to get to the stone. She had to find Adam. She tried the key again, wrenching it round, pressing the accelerator pedal to the floor. The car remained in total silence.

Where is A-dam? *A-dam hates you*!

'Leave me alone. Go away! I don't know where he is!' She could feel her panic growing. It was becoming airless in the car, but she didn't dare wind down the window. 'Go away!' Had she conjured Brid up herself? Why wouldn't the car start? 'Please, please, please God, let it start!' She tried the key again, conscious of the strong smell of petrol rising from the flooded engine.

There was a clatter behind her and she turned her head in terror. Another slate had tumbled from the roof. It had smashed on the rough stones of the drive near her. She stared at it incredulously. There was no wind now. In the mist the night was very still.

Help me!

Had she said it out loud, or did she just think the words? She put her head on her hands on the wheel and took a deep breath. Then she turned the key again. The engine started. She closed her eyes and breathed a quick prayer of thanks, then backed out of the driveway and headed back down the mountain road.

Behind her the cat stood for a moment on the track, swishing its tail with irritation. Then it turned and it vanished into the mist.

Beth drew up in the lay-by at the foot of the mountain track and sat for a moment staring out at the trees illuminated in the head-lights. She was more scared than she had ever been in her life. Turning them off, she swallowed hard. She waited a moment for her eyes to grow used to the dark and to summon up her courage, then, cautiously, she pushed the door open and swung her feet out. The air was very cold. The low cloud had lifted momentarily, drifting off out of sight and she could see the stars so close she felt she could reach out and touch them. The broad sweep of the Milky Way lay like a diaphanous gauze shawl overhead, and in the dis-tance, between the shoulders of two hills, she could see Orion appearing over the horizon. She pushed the car door closed quietly and locked it, then she turned towards the path, seeing her own breath a cloud of white in front of her as she began to walk into the darkness.

Where is A-dam?

She stopped, terrified. The woods were very quiet. Think. Think of the things Meryn had taught her. Draw the veil of protection around her.

And slowly force herself to move on.

'What if he dies, Ivor?'

Liza was sitting in the back of the ambulance, watching over Adam as the vehicle drove steadily north towards Pittenross.

'That will be my responsibility, not yours. I signed the forms.' He smiled at her encouragingly. 'He will die if he stays in hospital. This is his only chance. If it were summer, I would say we should get him up to the stone where it all started, but in this weather – well, at least here he is nearby. Wherever he is, he might think to come looking at home. And we shall leave him a sign.'

'How?'

He smiled again. 'That is your department. He told me you were psychic. Now is the time to prove it!'

It had taken a lot of persuasion to get the hospital authorities to allow Adam to go home for two or three days. Only Ivor Furness's reputation, and Liza's not quite true claim that she was next of kin and could sign any disclaimers necessary finally persuaded his consultant that there was nothing to lose by the experiment. If he had known they were considering for one instant taking their patient up a mountain and leaving him at the foot of a Pictish symbol stone they would have been certified on the spot. In the event the weather was so bad, Liza was not sure they should even be taking him back to Shieling House.

'Will she come to him?'

Liza shrugged. 'But it's not him, is it?'

Ivor bent and put his hand on Adam's forehead, then he took hold of his wrist and felt his pulse. 'It's the same. Weak but steady.' He straightened. 'It would be very interesting to meet Brid again. I always thought she trusted me, but I can't be sure. So, how are you going to send our two travellers a message?'

Liza shrugged. 'I wish I knew more about this. I think the only way is telepathically. Perhaps I should go to the stone first?'

'You're not afraid?' He looked at her shrewdly.

She raised an eyebrow. 'Yes, I'm afraid. I'm terrified. All I want to do is scoot back to Italy to my lovely down-to-earth husband

and hide behind him with a bottle of Chianti in the autumn sunshine. But I can't, can I?' She stooped and kissed Adam's forehead. It was very cold.

Her eyes screwed up against the freezing weather, Beth plodded on. Forcing herself to take every step, she kept her mind focused resolutely on Adam. She needed to find him. Nothing else mattered. She did not let herself think beyond that. The track was getting steeper and she was out of breath, but she could not allow herself to be distracted by the weakness of her own body. Cold and fear would debilitate her, make her vulnerable. She had to be strong.

She shone her torch ahead of her on the path, her throat tight with apprehension, waves of nausea flooding through her as she listened to the burn rushing down the rocks on her right, and heard the hiss of sleet on the branches of the trees. Keep the circle strong. She peered round nervously. Had the cat followed her? But there was no sign of the cat; no sound of anything at all up there on the hillside with her. She had never felt more alone.

Somehow she forced herself to keep climbing. Only once she stopped to catch her breath, hearing the blood pounding in her ears. Away to her right she could see the flash of water as the burn tipped over a rockface and turned to spray as it tumbled over the falls. Don't listen. Don't let your attention wander. Remember Meryn. Keep him there with her, a talisman within her circle of protection. The ground was levelling out now and she could feel the strength of the wind increasing. Once again the clouds had raced away, leaving the sky clear and frosty with glittering stars.

She could feel it now, the strength of the place beneath her feet as she drew nearer to the stone. She stopped, shocked, and immediately felt herself waver. There must be no emotion; no fear, no anger. She must remain calm and resolute. She stepped forward, off the track into the longer grass, and straightened her shoulders. There was nothing to fear, but fear itself. Who had said that? Some American. Was it Roosevelt? Never mind, keep it in her head firmly like a mantra. No fear. Just calm and strength.

She could see the stone itself now, standing windswept and free on the mountainside. Cautiously she stepped closer. She could feel the power coming off it in waves. It was conducting the special earth energies up from deep in the rocks beneath it, the energies which enabled the fabric of time to thin and distort enough for people to slip in and out. Beyond that spot time and space were flexible, anomalous and infinite.

Her mouth dry, she raised her hands and laid them on the stone so she could feel it, feel the power vibrating through it, will it into her body, feel it pouring up through her feet, through the palms of her hands, down into the top of her head. There was no wind to speak of now but the clouds were coming back, drifting up the broad valley below her, cutting off her view of the distant starlit mountains, circling lazily round the bushes, coming ever closer. In a moment it would be there. She took a deep breath. There was a formula Meryn had given her, a few simple words in Welsh to take her across the border. She frowned, not sure suddenly that she could remember them, then not giving herself time to think she began to recite out loud, quietly at first, then louder, hearing her voice ring out into the wind, and slowly she dropped onto her knees in the frozen mud as the fog closed in and she felt time itself take her.

Giles woke with a start. He sat up groggily. 'Beth?' The space beside him was empty. The house was silent. 'Beth, where are you?' He stared round the room. It was dark. Frowning, he brought his wrist up to his face and looked at his watch. He had been asleep for hours. 'Beth?'

Worried, he searched the house, then he opened the front door and glanced out. The mist seemed to have lifted a bit and now he could see quite clearly the track and even the first tree on the mound by the bend. His car had gone. Puzzled, he walked back into the cottage, closing the door. Only then did he spot the note on the kitchen table. He picked it up and read it: *Gone to the stone to look for Adam. Don't worry. I know what I'm doing. Love you always, B.*

Giles let out a groan. 'Silly, silly woman! Oh God, why did I fall asleep?' He ran back into the living room.

The mist was clearing fast. He could see the hedges now through the window, and the small garden in the starlight, the twisted crab apple tree and the thorn. It was very quiet. He shivered.

He had to follow her, somehow. A car. Any car. Adam's car. It was locked in the shed behind the house where it had stood since Adam had been taken to hospital. The keys. Where were the keys? He began to search frantically, first Adam's desk, then the table, the kitchen, then upstairs on the table in Adam's bedroom. No sign. 'Christ!' He was growing frantic. He was marooned here, with the sleet outside turning to snow and there was nothing he could do.

Pulling on his coat and boots he flung open the back door and made his way down the path. He had some faint notion of trying to hotwire the car after breaking down the door of the shed, but the door was not locked. Pulling it open he edged in along the narrow space between the small blue car and the lathe walls of the building and took hold of the car's door handle. The door opened. The keys were still in the ignition.

It took three goes to start it, then at last he was able to back it out, the engine coughing and sputtering, in a cloud of exhaust fumes. Turning on the headlights he glanced down at the petrol gauge, saw that the tank was half full and breathing a small prayer of thanks for that one small mercy, he reversed on out of the narrow gate and turned to hurtle down the mountain road. He had not thought to stop long enough even to lock the door of the house.

His own car was where Beth had left it, tucked into the hedge on the edge of the lay-by and he drew up behind it, leaping out and pulling on his coat as he set off at a run towards the track. The mist was returning and almost at once he lost his bearings, focusing as hard as he could on the barely marked path at his feet. He cursed his own stupidity. He had forgotten even to bring a torch.

He had a stitch and he was breathing heavily as he lumbered on up the steep track. His injured arm still ached as he swung it, and he could feel the needles of sleet in his face. Stop, retrace, careful. He had lost the path. He glanced round frantically, then he saw it again ahead of him, beside the burn, barely more than a track in the intense darkness.

'There's no one here.' Liza had returned to the ambulance after walking round the back of the house. 'The back door is unlocked and the place is reasonably warm, but there is no sign of Giles or Beth. The trouble is they may not be expecting us. I never got through, even though I left about six messages on Giles's mobile.'

'Can we bring him in?' Ivor was sitting with Adam in the back of the ambulance. With him was the driver and a nurse they had engaged for the journey.

Liza nodded. 'I've opened the front door. You can take him up to his bedroom straightaway. I'm sure the other two will be back soon.'

It was only after Adam had been settled at last in his own bed, and the ambulance had driven away that Liza found Beth's note lying on the kitchen table where Giles had thrown it. She stared at Ivor, white-faced. 'Beth's gone to the stone.'

Ivor read the note and sighed. 'Presumably Giles has gone after her?'

Liza nodded. 'If they could just have waited till we got here.'

'I think I've found the reason they didn't wait.' On the kitchen table, amongst the letters and papers scattered there, Ivor had uncovered Giles's phone. The battery, when he tried to switch it on, was flat. 'They never got your messages.'

'Dear God!' Liza sat down abruptly on a kitchen stool. 'What have we done, bringing Adam here?'

'We've brought him to the place where he needs to be.' He looked at her gravely. 'I'm sure we've done the right thing, but all we can do now is wait to see what Beth is doing.'

'To see if she survives,' Liza retorted sharply. 'She is facing Brid out there, don't forget.'

'I haven't forgotten.' Ivor patted her hand reassuringly. 'I think it is time we went up to Adam. Let's see if we can make ourselves heard.'

Meryn was standing in the shadows, watching the silhouette against the sun as it set behind the mountains. Broichan was there, his arms folded in the sleeves of his dark robe. He had tensed, his senses alert, aware suddenly that he was no longer alone, that the one who had been pursuing him through the ages was close. Turning slowly, his back to the crimson sky, Broichan surveyed the woods. Behind him in the hut Brid's sleeping form lay still, covered by a blanket of rich fur.

Meryn glided closer on silent feet, aware of the cold purity of the air around him, of the intense silence of time. He was so close now.

He drew his cloak of protection around him and felt himself grow strong.

Beth couldn't believe it was so easy. The hillside was sunlit and green, the heather purple, the vast backdrop of mountains grey against the blue of the sky. Looking round she could see the cross-slab, close beside her. She frowned, expecting to see the carvings – the zed rod, the serpent, the mirror – but instead all she could see was the huge wheel cross in relief on the granite, and below it the soft grass.

She heard herself sob out loud. It hadn't worked. She wasn't looking for a cross. She was in the wrong place.

She moved closer to the stone and then she saw them, the ancient symbols on the back of it, clear, newly drawn, strong.

So, the child of A-dam's child is here . . .

The voice was coming from immediately behind her. Beth

whirled round. Brid was standing near the stone, a shiny iron knife, newly honed, in her hand, the silver knife long-ago stolen from Catriona lost somewhere in the long grasses of a twentieth-century hillside. She was dressed in a long green gown, and a leather girdle. At her waist hung the empty sheath.

The child of A-dam's child.

It was like a mantra inside her head, but Brid's lips had not moved.

Beth took a deep breath, trying to steady herself. 'Adam? Where is Adam? Tell me where he is. I've come to find him.'

Panic was fogging her brain. Or was it sleep? Was she really just dreaming, still lying in the bed in the house beside Giles, as the mist lapped round the windows?

Remember what Meryn had told her. Picture her own neat notes, pages of them, fix them in her mind. Surround herself with light. Repeat her own mantra of protection, call on her own gods and angels. She squared her shoulders, trying to hide her fear, stepping forwards instead of back as Meryn had insisted she do.

'Brid, you must tell me where Adam is. He does not belong here –'

But suddenly Brid was looking beyond her towards the trees, her eyes enormous with fear. Beth could hear it now too, the rumble of thunder and the sizzle and crack of the lightning bolt.

Her concentration broke and she whirled round. A tall figure stood there, a man with a fine aquiline face and wild white hair. His robe of scarlet and gold thread was covered with a mantle of heavy black. In his hand he held a sword. Beth stared at him for a full second, Brid forgotten, then she turned and ran. Her feet slipped on the grass. She gasped for breath. Her terror was overwhelming.

Beth, stand firm. Do not be afraid. I'm here. It was Meryn's voice inside her head.

Where was he? Frantically she looked around her. 'Meryn!'

Beth, the barriers between the planes are open. Bring Adam through now whilst time stands still.

The sun had gone in and she was again surrounded by mist. It was so thick she could see nothing. The sleet beat against her face and she could feel the needle-sharp cut of ice.

Meryn, help me! Where is Adam? I can't see him! Her own voice seemed to be in her head. She was imprisoned in a nightmare, unable to free herself, running, but not moving, breathing, gasping for breath, but suffocating as her lungs locked.

Blindly she turned. There were other figures now in the mist near her. *Meryn? Grandfather?* She couldn't see properly. Her terror was too great. She saw another flash of lightning and heard a crack of thunder. The sleet cut more deeply. Then she felt a hand on hers.

Come. Quickly. Back to the stone. Back to your own time.

'Meryn?'

Brid was there again now, standing before her uncle. Her hair was flying, the small blade in her hand puny against Broichan's strength.

Traitor witch! Daughter of the hag! His voice echoed in the vastness of the storm. *You and Adam will die together on this night.*

'Grandfather! Meryn!'

Beth found herself turning round and round in despair. It was a dream; a nightmare. It had to be. In a moment they would all turn into a pack of cards and come tumbling down around her ears.

'Meryn, help me!' She screamed into the darkness. 'I need you . . . *Now!*'

The snow had begun to fall heavily. Giles bent closer to the ground, wishing again and again that he had brought a torch. He was out of breath, gasping, his eyes screwed up against the cold. The path disappeared again and he stooped closer, desperately hunting for it.

'Beth!' He stood upright and shouted into the murk. 'Beth, where are you?' There was no answer. He moved on, almost in despair. Hot tears mixed with the ice on his cheeks. 'Beth!'

He was at the top now, and the ground had levelled out. He stood still again and tried to look round. Was that a figure he could see near him? 'Beth?' Excitement gave his voice strength. 'Beth, I'm coming!'

He stumbled into a run, then he stopped. The figure was almost lost in the mist. But it was not Beth. It was a man, a man who appeared to be brandishing a sword.

'Christ Almighty!' Giles skidded to a halt. He had nothing to defend himself but his bare hands as Broichan moved towards him, his hair flying wildly round his head in the whirling snow.

In a second he had closed in on Giles and Giles found himself leaping sideways out of reach of the murderous blows. In a frantic, instinctive moment of self-protection he jumped forward under the blade and caught the other man's wrist, wrestling frantically, surprised that, in spite of his ferocity he seemed less strong than he had expected. 'Drop it, you bastard!' Giles gasped through gritted teeth. He shook the man's arm like a terrier.

Broichan!

The scream came from far away, but it was enough to make the man hesitate. Giles wrenched the sword out of his grasp and it flew through the air. He doubled his fist and aimed it at Broichan's chin. It made contact with a satisfying thump and Broichan reeled back. Giles turned, searching for the sword. He had a painful stitch and it seemed that blood was running into his eyes.

'Beth!' He screamed the name into the sleet. 'Beth, where are you? Adam?'

Someone was heading towards him. He recognised suddenly the slim figure, the flying hair, the wild stance, the long skirts, the brilliant eyes, the knife . . .

'Jesus Christ! Beth, look out!' He didn't seem to be able to move fast enough. He was locked into his nightmare. He couldn't see properly.

The yell from behind him caught him by surprise; he spun round in time to see the huge sword flash again across his vision. He ducked, slipped, fell to one knee and looked up in terror at the man standing above him. There was no mistaking the intention in those eyes as for one instant their gaze locked.

Then suddenly Meryn was there. Giles saw him facing Broichan, his hands upraised. He saw Broichan hesitate and step backwards, lowering his sword; he saw Gartnait, his arms reaching out towards his sister, and then Adam was there too.

'Grandfather! Adam!' Beth's scream brought them all to a standstill. 'Adam!'

He was standing a little way away staring at them all, a much younger Adam, his face alight with excitement and love.

Brid spun round.

A-dam!

She had seen him. At last she had seen him. Her face full of joy she was running towards him through the snow.

Beth closed her eyes. Meryn! What had Meryn told her to say?

And suddenly she too could see him in front of her with his gentle face, his strength, his certainty. *You can win, Beth. You can prevail! You can save Adam and Brid and yourself. You don't need me any more.* And at last she remembered the word. The word of power which cannot be spoken save *in extremis*.

She closed her eyes and raised her arms and shouted it across the hillside, her voice echoing and gaining in strength as the wind dropped and the snow began to slacken.

* * *

455

'Wake up!' Giles's voice, weak with relief, came to her from a long way away. 'Beth, wake up!'

She opened her eyes and looked round.

Broichan and Brid and Gartnait had disappeared.

The door to the past had closed.

She threw herself at Giles, shaking with cold and fear. 'They've gone! Oh my darling, I thought you were going to die!' She buried her face in his chest.

He closed his arms around her. 'Tell me I was dreaming, Beth!'

She gave a small, sad laugh. 'I don't think you were, Giles, look at you.'

Shaking the sleet from his eyes he stared down. His clothes were soaked in blood. Pushing back his sleeve he saw a vicious slice through his forearm just below the elbow.

'That came from Broichan's sword,' Beth said quietly.

'The arch Druid!' Giles gave a small groan. 'Who would believe me?'

'No one.' She had pulled off her scarf and was wrapping it tightly round his arm.

'Beth, where's your grandfather?'

Beth stopped and stared round. There was no one in sight in the mist. She rubbed her eyes and turned slowly. 'But he was here! I can't see him. Oh Giles, you don't think –'

'He's gone back with them.'

'No! Oh, Giles, no. Meryn said it would work. He said we would all go back to our own time!' Tears poured down her face.

Giles hugged her to him, biting his lip against the pain in his arm. 'I'm so sorry, sweetheart. I don't know what to say.'

'It didn't work.' She took one last despairing look around and stumbled back towards the path. 'It was all for nothing! Poor Grandfather. He's trapped with them, with that evil man Broichan. He will be killed.'

Liza had stood for a long time at the back door, staring out at the darkness, seeing, in her mind's eye, not the bitterly cold garden with its layer of light snow, but the stone with its cluster of ancient symbols. She was not afraid. She could sense now that it was over.

She sighed. 'God bless, wherever you are,' she murmured and at last she turned back into the house.

Ivor was sitting at Adam's table, his spectacles perched on the end of his nose, deep in Adam's papers.

'How is he?' She was tired and very cold.

'I've been checking every half an hour. No change.' He stood up. 'Go and have a look at him, and I'll make you a hot drink.'

Wearily Liza climbed the stairs, pulling off her wet coat as she went. She hung it from the banister at the top and walked along the landing to Adam's bedroom. Pushing open the door she walked in.

'Beth has gone up to the stone to look for you, you old reprobate,' she said quietly as she went up to the bed. She looked down at him fondly. 'I wish I knew where you were.'

'I'm here.' The whisper was so quiet she barely heard it. He reached out for her hand, his own so weak he could scarcely move. 'I saw Beth. She's coming home. And I saw Brid. She's safe. She has gone to her brother in her own time. He has rescued her from Broichan and he will take care of her. Meryn was there too.'

Liza sat down on the edge of the bed. She leaned forward and kissed him on the forehead. 'And you're sure she won't come back?'

'Not for a while, anyway.' He shook his head. 'Not for a while.'

Then he smiled.

As he had gathered her into his arms and touched the dark silky hair and kissed her cold lips under the whirling snow, Brid had made one last promise before she turned away from him and slipped out of sight:

One day, A-dam, I shall find you again. One day I shall see you in the mirror of my mind and I shall return. Then no one shall come between us. Ever.

24

The sun was going down. It was growing cold. With a groan Adam sat up and stretched. The shadow of the great Celtic cross lay across him like a swathe. Rubbing his eyes, he looked round. His stomach was rumbling and he could tell without looking at his watch that it must be time to go home.

He climbed uncomfortably to his feet. He felt disorientated; strange. Slowly the dream was coming back to him.

Was it a dream?

Had he dreamed his whole life?

He glanced back down the hill, trying to get a grip on himself, trying to remember. His mother and father had had another quarrel. He had run away, up the hillside, to his stone. And he had fallen asleep. That was it, surely.

He was a boy, wearing shorts and gym shoes with his binoculars and his life's dreams hanging round his neck.

Or was he, after all, an old man, a fool, who had gone back to the stone, looking for Brid, the beautiful nemesis of his dream; an old man, whose life was nearly over?

Cautiously, with a shiver of foreboding, he looked down at himself, wondering.

Which was he now, old man, or boy with his whole life still ahead of him? Could he believe his eyes, or had time played a trick on him again?

How would he ever know?

Author's Note

Of all the characters in the book only Broichan is based on fact. He appears in Adamnan's 'Life of Columba', the Druid of King Brude who opposed the Saint in his attempts to convert Pictland to Christianity. Naturally, in Adamnan's version, his pagan powers were vanquished and he vanishes from the story defeated, although history would seem to suggest that Christianity's spread was in fact a far more gentle and undramatic process than he relates. If I have taken Broichan's name in vain, and he was really a nice, gentle man, I hope he will forgive me. I should hate to incur his wrath.

There was a real Meryn, too. A healer and a mystic, he lived, when I knew him when I was a child, in Kensington rather than in his native Welsh hills, but he instilled in me a love of nature and of crystals and of the mysteries of things and for that I shall always remember him with affection and gratitude.

So many people help with stories and advice when one writes a book, but some have to be singled out for their special contribution. Dr John Waller went to endless trouble to describe for me his days as a medical student at Edinburgh University during the war and I thank him very much for all his help. Air Vice Marshal Sandy Johnstone sent me information and told me stories of his days in the RAF in Scotland in the early months of the war and about Edinburgh during that time, as did my father whose CO Sandy was in 602 Squadron. I am so grateful to them for their reminiscences. My son Adrian supplied me with information on mountain rescue techniques and Jo and Ian McDonald gave advice and hospitality on my tour of Pictish stones. A special thank you too, to Diana Currant who came with me on that trip, for her company and cheerful moral support climbing damp cold hillsides, peering through windows of closed museums and standing shivering whilst I photographed and sketched and made notes in the pouring rain and icy wind! And finally thanks as always to Carole Blake, and to Rachel Hore and Lucy Ferguson for their support and inspiration and patience!

459

A lost child in the Welsh borders;
a violent attack in London;
an epic battle between the Celts and the Romans.

What can possibly link them?

Read on for an extract from
BARBARA ERSKINE'S

thrilling new novel,

The
Warrior's Princess

Jess woke up late to the sound of the steadily beating rain. Pulling on jeans and a sweater after a hasty shower she ran down to find Dan's holdall standing by the front door. She glanced into the kitchen. There was a pot of coffee on the table and it was set for two but there was no sign of him.

'Dan?'

'I'm in here.' His voice came from the dining room. 'Come and look at this, Jess.'

Reluctantly she walked over to the doorway and glanced in. He was staring down at the table. 'It's gone,' he said softly. 'All gone.'

'What has?' She moved towards him.

'The damage. The scribbles. The blood. Look.'

He stood back, gesturing at the sketchbook in front of him. His face was white.

She glanced down and gasped out loud. He was right. The sketchbook was completely undamaged. Hardly daring to touch it she reached out and turned the pages. They were all the same. Her drawings and paintings were pristine.

'I don't understand.' She picked up the book and riffled through it. 'What's happened?'

'You tell me.'

She turned and stared round the dining room. Nothing had been touched. Everything was as neat and tidy as it had been before Rhodri arrived.

'We can't have dreamed it, can we?' She met his gaze at last.

Dan shrugged. 'All three of us?' He shivered. 'Let's go into the kitchen. I made coffee before I came in here.'

She followed him. 'We can't all have imagined what happened, Dan.'

'No?' He grabbed the coffee pot. 'Look in the bin.'

With a quick glance at him she peered in. 'What am I looking at?'

'Nothing. That's the point. Where is the broken glass?'

'Oh Dan!' She dropped the lid and went to sit down at the table, ramming her sleeves up to her elbows, then running her fingers through her hair. Two intact bottles of wine stood side by side on the draining board.

He pushed a mug of coffee towards her. 'It looks as though we all suffered some kind of hallucination,' he said thoughtfully. 'I don't see how or why, but there is no other explanation. If we had all eaten the same thing I could put it down to magic mushrooms or something, but Rhodri didn't eat with us.'

'And your hand. Where you cut it? Is the cut still there?' She reached out and touched his wrist.

He stretched out his right hand and turned it up to face her. There was no mark.

'Oh God!' She gave an involuntary shudder. 'What on earth has happened to us?'

'I'm afraid I am not going to be able to hang around to find out.' He glanced up at her again. 'I have to leave pretty soon, Jess. I've got a long drive ahead. Shall I ring up your mate Rhodri and get him to come over? You shouldn't be on your own to sort this out, but I don't know how my being here can help. Whatever it was it's over now.' He gave a small sharp bark of laughter. 'Next time I see you we'll joke about this!' Gulping back his coffee, he stood up.

For a moment she hadn't moved. She was still staring at his hand. Then she shook her head. 'Don't worry about me, Dan. I'll give Rhodri a ring later and tell him what has happened.'

She followed him out to his car and watched as he loaded his bag and his books. In minutes she was waving him out of sight as he headed down towards the lane, his car bumping over the ruts. Strangely she felt nothing but relief at his departure. Had he got up in the night and tested her door handle, she wondered? Probably not. She frowned suddenly. He hadn't offered to kiss her goodbye.

Walking back inside she went into the kitchen and straight to the sink. Without knowing why she turned on the tap and slowly rinsed her hands and face, then she reached for a towel.

Have the nasty men gone?

The voice was very close behind her. With a cry of fright she span round.

Can we stop playing now?

'Jesus!' She took a deep breath. 'Where are you?'

There was no reply.

'Eigon? Glads? Was it one of you who did that?' She was suddenly angry. 'Did you scribble over my drawings?' She scanned the room. 'Did you break all that glass?'

464

Outside the blackbird began to whistle from the roof of the studio. The rain had stopped and a stray ray of sunlight reflected off the wet paving stones. 'Did you hear me?' Jess called out again. She was suddenly every inch the schoolmistress. 'I want to see you. Now!' She held her breath, looking round. There was no sound. 'I mean it!'

Was that a gurgle of laughter? She ran to the window and stared out, scanning the courtyard. The house was full of sound. The creak of roof timbers, the rustle of leaves, the drip of rain down the gutters, birds, the baaing of sheep from the hillside on the far side of the track. 'Eigon?' Jess used the child's name without thinking, just as her mother, Cerys, had used it. 'Come here. I want to speak to you.'

But there was no response, as she had known there wouldn't be. She shook her head. Wandering back into the dining room she looked down at the table, half afraid that the sketchbook would once more be damaged. It wasn't. It lay there untouched.

'Shit!' She went to the phone, overcoming her reluctance to contact Rhodri again. After about twenty rings the answer service picked up. 'Rhodri? I'm sorry to disturb you, but can you come back here as soon as you can, there is something I need to show you.' She paused. 'Dan has gone. I'm on my own.'

Pulling the car into a gateway at the bottom of the lane, Dan turned off the engine and rested his forehead against the rim of the steering wheel. He was sweating hard. Fumbling blindly for the door handle he stumbled out into the long grass and nettles, dotted with campion, which fringed the trackway into the field and stood leaning on the gate waiting for the wave of nausea to pass. Then he turned and looked at the car.

It was empty. But someone had been in there, sitting behind him. Almost as soon as he had turned into the lane and pulled away from Ty Bran he had felt it. He could sense a presence. A solid threatening presence. A man. An angry, hate-filled man.

He had slammed on the brakes, staring into the mirror. Then he had turned, scanning the back seat. Nothing. Of course there was no one there. He accelerated away again, fast, over the roughly metalled lane, bumping the car over potholes and ridges, skidding over patches of red oozing mud which had leaked onto the road from the steep banks, growing more and more afraid until he had spotted the gateway, somewhere to pull up and throw himself out of reach of the malign shadow that was sharing his car.

Slowly the palpitations slowed. He wiped his face on his sleeve and turned, leaning on the gate, to stare at the vehicle. It sat there in the sunlight, the windows bright with reflections, the door hanging open as he had left it when he jumped out. Pushing himself away from the gate he forced himself to walk over and pull open the rear door. Leaning down, he peered in. Nothing. Cautiously he reached in, clawing at the empty air over the seat with his fingers as though to prove to himself the space was unoccupied. The film of sweat was drying on his face. He shivered, suddenly chilled. Somewhere in the distance he could hear the wild yapping cry of a buzzard, then near it, aggressive and primitive, the deep throaty croak of a raven. He peered up at the sky. It was up there. He could see it. The raven, a black silhouette against the blue, had set its sights on the buzzard. It was flying fast, on the attack, harrying, bullying, its call a sinister throbbing counterpoint to the alarmed yelp of the larger bird. Both birds angled their wings and swooped away over the fields and in a second they were out of sight over the shoulder of the hill.

Dan found he was breathing fast, as though he had been running. He swallowed hard, slamming the back door shut. Imagination. That was all. That damned haunted house and Jess with all her hysterical stories. They had got to him. He moved his head uncomfortably, his neck suddenly very stiff. For a moment he felt quite dizzy. He blinked. Something on the door had caught his eye. A smear of red. He held out his right hand and stared at it. A deep scar showed across his palm where he had cut it on the glass the night before. The cut that had disappeared. It was oozing blood. He shook his head. This was not happening! He straightened his back and squared his shoulders, furious with himself and with Jess. The sooner he got out of this god-forsaken place the better.

www.BarbaraErskine.co.uk

Have you logged in yet?

Visit Barbara's fantastic new website where you will find information about her novels, background, interest in writing and history. Read on for more information about Barbara's ongoing fascination with the supernatural and lose yourself in Barbara's exclusive monthly short stories.

You will also find details about this book, photographs of some of the locations visited by the characters in the story – both in the past and the present day – a bibliography and various items about the historical research involved. Further details on Barbara's upcoming appearances near you and events are also featured here.

Lady of Hay

Jo Clifford, successful journalist, is all set to debunk the idea of past-life regression. But when she submits to a simple hypnotic session, she suddenly finds herself reliving the experiences of Matilda, Lady of Hay, the wife of a baron at the time of King John. Jo's past and present become hopelessly entwined, and a story of secret passion and unspeakable treachery is about to begin again...

978 0 00 725086 8

Kingdom of Shadows

In a childless and unhappy marriage, Clare Royland is rich and beautiful – but lonely. And fuelling her feelings of isolation is a strange, growing fascination with an ancestress from the distant past. Troubled by inexplicable dreams that terrify her, Clare is forced to look back through the centuries for answers.

978 0 00 728866 3

Child of the Phoenix

In 1218 an extraordinary princess is born. Her mystical powers and unquenchable spirit will alter the course of history. Raised by her fiercely Welsh nurse to support the Celtic cause against the predatory English king, Princess Eleyne is taught to worship the old gods, to look into the future and sometimes the past. However, unable to identify time and place in her horrifying visions, she is powerless to avert forthcoming tragedy...

978 0 00 728079 7